MARY
HIGGINS
CLARK

THREE COMPLETE NOVELS

MARY HIGGINS CLARK

THREE COMPLETE NOVELS

Where Are The Children?
A Stranger Is Watching
The Cradle Will Fall

WINGS BOOKS

NEW YORK

This 1996 edition is published by Wings Books, a division of Random House Value Publishing, Inc., 201 East 50th Street, New York, New York 10022, by arrangement with Simon & Schuster, Inc.

Wings Books and colophon are trademarks of Random House Value Publishing, Inc.

Random House
New York • Toronto • London • Sydney • Auckland
http://www.randomhouse.com/

Printed and bound in the United States of America

Library of Congress Cataloging-in-Publication Data

Clark, Mary Higgins.
    [Novels. Selections]
    Mary Higgins Clark : three complete novels.
       p.   cm.
    Contents: The cradle will fall — A stranger is watching — Where are the children?
    ISBN 0-517-12315-0
    1. Detective and mystery stories, American.   I. Title.
PS3553.L287A6   1995   94-28075
813'.54—dc20   CIP

12 11 10

CONTENTS

INTRODUCTION
XI

WHERE ARE THE CHILDREN?
1

A STRANGER IS WATCHING
131

THE CRADLE WILL FALL
297

INTRODUCTION
by
MARY HIGGINS CLARK

Within these pages are my first three suspense novels. They've always been very special to me, and I was delighted when Wings Books at Random House wanted to gather them into a collection.

From age seven, starting with the Nancy Drew series, I virtually gulped down suspense novels. As the years passed, I became a devotee of Agatha Christie, Josephine Tey, Charlotte Armstrong, Mignon Eberhart, Daphne DuMaurier, Mary Roberts Rinehart . . . just to name a few.

I always knew I was going to grow up to be a writer and in my early twenties began to sell short stories. Ten years passed. Then I wrote an historical novel which no one read.

When I was trying to decide what my next project would be, I remembered that my first writing professor had said, "If you want a clue about what to write, take a look at your library shelves. What do you like to read?"

There on my shelves were those rows of suspense novels, some of them decades old. I reflected on the fact that besides loving to read them, I had come to understand why some of them worked and others didn't. I'd also become pretty good at deciphering clues.

That's important. You see, a suspense writer must play fair with the reader. Think about the legend of Hansel and Gretel. When they went into the forest, they dropped smooth stones and bread crumbs to leave a path that they could follow home. The birds ate the bread crumbs and ignored the stones.

In the same way, the suspense writer must offer legitimate clues—bread crumbs as a path to truth for the reader. Mixed in, of course, are the stones or red herrings in the plot.

After I decided to try my hand at writing suspense, the next problem was to determine what I would write about. Another piece of advice came to mind. In that first writing class, the professor had also suggested that we take a situation that particularly intrigued us and ask ourselves two questions: "Suppose?" and "What if?" Turn the facts into fiction.

At that time, a young woman was on trial for murdering her two children. I did not write about that case. I asked myself, "Suppose a beautiful young mother is accused of murdering her two small children? Suppose she is innocent and so heartbroken that she doesn't care what happens to her? Suppose she is found guilty of murder, goes to prison and then is released on a technicality? Suppose she remarries, has two more children and seven years later to the day, the children of her second marriage disappear?"

That was the premise of *Where Are The Children?* It became my first bestseller.

When I turned it into my publisher, I began a new book. There had just been a ransom drop in Grand Central Station. At the same time, the so-called Mad Bomber was setting off bombs all over New York City. I asked an FBI friend if it would be possible to hide kidnapping victims in Grand Central. His answer: "Mary, you could hide an army in that station."

I thought, "And suppose the kidnapper has a bomb ticking next to his victims."

That's how *A Stranger Is Watching* began to form.

When the first so-called test-tube baby was born in England, there was international excitement. Many editorials cautioned that soon there would be surrogate mothers, host mothers. What were the legal ramifications? I asked myself the "suppose" question. Suppose an unscrupulous doctor is experimenting on young women patients who long to become pregnant?

The Cradle Will Fall began to write itself.

Now I do hope that all of you will curl up in your favorite easy chair and enjoy reading these stories as much as I have enjoyed writing them.

Mary Higgins Clark

Mary Higgins Clark

THREE COMPLETE NOVELS

WHERE ARE THE CHILDREN?

To the memory of my mother,
Nora C. Higgins,
with love, admiration and gratitude

PROLOGUE

He could feel the chill coming in through the cracks around the window-panes. Clumsily he got up and lumbered over to the window. Reaching for one of the thick towels he kept handy, he stuffed it around the rotting frame.

The incoming draft made a soft, hissing sound in the towel, a sound that vaguely pleased him. He looked out at the mist-filled sky and studied the whitecaps churning in the water. From this side of the house it was often possible to see Provincetown, on the opposite shore of Cape Cod Bay.

He hated the Cape. He hated the bleakness of it on a November day like this; the stark grayness of the water; the stolid people who didn't say much but studied you with their eyes. He had hated it the one summer he'd been here—waves of tourists sprawling on the beaches; climbing up the steep embankment to this house; gawking in the downstairs windows, cupping their hands over their eyes to peer inside.

He hated the large FOR SALE sign that Ray Eldredge had posted on the front and back of the big house and the fact that now Ray and that woman who worked for him had begun bringing people in to see the house. Last month it had been only a matter of luck that he'd come along as they'd started through; only luck that he'd gotten to the top floor before they had and been able to put away the telescope.

Time was running out. Somebody would buy this house and he wouldn't be able to rent it again. That was why he'd sent the article to the paper. He wanted to still be here to enjoy seeing her exposed for what she was in front of these people . . . now, when she must have started to feel safe.

There was something else that he had to do, but the chance had never come. She kept such a close watch on the children. But he couldn't afford to wait anymore. Tomorrow . . .

He moved restlessly around the room. The bedroom of the top-floor apartment was large. The whole house was large. It was a bastardized evolution of an old captain's house. Begun in the seventeenth century on a rocky crest that commanded a view of the whole bay, it was a pretentious monument to man's need to be forever on guard.

Life wasn't like that. It was bits and pieces. Icebergs that showed in tips. He knew. He rubbed his hand over his face, feeling warm and uncomfortable even though the room was chilly. For six years now he'd rented this house in the late summer and fall. It was almost exactly as it had been when he had first come into it. Only a few things were different: the telescope in the front room; the clothes that he kept for the special times; the peaked cap that he pulled over his face, which shaded it so well.

Otherwise the apartment was the same: the old-fashioned sofa and pine tables and hooked rug in the living room; the rock maple bedroom set. This house and apartment had been ideal for his purpose until this fall, when Ray Eldredge had told him they were actively trying to sell the place for a restaurant and it could be rented only with the understanding it could be shown on telephoned notice.

Raynor Eldredge. The thought of the man brought a smile. What would Ray think tomorrow when he saw the story? Had Nancy ever told Ray who she was? Maybe not. Women could be sly. If Ray didn't know, it would be even better. How wonderful it would be to actually see Ray's expression when he opened the paper! It was delivered a little after ten in the morning. Ray would be in his office. He might not even look at it for a while.

Impatiently, he turned from the window. His thick, trunklike legs were tight in shiny black trousers. He'd be glad when he could lose some of this weight. It would mean that awful business of starving himself again, but he could do it. When it had been necessary he'd done it before. Restlessly he rubbed a hand over his vaguely itchy scalp. He'd be glad when he could let his hair grow back in its natural lines again. The sides had always been thick and would probably be mostly gray now.

He ran one hand slowly down his trouser leg, then impatientlly paced around the apartment, finally stopping at the telescope in the living room. The telescope was especially powerful—the kind of equipment that wasn't available for general sale. Even many police departments didn't have it yet. But there were always ways to get things you wanted. He bent over and peered into it, squinting one eye.

Because of the darkness of the day, the kitchen light was on, so it was easy to see Nancy clearly. She was standing in front of the kitchen window, the one that was over the sink. Maybe she was about to get something ready to put into the oven for dinner. But she had a warm jacket on, so she was probably going out. She was standing quietly, just looking in the direction of the water. What was she thinking of? Whom was she thinking of? The children—Peter . . . Lisa . . . ? He'd like to know.

He could feel his mouth go dry and licked his lips nervously. She looked very young today. Her hair was pulled back from her face. She kept it dark brown. Someone would surely have recognized her if she'd left it the natural red-gold shade. Tomorrow she'd be thirty-two. But she still didn't look her age. She had an intriguing young quality, soft and fresh and silky.

He swallowed nervously. He could feel the feverish dryness of his mouth, even while his hands and armpits were wet and warm. He gulped, then swallowed again, and the sound evolved into a deep chuckle. His whole body began to shake with mirth and jarred the telescope. Nancy's image blurred, but he didn't bother refocusing the lens. He wasn't interested in watching her anymore today.

Tomorrow! He could just see the expression she'd have at this time tomorrow. Exposed to the world for what she was; numbed with worry and fear; trying to answer the question . . . the same question the police had thrown at her over and over seven years ago.

"Come on, Nancy," the police would be saying again. "Come clean with us. Tell the truth. You should know you can't get away with this. Tell us, Nancy—where are the children?"

 *CHAPTER 1*

Ray came down the stairs pulling the knot closed on his tie. Nancy was sitting at the table with a still-sleepy Missy on her lap. Michael was eating his breakfast in his poised, reflective way.

Ray tousled Mike's head and leaned over to kiss Missy. Nancy smiled up at him. She was so darn pretty. There were fine lines around those blue eyes, but you'd still never take her for thirty-two. Ray was only a few years older himself, but always felt infinitely her senior. Maybe it was that awful vulnerability. He noticed the traces of red at the roots of her dark hair. A dozen times in the last year he'd wanted to ask her to let it grow out, but hadn't dared.

"Happy birthday, honey," he said quietly.

He watched as the color drained from her face.

Michael looked surprised. "Is it Mommy's birthday? You didn't tell me that."

Missy sat upright. "Mommy's birthday?" She sounded pleased.

"Yes," Ray told them. Nancy was staring down at the table. "And tonight we're going to celebrate. Tonight I'm going to bring home a big birthday cake and a present, and we'll have Aunt Dorothy come to dinner. Right, Mommy?"

"Ray . . . no." Nancy's voice was low and pleading.

"Yes. Remember, last year you promised that this year we'd . . ."

Celebrate was the wrong word. He couldn't say it. But for a long time he'd known that they would someday have to start changing the pattern of her birthdays. At first she'd withdrawn completely from him and gone around the house or walked the beach like a silent ghost in a world of her own.

But last year she'd finally begun to talk about them . . . the two other children. She'd said, "They'd be so big now . . . ten and eleven. I try to think how they would look now, but can't seem to even imagine. . . . Everything about that time is so blurred. Like a nightmare that I only dreamed."

"It's supposed to be like that," Ray told her. "Put it all behind you, honey. Don't even wonder what happened anymore."

The memory strengthened his decision. He bent over Nancy and patted her hair with a gesture that was at once protective and gentle.

Nancy looked up at him. The appeal on her face changed to uncertainty. "I don't think—"

Michael interrupted her. "How old are you, Mommy?" he asked practically.

Nancy smiled—a real smile that miraculously eased the tension. "None of your business," she told him.

Ray took a quick gulp of her coffee. "Good girl," he said. "Tell you what, Mike. I'll pick you up after school this afternoon and we'll go get a present for Mommy. Now I'd better get out of here. Some guy is coming up to see the Hunt place. I want to get the file together."

"Isn't it rented?" Nancy asked.

"Yes. That Parrish fellow who's taken the apartment on and off has it again. But he knows we have the right to show it anytime. It's a great spot for a restaurant and wouldn't take much to convert. It'll make a nice commission if I sell it."

Nancy put Missy down and walked with him to the door. He kissed her lightly and felt her lips tremble under his. How much had he upset her by starting this birthday talk? Some instinct made him want to say, *Let's not wait for tonight. I'll stay home and we'll take the kids and go to Boston for the day.*

Instead he got into his car, waved, backed up and drove onto the narrow dirt lane that wound through an acre of woods until it terminated on the cross-Cape road that led to the center of Adams Port and his office.

Ray was right, Nancy thought as she walked slowly back to the table. There was a time to stop following the patterns of yesterday—a time to stop remembering and look only to the future. She knew that a part of her was still frozen. She knew that the mind dropped a protective curtain over painful memories—but it was more than that.

It was as though her life with Carl were a blur . . . the entire time. It was hard to remember the faculty house on the campus, Carl's modulated voice . . . Peter and Lisa. What had they looked like? Dark hair, both of them, like Carl's, and too quiet . . . too subdued . . . affected by her uncertainty . . . and then lost—both of them.

"Mommy, why do you look so sad?" Michael gazed at her with Ray's candid expression, spoke with Ray's directness.

Seven years, Nancy thought. Life was a series of seven-year cycles. Carl used to say that your whole body changed in that time. Every cell renewed itself. It was time for her to really look ahead . . . to forget.

She glanced around the large, cheerful kitchen with the old brick fireplace, the wide oak floors, the red curtains and valances that didn't obstruct the view over the harbor. And then she looked at Michael and Missy. . . .

"I'm not sad darling," she said. "I'm really not."

She scooped Missy up in her arms, feeling the warmth and sweet stickiness of her. "I've been thinking about your present," Missy said. Her long strawberry-blond hair curled around her ears and forehead. People sometimes asked where she got that beautiful hair—who had been the redhead in the family?

"Great," Nancy told her. "But think about it outside. You'd better get some fresh air soon. It's supposed to rain later and get very cold."

After the children were dressed, she helped them on with their windbreakers and hats. "There's my dollar," Michael said with satisfaction as he reached into the breast pocket of his jacket. "I was sure I left it here. Now I can buy you a present."

"Me has money too." Missy proudly held up a handful of pennies. "Oh, now, you two shouldn't be carrying your money out," Nancy told them. "You'll only lose it. Let me hold it for you."

Michael shook his head. "If I give it to you, I might forget it when I go shopping with Daddy."

"I promise I won't let you forget it."

"My pocket has a zipper. See? I'll keep it in that, and I'll hold Missy's for her."

"Well . . ." Nancy shrugged and gave up the discussion. She knew perfectly well that Michael wouldn't lose the dollar. He was like Ray, well organized. "Now, Mike, I'm going to straighten up. You be sure to stay with Missy."

"Okay," Michael said cheerfully. "Come on, Missy. I'll push you on the swing first."

Ray had built a swing for the children. It was suspended from a branch of the massive oak tree at the edge of the woods behind their house.

Nancy pulled Missy's mittens over her hands. They were bright red; fuzzy angora stitching formed a smile face on their backs. "Leave these on," she told her; "otherwise your hands will get cold. It's really getting raw. I'm not even sure you should go out at all."

"Oh, please!" Missy's lip began to quiver.

"All right, all right, don't go into the act," Nancy said hastily. "But not more than half an hour."

She opened the back door and let them out, then shivered as the chilling breeze enveloped her. She closed the door quickly and started up the staircase. The house was an authentic old Cape, and the stairway was almost totally vertical. Ray said that the old settlers must have had a bit of mountain goat in them the way they built their staircases. But Nancy loved everything about this place.

She could still remember the feeling of peace and welcome it had given her when she'd first seen it, over six years ago. She'd come to the Cape after the conviction had been set aside. The District Attorney hadn't pressed for a new trial because Rob Legler, his vital prosecution witness, had disappeared.

She'd fled here, completely across the continent—as far away from California as she could get; as far away from the people she'd known and the place she'd lived and the college and the whole academic community there. She never wanted to see them again—the friends who had turned out not to be friends but hostile strangers who spoke of "poor Carl" because they blamed his suicide on her too.

She'd come to Cape Cod because she'd always heard that New Englanders and Cape people were reticent and reserved and wanted nothing to do with strangers, and that was good. She needed a place to hide, to find herself, to sort it all out, to try to think through what had happened, to try to come back to life.

She'd cut her hair and dyed it sable brown, and that was enough to make her look completely different from the pictures that had front-paged newspapers all over the country during the trial.

She guessed that only fate could have prompted her to elect Ray's real estate office when she went looking for a house to rent. She'd actually made an appointment with another realtor, but on impulse she'd gone in to see him first because she liked his hand-lettered sign and the window boxes that were filled with yellow and champagne mums.

She had waited until he finished with another client—a leathery-faced old man with thick, curling hair—and admired the way Ray advised him to hang on to his property, that he'd find a tenant for the apartment in the house to help carry expenses.

After the old man left she said, "Maybe I'm here at the right time. I want to rent a house."

But he wouldn't even show her the old Hunt place. "The Lookout is too big, too lonesome and too drafty for you," he said. "But I just got in a rental on an authentic Cape in excellent condition that's fully furnished. It can even be bought eventually, if you like it. How much room do you need, Miss . . . Mrs. . . . ?"

"Miss Kiernan," she told him. "Nancy Kiernan." Instinctively she used her mother's maiden name. "Not much, really. I won't be having company or visitors."

She liked the fact that he didn't pry or even look curious. "The Cape is a good place to come when you want to be by yourself," he said. "You can't be lonesome walking on the beach or watching the sunset or just looking out the window in the morning."

Then Ray had brought her up here, and immediately she knew that she would stay. The combination family and dining room had been fashioned from the old keeping room that had once been the heart of the house. She loved the rocking chair in front of the fireplace and the way the table was in front of the windows so that it was possible to eat and look down over the harbor and the bay.

She was able to move in right away, and if Ray wondered why she had absolutely nothing except the two suitcases she'd taken off the bus, he didn't show it. She said that her mother had died and she had sold their home in Ohio and decided to come East. She simply omitted talking about the six years that had lapsed in between.

That night, for the first time in months, she slept through the night— a deep, dreamless sleep in which she didn't hear Peter and Lisa calling her; wasn't in the courtroom listening to Carl condemn her.

That first morning here, she'd made coffee and sat by the window. It had been a clear, brilliant day—the cloudless sky purple-blue; the bay tranquil and still; the only movement the arc of sea gulls hovering near the fishing boats.

With her fingers wrapped around the coffee cup, she'd sipped and watched. The warmth of the coffee had flowed through her body. The sunbeams had warmed her face. The tranquility of the scene enhanced the calming sense of peace that the long, dreamless sleep had begun.

Peace . . . give me peace. That had been her prayer during the trial; in prison. *Let me learn to accept.* Seven years ago . . .

Nancy sighed, realizing that she was still standing by the bottom step of the staircase. It was so easy to get lost in remembering. That was why she tried so hard to live each day . . . not look back or into the future.

She began to go upstairs slowly. How could there ever be peace for her, knowing that if Rob Legler ever showed up they'd try her again for murder; take her away from Ray and Missy and Michael? For an instant, she dropped her face into her hands. *Don't think about it,* she told herself. *It's no use.*

At the head of the stairs she shook her head determinedly and walked quickly into the master bedroom. She threw open the windows and shivered as the wind blew the curtains back against her. Clouds were starting to form, and the water in the bay had begun to churn with whitecaps. The temperature was dropping rapidly. Nancy was enough of a Cape person now to know that a cold wind like this usually blew in a storm.

But it really was still clear enough to have the children out. She liked them to have as much fresh air as possible in the morning. After lunch, Missy napped and Michael went to kindergarten.

She started to pull the sheets from the big double bed and hesitated. Missy had been sniffling yesterday. Should she go down and warn her not to unzip the neck of her jacket? It was one of her favorite tricks. Missy always complained that all her clothes felt too tight at the neck.

Nancy deliberated an instant, then pulled the sheets completely back and off the bed. Missy had on a turtleneck shirt. Her throat would be covered even if she undid the button. Besides, it would take only ten or fifteen minutes to strip and change the beds and turn on a wash.

Ten minutes at the most, Nancy promised herself, to quiet the nagging feeling of worry that was insistently telling her to go out to the children *now*.

≈ CHAPTER 2

Some mornings Jonathan Knowles walked to the drugstore to pick up his morning paper. Other days he pedaled on his bike. His outing always took him past the old Nickerson house, the one that Ray Eldredge had bought when he married the pretty girl who was renting it.

When old Sam Nickerson had had the place it had begun to be run-down, but now it looked snug and solid. Ray had put on a new roof and had painted the trim, and his wife certainly had a green thumb. The yellow and orange mums in the window boxes gave a cheerful warmth even to the bleakest day.

In nice weather, Nancy Eldredge was often out early in the morning working on her garden. She always had a pleasant greeting for him and then went back to her work. Jonathan admired that trait in a woman. He'd known Ray's folks when they were summer people up here. Of course, the Eldredges had helped settle the Cape. Ray's father had told Jonathan the whole family line right back to the one who had come over on the *Mayflower*.

The fact that Ray shared enough love for the Cape to decide to build his business career here was particularly exemplary in Jonathan's eyes. The Cape had lakes and ponds and the bay and the ocean. It had woods to walk in, and land for people to spread out on. And it was a good place for a young couple to raise children. It was a good place to retire and live out the end of your life. Jonathan and Emily had always spent vacations here and looked forward to the day when they'd be able to stay here the year around. They'd almost made it, too. But for Emily it wasn't to be.

Jonathan sighed. He was a big man, with thick white hair and a broad face that was beginning to fold into jowls. A retired lawyer, he'd found inactivity depressing. You couldn't do much fishing in the winter. And poking around antique stores and refinishing furniture wasn't the fun it had been when Emily was with him. But in this second year of his permanent residency at the Cape, he'd started to write a book.

Begun as a hobby, it had become an absorbing daily activity. A publisher friend had read a few chapters of it one weekend and promptly sent him a contract. The book was a case study of famous murder trials. Jonathan worked on it five hours every day, seven days a week, starting promptly at nine-thirty in the morning.

The wind bit against him. He pulled out his muffler, grateful for the watery sunshine he felt on his face as he glanced in the direction of the bay. With the shrubbery stripped, you could see clear to the water. Only the old Hunt house on its high bluff interrupted the view—the house they called The Lookout.

Jonathan always looked at the bay right at this point of his trip. This morning again, he squinted as he turned his head. Irritated, he looked back at the road after barely registering the stormy, churning whitecaps. That fellow who rented the house must have something metallic in the window, he thought. It was a damn nuisance. He felt like asking Ray to mention it to him, then ruefully brushed the thought away. The tenant might just suggest that Jonathan check the bay somewhere else along the way.

He shrugged unconsciously. He was directly in front of the Eldredge house, and Nancy was sitting at the breakfast table by the window talking to the little boy. The little girl was on her lap. Jonathan glanced away quickly, feeling like an intruder and not wanting to catch her eye. Oh, well, he'd get the paper, fix his solitary breakfast and get to his desk. Today he'd begin working on the Harmon murder case—the one that he suspected would make the most interesting chapter of all.

CHAPTER 3

Ray pushed open the door of his office, unable to shake the nagging sensation of worry that like an unlocated toothache was throbbing somewhere inside him. What was the matter? It was more than just making Nancy acknowledge her birthday and risking the memories it aroused. Actually, she'd been pretty calm. He knew her well enough to understand when the tension was building about that other life.

It could be triggered by something like the sight of a dark-haired boy and girl together who were the age of her other children, or a discussion of the murder of that little girl who'd been found dead in Cohasset last year. But Nancy was all right this morning. It was something else—a feeling of foreboding.

"Oh, no! What does that mean?"

Ray looked up, startled. Dorothy was at her desk. Her hair, more gray than brown, casually framed her long, pleasant face. Her sensible beige sweater and brown tweed skirt had an almost studied dowdiness and signaled the wearer's indifference to frills.

Dorothy had been Ray's first client when he had opened this office. The girl he had hired didn't show up, and Dorothy had volunteered to help him out for a few days. She'd been with him ever since.

"You do realize that you're shaking your head and frowning," she told him.

Ray smiled sheepishly. "Just morning jitters, I guess. How are you doing?"

Dorothy immediately became businesslike. "Fine. I have the file all together on The Lookout. What time do you expect that fellow who wants to see it?"

"Around two," Ray told her. He bent over her desk. "Where did you ever dig out those plans?"

"They're on file in the library. Don't forget, that house was begun in sixteen-ninety. It would make a marvelous restaurant. If anyone is willing to spend money renovating it, it could be a showcase. And you can't beat that waterfront location."

"I gather Mr. Kragopoulos and his wife have built up and sold several restaurants and don't mind spending the dollars to do everything the way it should be done."

"I've never yet met a Greek who couldn't make a go of a restaurant," Dorothy commented as she closed the file.

"And all Englishmen are fags and no German has a sense of humor and most Puerto Ricans—I mean Spics—are on welfare. . . . God, I hate labels!" Ray took his pipe from his breast pocket and jammed it into his mouth.

"What?" Dorothy looked up at him bewildered. "I certainly was not labeling—or I guess, maybe I was, but not in the way you took it." She turned her back to him as she put the file away, and Ray stalked into his private office and closed the door.

He had hurt her. Stupidly, unnecessarily. What in the hell was the matter with him? Dorothy was the most decent, fair-minded, nonbiased person he knew. What a lousy thing to say to her. Sighing, he reached for the humidor on his desk and filled his pipe. He puffed thoughtfully on it for fifteen minutes before he dialed Dorothy's extension.

"Yes." Her voice was constrained when she picked up the phone.

"Are the girls in yet?"

"Yes."

"Coffee made?"

"Yes." Dorothy did not ask him if he was ready to have some.

"Would you mind bringing yours in here and a cup for me? And ask the girls to hold calls for fifteen minutes."

"All right." Dorothy hung up.

Ray got up to open the door for her, and when she came in with the steaming cups he carefully closed it.

"Peace," he said contritely. "I'm terribly sorry."

"I believe that," Dorothy said, "and it's all right, but what's the matter?"

"Sit down, please." Ray gestured to the rust-colored leather chair by his desk. He took his coffee to the window and stared moodily out at the graying landscape.

"How would you like to come to our house for dinner tonight?" he asked. "We're celebrating Nancy's birthday."

He heard her sharp intake of breath and spun around. "Do you think it's a mistake?"

Dorothy was the only one on the Cape who knew about Nancy. Nancy herself had told her and asked her advice before she had agreed to marry Ray.

Dorothy's voice and eyes were speculative as she answered. "I don't know, Ray. What's the thinking behind a celebration?"

"The thinking is that you can't pretend that Nancy doesn't have birthdays! Of course, it's more than just that. It's that Nancy has got to break with the past, to stop hiding."

"*Can* she break with the past? *Can* she stop hiding with the prospect of another murder trial always hanging over her?"

"But that's just it. The *prospect.* Dorothy, do you realize that that fellow who testified against her hasn't been seen or heard of for over six years? God knows where he is now or if he's even alive. For all we know, he's sneaked back into this country under another name and is just as anxious as Nancy not to start the whole business up. Don't forget, he's officially a deserter from the Army. There's a pretty stiff penalty waiting for him if he's caught."

"That's probably true," Dorothy agreed.

"It *is* true. And take it one step further. Level with me, now. What do people in this town think of Nancy?—and I include the girls in my own office here."

Dorothy hesitated. "They think she's very pretty . . . they admire the way she wears clothes . . . they say she's always pleasant . . . and they think she keeps to herself pretty much."

"That's a nice way of putting it. I've heard cracks about my wife thinking she's 'too good for the folks around here.' At the club I'm getting more and more ribbing about why I only have a golf membership and why I don't bring that beautiful wife of mine around. Last week Michael's school called and asked if Nancy would consider working on some committee. Needless to say, she turned them down. Last month I finally got her to go to the realtors' dinner, and when they took the group picture, she was in the ladies' room."

"She's afraid of being recognized."

"I understand that. But don't you see that that possibility gets less likely all the time? And even if someone said to her 'You're a dead ringer for that girl from California who was accused' . . . well, you know what I mean, Dorothy. For most people it would end there. A resemblance. Period. God, remember that guy who used to pose for all those whiskey and bank ads, the one who was a ringer for Lyndon Johnson? I was in the Army with his nephew. People do look like other people. It's that simple. And if there ever is another trial, I want Nancy to be entrenched with the people here. I want them to feel she's one of them and that they're rooting for her. Because after she's acquitted, she'll have to come here and take up life again. We all will."

"And if there's a trial and she *isn't* acquitted?"

"I simply won't consider that possibility," Ray said flatly. "How about it? Have we got a date tonight?"

"I'd like very much to come," Dorothy said. "And I agree with most of what you've said."

"Most?"

"Yes." She looked at him steadily. "I think you've got to ask yourself how much of this sudden desire to opt for a more normal life is just for Nancy and how much because of other motives."

"Meaning what?"

"Ray, I was here when the Secretary of State of Massachusetts urged you to go into politics because the Cape needs young men of your caliber to represent it. I heard him say that he'd give you any help and endorsement possible. It's pretty hard not to be able to take him up on that. But as things stand now, you can't. And you know it."

Dorothy left the room without giving him a chance to answer. Ray finished the coffee and sat down at his desk. The anger and irritation and tension drained from him, and he felt depressed and ashamed of himself. She was right, of course. He did want to pretend that there wasn't any threat hanging over them, that everything was just nifty. And he had a hell of a nerve, too. He'd known what he was getting into when he'd married Nancy. If he hadn't, she certainly had pointed it out. She'd done her best to warn him.

Ray stared unseeingly at the mail on his desk, thinking of the times in the last few months when he'd blown up unreasonably at Nancy just the way he had this morning at Dorothy. Like the way he had acted when she had shown him the watercolor she'd done of the house. She should study art. Even now she was good enough to exhibit locally. He'd said, "It's very good. Now which closet are you going to hide it in?"

Nancy had looked so stricken, so defenseless. He'd wanted to bite his tongue off. He'd said, "Honey, I'm so sorry. It's just that I'm so proud of you. I want you to show it off."

How many of these flare-ups were being caused because he was tired of the constant constriction on their activities?

He sighed and started going through his mail.

At quarter past ten, Dorothy threw open the door of his office. Her usually healthy pink complexion was a sickly grayish white. He jumped up to go to her. But shaking her head, she pushed the door closed behind her and held out the paper she'd been hiding under her arm.

It was the weekly *Cape Cod Community News.* Dorothy had it open to the second section, the one that always featured a human-interest story. She dropped it on his desk.

Together they stared down at the large picture that to anyone was unmistakably Nancy. It was one he'd never seen before, in her tweed suit, with her hair pulled back and already darkened. The caption under it said, CAN THIS BE A HAPPY BIRTHDAY FOR NANCY HARMON? Another picture showed Nancy leaving the courtroom during her trial, her face wooden and expressionless, her hair cascading down her shoulders. A third picture was a copy of a snapshot of Nancy with her arms around two young children.

The first line of the story read: "Somewhere today Nancy Harmon is celebrating her 32nd birthday and the seventh anniversary of the death of the children she was found guilty of murdering."

 *CHAPTER 4*

It was timing. The whole universe existed because of split-second timing. Now his timing would be perfect. Hurriedly, he backed the station wagon out of the garage. It was such a cloudy day it had been hard to see much through the telescope, but he could tell that she'd been putting the children's coats on.

He felt in his pocket and the needles were there—filled, ready to use, to produce instant unconsciousness; dreamless, absolute sleep.

He could feel the perspiration starting under his arms and in his groin, and great beads of it were forming on his forehead and rolling down his cheeks. That was bad. It was a cold day. Mustn't look excited or nervous.

He took a precious few seconds to dab his face with the old towel he kept on the front seat and glanced over his shoulder. The canvas raincoat was the kind many Cape men kept in their cars, especially around fishing season; so were the rods that showed against the back window. But that coat was big enough to cover two small children. He giggled excitedly and swung the car toward Route 6A.

Wiggins' Market was on the corner of this road and Route 6A. Whenever he was at the Cape he shopped there. Of course, he brought most of the staples he needed with him whenever he came to stay. It was too risky to go out much. There was always the chance that he'd run into Nancy and she'd recognize him even with his changed appearance. It had almost happened four years ago. He'd been in a supermarket in Hyannis Port and he'd heard her voice behind him. He was reaching for a jar of coffee, and her hand went right up next to his as she took a jar from the same shelf. She was saying, "Wait a minute, Mike. I want to get something here," and while he froze, she brushed against him and murmured "Oh, I'm sorry."

He didn't dare to answer—just stood there—and she moved on. He was positive she hadn't even looked at him. But after that he had never risked a meeting. It was necessary, though, for him to establish a casual routine in Adams Port, because someday it might be important for people to dismiss his comings and goings as routine. That was why he bought milk and bread and meat at Wiggins' Market always about ten in the morning. Nancy never left the house before eleven, and even then she always went to Lowery's market, down the road a half mile. And the Wigginses had begun to greet him as a customer of long standing. Well, he'd be there in a few minutes, right on schedule.

There wasn't anyone out walking at all. The raw wind was probably discouraging any inclination to go outdoors. He was almost to Route 6A and slowed to a full stop.

The incredible luck. There wasn't a car in either direction. Quickly he accelerated, and the station wagon shot across the main street and onto the road that ran along the back of the Eldredge property. Audacity—that was all it took. Any fool could try to come up with a foolproof plan. But to have a plan so simple that it was unbelievable even to call it a plan—a schedule timed to the split second—that was real genius. To willingly leave yourself open to failure—to tightrope-walk across a dozen pits so that when the act was accomplished no one even glanced in your direction—that was the way.

Ten minutes of ten. The children had probably been out one minute now. Oh, he knew the possibilities. One of them might have gone into the house to the bathroom or for a drink of water, but not likely, not likely. Every day for a month straight he'd watched them. Unless it was actually raining, they came out to play. She never came to check them for ten to fifteen minutes. They never went back into the house for those same ten minutes.

Nine minutes of ten. He steered the car into the dirt road on their property. The community paper would be delivered in a few minutes. That article would be out today. Motivation for Nancy to explode into violence . . . exposure of her part . . . all the people in this town talking in shocked tones, walking by this house, staring . . .

He stopped the car halfway into the woods. No one could see it from the road. She couldn't see it from the house. He got out quickly and, keeping close to the protection of the trees, hurried to the children's play area. The leaves were off most of the trees, but there were enough pines and other evergreens to shield him.

He could hear the children's voices before he saw them. The boy, his voice panting a little—he must be pushing the girl on the swing . . . "We'll ask Daddy what to buy for Mommy. I'll take both our money."

The girl laughed. "Good, Mike, good. Higher, Mike—push me higher, please."

He stole up behind the boy, who heard him in that last second. He had an impression of startled blue eyes and a mouth that rounded in terror before he covered both with one hand and with the other plunged the needle through the woolen mitten. The boy tried to pull away, stiffened, then crumpled noiselessly to the ground.

The swing was coming back—the girl calling, "Push, Mike—don't stop pushing." He caught the swing by the right side chain, stopped it and encircled the small, uncomprehending wiggly body. Carefully stifling the soft cry, he plunged the other needle through the red mitten that had a smiling kitten face sewn on the back. An instant later, the girl sighed and slumped against him.

He didn't notice that one mitten caught on the swing and was pulled off as he easily lifted both children in his arms and ran to the car.

At five minutes of ten they were crumpled under the canvas raincoat. He backed down the dirt road and onto the paved highway behind Nancy's property. He cursed as he saw a small Dodge sedan coming toward him. It slowed up slightly to let him pull into the right lane, and he turned his head away.

Damn the luck. As he passed, he managed a swift sidelong glance at the driver of the other car and got an impression of a sharp nose and thin chin silhouetted from under a shapeless hat. The other driver didn't seem to turn his head at all.

He had a fleeting feeling of familiarity: probably someone from the Cape, but maybe not aware that the station wagon he had slowed up for had come off the narrow dirt road leading from the Eldredge property. Most people weren't observant. In a few minutes this man probably wouldn't even have a recollection of having slowed for an instant to let a car complete a turn.

He watched the Dodge through the rearview mirror until it disappeared. With a grunt of satisfaction, he adjusted the mirror so that it reflected the canvas raincoat on the back deck. It was apparently tossed casually over fishing gear. Satisfied, he flipped the mirror back into place without looking into it again. If he had looked into it, he would have seen that the car he had just been watching was slowing, backing up.

At four minutes past ten he walked into Wiggins' Market and grunted a greeting as he reached into the refrigerator section for a quart of milk.

CHAPTER 5

Nancy came down the steep staircase precariously balancing an armful of towels and sheets, pajamas and underwear. On impulse she'd decided to do a wash that could be hung outdoors to dry before the storm broke. Winter was here. It was on the edge of the yard, forcing the last few dead leaves off the trees. It was settling into the dirt road that now was as hardened as concrete. It was changing the color of the bay into a smoky gray-blue.

Outside, the storm was building, but now, while there was still some weak sun, she'd take advantage of it. She loved the fresh smell of sheets dried outside; loved to pull them against her face as she drifted off to sleep with the way they captured the faint scent of cranberry bogs and pine and the salty smell of the sea—so different from the coarse, rough, dank smell of prison sheets. She pushed the thought away.

At the foot of the staircase she started to turn in the direction of the back door, then stopped. How foolish. The children were fine. They'd been out only fifteen minutes, and this frantic anxiety that was her constant albatross had to be conquered. Even now she suspected that Missy sensed it and was beginning to respond to her overprotection. She'd turn the wash on, then call them in. While they watched their ten-thirty television program, she'd have a second cup of coffee and look at the weekly *Cape Cod Community News*. With the season over, there might be some good antiques available and not at tourist prices. She wanted an old-fashioned settee for the parlor—the high-backed kind they used to call a "settle" in the seventeen-hundreds.

In the laundry room off the kitchen she sorted the wash, tossed the sheets and towels into the machine, added detergent and bleach and finally pushed the button to start the cycle.

Now it surely was time to call the children. But at the front door she detoured. The paper had just arrived. The delivery boy was disappearing around the curve in the road. She picked it up, shivering against the increasing wind, and hurried into the kitchen. She turned the burner jet under the still-warm coffeepot. Then, anxious to get a look at the classified page, she thumbed quickly to the second section of the paper.

Her eyes focused on the blaring headline and the pictures—all the pictures: of her and Carl and Rob Legler; the one of her with Peter and Lisa . . . that clinging, trusting way they'd always huddled up to her. Through a roaring in her ears she remembered vividly the time they'd posed for that one. Carl had taken it.

"Don't pay attention to me," he'd said; "pretend I'm not here." But they'd known he was there and had shrunk against her, and she had looked down at them as he snapped the picture. Her hands were touching their silky, dark heads.

"No . . . no . . . no . . . no . . . !" Now her body arched in pain. Unsteadily she reached out her hand, and it hit the coffeepot, knocking it over. She drew it back, only dimly feeling the searing liquid that splattered on her fingers.

She had to burn the paper. Michael and Missy mustn't see it. That was it. She'd burn the paper so that no one could see it. She ran to the fireplace in the dining room.

The fireplace . . . that wasn't cheery and warm and protecting anymore. Because there was no haven . . . there never could be a haven for her. She squeezed the paper together and reached unsteadily for the box of matches on the mantel. A wisp of smoke and a flame, and then the paper began to burn as she stuffed it between the logs.

Everyone on the Cape was reading that paper. They'd know . . . they'd all know. The one picture they'd surely recognize. She didn't even remember that anyone had seen her after she'd cut her hair and dyed it. The paper was burning brightly now. She watched as the picture with Peter and Lisa flamed, and charred and curled. Dead, both of them; and she'd be better off with them. There was no place to hide for her . . . or to forget. Ray could take care of Michael and Missy. Tomorrow in Michael's class the children would be looking at him, whispering, pointing their fingers.

The children. She must save the children. No, *get* the children. That was it. They'd catch cold.

She stumbled to the back door and pulled it open. "Peter . . . Lisa . . ." she called. No, no! It was Michael and Missy. *They* were her children.

"Michael. Missy. Come here. Come in now!" Her wail heightened to a shriek. Where were they? She hurried out to the backyard, unmindful of the cold that bit through her light sweater.

The swing. They must have gotten off the swing. They were probably in the woods. "Michael. Missy. Michael! Missy! Don't hide! Come here now!"

The swing was still moving. The wind was making it sway. Then she saw the mitten. Missy's mitten, caught in the metal loops of the swing.

From far off she heard a sound. What sound? The children.

The lake! They must be at the lake. They weren't supposed to go there, but maybe they had. They'd be found. Like the others. In the water. Their faces wet and swollen and still.

She grabbed Missy's mitten, the mitten with the smile face, and staggered toward the lake. She called their names over and over again. She pushed her way through the woods and out onto the sandy beach.

In the lake a little way out, something was glistening below the surface. Was it something red . . . another mitten . . . Missy's hand? She plunged into the icy water as far as her shoulders and reached down. But there wasn't anything there. Frantically Nancy clutched her fingers together so that they formed a strainer, but there was nothing—only the terrible numbing cold water. She looked down, trying to see to the bottom; leaned over and fell. The water gushed into her nostrils and mouth and burned her face and neck.

Somehow she staggered up and back before her wet clothes pulled her down again. She fell onto the ice-crusted sand. Through the roar in her ears and the mist that was closing in front of her eyes, she looked into the woods and saw him—his face . . . *Whose* face?

The mist closed over her eyes completely. Sounds died away: the mournful cackle of the sea gull . . . the lapping of the water . . . Silence.

It was there that Ray and Dorothy found her. Shivering uncontrollably, lying on the sand, her hair and clothes plastered to her head and body, her eyes blank and uncomprehending, angry blisters raised on the hand that clutched a small red mitten to her cheek.

CHAPTER 6

Jonathan carefully washed and rinsed his breakfast dishes, scoured the omelet pan and swept the kitchen floor. Emily had been naturally, effortlessly neat, and years of living with her had made him appreciate the intrinsic comfort of tidiness. He always hung his clothes in the closets, put his laundry in the bathroom hamper and cleared up immediately after his solitary meals. He even had an eye for the kind of detail that his cleaning woman missed and after she left on Wednesdays would do small jobs like washing canisters and bric-a-brac and polishing surfaces that she'd left cloudy with wax.

In New York he and Emily had lived on Sutton Place, on the southeast corner of Fifty-fifth Street. Their apartment building had extended over the F.D.R. Drive to the edge of the East River. Sometimes they had sat on their seventeenth-floor balcony and watched the lights of the bridges that spanned the river and talked about the time when they'd be retired at the Cape and looking out over Maushop Lake.

"You won't have Bertha in every day to keep the wheels spinning," he'd teased her.

"By the time we get up there, Bertha will be ready to retire and I'll break you in as my assistant. All we'll really need is a weekly cleaning woman. How about you? Will you miss having a car pick you up at the door anytime you want it?"

Jonathan had answered that he'd decided to buy a bicycle. "I'd do it now," he'd told Emily, "but I'm afraid some of our clients might get upset if the word was around that I arrived at work on a tenspeeder."

"And you'll try your hand at writing," Emily had prodded. "I sometimes wish you'd just taken a chance and done it years ago."

"Never could afford to, married to you," he'd said. "The one-woman war against recession. All Fifth Avenue stays in the black when Mrs. Knowles goes shopping."

"It's your fault," she'd retorted. "You're always telling me to spend your money."

"I like spending it on you," he'd told her, "and I have no complaints. I've been lucky."

If only they'd had even a few years up here together . . . Jonathan sighed and hung up the dish towel. Seeing Nancy Eldredge and her children framed in the window this morning had vaguely depressed him. Maybe it was the weather or the long winter setting in, but he was restless, apprehensive. Something was bothering him. It was the kind of itch he used to get when he was preparing a brief and some facts just didn't jibe.

Well, he'd get to his desk. He was anxious to start working on the Harmon chapter.

He could have taken early retirement, he thought, as he walked slowly into his study. As it turned out, that was just what he had done anyway. The minute he lost Emily, he'd sold the New York apartment, put in his resignation, pensioned off Bertha and, like a dog licking its wounds, had come here to this house that they'd picked out together. After the first bleak grief, he'd found a measure of contentment.

Now writing the book was a fascinating and absorbing experience. When he'd gotten the idea for doing it, he had asked Kevin Parks, a meticulous free-lance researcher and old friend, to come up for a weekend. Then he had outlined his plan to him. Jonathan had selected ten controversial criminal trials. He'd proposed that Kev take on the job of putting together a file of all available material on those trials: court transcripts; depositions; newspaper accounts; pictures; gossip—anything he could find. Jonathan planned to study each file thoroughly and then decide how to write the chapter—either agreeing with the verdict or rejecting it, and giving his reasons. He was calling the book "Verdict in Doubt."

He'd already finished three chapters. The first was called "The Sam Sheppard Trial." His opinion: not guilty. Too many loopholes; too much suppressed evidence. Jonathan agreed with the Dorothy Kilgallen opinion that the jury had found Sam Sheppard guilty of adultery, not murder.

The second chapter was "The Cappolino Trial." Marge Farger, in his opinion, belonged in a prison cell with her former boyfriend.

The just-completed chapter was "The Edgar Smith Trial." Jonathan's view was that Edgar Smith was guilty but deserved his freedom. Fourteen years constituted a life sentence today, and he had rehabilitated and educated himself in a grisly cell on Death Row.

Now he sat down at his massive desk and reached into the file drawer for the thick cardboard folders that had arrived the previous day. They were labeled THE HARMON CASE.

A note from Kevin was stapled to the first envelope. It read:

> Jon, I have a hunch you'll enjoy getting your teeth into this one. The defendant was a sitting duck for the prosecutor; even her husband broke down on the stand and practically accused her in front of the jury. If they ever locate the missing prosecution witness and try her again, she'd better have a stronger story than last time. The District Attorney's office out there knows where she is, but I couldn't get it from them; somewhere in the East is the best I can do.

Jonathan opened the file with the accelerating pulse that he always associated with the beginning of an interesting new case. He never allowed himself to do much speculating until he got the research all together, but his memory of this case when it was being tried six or seven years ago made him curious. He remembered how at that time just reading the trial testimony had left so many questions in his mind . . . questions he wanted to concentrate on now. He recalled that his overall impression of the Harmon case was that Nancy Harmon never had told all she knew about the disappearance of her children.

He reached into the folder and began to lay out the meticulously labeled items on the desk. There were pictures of Nancy Harmon taken during her trial. She certainly was a pretty little thing with that waist-length hair. According to the papers she was twenty-five at the time the murders were committed. She looked even younger—not much more than a teen-ager. The dresses she wore were so youthful . . . almost childish . . . they added to the overall effect. Probably her attorney had suggested that she look as young as possible.

Funny, but ever since he'd started planning this book he'd felt that he'd seen that girl somewhere. He stared at the pictures in front of him. Of course. She looked like a younger version of Ray Eldredge's wife! That explained the nagging resemblance. The expression was totally different, but wouldn't it be a small world if there was some family relationship?

His eye fell on the first typewritten page, which gave a rundown on Nancy Harmon. She had been born in California and raised in Ohio. Well, that let out any possibility of her being a close relative to Nancy Eldredge. Ray's wife's family had been neighbors of Dorothy Prentiss in Virginia.

Dorothy Prentiss. He felt a quick dart of pleasure at the thought of the handsome woman who worked with Ray. Jonathan often stopped by their office around five o'clock, when he picked up the evening paper, the Boston *Globe*. Ray had suggested some interesting land investments to him, and they had all proved sound. He'd also persuaded Jonathan to become active in the town, and as a result they'd become good friends.

Still, Jonathan realized that he went into Ray's office more often than necessary. Ray would say, "You're just in time for an end-of-the-day drink" and call out to Dorothy to join them.

Emily had liked daiquiris. Dorothy always had Jonathan's favorite drink—a Rob Roy with a twist. The three of them would sit for a half hour or so in Ray's private office.

Dorothy had a penetrating humor that he enjoyed. Her family had been show-business people, and she had countless great stories about traveling with them. She'd planned a career too, but after three small parts Off Broadway she had gotten married and settled down in Virginia. After her husband died she'd come up to the Cape planning to open an interior-decorating shop, then had gotten started working with Ray. Ray said that Dorothy was a hell of a real estate saleswoman. She could help people visualize the possibilities in a place, no matter how seedy it looked at first glance.

More and more often lately Jonathan had toyed with the idea of suggesting that Dorothy join him for dinner. Sundays were long, and a couple of Sunday afternoons recently he'd actually started to dial her number, then stopped. He didn't want to rush into getting involved with someone he'd run into constantly. And he just wasn't sure. Maybe she came on a little too strong for him. All those years of living with Emily's total femininity had made him somewhat unprepared for reacting on a personal level to a terribly independent woman.

God, what was the matter with him? He was so easily diverted into woolgathering this morning. Why was he letting himself get distracted from this Harmon case?

Resolutely he lit his pipe, picked up the file and leaned back in his chair. Deliberately he picked up the first batch of papers.

An hour and fifteen minutes passed. The silence was unbroken except for the ticking of the clock, the increasing insistence of the wind through the pines outside his window and Jonathan's occasional snort of disbelief. Finally, frowning in concentration, he laid the papers down and walked slowly to the kitchen to make coffee. Something smelled about that whole Harmon trial. From as much of the transcript as he'd read through so far it was evident that there was something fishy there . . . an undercurrent that made it impossible for the facts to hang together in any kind of reasonably cohesive way.

He went into the immaculate kitchen and absently half-filled the kettle. While he waited for it to heat, he walked to the front door. The *Cape Cod Community News* was already on the porch. Tucking it under his arm, he went back into the kitchen, poured a rounded teaspoon of Taster's Choice into a cup, added the boiling water, stirred and began to sip as with the other hand he turned the pages of the paper, scanning the contents.

He had almost finished the coffee when he got to the second section. His hand with the cup stopped in mid-air as his gaze froze on the picture of Ray Eldredge's wife.

In that first instant of realization, Jonathan sadly accepted two irrefutable facts: Dorothy Prentiss had deliberately lied to him about having known Nancy as a child in Virginia; and retired or not, he should have been enough of a lawyer to trust his own instincts. Subconsciously, he had always suspected that Nancy Harmon and Nancy Eldredge were one and the same person.

t was so cold. There was a gritty taste in her mouth. Sand—why? Where was she?

She could hear Ray calling her, feel him bending over her, cradling her against him. "Nancy, what's the matter? Nancy, where are the children?"

She could hear the fear in his voice. She tried to raise her hand, then felt it fall loosely by her side. She tried to speak, but no words formed on her lips. Ray was there, but she couldn't reach him.

She heard Dorothy say, "Pick her up, Ray. Take her to the house. We have to get help looking for the children."

The children. They must find them. Nancy wanted to tell Ray to look for them. She felt her lips trying to form words, but the words wouldn't come.

"Oh, my God!" She heard the break in Ray's voice. She wanted to say, "Don't bother with me; don't bother with me. Look for the children." But she couldn't speak. She felt him pick her up and hold her against him. "What's happened to her, Dorothy?" he asked. "What's the matter with her?"

"Ray, we've got to call the police."

"The police!" Vaguely Nancy could hear the resistance in his voice.

"Of course. We need help finding the children. Ray, hurry! Every moment is precious. Don't you see—you can't protect Nancy now. Everyone will know her from that picture."

The picture. Nancy felt herself being carried. Remotely she knew she was shivering. But that wasn't what she had to think about. It was the picture of her in the tweed suit she'd bought after the conviction was overturned. They'd taken her out of prison and brought her to court. The state hadn't tried her again. Carl was dead, and the student who'd testified against her had disappeared, and so she'd been released.

The prosecuting attorney had said to her, "Don't think this is over. If I spend the rest of my life, I'll find a way to get a conviction that sticks." And with his words beating against her, she'd left the courtroom.

Afterward, when she'd received permission to leave the state, she'd had her hair cut and dyed and gone shopping. She had always hated the kind of clothes Carl liked her to wear and had bought the three-piece suit and brown turtleneck sweater. She still wore the jacket and slacks; she'd worn them shopping only last week. That was another reason the picture was so recognizable. The picture . . . it had been taken in the bus terminal; that was where she'd been.

She hadn't known that anyone was taking a picture of her. She'd left on the last evening bus for Boston. The terminal hadn't been crowded, and no one had paid any attention to her. She'd really thought that she could just slip away and try to begin again. But someone had just been waiting to start it all over again.

I want to die, she thought. *I want to die.*

Ray was walking swiftly, but trying to shield her with his jacket. The wind was biting through the wet clothes. He couldn't shield her; not even he could shield her. It was too late. . . . Maybe it had always been too late. Peter and Lisa and Michael and Missy. They were all gone. . . . It was too late for all of them.

No. No. No. Michael and Missy. They were here a little while ago. They were playing. They were out on the swing and then the mitten was there. Michael wouldn't leave Missy. He was so careful of her. It was like last time. Last time, and they'd find them the way they found Peter and Lisa, with the wet seaweed and bits of plastic on their faces and in their hair and their bodies swollen.

They must be at the house. Dorothy was opening the door and saying, "I'll call the police, Ray."

Nancy felt the darkness coming at her. She began sliding back and away. . . . No . . . no . . . no. . . .

～ CHAPTER 8

Oh, the activity. Oh, the way they were all scurrying around like ants—all milling around her house and yard. He licked his lips anxiously. They were so dry when all the rest of him was wet—his hands and feet and groin and underarms. Perspiration was streaming down his neck and back.

As soon as he got back to the big house, he carried the children in and brought them right up to the room with the telescope. He could keep an eye on them here and talk to them when they woke up and touch them.

Maybe he'd give the little girl a bath and dry her off in a nice soft towel and rub baby powder on her and kiss her. He had all day to spend with the children. All day; the tide wouldn't come in until seven tonight. By then it would be dark, and no one would be nearby to see or hear. It would be days before they'd be washed in. It would be like last time.

It was so much more enjoyable touching them when he knew their mother was being questioned by now. "What did you do with your children?" they'd ask her.

He watched more police cars swarm up the dirt road into her back-yard. But some of them were passing the house. Why were so many of them going to Maushop Lake? Of course. They thought she had taken the children there.

He felt wonderfully gratified. Here he could see everything that was happening without risk, perfectly safe and comfortable. He wondered if Nancy was crying. She had never cried once at her trial until the very end—after the judge sentenced her to the gas chamber. She'd begun sobbing and buried her face in her hands to cover the sound. The court attendants had snapped handcuffs on her, and her long hair had spilled forward, covering the tearstained face that looked hopelessly out at the hostile faces.

He remembered the first time he'd seen her walking across the campus. He'd been immediately attracted to her—the way the wind blew her strawberry-gold hair around her shoulders; the delicately formed face; the small, even white teeth; the enchanting round blue eyes that looked gravely out from thick, sooty brows and lashes.

He heard a sob. Nancy? But of course not. It was coming from the girl. Nancy's child. He turned from the telescope and stared resentfully. But his expression changed to a smile as he studied her. Those damp ringlets on her forehead; the tiny, straight nose; the fair skin . . . she looked a lot like Nancy. Now she wailed as she started to wake up. Well, it was just about time for the drug to wear off; they'd been unconscious nearly an hour.

Regretfully, he left the telescope. He'd laid the children on opposite ends of the musty-smelling velour couch. The little girl was crying in earnest now. "Mommy . . . Mommy." Her eyes were squeezed shut. Her mouth was open. . . . Her little tongue was so pink! Tears were running down her cheeks.

He sat her up and unzipped her jacket. She shrank away from him. "There, there," he said soothingly. "It's all right."

The boy stirred and woke up too. His eyes were startled, just as they had been when he had seen him in the yard. Now he sat up slowly. "Who are you?" he demanded. He rubbed his eyes, shook his head and looked around. "Where are we?"

An articulate child . . . well spoken . . . his voice clear and well modulated. That was good. Well-trained children were easier to handle. Didn't make a fuss. Taught respect for older people, they tended to be pliable. Like the others. They'd come with him so quietly that day. They had knelt in the trunk of the car unquestioningly when he had said they were going to play a game on Mommy.

"It's a game," he told this little boy. "I'm an old friend of your mommy's and she wants to play a birthday game. Did you know it was her birthday today?" He kept patting the little girl while he spoke. She felt so soft and good.

The boy—Michael—looked uncertain. "I don't like this game," he said firmly. Unsteadily he got to his feet. He pushed aside the hands that were touching Missy and reached for her. She clung to him. "Don't cry, Missy," he said soothingly. "it's just a silly game. We'll go home now."

It was obvious that he wasn't going to be fooled easily. The boy had Ray Eldredge's candid expression. "We're not going to play any of your games," he said. "We want to go home."

There was a wonderful way he could make the little boy cooperate. "Let go of your sister," he ordered. "Here, give her to me." He yanked her from the boy. With the other hand he took Michael's wrist and pulled him over to the window. "Do you know what a telescope is?"

Michael nodded uncertainly. "Yes. It's like the glasses my daddy has. It makes things bigger."

"That's right. You're very smart. Now, look in here." The boy put his eye to the viewer. "Now tell me what you see . . . No, squeeze your other eye shut."

"It's looking at my house."

"What do you see there?"

"There are lots of cars . . . police cars. What's the matter?" Alarm made his voice quiver.

He looked down happily at the worried face. A faint pinging sound came from the window. It was starting to sleet. The wind was driving hard little pellets against the glass panes. The visibility would be very poor soon. Even with the telescope it would be hard to see much. But he could have a wonderful time with the children—the whole, long afternoon. And he knew how to make the boy obey. "Do you know what it's like to be dead?" he asked.

"It means to go to God," Michael answered.

He nodded approvingly. "That's right. And this morning your mother went to God. That's why all the police cars are there. Your daddy asked me to mind you for a while and said for you to be good and help me take care of your sister."

Michael looked as though he'd cry too. His lip quivered as he said, "If my mommy went to God, I want to go too."

Running his fingers through Michael's hair, he rocked the still-wailing Missy. "You will," he told him. "Tonight. I promise."

The first reports went over the wire-service tickers at noon, in time to make bulletins on the news broadcasts throughout the country. Newscasters, hungering for a story, seized upon it and sent researchers scurrying to the files for records of the Nancy Harmon murder trial.

Publishers chartered planes to send their top crime reporters to Cape Cod.

In San Francisco, two assistant district attorneys listened to the bulletin. One said to the other, "Have I always said that bitch was as guilty as if I'd seen her kill those kids myself? Have I said it? So help me, if they don't hang this one on her, I'll take a leave of absence and personally comb the globe to find that Legler slob and get him back here to testify against her."

In Boston, Dr. Lendon Miles was enjoying the beginning of his lunch break. Mrs. Markley had just left. After a year of intense therapy she was finally beginning to get pretty good insight. She'd made a funny remark a few minutes ago. She'd been discussing an episode from her fourteenth year and said, "Do you realize that thanks to you I'm going through adolescence and change of life all at once? It's a hell of a deal." Only a few months ago she hadn't been doing much joking.

Lendon Miles enjoyed his profession. To him the mind was a delicate, complicated phenomenon—a mystery that could be unraveled only by a series of infinitely small revelations . . . one leading slowly, patiently into the next. He sighed. His ten-o'clock patient was in early analysis and had been extremely hostile.

He switched on the radio next to his desk to catch the balance of the noon news and was just in time to hear the bulletin.

A shadow of an old pain crossed his face. Nancy Harmon . . . Priscilla's daughter. After fourteen years he could still see Priscilla so clearly: the slender, elegant body; the way she held her head; the smile that came like quicksilver.

She had started working for him a year after her husband's death. She'd been thirty-eight then, two years his junior. Almost immediately he began taking her out to dinner when they worked late, and soon he realized that for the first time in his life the idea of marriage seemed logical and even essential. Until he met Priscilla, work, study, friends and freedom had been enough; he'd simply never met anyone who made him want to alter his status quo.

Gradually she'd told him about herself. Married after her first year in college to an airline pilot, she had one child, a daughter. The marriage had obviously been a happy one. Then on a trip to India her husband had come down with viral pneumonia and had died within twenty-four hours.

"It was so hard to take," Priscilla told him. "Dave flew over a million miles. He brought 707's down in blizzards. And then something so totally unexpected . . . I didn't realize people still died of pneumonia. . . ."

Lendon never did meet Priscilla's daughter. She had left for school in San Francisco soon after Priscilla had come to work for him. Priscilla had talked out her reasons for sending her so far away. "She was growing too close to me," Priscilla had worried. "She's taken Dave's death so hard. I want her to be happy and young and to get away from the whole climate of grief that I think is closing in on us. I went to Auberley and met Dave while I was there. Nancy had been with me to reunions so it isn't as if it's too strange to her."

In November Priscilla had taken a couple of days off to visit Nancy at college. Lendon had driven her to the airport. For a few minutes they had stood in the terminal waiting for her flight to be called. "Of course you know I'll miss you terribly," he'd said.

She was wearing a dark brown suede coat that showed off her patrician blond beauty. "I hope so," she said, and her eyes were clouded. "I'm so worried," she told him. "Nancy's letters are so down lately. I'm just terribly afraid. Did you ever have a feeling of something awful hanging over you?"

Then when he stared at her, they both began to laugh. "You see why I didn't dare mention this before," she said. "I knew you'd think I was crazy."

"On the contrary, my training has taught me to appreciate the value of hunches, only I call it intuition. But why didn't you tell me you were so worried? Maybe I should be going with you. I only wish I'd met Nancy before she left."

"Oh, no. It's probably me being a mother hen. Anyhow, I'll pick your brains when I get back." Somehow their fingers had become entwined.

"Don't worry. Kids all straighten out, and if there are any real problems, I'll fly out over the weekend if you want me."

"I shouldn't bother you. . . ."

An impersonal voice came over the loudspeaker: "Flight Five-six-nine now boarding for San Francisco . . ."

"Priscilla, for God's sake, don't you realize that I love you?"

"I'm glad. . . . I think . . . I know . . . I love you too."

Their last moment together. A beginning . . . a promise of love.

She had called him the next night. To say that she was worried and had to talk to him. She was at dinner with Nancy, but would call as soon as she got back to her hotel. Would he be home?

He waited all night for the call. But it never came. She never got back to the hotel. The next day he learned about the accident. The steering apparatus of the car she'd rented had failed. The car had careened off the road into a ditch.

He probably should have gone to Nancy. But when he finally got through to where she was staying, he spoke to Carl Harmon, the professor who said he and Nancy were planning to marry. He sounded perfectly competent and very much in charge. Nancy wouldn't be returning to Ohio. They had told her mother of their plans at dinner. Mrs. Kiernan had been concerned about Nancy's youth, but that was natural. She would be buried out there, where her husband was interred; the family had, after all, been residents of California for three generations until Nancy was a baby. Nancy was bearing up well. He thought that it was best for them to have a quiet wedding immediately. Nancy should not be alone now.

There had been nothing for London to do. What could he do? Tell Nancy that he and her mother had been falling in love? The odds were that she would simply have resented him. This Professor Harmon sounded fine, and undoubtedly Priscilla had simply been worried about Nancy's taking such a decisive step as marriage at barely eighteen. But surely there was nothing that he, London, could do about that decision.

He'd been glad to accept the offer to teach at the University of London. That was why he'd been out of the country and had never learned of the Harmon murder trial until after it was over.

It was at the University of London that he had met Allison. She was a teacher there, and the sense of sharing that Priscilla had begun to show him had made it impossible to go back to his well-ordered, solitary—selfish—life. From time to time he had wondered where Nancy Harmon had vanished. He'd been living in the Boston area for the last two years, and she was only an hour and a half away. Maybe now he could somehow make up for the way he had failed Priscilla before.

The phone rang. An instant later, the intercom light blinked on his phone. He picked up the receiver. "Mrs. Miles is on the phone, Doctor," his secretary said.

Allison's voice was filled with concern. "Darling, did you by chance hear the news about the Harmon girl?"

"Yes, I did." He had told Allison about Priscilla.

"What are you going to do?"

Her question crystallized the decision he had already made subconsciously. "What I should have done years ago. I'm going to try to help that girl. I'll call you as soon as I can."

"God bless, darling."

Lendon picked up the intercom and spoke crisply to his secretary. "Ask Dr. Marcus to take over my afternoon appointments, please. Tell him it's an emergency. And cancel my four-o'clock class. I'm driving to Cape Cod immediately."

CHAPTER 10

"We've started dragging the lake, Ray. We've got bulletins going out on the radio and TV stations, and we're getting manpower from all over to help in the search." Chief Jed Coffin of the Adams Port police tried to adopt the hearty tone that he would normally use if two children were missing.

But even looking at the agony in Ray's eyes and the ashen pallor of his face, it was difficult to sound reassuring and solicitous. Ray had deceived him—introduced him to his wife, talked about her coming from Virginia and having known Dorothy there. He'd filled him with talk and never once told the truth. And the Chief hadn't guessed—or even suspected. That was the real irritation. Not once had he suspected.

To Chief Coffin, what had happened was very clear. That woman had seen the article about herself in the paper, realized that everyone would know who she was and gone berserk. Did to these poor kids the same thing she'd done to her others. Studying Ray shrewdly, he guessed that Ray was thinking pretty much the same thing.

Charred bits of the morning paper were still in the fireplace. The Chief realized Ray was looking at them. From the jagged way the unburned parts were torn, it was obvious they'd been pulled apart by someone in a frenzy.

"Doc Smathers still upstairs with her?" There was unconscious discourtesy in the question. He'd always called Nancy "Mrs. Eldredge" till now.

"Yes. He's going to give her a needle to relax her but not to put her out. We've got to talk to her. Oh, God!"

Ray sat down at the dining-room table and buried his face in his hands. Only a few hours ago Nancy had been sitting in this chair with Missy in her arms and Mike asking, "Is it really your birthday,

Mommy?" Had he triggered something in Nancy by demanding she celebrate? . . . And then that article. Had . . . ?

"No!" Ray looked up and blinked, turning his head away from the sight of the policeman standing by the back door.

"What is it?" Chief Coffin asked.

"Nancy is incapable of harming the children. Whatever happened, it wasn't that."

"Your wife when she's herself wouldn't harm them, but I've seen women go off the deep end, and there is the history . . ."

Ray stood up. His hands clenched the edge of the table. His glance went past the chief, dismissing him. "I need help," he said. "Real help."

The room was in chaos. The police had made a quick search of the house before concentrating on the outside. A police photographer was still taking pictures of the kitchen, where the coffeepot had fallen, spewing streams of black coffee onto the stove and floor. The telephone rang incessantly. To every call the policeman answering said, "The Chief will have a statement later."

The policeman at the phone came over to the table. "That was the A.P.," he said. "The wire services have gotten hold of this. We'll be mobbed in an hour."

The wire services. Ray remembered the haunted look that had only gradually left Nancy's face. He thought of the picture in this morning's paper, with her hand up as though trying to fend off blows. He pushed past Chief Coffin and hurried upstairs, opening the door of the master bedroom. The doctor was sitting next to Nancy, holding her hands. "You can hear me, Nancy," he was saying. "You know you can hear me. Ray is here. He's very worried about you. Talk to him, Nancy."

Her eyes were closed. Dorothy had helped Ray strip off the wet clothes. They'd put a fluffy yellow robe on her, but she seemed curiously small and inert inside it—not unlike a child herself.

Ray bent over her. "Honey, please, you've got to help the children. We've got to find them. They need you. Try, Nancy—please try."

"Ray, I wouldn't," Dr. Smathers warned. His lined, sensitive face was deeply creased. "She's had some kind of terrible shock—whether it was reading the article or something else. Her mind is fighting confronting it."

"But we've got to know what it was," Ray said intently. "Maybe she even saw someone take the children away. Nancy, I know. I understand. It's all right about the newspaper. We'll face that together. But darling, where are the children? You must help us find them. Do you think they went near the lake?"

Nancy shuddered. A strangled cry came from somewhere in her throat. Her lips formed words: "Find them . . . find them."

"We will find them. But you must help, please. Honey, I'm going to help you sit up. You can. Now, come on."

Ray leaned down and supported her in his arms. He saw the raw skin on her face where the sand had burned it. There was wet sand still clinging to her hair. Why? Unless. . . .

"I gave her a shot," the doctor said. "It should relieve the anxiety, but it won't be enough to knock her out."

She felt so heavy and vague. This was the way she'd felt for such a long time—from the night Mother died . . . or maybe even before that—so defenseless, so pliable . . . so without ability to choose or move or even speak. She could remember how so many nights her eyes would be glued together—so heavy, so weary. Carl had been so patient with her. He had done everything for her. She had always told herself that she had to get stronger, had to overcome that terrible lethargy, but she never could.

But that was so long ago. She didn't think about that anymore—not about Carl; not about the children; not about Rob Legler, the handsome student who'd seemed to like her, who made her laugh. The children had been so gay when he was there, so happy. She had thought he was a real friend—but then he sat on the witness stand and said, "She told me that her children would be smothered. That was exactly what she said, four days before they disappeared."

"Nancy. Please. Nancy. Why did you go to the lake?"

She heard the stifled sound she made. The lake. Did the children go there? She must search for them.

She felt Ray lifting her and slumped against him, but then forced her body to begin to sit up. It would be so much easier to slip away, to slide into sleep just as she used to do.

"That's it. That's right, Nancy." Ray looked at the doctor. "Do you think a cup of coffee . . . ?"

The doctor nodded. "I'll ask Dorothy to make it."

Coffee. She'd been making coffee when she saw that picture in the paper. Nancy opened her eyes. "Ray," she whispered, "they'll know. Everyone will know. You can't hide . . . you can't hide." But there was something else. "The children." She clutched his arm. "Ray, find them—find my babies."

"Steady, honey. That's where we need you. You've got to tell us. Every single thing. Just get your bearing for a few minutes."

Dorothy came in with a cup of steaming coffee in her hand. "I made the instant. How is she?"

"She's coming round."

"Captain Coffin is anxious to begin questioning her."

"Ray!" Panic made Nancy clutch Ray's arm.

"Darling, it's just that we have to have help finding the children. It's all right."

She gulped the coffee, welcoming the searing, hot taste as she swallowed it. If she could just think . . . just wake up . . . just lose this terrible sleepiness.

Her voice. She could talk now. Her lips felt rubbery, thick, spongelike. But she had to talk . . . make them find the children. She wanted to go downstairs. She mustn't stay here . . . like last time . . . waiting in her room . . . unable to go downstairs . . . to see all the people downstairs . . . the policemen . . . the faculty wives. . . . Are there any relatives? . . . Do you want us to call anyone? . . . No one . . . no one . . . no one . . .

Leaning heavily on Ray's arm, she stood up unsteadily. Ray. She had his arm to lean on now. His children. His children.

"Ray . . . I didn't hurt them. . . ."

"Of course not, darling."

The voice too soothing . . . the shocked sound. Of course he was shocked. He was wondering why she would deny it. No good mother spoke of hurting her children. Why then did she . . . ?

With a supreme effort she groped toward the door. His arm around her waist steadied her steps. She couldn't feel her feet. They weren't there. She wasn't there. It was one of the nightmares. In a few minutes she'd wake up, as she had so many nights, and slip out of bed and go in to see Missy and Michael and cover them and then get back into bed—softly, quietly, not waking Ray. But in sleep he'd reach out and his arms would pull her close, and against the warm scent of him she'd be calmed and sleep.

They started down the stairs. So many policemen. Everybody looking up . . . curiously still . . . suspended in time.

Chief Coffin was at the dining-room table. She could feel his hostility. . . . It was like last time.

"Mrs. Eldredge, how do you feel?"

A perfunctory question, noncaring. Probably he wouldn't have bothered to ask except that Ray was there.

"I'm all right." She had never liked this man.

"We're searching for the children. I have every confidence that we'll find them quickly. But you must help us. When did you last see the children?"

"A few minutes before ten. I put them outside to play and went upstairs to make the beds."

"How long were you upstairs?"

"Ten minutes . . . not more than fifteen."

"Then what did you do?"

"I came downstairs. I was going to turn on a wash and call the children. But after I started the wash, I decided to heat the coffee. Then I saw the boy deliver the community paper."

"Did you speak to him?"

"No. I don't mean I *saw* him. I went to get the paper and he was just going around the corner."

"I see. What happened then?"

"I went back into the kitchen. I turned on the coffeepot—it was still quite warm. I started turning the pages of the paper."

"And you saw the article about yourself."

Nancy stared straight ahead and nodded her head.

"How did you react to seeing that article?"

"I think I started to scream . . . I don't know. . . ."

"What happened to the coffeepot?"

"I knocked it over. . . . The coffee went all over. It burned my hand."

"Why did you do that?"

"I don't know. I didn't mean to. It was just that I was going to burst. I knew that everyone would start looking at me again. They'd stare and whisper. They'd say I killed the children. And Michael mustn't ever see that. I ran with the paper. I pushed it into the fireplace. I lit a match and it burned . . . it started to burn . . . and I knew I had to get Michael and Missy—I had to hide them. But it was the way it was last time. When the children were gone. I ran out to get Michael and Missy. I was afraid."

"Now, this is important. Did you see the children?"

"No. They were gone. I started calling. I ran to the lake."

"Mrs. Eldredge, this is very important: Why did you go to the lake? Your husband tells me the children have never once been disobedient about going there. Why didn't you look on the road for them, or in the woods, or see if they'd decided to walk into town to buy you a birthday present? Why the lake?"

"Because I was afraid. Because Peter and Lisa were drowned. Because I had to find Michael and Missy. Missy's mitten was caught on the swing. She's always losing a mitten. I ran to the lake. I had to get the children. It's going to be just like last time . . . their faces all wet and quiet . . . and they won't talk to me. . . ."

Chief Coffin straightened up. His tone became formal. "Mrs. Eldredge," he said, "it is my duty to inform you that you have a right to legal advice before you answer any further questions and that anything you say can be used against you."

Without waiting for her response, he got up and stalked out of the room and to the back door. A car with a policeman at the wheel was waiting for him in the rear driveway. As he stepped from the house, thin, driving pellets of sleet stung his face and head. He got into the car and the wind blew the door closed behind him, scraping it against his shoe. He winced at the short stab of pain in his ankle and growled, "The lake."

Fat chance they had of doing any searching if this weather got any worse. At noon it was already so dark you'd think it was nighttime. The diving operation was a mess under optimal conditions. Maushop was among the biggest lakes on the Cape and one of the deepest and most treacherous. That was why over the years there'd been so many drownings there. You could be wading up to your waist and at the next step be in forty feet of water. If those kids had been drowned, it might be spring before their bodies surfaced. The way the temperature was dropping, the lake would be fit for ice skating in a few days.

The lakeside, normally deserted at this time of the year and certainly in this kind of weather, was crowded with bystanders, who huddled together in small clusters, silently watching the roped-off area where the divers and their apparatus were flanked by police.

Chief Coffin jumped out of the squad car and hurried to the beach. He went directly to Pete Regan, the lieutenant who was supervising the operation. Pete's eloquent shrug answered his unasked question.

Hunching his shoulders inside his coat, the chief stamped his feet as the sleet melted into his shoes. He wondered if this was the spot from which Nancy Eldredge had dragged her kids into the water. Now men were risking their own lives because of her. God only knew where or when those poor little kids would be found. Shows what happens . . . A technicality . . . a convicted murderess gets off because a smart-ass lawyer gets a couple of bleeding-heart judges to declare a mistrial.

Angrily, he spat out Pete's name.

Pete turned to him quickly. "Sir?"

"How long are those guys planning to keep diving?"

"They've been down twice, and after this session, they'll try once more, then take a break and set up in a different location." He pointed to the television equipment. "Looks like we'll make the headlines tonight. You'd better have a statement ready."

With numbed fingers, the Chief dug into his coat pocket. "I've scribbled one down." He read it quickly. "We are conducting a massive effort to find the Eldredge children. Volunteers are making a block-by-block search of the immediate vicinity of her home as well as the neighboring wooded areas. Helicopters are conducting an air reconnaissance. The search of Maushop Lake, because of its proximity to the Eldredge home must be considered a normal extension of the investigation."

But a few minutes later, when he delivered that statement to the growing assemblage of reporters, one of them asked, "Is it true that Nancy Eldredge was found hysterical and drenched in this area of Maushop Lake this morning after her children disappeared?"

"That is true."

A thin, sharp-eyed reporter who he knew was connected with Boston Channel 5's news team asked, "In view of that fact and her past history, doesn't the search of the lake take on a new aspect?"

"We are exploring all possibilities."

Now the questions came thick and fast, the reporters interrupting one another to ask them. "In view of the past tragedy, wouldn't the disappearance of the Eldredge children be considered of suspicious origin?"

"To answer that question could prejudice Mrs. Eldredge's rights."

"When will you question her again?"

"As soon as possible."

"Is it known whether Mrs. Eldredge was aware of the article about her that came out this morning?"

"I believe she was."

"What was her reaction to that article?"

"I can't say."

"Isn't it a fact that most if not all of the people in this town were unaware of Mrs. Eldredge's past?"

"That is true."

"Were you aware of her identity?"

"No. I was not." The Chief spoke through clenched teeth. "No more questions."

Then, before he could get away, another question came. A reporter from the *Boston Herald* blocked his path. All the other news personnel stopped trying to get the Chief's attention when they heard him ask loudly, "Sir, in the past six years haven't there been several unsolved deaths of young children both on the Cape and on the nearby mainland?"

"That is true."

"Chief Coffin, how long has Nancy Harmon Eldredge been living on the Cape?"

"Six years, I believe."

"Thank you, Chief."

J onathan Knowles did not realize how much time was slipping by. Neither was he aware of the activity in the area near Maushop Lake. His subconscious had registered the fact that heavier-than-usual traffic was passing on the road in front of his house. But his study was to the back of the house, and much of the sound was filtered out before it came to his ears.

After the first shock of realizing that Ray Eldredge's wife was the notorious Nancy Harmon, he'd gotten another cup of coffee and settled down at his desk. He resolved to stick to his schedule—to begin to study the Harmon murder case just as he'd planned. If he found that knowing Nancy Harmon personally in some way clouded his ability to write about her, he'd simply eliminate this chapter from his book.

He began his research by carefully studying the sensational article in the Cape paper. With grim detail that insidiously evoked horror in the reader, it reviewed Nancy Harmon's background as the young wife of a college professor . . . two children . . . a home in the college campus. An ideal situation until the day Professor Harmon sent a student to his house to repair the oil burner. The student was good-looking, glib and experienced with women. And Nancy—barely twenty-five herself—had flipped over him.

Jonathan read excerpts from the trial testimony in the article. The student, Rob Legler, explained how he had met Nancy. "When Professor Harmon got that call from his wife about the oil burner not working, I was in his office. There's just nothing mechanical I can't fix, so I volunteered to go over. He didn't want me to do it, but he couldn't get the regular maintenance service and had to get the heat back on in his house."

"Did he give you any specific instructions concerning his family?" a district attorney asked.

"Yes. He said that his wife wasn't well and I shouldn't bother her; that if I needed anything, or wanted to discuss whatever problem I found, I should call him."

"Did you follow Professor Harmon's instructions?"

"I would have, sir, but I couldn't help the fact that his wife followed me around like a little dog."

"Objection! Objection!" But the defense attorney had been too late. The point had been made. And further evidence from the student had been totally damaging. He was asked if he had had any physical contact with Mrs. Harmon.

His answer was direct. "Yes, sir."

"How did it happen?"

"I was showing her where the emergency switch was on the oil burner. It was one of those old-fashioned hot-air-blower types, and the switch had caused the problem."

"Didn't Professor Harmon tell you not to trouble Mrs. Harmon with any questions or explanations?"

"She insisted on knowing about it. Said she had to learn how to manage things in her house. So I showed her. Then she was sort of leaning over me to try the switch, and . . . well, I figured, why not? . . . so I made a pass."

"What did Mrs. Harmon do?"

"She liked it. I could tell."

"Will you please explain exactly what happened?"

"It wasn't really what happened. 'Cause nothing much actually happened. It was just that she liked it. I sort of spun her around and grabbed her and kissed her—and after a minute she pulled away, but she didn't want to."

"What happened then?"

"I said something about that being pretty good."

"What did Mrs. Harmon say?"

"She just looked at me and said . . . almost like she wasn't talking to me . . . she said, 'I've got to get away.' "

"I figured I didn't want to get in any trouble. I mean, I didn't want to do anything to get kicked out of school and end up being drafted. That was the whole reason for the college scene. So I said, 'Look, Mrs. Harmon' . . . only then I decided it was about time to call her Nancy . . . so I said, 'Look, Nancy, this doesn't have to be a problem. We can work something out so we can get together without anyone ever guessing. You can't leave here—you've got the kids.' "

"How did Mrs. Harmon respond to that statement?"

"Well, it's funny. Just then the boy . . . Peter . . . came down the stairs looking for her. He was a real quiet kid—didn't say 'Boo.' She looked mad and said, 'The children'; then she sort of laughed and said, 'But they're going to be smothered.' "

"Mr. Legler, this is a crucial sentence you're quoting. Are you sure you are repeating Mrs. Harmon's exact phrasing?"

"Yes, sir, I am. It really made me feel spooky right then. That's why I'm so sure of it. But of course you don't really believe that anyone means it when they say something like that."

"On what date did Nancy Harmon make that statement?"

"It was on November thirteenth. I know because when I went back to school, Professor Harmon insisted on giving me a check for fixing the burner."

"November thirteenth . . . and four days later the Harmon children disappeared from their mother's automobile and eventually were washed in on the shores of San Francisco Bay with plastic bags over their heads—in effect, smothered."

"That's right."

The defense attorney had tried to reduce the impact of the story. "Did you continue to embrace Mrs. Harmon?"

"No. She went upstairs with the kids."

"Then we have only your statement that she enjoyed the kiss you forced on her."

"Believe me, I can tell a receptive babe when I'm with one."

And Nancy's sworn testimony when asked about that incident: "Yes, he did kiss me. Yes, I believe that I knew he was going to and I let him."

"Do you also remember making the statement that your children were going to be smothered?"

"Yes, I do."

"What did you mean by that statement?"

According to the article, Nancy simply looked past her attorney and stared unseeingly over the faces in the courtroom. "I don't know," she said in a dreamy voice.

Jonathan shook his head and swore silently. That girl should never have been permitted to take the witness stand. She did nothing except damage her own case. He continued reading and winced as he came to the description of the finding of those pathetic children. Washed in, both of them, two weeks and fifty miles apart. Bodies badly swollen, seaweed clinging to them, the little girl's body savagely mutilated— probably by shark bites; the handmade bright red sweaters with the white design still miraculously colorful against the small bodies.

After he'd finished reading the article, Jonathan turned his attention to the voluminous file Kevin had sent him. Leaning back in his chair, he began to read through it, starting with the first newspaper clipping headlining the disappearance of the Harmon children from their mother's automobile while she was shopping. Blowups of fuzzy snap-shots of both of the children; a minutely detailed description of their weight and size and what they were wearing; anyone with any informa-tion please call this special number. With his carefully trained mind and eyes, Jonathan read rapidly, assorting and assimilating information, lightly underlining cogent facts he wanted to refer to later. When he began reading the transcript of the trial, he understood why Kevin had referred to Nancy Harmon as a sitting duck for the prosecutor. The girl didn't even make sense. She had played so completely into the prose-cutor's hands the way she testified—without fight; her protestations of innocence sounding perfunctory and emotionless.

What had been the matter with her? Jonathan wondered. It was almost as though she didn't want to get off. At one point she'd even said to the husband right from the witness stand, "Oh Carl, can you forgive me?"

The creases along Jonathan's forehead deepened as he recalled that just a few hours before he'd passed the Eldredges' house and glanced in at that young family around the breakfast table. He'd compared them with his own solitary state and had been envious. Now their life was ripped apart. They'd never be able to stay in as insular a community as the Cape, knowing that everywhere they went people were pointing and talking. Anyone would instantly recognize Nancy from that one picture. Even he remembered her wearing that tweed suit—and recently, too.

Suddenly Jonathan recalled the occasion. It had been at Lowery's Market. He'd run into Nancy when they were both shopping and they'd stopped for a few minutes to talk. He'd admired the suit, telling her that there was nothing better-looking than a good tweed—and pure wool, of course; none of that synthetic junk that had no depth or sheen.

Nancy had looked very pretty. A yellow scarf knotted casually at her neck had picked up the glint of yellow in the predominantly brown and rust-colored material. She'd smiled—a warm, lovely smile that wrapped you in it. The children were with her—nice, polite children, both of them. Then the boy had said, "Oh, Mommy, I'll get the cereal," and as he reached for it, he knocked over a pyramid of soup cans.

The clatter had brought everyone in the store running, including Lowery himself, who was a sour, disagreeable man. Many young mothers might have been embarrassed and started berating the child. Jonathan had admired the way Nancy said very quietly, "We're sorry, Mr. Lowery. It was an accident. We'll take care of it."

Then she said to the little boy, who looked stricken and worried, "Don't be upset, Mike. You didn't mean it. Come on. Let's pile them back up."

Jonathan had helped with the restacking, after first shooting a menacing glare at Lowery, who'd obviously been about to make some kind of remark. It seemed so hard to believe that seven years ago today that same considerate young woman could have deliberately taken the life of two other children—children she had brought into life.

But passion was a powerful motive, and she had been young. Maybe her very indifference at her trial had been acceptance of guilt, even though she couldn't publicly bring herself to admit such a heinous crime. He'd seen that kind of thing happen too.

The doorbell rang. Jonathan got up from his chair, surprised. Few people visited unannounced at the Cape, and any door-to-door selling was absolutely forbidden.

As he walked to the door Jonathan realized how stiff he'd become from sitting. To his amazement, his visitor was a policeman, a young man whose face he only vaguely recognized from seeing him in a squad car. *Selling some kind of tickets* was Jonathan's immediate thought, but he discarded that idea at once. The young officer accepted his invitation to step inside. There was something crisply efficient and serious about his demeanor. "Sir, I'm sorry to bother you but we're investigating the disappearance of the Eldredge children."

Then, while Jonathan stared at him, he pulled out a notebook. His eyes darting around the orderly house, he began his questions. "You live alone here, sir, do you not?"

Without answering, Jonathan reached past him and opened the massive front door. At last he became aware of the presence of unfamiliar cars driving down the road toward the lake and the sight of grim-faced men in heavy rain gear swarming through the neighborhood.

 *CHAPTER 12*

"Just sip this, Nancy. Your hands are so cold. It will help you. You need your strength." Dorothy's voice was cajoling. Nancy shook her head. Dorothy set the cup on the table, hoping the aroma of the fresh vegetables, bubbling in a spicy base of tomato soup, might tempt her.

"I made that yesterday," Nancy said tonelessly, "for the children's lunch. The children must be hungry."

Ray was sitting next to her, his arm slung protectively across the back of her chair, an ashtray filled high with ground-out cigarettes in front of him.

"Don't torture yourself, dear," he said quietly.

Outside, over the rattling of the shutters and windowpanes, they could hear the staccato sound of helicopters flying low.

Ray answered the question he saw on Nancy's face. "They've got three helicopters scanning the area. They'll spot the kids if they just wandered away. They've got volunteers from every town on the Cape. There are two planes over the bay and sound. Everyone's helping."

"And there are divers in the lake," Nancy said, "looking for my children's bodies." Her voice was a remote monotone.

After giving the statement to the news media, Chief Coffin had gone back to the police station to make a series of phone calls. When they

were completed, he returned to the Eldredge house, coming in just in time to hear Nancy's words. His practiced glance took in the staring quality of her eyes, the ominous stillness of her hands and body, the facile expression and voice. Approaching a state of shock again, and they'd be lucky if she was able to answer to her own name before long.

He looked past her, his eyes seeking Bernie Mills, the policeman he'd left on duty in the house. Bernie was standing at the doorway of the kitchen, poised to pick up the telephone if it rang. Bernie's sandy hair was plastered neatly over his bony skull. His prominent eyes, softened by short, blond lashes, moved horizontally. Accepting the signaled message, Chief Coffin looked again at the three people around the table. Ray got up, walked behind his wife's chair and put his hands on her shoulders.

Twenty years disappeared for Jed Coffin. He remembered the night he'd gotten a call at the precinct house when he was a rookie cop in Boston that Delia's folks had been in an accident and it wasn't likely they'd make it.

He'd gone home. She'd been sitting in the kitchen in her nightgown and robe, sipping a cup of her favorite instant hot chocolate, reading the paper. She'd turned, surprised to see him early but smiling, and before he said one word, he'd done just what Ray Eldredge was doing now—pressed his hands on her shoulders, holding her.

Hell, wasn't that the guts of the departure speech stewardesses used to rattle off on airplanes? "In the event of an emergency landing, sit straight, grip the arms of your seats, plant your feet solidly on the floor." What they were saying was "Let the shock pass through you."

"Ray, can I see you privately?" he asked brusquely.

Ray's hands continued to steady Nancy's shoulders as her body began to shake. "Did you find my children?" she asked. Now her voice was almost a whisper.

"Honey, he'd tell us if he found the kids. Just sit tight here. I'll be right back." Ray bent down and for an instant laid his cheek on hers. Without seeming to expect a response, he straightened up and led the Chief through the connecting foyer into the large living room.

Jed Coffin felt an unwilling admiration for the tall young man who positioned himself by the fireplace before turning to face him. There was something so gut-level self-possessed about Ray even in these circumstances. Fleetingly he remembered that Ray had been decorated for outstanding leadership under fire in Vietnam and given a field promotion to captain.

He had class, no doubt about that. There was class inherent in the way Ray stood and talked and dressed and moved; in the firm contours of his chin and mouth; in the strong, well-shaped hand that rested lightly on the mantel.

Stalling to regain his sense of rightness and authority, Jed looked slowly around the room. The wide oak floorboards shone softly under oval hooked rugs; a dry sink stood between the leaded paned windows. The mellow, creamy walls were covered with paintings. Jed realized that the scenes in them were familiar. The large painting over the fireplace was Nancy Eldredge's rock garden. The country-graveyard scene over the piano was that old private cemetery down the road from Our Lady of the Cape Church. The pine-framed painting over the couch had caught the homecoming flavor of Sesuit Harbor at sundown as all the boats came sailing in. The watercolor of the windswept cranberry bog had the old Hunt house—The Lookout—barely outlined in the background.

Jed had occasionally noticed Nancy Eldredge sketching around town, but never dreamed that she was any good. Most women he knew who fooled around with that sort of thing usually ended up framing stuff that looked like exhibits from Show and Tell.

Built-in bookcases lined the fireplace. The tables made of heavy old distressed pine weren't unlike the ones he remembered they'd donated to the church bazaar after his grandmother died. Pewter lamps like hers were on the low tables next to comfortable overstuffed chairs. The rocker by the fireplace had a hand-embroidered cushion and back.

Somewhat uncomfortably, Jed compared this room with his own newly decorated living room. Delia had picked out black vinyl for the couch and chairs; a glass-topped table with steel legs; wall-to-wall carpeting—thick yellow shag that clawed at the shoes and faithfully preserved and displayed every drop of saliva or pee their still-untrained dachshund bestowed on it.

"What do you want, Chief?" Ray's voice was cold and unfriendly. The Chief knew that to Ray he was an enemy. Ray had seen through his routine admonition to Nancy about her rights. Ray knew exactly how he felt and was fighting him. Well if a fight was what he wanted . . .

With the ease born of experience garnered from countless similar sessions, Jed Coffin sought out the weakness and directed his attention to it. "Who is your wife's lawyer, Ray?" he asked curtly.

A flicker of uncertainty, a stiffening of the body betrayed the answer. Just as Jed had figured, Ray hadn't taken the decisive step. Still trying to pretend his wife was the average distraught mother of missing children. Christ, he'd probably want to put her on a television news show tonight, handkerchief twisting in her hands, eyes swollen, voice pleading, "Give me back my children."

Well, Jed had news for Ray. His precious wife had done that scene before. Jed could get copies of the seven-year-old film the newspapers had called "a moving plea." In fact, the assistant district attorney in San

Francisco had offered to provide it during their telephone conversation only half an hour ago. "It'll save that bitch the trouble of going through her act again," he'd said.

Ray was speaking quietly, his tone a hell of a lot more subdued. "We haven't contacted a lawyer," he said. "I hoped that maybe . . . with everyone searching . . ."

"Most of that search is going to be suspended pretty soon," Jed said flatly. "With this weather, there isn't going to be anyone able to see anything. But I've got to take your wife down to the station for questioning. And if you haven't arranged for a lawyer yet, I'll have the court appoint one for her."

"You can't do that!" Ray snapped the words furiously, then made an obvious effort to control himself. "What I mean is that you would destroy Nancy if you took her to a police-station setting. For years she used to have nightmares, and they were always the same: that she was in a police station being questioned and then that she was taken down a long corridor to the mortuary and made to identify her children. My God, man, she's in shock right now. Are you trying to make sure that she won't be able to tell us anything she may have seen?"

"Ray, my job is to get your children back."

"Yes, but you see what just reading that cursed article has done to her. And what about the bastard who wrote that article? Anyone vile enough to dig up that story and send it out might be capable of taking the children."

"Naturally we're working on that. That feature is always signed with a fictitious staff name, but the articles are actually free-lance submissions that if accepted involve a twenty-five-dollar payment."

"Well, who is the writer, then?"

"That was what we tried to find out," Jed replied. He sounded angry. "The covering letter instructed that the story was offered only on condition that if accepted, it would not be changed at all, that all the accompanying pictures would be used and that it would be published on November seventeenth—today. The editor told me that he found the story both well written and fascinating. In fact, he felt it was so good that he thought the writer was a fool to have submitted it to him for a lousy twenty-five dollars. But of course, he didn't say so. He dictated a letter accepting the conditions and enclosing the check."

Jed reached into his hip pocket for his notebook and flipped it open. "The letter of acceptance was dated October twenty-eighth. On the twenty-ninth the editor's secretary remembers receiving a phone call asking if a decision had been reached about the Harmon article. It was a bad connection and the voice was so muffled she could hardly hear the caller, but she told him—or her—that a check was in the mail, care of General Delivery, Hyannis Port. The check was made out to one J. R. Penrose. The next day it was picked up."

"Man or woman?" Ray asked quickly.

"We don't know. As you have to realize, a town like Hyannis Port has a fair number of tourists going through it even at this time of the year. Anyone requesting something from General Delivery would only have to ask for it. No clerk seems to remember the letter, and so far the twenty-five-dollar check hasn't been cashed. We can work our way back to J. R. Penrose when it is. Frankly, it wouldn't surprise me if the writer turns out to be one of our own little old ladies in town. They can be just wonderful at digging into gossip."

Ray stared into the fireplace. "It's cool in here," he said. "A fire will feel good." His eye fell on the cameos on the mantelpiece that Nancy had painted of Michael and Missy when they were babies. He swallowed over the stinging lump that suddenly closed his throat.

"I don't think you really need a fire in here now, Ray," Jed said quietly. "I asked you to step in here because I want you to tell Nancy to get dressed and come with us to the station house."

"No . . . no . . . please . . ." Chief Coffin and Ray whirled to face the archway leading into the room. Nancy was standing there, one hand leaning against the carved oak archway for support. Her hair had dried, and she had pulled it into a bun caught loosely against the nape of her neck. The strain of the past hours had turned her skin a chalky white that was accentuated by the dark hair. An almost detached expression was settling into her eyes.

Dorothy was behind her. "She wanted to come in." Dorothy's voice was apologetic.

Now she felt the accusation in Ray's eyes as he hurried over to them. "Ray, I'm sorry. I couldn't make her stay inside."

Ray pulled Nancy against him. "It's all right, Dorothy," he said briefly. His voice changed and became tender. "Honey, just relax. Nobody's going to hurt you."

Dorothy felt the dismissal in his tone. He had counted on her to keep Nancy away while he spoke to the Chief, and she couldn't even do that much. She was useless here—useless. "Ray," she said stiffly. "It's ridiculous to bother you about this, but the office just phoned to remind me that Mr. Kragopoulos, who wrote about the Hunt property, wants to see it at two o'clock. Shall I get someone else to take him up there?"

Ray looked over Nancy's head as he held her firmly against him. "I don't give a damn," he snapped. Then quickly he said, "I'm sorry, Dorothy. I would appreciate it if you showed the place; you know The Lookout and can sell it if there's real interest. Poor old Mr. Hunt needs the money."

"I haven't told Mr. Parrish that we might be bringing people in today."

"His lease clearly states that we have the right to show the house at any time with simply a half hour's telephone notice. That's why he has it so cheap. Give him a call from the office and tell him you're coming."

"All right." Uncertainly, Dorothy waited, not wanting to go. "Ray . . ."

He looked at her, understanding her unspoken wish but dismissing her. "There's nothing you can do here now, Dorothy. Come back when you've finished at The Lookout."

She nodded and turned to go. She didn't want to leave them; she wanted to stay with them, sharing their anxiety. Ever since that first day when she'd walked into Ray's office, he'd been a lifeline for her. After nearly twenty-five years of planning her every activity with Kenneth or around Kenneth's schedule, she'd been so rootless and, for the first time in her life, frightened. But working with Ray, helping him to build the business, using her knowledge of interior decorating to spark people to buy the houses, then invest in renovating them had filled so much of the void. Ray was such a fair, fine person. He'd given her such a generous profit-sharing arrangement. She couldn't have thought more of him if he'd been her own son. When Nancy had come, she'd been so proud that Nancy trusted her. But there was a reserve in Nancy that didn't permit any real intimacy, and now she felt like an unnecessary bystander. Wordlessly she left them, got her coat and scarf and went to the back door.

She braced herself against the wind and sleet as she opened it. Her car was parked halfway around the semicircular back driveway. She was glad she didn't have to go through the front drive. One of the networks had a television van parked in front of the house.

As she hurried toward her car, she saw the swing on the tree at the edge of the property. That was where the children had been playing and where Nancy had found the mitten. How many times had she herself pushed the children on that swing? Michael and Missy . . . The awful possibility that something might have happened to them—that they might be dead—gave her a terrible choking sensation. *Oh, please not that . . . almighty and merciful God, please not that.* She'd joked once about being their surrogate grandmother, and then the look of pain had been so unmistakable on Nancy's face that she had wanted to bite her tongue off. It had been a presumptuous thing to say.

She stared at the swing, lost in thought, unmindful of the wet sleet stinging her face. Whenever Nancy stopped in the office, the children made a beeline for her desk. She tried to always have a surprise for them. Just yesterday when Nancy had come in with Missy, she'd had tollhouse cookies she'd baked the night before as the special treat.

Nancy had been on her way to look at drapery material, and Dorothy had offered to mind Missy and pick up Michael at kindergarten. "It's hard to select material unless you can really concentrate," she'd said, "and I have to pick up some title-search papers at the courthouse. It will be fun to have company, and on the way back we'll get some ice cream, if that's all right." Only twenty-four hours ago. . . .

"Dorothy."

Startled, she looked up. Jonathan must have cut through the woods from his house. His face was deeply creased today. She knew he must be nearly sixty years old, and today he looked every bit of it. "I just heard about the Eldredge children," he said. "I've got to talk to Ray. Possibly I can help."

"That's nice of you," Dorothy said unsteadily. The concern in his voice was oddly comforting. "They're inside."

"No trace of the children yet?"

"No."

"I saw the article in the paper."

Belatedly, Dorothy realized that sympathy was not being offered to her. There was a coolness in Jonathan's tone, a reproof that clearly reminded her that she had lied to him about having known Nancy in Virginia. Wearily, she opened the door of her car. "I have an appointment," she said abruptly. Without giving him time to answer, she got in and started up the engine. It was only when her vision blurred that she realized that tears were swimming in her eyes.

 CHAPTER 13

The clatter of the helicopters pleased him. It reminded him of the last time, when everyone for miles around the University had fanned out looking for the children. He stared out the front window overlooking the bay. The gray water was caked with ice near the jetty. Earlier the radio had spoken of gale warnings and sleet or rain mixed with snow. For once, the weatherman had been right. The wind was whipping the bay into angry whitecaps. He watched as a flock of gulls flew unsteadily in a futile effort to make headway against the wind.

He carefully consulted the indoor-outdoor thermometer. Twenty-eight degrees out there now—a drop of twenty degrees since the

morning. The helicopters and search planes wouldn't be up much longer in this. There wouldn't be many searchers out on land either.

High tide was seven o'clock tonight. At that time he'd take the children up through the attic to the outer balcony they called the widow's walk. The water at high tide covered the beach below, broke furiously against the retaining wall and then, sucked by the violent undertow, rolled back to sea. That would be the time to drop the children . . . over . . . down . . . They might not be washed in for weeks. . . . But even if they were found in a few days, he'd prepared for that. He'd given them only milk and cookies. He wouldn't be fool enough to feed them anything that would suggest that a person other than Nancy had fed them a real meal after breakfast. Of course, hopefully they'd be beyond analysis when they were found.

He chuckled. In the meantime, he had five hours: five long hours to look at the floodlights that were being set up near Nancy's house and the lake; five hours to be with the children. Even the boy, come to think of it, was a beautiful child . . . such soft skin, and that perfectly formed body.

But it was the little girl. She looked so much like Nancy . . . that silky, beautiful hair and small, well-formed ears. He turned from the window abruptly. The children were lying together on the couch. The sedative he'd put in the milk had both of them sleeping. The boy's arm was protectively over his sister. But he didn't even stir when he picked up the little girl. He'd just take her inside and put her on the bed and undress her. She made no sound as he carefully carried her into the bedroom and laid her down. He went into the bathroom and turned on the faucets in the tub, testing the gushing water until it reached the temperature he wanted. When the tub was filled, he tested the water again with his elbow. A little hotter than it should be, but that was all right. It would cool in a few minutes.

He sucked in his breath. He was wasting time. Swiftly he opened the door of the medicine cabinet and pulled out the can of baby powder he'd slipped into his coat pocket at Wiggins' Market this morning. As he was about to close the door, he noticed the little rubber duck poked back behind the shaving cream. He'd forgotten about that . . . why it had been used the last time . . . how appropriate. Laughing softly, he reached for the duck; ran it under cold water, feeling the lack of elasticity and the cracking of the rubber; then tossed it into the tub. It was a good idea to distract children sometimes.

Grabbing the can of powder, he hurried back into the bedroom. Swiftly his fingers unbuttoned Missy's jacket and pulled it off. Easily, he slipped the turtleneck polo shirt over her head, bringing her undershirt with it. He sighed—a lingering, groaning sound—and picked up the little girl, hugging her limp body to him. Three years old. Just a beautiful age. She stirred and started to open her eyes. "Mommy, mommy . . ." It was a weak, lazy cry—so dear, so precious.

The phone rang.

Angrily he tightened his grip on the child, and she began to wail—a hopeless, lethargic cry.

He'd let the phone ring. He never, never got calls. Why now? His eyes narrowed. It might be a call from the town, asking him to volunteer in the search. He'd better answer. It might be suspicious not to answer. He tossed Missy back onto the bed and closed the bedroom door securely before he picked up the phone in the sitting room. "Yes." He made his voice sound formal and cold.

"Mr. Parrish, I hope I haven't disturbed you. This is Dorothy Prentiss of Eldredge Realty. I'm sorry to give you such short notice, but I'll be bringing a prospective buyer for the house over in twenty minutes. Will you be there or shall I use my passkey to show your apartment?"

CHAPTER 14

Lendon Miles turned right off Route 6A onto Paddock Path. All the way down on the trip from Boston he'd kept his radio at a news station, and most of the news was about Nancy Eldredge and the missing Eldredge children.

According to the bulletins, Maushop Lake had been divided into sections, but it would take divers at least three days to search it properly. Maushop Lake was filled with underwater ledges. Police Chief Coffin of Adams Port was quoted as explaining that at one point it was possible to walk halfway across the lake and still be in water only to the waist; a few yards away, only five feet from the shore, the water became forty feet deep. The underwater ledges caught and held objects and made the search hazardous and inconclusive. . . .

The bulletins announced that helicopters, small seaplanes and ground search parties had been out, but gale warnings for the Cape were in effect and the air search was being called off.

At the news that Nancy Eldredge was expected to be taken to Police Headquarters for questioning, Lendon unconsciously accelerated the car. He felt a desperate urgency about getting to Nancy. But he quickly found that he had to reduce his speed. Sleet was glazing the windshield so rapidly that the defroster was having trouble melting the crusting ice.

When at last he turned into Paddock Path, he had no trouble finding the Eldredge home. There was no mistaking the center of activity on the street. Halfway up the road, a television van was parked across the street from a house that had two police cars stationed in front of it. Private cars lined the road near the television van. Many bore special press identifications.

The entrance to the semicircular driveway was blocked by one of the police cars. Lendon stopped and waited for a policeman to come over to him. When one did, his tone was brusque. "State your business, please."

Lendon had anticipated the question and was ready. He handed out his card with a note scrawled on it. "Please take this to Mrs. Eldredge."

The policeman looked uncertain. "If you'll wait here, Doctor . . . I'll have to check." He returned promptly, his attitude subtly less hostile. "I'll move the squad car out of the way. Park in the driveway and go into the house, sir."

From across the street, reporters had been watching the byplay, and they hurried over. One of them thrust a microphone in front of Lendon's face as he got out of the car.

"Dr. Miles, may we ask you a few questions?"

Without waiting for an answer, he went on quickly, "Sir, you are a prominent psychiatrist on the staff of Harvard Medical School. Has the Eldredge family sent for you?"

"No one has sent for me," Lendon replied sharply. "I am a friend—was a friend—of Mrs. Eldredge's mother. I have come here because of personal friendship and that alone."

He tried to pass, but was blocked by the microphone-holding reporter. "You say you were a friend of Mrs. Eldredge's mother. Will you tell us this: Was Nancy Harmon Eldredge ever a patient of yours?"

"Absolutely not!" Lendon literally shoved his way through the reporters and onto the porch. The front door was being held open by another policeman. "Right in there," the man said, indicating the room to the right.

Nancy Eldredge was standing at the fireplace next to a tall young man, undoubtedly her husband. Lendon would have known her anywhere. The finely chiseled nose, the large midnight-blue eyes that looked straight out from under thick lashes, the widow's peak at the hairline, the profile that was so like Priscilla's . . .

Ignoring the openly hostile look of the police officer and the scrutiny of the craggy-faced man at the window, he went directly to Nancy. "I should have come before," he said.

The girl's eyes had a staring quality, but she knew what he meant. "I thought you would come last time," she told him—"when mother died. I was so sure you would come. And you didn't."

Expertly, Lendon measured the symptoms of shock that he could see: the enlarged pupils; the rigidity of her body; the low, monotone quality of her voice. He turned to Ray. "I want to help if there's any possible way," he said.

Ray studied him intently and instinctively liked what he saw. "Then as a doctor, try to persuade the Chief here that it would be a disaster to take Nancy to the police station," he said flatly.

Nancy stared into Lendon's face. She felt so detached—as though each minute she were slipping farther and farther away. But there was something about this Dr. Miles. Mother had liked him so much; Mother's letters had sounded so happy; more and more often his name had been in them.

When her mother had come out to visit her at college she'd asked about the doctor; how important was he? But Carl was with them, and Mother didn't seem to want to talk about him then. She just smiled and said, "Oh, terribly important, but I'll fill you in later, dear."

She could remember that so clearly. She had wanted to meet Dr. Miles. Somehow she'd been sure that when he heard about Mother's accident he would call her. She had needed to talk to someone who loved Mother too. . . .

"You loved my mother, didn't you?" It was her voice asking that question. She wasn't even aware that she had intended to ask it.

"Yes, I did. Very much. I didn't know that she had told you about me. I thought you might resent me. I should have tried to help you."

"Help me now!"

He took her hands in his, her terribly cold hands. "I'll try, Nancy, I promise." She sagged, and her husband put his arms around her.

Lendon liked the looks of Ray Eldredge. The younger man's face was gray with anxiety, but he bore himself well. His attitude toward his wife was protective. He obviously had a firm grip on his own emotions. Lendon noticed the small framed picture on the table next to the sofa. It was an outdoor snapshot of Ray holding a little boy and girl. . . . The missing children. Of course. What a handsome family. Interesting that nowhere in this room could he see a single picture of Nancy. He wondered if she ever allowed herself to be photographed.

"Nancy, come, honey. You've got to rest." Ray gently eased her down onto the sofa and lifted her feet. "Now, that's better." She obediently leaned back. Lendon watched as her eyes focused on the snapshot of Ray and the children and then closed in pain. A shiver made her entire body tremble.

"I think we'd better stir up this fire," he told Ray. He selected a medium-sized log from the basket on the fireplace and threw it onto the smoldering hearth. A shower of flames sprayed up.

Ray tucked a quilt around Nancy. "You're so cold, darling," he said. For an instant he held her face between his hands. Tears trickled from under her closed eyelids and dampened his fingers.

"Ray, have I your permission to represent Nancy as her legal counsel?" Jonathan's voice had subtly altered. It was infused with an authoritative crispness. Calmly he met the astonished stares. "I assure you I am well qualified," he said drily.

"Legal counsel," Nancy whispered. From somewhere she could see the colorless, frightened face of the lawyer last time. Domes, that had been his name—Joseph Domes. He'd kept saying to her, "But you must tell me the truth. You must trust me to help you." Even he hadn't believed her.

But Jonathan Knowles was different. She liked his bigness and the courtly way he always spoke to her, and he was so attentive to the children when he stopped to speak. . . . Lowery's Market—that was it. A couple of weeks ago, he'd helped her and Mike to stack up the cans that Mike had knocked over. He liked her, she was sure. Instinctively she knew it. She opened her eyes. "Please," she said, looking at Ray.

Ray nodded. "We'd be very grateful, Jonathan."

Jonathan turned to Lendon. "Doctor, may I have your medical opinion as to the advisability of allowing Mrs. Eldredge to be taken to the police station for questioning?"

"It is highly inadvisable," Lendon said promptly. "I would urge that any questioning be done here."

"But I can't remember." Nancy's voice was weary, as though she had said those same words too many times. "You say I know where my children are. But I don't remember anything from when I saw that paper in the kitchen this morning until I heard Ray calling me." She looked up at Lendon, her eyes clouded and staring. "Can you help me to remember? Is there any way?"

"What do you mean?" Lendon asked.

"I mean isn't there some way you can give me something so that if I know . . . or saw . . . or did . . . Even if I did something . . . I have to know . . . That isn't something you can hide. If there is some awful part of me that could hurt my children . . . we have to know that too. And if there isn't but if somehow I know where they might be, we're just wasting time now."

"Nancy, I won't let—" But Ray stopped when he saw the anguish in her face.

"Is it possible to help Nancy to remember what happened this morning, Doctor?" Jonathan asked.

"Perhaps. She is probably suffering from a form of amnesia which is not uncommon after what to her was a catastrophic experience. In medical terms, it's a hysterical amnesia. Under an injection of sodium amytal, she would be relaxed and probably able to tell us what happened—the truth as she knows it."

"Answers given under sedation would not be admissible in court," Jed snapped. "I can't have you questioning Mrs. Eldredge like that."

"I used to have such a good memory," Nancy murmured. "Once at college we had a contest to see who could recall what she'd done every day. You just kept going backwards day by day until you couldn't remember anymore. I won by so much that it was a joke in the dorm. Everything was so clear. . . ."

The telephone rang and had the effect of a pistol exploding in the room. Nancy shrank back, and Ray covered her hands with his. They all waited silently until the policeman on duty at the phone came into the room. He said, "Long distance for you, Chief."

"I can assure you that this is the call I've been trying to place," Jed told Nancy and Ray. "Mr. Knowles, I'd appreciate it if you'd come with me. You too, Ray."

"Be right back, darling," Ray murmured to Nancy. Then he looked into Lendon's face. Satisfied with what he saw, he followed the other men out of the room.

Lendon watched as relief drained from Nancy's expression. "Every time it rings, I think somebody has found the children and they're safe," she murmured. "And then I think it will be like last time . . . when the call came."

"Steady," Lendon said. "Nancy, this is important. Tell me when you started having trouble remembering specific events."

"When Peter and Lisa died . . . but maybe even before that. It's so hard to remember the years I was married to Carl."

"That could be because you associate those years with the children and it's too painful to remember anything about them."

"But during those five years . . . I was so terribly tired so much . . . after Mother died . . . always so tired. Poor Carl . . . so patient. He did everything for me. He got up with the children at night—even when they were babies. Everything was such an effort for me. . . . After the children disappeared, I couldn't remember . . . like now . . . I just couldn't." Her voice had begun to rise.

Ray came back into the room. Something had happened. Lendon could see it in the taut lines around Ray's mouth, the slight trembling of his hands. He found himself praying: *Please, don't let it be bad news.*

"Doctor, could you speak with Jonathan for a minute, please?" Ray was making a determined effort to keep his voice even.

"Certainly." Lendon hurried toward the arched doorway that led into the family and dining room, sure that the phone call had badly upset Ray.

When he got to the dining room, Chief Coffin was still on the phone. He was barking orders to the lieutenant on duty at the station: "Get the hell down to that post office and round up every clerk who was on duty October thirtieth and don't stop questioning them until somebody remembers who picked up that letter from the *Community News* addressed to J. R. Penrose. I need a full description, and I need it now." He slammed the receiver into its cradle.

There was new tension in Jonathan too. Without preamble, he said, "Doctor, we can't lose any time in trying to break through Nancy's amnesia. To fill you in, I have a very complete file on the Harmon case because of a book I'm writing. I've spent the last three hours studying that file and reading the article that appeared in today's paper. Something struck me that seemed of the greatest possible importance, and I asked Chief Coffin to phone the District Attorney in San Francisco and check my theory. His assistant has just returned the call."

Jonathan reached into his pocket for his pipe, clamped his teeth on it without lighting it and continued, "Doctor, as you may know, in cases of missing children where foul play is suspected, the police will often deliberately withhold a piece of information so that they have some help in sifting through the inevitable meaningless clues they receive after a publicized disappearance."

He began to speak more quickly, as though he felt he was letting too much time pass. "I noticed that all the newspaper accounts seven years ago described the missing children as wearing red cardigan sweaters with a white pattern when they disappeared. Nowhere in any of the extensive newspaper coverage is there an exact description of what that pattern was. I surmised—correctly—that the motif of the pattern had been deliberately withheld."

Jonathan looked directly at Lendon, wanting him to understand immediately the importance of what he was about to tell him. "The article which appeared in the *Cape Cod Community News* clearly states that when the Harmon children disappeared they were wearing red cardigan sweaters with an unusual white sailboat design, and that they were still wearing them when their bodies were washed ashore weeks later. Now, Nancy, of course, was aware of that sailboat design. She made those sweaters herself. But only one other person outside of the top people on the San Francisco investigative staff knew about that design." Jonathan's voice rose in pitch. "If we assume Nancy's innocence, that person was the one who kidnapped the Harmon children seven years ago—and who one month ago wrote the story that appeared in today's paper!"

"Then you mean—" Lendon began.

"Doctor, I mean, as Nancy's lawyer and friend, if you can break through her amnesia, do it—quickly! I have persuaded Ray that it is worthwhile to waive any immunity. The overriding necessity is to find out what Nancy may know; otherwise it will surely be too late to help her children."

"Can I telephone a drugstore and get something delivered?" Lendon asked.

"You call, Doctor," Jed ordered. "I'll send a squad car over to pick up whatever you need. Here—I'll dial the drugstore for you."

Quietly Lendon phoned his instructions and when he had finished went into the kitchen for a glass of water. *Oh, the waste,* he thought—*the awful waste.* The tragedy that had begun with Priscilla's accident . . . cause and effect . . . cause and effect. If Priscilla had not died, she probably would have persuaded Nancy not to marry so young. The Harmon children would never have been born. Sharply he pulled himself back from useless speculation. The kitchen had obviously been gone over for fingerprints. Grains of powder were still evident on the countertops, around the sink and on the stove. No one had wiped up the stain from where coffee had spilled.

He returned to the dining room to hear Chief Coffin say, "Remember, Jonathan, I may well be exceeding my authority as it is. But I'm going to have a tape recorder on in that room when that girl is questioned. If she confesses to anything under sedation, we may not be able to use it directly, but I'll know what to ask her under regular questioning later."

"She's not going to confess to anything," Jonathan said impatiently. "What concerns me is that if we accept her innocence as a fact—not only about Michael and Missy's disappearance but also her innocence in the murder of the Harmon children—then our next supposition becomes this: if the killer of the Harmon children wrote the article for the *Community News* and used a Hyannis post office, he has been here on the Cape for some time."

"And you are saying that he abducted the Eldredge children this morning," Chief Coffin finished.

Jonathan relit his pipe and puffed at it vigorously before answering. "I'm afraid so," he said. His tone of voice, deliberately devoid of expression, made Lendon understand what he meant. Jonathan believed that if the killer of the Harmon children had taken Michael and Missy Eldredge, they were probably dead.

"On the other hand," Jed theorized, "if we remove Mrs. Eldredge as a suspect, it is equally possible that someone who never came forward at the Harmon trial knew something about those murders, wrote that article and has now kidnapped the Eldredge children. A third possibility is that the two cases are unrelated except that someone reading that article and recognizing Nancy Eldredge has become involved in the disappearance this morning. The children may have been taken by a frustrated mother who feels Nancy doesn't deserve them. I've seen a lot screwier rationalizations than that in my day."

"Jed," snapped Jonathan, "what I'm trying to say is that no matter who else may have become involved, one fact is very clear: I don't believe there's any question but that Nancy knew more than she told about the disappearance of her children seven years ago."

Lendon raised an eyebrow. Jed frowned deeply. At the expressions on the faces of the two men, Jonathan slapped his hand impatiently on the table. "I'm not saying that that girl is guilty. I am saying that she knew more than she told; probably knew more than she was aware of knowing. Look at the pictures of her on the witness stand. Her face is an absolute blank. Read the testimony. For God's sake, man, read the trial testimony. That girl was out of it. Her lawyer may have upset her conviction on a technicality, but that doesn't mean that he didn't let that district attorney crucify her. That entire setup stank, and you're trying to reenact it here."

"I'm trying to get away from your theories . . . and that's all they are . . . and perform my job, which is to recover those children—dead or alive—and find out who abducted them." Jed was clearly out of patience. "In one breath you tell me she's too sick to be questioned and in the next one that she knows more than she ever let on. Look, Jonathan, you said yourself that writing a book about questionable verdicts is a hobby with you. But those lives aren't hobbies with me, and I'm not here to help you play chess with the law."

"Hold on." Lendon put a restraining hand on the Chief's arm. "Mr. Knowles . . . Jonathan . . . you believe that whatever knowledge Nancy has of the death of her first family may help us find the Eldredge children."

"Exactly. But the problem is to extract that knowledge, not drive it deeper into her subconscious. Dr. Miles, you are considered an expert in the use of sodium amytal in psychiatry, are you not?"

"Yes, I am."

"Is it possible you might be able to have Nancy reveal not only what she knows of this morning's events—which I suspect will be nothing— but also information about the past that she doesn't even know she has herself?"

"It's possible."

"Then unless she can tell us something tangible about Michael and Missy's whereabouts, I beg you to try."

When Dorothy was readmitted to the house an hour later, the family room and kitchen were deserted except for Bernie Miles, the policeman charged with answering the phones. "They're all in there," he said, jerking his head toward the front parlor. "Something pretty queer going on."

Dorothy hurried down the hall, but stopped at the doorway of the room. The greeting she was about to utter died on her lips as she took in the scene before her.

Nancy was lying on the couch, a pillow under her head, a quilt tucked around her. A stranger who looked like a doctor was sitting beside her, speaking softly. Nancy's eyes were closed. An anguished-looking Ray and grim-faced Jonathan were side by side on the love seat. Jed Coffin was sitting at a table behind the couch, holding a microphone pointed toward Nancy.

As Dorothy realized what was happening, she sank into a chair, not bothering to take off her coat. Numbly she slipped her chilled fingers into the deep side pockets, unconsciously gripping the scrap of damp, fuzzy wool that she felt in the right-hand pocket.

"How do you feel, Nancy? Are you comfortable?" Lendon's voice was tranquil.

"I'm afraid. . . ."

"Why?"

"The children . . . the children . . ."

"Nancy. Let's talk about this morning. Did you sleep well last night? When you woke up did you feel rested?"

Nancy's voice was reflective. "I dreamed. I dreamed a lot. . . ."

"What did you dream about?"

"Peter and Lisa. . . . They'd be so grown up. . . . They're dead seven years. . . ." She began to sob. Then, as Jonathan's iron grip held Ray back, she cried, "How could I have killed them? They were my children! How could I have killed them . . . ?"

CHAPTER 15

Before Dorothy had met John Kragopoulos at the office, she had tried to camouflage her red-rimmed eyes with a dusting powder. She'd tried to convince herself that after all, showing the Hunt place would be an outlet, an action that could be concentrated on for a little while and keep her mind from its endless squirreling for clues to the children's whereabouts. What clues?

Normally she took prospective clients on a brief tour of the area before showing a property, to let them see the beaches and lakes and marina; the stately old homes that were scattered between Cranberry Highway and the bay; the breathtaking view from Maushop Tower; the old town landmarks.

But today, with the sleet beating a sharp tattoo on the car roof and windows, with the sky filled with black fields of clouds and with the cold sea air chilling the very marrow of the bones, she headed directly for The Lookout.

It was so hard to keep her mind on what she was doing. She felt so distracted and shaken. She who hadn't cried in years was having to bite her lips to keep tears back. There was a crushing weight on her shoulders, a weight of grief and fear that she could not hope to support alone.

As she drove the car along the treacherously slick road, she stole an occasional glance at the swarthy-complexioned man beside her. John Kragopoulos was somewhere in his mid forties. He had the build of a weight lifter, yet there was an innate courtliness in his bearing that complemented his slightly accented manner of speaking.

He told Dorothy that he and his wife had just sold their restaurant in New York and agreed their next venture would be in an area where they would want to settle permanently. They were anxious to be where well-to-do retired people could be found for winter business, as well as the summer resort trade.

Mentally reviewing these points, Dorothy said, "I'd never recommend investing in a restaurant over on the other side of the Cape anymore; it's just one mass of motels and pizza parlors now—absolutely frightful zoning—but this side of the Cape is still lovely. The Lookout has unlimited possibilities as a restaurant and inn. During the thirties it was renovated extensively and turned into a country club. People didn't have money to join expensive country clubs at that time, and so it never caught on. Eventually Mr. Hunt bought the house and grounds—nine acres in all, including one thousand feet of waterfront property and one of the finest views on the Cape."

"The Lookout was originally a captain's house, was it not?"

Dorothy realized that John Kragopoulos had done some homework on the place—a sure sign of real interest. "Yes, it was," she agreed. "It was built by a whaling captain in the sixteen-nineties as a gift for his bride. The most recent renovation, forty years ago, added two floors, but the original roof was put back on, including one of those charming little balconies near the peak of the chimney—widow's walks they're called, because so many of the captains' wives used to watch in vain for their men to come back from a voyage."

"The sea can be treacherous," her passenger agreed. "By the way, is there a dock with the property? If I relocate up here, I plan to buy a boat."

"A very good one," Dorothy assured him. "Oh, dear!" She gasped as the car skidded dangerously when she turned onto the narrow, winding road that led up to The Lookout. She managed to straighten the wheels and glanced anxiously at her passenger. But he seemed unperturbed, and remarked mildly that she was a brave lady to risk driving on such icy roads.

Like a surgeon's knife the words penetrated to the core of Dorothy's misery. It was a frightful day. It would be a miracle if the car didn't skid right off this narrow road. Whatever interest she had talked herself into about showing the house vanished. If the weather were only decent, the beaches and streets and woods would be filled with men and boys looking for Missy and Michael; but in this weather only the heartiest would think of going out—especially since many felt it was a useless search.

"I don't mind driving," she said thickly; "I'm just sorry Mr. Eldredge isn't with us. But I'm sure you understand."

"I understand very well," John Kragopoulos said. "What an agonizing experience for the parents to have young children missing! I am only sorry to take your time today. As a friend and coworker, you must be concerned."

Determinedly, Dorothy did not let herself reply to the sympathy in the man's voice and manner. "Let me tell you more about the house," she said. "All the windows to the front look over the water. The front door has an exquisite fanlight, which was a feature on the finer houses of that period. The large downstairs rooms have wonderful gable-end fireplaces. On a day like this many people would enjoy going to a restaurant where they can watch the storm while they enjoy a good drink and good food and a warm fire. Here we are."

They rounded the curve, and The Lookout was in full view. To Dorothy it seemed strangely bleak and dreary as it loomed against the shrouded embankment. The weatherbeaten shingles were stark gray. The sleet slapping against the windows and porches seemed to reveal mercilessly the peeling shutters and sagging outside steps.

She was surprised to see that Mr. Parrish had left the garage doors open. Maybe he had been carrying groceries his last trip in and had forgotten to come out again to pull the door down. But it was a break for them. She'd drive right into the roomy garage and park her car beside his old station wagon, and they'd be able to make a run for the house with some protection from the garage overhang.

"I've got a key to the back door," she told John Kragopoulos after they'd gotten out of the car. "I'm so sorry I didn't think to bring Ray's golf umbrella. I hope you don't get too wet."

"Don't worry about me," he chided. "I'm pretty rugged. Don't I look it?"

She smiled faintly and nodded. "All right, let's make a dash for it." They ran out of the garage and kept close to the wall as they covered the fifty feet to the kitchen door. Even so, the sleet pelted their faces and the wind pulled at their coats.

To her annoyance, Dorothy found that the door was double-locked. Mr. Parrish might have been more considerate, she fumed. She rummaged through her bag for the key to the top lock and found it. She gave a quick yank at the bell to let Mr. Parrish know they had arrived. She could hear the ringing sound echoing upstairs as she pushed the door in.

Her prospective buyer seemed unperturbed as he brushed sleet from his coat and dried his face with a handkerchief. He was a low-keyed person, Dorothy decided. She had to will herself not to sound either nervous or overly talkative showing the place. Every fiber of her being made her want to rush this man through the house. *See this . . . and this . . . and this . . . Now let me go back to Ray and Nancy, please; maybe there's been some news of the children.*

She did notice that he was carefully studying the kitchen. Deliberately she reached for her own handkerchief to dab at her face, aware suddenly that she was wearing her new suede winter coat. This morning she'd decided to wear it because of this appointment. She knew it was becoming and that the gray shade complemented her pepper-and-salt-colored hair. The big deep pockets were what made her conscious that she wasn't wearing her old storm coat—but the storm coat would certainly have been a better choice today.

And there was something else. Oh, yes. When she had put on the coat, she had wondered if Jonathan Knowles would stop into the office this afternoon and maybe notice it. Maybe this would be the day when he'd suggest they might have dinner together. She had daydreamed like that only hours ago. How could everything change so quickly, so terribly . . . ?"

"Mrs. Prentiss?"

"Yes. Oh, I'm sorry. I guess I'm a bit distracted today." To her ears she sounded falsely cheery. "As you can see, this kitchen needs modernizing, but it is very well laid out and roomy. That fireplace is large enough to cook for a crowd—but I'm sure you'd settle for modern ovens."

Unconsciously she'd lifted her voice. The wind was howling around the house with a harsh, mournful sound. From somewhere upstairs she heard a door slam and, just for a second, a wailing sound. It was her nerves; this house upset her today. The kitchen was freezing, too.

Quickly she led the way into the front rooms. She was anxious that Mr. Kragopoulos have the important first impression of the water view.

The savagery of the day only enhanced the breathtaking panorama that met their eyes when they stood at the windows. Angry whitecaps churned, lifted, fell, crashed on the rocks, pulled back. Together they stared at the tumultuous beating of the water on the rocks at the base of the cliff below.

"At high tide these rocks are completely covered," she said. "But just down a little to the left, past the jetty, there's a beautiful big sandy beach that is part of the property, and the dock is just past that."

She took him from room to room, pointing out the magnificent wide oak floors, the massive fireplaces, the leaded pane windows, the way the overall layout lent itself to a fine restaurant. They went up to the second floor, and he examined the large rooms that could be rented to overnight guests.

"During the renovation, they changed the small bedrooms into baths and connected them with the large rooms," Dorothy explained. "As a result, you've got really beautiful units that only need painting and papering. The brass beds alone are worth a fortune. Really, most of the furniture is very good—look at that highboy, for example. I used to have an interior decorator's shop, and a house like this is my idea of a dream to work on. The possibilities are endless."

He was interested. She could tell by the way he took time to open closet doors, pound walls and turn on water taps.

"The third floor has more bedrooms, and then Mr. Parrish's apartment is on the fourth floor," she said. "That apartment was designed for the resident manager of the country club. It's quite spacious and has a wonderful view of the town as well as the water."

He was pacing off the room and did not answer. Feeling pushy and garrulous, Dorothy walked over to the window. She should give him a chance to consider the house quietly and come up with any questions that might occur to him. *Hurry, hurry,* she thought. She wanted to get out of here. The insistent need to be back with Ray and Nancy, to know what was happening, was overwhelming. Suppose the children were out somewhere, exposed to this weather? Maybe she should take the car and cruise up and down; maybe they had just wandered away. Maybe if she tried to look in the woods, if she called them . . . She shook her head. She was being so foolish.

When Nancy had left Missy at the office with her yesterday, she'd said, "Please make her keep her mittens on when you go out. Her hands get so cold." Nancy had laughed as she handed Dorothy the mittens, saying, "As you can see, they don't match—and I'm not trying to set a style. This kid is always losing mittens." She'd given her one red mitten with a smile face and a blue-and-green-checked one.

Dorothy remembered the cheerful smile with which Missy had held up her hands when they'd gone for their drive. "Mommy said don't forget my mittens, Aunt Dorothy," she'd warned reproachfully. Later on, when they'd picked up Mike and stopped for ice cream, she'd asked, "Is it all right if I take my mittens off when I eat my cone?" Blessed little baby. Dorothy dabbed at the tears that rushed to her eyes.

Determinedly she composed herself and turned back to John Kragopoulos, who had just finished making notes on the size of the room. "You don't get high ceilings like these anymore except in these wonderful old houses," he exulted.

She couldn't tolerate being here like this any longer. "Let's go upstairs now," she said abruptly. "I think you'll like the view from the apartment." She led the way back into the hall and to the front stair-case. "Oh, did you notice that there are four heat zones in this house? It saves a lot on fuel bills."

They walked up the two flights of stairs quickly. "The third floor is exactly like the second floor," she explained as they passed it. "Mr. Par-rish has been renting the apartment on and off for six or seven years, I guess. His rent is quite minimal, but Mr. Eldredge felt that the presence of a tenant discourages vandals. Here we are—just down the hall." She knocked at the door of the apartment. There was no answer. "Mr. Par-rish," she called. "Mr. Parrish."

She began to open her handbag. "That's strange. I can't imagine where he'd go without his car. But I've got a key here somewhere." She started to rummage through her bag, feeling unreasonable annoyance. Over the phone Mr. Parrish had obviously been unhappy that she was bringing someone over. If he had been going out, he might have told her. She hoped the apartment was tidy. There weren't that many people looking for a three-hundred-fifty-thousand-dollar investment. They hadn't had even a nibble on the property in nearly a year.

Dorothy did not realize that the handle was being turned from the inside. But when the door was pulled open abruptly, she looked up and gasped and stared into the searching eyes and perspiring face of the fourth-floor tenant, Courtney Parrish.

"What a dreadful day for you to have to come." Parrish's tone was courteous as he stepped aside to let them pass. By holding the door back and getting out of the way, he reasoned, he might be able to avoid shak-ing hands. He could feel that his hands were drenched in perspiration.

His eyes darted from one to the other. Had they heard the little girl—that one cry? He was such a fool . . . getting too eager. After the phone call, he'd had to hurry so much. Picking up the children's cloth-ing, in his excitement he'd almost missed the little girl's undershirt. Then the can of baby powder had spilled. He'd had to wipe that up.

He'd taped the children's hands and feet and mouths and hidden them in that secret room behind the fireplace downstairs that he'd discovered months ago in wandering through the house. He knew those hidden rooms were peculiar to many old Cape houses. The early settlers used to hide in them during Indian attacks. But then he'd panicked. Suppose that fool of a real estate woman knew about that room and decided to show it? It was reached by a spring in the built-in bookcase in the main room downstairs.

Suppose she knew about it; just suppose. Even as Dorothy's Buick sedan pulled up and into the garage, he had dashed from his watching point at the window and rushed down to get the children. He'd carried them up and thrown them into one of the deep closets in the bedroom. Better . . . much better. He could say that he used that closet for storage and couldn't find the key. Since he had put a new lock on, that fool of a real estate woman couldn't possibly have a duplicate. Besides, the other closet in the room was practically the same size. She could show that one. That was where he could make a mistake . . . by getting complicated.

They'd dallied downstairs long enough for him to make one last inspection of the apartment; he hadn't missed anything, he was sure. The tub was still full, but he'd decided to leave it. He knew he'd sounded too annoyed over the phone. Let Dorothy think that that was the reason; he'd been just about to bathe. That would justify annoyance.

He wanted so much to get back to the little girl that it was painful. From deep in his loins he felt frantic desire. Right now, there she was, just a few feet from them all, behind that door, her little body half-naked. Oh, he couldn't wait! Be careful. Be careful. He tried to pay attention to the voice of reason that kept cautioning him, but it was so hard. . . .

"John Kragopoulos." That damn fellow was insisting on shaking his hand. Clumsily he tried to dry his palm on his trouser leg before grasping the outstretched hand that he could not ignore. "Courtney Parrish," he said sullenly.

He could see the fleeting expression of distaste come over the other man's face when their hands touched. Probably a damned fag. Half the restaurants on this side of the Cape were run by fags. Now they wanted this house too. Well, fine. After today he wouldn't need it.

Suddenly he realized that if this house were sold, no one would ever find it suspicious if as Courtney Parrish he didn't come back to the Cape. Then he could lose weight and let his hair grow and totally change his appearance again, because he would want to be here for Nancy's trial, after they found the children's bodies and accused her. Why, this wasn't a problem at all. Fate was playing into his hands. This was meant to be.

He shuddered as a wave of exhilaration surged through his body. Why, he could even ask about Nancy. It would be only neighborly. Feeling suddenly confident, he said courteously, "I am pleased to meet you, Mr. Kragopoulos, and rue the weather in which you first observe this wonderful house." Miraculously, the dampness was leaving his hands and armpits and groin.

The tension in the small foyer relaxed tangibly. He realized that most of it was emanating from Dorothy anyway. Why not? He'd seen her countless times in these past years, in and out of the Eldredge house, pushing the children on the swing, taking them in her car. He had her number: one of those dreary middle-aged widows trying to be important to someone; a parasite. Husband dead. No children. A miracle she didn't have a sick old mother. Most of them did. That helped them to be martyrs to their friends. So nice to Mother. Why? Because they needed to be nice to someone. They had to be important. And if they had children, they concentrated on them. The way Nancy's mother had.

"I have been listening to the radio," he said to Dorothy, "and am so disturbed. Have the Eldredge children been found yet?"

"No." Dorothy felt all her nerve endings tingling. From inside she could hear that the radio was on. She caught the word "bulletin." "Excuse me," she cried, and hurried into the living room and over to the radio. Swiftly she turned up the volume. ". . . storm increasing. Gale winds from fifty to sixty miles an hour are predicted. Driving is hazardous. The air and water search for the Eldredge children has been suspended indefinitely. Special patrol cars will continue cruising in Adams Port and vicinity. Chief Coffin of Adams Port urges that anyone who believes he or she may have any information report it at once. He urges that any untoward incident be discussed with the police, such as a strange vehicle that may have been seen in the neighborhood of the Eldredge home; any unfamiliar person or persons in the area. Call this special number: KL five, three eight hundred. Your privacy will be respected."

The commentator's voice continued. "Despite the urgent appeal for clues to the missing children, we have it on good authority that Mrs. Nancy Harmon Eldredge will be taken to Police Headquarters for questioning."

She had to go to Nancy and Ray. Dorothy turned to John Kragopoulos abruptly. "As you can see, this is a charming apartment, quite suitable for two people. The view from both the front and back windows in this room is really spectacular."

"You are an astronomer, perhaps?" John Kragopoulos spoke to Courtney Parrish.

"Not really. Why do you ask?"

"It is just that magnificent telescope."

Belatedly, Parrish realized that the telescope was still positioned facing the Eldredge house. Seeing that John Kragopoulos was about to look through it, he gave it an abrupt push so that it tilted upward.

"I enjoy studying the stars," he volunteered hastily.

John Kragopoulos squinted as he looked through the lens. "Magnificent equipment," he cried. "Simply magnificent." Carefully he manipulated the telescope until it was pointing in the same direction as it had been when he had first noticed it. Then, sensing the other man's antagonism, he straightened up and began to study the room. "This is a well-laid-out apartment," he commented to Dorothy.

"I have been most comfortable here," Parrish volunteered. Inwardly he was fuming at himself. Once more he had suspiciously overreacted. The moisture was pouring from his body again. Had he forgotten anything else? Was there any sign of the children around? Frantically his eyes darted around the room. Nothing.

Dorothy said, "I'd like to show the bedroom and bath if it's all right."

"Of course."

He'd straightened the coverlet on the bed and shoved the can of baby powder into the night-table drawer.

"The bathroom is as large as most of today's second bedrooms," Dorothy told John Kragopoulos. Then, as she glanced around it, she said, "Oh, I'm so sorry." She stared down at the filled tub. "We did catch you at an inconvenient time. You were just about to bathe."

"I have no rigid schedule to follow." Despite the words, he managed to leave the impression that she had indeed inconvenienced him.

John Kragopoulos stepped back into the bedroom hastily. He realized that this man obviously resented their coming. Leaving the tub like that was a clumsy way of making the point. And that duck floating in the tub. A child's toy. He winced, disgusted. His hand touched the closet door. The satiny quality of the wood intrigued him. Really, this house was beautifully constructed. John Kragopoulos was a hard-headed businessman, but he also believed in instinct. His instinct told him that this house would be a good investment. They wanted three hundred and fifty thousand for it. . . . He'd offer two ninety-five and come up to three twenty. He was sure he could get it for that.

The decision finalized in his mind, he began to take a proprietary interest in the apartment. "May I open this closet?" he asked. The question was perfunctory. He was already turning the handle.

"I'm sorry. I changed the lock on that closet and can't seem to find the key. If you'll look in this other closet . . . they're practically identical."

Dorothy looked sharply at the new handle and lock. Both were run-of-the-mill low-priced hardware-store items. "I do hope you kept the original handle," she said. "All the doorknobs were specially cast solid brass."

"Yes, I have it. It needs fixing." God, would that woman insist on turning the handle? Suppose the new lock gave? It wasn't a very tight fit into the old wood. Suppose it slid open?

Dorothy relaxed her grip on the handle. The slight flare of annoyance she'd felt vanished as quickly as it had come. What, in the name of heaven, difference did it make if all the brass handles all over the universe were changed? Who cared?

Parrish had to clamp his lips together to keep from ordering that nosy woman and her prospective buyer out. The children were just on the other side of the door. Had he tightened their gags enough? Would they hear the familiar voice and try to make some kind of sound? He had to get rid of these people.

But Dorothy wanted to go too. She was aware of an indefinably familiar scent in the bedroom—one that made her acutely aware of Missy. She turned to John Kragopoulos. "Perhaps we should start . . . if you're ready."

He nodded. "I'm quite ready, thank you." He started to leave, this time obviously avoiding shaking hands. Dorothy followed him. "Thank you, Mr. Parrish," she said hastily over her shoulder. "I'll be in touch with you."

She led the way down the stairs to the main floor in silence. They went through the kitchen, and when she opened the back door she could see why the gale warnings were in effect. The wind had heightened sharply in the brief time they'd been in the house. Oh, God, the children would die of exposure if they were outside all this time.

"We'd better make a dash for the garage," she said. John Kragopoulos, looking preoccupied, nodded and took her arm. Together they ran, not bothering to stay under the overhang. With the increased wind velocity there was simply no protection from the sleet, which was now finely blended with snow.

In the garage, Dorothy walked between the station wagon and her car and opened the door on the driver's side. As she began to slide into her car, she glanced down. A bright red scrap of material on the garage floor caught her eye. Getting out of the car again, she bent down, picked it up, then slumped back into the car seat, holding the object against her cheek. John Kragopoulos, sounding alarmed, asked, "My dear Mrs. Prentiss, what is wrong?"

"It's the mitten!" Dorothy cried. "It's Missy's mitten. She was wearing it yesterday when I took her out for ice cream. She must have left it in the car. I guess I kicked it out when I got out of the car before. She was always losing her mittens. She never had two on that matched. We always joked about that. And this morning, they found the mate of this one on the swing." Dorothy began to sob—a dry, hacking sound that she tried to stifle by holding the mitten against her lips.

John Kragopoulos said quietly, "There is little that I can say except to remind you that a merciful and loving God is aware of your pain and the agony of the parents. He will not fail your need. Somehow I am confident of that. Now, please, wouldn't you like me to drive?"

"Please," Dorothy said in a muffled voice. She pushed the mitten deep into her pocket as she slid over. She wouldn't want Nancy or Ray to see it; it would be too heartbreaking. Oh Missy, Missy! She'd taken it off when she started to eat the cone yesterday. She could see her dropping it on the seat. Oh, the poor little kids.

John Kragopoulos was glad to be driving. A great restlessness had come over him in the room with that hideous man. There was something too slimy and sour-smelling about him. And that scent of baby powder in the bedroom and that incredible toy in the tub. How could a grown man need such trappings?

Upstairs, Parrish stood to one side and watched from the window until the car had disappeared around the bend in the lane. Then, with trembling fingers, he drew out the key from his pocket and unlocked the closet door.

The boy was conscious. His sandy hair fell on his forehead, and his large blue eyes were filled with terror as he stared mutely up. His mouth was still securely taped and his hands and legs still firmly tied.

Roughly he pushed the child aside and reached past him for the little girl. He lifted out her limp body and laid her on the bed—then shrieked in outrage and despair as he stared down at her closed eyes and pinched blue face. . . .

 CHAPTER 16

Nancy's hands were clenching and unclenching, pulling at the coverlet. Gently, Lendon covered her fingers with his own strong, well-shaped hands. Anxiety and agitation were causing her to breathe in harsh, labored breaths.

"Nancy, don't worry. Everyone here knows that you couldn't hurt your children. That's what you meant, isn't it?"

"Yes . . . yes . . . people think I could hurt them. How could I kill them? They are me. I died with them. . . ."

"We all die a little death when we lose the people we love, Nancy. Think back with me before all the trouble started. Tell me what it was like when you were growing up in Ohio."

"Growing up?" Nancy's voice trailed off into a whisper. The rigidity of her body began to relax.

"Yes, tell me about your father. I never knew him."

Jed Coffin moved restlessly, and the chair he was sitting on made a creaking sound against the wooden floor. Lendon shot him a warning glance. "I have reason for this," he said quietly. "Please bear with me."

"Daddy?" A lilt came into Nancy's voice. She laughed softly. "He was such fun. Mother and I used to drive to the airport to pick him up when he came in from a flight. In all those years he never came back from a trip without something for Mother and me. We used to go all over the world on his vacations. They always took me with them. I remember one trip . . ."

Ray could not take his eyes off Nancy. He had never heard her speak in that tone of voice—animated, amused, a ripple of laughter running through her words. Was this what he had been blindly trying to find in her? Was it more than being tired of living with the fear of discovery? He hoped so.

Jonathan Knowles listened intently to Nancy, approving of the technique Lendon Miles was using to gain her confidence and relax her before asking about the details of the day the Harmon children had vanished. It was agonizing to hear the soft ticking of the grandfather clock . . . a reminder that time was passing. He realized that he was finding it impossible not to look at Dorothy. He knew he had been harsh when he spoke to her as she was getting into her car. It was his disappointment that had reacted to her deliberate falsehood—the fact that she had made a point of telling him personally about knowing Nancy as a child.

Why had she done that? Was it perhaps that he had indicated somehow that Nancy looked familiar? Had it been simply an attempt to keep him from the truth because she couldn't trust him with the truth? Had he perhaps been displaying what Emily used to call his "Your witness, Counsel" manner?

In any event, he felt that he owed Dorothy an apology. She didn't look well. The strain was telling on her. She still was wearing her heavy coat, and her hands were jammed in her pockets. He decided that he wanted to talk to her at the first opportunity. She needed calming down. She certainly thought the world of those children.

The lights in the room flickered, then went off. "That figures." Jed Coffin propped the microphone on the table and searched for matches. Quickly Ray lighted the antique gas lamps on either side of the mantel.

They threw a yellow glow that melted and blended with the vivid red flames of the fireplace, bathing the couch where Nancy was lying in a rosy glow and throwing deep shadows on the corners of the dark room.

It seemed to Ray that the steady tattooing of the sleet against the house and the moaning of the wind through the pines had intensified. Suppose the children were out somewhere in this weather . . . ? Last night he'd awakened hearing Missy cough. But when he went into her room, she'd been settled again in deep sleep, her cheek cupped in her palm. As he bent over to pull up her covers, she'd murmured, "Daddy" and stirred, but at the touch of his hand on her back she'd settled down again.

And Michael. He and Mike had gone for milk to Wiggins' Market— was it just yesterday morning? They'd arrived just as that tenant at The Lookout, Mr. Parrish, was leaving. The man had nodded pleasantly, but when he got into that old Ford wagon of his, Michael's face had wrinkled with distaste. "I don't like him," he'd said.

Ray almost smiled at the memory. Mike was a rugged little guy, but he had something of Nancy's distaste for ugliness, and no matter how you sliced it, Courtney Parrish was a clumsy, slow-moving, unattractive man.

Even the Wigginses had commented on him. After he left, Jack Wiggins said drily, "That fellow's about the slowest-moving human being I ever bumped into. He meanders around shopping like he's got all the time in the world."

Michael had looked reflective. "I never have enough time," he said. "I'm helping my dad refinish a desk for my room, and every time I want to keep working on it, I have to get ready for school."

"You've got quite an assistant there, Ray," Jack Wiggins had remarked. "I'll give him a job anytime; he sounds like a worker."

Mike had picked up the package. "I'm strong, too," he'd said. "I can carry things. I can carry my sister for a long time."

Ray ground his hands into fists. This was unreal, impossible. The children missing. Nancy sedated. What was she saying?

Her voice still had that eager lilt. "Daddy used to call Mother and me his girls. . . ." Her voice faltered.

"What is it, Nancy?" Dr. Miles asked. "Your father called you his little girl? Did that upset you?"

"No . . . no . . . no . . . he called us his girls. It was different . . . it was different . . . not like that at all. . . ." Her voice rose sharply in protest.

Lendon's voice was soothing. "All right, Nancy. Don't worry about that. Let's talk about college. Did you want to go away to school?"

"Yes . . . I really did . . . except . . . I was worried about Mother. . . ."

"Why did you worry about her?"

"I was afraid she'd be lonely—because of Daddy . . . and we'd sold the house; she was moving into an apartment. So much had changed for her. And she'd started a new job. But she liked working. . . . She said she wanted me to go. . . . She liked to say that today . . . today . . ."

"Today is the first day of the rest of your life," Lendon finished quietly. Yes, Priscilla had said that to him too. The day she came into the office after she'd put Nancy on the plane for school. She told him about still waving goodbye after the plane had taxied away toward the runway. Then her eyes had filled, and she'd smiled apologetically. "Look how ridiculous I am," she'd said, trying to laugh; "the proverbial mother hen."

"I think you're doing fine," Lendon had told her.

"It's just that when you think how your life can change. . . . so incredibly. All of a sudden, a whole part, the most important part . . . is ended. But on the other hand, I think when you've had something quite wonderful . . . so very much happiness . . . you can't look back and regret. That's what I told Nancy today. . . . I don't want her worrying about me. I want her to have a wonderful time in school. I said that we should both remember that motto: 'Today is the first day of the rest of our lives.' "

Lendon remembered that a patient had come into the office. At the time, he'd considered it a blessing; he'd been dangerously close to putting his arms around Priscilla.

". . . but it was all right," Nancy was saying, her voice still hesitant and groping. "Mother's letters were cheerful. She loved her job. She wrote a lot about Dr. Miles. . . . I was glad. . . ."

"Did you enjoy school, Nancy?" Lendon asked. "Did you have many friends?"

"At first. I liked the girls, and I dated a lot."

"How about your schoolwork? Did you like your subjects?"

"Oh, yes. They all came pretty easily . . . except bio. . . ." Her tone changed—subtly became troubled. "That was harder. I never liked science . . . but the college required it . . . so I took it. . . ."

"And you met Carl Harmon."

"Yes. He . . . wanted to help me with bio. He had me come to his office and he'd go over the work with me. He said I was dating too much and that I must stop or I'd be sick. He was so concerned . . . he even started giving me vitamins. He must have been right . . . because I was so tired . . . so much . . . and started to feel so depressed. . . . I missed Mother. . . ."

"But you knew you would be home over Christmas."

"Yes . . . and it didn't make sense. . . . All of a sudden . . . it got so bad . . . I didn't want to upset her . . . so I didn't write about it . . . but I think she knew. . . . She came out for a weekend . . . because she was worried about me . . . I know it. . . . And then she was killed . . . because she came out to see me. . . . It was my fault . . . my fault. . . ." Her voice rose in a shriek of pain, then broke into a sob.

Ray started out of his chair, but Jonathan pulled him back. The oil lamp flickered on Nancy's face. It was contorted with pain. "Mother!" she cried, "Oh Mother . . . please don't be dead . . . live! Oh, Mother, please, please live. . . . I need you. . . . Mother, don't be dead . . . Mother . . ."

Dorothy turned her head, trying to bite back tears. No wonder Nancy had resented her remarks about being a surrogate grandmother to Missy and Michael. Why was she here? No one was even conscious or caring of her presence. She'd be more useful if she went out and made coffee. Nancy might want some later too. She should take off her coat. She couldn't. She felt too cold; so alone. She stared down for a moment at the hooked rug and watched as the pattern blurred before her eyes. Lifting her head, she met the inscrutable gaze of Jonathan Knowles and knew that he'd been watching her for some time.

". . . Carl helped you when your mother died. He was good to you?" Why was Lendon Miles dragging out this agony? What point was there in making Nancy relive this too? Dorothy started to her feet.

Nancy's answer was quiet. "Oh, yes. He was so good to me. . . . He took care of everything."

"And you married him."

"Yes. He said he'd take care of me. And I was so tired. He was so good to me. . . ."

"Nancy, you mustn't blame yourself for your mother's accident. That wasn't your fault."

"Accident?" Nancy's voice was speculative. "Accident? But it wasn't an accident. It wasn't an accident. . . ."

"Of course it was." Lendon's voice stayed calm, but he could feel the tightness of his throat muscles.

"I don't know . . . I don't know. . . ."

"All right; we'll talk about it later. Tell us about Carl."

"He was good to me. . . ."

"You keep saying that, Nancy. How was he good to you?"

"He took care of me. I was sick; he had to do so much for me. . . ."

"What did he do for you, Nancy?"

"I don't want to talk about that."

"Why, Nancy?"

"I don't. I don't. . . ."

"All right. Tell us about the children. About Peter and Lisa."

"They were so good. . . ."

"They were well behaved, you mean."

"They were so good . . . too good . . ."

"Nancy you keep saying 'good.' Carl was so good to you. And the children were good. You must have been very happy."

"Happy? I was so tired . . ."

"Why were you so tired?"

"Carl said I was so sick. He was so good to me."

"Nancy, you must tell us. How was Carl good to you?"

"He made sure I was getting better. He wanted me to get better. He said I had to be a good little girl."

"How did you feel sick, Nancy? What hurt you?"

"So tired . . . always so tired. . . . Carl helped me. . . ."

"Helped you how?"

"I don't want to talk about that."

"But you must, Nancy. What did Carl do?"

"I'm tired . . . I'm tired now. . . ."

"All right, Nancy. I want you to rest for a few minutes; then we'll talk some more. Just rest . . . just rest. . . ."

Lendon got up. Chief Coffin immediately took his arm and jerked his head toward the kitchen. As soon as they were out of the room, Chief Coffin spoke abruptly. "This isn't leading us anywhere. This could take hours and you're not going to find anything out. The girl blames herself for her mother's accident because the mother had made the trip to see her. It's that simple. Now, if you think you can find out anything else about the Harmon murders, get to it. Or else I question her at Head-quarters."

"You can't force . . . She's starting to talk. . . . There's a great deal that even her subconscious doesn't want to face."

The chief snapped: "And I don't want to face myself if there's any chance those kids are still alive and I've wasted precious time here."

"All right, I'll get to questioning her about this morning. But first, please, let me ask her about the day the Harmon children disappeared. If there is any link between the two, she may reveal it."

Chief Coffin looked at his watch. "God, it's almost four already. Whatever visibility there was all day will be gone in half an hour. Where is a radio? I want to hear the newscast."

"There's one in the kitchen, Chief." Bernie Mills, the patrolman on guard in the house, was an earnest, dark-haired man in his early thirties. He'd been on the force twelve years, and this was by far the most sensational case he'd ever known. Nancy Harmon. Nancy Eldredge was Nancy Harmon! Ray Eldredge's wife. It showed. You never knew what was going on inside people. Bernie had played on the same ball team summers with Ray Eldredge when they were little kids. Then Ray had gone to one of those fancy prep schools and Dartmouth College. He had never expected Ray would settle on the Cape when he finished service. But he did. When he married the girl who'd rented this house, everybody said that she was some looker. A few people commented that she kind of reminded you of someone.

Bernie remembered his own reaction to that talk. Lots of people look like someone else. His own uncle, a deadbeat and drunk who made his aunt's life miserable, was a dead ringer for Barry Goldwater. He glanced quickly out the window. The television news guys were all still out there, with their trucks and all their gear. Looking for a story. He wondered what they'd think if they knew Nancy Eldredge was injected with truth serum right now. Now, there was a story. He was anxious to get home to tell Jean about it. He wondered how she was doing. The baby had been teething last night; kept both of them up.

For a single, terrible minute Bernie wondered how it would feel if the little guy was missing on a day like this . . . out there somewhere . . . and he not knowing. The prospect was so awful, so breathtaking, so mind-shattering that he rejected it. Jean never took her eyes off Bobby. Sometimes she bugged Bernie the way she was always fussing about the kid. Right now her need to never take her eyes off their baby reassured him, assuaged his apprehensions. The little guy was fine—trust Jean.

Dorothy was in the kitchen filling the coffeepot. Bernie reflected that Dorothy bugged him a little. She had such a—well, guess you'd call it reserved—way. She could be nice and friendly—but, well, Bernie didn't know. He decided that Dorothy was just a little too highfalutin for his thinking.

He turned on the transistor radio, and instantly the voice of Dan Phillips, the newscaster for WCOD in Hyannis, filled the room. "The case of the missing Eldredge children has just taken a new twist," Phillips said, and his voice was pulsing with somewhat unprofessional excitement. "A mechanic, Otto Linden from the Gulf Station on Route Twenty-eight in Hyannis, has just phoned us to say that he can positively state that this morning at nine A.M. he filled the gas tank of Rob Legler, the missing witness in the Harmon murder case of seven years ago. Mr. Linden said that Legler appeared nervous and volunteered the information that he was on his way to Adams Port to visit someone who probably wouldn't be glad to see him. He was driving a late-model red Dodge Dart."

Jed Coffin swore softly. "And I'm wasting my time here listening to this claptrap." He started for the phone and picked it up just as it rang. After the caller identified himself, he said impatiently, "I heard it. All right. I want a roadblock on the bridges going to the mainland. Check with the FBI deserter file—find out what they may know about the latest whereabouts of Rob Legler. Put out a bulletin about a red Dodge." He slammed the receiver back onto the hook and turned to Lendon.

"Now I've got a simple, direct question for you to ask Mrs. Eldredge. It's whether or not Rob Legler got here this morning . . . and what he said to her."

Lendon stared. "You mean . . ."

"I mean that Rob Legler is the person who could dump Nancy Eldredge back into the middle of a murder trial. The Harmon case has never been closed. Now, suppose he's been hiding out in Canada for six years or so. He needs money. Didn't it come out at the Harmon trial that Nancy had inherited a fair amount of money from her parents?— some hundred and fifty thousand dollars. Now, suppose Rob Legler knows about that money and somehow finds out where Nancy is. The District Attorney's staff in San Francisco know where she's been. Now, suppose Legler decides he's sick of Canada and wants to come back here and needs a stake. How about going to Nancy Eldredge and promising to change his testimony if he's ever caught and there's a new trial? That's the same as making her give him a blank check for the rest of her life. He gets here. He sees her. The deal sours. She doesn't go for it . . . or he changes his mind. She knows that at any moment he may be caught or turn himself in and she's back in San Francisco on a murder charge, and she cracks. . . ."

"And murders her Eldredge children?" Lendon's voice was scornful. "Have you thought about the possibility that this student who nearly put Nancy in the gas chamber was in the vicinity when both sets of children disappeared?"

"Give me one more chance," Lendon pleaded. "Just let me ask her about the day the Harmon children disappeared. I want her to describe the events of that day first."

"You have thirty minutes—no more."

Dorothy began pouring coffee into cups that she'd already placed on a tray. Quickly she cut up a coffee cake that Nancy had baked the day before. "Perhaps coffee will help everyone," she said.

She carried the tray into the front room. Ray was sitting in the chair Lendon had drawn next to the couch. He was holding Nancy's hands in his, gently massaging them. She was very still. Her breathing was even, but as the others came into the room, she stirred and moaned.

Jonathan was standing by the mantel, staring into the fire. He had lighted his pipe, and the warm smell of the good tobacco he used had begun to penetrate the room. Dorothy breathed it in deeply as she set the coffee tray on the round pine table by the fireplace. A wave of pure nostalgia washed over her. Kenneth had smoked a pipe, and that had been his brand of tobacco. She and Kenneth used to love stormy winter afternoons like this. They would make a roaring fire and get out wine and cheese and books and sit contently together. Regret swept over her. Regret because you really can't control your life. Most of the time you don't act; you react.

"Will you have coffee and cake?" she asked Jonathan.

He looked at her thoughtfully. "Please."

She knew he took cream and one sugar. Without asking, she prepared the coffee that way and handed it to him. "Shouldn't you take your coat off?" he asked her.

"In a little while. I'm still so chilled."

Dr. Miles and Chief Coffin had followed her in and were helping themselves to the coffee. Dorothy poured another cup and carried it over to the couch. "Ray, please have some."

He looked up. "Thank you." As he reached for it, he murmured to Nancy, "Everything is going to be all right, little girl."

Nancy shuddered violently. Her eyes flew open and she threw up her arm, knocking the cup from Ray's hand. It fell and broke on the floor, spewing hot liquid over her robe and the blanket. Splashes of it spattered on Ray and Nancy. Simultaneously they winced as Nancy cried out in the desperate tone of a trapped animal, "I am not your little girl! Don't call me your little girl!"

CHAPTER 17

Courtney Parrish turned from the small unmoving figure on the bed, sighing heavily. He'd taken the adhesive from Missy's mouth and the cords from her wrists and ankles, and they made an untidy pile on the quilt. Her fine, silky hair was matted now. He'd been planning to brush it when he bathed her, but now there was no point. He needed her response.

The little boy, Michael, was still on the floor of the closet. His large blue eyes were terrified as Courtney picked him up and hugged him against his massive chest.

He laid Michael on the bed, undid the bindings on his ankles and wrists and with a quick pull yanked the adhesive off his mouth. The boy cried out in pain, then bit his lip. He seemed more responsive—infinitely wary, apprehensive, but with some of the courage of the trapped animal.

"What did you do to my sister?" The belligerent tone made Courtney realize that the boy hadn't drunk all the milk with the sedative he'd given him just before the meddling fools came along.

"She's asleep."

"Let us go home. We want to go home. I don't like you. I told my daddy I didn't like you, and Aunt Dorothy was here and you hid us."

Courtney lifted his right hand, curved it into the mitt-like shape and slapped Michael across the cheek. Michael jerked back in pain and then rolled out from under the man's grasp. Courtney reached for him, lost his balance and fell clumsily across the bed. His mouth touched Missy's tangled yellow hair, and for an instant he was distracted. Pulling himself up, he turned and was on his feet, crouching to spring at Michael. But Michael was backing away toward the bedroom door. With a swift movement he opened it and raced through the adjoining sitting room.

Courtney lunged after him, realizing that he hadn't locked the apartment door. He hadn't wanted Dorothy to hear the distinct ping of the lock turning as she went downstairs.

Michael threw open the door and raced for the staircase. His shoes clattered on the uncarpeted stairs. He moved swiftly, a slim shadow that darted down into the protecting gloom of the third floor. Courtney hurried after him, but in his frantic rush lost his balance and fell. He hurtled down six steps before he managed to stop the fall by grasping the heavy wooden banister. Shaking his head to clear it, he picked himself up, aware of a sharp pain in his right ankle. He had to make sure the kitchen door was locked.

There was no further sound of footsteps. The boy was probably hiding in one of the third-floor bedrooms, but he had plenty of time to look for him. First the kitchen door. The windows were no problem. They were all double-locked, and too heavy anyhow. The double lock on the front door was too high for the child. He'd just secure the kitchen door, then search for the boy—room by room. He'd call to him and warn him. The boy was so frightened. His eyes had been so terrified and wary. He looked more than ever like Nancy this way. Oh, this was so unexpectedly wonderful. But he had to hurry. He had to make sure the boy couldn't get out of the house.

"I'll be right back, Michael," he called. "I'll find you. I'll find you, Michael. You're a very bad boy. You must be punished, Michael. Do you hear me, Michael?"

He thought he heard a noise in the bedroom on his right and rushed in, favoring his ankle. But the room was empty. Suppose the boy had run through this hallway and used the front stairs? Suddenly panicking, he lumbered down the remaining two flights. From outside he could hear the waves from the bay crashing against the rocks. He raced into the kitchen and over to the door. This was the door he always used going into and out of the house. This one had not only a double lock but a high bolt. His breath came in quick furious gasps. With thick, trembling fingers, he shoved the bolt into place. Then he pulled over a heavy wooden kitchen chair and wedged it under the knob. The boy would never be able to move this. There was no other way out of the house.

The heavy storm had almost obliterated the remaining daylight. Courtney switched on the overhead light, but an instant later it flickered and went off. He realized that the storm had probably pulled down some wires. It would make it harder to find the boy. All the upstairs bedrooms were fully furnished. They all had closets, too—deep ones—and cupboards that he might hide in. Courtney bit his lip in fury as he reached for the hurricane lamp on the table, struck the match and lighted the wick. The glass was red, and the light cast an eerie reddish glow against the fireplace wall and faded planked floor and thick-beamed ceiling. The wind wailed against the shutters as Courtney called, "Michael . . . it's all right, Michael. I'm not angry anymore. Come out, Michael. I'll take you home to your mother."

CHAPTER 18

The chance to blackmail Nancy Harmon was the break Rob Legler had been needing for over six years—from the day he'd gotten on a plane to Canada after carefully shredding his embarkation orders for Vietnam. During those years, he'd worked as a farmhand near Halifax. It was the only job he'd been able to get, and he loathed it. Not for a minute did he regret his decision to bolt the Army. Who in the hell wanted to go to a filthy, hot hole to be shot at by a bunch of pint-sized bastards? He didn't.

He'd worked on the farm in Canada because he didn't have any alternative. He'd left San Francisco with sixty bucks in his pocket. If he went back home, he'd be tossed in jail. A conviction for desertion wasn't his idea of the way to spend the rest of his life. He needed a good stake to cut out for someplace like Argentina. He wasn't just one of the thousands of deserters who eventually might be able to slip back into the States with faked identification. Thanks to that blasted Harmon case, he was a hunted man.

If only that conviction hadn't been upset . . . that case would be finished. But that bastard of a D.A. had said if he spent twenty years he'd retry Nancy Harmon for the murder of those kids. And Rob was the witness, the witness who supplied the motive.

Rob couldn't let that scene happen again. As it was, the D.A. last time had told the jury that there was probably more to the killing than Nancy Harmon wanting to get out of a home situation. "She was probably in love," he'd said. "We have here a very attractive young woman who since the age of eighteen has been married to an older man. Her life might well be the envy of many a young woman. Professor Harmon's devotion to his young wife and family was an example for the community. But is Nancy Harmon satisfied? No. When a student-repairman comes in, sent by her husband so that she will not have to endure even a few hours' discomfort, what does she do? She follows him around, insists he have coffee, says it's nice to talk to someone young . . . says she has to get away . . . responds passionately to his overtures . . . and then when he tells her that 'raising kids isn't his bag' she calmly promises him that her children are going to be smothered.

"Now, ladies and gentlemen of the jury, I despise Rob Legler. I believe that he toyed with this foolish young woman. I don't for a minute believe that their unholy passion ended with a few kisses . . . but I do believe him when he quotes the damning phrases that fell from Nancy Harmon's lips."

Frig him. Rob felt sick fear in the pit of his stomach whenever he remembered that speech. That bastard would have given anything to have made him an accessory to murder. All because he'd been in old Harmon's office the day his wife phoned to tell him the heater had gone off. Rob wasn't usually given to volunteering his services. But he'd never seen a machine or engine or piece of equipment he couldn't fix, and he'd heard some guys talk about what a doll that creepy old drag had for a wife.

That piece of intriguing information had made him volunteer his services. At first Harmon had turned him down, but then when he couldn't get his regular maintenance man he'd said okay. He said he didn't want his wife taking the kids to a motel. That was what she'd suggested.

So Rob had gone over. Everything the guys had said about Nancy Harmon was true. She was a real looker. But she sure didn't seem to know it. She was kind of hesitant . . . unsure of herself. He'd gotten over about noon. She was just feeding the two little kids . . . a boy and a girl. Quiet kids, both of them. She didn't pay much attention to him, just thanked him for coming and turned back to the kids.

He realized that the only way to get her attention was through the kids and started talking to them. It was always easy for Rob to turn on the charm. He liked gals older than himself, too. Not that this one was older by much. But he'd learned from the time he was sixteen and screwing his next-door neighbor's wife that if you're nice to a woman's kids, she thinks you're A-okay and all the guilt goes down the drain.

Boy, Rob could write a book on the whole mother-complex rational-
ization.

In a couple of minutes he'd had the kids laughing and Nancy laughing, and then he'd invited the little boy down to be his helper fixing the
furnace. Just as he expected, the little girl asked to go too, and then
Nancy said she'd come along to make sure they didn't get in the way.
There wasn't much wrong with the furnace—just a clogged filter—but
he said it needed a part and he could get it working but he'd be back
and do the job right.

He got out fast the first day. No point in getting old Harmon upset.
Went straight back to his office. Harmon looked annoyed and worried
when he opened the door, but when he saw Rob he gave a big, relieved
smile. "So soon? You must be a whiz. Or couldn't you take care of it?"

Rob said, "I got it going. But you need a new part, sir, that I'll be glad
to pick up. It's one of those little things that if you call in a regular service, they'll make a big production over. I can get the part for a couple
of bucks. Be glad to do it."

Harmon fell for it, of course. Probably glad to save the money. And
Rob went back the next day and the next day. Harmon warned him that
his wife was very nervous and rested a lot and to please keep out of her
way. But Rob didn't see where she acted nervous. Timid, maybe, and
scared. He got her talking. She told him that she'd had a nervous breakdown after her mother died. "I guess I've been terribly depressed," she
said. "But I'm sure I'm getting better. I've even stopped taking most of
my medicine. My husband doesn't realize that. He'd probably be
annoyed. But I feel better without it."

Rob had told her how pretty she was, kind of feeling his way. He'd
begun to suspect that she might be a pushover. It was obvious she was
pretty bored with old Harmon and getting restless. He said maybe she
should get out more. She'd said, "My husband doesn't believe in company. He feels that at the end of the day he doesn't need to see any
more people—not after all the students he has to contend with."

That was when he'd known he'd try to make a pass at her.

Rob had an airtight alibi for that morning the Harmon kids had disappeared. He'd been in a class of only six students. But the D.A. had
told him that if he could find one shred of evidence that would help him
hang an accessory charge on Rob, it would be his pleasure to do it. Rob
had hired a lawyer. Plenty scared, he didn't want the D.A. poking into
his background and finding out about the time he'd been named in a
paternity suit in Cooperstown. The lawyer had told him that his posture
had to be that he was the respectful student of a distinguished professor; had been anxious to do a favor for him; had tried to stay away from
the wife, but she had kept following him around. That he never took it

seriously when she talked about the children being smothered. Actually, he'd thought she was just nervous and sick, the way the Professor had warned him.

But on the stand it didn't work like that. "Were you attracted to this young woman?" the D.A. asked smoothly.

Rob looked at Nancy sitting at the defendant's table next to her lawyer, looking at him through blank, unseeing eyes. "I didn't think in those terms, sir," he replied. "To me Mrs. Harmon was the wife of a teacher I admired greatly. I simply wanted to fix the furnace as I'd volunteered to do and get back to my room. I had a paper to write, and anyhow a sick woman with two children simply isn't my bag." It was that elaboration, that last damned phrase that the D.A. had pounced on. By the time he was finished with him, Rob was wringing with perspiration.

Yes, he'd heard the Professor's wife was a doll. . . . No, he wasn't given to volunteering his help. . . . Yes, he'd been curious to get a look at her. . . . Yes, he had made a pass at her. . . .

"But it stopped there!" Rob had shouted from the stand. "With two thousand coeds on campus, I didn't need problems." Then he'd admitted that he had told Nancy that she turned him on and he'd like to hustle her.

The D.A. had looked at him contemptuously, then read into the record the time Rob had been beaten up by an irate husband—the episode in Cooperstown when he'd been named in the paternity suit.

The D.A. said, "This philanderer was no willing volunteer. He went into that house to size up a beautiful young woman whom he'd heard about. He made a play for her. It succeeded beyond his wildest dreams. Ladies and gentlemen of the jury, I am not suggesting that Rob Legler was part of the scheme to murder Nancy Harmon's children. At least, in the legal sense he wasn't. But I am convinced that morally, before God, he is guilty. He let this gullible, ungrateful young woman know that he'd—and I use his words—'hustle her' if she were free, and she chose a freedom that is repugnant to the basic instincts of mankind. She murdered her children to be free of them."

After Nancy Harmon was sentenced to die in the gas chamber, Professor Harmon had committed suicide. He drove his car to the same beach where one of the kids had been found and left it by the shore. He pinned a note to the wheel saying that it was all his fault. He should have realized how sick his wife was. He should have taken his children from her. He was responsible for their deaths and her action. "I tried to play God," he wrote. "I loved her so dearly that I thought I could cure her. I thought bearing children would turn her mind from the grief of her mother's death. I thought love and care would heal her, but I was wrong; I meddled beyond my depth. Forgive me, Nancy."

There hadn't been any roar of approval when the conviction was overturned. It happened because two women jurors had been heard discussing the case in a bar midway through the trial and saying she was guilty as sin. But by the time a new trial was ordered Rob had graduated, been drafted, given Vietnam orders and bolted. Without him, the D.A. had no case and had to let Nancy go—but swore he'd retry her the day he could get hold of Rob again.

Over the years in Canada, Rob had thought of that trial often. There was something that bothered him about the whole setup. Taking himself out of it, he didn't buy Nancy Harmon as a murderess. She'd been like a clay pigeon in court. Harmon certainly hadn't helped her, breaking down on the stand when he was supposed to be in the midst of saying what a great mother she was.

In Canada, Rob was something of a celebrity among the draft evaders he hung out with whom he'd told about the case. They'd asked about Nancy, and Rob told them what a dish she was . . . hinting that he'd had a little action. He showed them the press clippings of the trial and Nancy's pictures.

He told them that she had to have some dough—that it came out at the trial that her folks left her over a hundred and fifty grand; that if he could find her he'd put the arm on her for money to split to Argentina.

Then he got his break. One of his buddies, Jim Ellis, who knew about his connection with the Harmon case, slipped home to visit his mother, who had terminal cancer. The mother lived in Boston, but because the FBI was watching the house hoping to pick up Jim, she met him in Cape Cod in a cottage she had hired on Maushop Lake. When Jim got back to Canada, he was bursting with news. He asked Rob what it would be worth to him to know where he could find Nancy Harmon.

Rob was skeptical until he saw the picture Jimmy had managed to snap of Nancy on the beach. There was no mistaking her. Jim had done some digging, too. The background checked. He'd found out that her husband was pretty prosperous. Quickly they worked out a deal. Rob would get to see Nancy. Tell her that if she'd stake him to fifty thousand bucks, he'd split to Argentina and she'd never have to worry about him testifying against her. Rob reasoned that she'd go for it, especially now that she was remarried and had more kids. It was a cheap price for her to know that someday she wouldn't be haul-assed back to California to stand trial.

Jim wanted a flat twenty percent for his share. While Rob was seeing Nancy, Jim would arrange for phony Canadian passports, identification and reservations to Argentina. They were available for a price.

They laid their plans carefully. Rob managed to rent a car from an American kid who was in school in Canada. He shaved his beard and cut his hair for the trip. Jim warned him that the minute you looked like a hippie, every damn cop in those crappy New England towns was ready to clock you with radar.

Rob decided to drive straight through from Halifax. The less time he spent in the States, the less chance of getting picked up. He timed his arrival at the Cape for early in the morning. Jim had found out that Nancy's husband always opened his office about nine-thirty. He'd get to her house around ten. Jim had made a map of her street for him, including that driveway through the woods. He could hide the car there.

He was running low on gas when he hit the Cape. That was why he got off at Hyannis to refuel. Jim had told him that even out of season there were a lot of tourists there. He'd be less likely to be noticed. All the way down he'd been nervous, trying to decide if he should offer his deal to Nancy and her husband together. Likely he'd have to know about her getting a bundle of cash. But suppose this guy called the cops? Rob would be convicted of desertion and blackmail. No, it was better to talk directly to Nancy. She must still remember sitting at that defendant's table.

The attendant at the gas station was helpful. Checked everything over, cleaned the windows, put air in the tires without being asked. That was why Rob was off guard. When he was settling the bill, the attendant asked if he was down for some fishing. That was when he babbled that he was actually doing some hunting—going to Adams Port to see an old girlfriend who might not be glad to see him. Then, cursing his talkiness, he bolted, stopping at a nearby diner for some breakfast.

He drove into Adams Port at quarter of ten. Slowly cruising around, studying the map Jim had drawn for him, he got a feel of the layout. Even so he almost missed the dirt road leading to the woods behind her property. He realized that after he slowed up for that old Ford wagon pulling out from it. Backing up, he turned into the dirt road, parked the car and started walking to the rear door of Nancy's house. That was when she'd come running out like a madwoman shrieking those names. Peter, Lisa, those were the dead kids. He followed her through the woods to the lake and watched when she threw herself into the water. He was just about to go after her when she dragged herself out and fell on the beach. He knew she looked in his direction. He wasn't sure if she saw him, but he did know that he had to get out of there. He didn't know what was happening, but he didn't want to get involved.

Back in the car, he'd cooled off. Maybe she'd turned into a drunk. If she was still screaming for the dead kids, chances were that she'd jump at the chance to know she didn't have to worry about a new trial. He decided to check into some motel in Adams Port and try to see her again the next day.

In the motel, Rob promptly went to bed and fell asleep. He awakened late in the afternoon and switched on the television set to catch the news. The screen focused in time for him to see a picture of himself and a voice describing him as the missing witness in the Harmon murder case. Numbly, Rob listened as the announcer recapped the disappearance of the Eldredge children. For the first time in his life he felt trapped. Now that he'd shaved off his beard and shortened his hair, he looked exactly the way he had in the picture.

If Nancy Eldredge had actually killed her new family, who would believe that he hadn't had something to do with it? It must have happened just before he got there. Rob thought of the old Ford wagon that had backed out from the dirt road just before he turned in. Massachusetts license, first two numbers 8—6- . . . heavyset guy behind the wheel.

But he couldn't talk about that even if he got caught. Couldn't admit being at the Eldredge house this morning. Who would believe him if he told the truth? Rob Legler's instinct for self-preservation told him to get off Cape Cod, and it was a cinch he couldn't go in a bright red Dodge that every cop was looking for.

He packed his bag and slipped out the back door of the motel. A Volks Beetle was parked in the stall next to the Dodge. Through the window he'd noticed the couple who had left it. They'd checked in just before he turned on the news. Chances were, if he was any judge, they were good for a couple of hours. No one else was outside braving the sleet and wind.

Rob opened the engine lid of the Volks, connected a few wires and drove away. He'd use Route 6A heading for the bridge. With any luck, in half an hour he'd be off the Cape.

Six minutes later, he ran a red light. Thirty seconds after that, he glanced in the rearview mirror and saw a flashing red light reflected there. He was being chased by a police car. For an instant he considered surrendering himself; then the overwhelming need to bolt from trouble overcame him. As he rounded a corner, Rob slipped open the door, wedged the accelerator down with his suitcase and jumped out. He was disappearing into the wooded area behind stately Colonial homes when the police car, its siren now screaming, chased the wildly careening Volkswagen down the sloping road.

W hen Michael began to run down the stairs, he was sure that Mr. Parrish would catch him. But then he heard the terrible thumping that meant Mr. Parrish had fallen down the stairs. Michael knew that if he wanted to get away from Mr. Parrish he mustn't make any noise. He remembered the time Mommy had had the carpet on the stairs at home taken off. "Now, until the new treads go down, you kids have to play a new game," she'd said. "It's called civilized walking." Michael and Missy had made a game of walking down the side of the stairs near the banister on tiptoe. They got so good at it they used to sneak down and scare each other. Now, walking lightly that same way, Michael slipped noiselessly down to the first floor. He heard Mr. Parrish calling his name, saying he would find him.

He knew he had to get out of this house. He had to run down the winding road to the long road that led to Wiggins' Market. Michael hadn't decided whether he'd go into Wiggins' Market or run past it across Route 6A up the road that led to his house. He had to get Daddy and bring him back here for Missy.

Yesterday in Wiggins' Market he had told Daddy he didn't like Mr. Parrish. Now he was afraid of him. Michael felt the choking fear as he ran through the dark house. Mr. Parrish was a bad man. That was why he had tied them up and hidden them in the closet. That was why Missy was so scared she couldn't wake up. Michael had tried to touch Missy in the closet. He knew she was scared. But he couldn't get his hands free. From inside the closet, he could hear Aunt Dorothy's voice. But she hadn't asked for them. She was right there and didn't guess that they were there. He was very angry that Aunt Dorothy didn't know they needed her. She should have guessed.

It was getting so dark. It was hard to see. At the bottom of the stairs, Michael looked around, confused, then darted toward the back of the house. He was in the kitchen. The outside door was over there. He rushed to it and reached for the knob. He was just about to turn the lock when he heard the footsteps approaching. Mr. Parrish. His knees trembled. If the door stuck, Mr. Parrish would grab him. Quickly, noiselessly, Michael raced out the other kitchen door, across the small foyer and into the little back parlor. He heard Mr. Parrish bolt the kitchen door. He heard him drag the chair over to it. The light in the kitchen was snapped on, and Michael shrank behind the heavy overstuffed couch. Crouching quietly, he barely fitted into the space between the couch and the wall. Dust from the couch tickled his nose. He wanted to sneeze. The light in the kitchen and hallway went out suddenly, and the house was black dark. He heard Mr. Parrish walking around, striking a match.

A moment later there was a reddish glow in the kitchen, and he heard Mr. Parrish call, "It's all right, Michael. I'm not angry anymore. Come out, Michael. I'll take you home to your mother."

CHAPTER 20

John Kragopoulos had intended to drive directly to New York after leaving Dorothy, but a vague sense of depression coupled with a headache over the bridge of his nose made the five-hour trip seem suddenly insurmountable. It was the frightful weather, of course, and the intense distress Dorothy was suffering couldn't help transmitting itself. She had shown him the picture she carried in her wallet, and the thought of those beautiful children having met with foul play left a sickening feeling in the pit of his stomach.

But what an incredible thought, he mused. There was still the possibility the children had simply wandered away. How could anyone hurt a child? John thought of his own twenty-eight-year-old twin sons—one an Air Force pilot, the other an architect. Fine young men, both of them. A source of pride for a father. Long after he and their mother were gone, they would live. They were a part of his immortality. Suppose when they were babies, he had lost them. . . .

He was driving down Route 6A toward the mainland. Ahead on the right an attractive restaurant was set back from the road. The lighted sign, THE STAGEWAY, was a welcoming beacon in the afternoon gloom. Instinctively, John swung off the road and into the parking lot. He realized that it was nearly three o'clock and he had had exactly one cup of coffee and one piece of toast all day. The bad weather had made the driving up from New York so slow he had been forced to skip lunch.

He rationalized that it was common sense to have a decent meal before he attempted the trip. And it was good business sense to try to strike up a conversation with the personnel of a large restaurant in a vicinity he was considering. He might be able to garner some useful information on the probable trade in the area.

Subconsciously approving of the rustic interior of the restaurant, he went directly to the bar. There were no customers at it, but that wasn't unusual before five o'clock in a town like this. He ordered a Chivas

Regal on the rocks; then, when the bartender brought it, he asked if it would be possible to get something to eat.

"No problem." The bartender was about forty, dark-haired, with exaggerated muttonchops. John liked both his obliging answer and the way he kept the bar immaculately neat. A menu was produced. "If you feel like steak, the special sirloin is great," he volunteered. "Technically, the kitchen is closed between two-thirty and five, but if you don't mind eating right here . . ."

"Sounds perfect." Quickly John ordered the steak rare and a green salad. The Chivas warmed his body, and some of his depression began to lift. "You make a good drink," he said.

The bartender smiled. "It takes real talent to put together a Scotch on the rocks," he said.

"I'm in the business. You know what I mean." John decided to be candid. "I'm thinking of buying the place they call The Lookout for a restaurant. What's your top-of-the-head opinion?"

The other man nodded emphatically. "Could work. A real class restaurant, I mean. Here we do fine, but we get the middle-buck crowd. Families with kids. Old ladies on pensions. Tourists heading for the beach or antique shops. We're right on the main drag. But a place like The Lookout overlooking the bay . . . good atmosphere, good booze, a good menu . . . you could charge top dollar and keep it packed."

"That's my feeling."

"Of course, if I was you, I'd get rid of that old creep on the top floor."

"I was wondering about him. He seems to be somewhat odd."

"Well, he's supposed to be up here every year around this time for the fishing. I know because Ray Eldredge happened to mention it. Nice guy, Ray Eldredge. He's the one whose kids are missing."

"I heard about that."

"Damn shame. Nice little kids. Ray and Mrs. Eldredge bring them in here once in a while. Some looker, Ray's wife. But like I was saying, I'm not a native. I quit bartending in New York ten years ago after the third time I was mugged going home late. But I always been crazy for fishing. That's how I ended here. And one day just a few weeks ago, this big guy comes in and orders a drink. I know who he is, I seen him around. He's the tenant at The Lookout. Well, I try to make anybody relax, get his beefs off his chest, so just to make conversation, I ask him if he was here in September when the blues were running. You know what that stupe said?"

John waited.

"Nothing. Blank. Zero. He didn't have a clue." The bartender stood with his hands on his hips. "Do you believe anyone can come fishing to the Cape seven years and not know what I meant?"

The steak arrived. Gratefully John began to eat. It was delicious. As the taste of the prime meat combined with the warm glow of the drink, he relaxed perceptibly and began to think about The Lookout.

What the bartender had told him had confirmed his decision to make an offer on the place.

He had enjoyed going through the house. The sense of discomfort he'd experienced had begun only on the top floor. That was it. He had been uneasy in the apartment of the tenant, Mr. Parrish.

John finished the steak thoughtfully and rather abstractedly paid his bill, remembering to tip the bartender generously. Turning up his collar, he left the restaurant and headed for his car. Now he should turn right and keep toward the mainland? But for minutes he sat irresolutely in the car. What was the matter with him? He was acting like a fool. What crazy impulse was forcing him to return to The Lookout?

Courtney Parrish had been nervous. John had been too many years in the business of sizing people up not to know nervous tension when he saw it. That man had been worried . . . desperately anxious for them to leave. Why? There had been a heavy, sour sweaty smell on him . . . the smell of fear . . . but fear of what? And that telescope. Parrish had rushed over to change the direction it was pointing in when John bent over it. John remembered that when he put it back to approximately where it had been, he'd been able to see the police cars around the Eldredge home. Such an incredibly powerful telescope. If it was directed into the windows of homes in the town, anyone looking into it could become a peeping tom . . . a voyeur.

Was it possible that Courtney Parrish had been looking through the telescope when the children disappeared from behind their home . . . that he had seen something? But if he had, of course he would have called the police.

The car was cold. John turned the ignition key and waited for the engine to warm up before switching on the heater. He reached for a cigar and lighted it with the small gold Dunhill lighter that had been his wife's anniversary present to him: an extravagant, deeply cherished gift. He puffed at the cigar until the tip began to glow.

He was a fool. A suspicious fool. What did one do? Phone the police and say that a man seemed nervous and they should look into it? And if they did, Courtney Parrish would probably say, "I was about to take my bath and disliked having such short notice of the house being shown." Perfectly reasonable. People who lived alone tended to become precise in their habits.

Alone. That was the word. That was what was nagging John. He had been surprised not to see someone else in the apartment. Something had made him sure that Courtney Parrish was not alone.

It was the child's toy in the tub. That was it. That incredible rubber duck. And the cloying scent of baby powder . . .

A suspicion so absurd that it would be impossible to vocalize took shape in John Kragopoulos' mind.

He knew what he had to do. Deliberately he took his gold lighter from his pocket and hid it in the glove compartment of his car.

He would drive back to The Lookout unannounced. When Courtney Parrish answered the door, he would ask permission to look for his valuable lighter, which he must have dropped somewhere in the house during his inspection. It was a plausible request. It would give him a chance to look around carefully and either allay what was probably a ridiculous suspicion or have something more than suspicion to discuss with the police.

Having made up his mind, John stepped on the accelerator and swung the car left on Route 6A, back toward the center of Adams Port and the curving, hilly road that led to The Lookout. Visions of a faded, peeling rubber duck bobbed in his head as he drove through the steadily pelting sleet.

⟨⟨⟨ *CHAPTER 21*

She didn't want to remember . . . there was only pain in going back. Once when she was very little, Nancy had reached up and pulled the handle of a pot on the stove. She could still remember how great torrents of bright red tomato soup had gushed over on her. She'd been in the hospital for weeks and still had faint scars on her chest.

. . . Carl had asked her about those scars . . . stroked them . . . "Poor little girl, poor little girl. . . ." He liked her to tell him about the incident over and over. "Did it hurt very much?" he would ask.

Remembering was like that. . . . Pain . . . only pain. . . . Don't remember . . . forget . . . forget. . . . Don't want to remember. . . .

But the questions, persistent, far away . . . asking about Carl . . . about Mother . . . Lisa . . . Peter . . . Her voice. She was talking. Answering.

"*No*, please, I don't want to talk about it."

"But you must. You must help us." That persistent voice. Why? Why?

"Why were you afraid of Carl, Nancy?"

She had to answer, if only to stop the questions.

She heard her voice, far away, trying to answer. . . . It was like watching herself in a play. . . . Scenes were taking shape.

Mother . . . the dinner . . . the last time she saw Mother . . . Mother's face so troubled, looking at her, at Carl. "Where did you get that dress, Nancy?" She could tell Mother didn't like it.

The white wool dress. "Carl helped me pick it out. Do you like it?"

"Isn't it a bit . . . young?"

Mother left to make a call. Was it to Dr. Miles? Nancy hoped so. She wanted Mother to be happy. . . . Maybe she should go home with Mother. . . . Maybe she would stop feeling so tired. Did she say that to Carl?

Carl left the table. "Excuse me, dear." . . . Mother back before him . . .

"Nancy, you and I must talk tomorrow . . . when we're alone. I'll pick you up for breakfast."

Carl came back. . . .

And Mother . . . kissing her cheek . . . "Good night, darling. I'll see you at eight." Mother getting in the rented car, waving good-bye, driving down the road . . .

Carl drove her back to school. "I'm afraid your mother doesn't approve of me yet, dear."

The call . . . "There's been an accident . . . Steering mechanism . . ."

Carl . . . "I'll take care of you, my little girl . . . "

The funeral . . .

The wedding. A bride should wear white. She'd wear the white wool dress. It would do for just going to the Mayor's office.

But she couldn't wear it . . . grease stain at the shoulder. . . . "Carl, where could I have gotten grease on this dress? I only wore it to have dinner with Mother."

"I'll have it cleaned for you." His hand, familiar, patting her shoulder . . .

"No . . . no . . . no. . . ."

The voice. "What do you mean, Nancy?"

"I don't know. . . . I'm not sure. . . . I'm afraid. . . ."

"Afraid of Carl?"

"No . . . he is good to me. . . . I'm so tired . . . always so tired. . . . Drink your medicine. . . . You need it. . . . The children . . . Peter and Lisa . . . all right for a while. . . . Carl was good. . . . Please, Carl, close the door. . . . Please, Carl, I don't like that. . . . Don't touch me like that. . . . Leave me alone. . . ."

"How should he leave you alone, Nancy?"

"*No* . . . I don't want to talk about it. . . ."

"Was Carl good to the children?"

"He made them obey. . . . He wanted them to be good. . . . He made Peter afraid . . . and Lisa. . . . 'So my little girl has a little girl' . . ."

"Is that what Carl said?"

"Yes. He doesn't touch me anymore. . . . I'm glad. . . . But I mustn't have medicine after dinner . . . I get too tired. . . . There's something wrong. . . . I must get away. . . . The children . . . Get away . . ."

"From Carl?"

"I'm not sick. . . . Carl is sick. . . ."

"How is he sick, Nancy?"

"I don't know. . . ."

"Nancy, tell us about the day Lisa and Peter disappeared. What do you remember about that?"

"Carl is angry."

"Why is he angry?"

"The medicine . . . last night. . . . He saw me pour it out . . . got more . . . made me drink it. . . . So tired . . . so sleepy. . . . Lisa is crying . . . Carl . . . with her. . . . I must get up . . . must go to her. . . . Crying so hard. . . . Carl spanked her . . . said she wet the bed. . . . I have to take her away . . . in morning. . . . My birthday . . . I'll tell Carl. . . ."

"Tell him what?"

"He knows . . . he's beginning to know. . . ."

"Know what, Nancy?"

"I'm going away . . . take the children. . . . Have to go away. . . ."

"Didn't you love Carl, Nancy?"

"I should. He said, 'Happy birthday.' . . . Lisa so quiet. I promised her we'd make a birthday cake for me . . . She and Peter and I. . . . We'd go out and get candles and chocolate for it. It's a bad day . . . starting to rain. . . . Lisa may be getting sick. . . ."

"Did Carl go to school that day?"

"Yes. . . . He phoned. . . . I said we were going to shopping center . . . that after that I was going to stop at the doctor's to let him see Lisa. . . . I was worried. I said I'd go to the Mart at eleven . . . after the children's television program. . . ."

"What did Carl say when you told him you were worried about Lisa?"

"He said it was a bad day . . . if Lisa was getting a cold, he didn't want her out. I said I'd leave them in the car while I shopped. . . . They wanted to help with the cake. . . . They were excited about my birthday. They never had fun. . . . I shouldn't have let Carl be so strict . . . my fault. . . . I'll talk to doctor . . . have to ask doctor . . . about Lisa . . . about me. . . . Why am I always so tired? . . . Why do I take so much medicine? . . . Rob made children laugh. . . . They were so different around him. . . . Children should laugh. . . ."

"Were you in love with Rob, Nancy?"

"No. . . . I was in cage . . . had to get out . . . wanted to talk to someone. . . . Then Rob said what I said to him. . . . Wasn't like that . . . wasn't like that. . . ." Her voice began to rise.

Lendon's voice became soothing. "Then you took the children to the store at eleven."

"Yes. It's raining. . . . I told children to stay in car. . . . They said they would. . . . Such good little children . . . I left them in back seat of car. . . . Never saw them again . . . never . . . never. . . ."

"Nancy, were there many cars in the lot?"

"No. . . . No one I knew in store. . . . So windy . . . cold . . . not many people. . . ."

"How long were you in the store?"

"Not long . . . ten minutes. . . . Couldn't find birthday candles. . . . Ten minutes. . . . Hurry back to car. . . . The children gone." Her voice was incredulous.

"What did you do, Nancy?"

"Don't know what to do. . . . Maybe they went to buy present for me. . . . Peter has money. . . . They wouldn't leave except for that. . . . They're so good. . . . That might make them leave. . . . Maybe in other store . . . the dime store. . . . Look in candy store . . . look in gift shop . . . hardware store . . . look back at car. . . . Look, look for children. . . ."

"Did you ask anyone if they'd been seen?"

"*No.* . . . Mustn't let Carl know. He'll be angry. . . . Don't want him to punish children. . . ."

"So you checked all the stores in the shopping center."

"Maybe they came looking for me . . . got lost. . . . Look in parking lot. . . . Maybe they couldn't find car again. . . . Begin calling them. . . . Frightened. . . . Someone said we'll call police and your husband. . . . I said, 'Don't tell my husband, please.' . . . Woman told about that at trial. . . . I just didn't want Carl to be angry. . . ."

"Why didn't you tell this at your trial?"

"Mustn't. . . . Lawyer said, Don't say Carl was angry. . . . Don't say you argued on phone. . . . Lisa didn't wet the bed . . . bed dry. . . ."

"What do you mean?"

"Bed dry. . . . Why did Carl hurt her? Why? Doesn't matter. . . . Nothing matters. . . . Children gone. . . . Michael . . . Missy gone too. . . . Look for them . . . have to look for them. . . ."

"Tell us about looking for Michael and Missy, this morning."

"I must look at the lake. . . . Maybe they went to the lake. . . . Maybe they fell into the water. . . . Hurry, hurry. . . . Something is in the lake. . . . Something is underwater. . . ."

"What was underwater, Nancy?"

"Red, something red. . . . Maybe it's Missy's mitten . . . I must get it. . . . Water is so cold. . . . I can't reach it. . . . It's not a mitten. . . . It's cold, cold. . . ."

"What did you do?"

"Children aren't here.... Get out ... get out of water.... So cold ... the beach ... I fell on the beach.... He was there ... in the woods ... watching me.... I saw him there ... watching me...."

Jed Coffin stood up. Ray jumped forward convulsively. Lendon held up a warning hand. "Who was there, Nancy?" he asked. "Tell us who was there."

"A man ... I know him.... It was ... it was ... Rob Legler.... Rob Legler was there.... He was hiding ... looking at me." Her voice rose, fell; her eyelids fluttered open, then closed again slowly. Ray paled. Dorothy inhaled sharply. So the two cases were linked.

"The amytal's about worn off. She'll be coming to soon." Lendon stood up, grimacing against the cramped sensation in his knees and thighs.

"Doctor, may I speak with you and Jonathan outside?" Jed's voice was noncommittal.

"Stay with her, Ray," Lendon cautioned. "She'll probably wake up any minute."

In the dining room, Jed faced Lendon and Jonathan. "Doctor, how long is this to go on?" Jed's face was impenetrable.

"I don't think we should attempt to question Nancy any further."

"What have we gotten from all this other than the fact that she was afraid of her husband; that she obviously did not love him and that Rob Legler may have been at the lake this morning?"

Lendon stared. "Good God, didn't you hear what that girl was saying? Don't you know what you were listening to?"

"I only know that I haven't heard one thing that will help me discharge my responsibility to find the Eldredge children. I heard Nancy Eldredge blaming herself for her mother's death, which is natural in a case where a visit to a child in school results in a parent's death. Her reactions to her first husband sound pretty hysterical. She's trying to blame him for the fact that she wanted out of their marriage."

"What impression did you get of Carl Harmon?" Lendon asked quietly.

"One of those possessive guys who marries a younger girl and wants the upper hand. Hell, he isn't any different than half the men on the Cape. I can cite you examples of guys who won't let their wives handle a dime except for food money. I know one who won't let his wife drive the family car. Another never lets his wife go out at night by herself. This kind of thing is common all over the world. Maybe that's why that Women's Lib bunch have something to beef about."

"Chief, do you know what pedophilia is?" Lendon asked quietly.

Jonathan nodded. "That's what I've been thinking," he said.

Lendon didn't give Jed time to answer. "In laymen's terms, it's a sexual deviation involving sexual activity of any type with a child who has not yet reached puberty."

"How does that fit in here?"

"It doesn't . . . not completely. Nancy was eighteen when she married. But in appearance she could look quite childish. Chief, is there any way you can run a check on Carl Harmon's background?"

Jed Coffin looked incredulous. When he answered, his voice was trembling with repressed fury. He pointed to the sleet that was beating a steady, sharp staccato against the window. "Doctor," he said, "do you see and hear that? Somewhere out there two kids are either wandering around freezing or they're in the hands of God knows what kind of kook and maybe they're dead. But it's my job to find them and find them now. We have one distinct lead to all this. That is that both Nancy Eldredge and a gasoline attendant have placed Rob Legler, a pretty unsavory character, in the immediate vicinity. That's the kind of information I can do something about." His voice bit off the words scornfully. "And you're asking me to waste my time running a check on a dead man to prove some cockeyed theory."

The telephone rang. Bernie Mills, who'd been standing unobtrusively in the room, hurried to answer it. Now they were talking about running a check on Nancy's first husband. Wait till he told this to Jean. He picked up the phone quickly. It was the station house. "Put the Chief on." Sergeant Poler at the desk spat the words.

Lendon and Jonathan watched while Chief Coffin listened, then asked quick, short questions. "How long ago? Where?"

The men looked at each other silently. Lendon realized he was praying—an inarticulate, fervent prayer that the message was not bad news about the children.

Jed slapped the receiver back into the cradle and turned to them. "Rob Legler checked into the Adams Port Motel right here in town around ten-thirty this morning. A car we believe he stole has just been smashed up on Route 6A, but he got away. He's probably heading for the mainland. We've got an all-out search for him and I'm going over to direct it. I'll leave Officer Mills here. We'll get that Legler bird, and when we do, I think we'll really have the answer to what happened to those kids."

After the door had closed behind the Chief, Jonathan spoke to Lendon. "What do you make of this so far?" he asked.

Lendon waited a long minute before answering. *I am too close to this,* he thought. *I see Priscilla at that phone . . . calling me. Carl Harmon left the table after her. Where did he go? Did he overhear what Priscilla said*

to me? Nancy said her dress was smeared with grease. Hadn't she been saying in effect that she believed Carl's hand must have been smeared and when he put his hand on her shoulder, her dress got dirty? Hadn't she been trying to say that she believed Carl Harmon might have done something to Priscilla's car? Lendon saw a violent pattern forming. But what purpose would this knowledge serve with Carl Harmon in his grave?

Jonathan said, "If your mind is running in the same direction as mine, going back to the disappearance of the Harmon children won't help us. You're thinking of the father."

"Yes," Lendon said.

"And since he is dead, we turn to Rob Legler, the man sent into the home by Carl Harmon and the one witness whose testimony convicted Nancy. How accurate is her statement about this morning under the amytal?"

Lendon shook his head. "I can't be sure. It's been known that even under sedation, some patients can resist and suppress. But I believe that she saw—or believes she saw—Rob Legler at Maushop Lake."

Jonathan said, "And at ten-thirty this morning he checked into a motel *alone.*"

Lendon nodded.

Without speaking again, the two men turned and looked out the window in the direction of the lake.

CHAPTER 22

The five-o'clock television news gave little coverage to the Mideastern crisis, spiraling inflation, the automobile workers' threatened strike or the dismal standing of the New England Patriots. Most of the half hour broadcast was devoted to the disappearance of the Eldredge children and old film clips from the sensational Harmon murder case.

The pictures that had appeared in the *Cape Cod Community News* were reproduced. Special attention was focused on the one of Rob Legler leaving the San Francisco courthouse with Professor Carl Harmon after Nancy Harmon's conviction for the willful murder of her children.

The commentator's voice was especially urgent when that picture was shown. "Rob Legler has been positively identified as being in the vicinity of the Eldredge home this morning. If you believe you have seen this man, please call this special number at once: KL five, three eight hundred. The lives of the Eldredge children may be at stake. If you believe you have any information which may lead to the person or persons responsible for the children's disappearance, we urge you to call this number: KL five, three eight hundred. Let me repeat it again: KL five, three eight hundred."

The Wigginses had closed their store when the power failed and were home in time to catch the broadcast on their battery-operated television set.

"That fellow looks kind of familiar," Mrs. Wiggins said.

"You'd say that anyhow," her husband snorted.

"No . . . not really. There's something about him . . . the way he bends forward . . . Certainly is nothing to look at."

Jack Wiggins stared at his wife. "I was just thinking he's the type that might turn a young girl's head."

"Him? Oh, you mean the young one. I'm talking about the other fellow—the professor."

Jack looked at his wife condescendingly. "This is why I say women don't make good witnesses and never should be jurors. Nobody's talking about that Professor Harmon. He committed suicide. They're talking about the Legler fellow."

Mrs. Wiggins bit her lip. "I see. Well, guess you're right. It's just . . . oh, well . . ."

Her husband got up heavily. "When'll dinner be ready?"

"Oh, not long. But it's hard to worry about food when you think about little Michael and Missy . . . God knows where. . . . You think you just want to help them. I don't care what they say about Nancy Eldredge. She never came in the store much, but when she did, I liked to watch her with her kids. She had such a nice way with them—never upset, never cranky, the way half these young mothers are. It makes our little annoyances so unimportant, you know."

"What little annoyances do we have?" His tone was sharply suspicious.

"Well . . ." Mrs. Wiggins bit her lip. They'd had so much trouble with shoplifters this past summer. Jack got so upset even discussing it. That was why, all day, it just hadn't seemed worthwhile to tell him that she was absolutely certain that Mr. Parrish had stolen a large can of baby powder from the shelf this morning.

The five o'clock news was on in a modest home down the block from St. Francis Xavier Church in Hyannis Port. The family of Patrick Keeney was about to start dinner. All eyes were glued on the small portable set in the crowded junior-size dining room.

Ellen Keeney shook her head as the picture of Michael and Missy Eldredge filled the screen. Involuntarily, she glanced at her own children—Neil and Jimmy, Deirdre and Kit . . . one . . . two. . . . three . . . four. Whenever she took them to the beach, that was the way it was. She never stopped counting heads. *God, don't let anything happen to them, ever, please.* That was her prayer.

Ellen was a daily communicant at St. Francis Church and usually went to the same Mass as Mrs. Rose Kennedy. She remembered the days after the President and then Bobby were killed when Mrs. Kennedy would come into the church, her face lined with grief but still serene and composed. Ellen never watched her during Mass. Poor lady, she had a right to some privacy somewhere. Often Mrs. Kennedy would smile and nod and sometimes say, "Good morning" if they happened to walk out after Mass at the same moment. *How does she stand it?* Ellen wondered. *How can she stand it?* Now she was thinking the same thing. *How can Nancy Eldredge stand it? . . . especially when you think that it happened to her before.*

The commentator was talking about the article in the *Community News*—that the police were trying to track down the author. His words barely registered on Ellen's mind as she decided that Nancy was not responsible for the death of her children. It simply wasn't possible. No mother murdered her flesh and blood. She saw Pat looking at her and smiled at him faintly—a communication that said, *We are blessed, my dear; we are blessed.*

"He got awful fat," Neil said.

Startled, Ellen stared at her oldest child. At seven, Neil worried her. He was so daring, so unpredictable. He had Pat's dark-blond hair and gray eyes. He was small for his age, and she knew that worried him a little, but from time to time, she reassured him. "Daddy's tall and your Uncle John's tall, and someday you will be too." Still, Neil did look younger than anyone else in his class.

"Who got fat, dear?" she asked absently, turning her back to gaze at the screen.

"That man, the one in front. He's the one who gave me the dollar to ask for his mail at the post office last month. Remember, I showed you the note he wrote when you wouldn't believe me."

Ellen and Pat stared at the screen. They were looking at the picture of Rob Legler following Professor Carl Harmon out of the courtroom.

"Neil, you're mistaken. That man has been dead for a long time."

Neil looked aggrieved. "See. You never believe me. But when you kept asking me where I got that dollar and I told you, you didn't believe me either. He's a lot fatter and his hair's all gone, but when he leaned out of the station wagon, he had his head kind of pulled down on his neck like that man."

The anchorman was saying, ". . . any piece of information, no matter how irrelevant you may consider it."

Pat scowled.

"Why do you look mad, Daddy?" five-year-old Deirdre asked anxiously.

His face cleared. Neil had said, "like that man." "I guess because sometimes I realize how hard it is to raise a bunch like you," he answered, running his hand through her short curly hair, grateful that she was here within his touch. "Turn off the television, Neil," he ordered his son. "Now, children, before we say grace, we will pray that God sends the Eldredge children safely home."

Through the prayer that followed, Ellen's mind was far away. They had pleaded for any information, no matter how irrelevant it seemed, and Neil had gotten that dollar tip to pick up a letter at General Delivery. She remembered the day exactly: Wednesday, four weeks ago. She remembered the date because there was a parents' meeting at school that night and she was annoyed that Neil was late for the early dinner. Suddenly she remembered something.

"Neil, by any chance, do you still have the note the man gave you to show the post office?" she asked. "Didn't I see you put it in your bank with the dollar?"

"Yes, I saved it."

"Will you get it, please?" she asked him. "I want to see the name on it."

Pat was studying her. When Neil left, he spoke over the heads of the other children. "Don't tell me you put any stock . . ."

She suddenly felt ridiculous. "Oh, eat up, dear. I guess I just have a case of nerves. It's people like me who are always wasting policemen's time. Kit, pass me your plate. I'll cut up the end piece of the meat loaf just the way you like it."

CHAPTER 24

It was all going so badly. Nothing was working as he'd expected. That foolish woman coming here and then the little girl; having to wait till she woke up, if she woke up, so that he could feel her twisting and pulling from him. Then the boy squirming away from him, hiding. He'd have to find him.

Courtney had a feeling of everything slipping away from him. His sense of pleasure and expectation had changed to disappointment and resentment. He wasn't perspiring anymore, but the heavy sweat still clung to his clothes and made them unpleasantly sticky against his body. The thought of the boy's big blue eyes, so like Nancy's, didn't give him anticipatory pleasure.

The boy was a threat. If he escaped, it would be the end. Better to finish with them both; better to do what he'd done before. In an instant he could remove the threat—seal off air so that lips and nostrils and eyes were covered—and then in a few hours—when the tide was high toss their bodies into the churning surf. No one would know. Then he'd be here safe again with nothing to threaten him; here to enjoy her torment.

And tomorrow night, with all the threat gone, he'd drive to the mainland. He'd go around dusk, and probably some little girl would be walking alone and he'd tell her he was the new teacher. . . . It always worked.

His decision made, he felt better. Now all he wanted was to be finished with this threat. That child, recalcitrant like Nancy . . . troublesome . . . ungrateful. . . . wanting to escape . . . he would find him. He'd tie him and then get the thin sheets of velvety plastic. He'd made sure to have a brand that Nancy could have bought at Lowery's. Then he'd seal it on the boy first, because the boy was so troublesome. And then . . . the little girl . . . right away too. It was too dangerous to even keep her.

The sense of danger always heightened his perception. Like last time. He hadn't really known what he would do when he had slipped across the campus to the shopping center. He'd only known that he couldn't let Nancy take Lisa to the doctor. He'd been there before she arrived, parked on that little supply road between the shopping center and the campus. He'd seen her drive in, speak to the children, go into the store. No cars nearby. Not a soul around. In a moment he'd known what to do.

The children had been so obedient. They'd looked startled and frightened when he opened the car door, but when he said, "Now, quickly—we're going to play a game on Mommy for her birthday," they'd gotten into the trunk and in an instant it was over. The plastic bags slipped over their heads, twisted tight, his hands holding them till they stopped squirming; the trunk shut and he back in school. Less than eight minutes gone in all; the students intent on their lab experiments, no one had missed him. A roomful of witnesses to testify to his presence if need be. That night he'd simply driven the car to the beach and dumped the bodies into the ocean. Opportunity seized, danger averted that day seven years ago, and now danger to be averted again. "Michael, come out, Michael. I'll take you home to your mother."

He was still in the kitchen. Holding the hurricane lamp up, he looked around. There was no place to hide here. The cupboards were all high. But finding the boy in this dark, cavernous house with only this lamp to see by would be infinitely difficult. It would take hours, and where should he begin?

"Michael, don't you want to go home to your mother?" he called again. "She didn't go to God . . . she's all better . . . she wants to see you."

Should he try the third floor and look in those bedrooms first? he wondered.

But the boy would probably have tried to get to this outside door. He was smart. He wouldn't have stayed upstairs. Would he have gone to the front door? Better to look there.

He started into the little hall, then thought of the small back parlor. If the boy had tried the kitchen and heard him coming, that would be the logical place to hide.

He walked to the doorway of the room. Was that breathing he was hearing, or only the wind sighing against the house? He walked a few steps farther, into the room, holding the kerosene lamp high above his head. His eyes darted, picking objects out of the gloom. He was about to turn around when he swung the lamp to his right.

Staring at what he was seeing, he let out a high-pitched, hysterical whinny. The shadow of a small figure huddled behind the couch was silhouetted like a giant crouched rabbit across the faded oak floor. "I found you, Michael," he cried, still giggling, "and this time you won't get away."

The power failure began as John Kragopoulos turned off Route 6A onto the road that led to The Lookout. Instinctively, he pressed the button under his foot to turn on the bright headlights. Vision was still poor, and he drove carefully, feeling the slick road under the tires and the tendency of the car to skid at the turns.

He wondered how he could possibly justify looking through that cavernous house for a small lighter. Mr. Parrish could reasonably suggest that he return in the morning or offer to search for it himself and give it to Dorothy if it was found.

John decided he would go to the door with his flashlight. He'd say that he was quite sure he remembered hearing something drop when he was bending over the telescope. He had meant to check to see if something had slipped out of his pocket. That was reasonable. It was the fourth-floor apartment that he wanted to see anyhow.

The hilly ascent to The Lookout was treacherous. At the last bend in the road, the front end of the car swayed precariously. John gripped the wheel as the tires grabbed and held the road. He had been within inches of veering onto the sloping embankment and would surely have hit the massive oak tree less than six feet away. A few minutes later, he turned the car into the back driveway of The Lookout, rejecting the alternative of pulling into the comparative shelter of the garage as Dorothy had done. He wanted to be casual, open. If anything his manner should be a bit irritated as though he were being inconvenienced too. He would say that since he had discovered his loss at dinner and was still in town, he'd decided to come right back rather than phone.

As he got out of the car, he was struck by the foreboding blackness of the big house. Even the top floor was completely dark. Surely the man had hurricane lamps. Power blackouts on the Cape in bad storms couldn't be unusual. Suppose Parrish had fallen asleep and didn't realize the electricity had failed? Suppose—just suppose—there'd been a woman visiting him who had not wanted to be seen. It was the first time the possibility had occurred to John.

Suddenly feeling foolish, he debated about getting back into the car. The sleet stung his face. The wind whipped it under the collar and sleeves of his coat, and the warm satisfaction of the dinner was dispelled. He realized he was chilled and tired and had a long, difficult drive ahead of him. He would look like a fool with his contrived story. Why hadn't he thought about the possibility that Parrish had a visitor who would be embarrassed at being seen? John decided he was a fool, a suspicious idiot. He and Dorothy had probably interrupted a liaison and nothing more. He'd get away from here before he made a further nuisance of himself.

He was about to get behind the wheel when he saw a glimmer of light from the far-left kitchen window. It moved swiftly, and a few seconds later he could see it reflected in the windows to the right of the kitchen door. Someone was walking around the kitchen with a lamp.

Carefully John closed the car door so that it made no slamming sound, only a soft click. Gripping the flashlight, he edged across the driveway to the kitchen window and peered in. The light seemed to be coming from the hall now. Mentally, he reviewed the layout of the house. The back staircase was reached through that hall, and so was the small parlor on the other side. Sheltering against the weathered shingles, he moved quickly along the back of the house, past the kitchen door, to the windows that should be those of the small parlor. The glow from the lamp was muted, but as he watched it grew stronger. He shrank back as the lamp became visible, held high by an outstretched arm. He could see Courtney Parrish now. The man was searching for something . . . for what? He was calling to someone. John strained to hear. The wind smothered sound, but he could make out the name "Michael." Parrish was calling, "Michael!"

John felt chilling fear race along his spinal column. He had been right. The man was a maniac, and those children were somewhere in the house. The lamp he was arching in circles was a spotlight that illuminated the solid thickness of Parrish's bulk. John felt totally inadequate, aware that he was no physical match for this man. He had only the flashlight as a weapon. Should he go for help? Was it possible Michael had gotten away from Parrish? But if Parrish found him, even a few minutes might make a difference.

Then, before his horrified eyes, John saw Parrish swing the lamp over to the right and reach behind the couch to pull out a small figure who tried desperately to escape. Parrish put down the lamp and, as John watched, closed both hands around the child's throat.

Acting as instinctively as he had when he'd been on combat duty in World War II, John pulled his arm back and smashed the window with his flashlight. As Courtney Parrish spun around, John reached his hand in and forced the lock open. With superhuman strength, he pushed the window up and vaulted over the sill into the room. He dropped the flashlight as his feet hit the floor, and Parrish grabbed for it. Still holding the hurricane lamp in his left hand, Parrish raised the flashlight in his right hand, holding it over his head like a weapon.

There was no way to escape the inevitable blow. But John ducked and weaved back against the wall for time. Shouting, "Run away,

Michael. . . . Call help," he managed to kick the kerosene lamp from Parrish's hand an instant before the flashlight crashed down on his skull.

⟨⟨⟩⟩ *CHAPTER 26*

I t had been a mistake to ditch the car. It had been an act of sheer, stupid panic. Rob believed in making your own luck. Today he had made every blunder in the book. When he saw Nancy at the lake, he should have gotten the hell off Cape Cod. Instead, he'd figured that she might be on a trip or stoned and all he had to do was lie low for a day and then go see her and her husband and get some money. Now he'd made a point of placing himself in the vicinity, and her kids were missing.

Rob had never really believed that Nancy had anything to do with the other kids' disappearance; but now, who could know? Maybe she did go haywire, just as Harmon used to tell him.

When he left the car, Rob had headed south toward the main expressway that ran through the center of the Cape. But when a police car whipped past him, he'd doubled back. Even if he could hitch a ride, the odds were they'd have a roadblock at the bridge. It would be better to head toward the bay. There had to be plenty of closed-up summer cottages there. He'd break into one of them and hole up for a while. Most of them probably had some staples left in the kitchen, and he was getting hungry. Then in a couple of days, when the heat was off, he'd find a truck, hide in the back and get off this damned island.

He shivered as he hurried down the narrow, darkened roads. One good thing: in this shit weather, there wasn't any danger of running into people out walking. Hardly any cars on the road, either.

But when he rounded a bend in the road, Rob barely had time to jump back into thick hedges to escape being revealed by the headlights of an approaching car. Breathing harshly, he waited till the automobile had screeched past him. Christ. Another cop car. The place was swarming with them. He'd have to get off the road. It couldn't be more than a couple of blocks to the beach now. Moving swiftly along the row of hedge, Rob headed toward the clump of woods that edged the back of the houses near him. Less chance of being spotted there, even if it took longer to wind through backyards.

Suppose Nancy had seen him at the lake? She did look in his direction . . . but maybe not. He'd deny he was there, of course. She was in no state to be a witness about seeing him. Nobody else had. He was sure of that. Except . . . the driver of that station wagon. Probably a local guy . . . Massachusetts plates . . . 8X642. . . . How did he remember that? The reverse . . . oh, sure . . . 2-4-6-8. He'd noticed that. If Rob did get caught, he could tell the cops about that station wagon. He'd seen it backing out of the dirt road leading from the Eldredge property, and that must have been just around the time the kids disappeared.

But on the other hand, suppose that station wagon was a regular delivery car that they already knew about? Rob hadn't seen the driver at all; hadn't paid attention, really . . . just noticed he was a big, fat guy. If he did get caught and told about the station wagon, he'd only nail himself as having been Johnny-on-the-spot at the Eldredge house.

No, he wouldn't admit anything if they got him. He'd say he had been planning to visit Nancy. Then he had seen his picture in that story about the Harmon case and decided to get away. The decision made, Rob felt better. Now if he could just get to the beach and into a cottage . . .

He hurried, careful to stay well in the shadows of the stark trees; stumbled; swore softly and recovered his balance. This sleet was making the whole damn place as slippery as a skating rink. But he couldn't have much farther to go. He had to get indoors somewhere, or someone would be sure to spot him. Steadying himself against the ice-crusted trees, he tried to move faster.

 CHAPTER 27

Thurston Givens sat quietly in his glassed-in back porch, watching the storm in the near dark. An octogenarian, he'd always found nor' easters fascinating and knew that he wouldn't be likely to see them for too many more years. The radio was on very low, and he'd just heard the latest bulletin about the Eldredge children. There was still no trace of them.

Now Thurston sat staring out toward the back, wondering why young people had to know so much misery. His only child had died at five from flu during the epidemic of 1917.

A retired realtor, Thurston knew Ray Eldredge well. He'd been a friend of Ray's father and grandfather, too. Ray was a fine fellow, the kind of man the Cape needed. He was a go-getter and a good realtor— not the kind out to turn a fast buck and the public be damned. Damn shame if anything happened to those little children of his. Nancy certainly didn't strike Thurston as the type to get mixed up with murdering any-one. There had to be a better answer than that.

He was drifting into a kind of reverie when some movement in the woods caught his attention. He leaned forward and peered through narrowed eyes. There was someone out there, sliding along, obviously trying to stay hidden. Nobody up to any good was in those woods in this kind of weather, and there'd been a lot of robberies on the Cape, and particularly in this area.

Thurston reached for the phone. He dialed Police Headquarters. Chief Coffin was an old friend, but, of course, the Chief probably wasn't there. He must be out on the Eldredge case.

The phone was answered at the other end, and a voice said, "Adams Port Police Headquarters. Sergeant Poler—"

Thurston interrupted impatiently. "Thurston Givens here," he said crisply. "I want you fellows to know there's a prowler in the woods behind my place and he's heading towards the bay."

～ *CHAPTER 28*

Nancy sat upright on the couch, staring straight ahead. Ray had lighted the fire, and the flames were beginning to lick at the thick twigs and broken pieces of branches. Yesterday. It was just yesterday, wasn't it? She and Michael had been raking the front lawn.

"This is the last time we'll have this job this winter, Mike," she'd said. "I guess just about all the leaves are down now."

He'd nodded soberly. Then, without her telling him, he'd picked out the biggest chunks of branch and thick twigs from the pile of leaves. "These are good for fires," he commented. He'd dropped the iron rake, and it had fallen with the metal prongs facing upward. But when Missy came running from the driveway, he'd quickly turned over the rake. With an apologetic half-smile he'd said, "Daddy always says it's dangerous to leave a rake like that."

He was so protective of Missy. He was so good. He was so like Ray. Nancy realized that in some incredible way there was comfort in know-ing that Mike was with Missy. If there was any way to do it, he'd take care of her. He was such a resourceful little kid. If they were outside somewhere now, he'd make sure that her jacket was zipped up. He'd try to cover her. He'd. . . .

"Oh, God."

She didn't know she'd spoken aloud until Ray looked up startled. He was sitting in his big chair. His face looked so strained. He seemed to know that she didn't want him to touch her now—that she needed to assimilate and evaluate. She must not believe that the children were dead. They could not be dead. But they must be found before anything happened.

Dorothy was watching her too. Dorothy, who suddenly looked so much older and so lost. She had taken Dorothy's affection and love without giving in return. She had held Dorothy at arm's length, made it clear that Dorothy was not to intrude on their closed family circle. She didn't want the children to have a grandmother substitute. She didn't want anyone to replace Mother.

I have been selfish, Nancy thought. *I have not seen her need.* How odd that it was so clear now. How odd to even think about that now when they were sitting here, so helpless, so powerless. Then why was something reassuring her? Why was she feeling some tiny lick of hope? What was the source of her comfort?

"Rob Legler," she said. "I told you that I saw Rob Legler at the lake this morning."

"Yes," Ray said.

"Is it possible I was dreaming? Does the doctor believe that I saw him—that I was telling the truth?"

Ray considered, then decided to be honest. There was a strength in Nancy, a directness that wouldn't tolerate evasion.

"I believe that the doctor feels that you gave an exact account of what happened. And Nancy, you should know, Rob Legler has definitely been seen near here both last night and this morning."

"Rob Legler would not hurt the children." Nancy's voice was matter-of-fact, flatly positive. That was her area of comfort. "If he took them, if he was responsible, he wouldn't hurt them. I know it."

Lendon came back into the room, Jonathan close behind him. Jonathan realized that he inadvertently looked for Dorothy first. Her hands were dug into her pockets. He suspected they were gripped into fists. She had always struck him as a remarkably efficient, self-sufficient person—traits that he admired without finding them necessarily endearing in a woman.

When Jonathan was honest with himself, he realized that an essential part of his relationship with Emily had been his constant awareness of her need for him. She never could unscrew the cap from a jar or find her car keys or balance her checking account. He had basked in his role as the indulgent, able, constant fixer, doer, solver. It had taken the past two years to make him begin to realize that he'd never understood the steel shaft of strength at the core of Emily's femininity: the way she'd accepted the doctor's verdict with only a sympathetic glance at him; the way she'd never once admitted to pain. Now, seeing Dorothy with her mute anguish so tangible, he ached somehow to comfort her.

He was diverted by a question from Ray. "What was the phone call?"

"Chief Coffin went out," Jonathan said evasively.

"It's all right. Nancy knows that Rob Legler has been seen near here."

"That's why the Chief left. Legler was chased and left a car he'd stolen two miles down on 6A. But don't worry, he won't get far on foot in this weather."

"How do you feel, Nancy?" Lendon studied her closely. She was more composed than he'd expected.

"I'm all right. I talked a lot about Carl, didn't I?"

"Yes."

"There was something I was trying to remember; something important I wanted to tell you."

Lendon kept his voice matter-of-fact. "Several times you said, 'I don't believe . . . I don't believe. . . .' Do you know why you would say that?"

Nancy shook her head. "No." She got up and walked restlessly to the window. "It's so dark, it would be hard to find anything or anybody now."

Movement was desirable. She wanted to try to clear her head to be able to think. She looked down, realizing for the first time that she was still wearing the fluffy woolen robe. "I'm going to change," she said. "I want to get dressed."

"Do you . . . ?" Dorothy bit her lip. She'd been about to ask if Nancy wanted her to go upstairs with her.

"I'll be all right," Nancy said gently. They were going to find Rob Legler. She was sure of it. When they did, she wanted to be dressed. She wanted to go to him wherever they took him. She wanted to say, "Rob, I know you wouldn't hurt the children. Do you want money? What do you need? Tell me where they are and we'll give you anything."

Upstairs in the bedroom, she took off her robe. Mechanically, she walked over to the closet and hung it up. For an instant, she felt light-headed and leaned her forehead against the coolness of the wall. The bedroom door opened, and she heard Ray cry, "Nancy!" His voice was startled as he hurried over to her, turned her to him and put his arms around her. She felt the scratchy warmth of his sports shirt against her skin and the growing intensity of his grasp.

"I'm all right," she said. "Really. . . ."

"Nancy!" He tilted her head up. His mouth closed over hers. As her lips parted, she arched her body against his.

It had been like this from the beginning. From that first night when he'd come to dinner and afterward they'd walked down to the lake. It had been chilly, and she'd shivered. His coat was open, and he'd laughed and pulled her against him, wrapping the coat around so that it covered her too. When he'd kissed her that first time, it had been so inevitable. She'd wanted him so much, right from the beginning. Not like Carl. . . . Poor Carl . . . she'd only tolerated him; felt guilty about not wanting him, and after Lisa was born, he had never again . . . not like a husband . . . Had he sensed her revulsion? She'd always wondered. It was part of her guilt.

"I love you." She didn't know she'd said it—words said so often, words she murmured to Ray even in her sleep.

"I love you too. Oh, Nancy. It must have been so bad for you. I thought I understood, but I didn't. . . ."

"Ray, will we get the children back?" Her voice shook, and she felt her whole body begin to tremble.

His arms tightened. "I don't know, darling. I don't know. But remember this: No matter what happens, we have each other. Nothing can change that. They've just come by for the Chief. They have Rob Legler at the station house. Dr. Miles went with them, and Jonathan and I are going over too."

"I want to go. Maybe he'll tell me . . ."

"No. Jonathan has an idea, and I think it could work. We've got to find out. Maybe Rob has an accomplice who has the children. If he sees you, he might refuse to say anything, especially if he was involved last time."

"Ray . . ." Nancy heard the despair in her voice.

"Darling, hang on. Just a little while longer. Take a hot shower and get dressed. Dorothy will stay with you. She's fixing a sandwich for you now. I'll be back as soon as I can." For an instant he buried his lips in her hair, then was gone.

Mechanically, Nancy walked into the bathroom off the bedroom. She turned on the water in the shower stall, then looked into the mirror over the washbasin. The face she saw looking back at her was pale and drawn, the eyes heavy and clouded. It was the way she had looked all those years with Carl, like the pictures of her in that article.

Quickly she turned away and, twisting her hair into a knot, stepped into the shower. The warm needle spray struck her body, making a steady assault against the rigid tension of her muscles. It felt good. Gratefully she lifted her face to the spray. A shower felt so clean.

She never, never took a tub bath anymore—not since the years with Carl. She didn't think about those baths anymore. A vivid shaft of recollection came as the water splashed against her face. The tub . . . Carl's insistence on bathing her . . . the way he had touched and examined her. Once when she'd tried to push him away, he'd slipped and his face had gone under the water. He'd been so startled that for a moment he couldn't pull up. When he did, he'd begun sputtering and trembling and coughing. He'd been so angry . . . but mostly so frightened. It had terrified him to have his face covered by the water.

That was it. That was what she had tried to remember: that secret fear of water. . . .

Oh, God. Nancy swayed against the side of the shower stall. She felt nausea rack her stomach and throat, stumbled out of the shower and began retching uncontrollably.

Minutes passed. She clung to the sides of the commode, unable to stem the violent waves of illness. Then, even when the vomiting finally stopped, icy chills still shuddered through her body.

 *CHAPTER 29*

"**R**ay, don't count on too much," Jonathan warned.

Ray ignored him. Through the streaked windowpane, he could see the station house. The glow from the gas lamps gave it the look of another century. Quickly parking the car, Ray threw open the door and darted across the macadam into the station. From behind he could hear Jonathan puffing as he tried to keep pace.

The desk sergeant looked surprised. "Didn't expect to see you here tonight, Mr. Eldredge. I'm sure sorry about the kids. . . ."

Ray nodded impatiently. "Where are they questioning Rob Legler?"

The sergeant looked alarmed. "You can't have anything to do with that, Mr. Eldredge."

"The hell I can't," Ray said evenly. "Go in and tell the Chief that I have to see him now."

The sergeant's protest died on his lips. He turned to a policeman who was coming down the corridor. "Tell the Chief that Ray Eldredge wants to see him," he snapped.

Ray turned to Jonathan. With the trace of a wan smile, he said, "Suddenly this seems like a farfetched, crazy idea."

"It isn't," Jonathan replied quietly.

Ray glanced around the room and realized for the first time that two people were sitting on a small bench near the door. They were just about as old as he and Nancy—a nice-looking couple. He wondered abstractedly what they were doing here. The guy looked embarrassed, the woman determined. What would bring anyone out on a night like this? Was it possible they had had a fight and she was pressing charges? The idea was wildly funny. Somewhere outside this room, outside this whole incredible day, people were home with their families; cooking dinner in candlelight, telling kids not to be scared of the dark, making love . . . having fights. . . .

He realized that the woman was staring at him. She started to get up, but the husband pulled her down. Quickly, Ray turned his back to her. The last thing in the world he wanted or needed was sympathy.

Footsteps hurried down the corridor. Chief Coffin rushed into the room. "What is it, Ray? Have you heard anything?"

Jonathan answered. "You have Rob Legler here?"

"Yes. We're questioning him. Dr. Miles is with me. Legler's asking for a lawyer. Won't answer any questions."

"I thought as much. That's why we're here." In a low voice, Jonathan outlined his plan.

Chief Coffin shook his head. "Won't work. This guy's a cool one. There's no way you'll get him to place himself at the Eldredge house this morning."

"Well, let us try. Can't you see how important time is? If he had an accomplice who has the children now, that person may panic. God knows what he might do."

"Well . . . come in here. Talk to him. But don't count on anything." With a jerk of his head, the Chief nodded to a room halfway down the corridor. As Ray and Jonathan started to follow him, the woman got up from the bench.

"Chief Coffin." Her voice was hesitant. "Could I speak to you for just a minute?"

The Chief looked at her appraisingly. "Is it important?"

"Well, probably not. It's just that I felt I wouldn't have any peace unless . . . It's something my little boy . . ."

The Chief visibly lost interest. "Just sit down please, ma'am. I'll be back with you as soon as I can."

Ellen Keeney sank down on the bench as she watched the three men leave. The sergeant at the desk sensed her disappointment. "Are you sure I can't help you, ma'am?" he asked.

But Ellen didn't trust the sergeant. When she and Pat had first come in, they had tried to tell him that they thought their little boy might know something about the Eldredge case. The sergeant had looked

pained. "Lady, do you know how many calls we've had today? Since the wire services got hold of this, we've had nothing but calls. Some jerk from Tucson phoned to say he thought he saw the kids in a playground across the street from his apartment this morning. No way they could have gotten there, even in a supersonic plane. So just take a seat. The Chief'll talk to you when he can."

Pat said, "Ellen, I think we should go home. We're only in the way here."

Ellen shook her head. She opened her pocketbook and took out the note the stranger had given Neil when he had sent him in for the mail. She had attached the note to her own scribblings about everything Neil had told her. She knew the exact time he had gone in for the letter. She had carefully written down his description of the man; his exact words when he'd said the man looked like the picture on television of Nancy Harmon's first husband; the kind of car the man was driving—"a real old station wagon just like Gramp's"—that sounded like a Ford. Last, Neil had said that the man had a fishing permit for Adams Port on his windshield.

Ellen was determined to sit here until she got a chance to tell her story. Pat looked so tired. Reaching over, she patted his hand. "Bear with me, dear," she whispered. "I suppose it doesn't mean anything, but something is making me wait. The Chief did say he'd talk to me soon."

The door to the station house opened. A middle-aged couple came in. The man looked thoroughly annoyed; the woman was visibly nervous. The desk sergeant greeted them. "Hi, Mr. Wiggins . . . Miz Wiggins. Anything wrong?"

"You won't believe it," Wiggins snapped. "On a night like this, my wife wants to report that somebody pilfered a can of baby powder from the store this morning."

"Baby powder?" The sergeant's voice ranged upward in astonishment.

Mrs. Wiggins looked more upset. "I don't care how stupid it sounds. I want to see Chief Coffin."

"He'll be coming out soon. These people are waiting for him too. Just sit down, won't you?" He pointed to the bench at a right angle to the one where the Keeneys were waiting.

They came over, and as they sat down, the husband muttered angrily, "I still don't know why we're here."

Ellen's ready sympathy made her turn to the couple. She thought that maybe just talking to someone would help the other woman to get over her nervousness. "We don't really know why we're here either," she said. "But isn't it an awful thing about those missing children. . . ."

Fifty feet away in the office down the corridor, Rob Legler stared through narrowed, hostile eyes at Ray Eldredge. The guy had class, he decided. Nancy had certainly done a lot better this time. That Carl Harmon had been some creep. Fear knotted Rob's stomach. The Eldredge kids hadn't been found. If anything had happened to them, they might try to pin something on him. But nobody had seen him near the Eldredge house ... nobody except that fat slob who'd been in the old station wagon. Suppose that guy had been a deliveryman or something and called the cops? Suppose he could identify Rob as being around the Eldredge house this morning? What excuse did he have for being there? No one would believe that he had sneaked into the country just to say hello to Nancy.

Mentally, Rob darted around for a story. There was none that made sense. He'd just keep his mouth shut until he got a lawyer—and maybe after that too. The older guy was talking to him.

"You are in a very serious situation," Jonathan was saying. "You are a deserter who has been taken into custody. Shall I remind you of the penalty the law holds for deserters? Your situation is far more serious than that of a man who left the country to avoid conscription. You were a member of the armed forces. No matter what has happened to the Eldredge children or how guilty or innocent you are in their disappearance, you stand right now to spend the better part of the next ten or twenty years in prison."

"We'll see about that," Rob muttered. But he knew Jonathan was right. *Christ!*

"But, of course, even the desertion charge isn't nearly so serious as a murder charge. . . ."

"I never murdered anyone," Rob snarled, jumping up from his chair.

"Sit down," Chief Coffin ordered.

Ray stood up and leaned across the table until his eyes were on a level with Rob's. "I'm going to lay it out for you," he said evenly. "I think you're a bastard. For two cents, I'd kill you myself. Your testimony almost put my wife in a gas chamber seven years ago, and right now you may know something that could save my children's lives if it isn't already too late. Now, listen, bum, and listen hard. My wife doesn't believe that you could or would harm our children. I happen to respect that belief. But she saw you there this morning. So that means you've got to know something about what went on. Trying to stall and say you never got to our house won't help. We'll prove you were there. But if you level with us now, and we get our kids back, we won't prosecute a kidnapping charge. And Mr. Knowles, who happens to be one of the top lawyers in the country, will be your lawyer, to get you off with as light a sentence as possible on the desertion charges. He has pull—plenty of it. . . . Now, which is it, punk? Do you take the deal?" The veins bulged out in Ray's forehead. He moved forward until his eyes

were inches away from Rob's. "Because if you don't . . . and if you know something . . . and if I find out that you could have helped us get our kids back and didn't . . . I don't care what jail they throw you in . . . I'll get to you and I'll kill you. Just remember that, you stinking bastard."

"Ray." Jonathan pulled him back forcibly.

Rob stared from face to face: The Chief . . . the doctor . . . Ray Eldredge . . . that Knowles guy, the lawyer. If he admitted being at the Eldredge house . . . but what good not to admit it? There was a witness. His instinct told him to take the offer that had been made. Rob knew when he had no cards left to play. At least by taking the offer, he had some leverage on the desertion business.

He shrugged and looked at Jonathan. "You'll defend me."

"Yes."

"I don't want any bum kidnapping rap."

"No one's trying to pin one on you," Jonathan said. "We want the truth—the simple truth, as you know it. And the deal's off unless we get it now."

Rob leaned back. He avoided looking at Ray. "Okay," he said. "This is how it started. My buddy up in Canada . . ."

They listened intently as he talked. Only occasionally did the Chief or Jonathan ask a question. Rob chose his words carefully when he said he was coming to ask Nancy for money. "See, I never believed she touched a hair on the head of those Harmon kids. She wasn't the type. But I got the word that they were trying to pin the rap on me out there and I'd better just answer questions and keep my opinions out of it. I felt kind of sorry for her; she was a scared kid in a big frame-up as far as I was concerned."

"A frame-up that was your direct responsibility," Ray said.

"Shut up, Ray," Chief Coffin said. "Get to this morning," he ordered Rob. "When did you arrive at the Eldredge home?"

"It was like a couple of minutes before ten," Rob said. "I had been driving real slow, looking for that dirt road my friend drew a picture of . . . and then I realized I'd missed it."

"How did you realize you missed it?"

"Well, this other car . . . I had to slow down for . . . Then I realized that the other car had come off that road, so I backed up."

"The other car?" Ray repeated. He jumped up. "*What* other car?"

The door of the interrogation room burst open. The sergeant hurried in. "Chief, I think it's real important you talk to the Wigginses and that other couple. I think they have something real important to tell you."

CHAPTER 30

Finally Nancy was able to get up, wash her face and rinse her mouth. She mustn't let them see that she'd been sick. She mustn't talk about it. They'd think she was crazy. They wouldn't believe or understand. But if the unbelievable was possible . . . The children. Oh, God, not again, not like that; please, not again.

She rushed into the bedroom and grabbed underwear from the drawer, slacks and a heavy sweater from the closet. She had to go to the station house. She had to see Rob, tell him what she believed, beg him for the truth. What did it matter if everyone thought she was crazy?

With lightning speed, she dressed, stuffed her feet into sneakers, laced them with trembling fingers and hurried downstairs. Dorothy was waiting for her in the dining room. The table was set with sandwiches and a pot of tea.

"Nancy, sit down. . . . Just try to have something. . . ."

Nancy cut her off. "I have to see Rob Legler. There's something I have to ask him." She clenched her teeth together, having heard the hysteria rising in her voice. She must not be hysterical. She turned to Bernie Mills, who was standing in the doorway of the kitchen.

"Please call the station," she begged him. "Tell Chief Coffin I insist on coming over . . . that it has to do with the children."

"Nancy!" Dorothy grabbed her arm. "What are you saying?"

"That I must see Rob. Dorothy, call the station. No, I will."

Nancy ran over to the phone. She was just reaching for it when it rang. Bernie Mills hurried to take it, but she picked it up.

"Hello?" Her voice was quick and impatient.

Then she heard. So low it was a whisper. She had to strain to make out his words. "Mommy. Mommy, please come and get us. Help us, Mommy. Missy is sick. Come and get us. . . ."

"Michael . . . Michael!" she screamed. "Michael, where are you? Tell me where you are!"

"We're at . . ." Then his voice faded and the line went dead.

Frantically, she jiggled the phone. "Operator," she shrieked, "don't break the connection! Operator . . ." But it was too late. An instant later, the monotonous dull, buzzing dial tone whined in her ear.

"Nancy, what is it? Who was it?" Dorothy was at her side.

"It was Michael. Michael phoned. He said Missy is sick." Nancy could see doubt on Dorothy's face. "In God's name, don't you understand? That was Michael!"

Frantically, she jiggled the phone, then dialed the operator and broke into her perfunctory offer of help when she responded. "Can you tell me about the call that just came here? Who handled it? Where did it come from?"

"I'm sorry, ma'am. We have no way of knowing that. In fact, we're having a lot of trouble generally. Most of the phones in town are out because of the storm. What is the problem?"

"I've got to know where that call came from. I've got to know."

"There is no way we can trace the call once the connection is broken, ma'am."

Numbly, Nancy put down the receiver.

"Somebody may have broken that connection," she said. "Whoever has the children."

"Nancy, are you sure?"

"Mrs. Eldredge, you're kind of strung-up and upset."

Bernie Mills tried to make his voice soothing.

Nancy ignored him. "Dorothy, Michael said, 'We're at . . .' He knows where he is. He can't be far away. Don't you see that? And he says Missy's sick."

From far off, she was hearing something else. Lisa is sick. . . . She doesn't feel right. She had said that to Carl long ago.

"What is the number of the police station?" Nancy asked Bernie Mills. She pushed back the waves of weakness that were like clouds of fog inside her head. It would be so easy to lie down . . . to slip away. Right now someone was with Michael and Missy . . . someone who was hurting them . . . maybe was doing to them what had happened before. No . . . no . . . she had to find them. . . . She mustn't get sick. . . . She had to find them.

She grasped the edge of the table to steady herself. She said quietly, "You may think I'm hysterical, but I am telling you that was my son's voice. What is the number of the police station?"

"Call KL five, three eight hundred," Bernie said reluctantly. *She's really flipped,* he thought. And the Chief would have his head for not having gotten to the phone. She imagined it was the kid . . . but it could have been anybody, or even a crank.

The number rang once. A crisp voice said, "Adams Port Police Headquarters. Sergeant . . . speaking." Nancy started to say, "Chief Coffin" and realized that she was speaking into nothingness. Impatiently, she jiggled the phone. "It's dead," she said. "The phone is dead."

Bernie Mills took it from her. "It's dead, all right. I'm not surprised. Probably half the houses don't have phones by now. This is some storm."

"Take me to the police station. No, you go if the phone comes back on and Michael can call again . . . Please go to the police station, or is someone outside?"

"I don't think so. The television van went to the station house too."

"Then you go. We'll stay here. Tell them Michael phoned. Tell them to bring Rob Legler here. We've got to wait."

"I can't leave you."

"Nancy, how sure are you it was Michael?"

"I'm sure. Dorothy, please believe me. I'm sure. It was Michael. It was. Officer. Please. How far is the station in your car? . . . Five minutes. You'll be gone ten minutes in all. —But make them bring Rob Legler here. Please."

Bernie Mills thought carefully. The Chief had told him to stay here. But with the phone out, there wouldn't be messages. If he brought Nancy with him, the Chief might not like it. If he left and came right back, he'd be gone a total of ten minutes, and if that ever was the kid on the phone and he didn't report it. . . .

He considered asking Dorothy to drive to the station, then discarded the idea. The roads were too icy. She looked so upset that the odds were she'd crack up her car.

"I'll go," he said. "Stay right here."

He didn't take time to look for his coat, but ran out the back door to the patrol car.

Nancy said, "Dorothy, Michael knew where he was. He said, 'We're at . . .' What does that mean to you? If you're on a street or a road, you say, 'We're *on* Route 6A,' or 'we're *on* the beach,' or 'we're *on* the boat'; but if you're in a house or store, you know you say, 'We're *at* Dorothy's house'; or 'We're *at* Daddy's office.' Do you see what I mean? Oh, Dorothy, there must be some way to know. I keep going over things. There must be something . . . some way to know.

"And he said that Missy is sick. I almost didn't let her go out this morning. I thought about it. I thought about it. Was it too cold; was it too windy? But I hate to think about them being sick or to baby them about being sick, and I know why now. It was because of Carl and the way he examined them . . . and me. He was sick. I know that now. But that's why I let Missy out. It was damp and too cold for her. But I thought just half an hour. And it was because of that. And I got her red mittens, the ones with the smile faces, and I told her to be sure to keep them on because it was so cold. I remember thinking that for a change she had a matching pair. But she did lose one by the swing. Oh, God, Dorothy, if I hadn't let them out! If I had kept them in because she was getting sick . . . But I didn't want to think about that. . . . Dorothy!"

Nancy spun around at Dorothy's strangled cry. Dorothy's face was working convulsively. "What did you say?" she demanded. "What did you say . . . about the mittens?"

"I don't know. Do you mean—that she lost one—or that they matched? Dorothy, what do you mean? . . . What do you know?"

With a sob, Dorothy covered her face. "I know where they are. Oh God, I know . . . and I was so stupid. Oh, Nancy, what have I done? Oh, what have I done?" She reached into her pocket and pulled out the mitten. "It was there . . . this afternoon on the floor of the garage . . . and I thought I'd kicked it out. And that awful man . . . I knew there was something about him; the way he smelled so sour . . . so evil . . . and that baby powder. Oh, my God!"

Nancy grabbed the mitten. "Dorothy, please help me. Where did you find that mitten?"

Dorothy sagged limply. "At The Lookout, when I was showing it today."

"The Lookout . . . where that Parrish man lives. I don't think I've ever seen him except from a distance. Oh, no!" In an instant of total clarity, Nancy saw truth and realized it might be too late. "Dorothy, I'm going to The Lookout. *Now* . . . the children are there. Maybe. Maybe I'll be in time. You go for Ray and the police. Tell them to come. Can I get into the house?"

Dorothy's shaking stopped. Her voice became as calm as Nancy's. Later—later, for the rest of her life—she could indulge in self-recrimination . . . but not this minute. "The kitchen door has a bolt. If he put it on, you can't get in. But the front door, the one on the bay side—he never uses it. I never gave him a key. This will open both locks." She dug into her pocket and came out with a set. "This one."

She did not question Nancy's decision to go alone. Together the women raced out the back door toward the cars. Dorothy let Nancy pull out first. She caught her breath as Nancy's car lurched, skidded and then righted itself.

It was almost impossible to see. The sleet had formed a thick ice shield against the window. Nancy rolled down her side window. Glancing out it, squinting against the pelting sleet, she raced the car down the road, across Route 6A and down the street that led to the cutoff for The Lookout.

As she started up the winding incline, the car began to slip. She floored the gas pedal and the front wheels skidded, twisting the car on the icy road. Nancy jammed on the brake. The car spun around. Too late, she tried to right it. A tree loomed ahead. She managed to yank the wheel in a half circle. The front end of the car pulled to the right and with a grinding crash hit the tree.

Nancy was thrown forward, then snapped back. The wheels were still spinning as she pushed open the door on the driver's side and stepped out into the pelting sleet. She hadn't put on a coat, but she barely felt the sleet go through her sweater and slacks as she tried to run up the precarious hill.

At the approach to the driveway, she slipped and fell. Ignoring the sharp pain in her knee, she ran toward the house. *Don't let me be too late. Please don't let me be too late.* Like clouds breaking before her vision, she could see herself staring down at the slabs at Lisa and Peter . . . their faces white and bloated from the water . . . the bits of the plastic bag still sticking to them. *Please,* she prayed. *Please!*

She got to the house and steadied herself against the shingles as she ran around it toward the front entrance. The key in her hand was wet and cold. She grasped it tightly. The house was completely dark except for the top floor. She could see a light coming through the shade on one of the windows. As she rounded the house, she could hear the harsh crashing sounds of the bay as the waves broke against the rocky shore. There was no beach—just piles of rock. The beach was over to the left.

She hadn't realized this property was so high. You could probably see the whole town from the back windows.

Her breath was coming in deep, sobbing gasps. Nancy felt her heart pounding. She couldn't breathe from running in the cold wind. Her numbed fingers fumbled with the key. *Let it turn; please, let it turn.* She felt resistance as the rusty lock grabbed at the key, then held it, and finally the lock turned and Nancy pushed open the door.

The house was dark—so terribly dark. She couldn't see. There was a musty smell, and it was so quiet here. The light had come from the top floor. That was where the apartment was. She'd have to find the stairs. She resisted the impulse to shriek Michael's name.

Dorothy had said something about two staircases in the foyer past the big front room. This was the front room. Uncertainly, Nancy started forward. In the pitch darkness, she reached her hands in front of her. She mustn't make noise; mustn't give warning. She tripped, fell forward and recovered herself by grabbing something. It was the arm of a couch or chair. She felt her way around it. If only she had matches. She strained to hear. . . . Had she heard something . . . a cry . . . or was it just the way the wind howled in the fireplace?

She had to get upstairs . . . had to find them. Suppose they weren't there? . . . Suppose she was too late? . . . Suppose it was like last time?— with those little faces so quiet, so distorted. . . . They had trusted her. Lisa had clung to her that last morning. "Daddy hurt me" was all she would say. Nancy was sure that Carl had spanked her for wetting the bed . . . had cursed herself for being too tired to wake up. She hadn't dared to criticize Carl . . . but when she made the bed, it wasn't wet; so Lisa hadn't wet the bed. She should have told them that at the trial, but she couldn't. She couldn't think, and she was too tired . . . and it didn't matter anymore.

The stairs . . . That was a post under her arm. . . . The stairs . . . three flights . . . Walk on the side . . . Be quiet. Nancy reached down and yanked off her sneakers. They were so wet they'd make a squishing noise. . . . *Important to be quiet. . . . Have to get upstairs . . . Mustn't be too late again. . . . Last time too late. . . . Shouldn't have left children in car. . . . Should have known . . .*

The stairs squeaked under her foot. *Mustn't let him panic. . . . Last time he panicked. . . . Maybe Michael's call panicked him. . . . Last time they said the children hadn't been thrown in the water till after they were dead. . . . But Michael was still alive just a few minutes ago . . . Twenty minutes ago . . . and he thought Missy was sick. . . . Maybe she was sick. . . . Have to get to her. . . . The first flight. . . . Bedrooms on this floor . . . but no light, no sound. . . .* Upstairs two more flights. . . . On the third floor there was no sound either.

At the base of the last staircase, Nancy stopped to control her harsh breathing. The door at the head of the stairs was open. She could see a shadow against the wall caused by a thin flicker of light. Then she heard it . . . a voice—Michael's voice . . . "Don't do that! Don't do that!"

She ran up the stairs blindly, furiously. Michael! Missy! She hurried, not caring about the noise, but her thick socks didn't make noise. Her hand grasping the banister was silent. At the top of the stairs she hesitated. The light was coming from down the hall. Silently, swiftly she hurried through the room, the living room probably, that was shadowy and quiet, toward the candlelight in the bedroom, toward the gross figure with its back to her that was holding a small struggling figure on the bed with one hand, giggling softly as with the other he pulled a shiny plastic bag over a blond head.

Nancy had an impression of startled blue eyes, of Michael's blond hair matting on his forehead, of the way the plastic clung to his eyelids and nostrils as she cried, "Let go of him, Carl! . . ." She didn't know she'd said "Carl" until she heard the name come from her lips.

The man spun around. Somewhere lurking in that gross mass of flesh, she could see eyes that darted and burned. Nancy had an impression of the plastic clinging, of Missy's tousled figure lying on the bed, her windbreaker a bright red heap beside her.

She saw the look of stupefaction replaced by cunning. "You." The voice was remembered. The voice that over seven years she'd tried to blot out. He started toward her menacingly. She had to get around him. Michael couldn't breathe.

He lunged for her. She pulled away, feeling his thick grasp on her wrist. They fell together, clumsily, heavily. She felt his elbow dig into her side. The pain was blinding, but his grip relaxed for an instant. His face was next to hers. Thick and white, the features bloated and broadened, but the sour, dank smell . . . the same as it had been before.

Blindly, she reached out with all her force and bit the thick, jowly cheek. With a howl of rage, he lashed out, but let her go, and she dragged herself up, feeling his hand pulling at her. She threw herself onto the bed, with her fingernails tearing at the tight plastic sheet that was making Michael's eyes bulge, his cheeks become blue. She heard his gasping breath as she twisted around to meet Carl's new attack. His arms pulled her tight against him. She felt the sick warmth of his exposed body.

Oh, God. She pushed back his face with her hands and felt him bend her backward. As she tried to pull away, she could feel Missy's foot under her, touching her, moving. It was moving. Missy was alive. She knew it; she could feel it.

She began to scream—a steady, demanding call for help; and then Carl's hand covered her mouth and nostrils, and futilely she tried to bite the thick palm that was choking out air and causing great black curtains to close in front of her eyes.

She was sinking into gasping unconsciousness when abruptly the hands loosened their pressure. She choked—great gurgling sounds. From somewhere, someone was shouting her name. Ray! It was Ray! She tried to call out, but no sound came.

Struggling up onto one elbow, she shook her head. "Mommy, Mommy, he's taking Missy!" Michael's voice was urgent, his hand shaking her.

She managed to sit up as Carl swooped. His arm passed her and grabbed the small figure that had begun to squirm and cry.

"Put her down, Carl. Don't touch her." Her voice was a croak now, but he looked at her wildly and turned. Holding Missy against him, he ran away, his gait awkward. In the dark of the next room, she heard him bumping into furniture, and she staggered after him, trying to shake the dizziness. There were footsteps on the stairs now—hard, racing footsteps coming up. Desperately she listened for Carl, heard him down the hall; saw his dark shadow silhouetted against the window. He was climbing up the stairs to the attic. He was going up to the attic. She followed him, caught up with him, tried to grasp his leg. The attic was cavernous, musty-smelling, thick-beamed with a low ceiling. And dark. So dark it was hard to follow him.

"Help!" she screamed. "Help!" At last she could make her voice carry. "Up here. Ray. Up here!" She stumbled blindly after the sound of Carl's footsteps. But where was he? The ladder. He was climbing the thin, rickety ladder that led from the attic straight up to the roof. The widow's walk. He was going onto the widow's walk. She thought of the narrow, perilous balcony that circled the chimney between the turrets of the house.

"Carl, don't go up there. It's too dangerous. Carl, come back, come back!"

She could hear his harsh breathing, the high-pitched sound that was between sob and giggle. She tried to grab his foot as she climbed after him, but he kicked savagely when he felt her hand. The thick sole of his shoe caught the edge of her forehead, and she slipped down the ladder. Ignoring the warm, gushing blood that streamed down her face, not feeling the force of the blow, she started up again, crying, "Carl, give her to me. Carl, stop!"

But he was at the top of the ladder, pushing up the door that led onto the roof. Thick sleet pelted down as the door creaked upward. "Carl, you can't get away," she pleaded. "Carl, I'll help you. You're sick. I'll tell them you're sick."

The wind caught the door, pulled it open till it thudded against the side of the house. Missy was crying now—a loud, frightened wail: "Mommmmmmmmy!"

Carl thrust his body onto the balcony. Nancy scrambled after him, bracing against the doorframe. It was so narrow. There was barely space for one person between the railing and the chimney.

Frantically she clawed at his clothes—trying to get a grip on him, to pull him back from the low railing. If he fell or dropped Missy . . . "Carl, stop. Stop!"

Sleet beat against him. He turned and tried to kick her again, but stumbled backward, grasping Missy against him. He lurched against the railing and regained his balance. His giggle was now a persistent, hiccuping sound.

The walk was covered with a layer of ice. He sat Missy on the railing, holding her with one hand. "Don't come any nearer, little girl," he said to Nancy. "I'll drop her if you do. Tell them they must let me go away. Tell them they must not touch me."

"Carl. I'll help you. Give her to me."

"You won't help. You'll want them to hurt me." He swung one foot over the rail.

"Carl. No. Don't do it. Carl, you hate water. You don't want water to cover your face. You know that. That's why I should have known you didn't commit suicide. You couldn't drown yourself. You know that, Carl." She made her voice calm, deliberate, soothing. She took one step toward the railing. Missy was reaching her arms out, pleading.

Then she heard it . . . a cracking, breaking sound. The railing was breaking! As she watched, the wooden posts gave way under Carl's weight. His head went backward; he swung his arms forward.

As he released his hold on Missy, Nancy darted forward and grabbed her baby. Her hands caught in Missy's long hair—caught and twisted and held. She was teetering on the edge of the walk; the rail was crumbling. She felt Carl grab her leg as he fell, screaming.

Then, as she was being dragged forward, firm arms came around her waist from behind—arms that held and supported her. A strong hand pulled Missy's head against her neck, pulled them both back, and she collapsed against Ray even as, with a last despairing scream, Carl slid off the balcony, across the icy, sloping roof and into the angry, rock-filled surf far below.

 CHAPTER 31

The fire licked hungrily at the thick logs. The warm hearth smell permeated the room and mingled with the scent of freshly made coffee. The Wigginses had opened the store and brought up cold cuts for sandwiches, and they and Dorothy had prepared a spread while Nancy and Ray were at the hospital with the children.

When they got home, Nancy insisted that the television crews and reporters be fed too, and Jonathan had thrown his home open to them. They had taken films of the homecoming of Nancy and Ray, carrying their children in from the car, and had been promised an interview the next day.

"In the meantime," Ray said into the microphones, "we want to thank everyone whose prayers through this day kept our children from harm."

The Keeneys had come back to the house too, wanting to be part of the gladness; frightened that they had waited to come forward with their information; sure that only prayer had made the rescue possible. *We are all so human, so foolish,* Ellen thought. She shuddered thinking that her Neil had talked to that insane man. Suppose he had asked Neil to get into his car that day . . . ?

Nancy sat on the couch, tightly holding a peacefully sleeping Missy. Missy, smelling of Vicks and soothed with warm milk and aspirin, the ragged blanket she called her "bee" held securely to her face as she nestled against her mother.

Michael was talking to a gently questioning Lendon—telling all about it, thinking it out. His voice, at first excitable and rapid, was calmer now, even a little boastful: ". . . I didn't want to go away from that house without Missy when the nice man started fighting with the other man and yelled at me to get help. So I ran back up to Missy and called Mommy on the phone. But then the phone stopped working. And I tried to carry Missy down the stairs, but the bad man came. . . ."

Ray's arms were around him. "Good boy. You're quite a guy, Mike." Ray couldn't keep his eyes off Nancy and Missy. Nancy's face was discolored and bruised, but so serenely beautiful that he had trouble swallowing over the lump in his throat.

Chief Coffin put down his coffee cup and reviewed the statement that he would make to the press: "Professor Carl Harmon, alias Courtney Parrish, was pulled out of the water still alive. Before he died, he was able to make a statement, confessing his sole guilt in the murder of his children, Lisa and Peter, seven years ago. He also admitted that he was responsible for the death of Nancy Eldredge's mother. Realizing that she would have prevented his marriage to Nancy, he jammed the steering mechanism of her car while she was in the restaurant with Nancy. Mr. John Kragopoulos, whom Professor Harmon assaulted today, is on the serious list in Cape Cod Hospital with a concussion, but is expected to recover. The Eldredge children have been examined and were not sexually molested, although the boy, Michael, suffered a bruise on the side of the face from a violent slap."

The Chief felt fatigue settling into the very marrow of his bones. He'd give the statement and get home himself. Delia would be waiting for him, wanting to know everything about what had happened. This, he reflected, was the kind of day that made police work worthwhile. There was so much grief in this job. There were the times you had to tell parents that their child was dead. Moments like the one in The Lookout when they knew they had found both kids safe were to be cherished.

Tomorrow. Jed reflected that tomorrow he would have to judge his own culpability. This morning he had prejudged Nancy because of pique that he hadn't recognized her. By prejudging her, he hadn't let his mind stay open; had ignored what Jonathan and Ray and the doctor and Nancy herself were telling him.

But at least he had driven the car that got Ray to the balcony on the roof of The Lookout in that split second of time. No one else could have gotten up that hill on that ice so fast. When they'd seen Nancy's car crashed into the tree at the bend of the road, Ray had wanted to stop. But Jed had kept going. Some instinct made him feel that Nancy had gotten out of the car and was in the house. His hunch had been right. For that he could defend himself.

Dorothy quietly refilled Lendon's cup at his affirmative nod. Michael would be all right, Lendon thought. He'd come down and see them again soon. He'd talk to the children and to Nancy—try to help her to completely see the past for what it was and then turn her back on it. Nancy wouldn't need too much help. It was a miracle that she'd had the toughness to survive the horror of everything that had happened to her. But she was a strong person and would emerge from this last ordeal, able to look forward to a normal life.

There was peace in Lendon. He had compensated at last for his neglect. If he had gone to Nancy when Priscilla died, so much could have been avoided. He would have realized there was something wrong with Carl Harmon and somehow gotten her away from him. But then she wouldn't be here now with this young man who was her husband. These children would not be in her arms.

Lendon realized how much he wanted now to get home to Allison.

"Coffee?" Jonathan repeated Dorothy's question. "Yes, thank you. I don't usually have any this late, but I don't think many of us will have trouble sleeping tonight." He studied Dorothy closely. "How about you? You must be pretty tired."

He watched as an indefinable sadness crept over her face and understood the reason for it. "I think I must tell you," he said firmly, "that any kind of self-recrimination you have is intolerable. We all ignored facts today in a way that might have contributed to disaster. One of the first of these is that every single morning as I walked past this house, I have been annoyed by the glint that hit my eyes. This very morning I considered asking Ray to speak to the tenant at The Lookout about whatever he had in the window. With my legal training, I should have remembered that. An investigation would have led us to The Lookout very quickly.

"And one irrevocable fact is that if you had not elected to keep that appointment and bring Mr. Kragopoulos to that house, Carl Harmon would not have been deterred in his evil intent. He would not have had his attention distracted from Missy. Surely you've been listening to Michael's description of what was happening before your call."

Dorothy listened, considered, and in basic honesty agreed. A weight of guilt and remorse dissolved, and she felt suddenly lighthearted and glad, able to rejoice fully in the reunion. "Thank you, Jonathan," she said simply. "I did need to hear that."

Unconsciously, she clasped his arm. Consciously, he covered her hand with his own. "The roads are still treacherous," he said. "When you're ready to go home, I'd feel better if I drove you."

It is over, Nancy thought. *It is over.* Her arms tightened around her sleeping child. Missy stirred, murmured "Mommy," and slipped back into even, soft breathing.

Nancy looked at Michael. He was leaning back against Ray. Nancy watched as Ray gently pulled him down on his lap. "You're getting tired, fellow," Ray said. "I think maybe you kids had better get to bed. It's been quite a day."

Nancy remembered the feeling when those strong arms had grabbed her, held her, kept her and Missy from falling. It would always be like that with Ray. She would always be safe. And today she'd seen and known and been in time.

From the wellsprings of her being, prayer permeated her mind and heart: *Thank You, thank You, thank You. You have delivered us from evil.*

She realized that the sleet was no longer pelting the windows, that the moaning sound of the wind had died.

"Mommy," Michael said, and now his voice was sleepy. "We didn't even have a birthday party for you, and I didn't get you your present."

"Don't worry, Mike," Ray said. "We'll celebrate Mommy's birthday tomorrow, and I know just the presents to get for her." Miraculously, the strain and fatigue left his expression, and Nancy saw a twinkle begin in his eye. He looked directly at her. "I'll even tell you what they are, honey," he volunteered. "Art lessons from a really good teacher from the kids and a color job at the beauty parlor from me."

He stood up, eased Michael back into the chair and came over to her. Standing over her, he studied the part in her hair carefully. "I have a hunch you make a hell of a redhead, honey," he said.

A STRANGER IS WATCHING

In joyful memory of Warren
and for
Marilyn, Warren, David, Carol, and Patricia

You are your parents' glass and I in you
Call back the lovely April of our prime.

CHAPTER 1

He sat perfectly still in front of the television set in room 932 of the Biltmore Hotel. The alarm had gone off at six but he was awake long before that. The wind, cold and forbidding, rattled the windowpanes and that had been enough to pull him out of the uneasy sleep.

The *Today* show came on but he didn't adjust the barely audible sound. He didn't care about the news or the special reports. He just wanted to see the interview.

Shifting in the stiff-backed chair, he crossed and uncrossed his legs. He'd already showered and shaved and put on the green polyester suit he'd worn when he'd checked in the night before. The realization that the day had come at last made his hand tremble and he'd nicked his lip when he shaved. It bled a little and the salty taste of blood in his mouth made him gag.

He hated blood.

Last night at the desk in the lobby, he'd seen the clerk's eyes sliding over his clothes. He'd carried his coat under his arm because he knew it looked shabby. But the suit was new; he'd saved up for it. Still the clerk looked at him like he was dirt and asked if he had a reservation.

He'd never checked into a real hotel before but knew how to do it. "Yes, I have a reservation." He said it very coldly and for a minute the clerk looked uncertain but when he didn't have a credit card and offered to pay cash in advance, the sneer was back. "I will check out Wednesday morning," he told the clerk.

The room cost one hundred forty dollars for the three nights. That meant he only had thirty dollars left. But that would be plenty for these few days and by Wednesday he'd have eighty-two thousand dollars.

Her face floated across his mind. He blinked to force it away. Because just as always the eyes came after it; the eyes like great lamps that followed him, that were always watching him, that never closed.

He wished he had another cup of coffee. He'd sent for room service, reading the instructions how to call for it very carefully. He'd had a large pot of coffee and there'd been a little left but he'd already washed the cup and saucer and orange juice glass and rinsed out the coffeepot before putting the tray on the floor in the hall.

A commercial was just ending. Suddenly interested he leaned forward to get nearer to the set. The interview should be next. It was. He twisted the volume knob to the right.

The familiar face of Tom Brokaw, the *Today* anchorman, filled the screen. Unsmiling, his voice subdued, he began to speak. "The restoration of capital punishment has become the most emotional and divisive issue in this country since the Vietnamese War. In just fifty-two hours, at eleven-thirty A.M. on March 24th, the sixth execution this year will take place when nineteen-year-old Ronald Thompson dies in the electric chair. My guests . . ."

The camera dollied back to include the two people seated on either side of Tom Brokaw. The man to his right was in his early thirties. His sandy hair was streaked with gray and somewhat disheveled. His hands were together, fingers spread apart and pointing upward. His chin rested on the fingertips, giving him a prayerful stance that was accentuated by dark eyebrows arcing over winter-blue eyes.

The young woman on the other side of the interviewer sat stiffly erect. Her hair, the color of warm honey, was pulled back in a soft chignon. Her hands were knotted into fists in her lap. She moistened her lips and pushed back a strand of hair from her forehead.

Tom Brokaw said, "On their previous appearance here, six months ago, our guests made a very strong case supporting their views on capital punishment. Sharon Martin, syndicated columnist, is also the author of the best-selling book, *The Crime of Capital Punishment.* Steven Peterson, the editor of *Events* magazine, is one of the most articulate voices in the media to urge restoration of capital punishment in this country."

His tone became brisk. He turned to Steve. "Let's start with you, Mr. Peterson. After having witnessed the emotional public reaction to the executions that have already taken place, do you still believe that your position is justified?"

Steve leaned forward. When he answered, his voice was calm. "Absolutely," he said quietly.

The interviewer turned to his other guest. "Sharon Martin, what do you think?"

Sharon shifted slightly in her chair to face her interrogator. She was achingly tired. In the last month she'd worked twenty hours a day, contacting prominent people—senators, congressmen, judges, humanitarians, speaking at colleges, at women's clubs, urging everyone to write and wire the Connecticut governor and protest Ronald Thompson's execution. The response had been enormous, overwhelming. She had been so sure that Governor Greene would reconsider. She found herself groping for words.

"I think," she said, "I *believe* that we, our country, has taken a giant step backwards into the Dark Ages." She held up the newspapers at her side. "Just look at this morning's headlines. Analyze them! They're blood-thirsty." Quickly, she leafed through them. "This one . . . listen . . . *Connecticut Tests Electric Chair,* and this . . . *19-Year Old Dies Wednesday,* and this, *Doomed Killer Protests Innocence.* They're all like that, sensational, savage!" She bit her lip as her voice broke.

Steve glanced at her swiftly. They'd just been told that the Governor was calling a press conference to announce her absolute refusal to grant Thompson another stay of execution. The news had devastated Sharon. It would be a miracle if she didn't get sick after this. They never should have agreed to come on this show today. The Governor's decision made Sharon's appearance pointless, and God knows Steve didn't want to be here. But he had to say something.

"I think every decent human being deplores sensationalism and the need for the death penalty," he said. "But remember it has been applied only after exhaustive consideration of extenuating circumstances. There is no *mandatory* death sentence."

"Do you believe that the circumstances in Ronald Thompson's case, the fact that he committed the murder only days after his seventeenth birthday, making him barely eligible for adult punishment, should have been considered?" Brokaw asked quickly.

Steve said, "As you know, I will not comment specifically on the Thompson case. It would be entirely inappropriate."

"I understand your concern, Mr. Peterson," the interviewer said, "but you had taken your position on this issue several years before . . ." He paused, then continued quietly, "before Ronald Thompson murdered your wife."

Ronald Thompson murdered your wife. The starkness of the words still surprised Steve. After two and a half years, he could still feel the sense of shock and outrage that Nina had died that way, her life snuffed out by the intruder who came into their home, by the hands that had relentlessly twisted her scarf around her throat.

Trying to blot the image from his mind, he looked directly ahead. "At one time, I had hoped that the ban on executions in our country might become a permanent one. But as you point out, long before the tragedy in my own family, I had come to the conclusion that if we were to preserve the most fundamental right of human beings . . . freedom to come and go without fear, freedom to feel sanctuary in our homes, we had to stop the perpetrators of violence. Unfortunately the only way to stop potential murderers seems to be to threaten them with the same harsh judgment they mete out to their victims. And since the first execution was carried out two years ago, the number of murders has dropped dramatically in major cities across the country."

Sharon leaned forward. "You make it sound so reasonable," she cried. "Don't you realize that forty-five percent of murders are committed by people under twenty-five years of age, many of whom have tragic family backgrounds and a history of instability?"

The solitary viewer in Biltmore's room 932 took his eyes from Steve Peterson and studied the girl thoughtfully. This was the writer Steve was getting serious about. She wasn't at all like his wife. She was obviously taller and had the slender body of someone who might be athletic. His wife had been small and doll-like with rounded breasts and jet black hair that curled around her forehead and ears when she turned her head.

Sharon Martin's eyes reminded him of the color of the ocean that day he'd driven down to the beach last summer. He'd heard that Jones Beach was a good place to meet girls but it hadn't worked out. The one he'd started to fool with in the water had called "Bob!" and a minute later this guy had been beside him, asking what his problem was. So he'd moved his blanket and just stared out at the ocean, watching the changing colors. Green. That was it. Green mixed with blue and churning. He liked eyes that color.

What was Steve saying? Oh yes, he'd said something about feeling sorry for the victims, not their murderers, "for people incapable of defending themselves."

"My sympathies are with them too," Sharon cried. "But it's not either/or. Don't you see that life imprisonment would be punishment enough for the Ronald Thompsons of this world?" She forgot Tom Brokaw, forgot the television cameras as once again she tried to convince Steve. "How can you . . . who are so compassionate . . . who value life so much . . . want to play God?" she asked. "How can anyone presume to play God?"

It was an argument that began and ended the same way as it had that first time six months ago when they'd met on this program. Finally Tom Brokaw said, "Our time is running out. Can we sum up by saying that notwithstanding the public demonstrations, prison riots and student rallys that are regularly occurring all over the country, you still believe, Mr. Peterson, that the sharp drop in random murder justifies execution?"

"I believe in the moral right . . . the duty . . . of society to protect itself, and of the government to protect the sacred liberty of its citizens," Steve said.

"Sharon Martin?" Brokaw turned quickly to her.

"I believe that the death penalty is senseless and brutalizing. I believe that we can make the home and streets safe by removing violent offenders and punishing them with swift, sure sentences, by voting for the bond issues that will build the necessary correctional institutions and will pay the people who staff them. I believe that it is our reverence for life, *all* life, that is the final test of us as individuals and as a society."

Tom Brokaw said hurriedly, "Sharon Martin, Steven Peterson, thank you for being with us on *Today*. I'll be back after this message . . ."

The television set in room 932 of the Biltmore was snapped off. For a long time the muscular, thick-chested man in the green-plaid suit sat staring straight ahead at the darkened screen. Once again he reviewed his plan, the plan that began with putting the pictures and the suitcase in the secret room in Grand Central Station and would end with bringing Steve Peterson's son Neil there tonight. But now he had to decide. Sharon Martin was going to be at Steve's house this evening. She would be minding Neil until Steve got home.

He'd planned simply to eliminate her there.

But should he? She was so beautiful.

He thought of those eyes, the color of the ocean, churning, caring.

It seemed to him that when she looked directly into the camera she had been looking at *him*.

It seemed as though she wanted him to come for her.

Maybe she loved him.

If she didn't it would be easy to get rid of her.

He'd just leave her in the room in Grand Central with the child on Wednesday morning.

Then at 11:30 when the bomb went off, she, too, would be blown to bits.

 *CHAPTER 2*

They left the studio together, walking a few inches apart. Sharon's tweed cape felt heavy on her shoulders. Her hands and feet were icy. She pulled on her gloves and noticed that the antique moonstone ring Steve had given her for Christmas had smudged her finger again. Some people had such a high acid content they couldn't wear real gold without that happening.

Steve reached past her and held the door open. They stepped into the windblown morning. It was very cold and just beginning to snow; thick, clinging flakes that chilled their faces.

"I'll get you a cab," he said.

"No . . . I'd rather walk."

"That's crazy. You look dead tired."

"It will help clear my head. Oh Steve, how can you be so positive . . . so sure . . . so relentless?"

"Don't let's start again, dear."

"We have to start again!"

"Not now." Steve looked down at her, impatience mingling with concern. Sharon's eyes looked strained, fine, red lines threaded through them; the on-camera makeup she was wearing had not covered the paleness that became accentuated as snow melted on her cheeks and forehead.

"Can you go home and get some rest?" he asked. "You need it."

"I have to turn in my column."

"Well, try to get a few hours' sleep. You'll get up to my place by about quarter of six?"

"Steve, I'm not sure . . ."

"I am. We haven't seen each other for three weeks. The Lufts are counting on going out for their anniversary and I want to be in my home tonight with you and Neil."

Ignoring the people scurrying into the Rockefeller Center buildings, Steve put his hands on Sharon's face and lifted it. Her expression was troubled and sad. He said gravely, "I love you, Sharon. You know that. I've missed you terribly these past weeks. We've got to talk about us."

"Steve, we don't think alike. We . . ."

Bending down he kissed her. Her lips were unyielding. He felt her body tense. Stepping back he raised his hand to signal a passing cab. When it pulled over to the curb, he held the door for her and gave the driver the address of the *News Dispatch* building. Before he shut the door, he asked, "Can I count on you for tonight?"

She nodded silently. Steve watched the cab turn down Fifth Avenue, then quickly walked west. He had stayed overnight at the Gotham Hotel because he had to be at the studio at 6:30, and was anxious to call Neil before he left for school. Everytime he was away from home, he worried. Neil still had nightmares, still woke up with suffocating attacks of asthma. Mrs. Lufts always called the doctor quickly but even so . . .

The winter had been so damp and cold. Maybe in the spring when Neil could get out more, he'd build up a little. He looked so pale all the time.

Spring! My God, it *was* spring. Sometime during the night the vernal equinox had taken place and winter had officially ended. You'd never guess it from the weather prediction.

Steve reached the corner and turned north, reflecting that he and Sharon had been seeing each other exactly six months now. When he picked her up at her apartment that first evening, she'd suggested walking through Central Park to the Tavern on the Green. He warned her that it had become much cooler in the last few hours and reminded her it was the first day of fall.

"Wonderful," she said. "I was just getting bored with summer." For the first few blocks they'd been almost silent. He studied the way she walked, easily in stride with him, her slender frame accentuated by the belted tawny gold suit that exactly matched the color of her hair. He remembered that the sharp breeze was pulling the first dead leaves from the trees and the setting sun accentuated the deep blue of the autumn sky.

"On a night like this, I always think of that song from *Camelot*," she told him. "You know the one, *If Ever I Would Leave You*." She sang softly, "How I'd leave in autumn, I never would know. I've seen how you sparkle when fall nips the air. I know you in autumn and I must be there . . ." She had a lovely contralto voice.

If ever I would leave you . . .

Was that the minute he fell in love with her?

That evening had been so good. They'd lingered over dinner talking while the people at other tables left, and new people came.

What had they talked about? Everything. Her father was an engineer for an oil company. She and her two sisters were born abroad. Both sisters were married now.

"How have you escaped?" It was a question that he had to ask. They both knew what he was really asking, "Is there anyone important in your life?"

But there wasn't. She'd traveled almost constantly for her last newspaper before she started writing the column. It was interesting and lots of fun and she didn't know where the seven years since college had vanished.

They walked back to the apartment and by the second block they were holding hands. She invited him up for a nightcap. There was the slightest emphasis on *nightcap*.

While he made drinks, she touched a match to the kindling in the fireplace and they sat side by side watching the flames.

Steven could still remember vividly the feeling of that night, the way the fire brought out the gold in her hair, threw shadows on her classic profile, highlighted her sudden beautiful smile. He'd ached to put his arms around her then but simply kissed her lightly when he left. "Saturday, if you're not busy . . ." He waited.

"I'm not busy."

"I'll call you in the morning."

And on the drive home, he'd known that the restless, ceaseless heart hunger of the last two years might be ending. *If ever I would leave you . . . Don't leave me, Sharon.*

It was quarter of eight when he turned into the building at 1347 Avenue of the Americas. *Events* magazine staffers were not noted for their early arrivals. The corridors were deserted. Nodding to the security guard at the elevator, Steve went up to his thirty-sixth-floor office and dialed his home.

Mrs. Lufts answered. "Oh, Neil's fine. He's just eating his breakfast, or picking at it, I should say. Neil, it's your dad."

Neil got on. "Hi, Dad, when are you coming home?"

"By eight-thirty sure. I have a five o'clock meeting. The Lufts still want to go to the movies, don't they?"

"I guess so."

"Sharon will be up before six so they can leave."

"I know. You told me." Neil's voice was noncommittal.

"Well have a good day, son. And dress warmly. It's getting pretty cold down here. Is it snowing up there yet?"

"No, it's just sort of cloudy."

"All right. See you tonight."

"Bye, Dad."

Steve frowned. It was hard to remember that at one time Neil had been such a vibrant, happy-go-lucky kid. Nina's death had changed that. He wished that Neil and Sharon would get closer. Sharon was trying, really trying, to break through Neil's reserve, but he just wouldn't give an inch, at least not so far.

Time. Everything took time. Sighing, Steve turned to the table behind his desk and reached for the editorial he had been working on the night before.

━━ *CHAPTER 3*

The occupant of room 932 left the Biltmore at 9:30 A.M. He exited by the Forty-fourth Street door and headed east toward Second Avenue. The sharp, snow-filled wind was hurrying pedestrians along, making them shrink within themselves, tuck their necks into upturned collars.

It was good weather for him, the kind of weather when people didn't bother to notice what other people were doing.

His first stop was a thrift shop on Second Avenue below Thirty-fourth Street. Ignoring the buses that passed every few minutes, he walked the fourteen blocks. Walking was good exercise and it was important to keep in shape.

The thrift shop was empty except for the elderly salesclerk who sat listlessly reading the morning paper. "Anything particular you want?" she asked.

"No. I'll just look around." He spotted the rack with the women's coats and went over to it. Pushing through the shabby garments, he selected a dark gray tent-shaped wool coat that looked long enough. Sharon Martin was fairly tall, he reflected. There was a tray of folded kerchiefs near the rack. He reached for the largest one, a faded bluish rectangle.

The woman stuffed his purchases in a shopping bag.

The Army-Navy store was next. That was easy. In the camping-gear section he bought a large canvas duffel bag. He selected it carefully, making sure it was long enough to hold the boy, thick enough that you couldn't tell from the shape what he'd be carrying, wide enough to let sufficient air in when the drawstring was loose.

In a First Avenue Woolworth's, he bought six rolls of wide bandage and two large spools of thick twine. He brought his purchases back to the Biltmore. The bed in his room was made and there were clean towels in the bathroom.

His eyes darted around for signs that the maid had gone through the closet. But his other pair of shoes was right there, exactly as he had left them, one a hairs-breadth behind the other, neither quite touching the old black double-locked suitcase that was standing in the corner.

Slipping the deadlock on the room door, he placed the bags with his purchases on the bed. With infinite care, he lifted the suitcase from the closet and laid it on the foot of the bed. Reaching into a compartment in his wallet, he extracted a key and opened the suitcase.

He made a thorough check of the contents, the pictures, the powder, the clock, the wires, the fuses, the hunting knife and the gun. Satisfied, he closed the bag again.

Carrying the suitcase and the shopping bag, he left the room. This time he went into the lower lobby of the Biltmore to the underground arcade which led to the upper level of Grand Central Station. The early morning commuter rush was over but the terminal was still filled with people scurrying to and from trains, people using the station as a short-cut to Forty-second Street or Park Avenue, people on their way to arcade shops, to the off-track betting center, the quick-service restaurants, the newsstands.

Moving quickly, he went down the stairs to the lower level and drifted over toward platform 112 from which Mount Vernon trains arrived and departed. There was no train due for eighteen minutes and the area was deserted. Glancing around swiftly, he made sure no guard was looking in his direction and disappeared down the stairs to the platform.

The platform extended in a U shape around the end of the tracks. From the other side a sloping ramp led into the depths of the terminal. Hurrying around the tracks, he made his way to that ramp. Now his movements became quicker, furtive. The sounds became different in this other world of the terminal. Overhead the station was bustling with the comings and goings of thousands of travelers. Here a pneumatic pump was throbbing, ventilating fans were rumbling, water was trickling across the damp floor. The silent, starved forms of beggar cats slithered in and out of the nearby tunnel under Park Avenue. A continuing dull railroad sound came from the loop where all the trains, beginning their outgoing journey, turned and chugged in gathering momentum away from the terminal.

He continued his gradual descent until he was at the foot of a steep iron staircase. He hurried up the metal steps, carefully placing one foot silently on the rung above. An occasional guard wandered through this area. The light was poor but even so . . .

At the head of the small landing there was a heavy metal door. Carefully depositing the suitcase and the shopping bag on the landing, he fished for and found the key in his wallet. Quickly, nervously, he inserted it in the lock. Reluctantly, the lock yielded its authority and the door swung open.

Inside it was pitch black. He fumbled for the light switch, found it, and keeping one hand firmly on it, reached down and lifted the suitcase and shopping bag into the room. He let the door close noiselessly.

The dark now was absolute. He could see the outlines of the room. The musty smell was overwhelming. Letting out a protracted sigh, the intruder consciously tried to relax. Deliberately he listened for the station sounds but they were far off, discernible only when a distinct effort was made to hear them.

It was all right.

He flicked the switch and the room became gloomy-bright. The dusty fluorescent lamps glared on the peeling ceiling and walls, casting deep shadows in the corners. The room was L-shaped, a cement room with cement walls from which thick layers of gray, moisture-repellent paint were hanging in jagged flaps. An ancient, outsize pair of laundry tubs were to the left of the door. Dripping water from the faucets had streaked their insides with canals of rust through thick layers of caked dirt. In the middle of the room, uneven, tightly nailed boards entombed a chimney-like object, a dumb-waiter. A narrow door off the far right of the L-shaped room was ajar, revealing a grimy toilet.

He knew the toilet worked. He'd come into this room last week for the first time in over twenty years and checked the lights and plumbing. Something had made him come here, had reminded him of this room when he was making his plan.

A rickety canvas army cot leaned lopsided against the far wall, an overturned orange crate next to it. The cot and crate worried him. Someone else, sometime, had stumbled onto this room and stayed in it. But the dust on the cot and the stale dampness could only mean the room had been unopened for months at least, maybe years.

He hadn't been here since he was sixteen, more than half a lifetime ago. That was when this room was used by the Oyster Bar. Located directly below the Oyster Bar kitchen, the old boarded-up dumbwaiter used to bring mounds of greasy dishes to be washed in the deep sinks and dried and sent back upstairs.

Years ago the Oyster Bar kitchen had been renovated and dishwashing machines installed. And this room sealed off. Just as well. No one would work in this smelly hole.

But it could still serve a purpose.

When he'd pondered where he could keep Peterson's son until the ransom was paid, he'd remembered this room. He'd investigated it and then realized how well it fit into his plan. When he'd been working here, with his hands all swollen from irritating detergents and scalding water and heavy wet towels, all through the terminal well-dressed people had been rushing home to their expensive houses and cars, or sitting in the restaurant eating the shrimp and clams and oysters and bass and snapper he'd had to scrape off their plates, never caring about him at all.

He'd make everyone in Grand Central, in New York, *in the world* notice him. After Wednesday they'd never forget him.

It had been simple to get into this room. A wax impression in the door of the rusty old lock. Then he'd made a key. Now he could come and go as he pleased.

Tonight Sharon Martin and the boy would be here with him. Grand Central Station. The world's busiest railroad terminal. The best place in the world to hide people.

He laughed aloud. Now that he was here, he could begin to laugh. He felt clear and brilliant and stimulated. The peeling walls and sagging cot and leaking water and splintered boards excited him.

Here he was the master, the planner. He'd arrange to get his money. He'd close the eyes forever. He couldn't stand dreaming about the eyes anymore. He couldn't stand it. And now they had become a real danger.

Wednesday. Eleven-thirty Wednesday morning was exactly forty-eight hours away. He'd be on a plane leaving for Arizona where no one knew him. It wasn't safe for him in Carley. There were too many questions being asked.

But out there, with the money ... and the eyes gone ... and if Sharon Martin was in love with him, he'd bring her with him.

He carried the suitcase past the army cot and carefully laid it flat on the floor. Opening it, he removed the tiny cassette recorder and camera and put them in the lefthand pocket of his shapeless brown overcoat. The hunting knife and gun went into the righthand pocket. No bulges showed through the deep, thick pockets.

He picked up the shopping bag and methodically spread its contents on the cot. The coat and scarf and twine and tape and bandage rolls, he stuffed into the duffel bag. Finally he reached for the packet of neatly rolled posters. He opened them, smoothing them down, bending them to reduce the curling. His eyes lingered on them. A smile, reminiscent, thoughtful, extended his narrow lips.

The first three pictures he hung on the wall, over the cot, securing them carefully with surgical tape. The fourth he studied, and slowly rolled up again.

Not yet, he decided.

Time was passing. Carefully he turned out the light before opening the door a few inches. He listened intently, but there were no footsteps in the area.

Slipping outside, he noiselessly descended the metal steps and hurried past the throbbing generator, the rumbling fans, the yawning tunnel, up the ramp, around the Mt. Vernon tracks, up the steps to the lower level of Grand Central Station. There he became part of the flow of people, a barrel-chested man in his late thirties with a muscular frame, a stiff, straight carriage, a chapped, puffy, high-cheekboned face with narrow lips that he pressed together and heavy lids that only partially concealed the pale eyes that darted from side to side.

A ticket in his hand, he hurried to the gate on the upper level where the train was leaving for Carley, Connecticut.

 *CHAPTER 4*

Neil stood on the corner waiting for the school bus. He knew Mrs. Lufts was watching him from the window. He hated that. None of his friends' mothers watched them like Mrs. Lufts did. You'd think he was a kindergarten baby instead of a first-grader.

Whenever it was raining, he had to wait in the house until the bus came. He hated that too. It made him look like a big sissy. He tried to explain that to his father but Dad hadn't understood. He'd just said that Neil had to take some special care because of his asthma attacks.

Sandy Parker was in the fourth grade. He lived on the next street but got on the bus at this stop. He always wanted to sit next to Neil. Neil wished that he wouldn't. Sandy always talked about things Neil didn't want to talk about.

Just as the bus turned the corner, Sandy came puffing up, his books sliding around in his arms. Neil tried to head for an empty seat near the back but Sandy said, "Here, Neil, here are two seats together." The bus was noisy. All the kids talked at the tops of their voices. Sandy didn't talk loud but you couldn't miss a single word he said.

Sandy was bursting with excitement. They'd barely sat down when he said, "We saw your father on the *Today* show when we were having breakfast."

"My father?" Neil shook his head. "You're kidding."

"No, I'm not. That lady I met at your house was on it too, Sharon Martin. They were arguing."

"Why?" Neil didn't want to ask. He was never sure if he should believe Sandy.

"Because she doesn't believe in killing bad people and your father does. My dad said that your dad's right. He said that the guy who killed your mother should fry." Sandy repeated the word with emphasis, "*Fry!*"

Neil turned to the window. He leaned his forehead against the cool glass. Outside it looked so gray and it was just starting to snow. He wished it were tonight. He wished his dad had been home last night. He didn't like being just with the Lufts. They were both nice to him but they argued a lot and Mr. Lufts went out to the bar and Mrs. Lufts was mad even though she tried not to show it in front of him.

"Aren't you glad they're going to kill Ronald Thompson Wednesday?" Sandy persisted.

"No . . . I mean . . . I don't think about it," Neil said in a low voice.

That wasn't true. He did think about it a lot. He dreamt about it all the time too, always the same dream about that night. He was playing with his trains up in his room. Mommy was in the kitchen putting away the shopping. It was just getting dark out. One of his trains went off the track and he switched off the power.

That was when he heard the funny sound, like a scream but not a loud scream. He'd run downstairs. The living room was almost dark but he'd seen her. Mommy. Her arms were trying to push someone back. She was making awful choking sounds. The man was twisting something around her neck.

Neil had stood on the landing. He wanted to help her but he couldn't move. He wanted to shout for help but he couldn't make his voice work. He started to breathe like Mommy, funny, gurgly sounds, then his knees went all crumbly. The man turned when he heard him and let Mommy fall.

Neil was falling too. He could feel himself falling. Then the room got brighter. Mommy was lying on the floor. Her tongue was sticking out, her face was blue, her eyes were staring. The man was kneeling beside her now; his hands were all over her throat. He looked up at Neil and started to run but Neil could see his face clearly. It was all sweaty and scared.

Neil had had to tell all about that to the policemen and point out the man at the trial. Then Daddy said, try to forget it, Neil. Just think of all the happy times with Mommy. But he couldn't forget. He kept dreaming about it all the time and he'd wake up with asthma.

Now maybe Daddy was going to marry Sharon. Sandy had told him that everybody said his dad would probably get married again. Sandy said that nobody wants other women's kids, especially kids who are sick a lot.

Mr. and Mrs. Lufts kept talking about wanting to move to Florida. Neil wondered if Daddy would give him to the Lufts if he married Sharon. He hoped not. Miserably, he stared out the window, so deep in thought that Sandy had to poke him when the bus pulled up in front of their school.

⮂ CHAPTER 5

The cab screeched to a stop at the *News Dispatch* building on East Forty-second Street. Sharon rummaged in her handbag, pulled out two dollars and paid the driver.

The snow flurry had stopped for the moment but the temperature was still dropping and the sidewalk felt slick underfoot.

She went directly to the newsroom that was already bustling with preparations for the afternoon edition. There was a note in her box to see the City Editor immediately.

Disturbed by the implied urgency, she hurried across the noisy room. He was alone in his small, cluttered office. "Come in and close the door." He waved her to a seat. "Got your column for today?"

"Yes."

"Any reference to telegraphing or phoning Governor Greene to commute Thompson's sentence?"

"Certainly. I've been thinking about it. I'll change the lead. The fact that the Governor said she won't stop the execution might be a break. It might jog a lot more people into action. We've still got forty-eight hours."

"Forget it."

Sharon stared. "What do you mean, 'forget it'? You've been right with me all through this."

"I said, forget it. After the Governor made her decision, she personally called the old man and blasted him. Said that we were deliberately creating sensationalism to sell papers. She said that she doesn't believe in capital punishment either but she has no right to interfere with the sentence of the court without new evidence. She said if we wanted to campaign to amend the Constitution, it was our right and she'd help us every step of the way, but to pressure her to interfere in one particular case had the effect of trying to apply justice capriciously. The old man ended up agreeing with her."

Sharon felt her stomach twist as though she'd been kicked. For an instant she was afraid she was going to get sick. Pressing her lips together, she tried to swallow over the sudden constriction in her throat. The editor looked at her closely. "You all right, Sharon? You look pretty pale."

She managed to force back the brackish taste. "I'm all right."

"I can get someone to cover that meeting tomorrow. You better take a few days off."

"No." The Massachusetts legislature was debating outlawing capital punishment in that state. She intended to be there.

"Have it your way. File your column and go home." His voice became sympathetic. "I'm sorry, Sharon. A constitutional amendment could take years to get passed and I thought if we got Governor Greene to be the first one to commute a death sentence, the same approach could be used case by case across the country. But I can understand her position."

Sharon said, "I understand that legalized murder is not to be protested anymore except in the abstract." Without waiting for his reaction, she abruptly got up and left the room. Going to her desk, she reached into the zipper compartment of her oversized shoulderbag and pulled out the folded typewritten pages that contained the article she had worked on most of the night. She carefully tore the pages in half, then in quarters, finally in eighths. She watched as they fluttered into the battered wastebasket next to her desk.

Putting a fresh sheet of paper in the typewriter, she began to write. "Society is again about to exercise its recently regained prerogative, the

right to kill. Almost four hundred years ago, the French philosopher Montaigne wrote, 'The horror of one man killing another makes me fear the horror of killing him.'

"If you agree that capital punishment should be outlawed by the constitution. . . ."

She wrote steadily for two hours, slashing whole paragraphs, inserting phrases, rewriting. When she had completed the column, she retyped it quickly, turned it in, left the building and hailed a cab. "Ninety-fifth Street just off Central Park West, please," she said.

The cab turned north at the Avenue of the Americas, entered the park at Central Park South. Sharon watched somberly as new snow flurries settled over the grass. If this kept up, by tomorrow, children would be sleighriding here.

Just last month Steve had brought his ice skates down and they'd gone skating at Wollman Rink. Neil was supposed to have come with him. Sharon had planned that after skating, they'd go to the zoo and then have dinner at the Tavern on the Green. But at the last minute, Neil claimed he didn't feel well and stayed home. He didn't like her, that was obvious.

"Okay, Miss."

"What? Oh, I'm sorry." They were turning onto Ninety-fifth Street. "The third house on the left." She lived in the ground-level-with-garden apartment of a renovated brownstone.

The cab pulled in front of it. The driver, a slight, graying man, looked over his shoulder at her quizzically. "It can't be all that bad, lady," he said. "You sure look down."

She attempted a smile. "It's that kind of day, I guess." Glancing at the meter, she fished in her pocket for money, making the tip generous.

The driver reached back and opened the door for her. "Boy, this weather is going to have a lot of people in the dumps by rush hour. Supposed to really start snowing. If you're smart, you'll stay inside from now on."

"I'm driving up to Connecticut later."

"Better you than me, lady. Thanks."

Angie, her two-mornings-a-week cleaning woman, had obviously just left. There was a faint smell of lemon polish; the fireplace had been swept; the plants trimmed and watered. As always the apartment offered a restful welcome to Sharon. The old oriental rug that had been her grandmother's had mellowed into soft shades of blue and red. She'd reupholstered in blue the couch and chair she bought secondhand, a labor of love that had taken the better part of four weekends but turned out well. The pictures and prints on the walls and over the fireplace she'd selected one by one, in small antique shops, at auctions, on trips abroad.

Steve loved this room. He always noticed even the smallest change in it. "You have a way with a home," he told her.

Mechanically, she walked into the bedroom and began to undress. She'd shower and change and make tea and try to sleep for a while. She couldn't even think coherently now.

It was nearly noon when she got into bed and she set the alarm for three-thirty. For a long time sleep didn't come. Ronald Thompson. She'd been so *sure* the Governor would commute his sentence. There was no question that he was guilty, and lying about it had certainly hurt him. But except for that one other serious episode when he was fifteen, his record was good. And he was so *young*.

Steve. It was people like Steve who were molding public opinion. It was Steve's reputation for integrity, for fair play that made people listen to him.

Did she love Steve?

Yes.

How much?

Very, very much.

Did she want to marry him? They were going to have to talk about that tonight. She knew that was why Steve wanted her to stay at his place. And he wanted so much for Neil to begin to accept her. But it wouldn't work; you can't force a relationship. Neil was so standoffish with her, so rejecting. Was it that he didn't like her or would he react the same way to any woman who took his father's attention from him? She wasn't sure.

Did she want to live in Carley? She loved New York so much, loved it seven days a week. But Steve would never agree to move Neil to the city.

She was just beginning to make it as a writer. Her book was in its sixth printing. It had been published as a paperback; no hardcover house had been interested, but the reviews and sales had been unexpectedly good.

Was this the time to get involved in marriage—marriage to a man whose child resented her?

Steve. Unconsciously she touched her face, remembering the feeling of those big, gentle hands warming it as he said goodbye to her this morning. They were so desperately attracted to each other . . .

But how could she accept the uncompromising, stubborn side of him when he made up his mind on an issue?

Finally she dozed off. Almost immediately she began to dream. She was writing a column. She had to finish it. It was important to finish it. But no matter how frantically she pressed the typewriter keys no impressions were being made on the paper. Then Steve was in the room. He was pulling a young man by the arm. She was still trying to make the words come out on the paper. Steve made the boy sit down. "I am so sorry," he kept saying to him, "but it is necessary. You must understand this is necessary." Then while Sharon tried to scream, Steve fastened the boy's arms and legs in shackles and reached for a switch.

Sharon was awakened by the sound of a hoarse voice, her own, shrieking, "No . . . No . . . No . . ."

CHAPTER 6

At five minutes of six the few people in the streets of Carley, Connecticut, were hurrying from cars to stores, heedless of anything except the bitter, snowy night.

The man standing in the shadows near the edge of the Cabin Restaurant parking lot was completely unobserved. His eyes constantly roved the area as pelting snow blew in his face. He'd been there nearly twenty minutes and his feet were freezing.

Impatiently, he shifted and his toe touched the duffel bag at his feet. He felt for the weapons in the pocket of his coat. They were at his fingertips and he nodded, satisfied.

The Lufts should be along any minute. He'd phoned the restaurant and confirmed the six o'clock reservation. They were planning to have dinner and then go to see the Selznick's *Gone With the Wind*. It was playing in the Carley Square Theater diagonally across the street. The 4:00 P.M. performance was on now. They were going to the 7:30 showing.

He stiffened. A car was coming down the block, was turning into the parking lot. He shrank behind the spruce trees edging the area. It was their stationwagon. He watched as they parked near the restaurant entrance. The driver got out and went around to help his wife who was clumsily stepping onto the slick tarpin. Their bodies bent against the wind, their gait awkward, his hand under her elbow, the Lufts moved with cautious haste toward the door of the restaurant.

He waited till they were safely inside before bending down and picking up the duffel bag. Moving swiftly, he circled the parking lot, keeping well behind the shrubbery. He cut across the street and hurried behind the moviehouse.

There were about fifty cars parked in the lot. He headed toward an eight-year-old dark-brown Chevrolet sedan parked unobtrusively in the far right corner.

In an instant he had the door unlocked. He slipped into the seat, put the key in the ignition and turned it. The engine purred with quiet pep. With a slight smile and a last overall glance at the deserted surroundings, he started the car. He did not turn the lights on as he drove past the theater into the quiet street. Four minutes later the shabby brown sedan pulled into the circular driveway of the Peterson home on Driftwood Lane and parked behind a small red Vega.

 ## CHAPTER 7

The drive from Manhattan to Carley usually took less than an hour but the ominous weather forecast had sent commuters scurrying to their cars early. The traffic buildup combined with icy spots on the parkways made Sharon's trip to Steve's house last nearly an hour and twenty minutes. But she was almost unaware of the maddening delays. All the way up, she rehearsed what she would say to Steve, "It won't work for us. . . . We don't think alike. . . . Neil will never accept me . . . it will be easier if we don't see each other any more. . . ."

Steve's house, a white clapboard colonial with black shutters, vaguely depressed Sharon. The porchlight was too bright. The foundation shrubs were too high. Sharon knew that Steve and Nina had lived in this house only a few weeks before her death and that he hadn't done any of the renovating they'd planned when they bought it.

She parked just past the porch steps and unconsciously braced herself for Mrs. Lufts' rapid-fire greeting and Neil's coolness. But this would be the last time. That thought deepened her depression.

Mrs. Lufts had obviously been watching for her. The front door was yanked open as she got out of the car. "Miss Martin, my, it's nice to see you." Mrs. Lufts' stocky frame filled the doorway. Her small-featured face was squirrel-like with bright, inquisitive eyes. She was wearing a heavy red-plaid coat and galoshes.

"How are you, Mrs. Lufts?" Sharon stepped past her into the house. Mrs. Lufts had a habit of always standing close to the person she was with so that contact with her invariably had a smothering effect. Now she moved back barely enough to let Sharon squeeze past.

"It's awfully nice of you to come," Mrs. Lufts said. "Here, let me take your cape. I love capes. Make you look sweet and feminine, don't you think?"

Sharon set her pocketbook and overnight bag down in the foyer. She pulled off her gloves. "I guess so. I've never really thought about it . . ." She glanced into the living room. "Oh . . ."

Neil was sitting, cross-legged, on the carpet, magazines scattered around him, a pair of blunt scissors in his hand. His sandy hair, exactly the shade of Steve's, fell over his forehead, leaving his bent neck thin and vulnerable. His bony shoulders stuck out under a brown-and-white flannel shirt. His face looked thin and pale except for the red streaks around the enormous dark brown eyes that were welling with tears.

"Neil, say hello to Sharon," Mrs. Lufts commanded.

He looked up, listlessly. "Hello, Sharon." His voice was low and quivering.

He looked so little and scrawny and woebegone. Sharon ached to put her arms around him but knew that if she did, he'd only pull away from her.

Mrs. Lufts made a clicking sound with her tongue. "I'll be blessed if I know what the trouble is. Just started crying a few minutes ago. Won't tell me why. You never can figure what goes on in that little head. Well, maybe you or his dad can get it out of him." Her voice rose an octave, "Billlllll . . ."

Sharon jumped, her eardrums ringing. Hastily she went into the living room and stood in front of Neil. "What are you supposed to cut out?" she asked.

"Just some dumb pictures with animals." Neil did not look at her again. She knew he was embarrassed to be seen crying.

"Why don't I get myself a sherry and then give you a hand. Want a Coke or something?"

"No." Neil hesitated, then reluctantly added, "Thank you."

"Just help yourself," Mrs. Lufts said. "Make yourself at home. You know where everything is. I got everything on the list Mr. Peterson left, steak and salad makings and asparagus and ice cream. It's all in the refrigerator. I'm sorry to be rushing but we do want to have dinner before the movie. Bill . . ."

"I'm coming, Dora." There was annoyance in the voice. Bill Lufts came up the stairway from the basement. "Just wanted to check on the windows," he said, "make sure they're locked. Hello, Miss Martin."

"How are you, Mr. Lufts?" He was a short, thicknecked man in his mid-sixties with watery blue eyes. Tiny broken capillaries formed tell-tale patches on his cheeks and nostrils, reminding Sharon that Steve was worried about Bill Lufts' heavy drinking.

"Bill, get a move on, will you?" His wife's voice was edged with impatience. "You know how I hate to gulp my food, and we're running late now. The only time you take me out is our anniversary, seems to me, and I do think you could hurry . . ."

"All right. All right." Bill sighed heavily and nodded to Sharon. "See you later, Miss Martin."

"Have a good time." Sharon followed him into the foyer. "And, oh yes, happy anniversary."

"Wear a hat, Bill. You'll catch your death . . . What? Oh, thank you, thank you, Miss Martin. Soon as I sit down and get a rest and something to eat, I'll start feeling like an anniversary. Right now with all this rushing . . ."

"Dora, you're the one who wants to see this movie . . ."

"All right. I've got everything. Have a nice time, together, you two. Neil, show your report card to Sharon. He's a real bright boy, no trouble either, are you, Neil? I gave him a snack to hold him over till dinner but he hardly touched it. Don't eat enough to keep a bird alive. All right, Bill, all right!"

They were finally off. Sharon shivered as a chilly blast of air rushed into the foyer before she could close the door after them. She went back into the kitchen, opened the refrigerator and reached for the bottle of Bristol cream sherry. She hesitated, then took out a carton of milk. Neil might have said he didn't want anything but she was going to make him some hot cocoa.

While she waited for the milk to heat, she sipped the sherry and glanced around. Mrs. Lufts did her best but she wasn't a good housekeeper and the kitchen had a vaguely untidy look. There were crumbs spilling around the toaster on the counter. The top of the stove needed a good scrubbing. Really the whole house needed a facelifting.

Steve's property backed onto Long Island Sound. "I'd cut all those trees that block the view," Sharon thought, "and enclose the back porch and make it part of the living room with floor-to-ceiling windows, and knock out most of the walls and put in a breakfast bar . . ." Sharply she checked herself. It was none of her business. It was just that the house and Neil and even Steve had such a neglected look.

But it was not for her to change. The thought of not seeing Steve again, not expecting his call, not feeling those strong, gentle arms around her, not watching that suddenly carefree look light up his face when she said something that amused him, filled her with bleak loneliness. This is how it feels to know you have to give up someone, she thought. How does Mrs. Thompson feel, knowing that her only child will die day after tomorrow?

She knew Mrs. Thompson's number. She'd interviewed her after deciding to get involved in Ron's case. A number of times during this

last trip, she'd tried to phone Mrs. Thompson to share the news that so many important people had promised to contact Governor Greene and urge clemency. But she'd never caught her home. Probably because Mrs. Thompson had been working on a petition for clemency from the people in Fairfield County.

That poor woman. She'd been so hopeful when Sharon visited her, then seemed so upset when she realized that Sharon didn't think Ron was innocent.

But what mother could believe her son was capable of murder? Maybe Mrs. Thompson was home now. Maybe it would help just to talk with someone who had worked to save Ronald.

Sharon lowered the flame under the saucepan, went over to the wall-phone and dialed the number. The phone was answered on the first ring. Mrs. Thompson's voice was surprisingly steady. "Hello."

"Mrs. Thompson, this is Sharon Martin. I had to call to tell you how sorry I am, to ask if there's anything I can do . . ."

"You've done enough, Miss Martin." The bitterness in the woman's voice stunned Sharon. "If my boy dies Wednesday, I want you to know that I hold you responsible. I begged you to keep out of this."

"Mrs. Thompson . . . I don't know what you mean . . ."

"I mean, that in all your columns you have over and over again written that there was no question of Ronald's guilt but that wasn't the issue. It *is* the issue, Miss Martin!" The woman's voice became high-pitched. "It *is* the issue. There were many people who know my boy, who know that he's incapable of hurting anyone, who were working to get him clemency. But you . . . you've forced the Governor not to examine his case just on its own merits . . . We're still trying, and I don't believe God will do this to me, but if my son dies, I don't think I'll be responsible for what I might do to you."

The connection was broken. Bewildered, Sharon stared at the receiver in her hand. Could Mrs. Thompson really believe . . . ? Numbly she replaced the receiver on the hook.

The milk was almost boiling in the saucepan on the stove. Mechanically, she reached for the box of Quik in the cabinet and scooped a heaping teaspoon of it into a mug. She poured the milk in, stirred it, and put the pot in the sink to soak.

Stunned by the implication of Mrs. Thompson's attack, she started for the living room.

The bell rang.

Neil scrambled for the door before she could stop him. "Maybe it's my dad." He sounded relieved.

He doesn't want to be alone with me at all, Sharon thought. She heard him click the double lock and a sense of alarm jangled through her. "Neil, wait a minute," she called. "Ask who it is. Your dad would have his key."

Hastily she set down the cocoa mug and sherry glass on a table near the fireplace and ran into the hall.

Neil obeyed her. He had one hand on the knob but hesitated and called, "Who is it?"

"Is Bill Lufts there?" a voice called. "I have the generator he ordered for Mr. Peterson's boat."

"Oh, that's all right," Neil told Sharon. "Mr. Lufts is waiting for that."

He turned the handle of the door and was starting to pull it open when it was pushed in with violent force, slamming Neil back against the wall. Stunned, Sharon watched as a man stepped into the foyer and with a lightning-quick movement closed the door behind him. Gasping, Neil fell to the floor. Instinctively, Sharon ran over to him. She helped him to his feet, and keeping one arm around him, turned to face the intruder.

Two distinctively separate impressions burned into her consciousness. One was the glittering stare in the stranger's eyes. The other was the thin, long-barreled pistol he was pointing at her head.

CHAPTER 8

The meeting in the conference room of *Events* magazine lasted until 7:10 P.M. The main topic of conversation was the just-released Nielson report that had been highly favorable. Two out of three of the surveyed college graduates in the twenty-five to forty age bracket preferred *Events* to *Time* or *Newsweek*. Besides that, the paid circulation was up fifteen percent over the previous year and the new regional advertising was working well.

At the end of the meeting, Bradley Robertson, the publisher, stood up. "I think we can all take a great deal of pride in these statistics," he said. "We've been working hard for nearly three years but we've done it. It's not easy to launch a new magazine these days and I, for one, want to say, that in my mind, the creative direction of Steve Peterson has been the decisive factor in our success."

After the meeting, Steve went down in the elevator with the publisher. "Thanks, again, Brad," he said, "that was very generous of you."

The older man shrugged. "It was honest of me. We've made it, Steve. We'll all be able to start taking some decent money soon. It's about time, too. I know it hasn't been easy for you."

Steve smiled grimly, "No, it hasn't."

The elevator door opened in the main lobby.

"Goodnight, Brad. I'm going to run. I want to catch the seven-thirty . . ."

"Wait a minute. Steve, I saw you on the *Today* show this morning."

"Yes."

"I thought you were excellent, but so was Sharon. And, personally, I confess I go along with her thinking."

"A lot of people do."

"I like her, Steve. She's as bright as they come . . . damn good-looking too. And a real lady."

"I agree."

"Steve, I know how much you've been through the last couple of years. I don't want to butt in, but Sharon would be good for you . . . and for Neil. Don't let issues, no matter how compelling, come between you."

"I pray they don't," Steve answered quietly. "And at least now I'll be able to offer Sharon something more than a financially strapped guy with a ready-made family."

"She'd be darn lucky to get both you and Neil! Come on, my car's outside. I'll drop you off at Grand Central."

"Great. Sharon is up at my place and I don't want to miss the train."

Bradley's limousine was at the door. The driver quickly began to thread through the snarled midtown traffic. Steve leaned back and unconsciously sighed.

"You look tired, Steve. This Thompson execution has got to be getting to you."

Steve shrugged. "It is. Naturally it brings everything back. Every paper in Connecticut is rehashing the . . . Nina's death. I know that the kids have to be talking about it in school. I worry about how much Neil is hearing. I'm desperately sorry for Thompson's mother . . . and for him too."

"Why don't you take Neil and get away for a few days until this is over?"

Steve considered. "I might do that. It probably would be a good idea."

The limousine pulled up to the Vanderbilt Avenue entrance to Grand Central. Bradley Robertson shook his head. "You're too young to remember, Steve, but during the thirties, Grand Central was the hub of transportation in this country. There even used to be a radio series . . ." He closed his eyes. " 'Grand Central Station, crossroads of a million private lives,' that was the blurb for it."

Steve laughed. "And then along came the jet age." He opened the door. "Thanks for the lift."

Pulling out his commuter book, he walked quickly down into the terminal. He had five minutes till train time and decided to phone home to tell Sharon he was definitely making the 7:30 train.

He shrugged. Don't kid yourself, he thought. You just want to talk to her, to make sure she didn't change her mind about coming. He stepped into a phonebooth. He didn't have much change and made the call collect.

The phone rang once . . . twice . . . three times.

The operator came in. "I am ringing your number but there is no answer."

"There has to be someone there. Keep trying, operator, please."

"Certainly, sir."

The jabbing sound continued. After the fifth time, the operator came back on. "There is no answer, sir. Will you place your call later, please?"

"Operator, would you mind checking the number? Are you sure we're ringing 203-565-1313?"

"I'll dial it again, sir."

Steve stared at the receiver in his hand. Where could they be? If Sharon hadn't come up, would the Lufts have perhaps asked the Perrys if Neil could stay with them?

No. Sharon would have phoned him if she decided not to go to his house. Suppose Neil had had an asthma attack . . . suppose he'd had to be rushed to the hospital again?

An attack wouldn't be surprising if he'd heard any talk in school about the Thompson execution.

Neil had been having more frequent nightmares lately.

It was 7:29. The train was leaving in one minute. If he tried to phone the doctor or the hospital or the Perrys, he'd miss the train and have to wait forty-five minutes for the next one.

Perhaps there was trouble with the phone lines because of the storm. That didn't always show up at once.

Steve started to dial the Perrys, then changed his mind. He replaced the phone on the hook, then raced across the station in long, sprinting strides. Taking the stairs down to the platform two at a time, he barely reached the train as the doors were closing.

At that same instant, a man and woman passed in front of the phonebooth he had just abandoned. The woman was wearing a long, shabby gray coat. Her head was covered with a soiled, bluish kerchief. The man's arm was through hers. Under his other arm, he clutched a heavy khaki duffel bag.

S haron stared at the powerful hands that held the gun, at the eyes that slithered from side to side, into the living room, up the staircase, over her body.

"What do you want?" she whispered. Within the crook of her arm, she could feel the violent trembling of Neil's body. She tightened her grip, pressed him to her.

"You're Sharon Martin." It was a statement. The voice was a monotone, without inflection. Sharon felt a pulse pounding in her throat, closing it. She tried to swallow. "What do you want?" she asked again. The persistent soft whistle in Neil's breathing . . . suppose he was frightened into one of his asthma attacks? She would offer cooperation. "I have about ninety dollars in my purse . . ."

"Shut up!"

The evenly spoken words chilled her. The stranger dropped the bag he was carrying. It was a large khaki duffel bag, the kind military personnel used. He reached into his pocket and pulled out a ball of thick twine and a roll of wide bandages. He dropped them next to her. "Blindfold the boy and tie him up," he ordered.

"No! I won't."

"You'd better!"

Sharon looked down at Neil. He was staring at the man. His eyes were cloudy; the pupils enormous. She remembered that after his mother's death he'd been in deep shock.

"Neil, I . . ." How could she help him, reassure him?

"Sit down." The intruder's voice was a sharp order to Neil. The child looked up beseechingly at Sharon, then obediently sat on the bottom step of the staircase.

Sharon knelt beside him. "Neil, don't be afraid. I'm with you." Her hands fumbled as she reached for one of the bandages and wound it around his eyes, tying it at the back of his head.

She looked up. The intruder was staring at Neil. The gun was pointed at him. She heard a click. She pulled Neil against her, shielding him. "No . . . no . . . don't."

The intruder looked at her; slowly he lowered the gun letting it dangle from his hand. He would have killed Neil, she thought. He was ready to kill him . . .

"Tie up the boy, Sharon." There was an intimacy about the command.

With hands that fumbled at the ropes, she obeyed. She tied Neil's wrists together, trying to leave the bindings loose enough to allow for circulation. After she fastened his wrists, she pressed her hands on his.

The stranger reached past her, cut the end of the twine with a knife. "Hurry up . . . tie his feet!"

She heard the edginess in the tone. Quickly she obeyed. Neil's knees were trembling so, making his legs jerk apart. She wound the twine around his ankles and knotted it.

"Gag him!"

"He'll choke; he has asthma . . ." The protest died on her lips. The man's face was different somehow, whiter, strained. His high cheekbones were throbbing under stretched skin. He was near panic. Desperately, she bound Neil's mouth, leaving the gag as loose as she dared. If only Neil didn't struggle . . .

A hand shoved her away from the child. She toppled to the floor. The man was leaning over her. His knee dug into her back. He pulled her arms behind her. She felt the twine biting her wrists. She opened her mouth to protest, felt a wad of cloth stuffed into it. He yanked a strip of gauze over her mouth and cheeks, knotted it at the back of her head.

She couldn't breathe. Please . . . No . . . Hands slid over her thighs, lingered. Her legs were pulled together; twine cut through the soft leather boots.

She felt herself being lifted. Her head fell backward. What was he going to do to her?

The front door was opened. Cold, wet air stung her face. She weighed 120 pounds but the abductor was rushing down the slippery porch steps as though she were weightless. It was so dark. He must have turned off the outside lights. She felt her shoulders hit against something cold, metallic. A car. She tried to inhale deeply through her nostrils; to adjust her eyes to the darkness. She must clear her head; stop panicking, think.

The grating sound of a door being opened. Sharon felt herself falling. Her head glanced against an open ashtray. Her elbows and ankles took the force of the jolt as she hit the musty smelling floor. She was in the back of a car.

She heard crunching footsteps retreating. The man was going back into the house. Neil! What would he do to Neil? Frantically Sharon tried to wrench her hands free. Pain shot through her arms. The rough twine bit deeply into her wrists. She thought of the way the intruder had stared at Neil, had released the safety catch on the gun.

Minutes passed. Please, dear God, please . . . The sound of a door opening. Crunching footsteps coming toward the car. The front right door swung open. Her eyes were adjusted to the darkness. Through the shadows, she could see his outline. He was carrying something . . . the canvas bag. Oh, God, Neil was in that bag! She knew it.

He was leaning into the car, dropping the bag onto the seat, pushing it down on the floor. Sharon heard the dull thud. He'll hurt Neil. He'll hurt him. A door closed. Footsteps scurried around the car. The driver's

door opened, clicked shut. The shadows moved. She heard harsh breathing. He was leaning down, looking at her.

Sharon felt something fall on her, something that scratched her cheek . . . a blanket or a coat. She moved her head trying to free her face from the choking, acrid smell of stale perspiration.

The engine started. The car began to move.

Concentrate on directions. Remember every detail. Later the police would want to know. The car was turning left onto the street. It was cold, so cold. Sharon shivered and the tremulous movement tightened the knots, causing the cords to dig tighter into her legs and arms and wrists. Her limbs shrieked a protest. Stop moving! Calm. Be calm. Don't panic.

Snow. If it was still snowing, there might be tracks for a while. But no. There was too much sleet mixed in with the snow. She could hear it on the windows. Where were they going?

The gag. It was choking her. Breathe slowly through the nostrils. Neil. How could he breathe inside that sack? He would suffocate.

The car picked up speed. Where was he taking them?

CHAPTER 10

Roger Perry stared unseeingly out the window of his living room on Driftwood Lane. It was a rotten night and it was good to be home. He became aware of how much faster the snow was falling even in the fifteen minutes since he'd been in.

Funny, all day a sense of apprehension had been making him edgy. Glenda hadn't looked well these past couple of weeks. That was it. He always teased her that she was one of those lucky women who grew better looking with every birthday. Her hair, now pure silver, strikingly accentuated her cornflower-blue eyes and lovely complexion. She'd been a size 14 when the boys were growing up but ten years ago had slimmed down to a size 8. Just want to look good in my declining years, she'd joked. But this morning when he'd brought coffee to her in bed, he noticed how deadly pale she was, how thin her face looked. He'd phoned the doctor from the office and they'd agreed that it was the execution Wednesday that was weighing on her mind. Her testimony had helped convict the Thompson boy.

Roger shook his head. It was a dreadful business. Dreadful for that unfortunate boy, for everyone connected with it. Steve . . . little Neil . . . the Thompson boy's mother . . . Glenda. Glenda couldn't take this kind

of strain. She'd had a coronary right after she testified at the trial.
Roger pushed back the fear that another attack might kill her. Glenda
was only fifty-eight. Now that their boys were raised, he wanted these
years with her. He couldn't do without her.

He was glad that she'd finally agreed to hiring a daily housekeeper.
Mrs. Vogler was to start in the morning and work weekdays from nine
till one. That way Glenda could rest more without worrying about the
house.

He turned when he heard Glenda come into the room: She was carrying a small tray.

"I was just about to do that," he protested.

"Never mind, you look as though you can use this." She handed him
a bourbon old-fashioned and stood companionably beside him at the
window.

"I do need it. Thank you, dear." He noticed that she was sipping a
Coke. If Glenda didn't have a predinner cocktail with him, it meant
only one thing. "Chest pains today?" But it was not a question.

"Just a few . . ."

"How many nitros did you take?"

"Only a couple. Don't worry, I'm fine. Oh look! That's funny."

"What is?" Don't change the subject, Roger thought.

"Steve's house. The outside lights are off."

"That's why it just seemed so dark to me," Roger said. He paused.
"I'm positive Steve's lights were on when I came home."

"I wonder why anyone would turn them off." Glenda's voice was
troubled. "Dora Lufts is so nervous. Maybe you should take a walk
over . . ."

"Oh, I don't want to do that, dear. I'm sure there's a simple explanation."

She sighed. "I suppose. It's just that . . . well, what happened . . . has
been on my mind so much these days."

"I know it has." He put a comforting arm around her shoulders, felt
the tension in her body. "Now, let's sit down and relax . . ."

"Wait, Roger, look!" She leaned forward. "There's a car pulling out
of Steve's driveway. The headlights aren't on. I wonder who . . ."

"Now you just stop wondering and sit down." Roger's tone was firm.
"I'll get some cheese."

"The Brie is out on the table." Ignoring the gentle tug of his arm on
her elbow, Glenda reached into the pocket of her long quilted skirt and
pulled out her glasses. Slipping them on, she bent forward again and
stared at the dark, quiet outline of the house diagonally across the road.
But the car she'd noticed coming from the Peterson driveway had
already passed her window and was disappearing down the block into
the swirling snow.

"After all, tomorrow is another day." Crouched on the staircase, a lilt of hope in her voice, Scarlett O'Hara murmured the final words and the music rose to a crescendo as the picture on the screen dissolved into a long view of Tara.

Marian Vogler sighed as the music faded out and the lights in the theater went up. They don't make pictures like that any more, she thought. She absolutely didn't want to see the sequel to *Gone With the Wind*. It would just have to be a letdown.

She got to her feet reluctantly. Time to come to earth. Her pleasant, freckle-spattered face slipped back into worried lines as she walked up the carpeted, sloping floor to the back of the theater.

Every one of the kids needed new clothes. Oh well, at least Jim had agreed that she could take the housekeeping job.

He'd arranged to get a ride to the plant so she could use the car. She'd have the kids off to school and time to tidy up before driving to the Perrys'. Tomorrow would be her first day on the job. She was a little nervous about it. She hadn't worked in twelve years . . . since young Jim was born. But if there was one thing she knew, it was how to keep a house shining.

She emerged from the warmth of the theater into the biting cold of the raw March evening. Shivering, she turned right and began walking briskly. Tiny pellets of sleet mixed with snow bit at her face and she huddled into the worn fur collar of her coat.

The car was in the parking lot behind the theater. Thank God they'd decided to spend the money and have it fixed. It was eight years old but the body still looked all right, and as Jim said, better to spend the four hundred dollars to get it shipshape than use the same money to buy another man's troubles.

Marian had walked so fast she was ahead of most of the movie crowd. Expectantly, she hurried into the parking area. Jim had promised to have supper ready and she was hungry.

But it had done her good to get out. He'd sensed her depression and said, "Three bucks won't make or break us and I'll take care of the kids. Enjoy yourself, Babe, and forget the bills."

His words echoed in Marian's ears as she slowed and frowned. She was sure that she'd parked the car over here to the right. She remembered that she'd been able to see the ad in the bank window, the one about "we want to say *yes* to your loan." Big deal, she thought. *Yes* if you don't need it, *no* if your guts are hanging out for it.

She *had* parked the car over here. She *had*. She could see the bank window, lighted up now, the ad prominent even through the snow.

Ten minutes later, Marian called Jim from the police station. Choking back the angry, despairing tears that crowded her throat, she sobbed, "Jim . . . Jim . . . no . . . I'm all right . . . but Jim, some . . . some *bastard* stole our car."

 # CHAPTER 12

As he drove through the thickening snow, he reviewed his timetable. Just about now this car should be missed. The woman would probably walk around a bit to be sure she hadn't made a mistake about where she'd left it. Then she'd start screaming for the police or call home. By the time the dispatcher put out a radio bulletin to squad cars, he'd be far away from the nosy Connecticut cops.

Not that anybody would look very hard for this heap. The cops would just roll their eyes when they heard an APB for a stolen car worth a couple of hundred bucks.

To have Sharon Martin in his possession! Excitement made his skin glisten. He remembered the rush of warmth he felt when he tied her up. Her body was so slender but her thighs and hips were curved and soft. He could feel that even through her heavy wool skirt. She had acted hostile and scared when he carried her to the car, but he was sure that she deliberately nuzzled her head against his side.

He had taken the Connecticut Turnpike to the Hutchinson River Parkway south to the Cross County to the Henry Hudson Parkway. He felt safe on the heavily traveled roads. But by the time he was approaching the West Side Highway into downtown Manhattan, he was behind schedule. Suppose, just suppose they *were* already watching for this car!

The other drivers were crawling along. Fools. Afraid of slippery roads, afraid to take a chance, delaying him, making problems. The pulse in his cheekbone started to throb. He felt the quickening, pressed one finger on it. He'd expected to go through the terminal by seven at the latest before the commuter rush was over. They'd be less noticeable then.

It was ten past seven when he exited from the West Side Highway at Forty-sixth Street. He drove a half block east, then made a quick right turn into a driveway that wound behind a warehouse. There were no guards here . . . and he only needed a minute.

Stopping the car, he turned off the lights. Fine, powdery snow stung his eyes and face when he opened the door. Cold. It was so damn cold.

With intense concentration, his eyes darted around the darkened parking area. Satisfied, he reached into the back of the car and lifted the coat he'd thrown over Sharon. He felt her eyes blazing up at him. Laughing softly, he pulled out a tiny camera and snapped her picture. The sudden flash made her blink. Now he extracted a pencil-thin flashlight from his inside pocket. He waited until his hand was deep in the car to flip it on.

Deliberately he shone the narrow beam of light in Sharon's eyes, moving it back and forth slowly, an inch from her face, until she squeezed her eyes shut and tried to turn her head.

It felt good to tease her. With a short, soundless laugh, he grabbed her shoulders and forced her to lie on her stomach. Quick strokes of the knife sliced the cords on her ankles and wrists. A faint sigh, muffled by the gag, a shuddering movement of her body . . .

"Feels pretty good, don't it, Sharon?" he whispered. "Now I'm going to take that gag off. If one scream comes out of you, the boy dies. Understand?"

He did not wait for the affirmative nod before he cut the knotted cloth at the back of her head. Sharon spat out the wad of gauze in her mouth. Desperately she tried not to moan. "Neil . . . please . . ." Her whisper was almost inaudible. "He'll suffocate . . ."

"That's up to you." The stranger pulled her up, stood her on her feet next to the car. Vaguely, Sharon felt the snow on her face. She was so dizzy. The muscles in her arms and legs were frantic with cramps. She staggered, was roughly grabbed.

"Put this on." The voice was different now . . . urgent.

She reached out, felt greasy, rough material . . . the coat that he'd thrown over her. She raised her arm. The man pulled the coat around her. Her other arm was thrust into it.

"Put this scarf on."

It felt so dirty. She tried to fold it. It was so big, woolly. Somehow her fingers managed to knot it under her chin.

"Get back in the car. The faster we move, the faster the boy has that gag off." Roughly, he pushed her into the front seat. The khaki bag was on the floor. She stumbled, trying to keep her boots from hitting it. Leaning down, she ran her hands over the bag, felt the outline of Neil's head. She realized that the drawstring wasn't tied. At least Neil was getting air—"Neil, Neil, I'm here. We'll be all right, Neil . . ."

Did she feel him moving? Oh God, don't let him strangle.

The stranger darted around the car, was in the driver's seat, turned the key in the engine. The car moved cautiously forward.

We're in midtown! The realization shocked Sharon, helped her to focus. She had to be calm. She had to do whatever this man ordered. The car approached Broadway. She saw the Times Square billboard clock: 7:20 . . . it was only 7:20.

At this time last night, she'd just gotten home from Washington. She'd showered and put chops on and sipped Chablis while they broiled. She'd been tired and uptight and trying to unwind before writing her column.

And she'd thought about Steve, how missing him had become a steady ache over the three weeks they'd been apart.

He'd phoned. The sound of his voice brought a peculiar combination of pleasure and anxiety. But he'd kept the conversation brief, almost impersonal. "Hi . . . just wanted to be sure you got in all right. Understand Washington has lousy weather and it's heading our way. I'll see you at the studio." Then he'd paused and added, "I've missed you. Don't forget you're staying with us tomorrow night."

She'd hung up, her need to see him intensified by talking with him and yet she'd somehow felt letdown and worried. What did she want, anyhow? What would he think when he got home and found them missing? Oh, Steve!

They stopped for a red light on Sixth Avenue. A patrol car drew up beside them. Sharon watched as the young driver pushed his peaked uniform hat back on his forehead. He glanced out the window and their eyes locked. Sharon felt the car begin to move. She kept her eyes directly on the policeman, willing him to keep looking at her, to sense something wrong.

She felt a sharp prodding against her side and looked down. The stranger had the knife in his hand. "If we get followed now, you get it first," he said. "I'll still have plenty of time for the boy."

There was icy matter-of-factness in his tone. The patrol car was directly behind them. Its dome light began flashing. Its siren began blasting. "No! Please . . ." In a burst of speed the police car sped around them and disappeared down the block.

They were turning south on Fifth Avenue. Pedestrian traffic was almost non-existent. It was too stormy, too icy to walk around New York.

The car made a quick left onto Forty-fourth Street. Where was he taking them? Forty-fourth wasn't a through street. It was blocked by Grand Central Station. Didn't he know that?

The stranger drove the two blocks to Vanderbilt Avenue and turned right. He parked near the entrance to the Biltmore Hotel, directly opposite the terminal.

"We're getting out," he said, his voice low. "We're going into the terminal. Walk next to me. Don't try anything. I'll be carrying the bag and

if anybody pays any attention to us, the boy gets the knife." He looked down at Sharon. His eyes were glittering again. A pulse throbbed in his cheek. "Understand?"

She nodded. Could Neil hear him?

"Wait a minute." He was staring at her. Reaching past her into the glove compartment, he pulled out dark glasses. "Put these on."

He pushed the door open, looked around, and stepped out quickly. The street was deserted. Only a few cabs were lined up in the enclosed driveway at the terminal. There was no one to see them or care . . .

He's taking us on a train, Sharon thought. We'll be miles away before anyone even begins to look for us!

She became aware of a stinging in her left hand. The ring! The antique moonstone ring Steve had given her for Christmas . . . it had turned sideways when her hands were tied. The raised gold setting had been cutting her. Almost without thinking, Sharon slipped the ring off. She just had time to force it partly down into the seat cushion before the car door opened.

Unsteadily, she got out and onto the slippery sidewalk. The man gripped her wrist with his hand and looked carefully around inside the car. He quickly leaned down and picked up the gag that had been on her mouth, the cords he had cut when releasing her. Sharon held her breath. But he didn't notice the ring.

He bent down and picked up the duffel bag, pulled the drawstring tight and knotted the ends. Neil could suffocate with that bag closed.

"Look." She stared at the blade in his hand that was nearly concealed by his loose overcoat sleeve. "This is pointed right at the kid's heart. You try anything and he gets it."

"Come on!" His other hand was at her elbow. He was forcing her to walk in step with him across the street. They were a man and woman hurrying out of the cold into the terminal, nondescript in every way, anonymous in their cheap clothes with duffel bag instead of suitcase.

Even behind the dark glasses, the brightly lit terminal made Sharon blink. They stood on the concourse overlooking the main terminal. There was a newsstand a few feet to their left. The vendor looked at them indifferently. They started down the steps to the first landing. The huge Kodak display caught Sharon's eye. It read, "Capture beauty where you find it . . ."

An hysterical laugh threatened to escape her lips. *Capture? Capture?* The clock. The famous clock over the center of the Information Booth in the middle of the terminal. It was harder to see now that the investment office counter had been built in front of it. Sharon had read somewhere that when the six red lights around the clock's base were flashing, it signaled an emergency to Grand Central's private police force. What would they think if they knew what was happening now?

It was 7:29. Steve. *Steve was catching the 7:30.* He was here right now . . . in a train in this terminal, a train that in a minute would be taking him away. Steve, she wanted to shriek . . . Steve . . .

Steely fingers bit into her arm. "Down here." He was forcing her to go down the stairs to the lower terminal. The rush hour was over. There weren't many people in the main terminal . . . there were even fewer going down the stairs. Should she try to fall . . . draw attention to them? No . . . she couldn't take the chance, not with that burly arm encircling the duffel bag, that knife ready to plunge into Neil . . .

They were on the lower level. Over to the right she could see the entrance to the Oyster Bar. She and Steve had met there for a quick lunch last month. They'd sat at the counter and had steaming bowls of oyster stew . . . Steve, find us, help us . . .

She was being pushed toward the left. "We're going down there . . . not so fast . . ." Track 112. The sign said "Mount Vernon—8:10." A train must have just left. Why would he go there?

To the left of the ramp leading down to the tracks Sharon saw a shabby old woman carrying a shopping bag. She was bundled in a man's jacket over a ragged woolen skirt. Thick cotton stockings drooped on her legs. The woman was staring at her. Did she realize something was wrong?

"Keep moving . . ."

They were going down the ramp on the 112 platform. Their footsteps echoed, a pinging sound on metal steps. The murmur of voices receded, the warmth of the terminal was vanquished by a clammy, cold draft.

The platform was deserted.

"Around here." He was forcing her to move faster now, around the end of the platform where the track terminated, down another ramp. Water was trickling nearby. Where were they going? The dark glasses made it hard to see here. A rhythmic, throbbing sound . . . a pump . . . a pneumatic pump . . . they were going down into the depths of the terminal . . . far underground. What was he going to do to them? She could hear the rumbling sounds of trains . . . there must be a tunnel nearby . . .

The concrete floor was still sloping down. The passage widened. They were in an area half the size of a football field; an area of thick pipes and shafts and rumbling motors. To the left, about twenty feet, there was a narrow staircase.

"Over there . . . hurry up!" Now his breath was coming in harsh gasps. She could hear him puffing as he followed her. She scrambled up the staircase, unconsciously counting the steps . . . ten . . . eleven . . . twelve. She was on a narrow landing, facing a thick metal door.

"Move over." She felt the heaviness of his body against her and shrank away. He set down the duffel bag, glanced at her quickly. In the dim light she saw shiny beads of perspiration glistening on his forehead.

He pulled out a key, put it in the lock. A grating sound and the handle turned. He pushed the door open, thrust her in before him. She heard him grunt as he picked up the duffel bag again. The door closed behind them. Through the clammy darkness she heard the snap of a switch.

A half-second delay and the dusty overhead fluorescent lights blinked on.

Sharon looked around at the filthy, damp room, at rusty sinks, a boarded-up shaft, a sagging cot, an overturned crate, an old black suitcase on the floor.

"Where are we? What do you want with us?" Her voice was a near-whisper but took on an echo sound in this dungeon-like room.

Her abductor didn't answer. Pushing her forward, he hurried toward the cot. He laid the duffel bag on it, then flexed his arms. Dropping to her knees, Sharon fumbled with the drawstring on the bag.

At last she had it untied, was pulling it apart, pulling the bag down, reaching for the small, crumbled figure. She freed Neil's head. Frantically, she tugged at the gag, pulling it down over his chin.

Neil gasped, clawing for air, his breath harsh and sobbing. She heard the wheeze in his breath, felt the jerking of his chest. Supporting his head with her arm, she began to tug at the blindfold.

"Let that alone!" The order was sharp, violent.

"Please," she cried, "he's sick . . . he's having an asthma attack. Help him."

She looked up, then bit her lips to force back a scream.

Over the army cot, three enormous pictures were taped to the wall.

A young woman running, hands outstretched, looking back over her shoulder, terror stamped on her face . . . her mouth a twisted, screaming arc.

A blond woman lying by a car, her legs jackknifed under her.

A dark-haired teenager with one hand raised to her throat, a look of puzzled detachment settling into her staring eyes.

⌇⌇⌇ CHAPTER 13

Long ago Lally had been a schoolteacher in Nebraska. Finally retired, alone, she had come to New York for a visit. She never went back home.

The night she'd arrived in Grand Central Station was the turning point. Bewildered and awed, she'd carried her one suitcase across the enormous Concourse, looked up, and stopped. She was one of the few to realize immediately that the sky on the great vaulted ceiling had been painted on backward. The eastern stars were in the west.

She'd laughed aloud. Her lips parted, revealing two enormous front teeth. People glanced her way, then hurried along. Their reaction had delighted her. At home if Lally were seen looking up and laughing by herself, it would be all over town the next day.

She checked her suitcase in a locker, and washed up in the main-floor ladies' room, smoothing her shapeless brown wool skirt, buttoning the thick cardigan sweater. Finally she combed the short gray hair, plastering it damply around her broad, chinless face.

For the next six hours Lally had toured the terminal, taking a childish delight in the bustling, rushing crowds. She ate at a counter in one of the small, cheap lunchstands, windowshopped in the corridors leading to the hotels, and finally returned to settle down in the main waiting room.

Fascinated, she watched a young mother breastfeed a screaming baby, stared at a young couple passionately embracing, followed the progress of a card game four men were playing.

The crowds thinned, swelled, thinned out again under the signs of the zodiac. It was nearly midnight when she noticed that one group had stayed a long time, six men and a tiny, birdlike woman who were clustered together, talking with the easy camaraderie of old friends.

The woman seemed to notice her watching them and came over to her. "You new here?" Her voice was raspy but kind. Earlier Lally had seen this woman take a newspaper from a disposal bin.

"Yes," she said.

"Got any place to go?"

Lally had a reservation at the Y but some instinct made her lie. "No."

"Just arrived here?"

"Yes."

"Got any money?"

"Not much." Another lie.

"Well, don't worry. We'll show you around. We're the regulars." Her arm jerked backward toward the group.

"You live near here then?" Lally asked.

A smile quirked the woman's eyes, revealed decaying teeth. "No, we live *here*. I'm Rosie Bidwell."

In all her cheerless sixty-two years, Lally had never had a close friend. Rosie Bidwell changed that. Soon Lally was accepted as one of the regulars. She got rid of the suitcase and like Rosie, kept all her possessions in shopping bags. She learned the routine . . . dawdling over cheap meals in the Automat, occasional showers in the public bath house in the Village, sleeping in flop houses, dollar a night hotels, or at the Salvation Army center.

Or . . . in her own room in Grand Central.

That was the one secret Lally kept from Rosie. A tireless explorer, she'd become familiar with every inch of her terminal. She climbed the stairs behind the orange doors on the platforms and wandered around the gloomy cavernous area between the floor of the upper level and the ceiling of the lower level. She found the hidden staircase that connected the two ladies' rooms and when the downstairs one was closed for repairs, she often slipped down that staircase and spent the night there with no one the wiser.

She even walked along the tracks of the tunnel that yawned under Park Avenue, flattening herself against the concrete wall when a train thundered by and sharing scraps of food with the hungry cats that prowled the tunnel.

But she was especially fascinated by the area right in the depths of the station that the guards called Sing-Sing. With its pumps and vents and airshafts and generators throbbing and creaking and groaning it was like being part of the very heartbeat of her station. The unmarked door at the head of a narrow staircase in Sing-Sing intrigued her. Cautiously, she'd mentioned it to one of the security guards who became a good friend. Rusty said that was only the miserable hole where they used to wash dishes for the Oyster Bar and she had no business in that area. But she'd worn him down until he took her to see the room.

She'd been delighted with it. The musty, peeling walls and ceilings didn't bother her at all. The room was large. The lights and sinks worked. There was even the tiny cubbyhole with the toilet. She'd known immediately that this place would fill her one remaining need, for occasional absolute privacy.

"Room and bath," she said. "Rusty, let me sleep here."

He'd looked shocked. "No way! It'd cost me my job." But she'd worn him down on that, too, and every once in a while he'd let her spend a night there. Then one day she managed to borrow his key for a few hours and secretly had another one made from it. When Rusty retired she made the room her own.

Little by little, Lally carried objects up the steps, a dilapidated canvas army cot, a lumpy mattress, an orange crate.

She began to stay there regularly. That was what she liked best of all, to sleep in the womblike darkness, tucked in the very depth of her station, to hear the faint roar and rumble of trains that became less and less frequent as the night grew late, then accelerated again into the morning frenzy.

Sometimes lying there, she thought about teaching *Phantom of the Opera* to her classes. "And under that beautiful, gilded opera house, there was another world," she'd told them, "a world dark and mysterious, a world of alleys and sewers and dampness where a man could hide away from everyone."

The only cloud on her horizon was the awful, gnawing fear that someday they'd tear her station down. When the Committee to Save Grand Central held the rally, she'd been there, unobtrusively in a corner, but applauding loudly when all the celebrities like Jackie Onassis said that Grand Central Terminal was a part of the tradition of New York and should never be destroyed.

But even though they had managed to get it designated as an historical landmark, Lally knew there were still plenty of people trying to get it pulled down. No, God, please, not my station!

She never used her room during the winter. It was too cold and damp. But from May till September she stayed there about twice a week, just infrequently enough so the cops didn't catch her, so Rosie didn't get curious.

Six years passed, the best six years of Lally's life. She came to know all the guards, the paper vendors, the countermen. She recognized the faces of commuters, knew which ones took which trains, at what time. She even grew to know the faces of the drinkers who usually caught the late trains home, hurrying unsteadily to their platforms.

That Monday evening, Lally was meeting Rosie in the main waiting room. She'd had severe arthritis over the winter. That was the only thing that had kept her from going to her room. But it had been six months now and suddenly she felt she couldn't wait any longer to use it again. "I'll just go down and see how it looks," she thought. Maybe if it wasn't too cold, she'd even sleep there tonight. But probably not.

She walked heavily down the stairs to the lower terminal. There weren't many people there. Carefully, she moseyed around, watching for the policemen. She couldn't take a chance of being spotted going to the room. They'd never let her stay there, not even the nice guys.

She noticed a family with three young children. Nice-looking, all of them. She liked children and she'd been a good teacher, too. After the class finished making fun of her homeliness, she usually got along well with her pupils. Not that she'd want those days back, not for anything.

She was about to drift down the ramp to track 112 when her attention was caught by a tattered, scarlet lining drooping below an old gray coat.

Lally recognized the coat. She'd tried it on in a Second Avenue thrift shop the week before. There couldn't be two like that, not with that lining. Her curiosity piqued, she studied the face of the woman wearing the coat and was surprised to see how young and pretty she was behind the scarf and dark glasses.

The man she was with . . . he was someone Lally had seen around the station lately. Lally noticed the expensive leather boots the girl was wearing; the kind the people wore who traveled the Connecticut line.

Funny combination, she thought. A thrift coat and those boots. Now fully interested, she watched the couple cross the terminal. The bag the man was carrying seemed pretty heavy. She frowned when she saw them go down to track 112. There wouldn't be a train for another forty minutes. Crazy, she thought. Why wait on the platform? It's cold and damp.

She shrugged. That settled that. She couldn't go to her room with them on the platform to see her. She'd have to wait until tomorrow.

Philosophically dismissing her disappointment, Lally headed for the main waiting room in search of Rosie.

～～～ CHAPTER 14

"Talk, Ron, talk, damn you!" The dark-haired attorney depressed the "record" button. The cassette player was on the bunk between the two seated young men.

"No!" Ron Thompson got up, walked restlessly across the narrow cell and stared out through the barred window. Quickly he turned away. "Even snow looks dirty here," he said, "dirty and gray and cold. Do you want to record that?"

"No, I don't." Bob Kurner stood up and put his arms on the boy's shoulders. "Ron, please . . ."

"What good? What good?" The nineteen-year-old's lip quivered. His expression changed, became young and defenseless. Quickly he bit his lip, brushed a hand across his eyes. "Bob, you did your best . . . I know you did. But there's nothing anyone can do now."

"Nothing except give the Governor a reason why she should grant executive clemency . . . even a stay . . . even a stay, Ron."

"But you've tried . . . that writer Sharon Martin . . . if she couldn't with all the important signatures she got . . ."

"Damn that stinking Sharon Martin to hell!" Bob Kurner clenched his hands into fists. "Damn all these do-gooders who don't know their way out of a paper bag. She loused you up, Ron. We had a petition going, a *real* one from people who know you, people who know you're incapable of hurting anyone, and she goes screaming all over the country that of course you're guilty but you shouldn't die. She made it impossible for the Governor to commute your sentence—*impossible.*"

"Then why waste your time? If it's no use, if it's hopeless, I don't want to talk about it anymore!"

"You've got to!" Bob Kurner's voice softened as he looked into the younger man's eyes. There was a compelling directness and honesty in them. Bob thought of himself at nineteen. Ten years ago he'd been a sophomore at Villanova. Ron had been planning to go to college . . . instead he was going to die in the electric chair. Even the two years in prison hadn't made his muscular body flabby. Ron exercised regularly in his cell, he was such a disciplined kid. But he'd lost twenty pounds and his face was chalk white.

"Look," Bob said, "there's got to be something somewhere that I missed . . ."

"You didn't miss anything."

"Ron, I defended you but you *didn't* kill Nina Peterson and you *were* convicted. If we can just find one piece of evidence to take to the Governor . . . one valid reason to make it possible for her to grant you a stay. We've got forty-two hours . . . only forty-two hours."

"You just said she won't commute any sentence."

Bob Kurner bent down and snapped off the cassette player. "Ron, maybe I shouldn't tell you this. God knows it's a long shot. But listen to me. When you were convicted of Nina Peterson's murder, a lot of people felt that you were guilty of committing those two other unsolved murders. You know that."

"They asked me enough about them . . ."

"You went to school with the Carfolli girl. You'd shoveled snow for Mrs. Weiss. It made sense to ask. That's just normal procedure. Then after you were arrested there weren't any more murders—*till now.* Ron, there have been two more murders of young women in Fairfield County in the last month. If we can just introduce something, some doubt, come up with something that might suggest a link between Nina Peterson's death and the others."

He put his arms around the boy. "Ron, I know how lousy this is for you. I can only guess what you're going through. But you've told me how often you go over that day in your mind. Maybe there's something . . . something that didn't seem important, some detail. If you'd just *talk.*"

Ron pulled himself away, walked over to the bunk and sat down. He depressed the "record" button on the cassette player and turned his head so that his voice would be picked up clearly. Frowning in concentration, his voice halting, he began to speak.

"I was working that afternoon after school in Timberly's Market. Mrs. Peterson was in shopping. Mr. Timberly had just told me that he was going to fire me because of the time I needed off for baseball practice. She heard him. When I helped her to the car with the groceries, she said . . ."

~~~~ *CHAPTER 15*

T
he train pulled into the Carley station at nine o'clock. By then Steve's frantic impatience had settled into deep, gnawing worry. He should have phoned the doctor. If Neil were sick Sharon might have taken him for an injection. Maybe that was why there was no answer.

Sharon had come. He was sure of that. She simply wouldn't have changed her mind without calling him.

Maybe it was just that the phones were going fluky. And if he'd missed this train, God knows when the next one would get in. The conductor said something about the tracks freezing.

Something was wrong. He felt it. He knew it.

But maybe it was the execution coming up that had him so rattled, so apprehensive. God, the paper tonight had rehashed the whole mess. Nina's picture on the front page. The caption "Youth to die for brutal murder of young Connecticut mother."

Thompson's picture next to hers. A nice-looking kid. Hard to believe he'd been capable of cold-blooded murder.

Nina's picture. Over and over on the long train ride, Steve found himself staring down at it. The reporters had all clamored for a photograph at the time of the murder, but he cursed himself for letting them make copies of this one. It had been his favorite; a snapshot he'd taken of her with the breeze blowing the dark curls around her face, and the small straight nose wrinkled a little the way it always had when she laughed. And the scarf tied loosely around her neck. It was only afterward that he'd realized that was the scarf Thompson had used to strangle her.

Oh Christ!

Steve was the first one waiting to rush out when the train finally arrived at Carley forty minutes late. Racing down the slippery platform stairs, he hurried into the parking lot and attempted to brush the snow from the windshield of his car. A thin, ice-crusted layer resisted his efforts. Impatiently, he opened the trunk and reached for the de-icer and scraper.

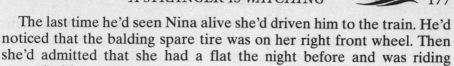

The last time he'd seen Nina alive she'd driven him to the train. He'd noticed that the balding spare tire was on her right front wheel. Then she'd admitted that she had a flat the night before and was riding around without a spare.

He'd been ticked off and exploded at her. "You shouldn't be riding on that lousy tire. Damn it, honey, your carelessness will get you killed." *Will get you killed!*

She'd promised to pick up the other tire right away. At the station, he'd started to get out of the car without kissing her goodbye. But she'd leaned over and her kiss had brushed his cheek, and with that familiar ripple of laughter in her voice, she'd said, "Have a good day, Grouchy. I love you."

He hadn't answered her, or looked back at her, just run for his train. He'd debated about calling her from the office but told himself that he wanted her to think he was really upset with her. He worried about her. She was careless in ways that mattered. A couple of nights, when he'd worked late, he'd come home to find her and Neil asleep and the door unlocked.

And so he hadn't called, hadn't made up with her. And when he got off the 5:30 train that night, Roger Perry was waiting for him at the station, waiting to ride home with him and tell him that Nina was dead.

And then nearly two years of bleak pain until that morning six months ago when he'd been introduced to the other guest on the *Today* show, Sharon Martin.

The windshield was clear enough. Steve got in the car, turned the key, and barely giving the engine time to catch, put his foot on the gas. He wanted to get home and find Neil all right. He wanted to make Neil happy again. He wanted to put his arms around Sharon and hold her. Tonight he wanted to hear her moving around in the guest room, know that she was near. They'd have to work it out. Nothing could be allowed to spoil it between them.

The five-minute drive took fifteen minutes. The roads were a sheet of ice. At one "stop" sign he put his foot on the brake and the car just slid onto the intersection. Thank God there was no one coming.

At last he turned onto Driftwood Lane. It seemed uncommonly dark to him. It was *his* place—the lights were off! A shock of fear tensed his body. Ignoring the slippery road, he floored the accelerator and the car shot forward, careened down the block. He turned into his driveway and jammed to a halt behind Sharon's car. Racing up the stairs, he thrust his key in the lock and pushed the front door open. "Sharon . . . Neil," he called. "Sharon . . . Neil . . ."

Chilling silence offset the warmth of the foyer, made his hands clammy. "Sharon . . . Neil," he called again.

He looked into the living room. Papers were scattered on the floor. Neil must have been doing cutouts; there were scissors and scraps on one open page. An untouched cup of cocoa and a glass of sherry were on the small end table near the fireplace. Hurrying over, Steve felt the cup. The cocoa was cold. He rushed into the kitchen, noticed the saucepan in the sink, then ran down the hall to the den. The sense of danger was overwhelming, stifling. The den was empty too. A fire was flickering in the hearth. He'd asked Bill to make one before he left.

Not knowing what he was looking for, Steve raced from the den back to the foyer and noticed Sharon's overnight bag and purse. He opened the door of the guest closet. Her cape was there! What would make her rush out without it? Neil! Neil must have had one of those violent attacks, the kind that come on so suddenly, that almost suffocated him.

Steve raced to the phone on the kitchen wall. The emergency numbers—hospital, police, fire, their own doctor—were clearly listed. He called the doctor's office first. The nurse was still there. "No, Mr. Peterson, we didn't get a call about Neil. Is there anything . . ."

He hung up without explaining.

He called the emergency room at the hospital. "We have no record . . ."

Where were they? What happened to them? His breath was coming in hard gasps. He looked at the wall clock. Nine-twenty. Nearly two hours since he'd tried to phone home. They'd been gone at least that long. The Perrys! Maybe they'd gone across the street to the Perrys. Sharon might have rushed over there with Neil if he started to get sick.

Steve reached for the phone again. Please God, please let them be at the Perrys'. Let them be all right.

And then he saw it. The message on the memo board. Printed in chalk. Thick, uneven lettering.

"If you want your kid and girlfriend alive, wait for instructions." The next three words were heavily underlined. *"Don't call police."* The message was signed "Foxy."

━━━ *CHAPTER 16*

In the midtown Manhattan office of the FBI, Hugh Taylor sighed as he closed the top drawer of his desk. God, it would be good to get home, he thought. Nearly 9:30, so traffic should be okay. But the storm would botch up the West Side Highway and the bridge was probably a mess by now.

He stood up and stretched. His shoulders and neck were tense and stiff. Pushing fifty and feel like I'm eighty, he thought. It had been a rotten day. Another attempted bank robbery, this time the Chase Bank at Forty-eighth and Madison. A teller had managed to sound the alarm and they'd rounded up the perpetrators, but not until the guard had been shot. Poor guy was in critical condition and probably wouldn't make it.

Hugh's face hardened. Criminals who could do that should be locked up for good.

But not executed. Hugh reached for his coat. That was one of the reasons he'd been so depressed today. That Thompson kid. He couldn't get him out of his mind: the Peterson case two years ago. Hugh had been in charge of the investigation. With his squad, he'd traced Thompson to the motel in Virginia where they'd nabbed him.

The kid had so persistently denied he'd murdered Nina Peterson. Even when he knew the only chance to save his skin was by throwing himself at the mercy of the court, he'd still denied the murder.

Hugh shrugged. It was out of his hands. That was for sure. And day after tomorrow Ronald Thompson would be electrocuted.

Hugh walked down the hall, pushed the button for the elevator.

Bone-tired. He really was bone-tired.

Half a minute later a car stopped at his floor. The door slid open. He stepped in, pushed the "M" button.

He heard his name being shouted. Automatically he reached out and held the door, keeping it from closing. Running feet raced to the elevator. His arm was grabbed by Hank Lamont, one of the younger agents.

"Hugh," he was out of breath. "Steve Peterson is on the phone . . . you know . . . Nina Peterson's husband . . . the Thompson kid . . ."

"I know who he is," Hugh snapped. "What does he want?"

"It's his son, he says his son and that writer, Sharon Martin, have been kidnapped."

 CHAPTER 17

"Who took those pictures?" Sharon heard the shrill fear in her voice, knew it was a mistake. She met his eye and saw that her tone had startled him. His lips narrowed, the pulse in his cheek quickened. Intuitively she said, "I mean, they're so realistic."

Something of the rigidity eased. "Maybe I found them."

She remembered the flash that had blinded her in the car.

"Or maybe you took them." There was a hint of a compliment.

"Maybe."

She felt his hand touch her hair, linger on her cheek. Don't act afraid, she thought frantically. She was still supporting Neil's head against her arm. He began to tremble. Sobs broke under the harsh asthmatic wheezing.

"Neil, don't cry," she implored. "You'll choke yourself." She looked up at their captor. "He's so frightened. Cut him loose."

"Will you like me if I do?" His leg was pressing against her side as she knelt by the cot.

"Of course I'll like you, but *please.*" Her fingers smoothed damp, sandy ringlets from the small forehead.

"Don't touch that blindfold!" His hand, steely on hers, pulling it away from Neil's face.

"I won't." Her voice was placating.

"All right. For a little while. But just his hands. First, you lay down." She stiffened. "Why?"

"I can't let both of you be untied. Let go of the boy."

There was nothing to do except obey. This time he tied her legs together from knees to ankles, then pulled her to a sitting position on the cot. "I won't tie your hands until I'm ready to go, Sharon." It was a concession. His voice lingered over her name.

Ready to go? Was he going to leave them here alone? He was bending over Neil, cutting the cords on his wrists. Neil pulled his hands apart. They flailed the air. His gasps were staccato-paced; the wheeze a constant, rising pitch.

Sharon pulled him on her lap. She was still wearing the gray coat. She wrapped him inside it with her. The shaking body struggled, trying to pull away.

"Neil, stop that! Calm down!" Her voice was firm. "Remember what your dad told you to do when you get asthma. Be very still and breathe very slowly." She looked up. "Please, will you get him a drink of water?"

In the uneven, dusty lighting, his shadow, dark and blotchy against the concrete wall, seemed fragmented by the peeling paint. He nodded and went over to the rusty sink. The dripping faucet sputtered in an uneven gurgling. While his back was turned, Sharon looked up at the posters. Two of those women were dead or dying; the other was trying to run from something or someone. Had he done that to them? What kind of madman was he? Why had he kidnapped her and Neil? It had taken daring to walk through the terminal with them. This man has planned this carefully. Why?

Neil's breath caught, choked. He began to cough a harsh, racking sound.

The abductor turned from the sink, a paper cup in his hand. The choking sound seemed to agitate him. When he handed Sharon the cup, his hand trembled. "Make him stop that," he said.

Sharon held the cup to Neil's lips. "Neil, sip this." He gulped the water. "No, slowly, Neil. Now lean back." The boy finished the water, sighed. She felt a faint relaxing of the slight body. "That's it."

The captor was leaning over her. "You're a very kind person, Sharon," he said. "That's why I fell in love with you. Because you're not frightened of me, are you?"

"No, of course not. I know you don't want to hurt us." Her tone was easy, conversational. "But why did you bring us here?"

Without answering, he walked over to the black suitcase, lifted it carefully and set it on the ground a few feet from the door. Crouching over the bag, he opened it.

"What is in there?" Sharon asked.

"Just something I have to make before I go."

"Where are you going to go?"

"Don't ask me so many questions, Sharon."

"I was just interested in your plans." She watched as his fingers moved among the contents of the suitcase. The fingers had a life of their own now, an existence in which they expertly handled wires and powder.

"I can't talk when I'm working like this. You have to be careful with nitroglycerin, even I do."

Sharon's arms tightened around Neil. This insane man was handling explosives a few feet away from them. If he made a mistake, if he jarred something . . . She remembered the story of the brownstone in Greenwich Village that had exploded. She'd been in New York on a school break that day and shopping a few blocks away when the deafening sound came. She thought of the mass of rubble, of the piles of broken stone and splintered wood. Those people thought they knew how to handle explosives too.

Prayerfully, she watched as he worked with painstaking care, watched as the circulation in her legs stopped, as the dampness penetrated her skin, as her ear became attuned to the faint rumbling sound of trains. The wheezing in Neil's chest developed a rhythm; fast, gasping, but not quite so frantic.

Finally the man straightened up. "It's all right." He sounded satisfied.

"What are you going to do with that?"

"It's your babysitter."

"What do you mean?"

"I have to leave you until morning. I can't take any chance of losing you, can I?"

"How can you lose us, if we're tied up alone here?"

"One in a million, one in ten million, someone tries to get in this room while I'm out . . ."

"How long are you going to keep us here?"

"Until Wednesday. Sharon, don't ask me questions. I'll tell you what I want you to know."

"I'm sorry. It's just that I don't understand."

"I can't let anyone find you. But I have to be away. So if the door is wired and someone tries to come in . . ."

She was not here. She was not hearing this. This could not be.

"Don't worry, Sharon. Tomorrow night Steve Peterson is going to give me eighty-two thousand dollars, and this will be all over."

"Eighty-two thousand dollars?"

"Yes. And then Wednesday morning you and I will go away and I'll leave word where they can find the boy." Somewhere far off there was a faint echo of a roar, a silence, another roar.

He came across the room. "I'm sorry, Sharon." In a sudden movement, he yanked Neil from her arms, dropped him on the cot. Before she could move, he pulled her hands behind her. He let the coat slide off before he tied her wrists together.

He reached for Neil. "Don't gag Neil, please," she begged. "If he chokes . . . you may not be able to get the money . . . you may have to prove he's alive. Please . . . I . . . I like you. Because you're so smart."

He was watching her, considering.

"You . . . you know my name but you haven't even told me your name. I'd like to be thinking about you."

His hands turned her face to him. They were calloused, rough. Impossible to think they were so dextrous with delicate wires. He bent down over her. His breath was stale, hot. She suffered his kiss, harsh on her lips, moist, lingering on her cheek and ear. "My name is Foxy," he said huskily. "Say my name, Sharon."

"Foxy."

He tied Neil's wrists and pulled him beside her. There was barely room for both of them lying sideways on the narrow cot. Sharon's hands were squeezed against the rough concrete wall. He covered them with the soiled gray coat, then stood over them. He looked from them to the boarded-up dumbwaiter.

"No." He looked dissatisfied, uncertain. "I can't take the chance that someone might hear you."

The gags were around their mouths again, but not quite so tight this time. She dared not protest any more. The nervousness was building up in him again.

And then she knew why. Because slowly, with agonizing care, he was fastening a slender wire to something in the suitcase and trailing it from

the suitcase to the door. He was going to attach that wire to the door. Then if anyone happened to come in here, the bomb would be triggered!

She heard the snap of the switch, and the dust-shrouded lights flickered away. The door opened and closed noiselessly. For an instant he was silhouetted against the outside gloom, and then he was gone.

The room was desperately dark now and the cavernous silence was broken only by Neil's labored breathing and the occasional muted rumble of a train entering the tunnel.

 *CHAPTER 18*

Roger and Glenda Perry decided to watch the eleven o'clock news in bed. She had already bathed and offered to make a hot toddy for him while he showered.

"Sounds good, but don't start puttering around." He checked the lock on the kitchen door and went upstairs. The shower was hot, needlesharp, infinitely satisfying. Quickly he got into blue-striped pajamas, folded back the heavy spread from the king sized bed, and turned on the reading lights that beamed on both pillows.

Just before getting into bed, he walked over to the front window. Even in weather like this, he and Glenda enjoyed the feel of fresh night air in the room. Automatically he glanced over at the Peterson house. It was lighted now, outside and in. Through the granular snow he could see cars parked in the driveway.

Glenda came into the bedroom carrying a steaming cup. "Roger, whatever are you looking at?"

He turned, sheepishly. "Nothing. But you don't have to worry about Steve's lights being off. His place is as bright as a Christmas tree now."

"He must have company. Well, thank heaven we're not out tonight." She put the cup down on his night table, slipped off her robe and got into bed. "Oh, I am tired." Her expression changed, became thoughtful. Her body stilled.

"A pain?"

"Yes."

"Lie still. I'll get you a pill." With fingers that tried not to fumble, he reached for the ever-present bottle of nitroglycerin tablets. He watched as she slipped one under her tongue and closed her eyes. A minute later, she sighed, "Oh, that was a pretty bad one. But it's all right now."

The phone rang. Roger reached for it, angrily. "If it's for you, I'll say you're asleep," he muttered. "Some people . . ." He picked up the receiver. His "yes" was curt.

Immediately his tone changed, became concerned. "Steve . . . is something wrong? No. No. Nothing. Of course. Oh, dear God! I'll be right over."

As Glenda stared, he replaced the receiver and reached for her hands. "Something's wrong at Steve's," he said carefully. "Neil and Sharon Martin are . . . missing. I'm going over there, but I'll be back as fast as I possibly can."

"Roger . . ."

"Please, Glenda. For my sake, stay calm. You know how you've been feeling lately. Please!"

He pulled a heavy sweater and slacks over his pajamas and stuffed his feet into moccasins.

He was just closing the front door when he heard the telephone ring again. Knowing Glenda would pick it up, Roger ran out into the swirling snow. He cut diagonally across his lawn, down the street, up the Peterson driveway. He was barely aware of the cold that chilled his bare ankles, that made his breath come harsh and uneven.

He was panting heavily, his heart racing when he hurried up the steps. The door was opened by a trim-looking man with bold features and graying hair. "Mr. Perry. I'm Hugh Taylor, FBI. We met two years ago . . ."

Roger thought of that day when Glenda had been knocked down by Ronald Thompson as he ran from this house, when she'd rushed in to find Nina's body.

"I remember." Shaking his head, he went into the living room. Steve was standing by the fireplace, his hands gripped together. Red-eyed and sobbing, Dora Lufts was seated on the couch. Beside her, Bill Lufts hunched forward helplessly.

Roger went directly to Steve and gripped his shoulders. "Steve, my God, I don't know what to say."

"Roger, thanks for coming so fast."

"How long have they been gone?"

"We're not sure. It happened sometime between six and seven-thirty."

"Sharon and Neil were alone here?"

"Yes. They . . ." Steve's voice broke. Quickly he recovered. "They were alone."

"Mr. Perry," Hugh Taylor interrupted. "Is there anything you can tell us? Did you notice any strangers in the neighborhood, strange cars or vans or trucks—anything? Can you think of anything unusual?"

Roger sat down heavily. Think. There *was* something. What was it? Yes. "Your outside lights!"

Steve turned to him, his expression intense. "Bill is positive they were on when he and Dora went out. They were off when I got home. What did you notice about them?"

Roger's analytical mind offered a precise timetable of his evening activities. He'd left the office at ten past five, driven into his garage at twenty of six. "Your lights must have been on when I got home at about twenty of six," he told Steve. "Otherwise I'd have noticed. Glenda made a cocktail. It wasn't more than fifteen minutes later that we were looking out our front window and she remarked that your place was dark."

He frowned. "As a matter of fact, the clock was chiming shortly before that so it must have been about five past six." He paused. "Glenda said something about a car coming from your driveway."

"A car! What kind of car?" Hugh Taylor snapped.

"I don't know. Glenda mentioned it to me. I had turned my back to the window."

"You're sure of the time?"

Roger looked directly at the FBI agent. "I'm positive." He realized that he was having difficulty making sense out of what he was hearing. Had Glenda actually watched a car drive away with Neil and Sharon in it? Neil and Sharon being abducted! Shouldn't some instinct have warned them that something was wrong? But it had. He remembered the feeling of alarm Glenda had at the window, how she'd wanted him to walk over here. And he'd cautioned her about overreacting.

Glenda!

How much could he tell her. He looked at Hugh Taylor. "My wife will be terribly upset."

Hugh nodded. "I understand. And Mr. Peterson feels she can be trusted to know the truth. But it is absolutely vital that there be no publicity about this. We don't want to scare the abductor or abductors off."

"I understand."

"Two lives depend on all of you acting as normally as possible."

"Two lives . . ." Dora Lufts broke into dry, racking sobs. "My little Neil . . . and that pretty girl. I can't believe this, not after Mrs. Peterson . . ."

"Dora, keep quiet." Bill Lufts' voice was a whiny plea.

Roger watched as Steve's face contorted into a spasm of pain.

"Mr. Perry, do you know Miss Martin?" Hugh Taylor asked.

"Yes. I've met Sharon several times both here and at my home. Now may I please go over for my wife?"

"Certainly. We want to speak with her about the car she saw. I have another agent with me. I can send him."

"No. I'd prefer to go myself. She's not well and Neil means a great deal to her."

Roger thought, I am making conversation. I don't believe this. I don't. Steve. How can Steve stand this? He looked at the younger man compassionately. Steve was outwardly calm but the bleak look of suffering that had been etched in his face, that had only begun to lighten in these last months, was there again in the gray pallor, in the suddenly deepened creases in his forehead, the taut lines around his mouth. "Why don't you have a drink or some coffee, Steve," he suggested. "You look pretty shaken."

"Maybe coffee . . ."

Dora looked up eagerly. "I'll make it, and some sandwiches. Oh my God, when I think . . . Neil . . . Why did I have to go to the movies tonight? If anything has happened to that boy, I can't take it. I can't take it!"

Bill Lufts put his hand over his wife's mouth. "For once in your life, shut up!" he barked. "Shut up!" There was ferocity, bitterness in his voice. Roger realized that Hugh Taylor was studying the couple intensely.

The Lufts? Could he suspect them? No. Never. Impossible.

He was in the foyer when the chimes began to peal frantically. They all jumped as an agent, who'd been in the kitchen, covered the length of the foyer in seconds, raced past Roger and pulled the door open.

Glenda stood in the doorway. Her hair and face were wet with snow. Her feet were in open satin slippers. Her pink wool dressing gown was her only protection against the sharp, wet wind. Her face was marble-white. The pupils of her eyes were dilated and staring. In her hand she was clutching a sheet of notepaper. She was trembling violently.

Roger ran to her, caught her just before she collapsed. He held her against him.

"Roger, the call, the phonecall . . ." She was sobbing now. "He made me write it down. He made me read it back to him. He said, get it right or . . . or . . . Neil . . ."

Hugh snatched the paper from her hand and read it aloud. "Tell Steven Peterson if he wants his son and girlfriend back to be in the telephone booth of the Exxon station at exit 22 of the Merritt Parkway tomorrow morning at eight o'clock. He'll get instructions for the ransom."

Hugh frowned. The last word was indistinguishable. "What is this word, Mrs. Perry?" he demanded.

"He made me read it back . . . I could hardly write . . . he was so impatient . . . it's 'Foxy.' That's it. He repeated it." Glenda's voice rose in pitch. Her face twisted in pain. She pulled away from Roger, clutching her chest. "He . . . he was trying to disguise his voice . . . but when he repeated that name . . . Roger, *I've heard that voice.* That man is someone I know."

CHAPTER 19

Before he left Somers State Prison, Bob Kurner phoned Kathy Moore and asked her to meet him in her office.

Kathy was an assistant prosecutor in Bridgeport assigned to Juvenile Court, and they'd met when he was serving as Public Defender there. They'd been going together for three months and Kathy had become deeply involved in his fight to save Ron Thompson.

She was waiting for him in the reception area with the typist he'd requested. "Marge said she'll stay all night if necessary. How much have you got?"

"A lot," Bob said. "I made him go over the story four times. There's a good two hours' worth."

Marge Evans stretched out her hand. "Just give it to me." Her tone was businesslike. She set the recorder on her desk, squeezed her massive body onto the swivel chair, inserted the cassette labeled "1" in the machine and ran it back to the beginning. Ron Thompson's voice, halting and low, began to speak: "I was working that afternoon after school in Timberly's Market . . ."

Marge snapped the "off" button and said, "Okay, you two get to something else. I'll take care of this."

"Thanks, Marge." Bob turned to Kathy. "Did you get those files?"

"Yes, they're inside." He followed her into her small crammed cubbyhole of an office. The desk was bare except for four manila folders labeled "Carfolli," "Weiss," "Ambrose," "Callahan."

"The police reports are right on top. Les Brooks wouldn't appreciate this, Bob. In fact, he'll probably fire me if he finds out about it."

Les Brooks was the prosecutor. Bob sat down at the desk and reached for the first file. Before he opened it he looked up at Kathy. She was wearing dungarees and a heavy sweater. Her dark hair was held back by a rubberband at the nape of her neck. She looked more like an eighteen-year-old co-ed than a twenty-five-year-old lawyer. But after the first time he'd been pitted against her in court Bob never made the mistake of underestimating Kathy. She was a good lawyer with a keen, analytical mind and a passion for justice.

"I know the chance you're taking, Kath. But if we can only find some thread between these murders and Nina Peterson's . . . Our one hope for Ron now is new evidence."

Kathy pulled a chair to the other side of the desk and reached for two of the files. "Well, God knows, if we can find any connection between these cases, Les will forget the irregularity in your seeing our files. The newspapers are really on his back. As of this morning they're calling these last two the 'Citizen Band Murders.' "

"How come?"

"Both the Callahan girl and Mrs. Ambrose had C.B. radios and had called for assistance. Mrs. Ambrose was lost and almost out of gas and Barbara Callahan had had a blowout."

"And two years ago Mrs. Weiss and Jean Carfolli were killed while driving alone at night on lonely roads."

"But that doesn't prove any connection. When Jean and Mrs. Weiss were killed the papers had started to write about the 'Highwayman Murders.' It's all catch phrases to make headlines."

"What do *you* think?"

"I don't know what I think. After Ron Thompson was arrested for the Peterson murder, we didn't have another woman killed in Fairfield County until last month. Now we have two unsolved deaths. But there have been other C.B.-related murders around the country. Those radios are great to have but it's insanity for a woman to get on the air and say she's alone on a deserted road and her car has broken down. It's an open invitation to every kook in the area who's listening to head straight to her. My God, they had a case in Long Island last year of a fifteen-year-old kid who used to listen to the police channel and head for trouble spots. They finally got him when he knifed a woman who'd called for assistance."

"I still say there's a connection between these four cases and that somehow Nina Peterson's case is linked with them," Bob said. "Call it a hunch. Call it grasping at straws. Call it anything. But help me."

"I want to. How do we go about it?"

"We'll start with a list: place, time, cause of death, weapon used, weather condition, kind of car, family background, witnesses' testimony, where victims were going, where they'd been that evening. In the last two cases, we'll measure the time elapsed between the message they sent out on the C.B. and the finding of the body. When we're finished, we'll compare everything with the circumstances of Mrs. Peterson's death. If there's nothing there, we'll start from another angle."

They began at ten past eight. At midnight, Marge came in with four sets of papers. "All finished," she said. "I typed them triple-spaced to make it easier to pick up discrepancies in any of the versions. You know, listening to that boy is enough to break your heart. I've been a legal stenographer for twenty years and I've heard an awful lot of stuff but I know the ring of truth when I hear it and that kid's telling the truth."

Bob smiled wearily. "I wish to God you were the Governor, Marge," he said. "Thanks so much."

"How're you two doing?"

Kathy shook her head. "Nothing. Absolutely nothing."

"Well, maybe these will show something. Why don't I get you some coffee. Bet neither one of you had dinner."

When she came back ten minutes later, Bob and Kathy were sitting with two sets of papers in front of each of them. Bob was reading aloud. They were making line by line comparisons of the transcripts.

Marge set the coffee down and left silently. A security guard let her out of the building. As she huddled into the warmth of her heavy storm-coat, bracing herself for the long walk across the snow-blown parking lot, she realized she was praying. "Please God, if there's anything there to find that will help that boy, let those kids find it."

Bob and Kathy worked until dawn. Then she said, "We've got to quit. I have to go home and shower and dress. I'm due in court at eight o'clock. And anyhow, I don't want anyone to see you here."

Bob nodded. The words he was reading were blurring in his mind now. Over and over they'd compared the four versions of Ron's account of his activities the day of the murder. They'd concentrated on the time Nina Peterson talked to him in Timberly's Market until he ran panic-stricken from her home. There wasn't a single meaningful discrepancy they could pick up. "There's got to be something here," Bob said stubbornly. "I'll take these home with me, and let me have the lists we made on the other four cases."

"I can't let you take the files."

"I know that. But maybe we missed some factor in comparing the cases."

"We didn't, Bob." Kathy's voice was gentle.

He stood up. "I'll go right to my office and start again. I'll compare these with the trial transcript now."

Kathy helped him to put the material in his briefcase. "Don't forget the recorder and the cassettes," she said.

"I won't." He reached his arm out and encircled her. For an instant she leaned against him. "Love you, Kath."

"Love you."

"If we only had more time," he cried. "It's this damn capital punishment. How the hell can twelve people have come in and said that kid has to die. When, and if, they get the real killer it will be too late for Ron."

Kathy rubbed her forehead. "At first, I was glad when capital punishment was reinstated. I'm sorry for victims, a lot sorrier for them than for perpetrators. But yesterday we had a kid in Juvenile. He's fourteen and looks about eleven; a skinny, small kid. Both parents are hopeless alcoholics. They signed a complaint against him as an incorrigible when he was seven years old, *seven years old.* He's been in and out of children's homes since then. He keeps running away. This time the mother signed the complaint and the father is fighting it. They're separated and he wants the kid with him."

"What happened?"

"I won, if you can call it that. I insisted that he be sent back to a juvenile home and the judge agreed. The father's so disoriented from booze that he's not much more than a vegetable. The boy tried to run out of the courtroom; the sheriff's officer had to tackle him to catch him. He got hysterical and kept screaming, 'I hate everybody. Why can't I have a home like other kids?' Psychologically, he's so damaged that it's probably already too late to save him. If in five or six years he kills someone, will we burn him? Should we?" Weary tears glistened in her eyes.

"I know, Kath. Why'd we get into law, anyhow? Maybe we should have been smarter. This tears your guts out." He bent down and kissed her forehead. "Talk to you later."

In his office, Bob put the kettle, brimming with water, on the hotplate. Four cups of Nescafé, strong and black, cleared the sensation of fogginess. He splashed cold water on his face and sat down at the long table in his office. Neatly, he laid out the rows of papers. He glanced at the clock over his desk. It was 7:30. He had just twenty-eight hours till the execution. That was why his heart was pounding, why his throat felt so constricted.

No. It was more than the frantic sense of urgency. Something was hammering at his consciousness. *There is something we have missed,* he thought.

This time it was not a hunch. It was certainty.

Long after the Perrys went home and the Lufts retired, Steve and Hugh Taylor sat at the dining-room table.

Quietly and efficiently, other agents had dusted the house for fingerprints and searched house and grounds for signs of the abductor. But the scrawled message was the only evidence to be found.

"The prints on the glass and cup will probably match the ones on Sharon Martin's purse," Hugh told Steve.

Steve nodded. His mouth felt dry and brackish. Four cups of coffee. Endless cigarettes. He'd given up smoking when he turned thirty. Then when Nina died he'd started again. It was Hugh Taylor who gave him the first one. Something like a smile, grim and humorless, tugged at the corners of his mouth. "You're the one who got me back on these weeds," he said as he lit another one.

Hugh nodded. If ever a guy needed a cigarette that last time, it was Steve Peterson. And now his child! Hugh remembered how he was sitting with Steve at this table when some crackpot mystic phoned to say Nina had a message for him. The message was, "Tell my husband to beware. My son is in danger." That was the morning of Nina's funeral.

Remembering the incident, Hugh flinched. He hoped Steve wasn't thinking about that. He studied the methodical notes he had made. "There's a pay telephone in an outside booth at that Exxon station," he told Steve. "We're putting a tap on it as well as on this house and the Perrys' line. The thing to remember when you talk to Foxy is to try to keep him on the phone. That'll give us a chance to run a trace and record his voice. Our big break may be that Mrs. Perry will be able to remember who he is if she hears him again."

"Do you really think it's possible that she isn't just imagining she recognized the voice? You saw how upset she was."

"Anything's possible. But she seems like a levelheaded woman to me and she's so *positive*. Anyhow, cooperate. Tell Foxy you want proof that Sharon and Neil are alive and unharmed, that you must have a message from them on a cassette or tape. Whatever money he asks for, promise to get it, but insist that you'll pay it only when you receive the proof."

"That won't antagonize him?" Steve wondered that he could sound so detached.

"No. But it will help insure that he won't panic and . . ." Abruptly Hugh clamped his lips together. But he knew Steve had gotten his meaning. He picked up his notebook.

"Let's start all over again. How many people knew the schedule of this house tonight, that the Lufts were planning to go out, that Sharon was coming up?"

"I don't know."

"The Perrys?"

"No. I hadn't seen them over the last week except to wave hello."

"Then it was just the Lufts and Sharon Martin and yourself?"

"And Neil."

"That's right. Is there any chance that Neil would have talked about Sharon's coming to other people, to his friends or his teachers at school?"

"It's possible."

"How serious is your friendship with Sharon? Sorry, but I have to ask."

"Very serious. I'm planning to ask her to marry me."

"I understand that you and Miss Martin were on the *Today* show this morning and that you disagreed strongly about the capital punishment issue and specifically that she was terribly upset about the Thompson execution."

"You work fast."

"We have to, Mr. Peterson. How much did that disagreement affect your personal relationship?"

"What's that supposed to mean?"

"Only this. As you know, Sharon Martin has been desperately trying to save Ronald Thompson's life. She's been in the Perry home and could have made a note of the phone number. Don't forget it's unlisted. Do you think there's a possibility that this kidnapping is a hoax, that she's hoping somehow to delay the execution?"

"No . . . no . . . no! Hugh, I understand you have to look at that angle, but please, for God's sake, don't waste your time on it. Whoever wrote that message could have copied the Perrys' number. It's right on that blackboard with the doctor's. Sharon would be incapable of doing this to me, incapable."

Hugh looked unconvinced. "Mr. Peterson, we've had some mighty unusual people breaking the law in the name of causes these last ten years. I only offer this thought, if Sharon Martin engineered this, your child is safe."

A tiny flicker of hope flared in Steve. This morning Sharon saying to him, "How can you be so positive, so sure, so relentless?" If that was the way she thought of him, could she . . . ? The hope died. "No," he said flatly. "That's impossible."

"Very well. We'll leave it at that for the moment. What about your mail—any threats, hate letters, anything at all?"

"Quite a few hate letters because of my editorial stand on capital punishment, especially with the Thompson execution so near. But that isn't surprising."

"You've received no direct threats?"

"No." Steve frowned.

"What are you thinking?" Hugh asked quickly.

"Just that Ronald Thompson's mother stopped me last week. I take Neil for antihistimine shots every Saturday morning. She was in the parking lot of the medical building when we came out. She asked me to beg the Governor to spare Thompson."

"What did you tell her?"

"I said I couldn't do anything. I was anxious to get Neil away. Naturally I didn't want him to be aware about Wednesday. I wanted to get him inside the car as quickly as possible so he wouldn't hear us talking and so I turned my back to her. But she seemed to think I was ignoring her. She said something like, 'How would you feel if it was your only son, how would you feel?' And then she walked away."

Hugh made a note in his book. "We'll check her out." Standing up, he flexed his shoulders, vaguely aware that hours ago he'd been looking forward to going to bed. "Mr. Peterson," he said, "try to hang on to the thought that our record of recovering kidnapping victims is a very good one and everything possible will be done. Now, I'd suggest that you try to get a few hours' sleep."

"Sleep?" Steve looked at him incredulously.

"Then rest. Go up to your room and lie down. We'll be right here and we'll call you if there's any reason. If the phone rings, you pick it up. We've got a tap on it now. But I don't think you'll get any further word from the abductor tonight."

"All right." Wearily, Steve walked out of the dining room. He stopped in the kitchen to get a glass of water and was sorry he had. The mug of cocoa and glass of sherry, smeared now with sooty powder, were on the kitchen table.

Sharon. Only a few hours ago she had been here in this house with Neil. He hadn't realized just how much he wanted Neil to trust and like Sharon until these last three weeks when she'd been away and he'd missed her so terribly.

Silently he left the kitchen, went into the foyer, up the stairs, down the hallway past Neil's room and the guest room to the master bedroom. Overhead, he could hear footsteps. The Lufts were walking around their third-floor room. Obviously they couldn't sleep either.

He switched on the light and stood near the door, studying the room. After Nina died, he'd refurnished it. He hadn't wanted to be around the antique white furniture she'd loved so much. He'd replaced the double bed with a twin-size brass fourposter, selected a color scheme of brown-and-white tweed. A man's room, the decorating shop had assured him.

He'd never cared for it. It was lonely and barren and impersonal, like a motel room. The whole house was like that. They'd bought it because they wanted waterfront property. Nina had said, "The house has real possibilities. Just wait and see. Give me six months with it." She'd had two weeks . . .

The last time he'd been in Sharon's apartment, he'd daydreamed about redoing this room, this house with her. She knew how to make a home charming and restful and inviting, too. It was the colors she used and the uncluttered look. And it was her presence.

Pulling off his shoes, he lay heavily across the bed. The room felt cool and he reached for the folded coverlet and drew it up. He touched the switch that turned off the overhead light.

The room was completely dark. Outside the wind was slapping branches of the dogwood trees against the house. The snow made a furry pelting sound against the windows.

Steve dozed off into a light, uneasy sleep. He began to dream. Sharon, Neil. They wanted him to help them. He was running through a thick fog . . . running down a long hallway. There was a room at the end of it. He was trying to get into the room. He *had* to get into the room. He reached it and threw the door open. And the fog cleared. The fog was gone. And Neil and Sharon were lying on the floor, scarves knotted around their throats and iridescent chalk marks outlining their bodies.

━━━ *CHAPTER 21*

I t was much too dangerous to be seen coming up from the Mount Vernon tracks alone late in the evening. The guards in the lower terminal had eyes for details like that. That was why he left Sharon and the boy at two minutes of eleven. Because at exactly eleven a train chugged into the station and he was able to go up the ramp and stairs with the eight or ten people who got off it.

He drifted near three of them who went to the Vanderbilt Avenue exit. He knew that to anyone watching he was one of a group of four people. He slipped away from the others when they turned left on Vanderbilt Avenue. He turned right, glanced across the street and stopped short. A police tow truck was there. Clanging chains were being attached to a shabby brown Chevrolet. They were just about to tow the car away!

Hugely amused, he started uptown. He was planning to make the phonecall from a booth in front of Bloomingdale's. The fifteen-block walk up Lexington Avenue chilled him and reduced some of the pulsing desire he'd experienced when he kissed Sharon. And she wanted him just as much. He could feel it.

He might have made love to Sharon then except for the boy. Even with the blindfold the eyes were there. Maybe the boy could see through the blindfold. The thought made him shiver.

The snow had tapered off some but the sky was still dark and heavy. He frowned, remembering how important it would be for the roads to be clear when he picked up the money.

He was planning to phone the Perrys and if they weren't home he'd call the Peterson house directly. But that could be risky.

He was lucky. Mrs. Perry picked up the phone on the first ring. He could tell by her voice that she was extremely nervous. Probably Peterson had called over there when he found the boy and Sharon missing. He gave Mrs. Perry the message in the low, gruff voice he'd practiced. It was only when she couldn't get the name that he exploded and raised his tone. Careless of him! Stupid! But she probably was too upset to notice.

Gently replacing the phone, he smiled. If the FBI had been called they'd tap the phone in the Exxon station. That was why in the morning when he called Peterson on that phone, he'd tell him to go right to the booth in the next service station. They wouldn't have time to put a tracer on it.

He left the phonebooth feeling exhilarated, brilliant. A girl was standing in the doorway of a small dress shop. In spite of the cold she was wearing a miniskirt. White boots and a white fur jacket completed an outfit he thought very attractive. She smiled at him. Her hair was thick and curly around her face. She was young, not more than eighteen or nineteen and she liked him. He could tell. Her eyes were smiling at him and he started walking toward her.

But then he stopped. She was undoubtedly a prostitute and even though she was sincere about liking him, just suppose the police were watching and arrested them both? He looked around fearfully. He'd read about great plans being ruined by a small mistake.

Stoically passing the girl, he permitted her a brief, skeletal smile before he put his head down into the frigid wind and hurried to the Biltmore.

The same sneering night clerk gave him his key. He hadn't had dinner and was very hungry. And he'd order two or three bottles of beer

from room service too. Around this time he always got thirsty for beer. Habit, maybe.

While he waited for the two hamburgers and french fries and apple pie, he soaked in the tub. It had felt so musty and cold and dirty in the room. After drying himself, he put on the pajamas he'd bought for this trip and examined his suit carefully. But it wasn't soiled.

He tipped the room service waiter generously. They always did that in the movies. The first bottle of beer he gulped down. The second he had with the hamburgers. The third he sipped listening to the midnight news. There was more about that Thompson kid. "The last possibility of a reprieve from death for Ronald Thompson was ended yesterday. Plans are being made to carry out the execution at 11:30 A.M. tomorrow as scheduled. . . ." But not a whisper about Neil or Sharon. Publicity was the one thing that he feared. Because someone might start putting two and two together.

The girls last month had been a mistake. It was just that he couldn't help it. He never went cruising around anymore. Too dangerous. But when he heard them on the C.B., something made him go to them.

The thought of the girls made him churn up inside. Restlessly, he switched off the radio. He really shouldn't . . . it might excite him.

He *had* to.

From his coat pocket he took out the expensive miniature recorder and the cassettes he always carried with him. Selecting one, he slipped it in the recorder, got into bed and turned out the light. He snuggled under the covers, appreciating the clean, crisp sheets, the warm blanket and coverlet. He and Sharon would stay in many hotels together.

Putting the earplug in his right ear, he cautiously deflected the "play" button of the machine. For several minutes there was only the sound of a car engine, then the faint squeal of brakes, a door opening and his own voice friendly and helpful as he got out of the Volks.

He let the cassette run until he got to the best part. That he kept replaying over and over again. Finally he had heard enough. He turned off the recorder, pulled out the earplug, and fell into a deep sleep, the sound of Jean Carfolli's sobbing scream, "Don't . . . please don't . . ." ringing in his ears.

Marian and Jim Vogler talked far into the night. Despite Jim's efforts to console her, something like despair had seeped into Marian's soul.

"I wouldn't mind so much if we hadn't just spent all that money! *Four hundred dollars!* If someone had to steal the car why didn't they take it last week before we fixed it? And it was running so well. Arty did such a good job on it. And now how can I get to the Perrys? I'll lose that job!"

"Babe, you won't have to give up the job. I'll get somebody to lend me a couple of hundred bucks and I'll look around for another jalopy tomorrow."

"Oh, Jim, would you?" Marian knew how Jim hated borrowing from friends, but if he would do it just this once . . .

It was too dark for Jim to see her face but he felt the faint relaxing of her body. "Babe," he reassured her, "someday we'll laugh about these lousy bills. Before you know it, we'll get caught up."

"I guess so," Marian agreed. Suddenly she felt desperately tired. Her eyes began to close.

They were just drifting off to sleep when the phone rang. Its jangle startled them. Marian pulled herself up on one elbow as Jim fumbled for the lamp on the night table and reached for the phone.

"Hello. Yeah, this is Jim—James Vogler. Tonight. That's right. Oh, that's good! Where? When can I get it? You're kidding. *You're kidding.* If that don't beat all! All right . . . Thirty-sixth Street and Twelfth Avenue. I know. Right. Thanks." He hung up the phone.

"The car," Marian cried. "They found our car!"

"Yeah, in New York City. It was parked illegally in midtown and the cops towed it away. We can get it in the morning. The cop said it was probably heisted by some fool kids joyriding."

"Oh, Jim, that's wonderful!"

"There's a hitch."

"What is it?"

Jim Vogler's eyes crinkled. His lips twitched. "Babe, can you believe . . . we're stuck with the fifteen-buck parking ticket and the sixty-buck tow charge?"

Marian gasped. "That's my first week's pay!" She began to laugh helplessly with him.

In the morning Jim took the 6:15 train to New York and was back with the car at five of nine. Marian was ready to leave. Promptly at nine o'clock she turned into Driftwood Lane. The car was none the worse

for its unauthorized trip into New York and she was grateful for the new snow tires. You sure needed them in this weather.

A Mercury was parked in the Perrys' driveway. It looked like the one she'd noticed in front of the house across the street when she'd come for the interview last week. The Perrys must have company.

Somewhat uncertainly she pulled up beside the Mercury taking care that her car didn't block access to the garage. Then she lingered a moment before opening the door. She was a little nervous . . . all that excitement with the car just when she was starting a job. Well, just get yourself together, she thought. Count your blessings. The car was back. Affectionately, she patted the seat beside her with her gloved hand.

Her hand stopped moving. One of the fingers had touched something hard. She looked down, and with two fingers tugged a shiny object from where it was wedged between the cushion and the backrest.

Why, it was a ring. She inspected it closely. How pretty—a pale, pink moonstone in a lovely raised antique gold setting. Whoever stole the car must have lost it.

Well, it was a cinch they wouldn't come around to claim it. As far as she was concerned the ring was hers. It made up for the seventy-five dollars Jim laid out for the ticket and towing fee. She pulled off her glove and slipped the ring on her finger. It fit perfectly.

It was a good omen. Wait until Jim found out about this. Suddenly confident, Marian opened the door of the car, stepped out into the snow, and walked briskly around to the kitchen door of the Perry home.

CHAPTER 23

The phone in the outside booth of the Exxon station rang promptly at eight o'clock. Swallowing over the convulsion of his throat muscles, the sudden, absolute dryness in his mouth, Steve picked up the receiver. "Hello."

"Peterson?" A voice so muffled, so low, he had to strain to hear it.

"Yes."

"In ten minutes I'll call you at the payphone of the service station just past exit twenty-one."

The connection was broken.

"Wait . . . wait . . ." A buzzing sound assaulted his ear.

Desperately he looked over to the service island. Hugh had driven into the station a few minutes before him. The hood of his car was up and he was standing outside with the attendant, pointing at one of the tires. Steve knew he was watching him. Shaking his head, he got back in his own car and careened onto the parkway. Before he turned, he caught a glimpse of Hugh, jumping into his car.

The traffic was creeping cautiously down the slippery road. Steve clenched the wheel. He'd never make it to the next station in ten minutes. Twisting the wheel, he rode down the right-hand shoulder of the parkway.

The voice. He could hardly hear it. The FBI wouldn't have a prayer of tracing the call.

This time he'd try to keep Foxy on the phone longer. Maybe it was a voice he'd recognize too. He felt for the pad and paper in his pocket. He had to write down everything Foxy said. In the rearview mirror, he could see a green car behind him, Hugh's car.

It was eleven minutes past eight when Steve pulled into the next service station. The public phone was ringing insistently. He raced into the booth, grabbed the receiver.

"Peterson?"

This time the caller spoke so softly that he had to cover his other ear to block out the highway sounds. "Yes."

"I want eighty-two thousand dollars in tens, twenties and fifties. *No new bills.* At two o'clock tomorrow morning be at the payphone on the southwest corner of Fifty-fifth and Lexington in Manhattan. Drive in your own car. Be alone. You'll be told where to leave the money."

"Eighty-two thousand dollars . . ." Steve began to repeat the instructions. The voice, he thought frantically. Listen to the intonation, try to memorize it, be able to mimic it.

"Hurry up, Peterson."

"I'm writing this down. I'll get the money. I'll be there. But how do I know my son and Sharon are still alive? How do I know that you have them? I need proof."

"Proof? What kind of proof?" The whisper was angry now.

"A tape . . . or a cassette . . . something with them talking."

"A *cassette!*"

Was that muffled sound a laugh? Was the caller *laughing?* "I must have it," Steve insisted. Oh God, he prayed, don't let this be a mistake.

"You'll get your cassette, Peterson." The receiver on the other end was slammed down.

"Wait!" Steve shouted. "Wait!"

Silence. The dial tone. He hung up slowly.

As they'd arranged, he drove directly to the Perrys' and waited for Hugh. Too restless to stay in the car, he got out and stood in the driveway. The icy, moisture-filled wind made him shiver. Oh God, was this happening? Was this nightmare real?

Hugh drove down the block, parked. "What'd he say?"

Steve pulled out the pad, read the instructions. The sense of unreality deepened.

"How about the voice?" Hugh asked.

"Disguised I think, very low. I don't think anybody could possibly identify it even if you had been able to tap that second phone." He stared unseeingly across the street, groped for comfort, found a slender thread.

"He promised the cassette. That means they're probably still alive."

"I'm sure of it." Hugh did not voice the gnawing worry that it would be virtually impossible for a cassette to reach Steve before he paid the ransom. There wasn't time to mail it even special delivery. A messenger service would be too easy to trace. The abductor didn't want the kidnapping publicized so he'd hardly leave a cassette at a newspaper or radio station. "How about the ransom?" he asked Steve. "Can you raise eighty-two thousand dollars today?"

"I couldn't raise five cents myself," Steve said. "I've invested so much in the magazine that I'm absolutely strapped. Second mortgage, you name it. But thanks to Neil's mother, I can get that much money."

"Neil's mother?"

"She inherited seventy-five thousand dollars from her grandmother just before she died. I put it in a trust fund for Neil for college. It's in a bank in New York. With the interest it comes to just over eighty-two thousand."

"*Just over eighty-two thousand.* Mr. Peterson, how many people are aware of that trust?"

"I don't know. Nobody except my lawyer and accountant. You don't go around talking about that."

"What about Sharon Martin?"

"I don't remember mentioning it to her."

"But it is possible you told her?"

"I don't think I did."

Hugh started to go up the porch steps. "Mr. Peterson," he said carefully, "you have got to go over in your own mind everyone who knows about that money. That and the possibility that Mrs. Perry can identify the kidnapper's voice are our only leads."

When they rang the front doorbell, Roger answered quickly. He put a finger to his lips as they came in. His face was pale and strained, his shoulders sagging. "The doctor just left. He's given Glenda a sedative. She refuses to go to the hospital but he thinks she's on the verge of another coronary."

"Mr. Perry, I'm sorry. But we have to ask her to listen to a recording of the first call the kidnapper made this morning."

"She can't! Not now! This is killing her. It's killing her!" Clenching his fists, he swallowed, "Steve, I'm sorry . . . what happened?"

Mechanically, Steve explained. He still had the feeling of unreality, of being an observer, watching a tragedy being acted out without power to interfere.

There was a long pause, then Roger said slowly, "Glenda refused to go to the hospital because she knew you'd need her to hear that tape. The doctor gave her a strong tranquilizer. If she just slept for a little while . . . Can you bring it over later? She absolutely can't get out of bed."

"Of course," Hugh said.

Chimes were an intrusion. "That's the back door," Roger said. "Who on earth . . . ? Oh my God, the new housekeeper. I forgot all about her."

"How long will she be here?" Hugh asked quickly.

"Four hours."

"No good. She might overhear something. Introduce me as the doctor. When we leave, send her home. Say you'll call her in a day or two. Where is she from anyhow?"

"Carley."

The chimes sounded again.

"She been in this house before?"

"Last week."

"We may want to check her out."

"All right." Roger hurried to the back door and returned with Marian. Hugh studied the pleasant-looking woman carefully.

"I've explained to Mrs. Vogler that my wife is ill," Roger said. "Mrs. Vogler, my neighbor, Mr. Peterson, and err . . . Doctor Taylor."

"How do you do?" Her voice was warm, a little shy. "Oh, Mr. Peterson, is that Mercury your car?"

"Yes."

"Then that must be your little boy. He's the dearest thing. He was out front when I came here last week and he pointed out this house to me. He was so polite. You must be very proud of him." Marian was peeling off her glove, reaching out her hand to Steve.

"I . . . am proud of Neil." Abruptly Steve turned his back to her and reached for the knob of the front door. Blinding tears stung his eyes. "Oh, God, please . . ."

Hugh jumped into the breach, shaking Marian's hand, careful not to squeeze the unusual ring she was wearing. Pretty fancy to do housework in, he thought. His expression had changed subtly. "I think it's a very good idea Mrs. Vogler is here, Mr. Perry," he said. "You know how concerned your wife gets about the house. I'd have her start today just as you originally planned."

"Oh . . . I see . . . very well." Roger stared at Hugh, understanding the implication. Did Hugh think this woman might be tied to Neil's disappearance?

Bewildered, Marian looked past Hugh and Roger and watched Steve open the front door. Maybe he thought she was too forward offering to shake hands. Maybe she should apologize. She'd better remember she was the housekeeper here. She started to touch his shoulder, thought better of it, and silently held the door open for Hugh. Embarrassed, she closed it quietly behind them and as she did the moonstone ring made a faint clinking sound on the knob.

〜〜 *CHAPTER 24*

He didn't want to be a crybaby. He tried so hard not to cry but it was like when the asthma came. He couldn't stop it. He'd get that gulpy feeling in his throat and his nose would start running and big baby tears would get his face all wet. He cried a lot in school. He knew the other kids thought he was a baby and the teacher did, too, even though she wasn't mean about it.

It was just that there was something inside him that kept bothering him all the time, some scared, worried feeling. It all began that day when Mommy got hurt and went to heaven. He'd been playing with his trains. He never played with them anymore.

The thought of that day made Neil's breath come faster. He couldn't breathe through his mouth because of the rag over it. His chest began to heave. He gulped and a piece of the rag went into his mouth. It tasted thick and raspy on his tongue. He tried to say, "I can't breathe." The rag went back further in his mouth. He was gagging. He was going to start crying . . .

"Neil, stop that." Sharon's voice sounded funny and low and hoarse like she was talking from somewhere down in her throat. But her face was right next to his and through some kind of cloth he could feel her face move when she talked. She must have something around her mouth too.

Where were they? It was so cold and so smelly here. There was something over him, a smelly blanket, he guessed. His eyes were so squeezed together and it was so dark.

The man had opened the door and knocked him down. He had tied them up and he'd taken Sharon away. Then he'd come back and Neil had felt himself being picked up and squished into some kind of bag. Once, over at Sandy's, they'd played hide-and-seek and he'd hidden in a big leaf bag that he found in the garage. It had felt like that. He didn't remember anything after the man put him in the bag, not until Sharon was pulling him out of it. He wondered why he didn't remember. It was like when Mommy fell.

He didn't want to think about that. Sharon was saying, "Breathe slowly, Neil. Don't cry, Neil, you're brave."

She probably thought he was a crybaby too. Tonight he'd been crying when she came. It was just that when he didn't eat the toast and tea Mrs. Lufts made for him she said, "Looks like we'll have to take you to Florida when we go, Neil. Got to fatten you up somehow."

See. That proved it. If Daddy married Sharon it was like Sandy said. Nobody wanted sick kids and they'd make him go with the Lufts.

And he'd started to cry.

But Sharon didn't seem to be mad that he was sick now. In that funny voice she was saying, "in . . . out . . . slowly breathe through your nose . . ." He tried to obey, in . . . out . . . "You're brave, Neil, think about when you tell all this to your friends."

Sometimes Sandy asked him about the day Mommy got hurt. Sandy said, "if anybody started to hurt my mother, I'd make them stop."

Maybe he should have been able to make the man stop. He wanted to ask Daddy about that but he never had. Daddy always told him not to think about that day anymore.

But sometimes he couldn't help it.

In . . . out . . . Sharon's hair was on his cheek. She didn't seem to mind that he was all squished against her. Why had that man brought them here? He knew who he was. He'd seen him a couple of weeks ago when Mr. Lufts took him to where the man worked.

He'd been getting a lot of bad dreams since that day. He'd started to tell Daddy about them but Mrs. Lufts came in and he felt stupid and didn't say anymore. Mrs. Lufts always asked so many dumb questions: "Did you brush your teeth? Did you keep your scarf on at lunch? Do you feel all right? Did you sleep well? Did you eat all your lunch? Did you get your feet wet? Did you hang up your clothes?" And she never let him answer really. She'd just rummage through his lunchbox to see if he'd eaten or make him open his mouth so she could look down his throat.

It was different when Mommy was there. Mrs. Lufts came in just one day every week to clean. It was after Mommy went to heaven that she and Mr. Lufts moved in upstairs and that was when everything changed.

Thinking about all that, listening to Sharon, had made the tears go away by themselves. He was scared now but it wasn't like that day when Mommy fell and he'd been alone. It wasn't like that . . .

The man . . .

His breathing got fast again, chokey. "Neil," now Sharon was rubbing her face against his. "Try to think about when we get out of here. Your dad will be so glad to see us. I bet he'll take us out. You know, I'd like to go ice-skating with you. You didn't come with us that time your dad came down to New York. And afterwards we were going to take you to the zoo next to the rink . . ."

He listened. Sharon sounded as though she really meant it. He'd been planning to go down that day, but when he told Sandy he was going, Sandy said that Sharon probably didn't want him but was just trying to make his father feel good by asking him along too.

"Your dad tells me that he wants to start taking you to football games at Princeton next fall," she said. "I used to go to Dartmouth games all the time when I was in college. Every year they played Princeton, but your dad had graduated by then. I went to a girls' college, Mount Holyoke. It was just two hours from Dartmouth and a whole bunch of us used to go up some weekends, especially in football season . . ."

Her voice sounded so funny, like a growly whisper, Neil decided.

"Lots of men bring their families to the games. Your dad's so proud of you. He says you're so brave when you get the asthma shots. He said most kids would be carrying on about having to have a shot every single week, but you never complain or cry. That's pretty brave."

It was so hard to talk. She tried to swallow.

"Neil, plan now. That's what I do when I'm scared or sick. I plan something nice that I know will be fun. Last year when I was in Lebanon—that's a country about five thousand miles from here—I was writing a story about the war they'd had, and I was staying in this ratty place, and one night I was so sick. I had flu and a fever and I was by myself and everything ached, my arms and legs, just the way they hurt now all tied up, and I made myself think of something nice that I'd do when I got home. And I remembered a painting that I wanted to buy. It was of a harbor with sailboats. And I promised myself that as soon as I got home, I'd treat myself to that picture. And I did."

Her voice was getting lower. He had to listen hard to catch every word.

"And I think we should plan a treat for you, a real treat. You know your dad says that the Lufts are really anxious to move to Florida now."

Neil felt a giant fist squeeze his chest.

"Easy Neil! Remember, in . . . out . . . breathe slowly. Well, when your dad showed me your house and I saw the Lufts' room and looked out the window, it was just like my painting. Because you can see all over the harbor and the boats and the Sound and the island. And if I were you, when the Lufts move to Florida, I'd take that room for myself. I'd put bookcases in it and shelves for your games and a desk.

The alcove is so big you could really put tracks all over it for your trains. Your dad said you loved your trains. I had them when I was little too. In fact, I've got some great Lionel trains that used to be *my* dad's. That's how old they are. I'd like you to have them."

When the Lufts move to Florida . . . when the Lufts move to Florida . . . Sharon didn't expect him to go with them. Sharon thought he should have their room.

"And I'm scared now and I'm uncomfortable and I wish I was out of here but I'm glad you're with me and I'm going to tell your dad how brave you were and how careful you were to breathe slowly and not get all chokey."

The heavy, black stone that always seemed to be lying on Neil's chest moved a little. Just the way he could wiggle a baby tooth when it got loose, Sharon's voice was moving the stone back and forth. Suddenly Neil felt desperately sleepy. His hands were tied but he could move his fingers and slide them along Sharon's arm until he found what he wanted, a piece of her sleeve that he could hold. Wrapping his fingers around the soft wool, he drifted into sleep.

The harsh, raspy breathing assumed an even pattern. Apprehensively, Sharon listened to the thick wheeze, felt the labored movement of Neil's chest. This room was so freezing, so damp, and Neil already had a cold. But at least lying this close together meant their shared body heat gave some warmth.

What time was it? They'd gotten to this place just past seven-thirty. The man . . . Foxy . . . had stayed at least a few hours with them. How long had he been gone? It must be past midnight. It was Tuesday now. Foxy had said that they'd be here till Wednesday. Where would Steve get eighty-two thousand dollars ransom money in one day? And why that crazy figure? Would he try to get in touch with her parents? It would be hard, with them living in Iran now. When Neil woke up, she'd tell him about that and about how her father was an engineer.

"Wednesday morning you and I are going away and I'll leave word where to find the boy." She explored the promise. She would have to act as though she wanted to go with him. As soon as Neil was safe and only she and the kidnapper were in the terminal, she'd start screaming. No matter what he might do to her, she'd have to take the chance.

Why in God's name had he kidnapped them? There was something about the way he looked at Neil. As though he hated him and was . . . frightened of him. But that was impossible.

Had he kept the blindfold on Neil because he was afraid Neil might recognize him? Maybe he was someone from around Carley. If that were true, how could he let Neil live? Neil had seen him when he pushed his way into the house. Neil had *stared* at him. Neil would

recognize this man if he saw him again. She was sure of it. He must realize that too. Was he planning to kill Neil as soon as he had the money?

Yes he was.

Even if he brought her out of this place, it might be too late for Neil.

A passion of fear and anger made her press closer to Neil, bend her legs against his, attempt to enfold him in the woman's arc of her body.

Tomorrow. Wednesday.

This must be the way Mrs. Thompson was feeling now, this minute. This sense of rage and fear and helplessness, this primal need to protect one's young. Neil was Steve's son and Steve had suffered so much already. Steve must be frantic. He and Mrs. Thompson were going through identical agony.

She didn't blame Mrs. Thompson for lashing out at her. She didn't mean what she said; she couldn't. Ron was guilty; there was no hope of anyone believing anything else. That was what Mrs. Thompson didn't understand; that the only possible hope of saving him was to have a massive outcry against the execution.

At least she, Sharon, had tried to help him. Steve, oh Steve, she cried silently, now do you understand? Now do you see?

She tried to rub her wrists against the wall. The cinderblocks were rough and jagged but the way the cords were tied, the knuckles and sides of her hand were taking the brunt of the contact.

When Foxy came back, she'd tell him she had to use the bathroom. He'd have to untie her. Maybe then, somehow . . .

Those pictures. He had killed those women. Only a madman would take pictures as he murdered and blow them up to that size.

He had taken *her* picture.

That bomb. Suppose someone did come near this room? If that bomb went off, she and Neil and how many others? How powerful was it?

She tried to pray, could only say over and over again, "Please, let Steve find us in time, please don't take his son from him."

That must be Mrs. Thompson's prayer. "Spare my son."

I blame you, Miss Martin . . .

Time moved agonizingly past. Her arms and legs subsided from pain into sudden numbness. Miraculously, Neil slept. Sometimes he'd moan and his breath would catch and he'd gasp, but then he'd sink back into fitful sleep.

It must be getting toward morning. The train sounds were becoming more frequent. What time did the station open? Five o'clock? It must be that now.

By eight this terminal would be swarming with people. Suppose that bomb went off?

Neil stirred restlessly. He muttered something. She couldn't make it out. He was waking up.

Neil tried to open his eyes and could not. He had to go to the bathroom. His arms and legs hurt. It was hard to breathe. Then he remembered what had happened. He'd run to the door and said, "Oh, that's all right," and opened it. Why had he said that?

He remembered.

He felt the rock moving back and forth in his chest. He felt Sharon's breath on his face. There was a far-off train sound.

A train sound.

And Mommy. He'd run downstairs.

And the man let Mommy drop and turned to him.

And then the man was bending over Mommy, looking all sweaty and scared.

No.

The man who pushed the door in last night, who stood over him and looked down at him; he'd done that before.

He'd come at him. He'd let Mommy drop and come at him. He'd put his hands out and looked right down at him.

And something happened.

The chimes. The chimes from the front door.

The man had run away. Neil had watched him run away.

That was why he couldn't stop dreaming about that day. Because of the part he forgot . . . the scary part when the man came to him and had his hands out and reached down to him.

The man . . .

The man who'd been talking to Mr. Lufts.

And last night had come pushing into the house and stood over him.

"Sharon," Neil's voice was muffled and hoarse as he struggled to speak through the thick wheeze . . .

"Yes, Neil. I'm here."

"Sharon, that man, the bad man who tied us up . . ."

"Yes, dear, don't be afraid, I'll take care of you."

"Sharon, that's the man who killed my Mommy."

~~~~ *CHAPTER 25*

The room. Lally *had* to go to her room. It didn't matter how cold it was. Newspapers between her two blankets would keep her warm enough. She missed it so much. The Tenth Avenue flop she and Rosie and some of the others had slept in most of the winter was too crowded. She needed her alone time. She needed her place to dream.

Years ago when she was young, after she read the Louella Parsons and Hedda Hopper columns, Lally would lull herself to sleep pretending that instead of being a homely spinster schoolteacher, she was a movie star coming into Grand Central Station with all the reporters and photographers waiting.

Sometimes she'd be in white fox when she stepped off the *Twentieth Century Limited;* or she'd be wearing a tailored silk suit, holding sable skins, and her secretary would be carrying the dressing case with her jewels.

Once she fantasized that she was already in an evening gown because she was going directly to the premiere of her movie on Broadway, wearing that ball gown Ginger Rogers wore in *Top Hat.*

After a while the dreams faded and she became used to life as it was; dreary, monotonous, lonely. But when she arrived in New York and began to spend all her time in Grand Central, it was as though she really was remembering her heyday as a star; not pretending at all.

Then when Rusty gave her the key to the room and she could sleep nestled in her station, listening to the faint sound of her trains coming and going, it made everything perfect.

At 8:30 Tuesday morning, armed with her shopping bags, she was heading toward the lower terminal to the Mount Vernon track. Her plan was to mosey down the ramp with the people who were taking the 8:50 and then slip around to her room. On the way she stopped at the Nedicks in the corridor leading from the Biltmore and ordered coffee and donuts. She had already finished the *Times* and *News,* which she had gotten out of a receptacle.

The man ahead of her at the takeout counter looked vaguely familiar. Why, he was the one who spoiled her plans last night by going down to the Mount Vernon platform with the girl in the gray coat! Resentfully, she heard him order two coffees and rolls and milk. With hostile eyes she watched him pay his bill and pick up his package. She wondered if he worked around here. Somehow she didn't think so.

After leaving Nedicks, she deliberately dawdled through the terminal so the cops who knew her wouldn't think she was doing anything out of the ordinary. But at last she was at the ramp to the Mount Vernon track. The train was loading. People were hurrying now. Delighted, Lally fell into step with them, moving down the platform. As the others rushed into the train, she slipped around the last car and turned right. In an instant she'd be out of sight.

And then she saw him. The man who'd just bought the coffee and milk and rolls. The man who'd come down here last night. His back was to her. He was hurrying now, disappearing into the gloom of the throbbing depths of the terminal.

There was only one place where he could be going.

Her room.

He had found it! That was why he went down on the platform last night. He wasn't waiting for the train. He had gone to her room with the girl.

And he had two coffees and milk and four rolls. So the girl must be there now.

Bitter, disappointed tears welled up in Lally's eyes. They had taken over her room! Then her lifelong ability to cope rescued her. She could handle this. She'd get rid of them! She'd watch and when she was sure he was out, she'd go into the room and warn the girl that the cops knew they were there and were coming to arrest them. That'd scare her off fast enough. He was a mean-looking one, but the girl wasn't the kind to be hanging around stations. Probably thought it was some kind of game being there. She'd probably clear out fast and take him with her.

Grimly satisfied at the prospect of tricking the interlopers, Lally turned around and headed for the upstairs waiting room. Her imagination leaped to the girl who was probably right now lying on *her* cot waiting for her boyfriend to bring in breakfast. "Don't get too comfortable in there, missy," she thought, "you're going to have company real soon."

~~~ *CHAPTER 26*

Steve, Hugh, the Lufts and agent Hank Lamont sat at the dining-room table. Dora Lufts had just brought a pot of coffee and freshly baked corn muffins to the table. Steve looked at them without interest. His chin was resting on his hand. Just the other night Neil had said to him. "You're always telling me not to put my elbows on the table and you always sit like that, Daddy."

He blinked away the thought. No use. No use. Keep concentrating on what could be done. Carefully, he studied Bill Lufts. Undoubtedly Bill had consoled himself with booze during the night. His eyes were blood-shot and his hands were shaking.

They had just heard the nineteen-word tape of the first phonecall. Muffled, indistinct, it was impossible to recognize the voice as familiar. Hugh played it three times, then snapped it off. "All right. We'll take it over to Mrs. Perry, as soon as Mr. Perry calls us, and see what she says about it. Now it's very, very important that we get a few things straight."

He consulted the list in front of him. "First, there'll be an agent here 'round the clock till this is settled. I think the man who calls himself Foxy is too clever to call this phone or the Perrys'. He'll guess that we have taps on them. But there's always the chance . . .

"Mr. Peterson has to go down to New York, so if the phone rings, Mrs. Lufts, you must answer it immediately. Agent Lamont will be on the extension and we'll be recording it as well. But if the abductor does call, you must not get rattled. You must try to keep him on the phone as long as possible. Can you do that?"

"I'll try," Dora quavered.

"What about Neil's school? Did you phone and report him ill?"

"Yes. Right at eight-thirty, just as you told me."

"Fine." Hugh turned to Steve. "Did you reach your office, Mr. Peterson?"

"Yes. The publisher had suggested I take Neil away for a few days until after the Thompson execution tomorrow. I left word I was doing that."

Hugh turned to Bill Lufts. "Mr. Lufts, I'd like you to stay right here in the house for today at least. Would anyone find that unusual?"

His wife laughed mirthlessly. "Only the regulars at the Mill Tavern," she said.

"All right, thank you both." Hugh's tone dismissed the Lufts. They got up and went into the kitchen, partially closing the door behind them.

Hugh leaned over and closed it with a decided thud. He raised one eyebrow to Steve. "I don't think the Lufts miss very much of what's said in this house, Mr. Peterson," he commented.

Steve shrugged. "I know. But ever since Bill retired the first of the year, they've really been staying on as a favor to me. They're very anxious to get to Florida."

"You said they've been here two years?"

"A little longer than that. Dora was our cleaning woman. She came in one day a week since before Neil was born. Our other house was only six blocks from here, you know. They were saving money for their retirement. When Nina was killed we'd just moved in here and I had to have someone to take care of Neil. I suggested that they take that large third-floor room. That way they could save the overhead they'd been paying, and I paid Dora as much as she was getting for all her cleaning jobs."

"How has it worked out?"

"Reasonably well. They're both very fond of Neil and she looks after him very carefully, too carefully maybe. She's always fussing over him. But since Bill's been hanging around with nothing to do, he's been into a lot of drinking. Frankly, I'll be glad when they do make the move."

"What's been holding them back?" Hugh asked sharply. "Money?"

"No. I don't think so. Dora would love to see me remarried so that Neil would have a mother again. Dora's really an awfully good soul."

"And you've been getting close to that with Sharon Martin?"

Steve's smile was wintry. "I hope so." Restlessly, he stood up and walked to the window. The snow was falling again, effortlessly, noiselessly. It seemed to him that he had as much control over his life as one of those snowflakes had over its ultimate destination . . . to fall, land on shrub or grass or street, to melt or freeze on contact, to be swept away, driven over, crunched down by boots.

He was getting fanciful, lightheaded. Deliberately he pulled his mind back to the present. He could not be helpless, waiting here immobilized. He had to *do* something.

"I'll get the bankbook and start down to New York," he told Hugh.

"Just a minute, Mr. Peterson. There are a few things we need to discuss."

Steve waited.

"What happens if you don't get a tape of your son and Sharon?"

"He *promised* . . ."

"He may not be able to deliver. How would he get it to you, assuming he makes it? The point is, are you prepared to pay the money without the proof?"

Steve considered. "Yes. I won't take the chance of antagonizing him. Maybe he'll leave a tape or cassette somewhere expecting it to be found, and then if I don't follow through . . ."

"All right. We'll face that later. If it hasn't come by two A.M. when he calls you at the Fifty-ninth Street payphone, you can consider stalling. Tell him you didn't get it. If he claims he left it somewhere, it's easy enough to pick it up.

"Now the next consideration. Do you want to give him real cash? We could get counterfeit money that would be easy to trace."

"I simply won't take that chance. The money in the trust is for Neil's education. If anything happens to him . . ."

"All right. So you'll get the money from your account and take it down to the Federal Reserve Bank. Get a cashier's check. Our men will be there photographing the ransom bills. That way at least we'll have some record."

Steve interrupted. "I don't want the money marked."

"I'm not talking about *marking* it. There's no way the abductor can possibly know if we've *photographed* it. But that will take time. Eighty-two thousand dollars in tens, twenties and fifties is a lot of bills to handle."

"I know."

"Mr. Peterson, there are several precautions I'm going to urge you to take. One, let us rig cameras into your car. That way we may have some kind of lead to follow after you make contact with the abductor. We may be able to get a picture of him or pick up the license number of the car he's driving. We'd also like to install a beeper device in your car so that we can follow you from a distance. I promise you they'll be impossible to detect. Last, and this is entirely up to you, we'd like to conceal an electronic tracer in the suitcase with the money."

"Suppose it's found. The abductor will know I brought you in."

"Suppose you *don't* put it in and you don't hear another word. You've paid the money and you don't have your child or Sharon. Believe me, Mr. Peterson, our first concern is to get them back safely. After that we'll pull out all the stops to find the perpetrators. But it's up to you."

"What would you do if it were your son and your . . . wife?"

"Mr. Peterson, we're not dealing with honorable people. It's not as simple as pay the money and you get them back. Maybe they'll release them. *Maybe.* But maybe they'll just abandon them somewhere unable to free themselves. That has to be considered. At least the area may be narrowed down if we can follow the kidnapper's trail electronically."

Steve shrugged helplessly. "Do what you have to. I'll take Bill's car to New York."

"No. I'd like to suggest that you take your own car and park it in the lot near the station as usual. It's very possible your movements are being watched. We'll have a loose tail on you, an agent following you from a distance. Leave your keys on the floor. We'll pick the car up and get the equipment installed and have it there when you come back. Now here's where you go with the money . . ."

Steve caught the 10:40 train to Grand Central Station. It was ten minutes behind schedule and he arrived at the terminal at 11:50. Electing to walk up Park Avenue, he carried a large, empty suitcase in his hand.

His sense of futility and misery deepened as he trudged the blocks between the terminal and Fifty-first Street. On this, the second day of the snowstorm, New Yorkers, exhibiting their customary resiliency, were out on the streets as usual. There was even a buoyancy about the way they stepped over icy curbs, maneuvered around drifts. Yesterday morning he and Sharon had stood in the falling snow a few blocks from here and he'd held her face in his hands and kissed her goodbye. Her lips had been unresponsive just as he'd been unresponsive when Nina kissed him goodbye that last day.

He arrived at the bank. The news that he wanted to withdraw all but two hundred dollars from Neil's account was greeted with a lifted eyebrow. The teller left her cage and consulted with a senior vice-president, who hurried over to Steve.

"Mr. Peterson," he asked, "is there any problem?"

"No, Mr. Strauss. I simply wish to make a withdrawal."

"I'll have to ask you to fill out state and federal forms. It's required for any withdrawal that large. I hope there has been no dissatisfaction with our handling of your son's account."

Steve struggled to keep his tone and expression even. "None at all."

"Very well." The vice-president's tone became coolly professional. "You can fill out the necessary forms at my desk. Follow me, please."

Mechanically, Steve scrawled the required information. By the time he was finished, the teller had brought the cashier's check to the desk.

Mr. Strauss quickly signed it, handed it to him and stood up. The man's face had become thoughtful. "I don't mean to intrude, but there isn't any trouble, is there, Mr. Peterson? Perhaps something we can help with?"

Steve stood up. "No, no, thank you, Mr. Strauss." To his own ears, he sounded strained, unconvincing.

"I hope not. We value you very much, as a client of this bank and, I hope, as a friend. If there *is* a problem and if we can help, please give us the chance." He held out his hand.

Steve grasped it. "You're very kind but it's quite all right, I assure you."

Carrying the suitcase, he went out, hailed a cab and directed it to the Federal Reserve Bank. There he was taken to a room where grim-faced FBI agents were busily counting and photographing the money he would exchange for the check he was carrying. Bleakly he watched them.

"The king was in the counting house, counting up his money." The nursery rhyme ran through his head. Nina used to singsong it to Neil when she was getting him ready for bed.

He returned to Grand Central just in time to miss the 3:05 train. The next train wouldn't leave for an hour. He called home. Dora answered and agent Lamont spoke from the extension. No further news. No sign of a cassette. Hugh Taylor would be back by the time he arrived.

The prospect of the hour to kill appalled Steve. His head was aching; a slow, burning ache that began in the center of his forehead and traveled back on each side like an ever tightening vise. He realized he'd eaten nothing since yesterday's lunch.

The Oyster Bar. He'd go down there and order a plate of oyster stew and a drink. He passed the phone he'd used last night when he tried to call Sharon. That had been the beginning of this nightmare. When he didn't get an answer, he'd known that something was wrong. That was only twenty hours ago. It seemed a lifetime.

Twenty hours. Where were Sharon and Neil? Had they been given anything to eat? It was so cold out. Were they in a place with heat? If there was any way possible, Sharon would take care of Neil, he knew that. Suppose Sharon had answered the phone when he'd called last night. Suppose the three of them had spent the evening together as they'd planned. After Neil went to bed, he was going to say, "You won't be getting much, Sharon. You probably could do a lot better if you waited, but don't wait. Marry me. We're good together."

She probably would have turned him down. She despised his position on capital punishment. Well, he'd been sure enough of it, relentless about it, positive he was right.

Was this the way Ronald Thompson's mother was feeling right this minute? Even when it was over for that boy, she'd go on suffering the rest of her life.

As he would, if anything happened to Sharon and Neil.

The pace of this terminal was beginning to quicken. Executives leaving early to avoid the commuter rush walked briskly to the New Haven trains that would take them to Westchester and Connecticut. Women in for a day of shopping crossed the terminal, consulting timetables, anxious to be home in time to start dinner.

Steve descended the stairs to the lower level and went into the Oyster Bar. It was nearly empty. The lunch rush was long since over. It was too early for the cocktail and dinner crowd. He sat at the bar and ordered, carefully keeping the suitcase right under his foot.

Last month he and Sharon had met here for lunch. She'd been exhilarated because of the overwhelming response to her campaign to have Thompson's sentence commuted to life imprisonment. "We're going to make it, Steve," she said confidently. She'd been so happy; she cared so much. She'd talked about her forthcoming trip to raise more support.

"I'll miss you," he'd said.

"I'll miss you, too."

I love you, Sharon. I love you, Sharon. I love you, Sharon. Had he said it then?

He gulped the martini the bartender put in front of him.

He sat in the Oyster Bar, the steaming, bubbling stew untouched, until at five minutes of four he paid his bill and went to the upper terminal and the Carley train. He didn't notice that as he made his way to the smoking car, a man seated in the rear of the car he entered, buried his face behind a newspaper. It was only after he had passed that the newspaper was lowered slightly and glittering eyes followed his progress through the coach with the heavy suitcase.

That same passenger got off at Carley, but carefully waited on the platform until Steve had entered the parking lot and driven away in the car which now had powerful cameras hidden in the headlights and behind the rearview mirror.

Glenda Perry slept until one o'clock. It was the sound of Marian's car pulling out of the driveway that brought her to full wakefulness. Before she opened her eyes she lay perfectly still, waiting. But the pain that often accompanied that first stirring did not come. It had been so bad during the night, worse than she had let on to Roger. Except he probably guessed, and she knew the doctor was concerned about the cardiogram.

She was *not* going to the hospital. They'd sedate her so much there that she'd be useless. She wouldn't let it happen. She knew why the pains had been so frequent lately. It was the Thompson boy. He was so young and her testimony had helped condemn him.

"He knocked you down, Mrs. Perry . . ."

"Yes, he was running from the house."

"It was dark, Mrs. Perry. Can you be sure it wasn't somebody else running away?"

"Positive. He hesitated in the doorway before he collided into me. The kitchen light was on."

And now Neil and Sharon. Oh God, let me remember. She bit her lip . . . a flicker of pain . . . no, don't get upset. That won't do any good. For God sake, *think*. She slipped a nitro under her tongue. That would ward off the pain before it became acute. Foxy. The way he said it. What was the association? It wasn't that long ago, either.

The door opened a crack and she saw Roger looking in at her. "It's all right, dear, I'm awake."

"How do you feel?" He hurried over to the bed, touched her hand.

"Not bad. How long have I been asleep?"

"Over four hours."

"Whose car just left?"

"That was Mrs. Vogler."

"Oh, I forgot. What did she do?"

"She seemed to keep herself pretty busy in the kitchen. Was on the stepladder taking things from the top shelves."

"Thank heaven. I've been afraid to stretch up there and they're so dusty. Roger, what happened? Did Steve talk to . . . Foxy?"

Roger explained—". . . so they only have a few words. Are you up to listening to them?"

"Yes."

Fifteen minutes later, propped up on pillows, a cup of tea in her hand, Glenda watched Hugh Taylor enter her bedroom.

"This is good of you, Mrs. Perry. I understand that it's a strain for you."

She waved away his concern. "Mr. Taylor, I'm just ashamed I've wasted the whole morning. Please turn that on."

She listened intently as Hugh ran the cassette.

"Oh, it's so low. It's impossible . . ."

The tense expectancy slid from Hugh's face. His tone was emotionless as he said, "Well, thank you very much for listening, Mrs. Perry. We're going to analyze this for voice pattern. It isn't admissible evidence, but when we get the abductor it may help to confirm the identification." He picked up the recorder.

"No . . . wait!" Glenda put her hand on the machine.

"Is this your only record of the call?"

"No. We ran both a tape and cassette during the wiretap."

"Will you leave this with me?"

"Why?"

"Because I *know* the person I spoke to last night. I know him. I'm going to try now to retrace every single thing I've done in the last few weeks. Maybe something will come to me. And I'd like to be able to hear that tape again."

"Mrs. Perry, if you could only remember . . ." Hugh bit his lip as Roger Perry shot a warning glance at him. Quickly he left the room, followed by Roger.

When they were downstairs, Roger asked, "Why did you have me keep Mrs. Vogler here today? Surely you don't suspect . . . ?"

"We can't let any possibility pass. But she seems all right. Good character, good family situation, well-liked. It's just coincidence that she talked about Neil this morning. And anyhow, she's got the best alibi of anyone last night and so does her husband."

"Why is that?"

"She was seen by the cashier both entering and leaving the movie. Her husband was seen by his neighbors at home with their kids. And shortly after seven o'clock they were in the police station reporting a stolen car."

"Oh yes. She did mention that. Lucky she got it back."

"Yeah. She gets a lousy eight-year-old car back and we haven't got a trace of two kidnap victims. Mr. Perry, what *is* your impression of Sharon Martin? Do you think she's capable of planning this?"

Roger considered. "Every instinct says no."

"How do you size up her relationship with Mr. Peterson?"

Roger thought of the last time Sharon and Steve had been over. She'd seemed a little depressed and Glenda asked her if anything was wrong. Steve had gone into the kitchen for ice and she'd said, "Oh, it's just that Neil shuts me out so." Then when Steve came back, he'd ruffled her hair as he passed her. Roger remembered the expression on both their faces. "I think they were . . . are . . . very much in love, more than either one of them realizes. I think Sharon has been troubled by Neil's rejection, and of course Steve is worried about it too. Then he's been pretty strapped financially. He sank everything he had into *Events.* I'm sure it will pay off, but that's had him concerned. He's said as much to me."

"And there was the Thompson execution."

"Yes. Glenda and I both hoped that Sharon would succeed in saving him. Glenda is heartsick over her role in that case."

"Did Sharon want Mr. Peterson to intercede with the Governor?"

"I think she realized that he wouldn't do it and that the Governor would only resent a purely emotional appeal. Don't forget, she's been bitterly criticized for the two stays she's already granted Thompson."

"Mr. Perry, what do you think of the Lufts? Is it possible that they might be part of this? They're trying to save money; they've had access to your private number. They could have known about the trust fund."

Roger shook his head. "Not a chance. If Dora ever picks up anything for Glenda at the store, she spends twenty minutes making sure she's given her the exact change. He's like that too. Sometimes he takes my car to be serviced and always brags about how much he saves me. Neither one of them has the capacity to be anything except painfully honest."

"Okay. I know you'll call us at the Peterson's immediately if Mrs. Perry has anything to tell us."

Hank Lamont was waiting for Hugh. Something in his manner telegraphed the fact that he had news. Hugh didn't waste time on preliminaries. "What have you got?"

"Mrs. Thompson . . ."

"What about her?"

"Last night. She talked to Sharon Martin!"

"She *what?*"

"The Thompson kid told us. Don and Stan interviewed him in his cell. Said there'd been some threats against the Peterson boy and warned him that if his friends were pulling something, we'd better get their names before they got into deep trouble."

"They didn't admit Neil and Sharon were kidnapped?"

"Of course not."

"What did he say?"

"He's clean. The only visitors he's had in the last year are his mother, his lawyer and the parish priest. His closest friends from high school are in college now. He gave us their names. Everyone of them is away. But he did tell us that Sharon called his mother."

"Did they talk to the mother?"

"Yes. She's staying at a motel near the prison. They found her."

"In the motel?"

"No, in church. God help her, Hugh, she's just kneeling there praying. Won't believe the kid's going to be executed tomorrow. Won't believe it. She says Sharon called her a few minutes before six. Wanted to know if she could do anything. Admitted she blew up at her, blamed her for running around the country saying the boy is guilty. Threatened that she wouldn't know what she'd do to Sharon if the boy dies. What do you make of it?"

"Let's try this," Hugh said. "Sharon Martin is upset by the phonecall, maybe even thinks there's some validity in what the mother said. She's desperate and calls someone to come for her and the boy. She's planning a grandstand stunt, make it look like a bona fide kidnapping and then make Neil a hostage for Thompson's life."

"It's a possibility," Hank said.

Hugh's face hardened. "I think it's more than a possibility. I think that poor guy, Peterson, is having his guts torn out and Mrs. Perry is verging on a coronary because Sharon Martin thinks she can manipulate justice."

"What do we do now?"

"Continue to treat this as a real snatch. And dig up everything we can about Sharon Martin's associates, particularly anyone she knows in this area. If only Mrs. Perry can remember where she heard that voice, we'll crack this wide open."

In her room, Glenda was playing the cassette over and over. ("Peterson? In ten minutes I'll call you at the payphone of the service station just past exit twenty-one.") Helplessly, she shook her head and turned off the machine. That wasn't the way to do it. Start retracing this last couple of weeks. *But what was it about that cassette?*

Yesterday she hadn't gone out at all. She'd talked on the phone to the drugstore, and to Agnes and then to Julie about the hospital benefit. Chip and Maria had called from California and put the baby on. That was the last time she was on the phone yesterday until Foxy called.

Sunday she and Roger drove to New York right after church and had brunch in the Pierre and went to Carnegie Hall to hear Serkin. She hadn't spoken to anyone on the phone at all.

Saturday, she'd been at the decorator's about the slipcovers. And she'd had her hair done, or was that Friday? She shook her head impatiently. This wasn't the way to go about it at all. Getting out of bed, she walked slowly over to her desk and reached for her appointment book.

She'd ask Roger to bring up the calender from the kitchen wall too. Sometimes she jotted notes on it. And her charge slips. She kept them together. They were all dated. They'd help her to remember where she'd stopped. And her checkbook. She pulled the checkbook out of a compartment, the charge slips out of a drawer.

Carrying the items, she got back into bed, sighing as a constriction began in her chest and mounted into sharp pain. As she reached for a nitroglycerin pill she pushed the button of the recorder and began running the cassette. Once again, the muffled, throaty whisper filled her ears. "Peterson? In ten minutes I'll call you at the payphone of the service station just past exit twenty-one."

⤳ CHAPTER 28

W alking back from the phonebooth, he thought about the cassette. After he recorded Sharon and the boy, should he do it? Why not?

He went directly to Grand Central. Better to go to them while there was still some commuter activity. Those guards had a sixth sense about people who didn't belong in the terminal.

Sharon and the kid probably hadn't had any dinner last night. They'd be hungry. He didn't want her to be hungry. But she probably wouldn't eat if he didn't feed the boy too. Thinking of the boy always made him nervous. A couple of weeks ago, he'd almost panicked when he'd looked out and seen the boy staring at him from the car. Just the way he did in the dream, those round brown eyes, pupils so wide they looked black, accusing, always accusing.

Tomorrow it would be all over. He'd have to buy Sharon a ticket on the plane. He didn't have enough money now but after tonight he would. He could make a reservation. But what name would he use? He'd have to make up a name for her.

Yesterday on the *Today* show, she'd been introduced as the author and columnist. She was very well known and very popular. That's why it was so wonderful that she was so much in love with him.

She was very well known.

She'd been on the *Today* show.

Lots of people would recognize her.

Frowning, he stopped short, was jostled by the woman hurrying along behind him. He glowered at her and she said, "Oh, excuse me," and hurried past him down the street. He softened. She hadn't meant to be rude. In fact, she had smiled at him, really smiled at him. Lots of women would smile at him when they knew how wealthy he was.

Slowly he resumed the walk along Lexington Avenue. Buses had ground the fallen snow into filthy slush. Even that was freezing except what was directly in the path of buses and cars. He wished he were going to the Biltmore. That room was so comfortable. He'd never been in a place quite like that.

He'd stay with Sharon and the child until this afternoon. Then he'd take the train up to Carley. He'd go over to his place and see if there were any messages. No point in having people wondering why he wasn't around. He struggled to think of where he could leave the cassette. Maybe Peterson wouldn't pay if he didn't get it.

He had to have the money. It was too dangerous for him to stay in Fairfield County now. And he had a good reason to leave. Everyone expected him to leave.

"Any unexpected departures in this area?" the cops might start asking.

"Him? No. He's been complaining about losing the place; begged the old man to renew his lease."

But that was before the last two girls. "The C.B. Murderer," the papers were calling him. If they only knew . . .

He had even gone to the Callahan funeral service. The funeral service!

Suddenly he knew where to leave the cassette, where he could be sure it would be found that evening and delivered.

Satisfied, he walked briskly into Nedicks, ordered coffee, milk and rolls. He'd be staying a while so they might as well have some food right away and some later before he left. He didn't want Sharon to think he was unkind.

When he left the area of the Mount Vernon track he had an odd sense of being watched. His instinct was very good about that. He stopped and listened. He thought he heard something and tiptoed back. But it was just one of those shopping bag ladies making her way up the ramp to the terminal. She'd probably been sleeping on the platform.

With infinite care he released the sliver of wire that was taped to the door of the room. Gingerly, he took out his key and inserted it in the lock. Opening the door a hairsbreadth at a time to keep from jerking the wire, he slipped into the room and closed the door.

He switched on the fluorescent lights and grunted in satisfaction. Sharon and the boy were just as he left them. The boy couldn't see him because of the blindfold of course, but behind him, Sharon lifted her

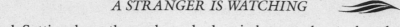

head. Setting down the package, he hurried over to her and yanked the gag from her mouth.

"It wasn't very tight this time," he told her. He thought that he'd seen a kind of reproach in her eyes.

"No." She was very nervous, nervous in a different way. Her eyes were very scared now. He didn't want her to be scared of him.

"Are you afraid, Sharon?" His voice was horribly gentle.

"Oh, no . . . not at all."

"I brought you some food."

"Oh, I'm glad, but won't you please take the gag off Neil? And please, won't you untie us, even just our hands, like before?"

His eyes narrowed. There was something different about her. "Certainly, Sharon." He nuzzled his nose against her face. His fingers were very strong. He could untie the knots very quickly. In a minute her hands were free and he reached for the boy.

The child shrank against Sharon. "It's all right, Neil," she said, "remember what we talked about."

"What did you talk about, Sharon?"

"Just that Neil's dad would give you the money you want and that tomorrow you'd tell his dad where to find him. I said that I was going away with you but that his dad would be here very soon after we left. Isn't that right?"

The voice was thoughtful, the glittering eyes speculative. "You're sure you want to go, Sharon?"

"Oh yes, very much. I . . . I like you, Foxy."

"I brought some rolls and coffee and some milk for the boy."

"That's very nice of you." She was flexing her fingers. He watched as she began to rub Neil's wrists, as she smoothed his hair back from his forehead. The way she was pressing the boy's hands, like a signal, like a secret pact.

He pulled over the orange crate and deposited the bag on it. He gave Sharon a container of coffee.

"Thank you." She put the container down without sipping from it. "Where is Neil's milk?"

He handed it to her, watched as she put it in Neil's hands. "There it is; hold onto it, Neil. Drink slowly." The boy's raspy breathing was irritating, worrisome, evoked memories.

He brought out the rolls. He'd had them thickly buttered the way he liked them. Sharon broke off a piece of one of them and handed it to the boy. "Here, Neil, it's a roll." Her voice was soothing. It was like she and the boy were in a conspiracy against him. Sullenly, he watched them eat. He gulped his own coffee, barely tasting it. They both ate one roll, finished the coffee and milk.

He hadn't taken his coat off. It was so cold in here and anyhow he didn't want to take the chance of getting his new suit dirty. He cleared off the orange crate, putting the bag with the remaining rolls on the floor, sat down on the crate and stared at them.

When they were finished eating, Sharon pulled Neil over on her lap. The boy's breathing was loud and strained. The sound irritated Foxy, jangled his nerves. Sharon didn't look at him at all. She just kept rubbing the boy's back, talking to him softly, telling him to try to sleep. Foxy watched as she kissed Neil's forehead, then pressed his head down on her shoulder.

She was a very young girl, Foxy thought, and probably was just trying to be nice to the boy. Maybe he should get rid of the boy right now and let her start being nice like that to him. The expression in his eyes changed, a little smile played on his lips as he began thinking about the ways Sharon could be nice to him. Anticipation flooded his body with warmth. He realized that Sharon was staring at him now and he watched as her arms tightened around the boy. He wanted to have those arms around *him*.

He started to get up to go over to the cot. His foot struck the recorder. The recorder! The cassette Peterson had demanded. It was too soon to get rid of the boy. Disappointed and angry, he sat down again. "You're going to make a recording for Peterson now," he told Sharon.

"A recording?" Sharon's voice was quick and nervous. A second ago she'd have sworn that he was planning to do something to them; there was something about the way he was looking at them, the expression on his face. She tried to think. Was there a chance, was there any way? Ever since Neil had told her that this man murdered his mother, she'd been even more frantic to find a way to get out of here. Tomorrow might be too late for Ronald Thompson as well as for Neil. She didn't know what time Foxy was planning to come for her. *If* he came for her. He was cunning. He'd surely realize that sooner or later she'd be recognized. The memory of her quest to save Ronald tortured and mocked her. His mother had been right. By insisting on his guilt, she had helped condemn him. Nothing mattered except to save Neil's life, to save Ronald's life. Whatever happened to her, she deserved. And she had been the one to tell Steve *he* was trying to play God.

Foxy had a gun. It was in the pocket of his coat. If she could get him to put his arms around her, she could reach for it.

If she had a chance, could she kill him?

She looked down at Neil, thought of the condemned boy in the prison cell. Yes, she could kill this man.

She watched as he expertly handled the recorder, inserted the cassette. It was a TWX cassette, the most common kind. They'd never be able to trace it. He pulled the crate over to the cot.

"Here, Sharon, you read this." He had a message written down. "Steve, pay the ransom if you want us back. The money must be in tens, twenties and fifties. Eighty-two thousand dollars. Don't fail to have it; don't let it be marked. Go to the phonebooth at Fifty-ninth and Lexington at two A.M. in your car. Be alone. Don't call the police."

She looked up at him. "Can I add anything? I mean, we had a quarrel. We broke off. Maybe, maybe he wouldn't pay money for me, if I don't apologize. You see, he's very stubborn. Maybe he'll only pay half the money, for Neil, because he knows I don't love him. But we'll need all the money, won't we?"

"What do you want to say, Sharon?" Was he toying with her? Did he believe her?

"Just an apology, that's all." She tried to smile. She slid Neil off her lap, reached over and stroked Foxy's hand.

"No tricks, Sharon."

"Why would I trick you? What do you want Neil to say?"

"Just that he wants to come home. Nothing else." His finger was poised over the "record" button. "When I push this down, start talking. The mike is built in."

She swallowed, waited until the cassette began to wind. "Steve . . ." she read the message slowly, trying to buy time, trying to phrase what she would say next. She finished reading the message ". . . don't call the police." She paused.

He was looking at her intently.

"Steve," she had to begin, "Steve, Neil is going to talk to you now. But first, I was wrong, I hope you'll forgive me . . ." The recorder clicked off. She was about to say, "I made a terrible mistake . . ."

"That's enough, Sharon. That's enough apology." He pointed at Neil. She put her arm around the child.

"All right, Neil, now talk to your dad."

The wheezing was accentuated by his effort to speak. "Dad, I'm all right. Sharon is taking care of me. But Mommy wouldn't want me to be here, Dad."

The recorder stopped. *Neil had tried to give Steve a message,* had tried to connect their kidnapping to his mother's death.

The man rewound the cassette, played it back. He smiled at Sharon. "Very nice. I'd pay to get you two back if I was Peterson."

"That's good. I'm glad if you're satisfied." Was he deliberately baiting her?

"Sharon." Neil groped for her sleeve, tugged it. "I have to . . ."

"You want to go to the john, kid?" Foxy's voice was matter of fact. "Guess you have to by now." He went over to Neil, picked him up and walked into the toilet with him, closing the door. Sharon froze, waiting, but almost immediately he was back, carrying Neil under his arm. She

noticed that he had Neil's face turned away from him, almost as though he were afraid that Neil could see through the blindfold. He dropped Neil on the cot. The boy was trembling. "Sharon."

"I'm here." She moved her hand against his back.

"Sharon, you want to?" The captor nodded his head toward the toilet. "Yes."

He took her by the arm and half-carried her into the musty cubby-hole. The cords bit through her legs and ankles making her wince with pain. "There's a bolt up there, Sharon," he said. "I'll even let you put it on, if you want while you're here, 'cause otherwise the door don't stay shut. But you better come right out." His hand caressed her cheek. "Because if you don't and I get mad, the boy gets it now." He stepped out, pulling the door closed behind him.

Quickly she slid the bolt and looked around. In the darkness inside the small compartment, she ran her hands down the walls, along the tank. Maybe there was something here, some piece of piping, something sharp. She felt along the floor.

"Hurry up, Sharon."

"All right."

When she started to open the door, the handle felt loose in her hand. Instantly she tried to twist it completely around. Maybe if she could get it off, she could slip it in the deep pocket of her skirt. It might have a sharp edge. But she couldn't wrest it free.

"Come out of there!" His voice was edgy now. Quickly she opened the door, tried to hobble out, stumbled, grabbed the metal frame of the doorway. He came over to her. Deliberately she put her arms around his neck. Forcing back revulsion, she kissed his cheek, his lips. His arms tightened. She felt the sudden racing of his heart. Oh, God, please . . .

She slid her arms down around his shoulders, his back. Her fingers made soft, petting motions on his neck. Her right hand moved forward, slipped into his coat pocket, felt steel.

He shoved her backward. She slammed onto the concrete floor, her tightly bound legs buckling under her. Blinding, shocking pain shot through her right ankle.

"You're like the rest, Sharon," he screamed. He was standing over her. From the floor, through the waves of pain that were causing the food she'd just eaten to gag her, she could see him. His face seemed disembodied as he leaned over her. The pulse under his eye was throbbing. Red spots accentuated the sharp lines of his cheeks. His eyes were black narrow pits spewing over with rage. "You bitch," he said, "you bitch."

Yanking her up, he threw her on the cot and slapped her arms behind her. Pain made great foggy blackness close over her. "My ankle." Was that her voice?

"Sharon, Sharon, what happened?" Neil's voice was terrified.

With a tremendous effort, she bit back a moan. "I fell."

"Like all the others ... pretending ... but worse ... trying to trick me. I could tell you were fooling, lying, I could tell ..." She felt hands close on her throat. Oh God! Powerful fingers were pressing into her neck ... God ... help ...

"No." The pressure vanished. Her neck fell backward.

"Sharon, Sharon," Neil was crying, his voice agitated choking.

Gulping in air, she moved her face to his. Her eyelids felt so heavy. She forced them open. Foxy was at the rusty sink, splashing water in his face. The water must be freezing. Fearfully, she watched. He was trying to calm himself. He'd been about to kill her. What stopped him? Maybe he was afraid he'd still need her.

She bit her lip against the pain. There was no way out, no way. Tomorrow when he got the money he'd kill her and Neil. And Ronald Thompson would die for a crime he didn't commit. She and Neil were the only ones who could prove his innocence. Her ankle was swelling, pressing out against the leather boot. The cords were biting into it. Oh, God, please. Pain made her shiver even while it brought perspiration to her face.

She watched as he dried his face with a handkerchief. He came over and methodically retied Neil's hands, put tight gags on both of them. He adjusted the wire from the suitcase to the door. "I'm leaving, Sharon," he said. "I'll be back tomorrow. I'll be back just once more ..."

He hadn't planned to leave this early but he knew if he stayed any longer, he'd kill her. And he might need her again. They might demand more proof that she and the boy were alive. He had to have the money. He couldn't take the chance of killing her yet.

There was a train coming in from Mount Vernon at eleven o'clock. He'd just have to wait a few minutes before it arrived. He stayed near the entrance to the tunnel. It was dark there.

Footsteps. He shrank against the wall, peered out cautiously. A guard! The man looked around carefully, walked up and down the area, stared curiously at the pipes and valves, glanced up at the stairs leading to the room, and then walked slowly back onto the Mount Vernon platform.

He felt the freezing sweat drip all over his body. His luck was running out. He could feel it. He had to finish all this and get away. There was a rumbling sound, the squealing of brakes. Carefully he slipped around the ventilating shafts, the sewer pumps, to the ramp, gratefully melting in with the disembarking passengers.

It was just eleven o'clock. He didn't want to sit in the hotel room. He was too restless. Walking west across Forty-second Street, he went into a movie. For four and a half hours he stared fascinated as three porno films titillated his senses, satisfied his needs. At 4:05 he was on the train to Carley.

He did not see Steve Peterson until he was already seated on the train. He happened to look up as Peterson was passing. Fortunately, he already was buried behind the papers, a precaution against being recognized and having someone he knew sit beside him.

Steve was carrying a heavy suitcase.

It was the money! He knew it! And tonight he'd have it. The sensation of impending disaster left him. It was with high confidence and good humor that he left the Carley station after he was sure Steve had driven away. He walked briskly through the snow the eight blocks to his place, a shabby garage on a dead-end street. The sign said "A. R. Taggert—Auto Repairs."

Unlocking the door, he went inside quickly. There were no messages shoved under the door. Good. Nobody had come looking for him. But even if someone had, it wouldn't be unusual not to find him. He often fixed people's cars right in their own driveways.

The garage looked cold and dirty, not much better than the place in Grand Central. He'd certainly always worked in stinking holes.

His car was there, ready to go. He'd filled it with gas from the pump in the corner. Installing that pump had been the best idea he'd ever had. Handy for the customers; they loved that touch of having their cars all gassed up. Handy for him too. Easy to go around cruising the highways at night. "You're out of gas, ma'am? Why, I've got some right in my trunk. Cars are my business . . ."

The car was already equipped with an old set of license plates he'd changed for a customer a couple of years ago; just in case any prying eyes jotted down a number tonight.

He'd unhooked the C.B. radio and it was crated on the front seat.

He'd gotten rid of all the other license plates he'd accumulated over the last six years and the extra sets of car keys he'd made. They'd been tossed in a dump near Poughkeepsie.

There were some odd tools and parts on the shelves, some tires stacked in the corner. Let old man Montgomery worry about getting rid of them. He was going to tear down this place anyhow. He'd have plenty of crap to haul away.

This was his last time here ever. Just as well. He hadn't been able to work much the past couple of months. He'd gotten too nervous. Lucky he'd had that big job on the Vogler car. Just tided him over.

That's that.

He went into the small shabby room in the rear, took a battered suitcase out from under the single bed. From an unsteady old maple dresser he extracted his meager collection of underwear and socks and placed them in the suitcase.

A badly cut fraying red sports jacket and plaid pants were lifted off a hook on the back of the door and folded into the suitcase. His overalls, thick with grease, he tossed onto the bed. He'd leave them here. With all the money he wouldn't need them again.

He took his recorder from his coat pocket and listened again to the cassette he had made with Sharon and Neil. His other recorder, the Sony, was on top of the dresser. He put it on the bed, rummaged through his cassettes, selected one, and put it on. He just needed the beginning part.

That was it.

Again he played the cassette with Sharon and Neil, letting it run just past the trailing off of Neil's voice. Then he pressed the "record" button. On the other machine, the Sony, he deflected the "play" button.

It only took a minute. When he was finished, he re-ran the revised cassette he was sending to Peterson. Perfect. Perfect. He wrapped it in a piece of brown paper, fastened it with Scotch tape. With a red magic marker, he wrote a message across the front of the package.

The other cassettes and the two recording machines were placed in the suitcase between his folded clothes. The suitcase was closed, locked, and carried to the car. He'd have enough to manage the suitcase with the money in the cabin of the plane. This one and his C.B. could go in the baggage compartment.

He opened the garage door, got into the car and turned on the engine. As it idled, he smiled, a musing, secret smile. "Now for a visit to church and a beer," he said.

 *CHAPTER 29*

"I don't believe it," Steve told Hugh flatly, "and you are endangering the lives of Neil and Sharon if you treat this as a hoax."

Just back from New York, he was pacing the living room, his hands thrust in his pockets. Hugh watched him with a mixture of compassion and irritation. The poor guy had himself in such iron control but he'd aged ten years in as many hours. Even since morning, Hugh could see new lines of anguish around Steve's eyes and mouth.

"Mr. Peterson," he said crisply, "I assure you we are presuming this is a bona fide kidnapping. However, we are beginning to believe that Sharon and Neil's . . . disappearance is going to be directly tied into an attempt to bargain for clemency for Ronald Thompson."

"And I say it won't! There's been no word from Glenda?"

"I'm afraid not."

"And no sign of a tape or cassette from Foxy?"

"I'm sorry."

"Then we can only wait."

"Yes. You'd better plan to leave for New York by midnight."

"The phonecall isn't till two."

"The road conditions, Mr. Peterson, are pretty grim."

"Do you think that Foxy might be afraid to meet me, afraid of not being able to make a getaway?"

Hugh shook his head. "Your guess is as good as mine. We've put a tap on the phone at Fifty-ninth Street, of course. But I suspect that he'll direct you immediately to another phonebooth just as he did before. We can't risk putting a mike in your car because for all we know he might plan to get in your car with you. We'll have agents in surrounding buildings who will be able to follow your progress. We'll have the area covered with cars which will keep you in sight and then radio other cars to pick you up. Don't worry, we won't give the appearance of following you. The beeper in the suitcase will let us track you within a few blocks."

Dora put her head into the living room. "Excuse me." Her voice was different. Something in Hugh's steely manner intimidated her. She didn't like the way he kept studying her and Bill. Just because Bill liked his liquor didn't mean he wasn't a good man. The strain of the past twenty-four hours was too much for her. Mr. Peterson would get Neil and Sharon back safely. She had to believe that; he was too good a man to suffer any more than he had these two years.

Then she and Bill were going to leave. It was time to go to Florida. She was getting too old, too tired to take care of a child and this house. Neil needed someone young, someone he could talk to. She knew she fussed over him too much. It doesn't do a child good to be jumping every time he sniffles.

Oh, Neil. He used to be such a happy little boy when his mother was alive. He never had asthma then and hardly ever a cold and those big brown eyes were always twinkling, not lost and sad the way they looked now.

Mr. Peterson should get married again soon; if not to Sharon, to someone who would make this a real home.

Dora realized that Steve was looking at her questioningly, that she'd spoken to him. It was just that she couldn't function with this kind of worry; she hadn't closed her eyes all night. What did she want to say to him? Oh, yes, "I know you don't want much," she said, "but couldn't I just fix a club steak for you and Mr. Taylor?"

"Not for me, thank you, Dora. Maybe, Mr. Taylor . . ."

"Put on steaks for both of us if you don't mind, Mrs. Lufts." Hugh put his hand on Steve's arm. "Look, you haven't eaten anything since yesterday. You'll be up all night. You need to be alert and able to drive and follow directions."

"I guess you're right."

They were barely at the dining-room table when the bell rang. Hugh jumped up. "I'll get it."

Steve wadded the napkin he'd been about to put on his lap. Was it the proof he had demanded? Would he hear Neil's voice, Sharon's voice?

Hugh was coming back, followed by a young, dark-haired man. He was familiar—of course, it was Ronald Thompson's defense attorney. Kurner. That was his name, Robert Kurner. He looked agitated, somehow unkempt. His coat was open, his suit was rumpled as though he'd slept in it. Hugh's face was inscrutable.

Bob did not apologize for interrupting their dinner. "Mr. Peterson," he said, "I've got to talk about your son."

"My son?" Steve felt the warning glance Hugh shot at him. Under the table he clenched his hands into fists. "What about my son?"

"Mr. Peterson, I defended Ron Thompson. I did a lousy job."

"It isn't your fault Ronald Thompson was convicted," Steve said. He did not look at the young man. Instead he stared down at the steak, watching the bubbling strip of fat at the edge begin to congeal. He pushed it away. Was Hugh right? Was the kidnapping a hoax after all?

"Mr. Peterson, Ron did not kill your wife. He was convicted because most of those jurors, consciously or unconsciously, thought he also killed the Carfolli girl and Mrs. Weiss."

"He had a record . . ."

"A *juvenile* record, a single occurrence."

"He attacked a girl before, was choking her . . ."

"Mr. Peterson, he was a fifteen-year-old kid at a party. He got into a beer drinking contest. What kid doesn't do that at some point in high school? When he was absolutely out of it, somebody slipped him cocaine. He didn't know what he was doing. He had absolutely no memory of putting his hands on that girl. We all know what a combination of drugs and alcohol can do to the mind. Ron was a kid with the lousy, hard luck to get in serious trouble the first and only time he ever got drunk. He never even had a beer for the next two years. And he had the incredibly bad luck to come into your house right after your wife was murdered."

Bob's voice was trembling now; his words rushing out. "Mr. Peterson, I've been studying the trial transcript. Then yesterday I had Ron repeat over and over again every single thing he said or did between the time he spoke to Mrs. Peterson in Timberly's Market and when he found her body. And I realized a mistake I made.

"Mr. Peterson, your son, Neil, told about coming downstairs when he heard your wife gasping, seeing a man strangle her and then seeing the man's face . . ."

"Ron Thompson's face."

"No! No! Don't you see. Here, look at the transcript." Bob slammed his briefcase on the table, pulled out a thick sheaf of legal-sized papers, raced through them until he came to a page near the center. "Here it is. The prosecutor asked Neil why he was so sure it was Ron. And Neil said, '*It got light so I'm sure.*'

"I missed that. I missed it. Because when Ron was going over and over his testimony yesterday, he said that he rang the front doorbell. Then he waited a couple of minutes and rang it again. Neil didn't say one word about hearing chimes, not one word."

"That proves nothing," Hugh interrupted. "Neil was upstairs playing with his trains. He was probably quite absorbed and the trains were noisy."

"No, no. Because he said, '*It got light.*' Mr. Peterson, this is my point. Ron rang the front doorbell. He waited, rang it again, walked around the house. He gave the killer time to escape. That's why the back door was open.

"Ron turned on the kitchen light. Don't you see? The reason Neil saw Ron's face clearly was because the light was coming in from the kitchen. Mr. Peterson, a little boy comes running downstairs and sees his mother being strangled. The living room was dark. Remember that. Only the foyer light was on. Isn't it possible that he went into some kind of shock, that he maybe even passed out? Adults have been known to do that. Then when he comes to, he sees. *Sees,* because now the light is coming from the kitchen through to the living room. Neil sees someone bending over his mother, someone tugging at her throat. Ron was trying to get the scarf off. But it was impossible. It was knotted so tightly. And he realized she was dead and how it would look for him. So he panicked and ran.

"If he were a killer would he have left an eyewitness like Neil? Would he have left Mrs. Perry alive knowing she probably recognized him? She shops in Timberly's. A killer doesn't leave witnesses, Mr. Peterson."

Hugh shook his head. "It doesn't wash. It's all conjecture. There isn't a scrap of proof in this."

"But Neil can give us the proof," Bob begged. "Mr. Peterson, would you consent to his being hypnotized? I've spoken today to several doctors. They say if he's suppressing something it might very well be revealed through hypnosis."

"That's impossible!" Steve bit his lip. He'd been about to blurt out that you can't hypnotize a kidnapped child. "Get out," he said, "just get out of here."

"No, I won't get out!" Bob hesitated, then reached into his briefcase again. "I'm sorry to show these to you, Mr. Peterson. I didn't want to. I've been studying them. They're the pictures taken of this house after the murder."

"Are you nuts?" Hugh grabbed for the photos. "Where the hell did you get them? They're state's evidence."

"Never mind where I got them. Look at this one. See? The kitchen. The globe isn't on the ceiling fixture. That means the light might have been unusually strong."

Bob thrust open the kitchen door almost knocking down Dora and Bill Lufts who were standing right behind it. Ignoring them, he dragged a chair over to the light fixture, jumped on it, quickly unscrewed the globe. The room brightened measurably. He ran back into the dining room, snapped off the light. He hurried into the foyer and turned that light on. Finally he switched off the living room lamps.

"Look, look into the living room. Now it's perfectly possible to see into it. Now wait." He rushed back into the kitchen and turned off the light. Steve and Hugh sat mesmerized at the table watching him. Under Steve's hand was the photograph of Nina's body.

"Look," Bob pleaded. "With the kitchen light out, the living room is almost dark. Suppose you're a child coming down the stairs. Please, stand in the foyer on the landing. Look into the living room. What could Neil have seen? Not much more than a silhouette. Someone is attacking his mother. He passes out. He never heard the bell. Remember that, *he never heard the bell.* The killer escapes. By the time Ron had rung the bell, and waited and rung it again and walked around the house, the killer is gone. And Ron probably saved your child's life by coming here that day."

Is it possible? Steve wondered. Is it possible that boy is innocent? He stood in the foyer, staring into the living room. How much had Neil seen? Could he have blacked out for a few moments?

Hugh strode past him into the living room, snapped on a lamp. "It's not good enough," he said flatly. "It's conjecture, pure and simple conjecture. There's not a shred of evidence to back it up."

"Neil is the one who could give us the evidence. He's our only hope. Mr. Peterson, I beg you to let him be questioned. I've been on the phone with Dr. Michael Lane. He's willing to come up tonight to question Neil. He's on the staff of Mount Sinai. Mr. Peterson, please, give Ron that chance."

Steve looked at Hugh, saw the faint, negative movement of his head. If he admitted Neil had been kidnapped, this lawyer would grasp at the excuse to suggest that it was tied into Nina's death. It would mean publicity; it might mean the end of any hope of getting Neil and Sharon back safely.

"My son is away," he said. "There have been threats against me, because of my stand on capital punishment. I will not divulge his whereabouts to anyone."

"*You will not divulge his whereabouts!* Mr. Peterson, an innocent nineteen-year-old kid is going to die tomorrow morning for something he didn't do!"

"I can't help you." Steve's calm snapped. "Get out of here. Get out and take those cursed pictures with you!"

Bob knew it was hopeless. Striding into the dining room, he jammed the trial transcript into his briefcase and scooped up the pictures. He started to close the bag, then reached in and yanked out the copies of the statements Ron had made the day before. He slammed them on the table.

"Read these, Mr. Peterson," he said. "Read them and see if you can find a killer talking. Ron was sentenced to the electric chair because Fairfield County was shocked by the Carfolli and Weiss murders as well as your wife's. There have been two more murders of women alone in their cars on lonely roads in the last few weeks. You know that. I swear to God those four murders are linked and I swear that somehow your wife's murder is connected to them. They were strangled with their scarves or belts. Don't forget that. The only difference is that for some reason, the killer chose to come into your home. But every one of those five women died the same way."

He was gone, slamming the front door behind him. Steve looked at Hugh. "What about your theory, that the kidnapping is tied into the execution tomorrow?" he asked accusingly.

Hugh shook his head. "We only know that Kurner isn't part of any conspiracy, but we never suspected that he was."

"Is there any chance, any chance at all, that he's right about Nina's death?"

"He's grasping at straws. It's all 'maybe' and conjecture. He's a lawyer trying to save his client."

"If Neil were here I would have allowed that doctor to talk with him, to hypnotize him, if necessary. Neil has had recurring nightmares since that night. Just last week he started talking about it again."

"What did he say?"

"He said something about being scared and not being able to forget. I've actually spoken to a psychiatrist in New York who suggested that there may be some repression there. Hugh, tell me honestly, are you *convinced* Ronald Thompson killed my wife?"

Hugh shrugged. "Mr. Peterson, when the evidence is as clearcut as it is in this case, it's impossible to come to any other conclusion."

"You haven't answered my question."

"I've answered it the only way I can. Please, that steak's probably not worth eating by now, but have *something.*"

They went into the dining room. Steve crumbled a piece of roll, reached for the coffee. The transcripts of Ron's statement were at his elbow. He picked up the top sheet, started to read it:

> I was pretty down about losing the job, but I understood. Mr. Timberly needed someone who could work more hours. I knew that being on the varsity would help me get into college and maybe get a scholarship. So I couldn't work more. Mrs. Peterson heard Mr. Timberly. She said she was sorry and that I was always so nice about bringing her packages to the car. She asked me what kind of job I'd get. I said I'd done housepainting during the summer. That was when we were walking out to the car. She told me that they'd just moved and there was a lot of painting to do, inside and out, and asked me to come over and look at the house. I was putting her groceries in the trunk. I said I guess this is my lucky day and it's just like my mom's always saying, bad luck can turn into good luck. Then we joked because she said, "It's my lucky day that way too. At least there's room in the trunk for all these darn groceries." She said she really didn't like grocery shopping, that's why she always bought so much at one time. That was at four o'clock. Then . . .

Steve stopped reading. Nina's lucky day. *Lucky day!* He pushed the transcript away.

The phone rang. He and Hugh both jumped. He rushed to the kitchen phone. Hugh hurried to the extension in the den. "Steve Peterson?" His voice was guarded. Let it be good news, please.

"Mr. Peterson, this is Father Kennedy from St. Monica's Church. I'm afraid something quite unusual has happened."

Steve felt his throat muscles close. It was an effort to speak. "What is it, Father?"

"Twenty minutes ago when I went on the altar to offer the evening mass, I found a small package propped against the door of the sanctuary. Let me read exactly what it says. 'Deliver to Steve Peterson at once—life or death.' And your phone number. Could it possibly be some sort of joke?"

Steve heard the hoarseness in his voice, felt the clammy sweat in his hands. "No, it's not a joke. It may be important. I'll be right down for it, Father, and please, don't say anything about this to anyone."

"Of course, Mr. Peterson. I'll wait for you in the rectory."

When Steve got back to the house half an hour later, Hugh was waiting with the recorder. Grimly they leaned over the machine as the spool began to turn.

For an instant they heard just a muted, rasping sound, then Sharon's voice. Steve paled and Hugh gripped his arm. The message. She was repeating the message the kidnapper had given him. What did she mean about being wrong? What was he supposed to forgive her for? There was something so abrupt about the way she stopped. As though she'd been cut off. Neil. That was the rasping sound. Neil, choked with asthma. Steve listened to his son's halting voice. Sharon was caring for him. Why did he mention his mother? Why now?

He gripped his fists until his knuckles were white, held them to his lips to push back the sobs that he felt shaking his chest.

"That's it," Hugh said. He reached out his hand. "We'll run it through again."

But before he could press the "stop" button it came. A warm, bubbly voice, melodic, welcoming. "Why, how nice of you," it was saying, "do come in."

Steve jumped up as an anguished cry broke from his lips.

"What is it?" Hugh shouted. "Who is that?"

"Oh Christ . . . oh Christ," Steve cried, "that's my wife, that's Nina!"

◅━━ CHAPTER 30

Hank Lamont parked his car in front of Mill Tavern on Fairfield Avenue in Carley. The snow was falling hard again and sharp gusts of wind were slapping it against the windshield. His large innocent-looking blue eyes narrowed as he studied the dimly lit interior of the tavern. It seemed pretty empty. Probably the weather had kept people home, but that was just as well. He'd get more chance to talk to the bartender. Let's hope he was the kind who liked to chew the rag.

He stepped out of the car. God, it was cold. Lousy, lousy night. It would be hard to keep a tail on Peterson's car later on. There'd probably be so few cars on the road, the ones that were there would stick out like sore thumbs.

He pushed open the door and stepped inside the bar. Warm air embraced him and a not unpleasant beer and food smell filled his nostrils. Blinking to clear his eyes of snow, he glanced at the bar. There were only four men at it. He ambled up, heaved his bulk onto a stool, and ordered a Michelob.

While he sipped it, his eyes flitted from side to side. Two of the patrons were watching a hockey game on television. Halfway down the bar, a well-dressed glassy-eyed executive-type with a fringe of white hair was sipping a martini. He caught Hank's gaze. "Do you agree with me, sir, that it's the mark of a sensible man not to drive ten miles in these adverse conditions; that it is far more expedient to call a cab?" He considered his own premise. "Especially with a snootful," he added unnecessarily.

"You're right, mister," Hank said heartily. "I just drove down from Peterboro and let me tell you these roads are *bad*." He swallowed a large gulp of beer.

The bartender was drying glasses. "You from Peterboro? Never seen you around here, have I?"

"No. Just passing through. Wanted to take a break and remembered my old buddy, Bill Lufts, says he's usually here about this time."

"Yeah, Bill's here just about every night," the bartender agreed. "But you might be out of luck. Last night he didn't make it 'cause he was taking his wife out for their anniversary; going to dinner and the movies. We figured he'd drop her off home and come on down for a nightcap, but he never did show up. Really surprising he's not here again tonight, unless she's giving him a lot of flak again. And if she does, we'll hear about it, right Arty?"

The other solitary drinker looked up from where he was hunched over a beer. "In one ear and out the other," he said, "who wants to listen to that stuff?"

Hank laughed. "Well, what's a bar for if not to get your beefs out of your system?"

The men watching the hockey game switched it off. "Lousy game," one of them commented.

"Stinks," the other agreed.

"This here's a friend of Bill Lufts'," the bartender jerked his head toward Hank.

"Les Watkins," the taller man said.

"Pete Lerner," Hank lied.

"Joe Reynolds," the plump man volunteered. "What's your work, Pete?"

"Plumbing supply house in New Hampshire; on my way to New York to pick up some samples. Say, how about everyone having a beer on me?"

An hour passed. Hugh learned that Les and Joe were salesmen in the Modell discount house on Route 7. Arty repaired cars. The bald-headed executive, Allan Kroeger, worked in an advertising agency.

A number of the regulars weren't around, thanks to the weather. For instance, Bill Finelli hadn't been by tonight, neither had Don Branni-gan. Charley Pincher usually drifted in, but he and his wife were active in the Little Theatre group and were probably rehearsing a new play.

Kroeger's cab arrived. Les was giving Joe a ride. They asked for their bill. Arty got up to go. The bartender waved away his money. "This one's on me," he said. "We'll miss you."

"That's right," Les said, "good luck, Arty. Let us know how you're doing."

"Thanks: If it don't work I'll come back and take the job at Shaw's. He's always bugging me to go with him."

"Why wouldn't he? He knows a good mechanic," Les said.

"Where'ye heading for?" Hank asked.

"Rhode Island—Providence."

"Too bad you didn't get a chance to say goodbye to Bill," Joe commented.

Arty laughed cynically. "Rhode Island ain't Arizona," he said. "I'll be back. Well, better get some sleep. Want to get an early start in the morning."

Allan Kroeger wove unsteadily toward the door. "Arizona," he said, "home of the painted desert." The four men went out together, letting in a sharp blast of cold air.

Hank studied Arty's retreating back. "That Arty, he a particular friend of Bill Lufts'?"

The bartender shook his head. "Nah. Anybody who can *hear* is a friend of Bill's after he gets a couple of boilermakers. You should know that. The way the guys have it figured, Bill's wife yaks in his ear all day and he comes here at night and yaks in everyone else's ear."

"I see." Hank shoved his glass across the bar. "Have one yourself."

"Don't mind if I do. Don't usually if it's busy, but you could swing a cat around here. Lousy kind of night anyhow. Kind of gives you the creeps. Guess everybody feels that way. That Thompson kid, you know. His mother lives two blocks from me."

Hank's eyes narrowed. "That's what happens when you go around murdering people," he suggested.

The bartender shook his head. "Most of us can't imagine that kid murdering anyone. 'Course he did go off the deep end once before, so maybe it's possible. They say some of the most vicious killers are real ordinary on the surface."

"That's what I hear."

"You know Bill and his missus live at the house of the woman who was murdered—the Peterson house."

"Yeah, I did know that."

"They took it awful hard. Dora Lufts worked for the Petersons for years. Bill says the little kid is still like a ghost of himself, cries a lot, has nightmares."

"It's tough," Hank agreed.

"Bill and the missus really want to get down to Florida. They're hanging around hoping the kid's father will get married. He's going with some writer; good-looking, Bill says. She was coming up last night."

"Was she?"

"Yeah. The little kid is pretty cool about her, probably scared about having his mother replaced. Kids are like that."

"Guess so."

"The father's the editor of *Events* magazine, you know, that new one, just a couple of years old. Guess he sunk a lot of dough into it. Second mortgage, you name it. But it's coming along pretty well now. Well, guess I'll start closing up. It's a cinch nobody else is coming around here tonight. Want another?"

Hank considered. He needed answers. There was no more time to waste. He set his glass down, reached for his wallet, flipped out his badge. "FBI," he said.

An hour later he was back at the Peterson house. After conferring with Hugh, he called FBI headquarters in Manhattan. Making sure the den door was securely closed, he spoke softly into the phone. "Hughie was right. Bill Lufts is a bigmouth. Everyone in the Mill Tavern has known for two weeks that he and Mrs. Lufts would be out last night, that Peterson had a late meeting and that Sharon Martin was expected up. The bartender gave me a list of ten regulars who are always talking to Bill. Some of them were there tonight. They all seemed okay. You might check on a Charley Pincher though, he and his wife are in theatricals; maybe one of them could mimic a voice they'd heard a couple of years ago. There's an Arty Taggert who'll be pulling out tomorrow for Rhode Island. Seems harmless. Two salesmen, Les Watkins and Joe Reynolds—wouldn't waste time on them. Here are the rest of the names . . ."

When he'd concluded the list, he added, "Another thing. Bill Lufts told the whole bar about Neil's trust fund less than a month ago; overheard Peterson talking to his accountant. So everyone in the Mill Tavern

and God knows where else knows about it. Okay. I'll start down with the cassette. Have you reached John Owens?"

He hung up the phone, walked thoughtfully past the living room. Hugh Taylor and Steve were talking in muted tones. Steve was just putting on his coat. It was nearly midnight and time for him to leave for the rendezvous with Foxy.

CHAPTER 31

Lally was so upset over the intruders that when she met Rosie in the main waiting room she blurted out the story to her and immediately was sorry. "It's kind of a special place for me," she finished lamely. Now what would she say if Rosie wanted to share it? She couldn't let her. She just couldn't.

She needn't have worried. "You mean you bed down in Sing Sing?" Rosie asked incredulously. "You couldn't get me near there with a ten-foot pole. You know how I hate cats."

Of course. She'd never thought. Rosie was frightened of cats, would walk across the street to avoid one.

"Well, you know me," Lally said. "I love them. Poor things get so hungry. There're more slithering around that tunnel than ever," she exaggerated. Rosie shuddered.

"So I figure the two of them are staying there," Lally concluded, "and I'll scare off the girl when he's out."

Rosie was deep in thought. "Suppose you make a mistake," she suggested. "Suppose he's there. You say he looks mean."

"More than mean. Maybe, maybe you could help me keep an eye on him."

Rosie loved intrigue. She smiled widely, revealing broken yellow teeth. "Sure."

They finished their coffee, carefully putting leftover pieces of the donuts in their shopping bags, and headed for the lower level.

"Might take a long time," Lally fretted.

"It don't matter, except Olendorf's on today," Rosie said.

He was one of the strictest guards. He didn't believe in letting the regulars hang around the station; he was always chasing them and watching to see they didn't panhandle or litter.

Somewhat nervously, they took up a position near the *Open Book* display windows. Time passed. They waited patiently, almost motionlessly. Lally had a story ready if Olendorf came over to them. She'd say she had a friend coming to New York and had promised to meet her right here.

But the guard ignored them. Lally's feet and legs began to throb. She was about to suggest to Rosie that they give up the vigil when a stream of people came up the steps of the Mount Vernon platform. One of them had dark hair, a stiff way of walking.

She grabbed Rosie's arm. "That's him," she cried. "See, he's going toward the stairs, brown coat, green pants."

Rosie's eyes narrowed. "Oh yeah, I see him."

"Now I can go down," Lally exulted.

Rosie looked doubtful. "Not with Olendorf around, I wouldn't. He just looked over here."

But Lally was not to be dissuaded. She waited until she saw Olendorf leave for his lunch break, then slipped down to the platform. The 12:10 was starting to load; she knew she wasn't too conspicuous. She disappeared around to the other side of the track, hurried down the ramp as fast as her arthritic knees would allow. She really didn't feel well. This had been the hardest winter ever. The arthritis was in her back now and in the soles of her feet. Her whole body was hurting a lot. She couldn't wait to lie down and have a rest on her own cot. She'd have the girl out of there in the next two minutes.

"Missy," she'd say, "the cops are wise. They're on their way to arrest you. Get out and warn your boyfriend."

That would do it.

She shuffled past the generator, around the sewer pipes. The tunnel loomed dark and still at the far end of the area.

She looked up at the door of her room and smiled happily. Eight more shuffling movements and she was at the base of the steps leading to it. Shifting the handles of her shopping bag over one arm, she fished her key out of her jacket. With the other hand she gripped the railing and began to pull herself up the steep steps.

"Where do you think you're going, Lally?" The voice was sharp. Lally let out a frightened cry and almost tumbled over backward. She regained her balance, and fighting for time, turned around slowly to face the menacing form of Officer Olendorf. So he'd been keeping an eye on her, just like Rosie warned; he'd tried to trap her by pretending to go to lunch. She let the key slide into the shopping bag. Had he seen it?

"I asked, where are you going, Lally?"

Near her the generators throbbed. There was a rushing, squealing sound as a train entered a platform somewhere overhead. She was silent, helpless.

A sudden, sharp spitting sound, a snarling yowl came from a shadowy corner and inspiration struck Lally. "The cats!" With a trembling hand she pointed to the moving skeletal forms. "They're starving! I wanted to bring them something to eat. I was just getting it out." Eagerly, she yanked the crumpled napkin with the bits of donut from her shopping bag.

The guard examined the greasy napkin with distaste, but his tone was somewhat less hostile when he spoke. "I'm sorry for them too, but you've no business here, Lally. Throw that stuff to them and clear out." His glance passed her, eyed the steps, moved upward, lingered thoughtfully on the door of her room. Lally's heart beat wildly. She picked up her bag, hobbled over to the cats, tossed the meager scraps, watched as they fought over them.

"See how hungry they are." Her voice was placating. "You got cats home, Mr. Olendorf?" She was moving out of the area, willing him to follow her. Suppose he used his passkey and checked her room? If he found the girl there, they'd surely change the lock. Maybe padlock it.

He hesitated, shrugged, decided to follow her. "Used to, but my wife isn't much for cats anymore, not since we lost the one she was crazy about."

Safely back in the waiting room, Lally realized her heart was still beating wildly. That was that. She wouldn't go near her place again until tonight when Olendorf went home. Thanking her stars that the cats had staged their fights, she went over to a bin and plucked out a discarded copy of *People* magazine and the crumpled first section of the *Village Voice*.

CHAPTER 32

Neil knew Sharon was hurt. She hadn't fooled him when she said she fell. The man must have pushed her down. He wanted to talk to Sharon but the rag on his mouth was so tight he couldn't. It was much tighter than before. He wanted to tell Sharon how brave she was to try to fight that man. He'd been too scared to fight him when he was hurting Mommy. But even Sharon, who was almost as tall as the man, wasn't strong enough to beat him.

Sharon had told him that she was going to try to get the man's gun. She had said, "Don't be scared if you hear me talking about leaving you. I won't leave you. But if I can get his gun, maybe we can make him

take us out of here. We both made a mistake and we're the only ones who can save Ronald Thompson."

Her voice had been all funny and growly trying to talk and his had too, but somehow he'd been able to tell her about it . . . how Sandy said that he should have helped Mommy; how he kept dreaming about that day; how Sandy said the Lufts would probably take him to Florida; how the kids asked him if he wanted Ronald Thompson to fry.

Even though it was hard to talk with the gag on it was easier to breathe after he talked. He knew what Sharon meant. They were going to kill Ronald Thompson for hurting Mommy and he hadn't done it. But Neil said he had. Neil hadn't meant to lie. That was what he was trying to tell Daddy on the message.

Now he had to be careful to breathe very slowly through his nose and not get scared or cry because then he wouldn't be able to breathe.

It was cold and his arms and legs hurt so much. But even so, something inside him had stopped hurting. Sharon would figure a way to get them out of here away from the man so they could tell about Ronald. Or Daddy would come and get them. Neil was sure of that.

He could feel Sharon's breath on his cheek. His head was right under her chin. Sometimes she made a funny sound, like something was hurting her. But being squished against her made him feel better. It was like when he was a little kid and sometimes woke up in the middle of the night with a bad dream and used to get into bed with Mommy and Daddy. Mommy would pull him close and say, "stop wiggling" in a sleepy voice, and he'd go back to sleep all tucked against her.

Sharon and Daddy would take care of him. Neil wiggled a fraction closer to Sharon. He wished he could tell her not to worry about him. He'd take long, slow breaths through his nose. His arms hurt so much. Determinedly he pushed that thought away. He'd think about something nice . . . the room on the top floor and the Lionel trains Sharon would give him.

CHAPTER 33

"For God's sake, dear, it's nearly midnight. Give it up." Roger watched helplessly as Glenda shook her head. Alarmed, he saw that the vial of nitroglycerin tablets on her night table was nearly empty. It had been full only this morning.

"No. I'll get it. I know I will. Roger, here . . . let's try this. I'll tell you everything I did over the past month. I've been going back day by day but I still have missed something. Maybe if I tell it to you . . ."

He knew it was useless to protest. Pulling up a chair close to the bed, he prepared to concentrate. His head was throbbing. The doctor had come back and been furious that Glenda was upsetting herself so much. Of course they hadn't been able to explain why she was so agitated.

The doctor wanted to give her a strong shot, but Roger knew she'd never forgive him if he okayed it. Now, watching her ashen pallor and the telltale purplish-blue lips, he thought of that day when she'd had the coronary: . . . we're doing everything we can, Mr. Perry . . . it's touch and go . . . it might be wise to send for your sons . . .

But she'd pulled out of it. Oh God, if she knows anything let her remember, Roger prayed. Let me help her remember. If Neil and Sharon died and afterward Glenda felt she could have saved them, it would kill her too.

What was Steve feeling right now? It would soon be time for him to leave for New York with the ransom money.

Where was Ronald Thompson's mother now? What was she thinking? Did she know this same futile anguish? Of course she did.

What about Sharon and Neil? Were they terrified, had they been abused? Were they still alive or was it already too late?

And Ronald Thompson. At the trial, Roger had been able to think only of how much he resembled Chip and Doug at that age. At nineteen, his boys had been sophomores in college; Chip at Harvard, Doug at the University of Michigan. That's where nineteen-year-olds belong—in college, not in prison cells on Death Row.

"Roger." Glenda's voice was remarkably steady. "Maybe if you make a diagram of each day, nine o'clock, ten o'clock, that kind of thing, it will help to point up whatever I'm missing. There's a pad in my desk."

He walked over and got it. "All right," she said, "I'm sure of yesterday and Sunday, so we won't waste time on them. Let's start with last Saturday . . ."

 *CHAPTER 34*

"N o questions, Mr. Peterson? You're sure you've got it straight?" Hugh and Steve were in the foyer. Steve had the heavy suitcase containing the ransom money gripped in his hand.

"I think so." Steve's voice was even, almost a monotone. Somewhere in the past hours, the fatigue had retreated; overwhelming numbness had anesthetized pain and worry. He could think clearly, almost abstractly. He was standing on a high hill overlooking a drama. He was viewer as well as participant.

"All right. Run it down for me." Hugh recognized the symptoms in the other man. Peterson was coming to the end of his emotional tether. Already he was in some kind of shock, of course. That business of imitating his wife's voice had been the limit. And the poor guy kept insisting it was her. What a cheap, clumsy way to try to link the abduction to Nina Peterson's death. There were a couple of other things Hugh had noticed; Sharon's request for Steve to forgive her. Neil saying, "Sharon is taking care of me." Wasn't that the tip-off that this was a fraud?

Was it?

Maybe John Owens could help them. They'd located him and he was meeting Hugh at headquarters in New York.

Steve said, "I go directly to the Fifty-ninth Street phonebooth. If I'm early, I sit and wait in the car until just before two A.M., then get out of the car and stand at the phone. I'll probably be directed to another phone. I go there. Then hopefully I make direct contact and turn the suitcase over to the abductor. After I leave him, I drive to FBI headquarters on Sixty-ninth Street and Third Avenue. You'll be waiting to take the cameras out of the car and develop the film."

"That's it. We'll be trailing you from a distance. The beeper in your car will keep us informed of your movements. One of our men is waiting to follow you down the parkway now to make sure you don't get stuck or delayed. Mr. Peterson . . ." Hugh reached out his hand, "good luck."

"Luck?" Steve said the word with wonderment as though he were hearing it for the first time. "I haven't been thinking of luck so much as I have of an old Wexford curse. Do you know it by any chance?"

"I don't think so."

"I can't remember all of it, but it's something like this, 'May the fox build his nest on your hearthstone. May the light fade from your eyes so you never see what you love. May the sweetest drink you take be the bitterest cup of sorrow . . .' There's more, but that pretty much sums it up. Rather appropriate, isn't it?"

Without waiting for an answer, Steve left. Hugh watched the Mercury pull out of the driveway, turn left toward the parkway. *May the fox build his nest on your hearthstone.* God help that guy Peterson. Shaking his head to try to relieve the persistent sense of impending doom, Hugh grabbed his own coat. None of the FBI cars were in the driveway. He and the other agents were slipping out the back door, across the two acres of vacant woods next to Steve's place. Their cars were parked on the narrow road that had been made in the woods when sewer lines were laid. There they were invisible from the street.

Maybe John Owens could make something of the cassette the kidnapper had sent. A retired agent who'd gone blind from glaucoma twenty years before, John had developed his hearing so keenly that he could interpret background sounds on recordings with remarkable accuracy. They brought him in whenever this kind of evidence came into a case. Later on of course, they'd run the cassette through regular lab tests, but that would take days.

Without explaining his reason, Hugh had asked Steve about Nina's background: Philadelphia Main Line family, fourth generation. Nina had attended a Swiss boarding school, Bryn Mawr College. Her parents spent most of their time now in their home in Monte Carlo. Hugh remembered meeting them at Nina's funeral. They'd flown in for the service and interment; hardly spoken to Steve, a pair of cold potatoes if ever he saw them.

But the information would be enough for Owens to give a pretty accurate opinion whether that voice actually was Nina's or an impersonation. Hugh had little doubt about the outcome.

The Merritt Parkway had been sanded and even though fresh snow was still falling, the driving was better than Steve had expected. He'd been fearful that the abductor might call off meeting him if the roads were hazardous. Now he was sure they'd somehow make contact.

He wondered why Hugh had queried him about Nina's background. He'd only wanted a few basic facts. "What college did your wife go to, Mr. Peterson? Where was she raised?"

"She went to Bryn Mawr." They'd met when they were both seniors. He was at Princeton. It was love at first sight. Corny but true.

"Her family is fourth generation Philadelphia Main Line." They were outraged about him. They wanted Nina to "marry her own kind," as they put it. Someone with good family and money and a preppie background. Not an impoverished student who waited table at the Nassau Inn to stretch his scholarship, who'd graduated from Christopher Columbus High School in the Bronx.

God, they'd been formidable when he and Nina were going around together. He'd said to Nina, "How did you ever get to be *their* daughter?" She was so funny, so bright, so unpretentious. They'd been married right after graduation. Then he'd gone into service, been commissioned and sent to Vietnam. They didn't see each other for two years. Finally he'd gotten an R and R and she'd met him in Hawaii. She'd been so beautiful, running down the steps of the plane, tumbling into his arms.

After he was discharged, he'd gone to Columbia for a Master's in Journalism. Then he got the job at *Time* and they moved up to Connecticut and she became pregnant with Neil.

He'd bought her the Karman Ghia when Neil was born, and you'd have thought it was a Rolls. Which, of course, was what her father had.

He'd sold Nina's car the week after the funeral. It was impossible to see it parked next to his Mercury in the garage. That night when he'd come home to find her dead, he'd walked out to it, hoping against hope. "Your carelessness will get you killed!" But the new radial was back on the front wheel; the balding spare was in the trunk. If she hadn't bothered to have it changed that day, it would have meant that she didn't take his annoyance too seriously.

Nina, Nina, I'm sorry.

Sharon. She'd made him come alive again. Because of her the numbness and pain had dissolved like ice gradually melting in a spring thaw. These six months had been so good. He'd started to believe that he'd been given a second chance at happiness.

You didn't fall in love the first time you met someone. He was thirty-four now, not twenty-two.

Or didn't you?

That first meeting on the *Today* show. After it was over they walked out of the studio together and stood talking in front of the building. He hadn't been even vaguely interested in any woman after Nina died, but that morning he'd found himself reluctant to let Sharon go. He was due at an early meeting and couldn't suggest having breakfast with her. Finally he'd blurted out, "Look, I have to run now but how about dinner tonight?"

Sharon said yes, quickly, almost as though she'd been hoping he'd ask. The whole day had seemed interminably long before he was finally at her apartment ringing her doorbell. At that time their debate over capital punishment was more ideological than personal. It was only when Sharon began to feel that she couldn't save Ronald Thompson that she started to turn on him.

He was on the Cross County Parkway. His hands were working independently, selecting the roads without his conscious awareness.

Sharon. It was so good to talk to someone again, over dinner, over a nightcap at her place. She understood the problems of launching a new magazine, the struggle to get advertisers, to get readership. The nearest thing to pillowtalk, he'd joked.

He'd left his job at *Time* to go with *Events* a few months before Nina died. It had been a real gamble. He was making important money at *Time*. Part of it had been pride. He was going to help create the best magazine in the country. He was going to be a rich, hotshot editor and show Nina's father. He'd make him eat his words.

Nina's parents blamed him for her death. "If she'd been in a properly staffed, properly secured house, this never would have happened," they said. They'd wanted to take Neil back with them to Europe. Neil, with those two!

Neil. The poor little kid. Like father, like son. Steve's mother had died when he was three. He didn't remember her at all. His father had never remarried. That was a mistake. Steve had grown up wanting a mother. He remembered when he was seven, there'd been a substitute teacher in his class and she'd had them draw Mother's Day cards.

At the end of the day she noticed that he didn't put his in his schoolbag. "You're not going to leave that here, are you?" she'd asked. "Your mother will be so pleased to have it Sunday."

He'd torn it up and run out of the room.

He didn't want that for Neil. He wanted Neil to grow up in a happy home, a home with brothers and sisters. He didn't want to live the way his father had, alone, making Steve his whole life, bragging to everybody in the post office about his son in Princeton. A lonely man in a lonely apartment. One morning he hadn't awakened. When he didn't show up for work, they'd investigated. And Steve had been called out of class.

Maybe that was why over the past years he'd taken the stand on capital punishment. Because he knew how elderly, poor people lived, how little they had. Because it sickened him to think of any of them being brutally murdered by thugs.

The suitcase was on the front seat next to him. Hugh had assured him the electronic device wouldn't be detected. Now he was glad that he'd let them put it in.

At 1:30 Steve pulled off the Fifty-seventh Street exit of the West Side Highway. At twenty of two, he was parked in front of the payphone outside Bloomingdale's. At ten of two he got out of the car and, unmindful of the wet, icy wind, stood in the booth.

At precisely 2:00 A.M. the phone rang. The same muffled, whispering voice instructed him to go immediately to a phone on Ninety-sixth Street and Lexington Avenue.

At 2:15 that phone rang. Steve was told to drive over the Triborough Bridge, take the Grand Central Parkway to the Brooklyn Queens Expressway exit. He was to drive on the BQE to Roosevelt Avenue, turn left to the end of the first block, and park immediately. He was to turn out his headlights and wait. "Be sure to have the money. Be alone."

Frantically, Steve scribbled, repeated the instructions. The abductor hung up.

At 2:35 he turned off the BQE onto Roosevelt Avenue. A large sedan was parked halfway down the block on the other side of the street. As he passed it, he twisted the wheel a fraction, hoping the hidden cameras might be able to pick up the make and license number; then he pulled over to the curb and waited.

It was a dark street. The doors and windows of the shabby old stores were protected with chains and bars; the elevated tracks helped cut off the street lights; the snow blocked remaining visibility.

Were the FBI agents able to trace his course through the beeper? Suppose it stopped working. He hadn't noticed any cars following him. But they'd said they wouldn't get too close.

There was a thump at the driver's door. Steven spun his head around, felt his mouth go dry. A gloved hand was gesturing for him to pull the window down. He switched the ignition key on, deflected the window button.

"Don't look at me, Peterson."

But he'd already glimpsed a brownish coat, a stocking mask. Something was dropped on his lap, some large canvas bag—a duffel bag. He felt a sick feeling in the pit of his stomach. This man was not going to take the suitcase with the tracer. He knew it.

"Open that suitcase and put the money in the bag. Hurry up."

He tried to stall for time. "How do I know that you'll return my son and Sharon unharmed?"

"Fill that bag!" He could hear the high-pitched undercurrent in the voice. The man was violently nervous. If he panicked and ran off without the money, he might kill Sharon and Neil. With fumbling hands, Steve wrenched the neat packets of money from the suitcase, jammed them into the duffel bag.

"Close it!"

He drew the strings tightly together, knotted them.

"Hand it over. Don't look at me."

He stared straight ahead. "What about my son and Sharon?"

Gloved hands reached in through the window, yanked the bag away from him. The gloves. He tried to notice them. Stiff-looking, cheap imitation leather, dark gray or brown, large. The sleeve of the coat was frayed; broken pieces of thread spidered out from it.

"You're being watched, Peterson." The abductor's voice was hurried, almost trembling. "Don't leave here for fifteen minutes; remember that, *fifteen minutes.* If I'm not followed and the money is all here, you'll be told where to pick up your son and Sharon at eleven-thirty this morning."

Eleven-thirty. The exact minute of Ronald Thompson's execution. "Did you have anything to do with my wife's death?" Steve burst out.

There was no answer. He waited, then cautiously turned his head. The abductor had slipped away. Across the street, a car started.

His watch said 2:38. The entire meeting had taken place in less than three minutes. Was he being watched? Was there an observer on the roof of one of those buildings ready to report if he moved? The FBI wouldn't get any signal of location change from the suitcase. Did he dare start sooner?

No.

At 2:53 Steve made a U turn and headed back toward Manhattan. At 3:10 he was at the FBI headquarters on Sixty-ninth Street and Third Avenue. Grim-faced agents rushed to his car and began unscrewing the headlights. A somber-looking Hugh listened to his explanation as they rode up to the twelfth floor. There he was introduced to a man with snow-white hair and a patient, intelligent expression that was not concealed by dark glasses.

"John has been listening to the cassette," Hugh explained. "From the quality of their voices and a certain echo, he concludes that Sharon and Neil are being kept in a nearly empty, cold room, about eleven by twenty-three feet in size. They may be in the basement of a freightyard; there's a continuing faint sound of trains pulling in and leaving from somewhere nearby."

Steve stared.

"I'll be able to be considerably more specific later," the blind agent said. "There's no magic to this. It's simply a case of listening with the same degree of intensity with which you'd study a specimen under a microscope."

A cold room, nearly empty. A freightyard. Steve looked accusingly at Hugh. "What does this do to your theory that Sharon may have planned this?"

"I don't know," Hugh replied simply.

"Mr. Peterson, about the last voice on the cassette," John Owens' manner was hesitant, "by any chance was your late wife's first tongue French rather than English?"

"No, not at all. She was raised in Philadelphia till she went to boarding school at ten. Why?"

"There's an intonation in that voice that to an expert definitely suggests that English was not the first language."

"Wait a minute! Nina did tell me that she'd had a French nurse, that as a young child she actually thought in French rather than English."

"That's exactly what I'm talking about. Then that was no imposter or mimic. You are correct in identifying your wife's voice."

"All right. I was wrong about that," Hugh said. "But John says that last voice was definitely added to the cassette after Neil and Sharon were recorded. Think, Mr. Peterson. Somebody who knows a great deal about your personal life has planned this. Were you ever at a party, maybe, where people were doing home movies, where someone might have recorded a voice track of your wife and excerpted those few words from it?"

It was so hard to think . . . Steve frowned. "The country club. When it was renovated and redecorated four years ago, they made a film for some charity. Nina was the narrator, going from room to room, explaining what had been done."

"Now we're getting somewhere," Hugh said. "Might she have used those words within the framework of that film?"

"Possibly."

The phone rang. Hugh grabbed it, identified himself, listened intently. "Good. Get right on it!" He slammed the receiver down; he had the look of a hunter on a fresh scent. "Things are beginning to break, Mr. Peterson," he said. "You got a clear picture of the car and license plate. We're tracing it now."

The first faint hope he'd been offered! Then why was the knot in his throat still choking him? It's too easy, something was saying; it's not going to work out.

John Owens stretched out his hand in the direction of Steve's voice. "Mr. Peterson, just one question. My impression is that, if that actually is your wife on the cassette, she spoke while she was in the process of opening a door. Are you aware by any chance of a particular door with a faint squealing sound when it opens, something like this—'eerkkk'?" He gave a startling imitation of a rusty hinge moving.

Hugh and Steve stared at each other. It is a mockery, Steve thought dully. It is a farce; it is already too late for everybody.

Hugh answered for him. "Yes, John," he said. "That's exactly the way Mr. Peterson's kitchen door sounds as it's being opened."

A rty drove away from the Mill Tavern, a nagging worry sending out alarm signals through his body, dissolving the euphoric sense of infallibility he'd been enjoying.

He'd really counted on Bill Lufts being in the bar; it would have been helpful to pump Bill. Oh, the boy's away? Where is he? How's Mr. Peterson? Has he had any company?

He'd figured that Peterson wouldn't admit to the Lufts that Neil and Sharon were missing. He'd figured Peterson knew that the Lufts shot their mouths off about everything.

So if Bill wasn't there, it was because Peterson had called the cops—, no, not the cops, the FBI.

That guy who called himself Pete Lerner, who asked so many questions. He was an FBI agent. Arty knew it.

He steered the dark-green Beetle onto the Merritt Parkway south. Anxiety made perspiration ooze from his forehead and armpits and hands.

Twelve years slipped away. He was being grilled in FBI headquarters in Manhattan. "Come on, Arty, the news vendor saw you leave with that kid. Where'd you take her?"

"I put her in a cab. She said she was meeting some guy."

"What guy?"

"How do I know? I carried her bag out, that's all."

They couldn't prove anything. But they tried. God, they tried.

"How about the other girls, Arty. Take a look at these pictures. You're always hanging around the Port Authority. How many of them did you carry bags for?"

"I don't know what you mean."

They were coming too close. It was too dangerous. That was when he left New York, drifted up to Connecticut, got a job pumping gas. Six years ago he'd taken over the repair shop in Carley.

Arizona. That had been a bad mistake. Why did he say, "Rhode Island ain't Arizona?" Probably that guy who called himself Pete Lerner hadn't noticed, but even so it had been a mistake.

They had nothing on him unless they started checking way back, unless they came up with the time they questioned him about the kid from Texas. "Come on down to my place in the Village," he'd told her. "I have a lot of artist friends who can use a good-looking model."

But they didn't have proof then and they didn't have it now. Nothing. There hadn't been any slip-ups. He was sure of it.

"*Is this your place,*" she'd asked, "*this dump?*"

The Merritt faded into the Hutchinson River Parkway. He followed the signs leading to the Throgs Neck Bridge. His plan was ingenious. Stealing a car was dangerous. There was always the chance that the owner might come back in ten minutes; that the cops would have an alert before it had gone five miles. You shouldn't steal a car unless you're sure the owner is out of the way—like sitting, watching a thirty-year-old movie, or taking off on a plane.

The Throgs Neck Bridge had caution signs flashing. Ice. Wind. But that was all right. He was a good driver and tonight the chicken drivers would be staying home. That would make it easy for him to move around later.

At 11:20 he drove into LaGuardia Airport into parking lot five, the one with special rates for long-term parkers.

He took a ticket from the machine; the gate lifted and he drove slowly through the lot, taking care to get well away from the view of the cashier in the exit line next to the automatic check-in. He pulled into an empty space in section nine, between a Chrysler and a Cadillac, behind an Oldsmobile wagon. In the midst of them the Beetle was diminished and hidden.

He leaned back in the seat and waited. Forty minutes passed. Two cars came into the lot, one a flashy red, the other a yellow station wagon. Both too easy to spot. He was glad when they ignored the empty spaces near him and drove further down into the far-left section.

Another car drove slowly by. A dark-blue Pontiac that pulled into a spot three rows ahead. The lights went off. He watched as the driver got out, walked around to the trunk and extracted a large suitcase. This guy would be away for a while.

Slumped in the Volks, only the top of his head above the level of the windshield, he watched as the man slammed the trunk down, picked up the suitcase and made his way to the nearest bus shelter from which the courtesy airport bus would take him to the departure terminal.

The bus came in a few minutes. Foxy observed the silhouetted figure get on the vehicle. The bus pulled away.

Slowly, quietly, he got out of the Beetle and looked around. There were no headlights approaching. In quick strides he was at the side of the Pontiac. The second key he tried opened the door. He was in the car.

It was still comfortably warm. He put the key he was holding in the ignition. The engine turned over almost noiselessly; the tank was three-quarters full.

Perfect.

He'd have to wait. The guard would be suspicious if he collected on a ticket with less than a couple of hours' parking in this lot. But he had plenty of time and he wanted to think. He leaned back, closed his eyes, and Nina's image floated across his mind, the way she'd looked that first night . . .

He'd been cruising around, knowing he shouldn't be out, knowing it was too soon after Jean Carfolli and Mrs. Weiss, but not able to stay in. And he'd seen her. The Karmann Ghia pulled over on Route 7 in that quiet, lonely spot. The slender, small body caught up in his headlights. The dark hair. The little hands that were struggling with the jack. The enormous brown eyes that looked startled when he slowed down and pulled over. Probably hearing in her head all the talk about the highwayman murders.

"Can I help you, miss? That's rough work for you, but it's my job. I'm a mechanic."

The worried look disappeared. "Oh, great," she said. "I don't mind telling you that I'm a bit nervous . . . of all the crazy places to get a flat."

He never glanced at her; just at the tire, like she didn't exist, like she was nine hundred years old. "You've picked up some glass, no big deal." Quickly, effortlessly, he changed it. Less than three minutes. No cars coming in either direction. He stood up.

"How much do I owe you?" Her purse open, her neck bent. Her breast rising and falling under the suede coat. Class. Something about her that showed it. Not a scared kid like Jean Carfolli, not an outraged old bitch like Weiss, just a beautiful young woman who was very grateful to him. He reached out his hand to touch her breast.

The light began on the tree across the road, swung around, illuminated the two of them. A cop car. He could see the dome. "It's three dollars to change the tire," he said briskly, "and I can fix your flat if you want." He had his hand in his pocket now. "I'm Arty Taggert, I have a repair shop in Carley on Monroe Street, about half a mile from Mill Tavern."

The police car was coming up, pulling toward them. The trooper got out. "You all right, ma'am?" His look at Arty was very funny, very suspicious.

"Oh, fine, officer, I certainly was in luck. Mr. Taggert is from my town and he came along just as I got the flat."

She made it sound like she knew him. What a break! The policeman's expression changed. "You're lucky ma'am to be helped by a friend. It's not safe for women to be alone in disabled cars these days."

The cop got back in the patrol car but stayed there watching. "Will you fix the tire for me?" she asked. "I'm Nina Peterson. We live on Driftwood Lane."

"Sure. Be glad to." He got back in his car, very indifferent, very casual, like this was just another cheap repair job, never showing that he *had* to see her again. He could tell the way she looked at him that she was sorry the cop had come along too. But it was important to get away before the cop started thinking about Jean Carfolli and Mrs. Weiss; before the cop asked, "You in the habit of stopping to help out ladies who are alone, mister?"

So he'd driven away and the next morning just when he was thinking about calling her, she called him. "My husband just gave me what-for about driving on the spare," she said, and her voice was very warm and intimate and amused like they had a private joke. "When can I pick up my tire?"

He thought fast. Driftwood Lane was in a quiet area; the houses weren't close together. If she came to his place, there'd be no way of getting friendly with her. That would be too dangerous.

"I have to go out on a job right now," he lied, "I'll bring it by late this afternoon, maybe about five." It got dark by five.

"Wonderful," she said, "just as long as the darn thing is back on the car before I go to pick up my husband at half-past six."

He was so excited that day that he could hardly think. He went out for a haircut and bought a new checkered sportshirt. When he got back he didn't bother at all with work. He just showered and dressed and while he waited he listened to some of his cassettes. Then he put a fresh new cassette in the recorder and labeled it "Nina." He made sure his camera was loaded and reflected on the pleasure of developing pictures, watching the images forming on the prints . . .

At ten after five he left for Driftwood Lane. He cruised her street before deciding to park in the woods next to her house. Just in case . . .

He walked through the woods near the shore. He remembered how the water was lapping on the beach, a friendly sound that thrilled and warmed him even on the cold night.

Her car was in the driveway behind the house; her keys were in the ignition. He could see Nina through the kitchen window; moving around, unpacking groceries. The globe was off the fixture so the room was very bright. And she was so beautiful with that pale blue sweater over her slacks and that scarf knotted at her throat. He changed the tire very fast, keeping an eye out for any signs of other people in the house. He knew he'd make love to her and that secretly she wanted him to. Just the way she hinted that her husband had been angry at her showed she needed a sympathetic man. He turned on the recorder and began to whisper into it his plans for making Nina happy when he told her his feelings about her.

He went up to the kitchen door and knocked on it softly. She ran over, looked startled, but he held up her keys, smiling at her through the glass. Right away she began to smile and opened the door, all warm

and friendly, her voice like arms around him, inviting him in, telling him how nice he was.

Then she asked him what she owed him. He reached his hand up, he had his gloves on, of course, and switched off the kitchen light. He put his hands on her face and kissed her. "Pay me like this," he whispered.

She slapped him, a stunning slap, impossibly hard from that small hand. "Get out of here," she said, spilling the words out like he was dirt, like he hadn't gotten all dressed up for her, like he hadn't done her a favor.

He went wild. Like the other times. Rejection did that to him. She should have known better than to lead him on like that. He stretched out his hands, wanting to hurt her, to squeeze that nastiness out of her. He reached for her scarf. But somehow she slipped away from him and ran into the living room. She never uttered a sound, never screamed for help. Afterward he understood why. She didn't want him to know the child was in the house. But she tried to pick up a poker from the fireplace.

He just laughed. He talked to her very low telling her what he would do. He held both her hands in one of his and put the poker back. Then he grabbed her scarf and twisted it around her neck, twisted while she gurgled and gagged, and her hands like a doll's hands waved and dropped and went limp, while her great brown eyes widened and glazed and accused, while her face turned blue.

The gurgling stopped. He was holding her with one hand, snapping the picture, wishing her eyes would close, when somewhere behind him the gurgling, choking sound began again.

He swung around. The boy was standing in the foyer, staring at him with huge brown eyes that burned through him. The boy was gasping just like she'd been gasping.

It was like he hadn't killed her at all; like she'd moved into the boy's body and was going to punish him, was taunting him, promising revenge.

He started across the room for the boy. He'd make him stop that noise, he'd close those eyes. He cupped his hands, bent over the boy . . .

The bell rang.

He had to run. He raced through the foyer into the kitchen, slipped out the back door while he heard the bell ring again. He was out through the woods, in his car, back in his shop in a few minutes. Calm. Be calm. He went to the Mill for a hamburger and beer, was there when the news of the murder on Driftwood Lane swept through the town.

But he was scared. Suppose that trooper recognized Nina's picture in the paper, said at headquarters, "Funny thing, last night I saw her on the road, some guy named Taggert was fixing her car . . ."

He decided to get out of town. But when he was packing he heard on the news that an eyewitness, a neighbor, had been knocked down by someone running out of the Peterson house, that she had positively identified him as Ronald Thompson, a local seventeen-year-old, and that Thompson had been seen talking to Mrs. Peterson a few hours before the crime.

Arty put his camera and recorder and prints and film and cassettes inside a metal box and buried it under a bush behind his shop. Something told him to wait.

Then Thompson was caught at that motel in Virginia, and the kid identified him, too.

The luck. The incredible luck. The living room had been dark. The boy might not have seen his face clearly and then Thompson had gone into the house.

But he'd started to go for the kid; he'd gotten close to him. Neil must have been in shock. But suppose he remembered some day.

The thought haunted Arty's dreams. The eyes followed him all through his restive nights. Sometimes he woke up in the middle of the night, sweating, trembling, thinking the eyes were looking in his bedroom window, or the wind would be making that same gurgling sound.

He never went looking for girls after that. Never. He just went to the Mill Tavern most nights and got friendly with the guys there and especially with Bill Lufts. Bill talked a lot about Neil.

Until last month; until he knew he had to dig out his cassettes from where he'd buried them and listen to them again.

That night on his C.B. he heard the Callahan girl saying she had a blowout, and he went looking for her. Two weeks later he went out when Mrs. Ambrose got on the C.B. looking for directions, saying she was almost out of gas.

Now Fairfield County was in an uproar again, looking for a guy they called the C.B. killer. You didn't leave any trace, he told himself.

But after these last two, the dreams of Nina came every single night. Accusing. Then a couple of weeks ago, Bill Lufts drove up to his place with the boy Neil beside him in the wagon. Neil stared at Arty.

That was when he knew he had to kill Neil before he left Carley. And when Lufts bragged about the trust fund in Neil's name—his wife had seen the bank statement on Peterson's desk—he'd known how to get the money he needed.

Whenever he thought about Nina, he hated Steve Peterson more. Peterson had been able to touch her without getting slapped; Peterson was a big-shot editor; Peterson had people to wait on him; Peterson had a good-looking new girlfriend. He'd show him.

The room in Grand Central had always been there in his consciousness. A place to hide if ever he needed it, or a place to take a girl where no one would find her.

He used to think all the time about blowing up Grand Central Station when he was working in that room. He'd think about how scared and shocked the people would be when a bomb went off, when they felt

the floor give way under them and the ceilings fall in; all those people who ignored him when he was trying to be friendly, who never smiled at him, who rushed past him, who looked through him, who ate off the dishes he had to wash and left them greasy with shells and salad dressing and smears of butter.

Then everything came together. The plan. The August *Rommel* Taggert plan. A fox's plan.

If only Sharon didn't have to die; if only she'd loved him. But in Arizona many girls would be friendly. He'd have so much money.

It was a good idea to have Sharon and Neil die just at the minute the Thompson kid was executed. Because he was executing them, too, and Thompson deserved to die for having interfered that night.

And all those people in Grand Central—tons of rubble falling on them! They'd know how it felt to be trapped.

And he'd be free.

Soon. Soon it would be over.

Arty narrowed his eyes realizing that much time had passed. It was always like that when he began to think of Nina. It was time to go.

He turned the ignition key in the Pontiac. At quarter of two he drove to the tollbooth and handed over the ticket he'd taken at the automatic gate for his Volks. The collector looked sleepy. "Two hours and twenty-five minutes—that'll be two bucks, mister."

He drove out of the airport to a phone on Queens Boulevard. Promptly at two, he called the payphone outside Bloomingdale's. As soon as Peterson answered, he directed him to the public phone at Ninety-sixth Street.

He was getting hungry and he had fifteen minutes.

In an all-night diner, he gulped down coffee and some toast as he watched the clock.

At 2:15, he dialed the Ninety-sixth Street public phone and tersely directed Steve to the meeting place he'd selected.

Now for the really dangerous part.

At 2:25 he began driving toward Roosevelt Avenue. The streets were nearly deserted. There was no sign of unmarked cop cars. He'd be able to pick them out; he was the master of cruising around on roads without looking suspicious.

Last week he'd selected Roosevelt Avenue for the meeting place. He'd timed how long it would take to get back to LaGuardia Airport from there. Exactly six minutes. Just in case the cops came along with Peterson, he'd have a good chance of getting away from them.

Because of the elevated train, Roosevelt was filled with pillars that obstructed the view, that made it hard to see what was happening across the street or down the block. It was the best place to make contact.

At exactly 2:35 he parked on Roosevelt Avenue, facing the Brooklyn Queens Expressway, less than half a block to the access road.

At 2:36, he saw the lights of a car coming off the BQE from the opposite direction. Instantly he slipped the stocking mask over his face.

It was Peterson's Mercury. For a second he thought Peterson was going to pull up to him, the car swerved right at him. Or was he trying to take a picture of the Pontiac? A lot of good that would do.

Peterson's car stopped almost directly across the street. He swallowed nervously. But there were no other headlights coming off the expressway. He had to move fast. He reached for the duffel bag. In his electronics magazine he'd read that in payments of ransom, suitcases were usually bugged. He wasn't taking any chances.

The feel of the duffel bag, light, empty, ready to be filled, was reassuring. He opened the car door and crossed the street noiselessly. He needed just sixty seconds and then he'd be safe. He tapped on the window of Peterson's car, motioned him to open it. As the window slid down he looked quickly into the car. Peterson was alone. He shoved in the duffel bag.

The dim street lights threw shadows of the pillars against the car. In the soft, whispery voice he'd practiced, he told Peterson not to look at him, to put the money in the duffel bag.

Peterson didn't argue. Behind the stocking mask, Foxy's eyes roamed the area. His ears strained. But there was no sound of anyone coming. The cops had to be tailing Peterson, but probably wanted to be sure he made contact.

He watched Peterson drop the last packet of bills in the duffel bag and told him to close it and hand it over. Greedily, he felt its weight. Remembering to speak very low, he warned Peterson to wait fifteen minutes and told him that Sharon and Neil could be picked up at 11:30.

"Did you have anything to do with my wife's death?"

The question startled Foxy. How much were they beginning to suspect? He had to get away. He was sweating now, heavy beads of perspiration that soaked his suit under the brown coat, that warmed the soles of his feet even while the sharp wind bit at his ankles.

He crossed the street, got back in the Pontiac. Would Peterson dare to follow him?

No. He was still parked in the dark, silent car.

Foxy floored the accelerator of the Pontiac, shot onto the access road to the Brooklyn Queens Expressway, drove on that two minutes to the Grand Central Parkway, slipped into the light eastbound traffic and three minutes later exited at LaGuardia Airport.

At 2:46 he was reaching for a parking ticket at the automatic entry to parking lot five.

Ninety seconds later, the Pontiac was parked exactly where he'd found it, the only perceptible difference a fraction less gas and six more miles registered on the odometer.

He got out of the Pontiac, carefully locked it, and carried the duffel bag to the dark-green Beetle. His first easy breath came when he was inside the Volks and clawing at the cord of the duffel bag.

Finally he had it loose. He switched the beam of his flashlight inside the bag. A smile, humorless as a jack-o'-lantern's, played on his lips. He reached for the first packet of money and began to count.

It was all there. Eighty-two thousand dollars. He reached for the empty suitcase in the back seat and neatly began to pile the packets inside it. This bag he'd carry on the plane.

At 7:00 A.M. he pulled out of the parking lot, blended with the early morning commuter traffic into Manhattan, parked the car in the Biltmore garage, and hurried upstairs to his room for a shave and shower and room service.

◠ CHAPTER 36

By 4:00 A.M. it was clear that the one lead they had, the license number of the car the abductor had used, was going sour.

The first blow was to find that the car was registered to Henry A. White, a vice-president of the International Food Company of White Plains.

Agents rushed to White's home in Scarsdale and put it under surveillance. But the Pontiac was not in the garage and the house had a closed-up look. Not one window in the sprawling house was open even a fraction and the single light shining through the drawn drapes was probably on a timer.

The security guard at International Food was contacted. He called the head of the personnel department. In turn a product manager from White's department was reached. In a sleepy voice, he told investigators that White had just returned from a three-week stay at their world headquarters in Switzerland; that he'd had dinner with two of his staff in Pastor's Restaurant in White Plains and was leaving directly from there to join his wife for a brief skiing vacation. She was staying either in Aspen or Sun Valley with friends.

At five o'clock, Hugh and Steve started for Carley. Hugh drove. Steve watched the road thread through Westchester, approach Connecticut. There were so few cars out. Most people were in bed, able to reach for their wives, able to make sure their children were covered, that open windows weren't too drafty. Were Neil and Sharon in a drafty, cold place now?

Why am I thinking that? he wondered. Vaguely he remembered reading that when people couldn't control overwhelming events, they became concerned about small problems. Were Sharon and Neil still alive? That's what he should be worrying about. Spare them, oh Lord in mercy, spare them . . .

"What do you make of the Pontiac?" he asked Hugh.

"It'll probably turn out that White's car was stolen from wherever he left it," Hugh replied.

"What do we do next?"

"We wait."

"For what?"

"He may release them. He did promise. He has the money."

"He's covered his tracks so carefully. He's thought of everything. You don't really expect him to release two people who could identify him, do you?"

"No," Hugh admitted.

"Is there nothing else we can do?"

"If he doesn't keep his word and let them go, we have to consider blowing this open, releasing it to the media. Maybe somebody saw or heard something."

"What about Ronald Thompson?"

"What about him?"

"Suppose he's been telling the truth. Suppose we find that out after eleven-thirty?"

"What is your point?"

"My point is, do we have the right not to admit that Neil and Sharon have been kidnapped?"

"I doubt that it would affect the Governor's decision about Thompson. There's absolutely no proof that this is a hostage situation but if she thinks it is, it might only make her anxious to get the execution over with. She's already been criticized for granting Thompson two stays. Those kids in Georgia had the switch pulled on them right on the dot. And there still may be a simple explanation of how Foxy managed to get a tape or cassette with your wife's voice on it . . . an explanation that has nothing to do with her death."

Steve stared ahead. They were passing Greenwich. He and Sharon had been at a party in Brad Robertson's house in Greenwich during the

holidays. Sharon wore a black velvet skirt, a brocaded jacket. She looked lovely. Brad said to him, "Steve, if you have any sense, you'll latch onto that girl."

"Could publicity panic the kidnapper?" He knew the answer. Even so he had to ask.

"I would say so." Hugh's inflection was different, crisper. "What's on your mind, Mr. Peterson?"

The question. Flat. Direct. Steve felt his mouth go dry. It's only a hunch, he told himself. It's probably irrelevant. If I begin this, I can't stop it. It may cost Neil and Sharon their lives.

Bleakly, miserably, he waited, poised like a diver for a leap that would throw him into an uncontrollable current. He thought of Ronald Thompson at the trial, the young face, scared but adamant. "I didn't do it. She was dead when I got there. Ask the kid. . . ."

"How would you feel if it were your only child? How would you feel . . ."

It is my only child, Mrs. Thompson, he thought.

He began to speak. "Hugh, do you remember what Bob Kurner said, that he thought the murders of those four women and Nina's murder were tied together?"

"I heard him and I told you what I think. He's grasping at straws."

"Suppose I told you that Kurner may be right, that there may be a link between Nina's death and the others."

"What are you talking about?"

"Remember Kurner said that the only thing he couldn't understand is that the others had car trouble and Nina didn't; that she'd been strangled at home, not somewhere on the road?"

"Go on."

"The night before she was murdered, Nina got a flat. I was at a late meeting in New York and didn't get home till well after midnight. She was asleep. But the next morning when she drove me to the train, I noticed the spare was on her car . . ."

"Go on."

"Remember that transcript Kurner left? The Thompson boy said something about joking with Nina about bad luck turning into good luck and she said something about the groceries all fitting in the trunk."

"What are you saying?"

"Her trunk was small. If she had extra room in it, it can only mean that the spare tire hadn't been put back. That was after four o'clock and she must have gone directly home. Dora was at the house cleaning that day and she said Nina drove her home shortly before five."

"Then she and Neil went straight back to your house?"

"Yes, and he went up to play with his trains. Nina unloaded the car. Remember all those bundles were on the table? We know she died in the next few minutes. I looked at her car that night. The spare tire was in the trunk. The new radial was back on her front wheel."

"You're saying that someone brought the tire back, changed it, then killed her?"

"When else could the tire have been changed except right at that time? And if that happened, that Thompson boy may be innocent. He may even have frightened off the killer by ringing the bell. For God's sake, find out if he remembers whether the spare was in the trunk when he loaded those groceries. I should have realized that tire might be important when I checked it that night. But I hated remembering that I'd blown up at Nina the very last minute I was with her."

Hugh pressed his foot on the accelerator. The speedometer climbed from sixty to seventy to eighty. The car screeched into the driveway as the first hint of dawn cut across the somber sky. Hugh rushed to the phone. Before he took off his coat, he dialed the prison at Somers and demanded to speak to the warden. ". . . no, I'll hold on." He turned to Steve. "The warden's been in his office all night, just in case the Governor decided to call. They're shaving the kid now."

"Good God."

"Even if he claims that the trunk was empty, it's not proof. Everything is still supposition. Somebody could have dropped off that tire, changed it for her, been gone. It still doesn't let Thompson off the hook."

"We both believe Thompson is innocent," Steve said. Dully he thought, I have always believed it. Dear God, in my heart I have always believed it, and never faced it.

"Yes, I'm here . . ." Hugh listened. "Thank you very much." He slammed down the phone. "Thompson swears the spare was missing when he loaded the groceries."

"Call the Governor," Steve pleaded. "Tell her, beg her, to at least delay the execution. Put me on if it will help."

Hugh was dialing the State House. "It's not evidence," he said. "It's a string of coincidences. I doubt she'll postpone it on this. When she hears that Sharon and Neil are missing—and you have to tell her that now—she may be convinced this is some kind of last-ditch trick."

The Governor absolutely could not be reached. She had referred all requests for further postponements of the execution to the Attorney General to appraise. He would be in his office at eight o'clock. No, his private phone number would not be given out.

There was nothing to do except wait. Steve and Hugh sat silently in the den as faint, watery light began to filter through the window. Steven

tried to pray, could only think Dear God, they are so young, all three so young, please . . .

At six o'clock Dora came down the stairs, her footsteps heavy and unsteady. Looking aged and infinitely weary, she silently began to make coffee.

At six-thirty Hugh spoke to FBI headquarters in New York. There were no new leads. Henry White had taken a 1:00 A.M. flight to Sun Valley. They'd been too late to catch him at the airport there. He'd been driven away in a private car. They were checking motel registrations and condominium rentals. The APB for the Pontiac hadn't produced any results. They were still checking the regulars from the Mill Tavern.

At seven-thirty-five Bob Kurner's car plummeted down the road and pulled into the driveway. He rang the bell furiously, stalked past Dora and demanded to know why Ronald had been asked about the spare tire.

Hugh glanced at Steve. Steve nodded. Tersely Hugh explained.

Bob paled. "Do you mean to say that your son and Sharon Martin were kidnapped, Mr. Peterson, and you've been covering it up?" he demanded. "When the Governor knows this, she'll have to postpone the execution. She has no choice."

"Don't count on it," Hugh warned.

"Mr. Peterson, I'm sorry for you, but you had no right not to tell me about this last night," Bob said bitterly. "My God, can't we reach the Attorney General before eight?"

"That's only twenty minutes."

"Twenty minutes is a lot when you've got only three hours and fifty minutes left to live, Mr. Taylor."

At exactly eight o'clock Hugh reached the Attorney General. He spoke for thirty-five minutes, his voice forceful, arguing, pleading. "Yes sir, I realize the Governor has already granted two stays. . . . I understand that the Connecticut Supreme Court unanimously confirmed the verdict. . . . No sir, we don't have *proof.* . . . It's more than *speculation* though . . . the cassette. . . . Yes sir, I'd appreciate if you'll call the Governor. . . . May I put Mr. Peterson on . . . ? All right, I'll hold."

Hugh cupped his hand over the phone. "He's going to call her but let me tell you, he's not going to recommend a stay."

Three minutes passed slowly. Steve and Bob did not look at each other. Then Hugh said, "Yes, I'm here . . . but . . ."

He was still protesting when Steve heard the unmistakable sound of the dial tone. Hugh let the phone drop. "The execution's on," he told them flatly.

CHAPTER 37

The pain. It was so hard to think with the pain shooting up through her body. If she could only unzip her boot. Her ankle was a mass of burning concrete, swelling against the boot, against the biting twine.

She should have taken a chance and screamed when they were going through the terminal. Better to have risked it then. What time was it? Time didn't exist. Monday night. Tuesday. Was it still Tuesday? Was it Wednesday yet?

How could they get out of here?

Neil. She could hear the rasping breath close to hers. He was trying to breathe slowly, trying to obey her. Sharon heard the moans coming from her lips, tried to bite them back.

She felt Neil sliding closer to her, trying to comfort her. Neil would be so like Steve when he grew up. *If* he grew up . . .

Steve. What would it be like to live with Steve, to make a life with him and Neil? Steve who had known so much pain.

Everything had always been so easy for her. Her father saying, "Sharon was born in Rome, Pat in Egypt, Tina in Hong Kong." Her mother, "We have friends all over the world." Even when they found out that she was dead, they'd have each other. When Steve lost Neil, he'd have no one.

Steve asking, "How come you're still single?" Because she hadn't wanted the responsibility of loving someone else.

Neil. So afraid that the Lufts would take him with them. So afraid that she'd take Steve away from him.

She had to get him out of here.

Again she tried rubbing her wrists against the cinderblock wall. But the cords were too tight, biting into her wrists. She couldn't get them in contact with the wall.

She tried to think. Her only hope was to get Neil free, to get him out of this room. If he opened the door from the inside, would the bomb explode?

The knob in the bathroom. If Foxy came back, if he let her go into the bathroom again, maybe she could pull the knob, break it off.

What would he do with them when he got the money? She was drifting off. Time . . . how much time . . . time passing . . . was it day or night? . . . muted train sounds . . . come for us, Steve . . . I blame you, Miss Martin . . . it is the issue, Miss Martin . . . none so blind as those who will not see . . . I love you, Sharon, I've missed you terribly . . . big, gentle hands on her face . . .

Big gentle hands on her face. Sharon opened her eyes. Foxy was bending over her. With horrible gentleness his hands were running over her face, her neck. He slipped the gag from her mouth and kissed her. His lips were pokerhot, his mouth mushy. She tried to turn her head. It was such an effort.

He whispered, "It's all finished, Sharon. I have the money. I have to go now."

She tried to focus her eyes. His features emerged from the blur, glittering eyes and a throbbing pulse and narrow lips.

"What are you going to do to us?" It was so hard to talk.

"I'm going to leave you right here. I'll tell Peterson where to pick you up."

He was lying. It was like before, when he'd been leading her on, toying with her. No, she'd tried to trick him and then he'd pushed her down.

"You're going to kill us."

"That's right, Sharon."

"You killed Neil's mother."

"That's right, Sharon. Oh, I almost forgot." He was moving away from her, reaching down, unfolding something. "I'll put this picture up with the others." Something was floating over her head. Neil's eyes were staring down at her, eyes that were part of a sprawled body, a body with a scarf around its neck. A shriek tore her throat, pushing back pain and dizziness. Suddenly she was completely rational, focusing, looking at the picture, at the glittering, mad eyes of the man holding it.

He was hanging it next to the others on the wall over the cot, hanging it carefully, ritualistic in his exactness.

Fearfully, she watched him. Would he kill them now, strangle them as he'd strangled those women?

"I'm going to set the clock for you now," he told her.

"The clock?"

"Yes. It will make the bomb go off at eleven-thirty. You won't feel anything, Sharon. You'll just be gone, and Neil will be gone, and Ronald Thompson will be gone."

Carefully, delicately, he was opening the suitcase. She watched as he took a clock out, as he consulted his wristwatch and set the clock to 8:30. It was 8:30 Wednesday morning. The alarm—he was setting the alarm to 11:30. Now he was attaching wires to the clock.

Three hours.

Carefully, he lifted the suitcase, put it on top of the deep sinks near the door. The face of the clock was directly opposite her across the room. The hands and numerals glowed.

"Do you want to have anything before I go, Sharon, a glass of water? Would you like me to kiss you good-bye?"

"Could I . . . would you let me go into the bathroom?"

"Sure, Sharon." He came over, untied her hands, picked her up. Her legs crumbled under her. Pain made her shiver. Black curtains closed over her eyes. No . . . no . . . no . . . she could not faint.

He left her inside the dark cubbyhole, holding onto the doorknob. She twisted it around, around, around, praying the sound wasn't carrying. A faint cracking sound. The handle broke off.

Sharon ran her fingers over the separated end, felt the jagged edge of the broken metal. She slipped the handle in the deep pocket of her skirt. When she opened the door she had one hand in her pocket. If he felt anything when he carried her back to the cot, he'd think it was her fist.

It worked. He was hurrying now, anxious to be out of there. He tossed her back down; retied her hands quickly. She was able to keep them a little separated, those cords were not as tight as the others. The gag was yanked over her mouth.

He was bending over her. "I could have loved you very much, Sharon, as I think you could have loved me."

With a quick movement he pulled off Neil's blindfold. Neil blinked, his eyes swollen, his pupils enormous.

The man looked directly into the eyes; his gaze slid to the picture on the wall then back to Neil's face.

Abruptly he dropped the child's head, turned and clicked off the lights as for the last time he slipped out of the room.

Sharon stared at the glowing face of the clock. It was 8:36.

CHAPTER 38

Glenda's bed was strewn with pages, pages crumpled, begun again. "No . . . on the fourteenth I didn't go straight to the doctor. I stopped at the library . . . put that in, Roger, I spoke to a couple of people there. . . ."

"I'll start a new sheet. This one's too cluttered. Who did you talk to in the waiting room at the doctor's?"

Minutely, they reviewed every detail of the past month. Nothing triggered awareness in Glenda of the man who called himself Foxy. At 4:00 A.M. at her persuasion, Roger called FBI headquarters and asked to speak to Hugh. Hugh told him about the contact.

"He says that the kidnapper has promised that Sharon and Neil can be picked up at eleven-thirty," Roger told her.

"They don't trust him, do they?"

"No, I don't think they do."

"If it is someone familiar to me, it might be someone Neil knows from this area. He couldn't let Neil go."

"Glenda, we're both so tired we're incapable of thinking. Let's try to sleep for a few hours. Then maybe something will come to you. Your subconscious works when you're sleeping. You know that."

"All right." Wearily, she started to stack the sheets of paper in chronological order.

He set the alarm for seven. For three hours they slept—exhausted, troubled sleep.

At seven Roger went down to make tea. Glenda slipped a nitroglycerin tablet under her tongue, went into the bathroom, washed her face, got back into bed and picked up her pad.

At nine Marian arrived. At 9:15 she came up to see Glenda. "I'm sorry you're not feeling well, Mrs. Perry."

"Thank you."

"I'll stay out of your way. If it's all right, I'll concentrate on one room at a time downstairs."

"That would be fine."

"That way by the end of the week, downstairs will be shipshape. I can tell you like a house kept nice."

"Yes, I do. Thank you."

"I'm just glad to be here, that I didn't have to disappoint you with the trouble we had over our car . . ."

"My husband mentioned something." Deliberately, Glenda raised her pen, held it poised.

"Really awful. After just spending four hundred dollars to get it fixed. Normally we wouldn't spend that much on an old car, but Arty's such a good mechanic that my husband said it was worth it. Well, I see you're busy. I shouldn't be gabbing. Would you like a little breakfast?"

"No thank you, Mrs. Vogler."

The door closed behind her. A few minutes later Roger came back in. "I spoke to a couple of people at the office. Said I had a touch of flu."

"Roger . . . wait a minute." Glenda depressed the button on the recorder. The now familiar sentence filled their ears: *Be at the Exxon service station. . . .* Glenda snapped the machine off. "Roger, when did we get my car serviced?"

"A little over a month ago, I think. Bill Lufts took it over to that place he recommended."

"Yes, and you dropped me off on your way to work when it was ready. *Arty,* that was the name wasn't it?"

"I believe so. Why?"

"Because the car was ready but he was just about to fill it with gas. I was talking to him, standing next to it. I noticed his sign said 'A. R. Taggert' and asked if the 'A' stood for Arthur, because I'd heard Bill call him Arty.

"Roger," Glenda's voice became high-pitched. She sat up and grabbed his hand, "Roger, he told me that people around here started to call him Arty because of the sign 'A. R. Taggert,' but that his name really was August Rommel Taggert.

"And I said, 'Rommel—wasn't he the famous German General?'

"And he said, 'Yes, Rommel was the Desert *Fox.*' The way he said *fox* . . . and the way he said *foxy* on the phone the other night. Roger, I swear to you, that mechanic is Foxy and he's the one who kidnapped Neil and Sharon!"

It was 9:31 A.M.

~~~ *CHAPTER 39*

She was going to her room. Olendorf was off today and the other guard would never bother her. Lally hadn't slept all night. She was getting sick. The arthritis was murder, but it was more than that. There was something inside her winding down. She could feel it. She just wanted to get into her room and lie down on the cot and close her eyes.

She *had* to.

She drifted down with the 8:40 Mount Vernon passengers and slipped around to the ramp. She had extra newspapers in her shopping bag to cover herself, but she didn't stop for coffee. She wasn't hungry for anything, just her room.

It didn't even matter if the man was there. She'd take her chances. The comforting noise of the generators and vents greeted her. It was gloomy here like always, and that was good with her. Her heavy sneakers were silent as she padded across to the staircase.

And then she heard it.

The muffled sound of a door opening slowly. Her door. Lally shrank behind the generator into the shadows.

Soft, low footsteps. He was coming down the metal steps, the same man. She melted back, pressed her bulk against the wall. Should she confront him? No . . . no. Every instinct warned her to hide. She watched him stand, listen intently, then move swiftly toward the ramp.

In a minute he'd be gone and she'd be in her room. If the girl was still there, she'd scare her off.

Her arthritic fingers started to pull the key from her pocket, fumbled. It fell with a ping at her feet.

She held her breath. Had he heard? She didn't dare to look out. But the footsteps were completely gone. There was no sound of anyone coming back. She waited ten minutes, ten long minutes, trying to calm the pounding of her heart. Then slowly, painfully, she bent down, felt on the ground for her key. It was so dark here; her eyes were so bad now. She felt the outline of the key and sighed with relief.

Lally was just beginning to straighten up when something grazed against her back, something shivery cold. She gasped as it touched her skin, touched and slipped in, so sharp, so quickly that she barely felt the blinding pain, the warm gushing of her blood as she clumsily sank to her knees and slumped forward. Her forehead took the impact of the fall; her left arm arced out. As she slipped into unconsciousness, her right fist closed around the key to her room.

⬱ *CHAPTER 40*

At 9:30 an agent from FBI headquarters phoned Hugh Taylor at Steve's home. "We think we have something, Hughie."

"What is it?"

"That Arty—the mechanic, Arty Taggert."

"Yeah."

"There used to be a guy known as Gus Taggert who got picked up for hanging around the Port Authority about twelve years ago. Suspect in disappearance of some sixteen-year-old runaway. We couldn't pin anything on him, but a lot of guys thought he did something to her. He was questioned about disappearances of other young girls, too. His description matches the one you gave us."

"Good work. What else have you got on him?"

"We're trying to check out where he used to live. He had a bunch of jobs in New York, pumping gas on the west side, busboy in an Eighth Avenue joint, dishwasher in the Oyster Bar . . ."

"Concentrate on where he lived; find out if he has any family."

Hugh hung up the phone. "Mr. Peterson," he said carefully, "there's a chance we have a new lead. A mechanic who hangs around Mill Tavern seems to have been a suspect in several cases of young girls disappearing about twelve years ago. Name of Arty Taggert."

"A mechanic." Steve's voice rose. "*A mechanic.*"

"Exactly. I know what you're thinking. It's a slim chance, but if someone fixed your wife's tire that day, is it possible she'd have written a check in payment? Do you have your canceled checks or stubs from January two years ago?"

"Yes, I'll look."

"Remember, we're only examining any lead we can. We have no proof at all of anything about this Arty except that he was questioned once years ago."

"I see." Steve walked over to his desk.

The phone rang. It was Roger Perry shouting the news that Glenda was positive a mechanic called A. R. Taggert was Foxy.

Hugh slammed the phone down, was about to pick it up to dial New York when it rang again. Impatiently he barked "Yes." His expression changed, became inscrutable. "What? Hold it, start again."

Steve watched as Hugh's eyes hardened into slits of concentration. When Hugh whipped out a pen, he held the memo pad for him. Ignoring the other man's attempt to screen what he was writing, Steve stared at the pad, digesting the words as they went down.

> Thank you for the money. It is all there. You have kept your promise. Now I will keep mine. Neil and Sharon are alive. At 11:30 they will be executed during an explosion in New York State. In the rubble from that explosion you can dig for their bodies.
>
> FOXY

Hugh said, "Repeat that again so I'm sure I have it straight." A moment later he said, "Thank you. We'll be in touch with you shortly." He hung up the phone.

"Who took the call?" Steve asked. Merciful numbness was paralyzing his capacity to think, to fear.

Hugh waited a long minute before answering. When he did his voice was infinitely weary. "The mortician in Carley who handled your wife's funeral arrangements," he said.

It was 9:35 A.M.

f that old hag hadn't made that noise! Arty was drenched in perspiration. His new green suit smelled really bad now, just the way it always did after . . .

Suppose he hadn't heard her? She must be the one who'd been staying in the room, who dragged that cot in. That meant she must have a key. If he hadn't heard her, she'd have gone in, found them. They'd have time to get experts to deactivate the bomb.

He walked rapidly through the terminal to the arcade that led to the Biltmore and picked up the car from the Biltmore garage. The suitcase and radio were already packed in it. He drove swiftly up the East Side Drive to the Triborough Bridge. It was the quickest way to LaGuardia. He was frantic now to get out of New York. The plane to Phoenix left at 10:30.

He returned to the parking lot he'd left only hours before. The thought of how successful his plan had been to pick up the ransom soothed him. This time he parked the Volks far away from the tollgate in the area where people parked for the Eastern Shuttle. That section was always crowded. He'd filed the engine number off the Volks and the license plate could never be traced to him. He'd taken it off a junked car five years ago. Anyhow, it might be a month before someone noticed that the Volks had been here a long time.

He pulled his two suitcases, the light one with the clothes and cassettes and the heavy one with his money, and the crated C.B. radio out of the trunk. Now there was absolutely nothing to link him with the car.

He walked swiftly over to the bus stop. The courtesy airport bus came along and he got on it. The other passengers glanced at him indifferently. He could feel their dismissal. Just because he wasn't all dressed up. He sat next to a girl about nineteen years old, a very attractive girl. He didn't miss the wrinkle of distaste, the way the girl turned away from him. Bitch. Little did she know that he was a clever, wealthy man.

The bus stopped at the domestic terminal. He walked two hundred feet to the American Airlines special entrance. An attendant was checking in luggage. He wouldn't have to drag all this stuff around. He yanked out his ticket. The name on the ticket was Renard. That meant fox in French. It was the name he planned to use in Arizona.

"Check all three pieces, sir?"

"No! Not that one." He yanked the suitcase with the money out of the reach of the attendant.

"Sorry, sir. I'm not sure you can carry one that big on board."

"I must!" Deliberately, he tried to curb the intensity in his voice. "I have papers I have to work on."

The attendant shrugged. "All right, sir. I guess the stewardess can always put it in the cabin closet if necessary."

It was 9:28 and he was hungry again. But first he had the call to make. He selected a phonebooth in a far corner of the terminal and wrote down what he wanted to say so there'd be no mistake. He pictured what Steve Peterson would think when he got the message.

The funeral home phone was picked up promptly. His voice low, Foxy said, "You will be needed to pick up remains."

"Of course, sir. Who is calling?" The other voice was subdued.

"Are you ready to write this down?"

"Certainly."

Foxy's voice changed, became harsh. "Write it down, then read it right back to me and make sure you have it straight." He began to dictate, enjoying the shocked gasp he heard on the other end of the phone. "Now read it back," he demanded. A trembling voice obeyed then said, "My God, please. . . ."

Smiling, Foxy hung up.

He went into a cafeteria in the terminal and selected bacon, rolls, orange juice and coffee. He ate slowly, watching the people hurrying past.

Now he was beginning to relax. The thought of the phone call to the funeral home made him chuckle deep in the pit of his stomach. At first he was going to warn them of an explosion in New York *City*. At the very last minute he'd changed it to New York *State*. He could just imagine the cops going nuts now. A lot of good it would do them.

Arizona, land of the painted desert.

Looking into the boy's eyes had been necessary. He wouldn't have to run away from them ever again. He imagined what it would be like at 11:30 in Grand Central. The explosion would go upward. The whole ceiling would come crashing down on Neil and Sharon, tons and tons and tons of cement.

It was easy to make a bomb just like it was easy to fix an engine. All you did was read everything about it. Now the whole world would want to know who Foxy was. They'd probably write about him the way they did about Rommel.

He finished his coffee, wiped the back of his hand over his mouth. From the window he watched as people carrying bags hurried across the terminal to departure gates. He remembered the bombing of LaGuardia at Christmastime a couple of years before. That had caused panic, closed the airport. He's seen it on television.

He was already looking forward to being in a bar tonight in Phoenix watching the news reports of the explosion in Grand Central. It would be on television all over the world. But it would be even better if the cops had some place to start looking. The people who put those bombs in the office buildings did it that way. They called up and gave a big list of where they'd put bombs and the cops didn't know where to go first. They'd had to make people leave every building they talked about.

He could still do something like that. What should he tell them? He stared out. This was a busy airport. People running back and forth all over the place and it wasn't even as big as Kennedy.

Just like Grand Central. Or the bus terminal. Everybody rushing. Paying no attention to anybody. Just wanted to get where they were going. Didn't notice anybody. Didn't smile back.

An idea slowly took shape. Suppose he warned the cops. Suppose he told them that Sharon and Neil and the bomb were in a transportation center in New York City. That would mean they'd have to clear out both airports and the two bus terminals and Penn Station as well as Grand Central. They'd start searching under seats in the waiting rooms and opening lockers. They wouldn't know where to start. And all these people, these lousy people would be made to get out of all those places, to miss their trains and planes and buses.

They'd never find Sharon and Neil. Never. The only one who knew about that room was the old hag and he'd taken care of her. All by himself he could keep people in or out of the biggest city in the world with one more phone call. Peterson thought he was a big shot with his magazine and his trust fund and his girlfriend. Foxy laughed aloud. The couple sitting at the next table looked at him curiously.

He *would* call, just before he got on the plane. Who would he call?

The funeral home again? No.

Who else would be sure the call wasn't a fake?

He knew! Smiling, anticipating the reaction he'd get, he went for another coffee. At twelve minutes past ten he left the cafeteria, the suitcase gripped in his hand. He deliberately waited that long so that when they were x-raying the carry-on luggage they'd be hurrying. No one would be curious about his suitcase. Airlines loved to keep to their schedules.

At 10:15 he slipped into a phonebooth near departure gate 9, pulled out quarters and dimes and dialed a number. When the receiver at the other end was picked up, he whispered a message. He replaced the receiver gently, walked to the check-in desk and went through the inspection without a hitch.

The "boarding" sign was flashing as he walked across the waiting area to the covered ramp leading to the plane.

It was 10:16 A.M.

CHAPTER 42

Her clothes felt wet and warm and sticky. Blood. She was bleeding to death.

Death. She was going to die. Lally knew it. Through the dim fading light in her mind, she sensed it. Someone had killed her . . . the man who had taken her room had taken her life.

The room. Her room. She wanted to die in it. She wanted to be there. He'd never come back. He'd be afraid. Maybe no one would find her. Entombed. She'd be entombed in the only home she'd ever had. She'd be here sleeping forever with the comforting roar of her trains. Her mind was clearing . . . but she didn't have long. She knew it. She had to get to her room.

Aware of the key in her right fist, Lally tried to drag herself up. Something was pulling . . . the knife . . . the knife was still plunged into her. She couldn't reach it. She began to crawl . . .

She had to arc around. She'd been lying facing away from where the room was. The effort of turning her body . . . too much, too much. Slowly, inch by inch, she crawled until she was in the direction of her room. Twenty feet at least to the staircase. And then the stairs. Could she? Lally shook her head trying to clear away the darkness. She could feel blood running from her mouth. She tried to clear it from her throat.

Right hand . . . keep gripping the key . . . left hand forward . . . right knee, drag it forward . . . left knee . . . right hand . . . She would do it. Somehow she would manage to get up those stairs.

She kept in her mind the vision of opening the door, closing it . . . crawling inside . . . pulling herself up on the cot . . . lying there . . . closing her eyes . . . waiting.

In her room death would come as a friend, a friend with cool and gentle hands . . .

CHAPTER 43

They are dead, Steve thought. When you are condemned you are already dead. This afternoon Ronald Thompson's mother would claim her son's body. This afternoon the Sheridan Funeral Home would go to the site of an explosion and wait for Sharon's and Neil's bodies.

Somewhere in New York State, digging in the rubble . . . He was standing by the window. A knot of reporters and television cameras was grouped outside. "The word goes fast," he said. "We vultures of the media love a good story."

Bradley had just phoned. "Steve, what can I do?"

"Nothing. Nothing. Just let me know if you happen to see a Volks beetle, dark green, with a guy about thirty-eight years old in it. He probably has the license plates changed so that won't help. We have an hour and twenty minutes—an hour and twenty minutes."

"What have you done about the bomb threat?" he had asked Hugh.

"Alerted every major city in the state to stand by for an emergency. There's nothing more we can do. An explosion in New York State, *New York State*. Do you know how many thousands of square miles that covers? Mr. Peterson, there's still a chance this is a hoax. I mean, the threat of the explosion, the call to the funeral parlor."

"No, no, it's too late for them, too late." Steve thought, Bill and Dora Lufts moved in because of Nina's death. They were staying here to do him a favor, to take care of Neil for him. But Bill Lufts discussing his affairs may have caused Neil and Sharon's kidnapping—their death. Circle of death. No, please let them live, help us to find them . . .

Restlessly, he turned from the window. Hank Lamont had just come in with Bill. They were going over his story again. Steve knew it by heart.

"Mr. Lufts, you've talked to this Arty a lot. Please try to remember. Has he ever mentioned wanting to go some particular place? Has he ever talked about some place a lot, like Mexico . . . or Alaska?"

Bill shook his head. All this was too much for him. He knew that they thought Arty had kidnapped Neil and Sharon. Arty, a quiet fellow, a good mechanic. Just a couple of weeks ago he'd driven over to his place. Neil rode with him. He could remember the day exactly because Neil had a bad asthma attack that night. Desperately, he tried to remember what Arty talked about, but it seemed as though he never said much, just seemed real interested in Bill's stories.

Hank was furious at himself. He'd been sitting in the Mill Tavern buying that guy beers. He'd even told the office not to bother much about checking him. Lufts *had* to remember something. Like Hughie said, everything a man does leaves traces. He could see that guy walking out of the Mill—and he, Hank, not suspecting. Hank frowned. There had been some kind of crack Arty made when he said goodbye. What was it?

Bill was saying, ". . . and a nice quiet fellow, like I tell you. Minds his business. Maybe he did ask questions, just seemed friendly and interested like . . ."

"Hold on." Hank interrupted.

"What is it?" Hugh turned quietly to the younger agent. "You've got something?"

"Maybe. When Arty left with the others . . . and they said something about not having the chance to see Bill before he left for Rhode Island . . ."

"Yeah. And in a pig's eye Arty's heading for Rhode Island."

"That's what I mean. He said something else . . . and that advertising guy Allan Kroeger made a crack on top of it. A crack about . . . about the painted desert. That's it!"

"What?" Hugh demanded.

"When they said, 'too bad Bill Lufts isn't around to say goodbye,' Arty said, 'Rhode Island's not Arizona.' Could that have been a slip?"

"We'll find out soon." Hugh ran for the phone.

Roger came in, put his hand on Steve's shoulder and listened with him as Hugh barked orders into the phone, putting the awesome power of the Federal Bureau of Investigation into tracking down the new lead.

Finally Hugh put the phone down. "If he's heading for Arizona, we'll get him, Mr. Peterson. I can promise you that."

"When?"

Roger's face was the color of the bleak morning. "Steve, get out of here," he said. "Glenda wants you to come over. Please."

Steve shook his head.

"We'll both go," Hugh said briskly. "Hank, take over here."

Steve considered. "All right." He started toward the front door.

"No, let's go out the back way and through the woods. You'll be able to avoid the reporters."

A ghost of a smile touched Steve's lips. "But that's just it. I don't intend to avoid them."

He opened the door. The cluster of reporters broke past the agents stationed on the walk and raced to him. Microphones were shoved in front of his face. Television cameras angled to catch his drawn, tired face.

"Mr. Peterson, has there been any further word?"

"No."

"Do you think the kidnapper will carry out his threat to execute your son and Sharon Martin?"

"We have every reason to believe he's capable of this kind of violence."

"Do you think it's more than coincidence that the threatened explosion will occur at the exact minute Ronald Thompson is executed?"

"I do not think it is coincidence. I think the kidnapper Foxy may very well have been involved in my wife's death. I have tried to get that word

to the Governor, who refuses to speak with me. I now publicly implore her to delay the Thompson execution. That boy may very well be innocent—I think he is."

"Mr. Peterson, has your position on capital punishment changed in view of your terrible worry over your son and Miss Martin? When this kidnapper is apprehended would you want to see him executed?"

Steve reached down and pushed the microphones back from his face. "I want to answer your questions. Please give me the opportunity." The reporters became quiet. Steve looked directly into the camera. "Yes. I have changed my mind. I say this knowing that it is very unlikely that my son and Sharon will be found alive. But even if their kidnapper is apprehended too late to save them, I have learned something in these past two days. I have learned that no man has the right to determine the time of death of one of his fellow human beings. I believe that power rests only with Almighty God and . . ." his voice broke, "I only ask you to pray to God that Neil and Sharon and Ronald will be spared this morning."

Tears streamed down his cheeks. "Let me pass."

Quietly the reporters separated. Roger and Hugh ran behind him as he darted across the street.

Glenda was watching at the door. She opened it for them, put her arms around Steve. "Let it out, dear," she said quietly. "Go ahead."

"I can't let them go," he cried brokenly. "I can't lose them . . ."

She let him cry, hugging him as the broad shoulders heaved. If I had only remembered sooner, she agonized. Oh God, I've been too late to help him. She felt the shuddering of his body as he tried to stifle his sobs.

"Sorry, Glenda, you've had enough . . . you're not well."

"I'm all right," she said, "Steve, like it or not, you're going to have a cup of tea and some toast. You haven't eaten or slept in two days."

Somberly, they went into the dining room.

"Mr. Peterson," Hugh said carefully, "remember that pictures of Sharon and Neil are coming out on special editions of morning newspapers; they're being shown on every television station. Someone may have seen them, seen something."

"Do you think whoever has them paraded them in public?" Steve asked bitterly.

"Someone may have seen unusual activity; someone may have heard one of those phone calls being made; may have heard people talking in a bar . . ."

Marian poured water from the kettle into the teapot. The door between the kitchen and dining room was open and she could overhear the conversation. That poor, poor, Mr. Peterson. No wonder he'd seemed so rude when she spoke to him. He'd been all choked up about the little boy being kidnapped and she'd only upset him by talking about Neil. Shows you should never judge people. You don't know what kind of grief they're carrying around inside them.

Maybe if he'd just have some tea.

She brought in the teapot. Steve's face was buried in his hands.

"Mr. Peterson," she said gently, "let me fix you a nice hot cup of tea."

She picked up his cup. With the other hand she began to pour.

Slowly Steve lowered his hands from his face. The next instant the teapot was flying across the table; spilling down into the sugar bowl, running across the flowered placemats, a bubbling, tawny stream.

Glenda, Roger and Hugh jumped up. Shocked, they stared at Steve, who was gripping a terrified Marian's arms. "Where did you get that ring?" he shouted. "Where did you get that ring?"

CHAPTER 44

At Somers State Prison, Kate Thompson kissed her son goodbye. She stared unseeingly at the shaven spot like a monk's tonsure on his head, the slits in the side of his trousers.

She was dry-eyed as she felt his strong young arms around her. She pulled his face down. "Be brave, dear."

"I will. Bob said he'd look out for you, Mama."

She left him. Bob was going to stay until the end. She knew it was easier if she went now . . . easier for him.

She walked out of the prison, along the cold, windswept road to town. A police car came by. "Let me drop you, ma'am."

"Thank you." With dignity, she got in the car.

"You're staying at the motel, Mrs. Thompson?"

"No. Take me to St. Bernard's, please."

The morning masses were over; the church was empty. She knelt at the statue of the Virgin. "Be with him at the end. Take the bitterness from my heart. You who gave up your innocent Son, help me if I must give up mine. . . ."

A trembling Marian tried to speak. But she couldn't talk over the dryness in her mouth, the knot in her throat. Her tongue was so heavy. The tea had burned her hand. Her finger hurt where Mr. Peterson had wrenched the ring from it.

They were all looking at her as though they hated her. Mr. Peterson's grip on her wrist tightened. "Where did you get that ring?" he shouted again.

"I . . . I . . . I found it." Her voice quivered, broke.

"You *found* it!" Hugh shoved Steve away from Marian. His voice dripped with scorn. "You *found* it."

"Yes."

"Where?"

"In my car."

Hugh snorted and looked directly at Steve. "Are you positive this is the ring you gave Sharon Martin?"

"Absolutely. I bought it in a village in Mexico. It's one of a kind. Look!" He tossed it at Hugh. "Feel for a ridge on the left side of the band."

Hugh ran his finger over the ring. His expression hardened. "Where's your coat, Mrs. Vogler? You're coming in for questioning." Rapidly he spat out the Miranda warning. "You are not obliged to answer questions. Anything you say may be used against you. You have the right to call a lawyer. Let's go."

Steve shouted, "Damn you! Don't tell her she doesn't have to answer questions! Are you crazy? She's *got* to answer questions!"

Glenda's face was stony. She stared at Marian with angry disgust. "You talked about Arty this morning," she accused. "You talked about him fixing your car. How *could* you? How could you, a woman with children of her own, be part of this?"

Hugh spun around. "She talked about Arty?"

"Yes."

"Where is he?" Steve demanded. "Where has he got them? My God, the first minute I met you, you talked about Neil."

"Steve, Steve, calm down." Roger gripped his arm.

Marian knew she was going to faint. She had kept the ring and it wasn't hers. Now they thought she had something to do with the kidnapping. How could she make them believe her? Waves of dizziness made her vision cloudy. She'd make them call Jim. They had to call Jim. He'd help her. He'd come here and tell them about the car being stolen and that she'd found the ring in it. He'd *make* them believe her. The room started spinning. She clutched at the table.

Steve jumped forward to catch her before she fell. Through blurring eyes, she looked into his eyes, saw the agony in them. Pity for him calmed her. She grabbed him for support, forced herself to push back the dizziness. "Mr. Peterson." She could speak now. She had to speak. "I couldn't harm anybody. I want to help you. I *did* find the ring. In our car. Our car was stolen Monday night. Arty had just fixed it for us."

Steve looked down into the frightened, earnest face, the truthfilled eyes. Then the impact of what he had just heard sank into him. "Stolen! Your car was stolen Monday night?" Oh God, he thought, is there still a chance to find them?

Hugh snapped. "Let me handle this, Mr. Peterson." He pulled over a chair, helped Marian into it. "Mrs. Vogler, if you are telling the truth, you must help us. How well do you know Arty?"

"Not well. He's a good mechanic. I picked the car up from him on Sunday. Then on Monday I went to the four o'clock movie at the Carley Square. I parked it in the movie lot. It was gone when I got out just before seven-thirty."

"So he knew the condition of the car," Hugh said. "Did he know you'd be going to the movie?"

"He might have." Marian frowned. "Yes, we were talking about it at his place. And then he filled up the car with gas. He said it was a bonus because it was such an expensive job."

Glenda murmured, "Remember I said that it was a dark car, a wide one."

"Mrs. Vogler," Hugh said, "this is very important. Where was your car recovered?"

"In New York City. The police towed it. It was illegally parked."

"*Where?* By any chance do you know where they found it?"

Marian tried to think. "By a hotel, by some hotel."

"Mrs. Vogler, try to remember. Which hotel? You can save us so much time."

Marian shook her head. "I can't."

"Would your husband remember?"

"Yes, but he's on an outside job today. You'll have to phone the plant and see if they can reach him."

"What is the license number of your car, Mrs. Vogler?"

Quickly Marian gave it to him. What hotel? Jim had said something about the street it was on? Why? It would take them so long to reach Jim . . . to check the towing records . . . She had to remember. It was something about an old car on easy street. That's what Jim said. No, he said the *block* was named after a family that's always been on easy street. "Vanderbilt Avenue," she cried, "that's it. My husband told me the car was parked on Vanderbilt Avenue in front of some hotel ... the ... the *Biltmore* Hotel."

Hugh grabbed the phone and dialed FBI headquarters in New York. He issued rapidfire orders. "Get back to me fast." He hung up the phone.

"An agent is rushing over to the Biltmore with an old mug shot we have of Taggert," he said. "Let's hope it still looks like him and let's hope they can tell us something."

Tensely they waited.

"Please," Steve prayed. "Dear God, please!" The phone rang.

Hugh yanked the receiver off the hook. "What have you got?" He listened, then yelled, "Sweet Jesus. I'll take the copter down." He dropped the phone, looked at Steve. "The room clerk positively identified the picture as an A. R. Renard who checked in on Sunday night. He had a dark green Beetle in the Biltmore garage. He checked out this morning."

"*Renard*. That's French for fox!" Glenda cried.

"Exactly," Hugh said.

"Was he?" Steve gripped the table.

"He was alone. But the clerk remembers that he's been going in and out of the hotel at odd hours. Sometimes he's only been gone a short time, which could mean that he's been keeping Neil and Sharon somewhere in midtown. Remember that John Owens picked up a lot of train noises in the background of the cassette.

"We've got no time, no time." Steve's voice was bitter. "What good will knowing this do?"

"I'm taking the copter down to the Pan Am building. They'll clear us for an emergency landing there. If we can get Taggert in time, we'll make him talk. If we don't our best bet is still to concentrate our search in the area of the Biltmore. Do you want to come?"

Steve didn't bother to answer. He ran to the front door.

Glenda looked at the clock. "It is half past ten," she said tonelessly.

CHAPTER 46

Father Kennedy sat at his desk in St. Monica's rectory listening to the news bulletins. He shook his head thinking of the agonized face of Steven Peterson when he picked up the package at the rectory last night. No wonder he'd been so upset.

Could they possibly find that child and young woman in time? Where would that explosion occur? How many others would be killed?

The phone rang. Wearily, he picked it up. "Father Kennedy."

"Thanks for delivering the package I left on your altar last night, Father. This is Foxy."

The priest felt his throat constrict. The press had been told only that the cassette was found in the church. "What . . ."

"Never mind any questions. You just call Steve Peterson for me and give him another hint. Tell him I said the bomb will go off at a major transportation center in New York City. He can do his digging there."

The phone went dead.

CHAPTER 47

Foxy moved slowly across the waiting area of gate 9 toward the enclosed ramp that led to the plane. A presentiment of danger as definite as a tripped alarm was jangling nerves through his entire system. His eyes moved restlessly around the area. His fellow passengers were ignoring him, intent on juggling on-board luggage with pocketbooks or attaché cases while preparing to present boarding passes.

He glanced down at his own boarding pass neatly protruding from the ticket envelope he'd presented at the desk. In his other hand he was firmly gripping the old black suitcase.

Sound! That was it. The sound of running feet. Police! He dropped the ticket, vaulted the low divider between the boarding area and corridor. Two men were running swiftly down the corridor toward him. Desperately, he glanced around and noticed an emergency exit door some fifty feet away. It had to lead to the field.

The suitcase. He couldn't run with the suitcase. With only the briefest hesitation, he threw it backward. It thumped against the stone floor, slid a few inches and burst open. Money scattered over the corridor.

"Stop or we'll shoot!" a commanding voice shouted.

Foxy threw open the emergency door, setting off a loud pealing sound. He yanked it closed behind him and wove across the field. The Phoenix-bound plane was in his path. He ran around it. A small service van, its engine running, was near the left wing of the plane. The driver was just getting back in. Foxy grabbed him from behind, punched him viciously in the neck. The man grunted and collapsed. Foxy shoved him aside and jumped into the van. Pressing his foot down on the accelerator, he zigzagged around the plane. They wouldn't dare shoot with that plane in the way.

The cops would be following him in a car any second. Or they'd send cars from other areas to head him off. It was risky to get out of this car, more risky to stay in it. The runways were fenced off or ended at the Sound. If he drove down one of them, he'd be trapped.

They were looking for a man driving a service van on the field. They'd never look for him in the terminal. He spotted an identical van parked near a hangar, swung next to it and stopped. On the seat beside him a looseleaf book was open. He glanced at it swiftly. Something about requisitions, supplies. He grabbed it and got out of the van. A door marked "authorized personnel only" was opening. Bending his head over the book, he reached for it, prevented it from closing. A brisk-looking young woman in an airline uniform came out, glanced at the book in his hand, and sped past him.

Now his walk became authoritative, swift. He strode through the small corridor with the individual offices and an instant later was in the departure area. Airport police were running past him toward the field. Ignoring them, he walked through the terminal, out to the curb and hailed a cab.

"Where to?" the driver asked.

"Grand Central Station." He pulled out a twenty-dollar bill, the last of his money. "How fast can you get there? My plane's been canceled and I gotta make a train before eleven-thirty."

The driver was a kid, not more than twenty-two. "Mister, that's calling it a little close, but I'll do it. The roads are pretty good now and the traffic is real light." He pressed his foot on the gas pedal. "Hang on."

Foxy leaned back. Icy perspiration chilled his body. They knew who he was now. Suppose they'd looked up his old record. Suppose someone said, "He used to work in the Oyster Bar. He was a dishwasher." Suppose they thought about the room and went to look in it.

The bomb was attached to the clock now. That meant that if anyone went into the room, they'd have time to get Sharon and Neil out; maybe time to deactivate the bomb. No, it would probably go off if anyone touched it; it was that sensitive. But what good if Sharon and Neil got out?

He shouldn't have made that last phonecall. It was Sharon's fault. He should have strangled her yesterday. He remembered the feeling of his hands squeezing her neck, reaching for the soft pulse in her throat. He hadn't touched any of the others with his hands; he'd just knotted and twisted their scarves or belts. But her! His hands burned with the need to surround that throat. She had ruined it for him. She had tricked him, pretending to be in love with him. The way she'd looked at him, even from the television, acting like she wanted him, wanted him to take her away. Then yesterday she'd put her arms around him and tried to get his gun. She was no good. She was the worst of all of them, all the women in the foster homes, the matrons in the detention homes, all of them, pushing him away when he tried to kiss them. "Stop that! Don't do that!"

He shouldn't have taken Sharon to the room. If he'd just taken the boy, this wouldn't have happened. She'd made him take her, and now the money was gone and they knew who he was and he'd have to hide somewhere.

But he'd kill her first. By now they were probably just starting to evacuate the terminals and airports. They probably wouldn't think of the room this fast. The bomb was too good for her. She had to look up and see him and feel his hands on her throat. He had to look down at her and see her die. He had to talk to her and tell her what he was going to do and listen to her beg him not to, and then he'd squeeze.

He closed his eyes and swallowed over the dryness in his mouth, the shiver of ecstasy that made the perspiration tingle.

He only needed four or five minutes inside the terminal. If he got into the room by 11:27, he'd have enough time. He'd get away through the Park Avenue tunnel.

And even though he didn't have his recorder, he'd remember how Sharon sounded. He wanted to remember. He'd fall asleep remembering how she sounded when she died.

The boy. He'd just leave him there. Let the bomb take care of him, him and all the stinking cops and all the people who wouldn't get out in time. Didn't even know what was going to happen to them.

They were entering the midtown tunnel. This kid was a good driver. It was only ten minutes of eleven. Another ten or fifteen minutes and he'd be on Forty-second Street. He'd have plenty of time. Plenty of time for Sharon.

The cab came to an abrupt halt halfway through the tunnel. Foxy looked up from his meditation. "What's the matter?"

The cabby shrugged. "Sorry, mister. There's a disabled truck up there. Looks like he lost some of his cargo too. Both lanes are blocked. But it shouldn't take long. Don't worry I'll get you there for your train."

Frantic with impatience to get to Sharon, Foxy waited. His hands were burning so much now, like they were on fire. He thought about getting out and walking the rest of the way but rejected the idea. The cops would stop him sure.

It was seventeen minutes past eleven when they inched out of the tunnel and turned north. The traffic began to back up at Fortieth Street. The driver whistled. "This is some mess. I'll try cutting west here."

At Third Avenue they came to a complete stop. Motionless cars blocked the intersections. Horns tooted angrily. Tense-looking pedestrians, scurrying east, tried to make their way around the cars. "Mister, there must be something wrong. Looks like some streets are closed off up there. Wait. I'll turn on the radio. Maybe it's another bomb threat."

They were probably clearing out the terminal. Foxy tossed the twenty-dollar bill at the driver, opened the door and slid out into the traffic.

At Forty-second Street he saw them. Cops. Cops all over the place. Forty-second Street closed off. He pushed and shoved his way through. Bomb. Bomb. He stopped. People were talking about a bomb in the station. Had they found Sharon and the boy? The thought sent black fury gushing through him. He shouldered people aside, forced his way through the crowd.

"Stand back, buddy. You can't go any further." A burly, young policeman tapped his shoulder as he tried to cross Third Avenue.

"What's the matter?" He had to know.

"Nothing, we hope, sir. But there's been a bomb threat phoned in. We have to take precautions."

Phoned in. His phonecall to that priest. *Threat!* That meant they hadn't found the bomb. It was all right. Exultation leaped through him. His fingers and palms tingled the way they always did when he started to go to a girl and knew nothing could stop him. His voice was smooth, his expression concerned when he spoke to the cop. "I'm a surgeon. I'm joining the emergency medical squad in case it's needed."

"Oh, sorry, Doctor. Go right through."

Foxy ran up Forty-second Street, taking care to keep close to the buildings. The next cop who stopped him might be smart enough to ask for identification. People were streaming out of office buildings and shops, prodded by the urgency of the bullhorns the police were using. "Move quickly but do not panic. Walk to Third or Fifth Avenue. Your cooperation may save your life."

It was exactly 11:26 when Foxy, pushing his way through the confused and frightened crowds, reached the main entrance to the terminal. The doors had been wedged open to speed the exodus. A veteran policeman was standing guard at the far left door. Foxy tried to duck past him. His arm was grabbed. "Hey, you can't go in there!"

"Terminal engineer," Foxy said crisply. "I've been sent for."

"You're too late. The searchers will be clearing out in a minute."

"I've been sent for," Foxy repeated.

"Suit yourself." The cop dropped his arm.

The deserted newsstand beyond the doors was piled with morning papers. Foxy saw the huge black headline. *Kidnap.* It was about him, what he'd done—the fox.

He ran past the stand and looked down into the main terminal. Grim-faced policemen with construction hats were searching behind counters and booths. There were probably dozens more all over the station. But he'd outsmarted them! All of them!

A small group of people was clustered near the information desk. The taller one, a broad-shouldered, sandy-haired man, hands shoved in his pockets, was shaking his head. Steve Peterson! It was Steve Peterson! Sucking in his breath, Foxy raced down to the main floor and dashed for the staircase to the lower level.

Now he only needed two more minutes. His fingers throbbed and burned. He curled and uncurled them as he rushed down the stairs. Only his thumbs were rigid as he ran, unchallenged, across the lower terminal and disappeared down the steps leading to the Mount Vernon platform and the room beyond it.

CHAPTER 48

The news of Foxy's phonecall reached Hugh and Steve as the helicopter passed over the Triborough Bridge.

"*Major transportation center, New York City,*" Hugh snapped into the phone. "Christ, that includes both airports, both bus terminals, Penn Station, and Grand Central. Have you started evacuating them?"

Steve listened, his shoulders slumped forward, his hands restlessly clasping and unclasping. Kennedy Airport! LaGuardia Airport! The Port Authority bus terminal took up a square block; the one at the bridge was probably bigger. Sharon . . . Neil . . . oh God, it was hopeless . . . may the fox build his nest on your hearthstone. . . .

Hugh hung up the phone. "Can't you push this thing any faster?" he urged the pilot.

"That wind is getting awful strong," the pilot replied, "I'll try going lower."

"Wind velocity, just what we need if there's a fire when that thing goes off," Hugh muttered. He looked over at Steve. "There's no use kidding. It's bad. We have to assume he's carried out his threat to set that bomb."

"With Sharon and Neil somewhere near it?" Steve's voice was ragged. "Where do you start looking?"

"We're gambling," Hugh said tersely. "The main search will be in Grand Central. Remember, he parked the car on Vanderbilt and stayed at the Biltmore. He knows the terminal like a book. And John Owens says the train sounds he heard on the cassette are more consistent with commuter trains than subways."

"What about the Thompson boy?"

"If we don't catch Foxy and get a confession out of him, he's finished."

At 11:05 the helicopter landed on the Pan Am building. Hugh threw open the door. A thin-faced agent ran over to them as they jumped to the ground. White with anger, lips tightly compressed, he briefed them on Foxy's escape.

"What do you mean, *escaped*?" Hugh exploded. "How the hell did that happen? How sure are you that it was Foxy?"

"Absolutely sure. He dropped the ransom. They're searching the field and terminal for him now. But the whole airport is being evacuated so it's a mess out there."

"The ransom doesn't tell us where he set that bomb and it can't help the Thompson kid," Hugh snapped. *"We've got to find Foxy and make him talk."*

Foxy escaped. With numb disbelief, Steve absorbed the words. Sharon. Neil. "Steve, I was wrong, forgive me." "Mommy wouldn't want me to be here." Was that bizarre cassette to be his last contact with them?

The cassette. Nina's voice . . .

He grabbed Hugh's arm. "That cassette he sent. He must have dubbed Nina's voice on it. You said he'd cleared everything out of the garage. Did he have any luggage? He may have been carrying a suitcase, something with him. Maybe he still has the other cassette with Nina's voice, maybe he has something that would show where Sharon and Neil are."

Hugh spun around to the other agent. "What about any luggage?"

"There are two stubs clipped onto the ticket he dropped. But the plane took off about twenty-seven minutes ago. No one thought to stop it. We'll get those bags in Phoenix."

"That's not good enough," Hugh shouted. "Sweet Christ, that's not good enough. Get that goddamn plane back. Have every baggage handler in LaGuardia ready to unload it. Tell the control tower to clear a runway. Don't let any dumb ass stand in your way. Where's a phone?"

"Inside."

Hugh pulled out his notebook as he ran. Rapidly he dialed Somers prison and got the Warden's office. "We're still trying to locate evidence to prove Thompson's innocence. Have a phone manned to the last split second."

He called the Governor's office, got through to her private secretary. "Make damn sure the Governor's available and that you have a phone open to our guys in LaGuardia and another to the prison. Or else, the Nutmeg State may go down in history for frying an innocent kid." He dropped the phone. "Let's go," he told Steve.

Nineteen minutes, Steve thought as they plummeted down in the elevator. Nineteen minutes.

The lobby of the Pan American building was jammed with people streaming from the terminal. Bomb threat . . . bomb threat . . . The words were on everyone's lips.

Steve and Hugh shoved their way through the surging bodies. How can anyone know where to search? Steve agonized. He'd been here only yesterday. Sitting in the Oyster Bar, waiting for his train. Had Sharon and Neil been here all along, helpless? Over the loudspeaker an urgent voice kept repeating, "Leave the buildings immediately. Walk to the nearest exit. Do not panic. Do not congregate at exits. Leave the area . . . leave the area. . . ."

The Information Booth on the upper level of the terminal, its red emergency lights flashing ominously, was the command desk for the investigators. Engineers were poring over charts and diagrams, issuing rapidfire orders to searching parties.

"We're concentrating on the area between the floor of this level and the ceiling of the lower level now," a supervisor told Hugh. "It's accessible from all the platforms and a good hiding place. We've done a fast check on the platforms and we're hitting all the lockers. We figure that even if we find the bomb, it's probably too risky to try to dismantle it. The bomb squad brought over all the bomb blankets they could lay their hands on. They're distributed among the searching parties. We can count on one of them being ninety percent effective in containing an explosion."

Steve's eyes swept the terminal. The loudspeaker was off now and the vast area was becoming quiet, a hushed, mocking silence. The clock. His eyes searched out the clock over the information desk. Relentlessly the hands kept moving: 11:12 . . . 11:17 . . . 11:24 . . . He wanted to hold those hands back. He wanted to run into every platform, every waiting room, every cubicle. He wanted to shout their names, Sharon! Neil!

Frantically, he turned his head. He had to *do* something, search for them himself. His gaze fell on a tall, bony man who rushed in from the

Forty-second Street entrance, ran down the stairs and disappeared down the second staircase that led to the lower level. There was something vaguely familiar about him—one of the agents maybe? What good could he do now?

The loudspeaker went on. "It is eleven-twenty-seven. All searchers immediately proceed to the nearest exit. Leave the terminal immediately. Repeat. Leave the terminal immediately."

"No!" Steve clutched Hugh's shoulders, spun him around. "No!"

"Mr. Peterson, make sense. If that bomb goes off, we may all be killed. Even if Sharon and Neil are here, we can't help them that way."

"I'm not leaving," Steve said.

Hugh grabbed his arm. Another agent took the other one. "Mr. Peterson, be reasonable. It may only be a precaution."

Steve wrenched himself free. "Let go of me, damn you," he shouted. "Let go of me."

CHAPTER 49

It was no use, no use, no use. Her eyes magnetized to the clock, Sharon frantically tried to jab the broken edge of the handle into the cords of her wrists. It was so hard to hold the handle in one fist, to try to push at the cords of the other.

More times than not, she missed the cords completely, and the metal cut into her hand. She could feel the warm, soft, sticky blood, running, crusting. She was beyond pain. But what if she jabbed an artery and passed out?

The blood was making the cord softer, more resilient. The metal jabbed at it, not in it. She'd been trying for over an hour now . . . it was twenty-five of eleven.

Twenty of eleven.

Ten of . . . five of . . . five after . . .

She worked on, her face clammy with perspiration, her hands sticky with blood, not feeling pain anymore. She felt Neil's eyes watching her. Pray, Neil.

At ten after eleven, she felt the cord weakening, giving. Summoning up a last reserve of energy, Sharon pulled her hands apart. They were free; the cords were dangling from them.

She held them up, shook them, tried to get feeling back into them. Fifteen minutes.

Leaning on her left elbow, Sharon dragged herself up. She swung just enough to support her back against the wall and managed to squirm to a sitting position. Her legs fell over the side of the cot. Raw pain screeched through her ankle.

Fourteen minutes.

Her fingers trembled with weakness as she tugged at the gag. The gauze was so tightly knotted. She couldn't get it loose. Tugging frantically, she managed to pull the gag down. Great gulping breaths of air helped to clear her head.

Thirteen minutes.

She couldn't walk. Even if she could drag herself over to the bomb she might jar it, trying to pull up on the sink, to reach it. Or she might set it off just by touching it. She remembered the infinite care Foxy had shown when he touched the wires.

There was no hope for her. She had to try to free Neil. If she could get him loose, he could get out, could warn people. She yanked his gag off.

"Sharon . . ."

"I know. I'm going to untie you. I can't help it if I hurt you."

"All right, Sharon."

And then she heard it. The sound. Something thudding against the door. Was he coming back? Had he changed his mind? Clutching Neil to her, Sharon stared at the door. It was opening. The light switch clicked.

In the dusty light, she saw what seemed to be an apparition stumbling toward her, a woman, an old woman with a trickle of blood coming from her mouth with deep sunken eyes that were out of focus.

Neil shrank back against her as the woman came toward them, stared in horror as the woman began to fall forward, to slump downward like an unsupported laundry bag.

The woman fell on her side, tried to speak, "Knife . . . still in my back . . . help . . . please . . . take it out . . . hurts . . . want to die here . . ."

The woman's head was against her foot. Her body angled grotesquely out. Sharon saw the handle of the knife between her shoulder blades.

She could free Neil with the knife. Shuddering, Sharon put both hands around the handle, pulled.

The knife held, then suddenly came free. She was holding it, the blade wickedly sharp, matted with blood.

The woman whimpered.

In an instant Sharon had cut Neil's bindings. "Neil . . . run . . . get out of here . . . yell to people that there's going to be an explosion . . . hurry . . . down those stairs . . . and there's a big ramp . . . run toward it . . . at the train platform, go up the stairs . . . you'll see people there . . . Daddy will come for you . . . hurry . . . get out of this building . . . get people out of it . . ."

"Sharon," Neil's voice was pleading. "What about you?"

"Neil . . . just go. Go!"

Neil slid off the cot. He tried to walk, stumbled, righted himself. "My legs . . ."

"Neil, hurry. Run! Run!"

With a last beseeching glance at her, Neil obeyed. He ran out of the room, onto the landing. Down the stairs. Sharon had said to go down the stairs. It was so quiet here, so spooky. He was so afraid. The bomb. Maybe if he could find someone, they'd help Sharon. He had to make someone help Sharon.

He was at the foot of the stairs. Which way should he go? There were so many pipes around here. A ramp. Sharon said a ramp. That must be it. Like the ramp they had in school between the classrooms and the auditorium.

He raced along it. He wanted to shout for help. But he had to hurry. He had to find someone. He was at the end of the ramp. He was in a station, a train station. The tracks were right there. Sharon said to go upstairs. He ran around the platform where the tracks ended.

A voice started to talk. It sounded like when the principal talked on the loudspeaker at school. It was telling everyone to get out. Where was the man who was talking?

He could hear footsteps coming down a staircase. Someone was coming, someone who would help Sharon. He was so relieved he tried to yell and couldn't. He had no breath from running. His legs hurt so much it was hard to run. He stumbled toward the stairs and began to climb. He had to tell whoever was coming about Sharon.

Neil looked up and saw the face that had stalked his dreams rushing down at him.

Foxy saw Neil. His eyes narrowed. His mouth twisted. He stretched out his hands . . .

Neil jumped to one side, stuck out his foot. The man's flailing leg jammed against his sneaker. The man sprawled down the last three steps. Eluding the arms that swung out at him, Neil ran up the steps. He was in a big, empty place. There was no one here. Another staircase. Over there. Maybe there were people upstairs. The bad man was going to Sharon.

Sobbing, Neil ran up the stairs. Daddy, he tried to yell, Daddy. Daddy. He was on the last step. There were policemen all over here. They were all running away from him. Some of them were pushing another man.

They were pushing Daddy.

"Daddy," Neil shouted. "Daddy!"

With a last, final burst of energy, he stumbled across the terminal. Steve heard him, turned, ran to him, grabbed him.

"Daddy," Neil sobbed, "that man is going to kill Sharon now . . . just like he killed Mommy."

CHAPTER 50

A determined Rosie was fighting the efforts to put her out. Lally was down in Sing Sing. She knew it. Cops were all over the place. There was a bunch of them right at the Information Desk. Rosie spotted Hugh Taylor. He was the nice FBI guy who always talked to her when he was around the station. She ran to him, tugged his arm. "Mr. Taylor, Lally . . ."

He glanced down at her, pulled his arm free. "Get the hell out of here, Rosie," he ordered.

A loudspeaker came on, ordering everyone out. "No!" Rosie sobbed.

The tall man near Hugh Taylor grabbed him, turned him around. She watched as Hugh and another cop wrestled with him.

"Daddy! Daddy!"

Was she hearing things? Rosie spun around. A little boy was weaving across the terminal. Then the big guy who was shouting at Mr. Taylor ran past her to the child. She heard the boy say something about a bad man and rushed over. Maybe he'd seen the guy she and Lally were watching.

The boy was crying. "Daddy, help Sharon. She's hurt. She's all tied up and there's a sick old lady . . .

"Where, Neil, where?" Steve begged.

"A sick old lady," Rosie shrieked. "That's Lally. She's in her room. You know it, Mr. Taylor, in Sing Sing—the old dishwasher room."

"Come on," Hugh shouted.

Steve thrust Neil at a policeman. "Get my son out of here," he ordered. He ran behind Hugh. Two men struggling with a heavy metal sheet followed them.

"Christ, let's get out of here!" Someone thrust an arm around Rosie's waist and dragged her toward an exit. "That bomb will go off any minute!"

CHAPTER 51

S haron heard the padding of Neil's sneakers as he ran down the steps. Please God, let him be safe. Let him get away.

The old woman's moans stopped, resumed, stopped for a longer instant. When the sound began again, it was lower, softer; it had a fading quality.

With detached clarity, Sharon remembered what this woman said about wanting to die here. Leaning down, she felt the matted hair, patted it gently. Her fingertips smoothed the wrinkled forehead. The skin felt damp and cold. Lally shuddered violently. The moaning stopped.

Sharon knew the woman was dead. And now she was going to die. "I love you, Steve," she said aloud. "I love you, Steve." His face filled her mind. Her need for him was physical pain; primal, acute, transcending the throbbing agony of her leg and ankle.

She closed her eyes. "Forgive us our trespasses as we forgive those who trespass against us . . . Into Your Hands, I commend my spirit."

A sound.

Her eyes flew open. Foxy was framed in the doorway. An ear to ear smile slashed his face. His fingers curved, his thumbs rigid, he started toward her.

CHAPTER 52

Hugh led the way down to the Mount Vernon platform, around the tracks, down the ramp into the lowest depths of the terminal. Steve raced beside him. The men carrying the bomb blanket struggled to keep up with them.

They were on the ramp when they heard the screaming.

"No . . . no . . . no . . . Steve . . . help me . . . Steve . . ."

Steve's track team days were twenty years in the past. But once again he felt that tremendous surge of power, that terrible burst of energy he had always summoned in a race. Crazed with the need to reach Sharon in time, he flew past the others.

"Steeeeeevvvvveeee . . ." The scream choked off.

Stairs. He was at the foot of a staircase. He lunged up it, burst through an open door.

His brain absorbed the nightmarish quality of the scene, the body on the floor, Sharon half-lying, half-sitting, her legs tied, her hair dangling behind her, trying to pull away from the figure bent over her, the figure with the thick fingers that were squeezing her throat.

Steve threw himself on the man, butted his head into the arched back. Foxy sprawled forward. They both fell on Sharon. Under their weight, the sagging cot broke and they rolled together on the floor. The hands were still on Sharon's throat but broke loose under the impact of the fall. Foxy stumbled to his feet, crouched. Steve tried to leap up, tripped on Lally's body. Sharon's breathing was a tortured, choking gasp.

Hugh raced into the room.

Cornered, Foxy backed away. His hand found the door to the toilet cubicle. He jumped past it, slammed it shut. They heard the bolt slide into place.

"Get out of there, you crazy fool," Hugh shouted.

The agents carrying the bomb blanket were in the room. With infinite care, they draped the black suitcase with the heavy metal sheet.

Steve reached for Sharon. Her eyes were closed. Her head flopped backwards as he picked her up. Ugly welts were rising on her throat. But she was alive; she was alive. Holding her to him, he turned to the door. His eyes fell on the posters, on Nina's picture. He hugged Sharon tightly.

Hugh bent over Lally. "This one's gone."

The large hand of the clock was moving to six.

"Get out of here!" Hugh shouted.

They tumbled down the stairs.

"The tunnel. Head for the tunnel!"

They raced past the generator, past the vents, onto the tracks, through the darkness . . .

Foxy heard the retreating steps. They were gone. They were gone. He slid the bolt and opened the door. Seeing the metal blanket over the suitcase, he began to laugh, a deep, rumbling, staccato sound.

It was too late for him. But it was too late for them too. In the end the Fox always won.

He reached his hand to the metal blanket, tried to tug it off the suitcase.

A blinding flash, a roar that shattered his eardrums hurtled him into eternity.

11:42 A.M.

Bob Kurner burst into St. Bernard's Church, raced up the aisle and threw his arms around the kneeling figure.

"Is it over?" Her eyes were tearless.

"*Is it over!* Mamma, come on and take your kid home. They've got absolute proof that another guy committed the murder; they've got a tape of him doing it. The Governor said to get Ron out of that prison *now.*"

Kate Thompson, mother of Ronald Thompson, staunch believer in the goodness and mercy of her God, fainted.

Roger Perry hung up the phone, turned to Glenda. "They were on time," he said.

"Sharon, Neil, both safe?" Glenda whispered.

"Yes, and the Thompson boy is going home."

Glenda raised her hand to her throat. "Thank God." She saw his expression. "Roger, I'm fine. Put away those damn pills and make me a good stiff old-fashioned!"

Hugh had his arm around a softly weeping Rosie. "Lally saved her station," he said. "And we're going to start a petition to put up a plaque for her. I'll bet Governor Carey himself will unveil it. He's a nice guy."

"A plaque for Lally," Rosie whispered. "Oh, she'd love that!"

A face was floating somewhere above her. She was going to die and never see Steve again. "No . . . no . . ."

"It's all right, darling. It's all right."

Steve's voice. It was Steve's face she was seeing.

"It's all over. We're on the way to the hospital. They'll fix up that leg."

"Neil . . ."

"I'm here, Sharon." A hand butterfly soft in hers.

Steve's lips on her cheeks, her forehead, her lips.

Neil's voice in her ear. "Sharon, just like you told me, I kept thinking the whole time about the present you promised me. Sharon, exactly how many Lionel trains have you got for me?"

THE CRADLE
WILL FALL

". . . for some patients, though conscious that their condition is perilous, recover their health simply through their contentment with the goodness of the physician."

—HIPPOCRATES

≈ CHAPTER 1

I f her mind had not been on the case she had won, Katie might not have taken the curve so fast, but the intense satisfaction of the guilty verdict was still absorbing her. It had been a close one. Roy O'Connor was one of the top defense attorneys in New Jersey. The defendant's confession had been suppressed by the court, a major blow for the prosecution. But still she had managed to convince the jury that Teddy Copeland was the man who had viciously murdered eighty-year-old Abigail Rawlings during a robbery.

Miss Rawlings' sister, Margaret, was in court to hear the verdict and afterward had come up to Katie. "You were wonderful, Mrs. DeMaio," she'd said. "You look like a young college girl. I never would have thought you could, but when you talked, you *proved* every point; you made them *feel* what he did to Abby. What will happen now?"

"With his record, let's hope the judge decides to send him to prison for the rest of his life," Katie answered.

"Thank God," Margaret Rawlings had said. Her eyes, already moist and faded with age, filled with tears. Quietly she brushed them away as she said, "I miss Abby so. There was just the two of us left. And I keep thinking how frightened she must have been. It would have been awful if he'd gotten away with it."

"He didn't get away with it!" The memory of that reassurance distracted Katie now, made her press her foot harder on the accelerator. The sudden increase in speed as she rounded the curve made the car fishtail on the sleet-covered road.

"Oh . . . no!" She gripped the wheel frantically. The country road was dark. The car raced across the divider and spun around. From the distance she saw headlights approaching.

She turned the wheel into the skid but could not control the car. It careened onto the shoulder of the road, but the shoulder too was a sheet of ice. Like a skier about to jump, the car poised for an instant at the edge of the shoulder, its wheels lifting as it slammed down the steep embankment into the wooded fields.

A dark shape loomed ahead: a tree. Katie felt the sickening crunch as metal tore into bark. The car shuddered. Her body was flung forward against the wheel, then slammed backward. She raised her arms in front of her face, trying to protect it from the splinters of flying glass that exploded from the windshield. Sharp, biting pain attacked her wrists and knees. The headlights and panel lights went out. Dark, velvety blackness was closing over her as from somewhere off in the distance she heard a siren.

The sound of the car door opening; a blast of cold air. "My God, it's Katie DeMaio!"

A voice she knew. Tom Coughlin, that nice young cop. He testified at a trial last week.

"She's unconscious."

She tried to protest, but her lips wouldn't form words. She couldn't open her eyes.

"The blood's coming from her arm. Looks like she's cut an artery."

Her arm was being held; something tight was pressing against it.

A different voice: "She may have internal injuries, Tom. Westlake's right down the road. I'll call for an ambulance. You stay with her."

Floating. Floating. I'm all right. It's just that I can't reach you.

Hands lifting her onto a stretcher; she felt a blanket covering her, sleet pelting her face.

She was being carried. A car was moving. No, it was an ambulance. Doors opening and closing. If only she could make them understand. I can hear you. I'm not unconscious.

Tom was giving her name. "Kathleen DeMaio, lives in Abbington. She's an assistant prosecutor. No, she's not married. She's a widow. Judge DeMaio's widow."

John's widow. A terrible sense of aloneness. The blackness was starting to recede. A light was shining in her eyes. "She's coming around. How old are you, Mrs. DeMaio?"

The question, so practical, so easy to answer. At last she could speak. "Twenty-eight."

The tourniquet Tom had wrapped around her arm was being removed. Her arm was being stitched. She tried not to wince at the needles of pain.

X-rays. The emergency-room doctor. "You're quite fortunate, Mrs. DeMaio. Some pretty severe bruises. No fractures. I've ordered a transfusion. Your blood count is pretty low. Don't be frightened. You'll be all right."

"It's just . . ." She bit her lip. She was coming back into focus and managed to stop herself before she blurted out that terrible, unreasoning, childish fear of hospitals.

Tom asking, "Do you want us to call your sister? They're going to keep you here overnight."

"No. Molly's just over the flu. They've all had it." Her voice sounded so weak. Tom had to bend over to hear her.

"All right, Katie. Don't worry about anything. I'll have your car hauled out."

She was wheeled into a curtained-off section of the emergency room. Blood began dripping through a tube inserted into her right arm. Her head was clearing now.

Her left arm and knees hurt so much. Everything hurt. She was in a hospital. She was alone.

A nurse was smoothing her hair back from her forehead. "You're going to be fine, Mrs. DeMaio. Why are you crying?"

"I'm *not* crying." But she was.

She was wheeled into a room. The nurse handed her a paper cup of water and a pill. "This will help you rest, Mrs. DeMaio."

Katie was sure this must be a sleeping pill. She didn't want it. It would give her nightmares. But it was so much easier not to argue.

The nurse turned off the light. Her footsteps made soft padding sounds as she left the room. The room was cold. The sheets were cold and coarse. Did hospital sheets always feel like this? Katie slid into sleep knowing the nightmare was inevitable.

But this time it took a different form. She was on a roller coaster. It kept climbing higher and higher, steeper and steeper, and she couldn't get control of it. She was trying to get control. Then it went around a curve and off the tracks and it was falling. She woke up trembling just before it hit the ground.

Sleet rapped on the window. She pulled herself up unsteadily. The window was open a crack and making the shade rattle. That was why the room was so drafty. She'd close the window and raise the shade and then maybe she'd be able to sleep. In the morning she could go home. She hated hospitals.

Unsteadily she walked over to the window. The hospital gown they'd given her barely came to her knees. Her legs were cold. And that sleet. It was mixed with more rain now. She leaned against the windowsill, looked out.

The parking lot was turning into streams of gushing water.

Katie gripped the shade and stared down into the lot two stories below.

The trunk lid of a car was going up slowly. She was so dizzy now. She swayed, let go of the shade, and it snapped up. She grabbed the windowsill. She stared down into the trunk. Was something white floating down into it? A blanket? A large bundle?

She must be dreaming this, she thought, then Katie pushed her hand over her mouth to muffle the shriek that tore at her throat. She was staring down into the trunk of the car. The trunk light was on. Through the waves of sleet-filled rain that slapped against the window, she watched the white substance part. As the trunk closed she saw a face—the face of a woman grotesque in the uncaring abandon of death.

⌐⌐⌐ *CHAPTER* 2

The alarm woke him promptly at two o'clock. Long years of learning to awake to urgency made him instantly alert. Getting up, he went over to the examining-room sink, splashed cold water on his face, pulled his tie into a smooth knot, combed his hair. His socks were still wet. They felt cold and clammy when he took them off the barely warm radiator. Grimacing, he pulled them on and slipped his feet into his shoes.

He reached for his overcoat, touched it and winced. It was still soaked through. Hanging it near the radiator had been useless. He'd end up with pneumonia if he wore it. Beyond that, the white fibers of the blanket might cling to the dark blue. That would be something to explain.

The old Burberry he kept in the closet. He'd wear that, leave the wet coat here, drop it off at the cleaner's tomorrow. The raincoat was unlined. He'd freeze, but it was the only thing to do. Besides, it was so ordinary—a drab olive green, outsized now that he'd lost weight. If anyone saw the car, saw him *in* the car, there was less chance of being recognized.

He hurried to the clothes closet, pulled the raincoat from the wire hanger where it was unevenly draped and hung the heavy wet Chesterfield in the back of the closet. The raincoat smelled unused—a dusty, irritating smell that assailed his nostrils. Frowning with distaste, he pulled it on and buttoned it.

He went over to the window and pulled the shade back an inch. There were still enough cars in the parking lot so that the presence or absence of his would hardly be noticed. He bit his lip as he realized that the broken light that always made the far section of the lot satisfactorily dark had been replaced. The back of his car was silhouetted by it. He would have to walk in the shadows of the other cars and get the body into the trunk as quickly as possible.

It was time.

Opening the medical supply closet, he bent down. With expert hands he felt the contours of the body under the blanket. Grunting slightly, he slipped a hand under the neck, the other under the knees, and picked up the body. In life she had weighed somewhere around one hundred ten pounds, but she had gained weight during her pregnancy. His muscles felt every ounce of that weight as he carried her to the examining table. There, working only from the light of the small flashlight propped on the table, he wrapped the blanket around her.

He studied the floor of the medical supply closet carefully and relocked it. Noiselessly opening the door to the parking lot, he grasped the trunk key of the car in two fingers. Quietly he moved to the examining table and picked up the dead woman. Now for the twenty seconds that could destroy him.

Eighteen seconds later he was at the car. Sleet pelted his cheek; the blanket-covered burden strained his arms. Shifting the weight so that most of it rested on one arm, he tried to insert the key into the trunk lock. Sleet had glazed over the lock. Impatiently he scraped it off. An instant later the key was in the lock and the trunk door rose slowly. He glanced up at the hospital windows. From the center room on the second floor a shade snapped up. Was anyone looking out? His impatience to lay the blanketed figure in the trunk, to have it out of his arms, made him move too quickly. The instant his left hand let go of the blanket, the wind blew it apart, revealing her face. Wincing, he dropped the body and slammed the trunk closed.

The light had been on the face. Had anyone seen? He looked up again at the window where the shade had been raised. Was someone there? He couldn't be sure. How much could be seen from that window? Later he would find out who was in that room.

He was at the driver's door, turning the key in the car. He drove swiftly from the lot without turning on the headlights until he was well along the county road.

Incredible that this was his second trip to Chapin River tonight. Suppose he hadn't been leaving the hospital when she burst out of Fukhito's office and hailed him.

Vangie had been close to hysteria, favoring her right leg as she limped down the covered portico to him. "Doctor, I can't make an appointment with you this week. I'm going to Minneapolis tomorrow. I'm going to see the doctor I used to have, Dr. Salem. Maybe I'll even stay there and let him deliver the baby."

If he had missed her, everything would have been ruined.

Instead he persuaded her to come into the office with him, talked to her, calmed her down, offered her a glass of water. At the last minute she'd suspected, tried to brush past him. That beautiful, petulant face had filled with fear.

And then the horror of knowing that even though he'd managed to silence her, the chance of discovery was still so great. He locked her body in the medical supply closet and tried to think.

Her bright red car had been the immediate danger. It was vital to get it out of the hospital parking lot. It would surely have been noticed there after visiting hours ended—top-of-the-line Lincoln Continental with its aggressive chrome front, every arrogant line demanding attention.

He knew exactly where she lived in Chapin River. She'd told him that her husband, a United Airlines pilot, wasn't due home until tomorrow. He decided to get the car onto her property, to leave her handbag in the house, make it seem as though she'd come home.

It had been unexpectedly easy. There was so little traffic because of the vile weather. The zoning ordinance in Chapin River called for homesites with a minimum of two acres. The houses were placed far back from the road and reached by winding driveways. He opened her garage door with the automatic device on the dashboard of the Lincoln and parked the car in the garage.

He found the door key on the ring with the car keys, but did not need it; the interior door from the garage to the den was unlocked. There were lamps on throughout the house, probably on a timing device. He'd hurried through the den down the hall into the bedroom wing, looking for the master bedroom. It was the last one on the right and no mistaking it. There were two other bedrooms, one fitted as a nursery, with colorful elves and lambs smiling out from freshly applied wallpaper and an obviously new crib and chest.

That was when he realized he might be able to make her death look like a suicide. If she'd begun to furnish the nursery three months before the baby was expected, the threatened loss of that baby was a powerful motive for suicide.

He'd gone into the master bedroom. The king-sized bed was carelessly made, with the heavy white chenille bedspread thrown unevenly over the blankets. Her nightgown and robe were on a chaise longue near it. If he only could get her body back here, put it on top of her own bed! It was dangerous, but not as dangerous as dumping her body in the woods somewhere. That would have meant an intensive police investigation.

He left her handbag on the chaise longue. With the car in the garage and the handbag here, at least it would look as though she'd returned home from the hospital.

Then he walked the four miles back to the hospital. It had been dangerous—suppose a police car had come down the road of that expensive area and stopped him? He had absolutely no excuse for being there. But he'd made the trip in less than an hour, skirted the main entrance to the hospital and let himself into the office through the back door that led from the parking lot. It was just ten o'clock when he got back.

His coat and shoes and socks were soaked. He was shivering. He realized it would be too dangerous to try to carry the body out until there was a minimal chance of encountering anyone. The late nursing shift came on at midnight. He decided to wait until well after midnight before going out again. The emergency entrance was on the east side of the hospital. At least he didn't have to worry about being observed by emergency patients or a police car rushing a patient in.

He'd set the alarm for two o'clock and lain down on the examining table. He managed to sleep until the alarm went off.

Now he was turning off the wooden bridge onto Winding Brook Lane. Her house was on the right.

Turn off the headlights; turn into the driveway; circle behind the house; back the car against the garage door; pull off driving gloves; put on surgical gloves; open the garage door; open the trunk; carry the wrapped form past the storage shelves to the inside door. He stepped into the den. The house was silent. In a few minutes he'd be safe.

He hurried down the hall to the master bedroom, straining under the weight of the body. He laid the body on the bed, pulling the blanket free.

In the bathroom off the bedroom he shook crystals of cyanide into the flowered blue tumbler, added water and poured most of the contents down the sink. He rinsed the sink carefully and returned to the bedroom. Placing the glass next to the dead woman's hand, he allowed the last drops of the mixture to spill on the spread. Her fingerprints were sure to be on the glass. Rigor mortis was setting in. The hands were cold. He folded the white blanket carefully.

The body was sprawled face up on the bed, eyes staring, lips contorted, the expression an agony of protest. That was all right. Most suicides changed their minds when it was too late.

Had he missed anything? No. Her handbag with the keys was on the chaise; there was a residue of the cyanide in the glass. Coat on or off? He'd leave it on. The less he handled her the better.

Shoes off or on? Would she have kicked them off?

He lifted the long caftan she was wearing and felt the blood drain from his face. The swollen right foot wore a battered moccasin. Her left foot was covered only by her stocking.

The other moccasin must have fallen off. Where? In the parking lot, the office, this house? He ran from the bedroom, searching, retracing his steps to the garage. The shoe was not in the house or garage. Frantic at the waste of time, he ran out to the car and looked in the trunk. The shoe was not there.

It had probably come off when he was carrying her in the parking lot. He'd have heard it fall in the office, and it wasn't in the medicine closet. He was positive of that.

Because of that swollen foot she'd been wearing those moccasins constantly. He'd heard the receptionist joke with her about them.

He would have to go back, search the parking lot, find that shoe. Suppose someone picked it up who had seen her wearing it? There would be talk about her death when her body was discovered. Suppose someone said, "Why, I saw the moccasin she was wearing lying in the parking lot. She must have lost it on her way home Monday night"? But if she had walked even a few feet in the parking lot without a shoe, the sole of her stocking would be badly soiled. The police would notice that. He had to go back to the parking lot and find that shoe.

But now, rushing back to the bedroom, he opened the door of the walk-in closet. A jumble of women's shoes were scattered on the floor. Most of them had impossible high heels. Ridiculous that anyone would believe she had been wearing them in her condition and in this weather. There were three or four pairs of boots, but he'd never be able to zip a boot over that swollen leg.

Then he saw them. A pair of low-heeled shoes, sensible-looking, the kind most pregnant women wore. They looked fairly new, but had been worn at least once. Relieved, he grabbed them. Hurrying back to the bed, he pulled the one shoe from the dead woman's foot and slipped her feet into the shoes he had just taken from the closet. The right one was tight, but he managed to lace it. Jamming the moccasin she had been wearing into the wide loose pocket of his raincoat, he reached for the white blanket. With it under his arm he strode from the room, down the hall, through the den and out into the night.

By the time he drove into the hospital parking lot, the sleet and rain had stopped falling but it was windy and very cold. Driving to the farthermost corner of the area, he parked the car. If the security guard happened to come by and spoke to him, he'd simply say that he'd received a call to meet one of his patients here; that she was in labor. If for any reason that story was checked, he'd act outraged, say it was obviously a crank call.

But it would be much safer not to be seen. Keeping in the shadow of the shrubbery that outlined the divider island of the lot, he hurried to retrace his steps from the space where he'd kept the car to the door of the office. Logically the shoe might have fallen off when he'd shifted the body to open the trunk. Crouching, he searched the ground. Quietly he worked his way closer to the hospital. All the patients' rooms in this wing were dark now. He glanced up to the center window on the second floor. The shade was securely down. Someone had adjusted it. Bending forward, he slowly made his way across the macadam. If anyone saw him! Rage and frustration made him unaware of the bitter cold. Where was that shoe? He had to find it.

Headlights came around the bend into the parking lot. A car screeched to a halt. The driver, probably heading for the emergency room, must have realized he'd taken the wrong turn. He made a U-turn and raced out of the lot.

He had to get out of here. It was no use. He fell forward as he tried to straighten up. His hand slid across the slippery macadam. And then he felt it: the leather under his fingers. He grabbed it, held it up. Even in the dim light he could still be sure. It was the moccasin. He had found it.

Fifteen minutes later, he was turning the key in the lock of his home. Peeling off the raincoat, he hung it in the foyer closet. The full-length mirror on the door reflected his image. Shocked, he realized that his trouser knees were wet and dirty. His hair was badly disheveled. His hands were soiled. His cheeks were flushed, and his eyes, always promi nent, were bulging and wide-lensed. He looked like a man in emotional shock, a caricature of himself.

Rushing upstairs, he disrobed, sorted his clothing into the hamper and cleaning bag, bathed and got into pajamas and a robe. He was far too keyed up to sleep, and besides, he was savagely hungry.

The housekeeper had left slices of lamb on a plate. There was a fresh wedge of Brie on the cheese board on the kitchen table. Crisp, tart apples were in the fruit bin of the refrigerator. Carefully he prepared a tray and carried it into the library. From the bar he poured a generous whiskey and sat at his desk. As he ate, he reviewed the happenings of the night. If he had not stopped to check his calendar he would have missed her. She would have been gone and it would have been too late to stop her.

Unlocking his desk, he opened the large center drawer and slid back the false bottom where he always kept his current special file. A single manila expansion file was there. He reached for a fresh sheet of paper and made a final entry:

February 15

     At 8:40 p.m. this physician was locking the rear door of his office. Subject patient had just left Fukhito. Subject patient came over to this physician and said that she was going home to Minneapolis and

would have her former doctor, Emmet Salem, deliver her baby. Patient was hysterical and was persuaded to come inside. Obviously patient could not be allowed to leave. Regretting the necessity, this physician prepared to eliminate patient. Under the excuse of getting her a glass of water, this physician dissolved cyanide crystals into the glass and forced patient to swallow the poison. Patient expired at precisely 8:15 p.m. The fetus was 26 weeks old. It is the opinion of this physician that had it been born it might have been viable. The full and accurate medical records are in this file and should replace and nullify the records at the Westlake Hospital office.

Sighing, he laid down the pen, slipped the final entry into the manila envelope and sealed the file. Getting up, he walked over to the last panel on the bookcase. Reaching behind a book, he touched a button, and the panel swung open on hinges, revealing a wall safe. Quickly he opened the safe and inserted the file, subconsciously noting the growing number of envelopes. He could have recited the names of them by heart: Elizabeth Berkeley, Anna Horan, Maureen Crowley, Linda Evans—over six dozen of them: the successes and failures of his medical genius.

He closed the safe and snapped the bookcase back into place, then went upstairs slowly. He took off his bathrobe, got into the massive four-poster bed and closed his eyes.

Now that he was finished with it, he felt exhausted to the point of sickness. Had he overlooked anything, forgotten anything? He'd put the vial of cyanide in the safe. The moccasins. He'd get rid of them somewhere tomorrow night. The events of the last hours whirled furiously through his mind. When he had been doing what must be done, he'd been calm. Now that it was over, like the other times, his nervous system was screaming in protest.

He'd drop his own cleaning off on the way to the hospital tomorrow morning. Hilda was an unimaginative housekeeper, but she'd notice the mud and dampness of his trouser knees. He'd find out what patient was in the center room on the second floor of the east wing, what the patient could have seen. Don't think about it now. Now he must sleep. Leaning on one elbow, he opened the drawer of his night table and took out a small pillbox. The mild sedative was what he needed. With it he'd be able to sleep for two hours.

His fingers groped for and closed over a small capsule. Swallowing it without water, he leaned back and closed his eyes. While he waited for it to take effect, he tried to reassure himself that he was safe. But no matter how hard he tried, he could not push back the thought that the most damning proof of his guilt was inaccessible to him.

"If you don't mind, we'd like you to leave through the back entrance," the nurse said. "The front driveway froze over terribly, and the workmen are trying to clear it. The cab will be waiting there."

"I don't care if I climb out the window, just as long as I can get home," Katie said fervently. "And the misery is that I have to come back here Friday. I'm having minor surgery on Saturday."

"Oh." The nurse looked at her chart. "What's wrong?"

"I seem to have inherited a problem my mother used to have. I practically hemorrhage every month during my period."

"That must have been why your blood count was so low when you came in. Don't worry about it. A D-and-C is no big deal. Who's your doctor?"

"Dr. Highley."

"Oh, he's the best. But you'll be over in the west wing. All his patients go there. It's like a luxury hotel. He's top man in this place, you know." She was still looking at Katie's chart. "You didn't sleep much, did you?"

"Not really." Katie wrinkled her nose with distaste as she buttoned her blouse. It was spattered with blood, and she let the left sleeve hang loosely over her bandaged arm. The nurse helped her with her coat.

The morning was cloudy and bitterly cold. Katie decided that February was getting to be her least-favorite month. She shivered as she stepped out into the parking lot, remembering her nightmare. This was the area she had been looking at from her room. The cab pulled up. Gratefully she walked over to it, wincing at the pain in her knees. The nurse helped her in, said good-bye and closed the door. The cabdriver pressed his foot on the accelerator. "Where to, lady?"

From the window of the second-floor room that Katie had just left, a man was observing her departure. The chart the nurse had left on the desk was in his hand. *Kathleen N. DeMaio, 10 Woodfield Way, Abbington. Place of Business: Prosecutor's office, Valley County.*

He felt a thrill of fear go through him. *Katie DeMaio.*

The chart showed she had been given a strong sleeping pill.

According to her medical history, she took no medication regularly, including sleeping pills or tranquilizers. So she'd have no tolerance for them and would have been pretty groggy from what they'd given her last night.

There was a note on the chart that the night nurse had found her sitting on the edge of the bed at 2:08 A.M. in an agitated state and complaining about nightmares.

The shade in the room had snapped up. She must have been at the window. How much had she seen? If she'd observed anything, even if she thought she'd been having a nightmare, her professional training would nag at her. She was a risk, an unacceptable one.

~~~~~ # CHAPTER 4

Shoulders touching, they sat in the end booth of the Eighty-seventh Street drugstore. Uneaten English muffins had been pushed away, and somberly they sipped coffee. The arm of her teal-blue uniform jacket rested on the gold braid on his sleeve. The fingers of his right hand were entwined with those of her left hand.

"I've missed you," he said carefully.

"I've missed you too, Chris. That's why I'm sorry you met me this morning. It just makes it worse."

"Joan, give me a little time. I swear to God we'll work this out. We've got to."

She shook her head. He turned to her and with a wrench noticed how unhappy she looked. Her hazel eyes were cloudy. Her light brown hair, pulled back this morning in a chignon, revealed the paleness of her usually smooth, clear skin.

For the thousandth time he asked himself why he hadn't made the clean break with Vangie when he was transferred to New York last year. Why had he responded to her plea to try just a little longer to make a go of their marriage when ten years of trying hadn't done it? And now a baby coming. He thought of the ugly quarrel he'd had with Vangie before he left. Should he tell Joan about that? No, it wouldn't do any good.

"How did you like China?" he asked.

She brightened. "Fascinating, completely fascinating." She was a flight attendant with Pan American. They'd met six months ago in Hawaii when one of the other United captains, Jack Lane, threw a party.

Joan was based in New York and shared an apartment in Manhattan with two other Pan Am attendants.

Crazy, incredible, how right some people are together from the first minute. He'd told her he was married, but also was able to say honestly that when he transferred from the Minneapolis base to New York he had wanted to break with Vangie. The last-ditch attempt to save the marriage wasn't working. No one's fault. The marriage was something that never should have happened in the first place.

And then Vangie had told him about the baby.

Joan was saying, "You got in last night."

"Yes. We had engine trouble in Chicago and the rest of the flight was cancelled. We deadheaded back. Got in around six and I checked into the Holiday Inn on Fifty-seventh Street."

"Why didn't you go home?"

"Because I haven't seen you for two weeks and I wanted to see you, *had* to see you. Vangie doesn't expect me till about eleven. So don't worry."

"Chris, I told you I put in an application to transfer to the Latin American Division. It's been approved. I'll be moving to Miami next week."

"Joan, no!"

"It's the only way. Look, Chris, I'm sorry, but it's not my nature to be an available lady for a married man. I'm not a home wrecker."

"Our relationship has been totally innocent."

"In today's world who would ever believe that? The very fact that in an hour you'll be lying to your wife about when you got in says a lot, doesn't it? And don't forget, I'm the daughter of a Presbyterian minister. I can just see Dad's reaction if I tell him that I'm in love with a man who not only is married but whose wife is finally expecting the baby she's prayed for for ten years. He'd be real proud of me, let me tell you."

She finished the coffee. "And no matter what you say, Chris, I still feel that if I'm not around, there's the chance that you and your wife will grow closer. I'm occupying your thoughts when you should be concerned about her. And you'll be amazed how a baby has a way of creating a bond between people."

Gently she withdrew her fingers from his. "I'd better get home, Chris. It was a long flight and I'm tired. You'd better get home too."

They looked directly at each other. She touched his face, wanting to smooth away the deep, unhappy creases in his forehead. "We really could have been awfully good together." Then she added, "You look terribly tired, Chris."

"I didn't sleep very much last night." He tried to smile. "I'm not giving up, Joan. I swear to you that I'm coming to Miami for you, and when I get there I'll be free."

The cab dropped Katie off. She hurried painfully up the porch steps, thrust her key into the lock, opened the door and murmured, "Thank God to be home." She felt that she'd been away weeks rather than overnight and with fresh eyes appreciated the soothing, restful earth tones of the foyer and living room, the hanging plants that had caught her eye when she'd visited this house for the first time.

She picked up the bowl of African violets and inhaled the pungent perfume of their leaves. The odors of antiseptics and medicines were trapped in her nostrils. Her body was aching and stiff, even more now than it had been when she got out of bed this morning.

But at least she was home.

John. If he were alive, if he had been here to call last night. . . .

Katie hung up her coat and sank down on the apricot velvet couch in the living room. She looked up at John's portrait over the mantel. John Anthony DeMaio, the youngest judge in Essex County. She could remember so clearly the first time she'd seen him. He'd come to lecture to her Torts class at Seton Hall Law School.

When the class ended, the students clustered around him. "Judge DeMaio, I hope the Supreme Court turns down the appeal on the *Collins* case."

"Judge DeMaio, I agree with your decision on *Reicher versus Reicher*."

And then it had been Katie's turn. "Judge, I have to tell you I don't agree with your decision in the *Kipling* case."

John had smiled. "That obviously is your privilege, Miss. . . ."

"Katie . . . Kathleen Callahan."

She never understood why at the moment she'd dragged up the Kathleen. But he'd always called her that, Kathleen Noel.

That day they'd gone out for coffee. The next night he'd taken her to the Monsignor II restaurant in New York for dinner. When the violinists came to their table, he'd asked them to play "Vienna, City of My Dreams." He'd sung it softly with them: "*Wien, Wien, nur Du allein . . .*" When they finished he asked, "Have you ever been to Vienna, Kathleen?"

"I've never been out of the country except for the school trip to Bermuda. It rained for four days."

"I'd like to take you abroad someday. But I'd show you Italy first. Now, there's a beautiful country."

When he dropped her off that night he'd said, "You have the loveliest blue eyes I've ever had the pleasure of looking into. I don't think a twelve-year age difference is too much, do you, Kathleen?"

Three months later, when she was graduated from law school, they married.

This house. John had been raised in it, had inherited it from his parents.

"I'm pretty attached to it, Kathleen, but be sure you are. Maybe you want something smaller."

"John, I was raised in a three-room apartment in Queens. I slept on a daybed in the living room. 'Privacy' was a word I had to look up in the dictionary. I *love* this house."

"I'm glad, Kathleen."

They loved each other so much—but besides that, they were such good friends. She'd told him about the nightmare. "I warn you that every once in a while, I'll wake up screaming like a banshee. It started when I was eight years old after my father died. He'd been in the hospital recovering from a heart attack and then he had a second attack. Apparently the old man in the room with him kept pressing the buzzer for the nurse, but no one came. By the time someone got around to answering the buzzer, it was too late."

"And then you started having nightmares."

"I guess I heard the story so much it made an awful impression on me. In the nightmare I'm in a hospital going from bed to bed, looking for Daddy. I keep seeing faces of people I know in the beds. They're all asleep. Sometimes it would be girls from school, or cousins—or just anybody. But I'd be trying to find Daddy. I knew he needed me. Finally I see a nurse and run up to her and ask her where he is. And she smiles and says, 'Oh, he's dead. All these people are dead. You're going to die in here too.' "

"You poor kid."

"Oh, John, intellectually I know it's nonsense not to get over it. But I swear to you I'm scared silly at the thought of ever being a patient in a hospital."

"I'll help you get over that."

She'd been able to tell him how it really was after her father died. "I missed him so much, John. I was always such a daddy's girl. Molly was sixteen and already going around with Bill, so I don't think it hit her as hard. But all through school, I kept thinking what fun it would be if he were at the plays and the graduations. I used to dread the Father and Daughter Dinner every spring."

"Didn't you have an uncle or someone who could have gone with you?"

"Just one. It would have taken too long to sober him up."

"Oh, Kathleen!" The two of them laughing. John saying, "Well, darling, I'm going to uproot that core of sadness in you."

"You already have, Judge."

They'd spent their honeymoon traveling through Italy. The pain had begun on that trip. They'd come back in time for the opening of court. John presided on the bench in Essex County. She'd been hired to clerk for a criminal judge in Valley County.

John went for a checkup a month after they got home. The overnight stay at Mt. Sinai stretched into three days of additional tests. Then one evening he'd been waiting for her at the elevator, impeccably elegant in the dark red velour robe, a wan smile on his face. She'd run over to him, aware as always of the glances the other elevator passengers threw at him, thinking how even in pajamas and a robe, John looked impressive. She'd been about to tell him that when he said, "We've got trouble, darling."

Even then, just the way he said, "*We've* got trouble." In those few short months, in every way, they had become one. Back in his room he'd told her. "It's a malignant tumor. Both lungs, apparently. And for God's sake, Kathleen, I don't even smoke."

Incredulously they had laughed together in a paroxysm of grief and irony. John Anthony DeMaio, Superior Court Judge of Essex County, Past President of the New Jersey Bar Association, not thirty-eight years old, had been condemned to an indeterminate sentence of Six Months to Life. For him there would be no parole board, no appeal.

He'd gone back on the bench. "Die with your robes on—why not?" he'd shrugged.

"Promise me you'll remarry, Kathleen."

"Someday, but you'll be a hard act to follow."

"I'm glad you think so. We'll make every minute we have count."

Even in the midst of it, knowing their time was slipping away, they'd had fun.

One day he came home from court and said, "I think that's about it for the bench."

The cancer had spread. The pain got steadily worse. At first he'd go to the hospital for a few days at a time for chemotherapy. Her nightmare began again; it came regularly. But John would come home and they'd have more time. She resigned her clerkship. She wanted every minute with him.

Toward the end, he asked, "Would you want to have your mother come up from Florida and live with you?"

"Good Lord, no. Mama's great, but we lived together until I went to college. That was enough. But anyhow, she loves Florida."

"Well, I'm glad Molly and Bill live nearby. They'll look out for you. And you enjoy the children."

They'd both been silent then. Bill Kennedy was an orthopedic surgeon. He and Molly had six kids and lived two towns away in Chapin River. The day Katie and John were married, they'd bragged to Bill and Molly that they were going to beat their record. "We'll have seven offspring," John had declared.

The last time he went in for chemotherapy, he didn't come back. He was so weak they had him stay overnight. He was talking to her when he slipped into the coma. They'd both hoped that the end would come at home, but he died in the hospital that night.

The next week Katie applied to the Prosecutor's office for a job and was accepted. It was a good decision. The office was chronically short-handed, and she always had more cases than she could reasonably handle. There wasn't any time for introspection. All day, every day, even on many weekends, she'd had to concentrate on her case load.

And in another way it was good therapy. That anger which had accompanied the grief, the sense of being cheated, the fury that John had been cheated of so much of life, she directed into the cases she tried. When she prosecuted a serious crime, she felt as though she were tangibly fighting at least one kind of evil that destroyed lives.

She'd kept the house. John had willed her all of his very considerable assets, but even so, she knew it was silly for a twenty-eight-year-old woman on a twenty-two-thousand-dollar salary to live in a home worth a quarter of a million dollars with five acres surrounding it.

Molly and Bill were always urging her to sell it.

"You'll never put your life with John behind you until you do," Bill had told her.

He was probably right. Now Katie shook herself and got up from the couch. She was getting downright maudlin. She'd better call Molly. If Molly had tried to get her last night and not received an answer she'd have been delighted. She was always making a novena that Katie would "meet someone." But she didn't want Molly to try to reach her at the office and find out that way that she'd been in an accident.

Maybe Molly would come over and they'd have lunch together. She had salad makings and Bloody Mary ingredients. Molly was perpetually on a diet, but would not give up her lunchtime Bloody Mary. "For God's sake, Kate, how could anyone with six kids *not* have a belt at lunch?" Molly's cheerful presence would quickly dispel the sense of isolation and sadness.

Katie became aware of the bloodstained blouse she was wearing. After she'd talked to Molly, while she was waiting for her to come over, she'd bathe and change.

Glancing into the mirror over the couch, she saw that the bruise under her right eye was assuming a brilliant purple color. Her naturally olive complexion, which Mama called the "Black Irish" look from her father's side, was a sickly yellow. Her collar-length dark brown hair, which usually bounced full and luxuriant in a natural wave, was matted against her face and neck.

"You should see the other guy," she murmured ruefully.

The doctor had told her not to get her arm wet. She'd wrap the bandage in a Baggie and keep it dry. Before she could pick up the phone, it began to ring. Molly, she thought. I swear she's a witch.

But it was Richard Carroll, the Medical Examiner. "Katie, how are you? Just heard that you'd been in some kind of accident."

"Nothing much. I took a little detour off the road. The trouble is there was a tree in the way."

"When did it happen?"

"About ten last night. I was on my way home from the office. I'd worked late to catch up on some files. Spent the night in the hospital and just got home. I look a mess, but I'm really okay."

"Who picked you up? Molly?"

"No. She doesn't know yet. I called a cab."

"Always the Lone Ranger, aren't you?" Richard asked. "Why the blazes didn't you call *me?*"

Katie laughed. The concern in Richard's voice was both flattering and threatening. Richard and Molly's husband were good friends. Several times in the last six months Molly had pointedly invited Katie and Richard to small dinner parties. But Richard was so blunt and cynical. She always felt somewhat unsettled around him. Anyhow, she simply wasn't looking to get involved with anyone, and especially anyone she worked with so frequently. "Next time I run into a tree I'll remember," she said.

"You're going to take a couple of days off, aren't you?"

"Oh, no," she said. "I'm going to see if Molly's free for a quick lunch; then I'll get in to the office. I've got at least ten files to work on, and I'm trying an important case on Friday."

"There's no use telling you you're crazy. Okay. Gotta go. My other phone's ringing. I'll poke my head in your office around five-thirty and catch you for a drink." He hung up before she could reply.

Katie dialed Molly's number. When her sister answered, her voice was shaken. "Katie, I guess you've heard about it."

"Heard about what?"

"People from your office are just getting there."

"Getting where?"

"Next door. The Lewises. That couple who moved in last summer. Katie, that poor man; he just came home from an overnight flight and found her—his wife, Vangie. She's killed herself. Katie, she was six months pregnant!"

The Lewises. *The Lewises.* Katie had met them at Molly and Bill's New Year's Day open house. Vangie a very pretty blonde. Chris an air-line pilot.

Numbly she heard Molly's shocked voice: "Katie, why would a girl who wanted a baby so desperately kill herself?"

The question hung in the air. Cold chills washed over Katie. That long blond hair spilling over shoulders. Her nightmare. Crazy the tricks the mind plays. As soon as Molly said the name, last night's nightmare had come back. The face she'd glimpsed through the hospital window was Vangie Lewis'.

➤ CHAPTER 6

Richard Carroll parked his car within the police lines on Winding Brook Lane. He was shocked to realize that the Lewises lived next door to Bill and Molly Kennedy. Bill had been a resident when Richard interned at St. Vincent's. Later he'd specialized in foren-sic medicine and Bill in orthopedics. They'd been pleasantly surprised to bump into each other in the Valley County courthouse when Bill was appearing as an expert witness in a malpractice trial. The friendship that had been casual in the St. Vincent's days had become close. Now he and Bill golfed together frequently, and Richard often stopped back to their house for a drink after the game.

He'd met Molly's sister, Katie DeMaio, in the Prosecutor's office and had been immediately attracted to the dedicated young attorney. She was a throwback to the days when the Spanish invaded Ireland and left a legacy of descendants with olive skin and dark hair to contrast with the intense blue of Celtic eyes. But Katie had subtly discouraged him when he'd suggested getting together, and he'd philosophically dis-missed her from his thoughts. There were plenty of mighty attractive ladies who enjoyed his company well enough.

But hearing Molly and Bill and their kids talk about Katie, what fun she could be, how chopped up she was over her husband's death, had rekindled his interest. Then in the past few months he'd been at a couple of parties at Bill and Molly's and found to his chagrin that he was far more intrigued by Katie DeMaio than he wanted to be.

Richard shrugged. He was here on police business. A thirty-year-old woman had committed suicide. It was his job to look for any medical signs which might indicate that Vangie Lewis had not taken her own life. Later today he'd perform an autopsy. His jaw tightened as he thought of the fetus she was carrying. Never had a chance. How was that for motherly love? Cordially, objectively, he already disliked the late Vangie Lewis.

A young cop from Chapin River let him in. The living room was to the left of the foyer. A guy in an airline captain's uniform was sitting on the couch, hunched forward, clasping and unclasping his hands. He was a lot paler than many of the deceased Richard dealt with and was trembling violently. Richard felt a brief twinge of sympathy. The husband. Some brutal kick to come home and find your wife a suicide. He decided to talk with him later. "Which way?" he asked the cop.

"Back here." He nodded his head to the rear of the house. "Kitchen straight ahead, bedrooms to the right. She's in the master bedroom."

Richard walked quickly, absorbing as he did the feel of the house. Expensive, but carelessly furnished, without flair or even interest. The glimpse of the living room had shown him the typical no-imagination interior-designer look you see in so many Main Street decorator shops in small towns. Richard had an acute sense of color. Privately he thought it helped him considerably in his work. But clashing shades registered on his consciousness like the sound of discordant notes.

Charley Nugent, the detective in charge of the Homicide Squad, was in the kitchen. The two men exchanged brief nods. "How does it look?" Richard asked.

"Let's talk after you see her."

In death Vangie Lewis was not a pretty sight. The long blond hair seemed a muddy brown now; her face was contorted; her legs and arms, stiff with the onslaught of rigor mortis, had the appearance of being stretched on wires. Her coat was buttoned and, because of her pregnancy, hiked over her knees. The soles of her shoes were barely showing under a long flowered caftan.

Richard pulled the caftan up past her ankles. Her legs, obviously swollen, had stretched the panty hose. The sides of her right shoe bit into the flesh.

Expertly he picked up one arm, held it for an instant, let it drop. He studied the mottled discoloration around her mouth where the poison had burned it.

Charley was beside him. "How long you figure?"

"Anywhere from twelve to fifteen hours, I'd guess. She's pretty rigid." Richard's voice was noncommittal, but his sense of harmony was disturbed. The coat on. Shoes on. Had she just come home, or had she been planning to go out? What had suddenly made her take her own life? The tumbler was beside her on the bed. Bending down, he sniffed it. The unmistakable bitter-almond scent of cyanide entered his nostrils. Incredible how many suicides took cyanide ever since that Jones-cult mess in Guyana. He straightened up. "Did she leave a note?"

Charley shook his head. Richard thought that Charley was in the right job. He always looked mournful; his lids drooped sadly over his eyes. He seemed to have a perpetual dandruff problem. "No letters; no nothing. Been married ten years to the pilot; he's the guy in the living room. Seems pretty broken up. They're from Minneapolis; just moved east less than a year ago. She always wanted to have a baby. Finally got pregnant and was in heaven. Started decorating a nursery; talks baby morning, noon and night."

"Then she kills it and herself?"

"According to her husband, she'd been nervous lately. Some days she had some sort of fixation that she was going to lose the baby. Other times she'd act scared about giving birth. Apparently knew she was showing some signs of a toxic pregnancy."

"And rather than give birth or face losing the baby, she kills herself?" Richard's tone was skeptical. He could tell Charley wasn't buying it either. "Is Phil with you?" he asked. Phil was the other senior member of the Homicide team from the Prosecutor's office.

"He's out around the neighborhood talking to people."

"Who found her?"

"The husband. He just got in from a flight. Called for an ambulance. Called the local cops."

Richard stared at the burn marks around Vangie Lewis' mouth. "She must have really splashed that in," he said meditatively, "or maybe tried to spit it out but it was too late. Can we talk to the husband, bring him in here?"

"Sure." Charley nodded to the young cop, who turned and scampered down the long hallway.

When Christopher Lewis came into the bedroom, he looked as though he were on the verge of getting sick. His complexion was now a sickly green. Perspiration, cold and clammy, beaded on his forehead. He had pulled open his shirt and tie. His hands were shoved into his pockets.

Richard studied him appraisingly. Lewis looked distraught, sick, nervous. But there was something missing. He did not look like a man whose life has been shattered.

Richard had seen death countless times. He'd witnessed some next of kin grieving in dumbstruck silence. Others shrieked hysterically, screamed, wept, threw themselves on the deceased. Some touched the dead hand, trying to understand. He thought of the young husband whose wife had been caught in a shoot-out while they were getting out of their car to do the grocery shopping. When Richard got there, he was holding the body, bewildered, talking to her, trying to get through to her.

That was grief.

Whatever emotion Christopher Lewis was experiencing now, Richard would stake his life on the fact that he was not a heartbroken husband.

Charley was questioning him. "Captain Lewis, this is tough for you, but it will make it easier all around if we can ask you some questions."

"Here?" It was a protest.

"You'll see why. We won't be long. When was the last time you saw your wife?"

"Two nights ago. I was on a run to the Coast."

"And you arrived home at what time?"

"About an hour ago."

"Did you speak with your wife in those two days?"

"No."

"What was your wife's mental state when you left?"

"I told you."

"If you'd just tell Dr. Carroll."

"Vangie was worried. She'd become quite apprehensive that she might miscarry."

"Were you alarmed about that possibility?"

"She'd become quite heavy, looked like she was retaining fluid, but she had pills for that and I understand it's quite a common condition."

"Did you call her obstetrician to discuss this with him, to reassure yourself?"

"No."

"All right. Captain Lewis, will you look around this room and see if you notice anything amiss. It isn't easy, but will you study your wife's body carefully and see if there's anything that in some way is different. For example, that glass. Are you sure it's the one from your bathroom?"

Chris obeyed. His face going progressively whiter, he carefully looked at every detail of his dead wife's appearance.

Through narrowed eyes, Charley and Richard watched him.

"No," he whispered finally. "Nothing."

Charley's manner became brisk. "Okay, sir. As soon as we take some pictures, we'll remove your wife's body for an autopsy. Can we help you get in touch with anyone?"

"I have some calls to make. Vangie's father and mother. They'll be heartbroken. I'll go into the study and phone them now."

After he'd left, Richard and Charley exchanged glances.

"He saw something we missed," Charley said flatly.

Richard nodded. "I know." Grimly the two men stared at the crumpled body.

 CHAPTER 7

Before she'd hung up, Katie had told Molly about the accident and suggested lunch. But Molly's twelve-year-old Jennifer and her six-year-old twin boys were home from school recovering from flu. "Jennifer's okay, but I don't like to leave those boys alone long enough to empty the garbage," Molly had said, and they'd arranged that she would pick Katie up and bring her back to her own house.

While she waited, Katie bathed quickly, managing to wash and blow-dry her hair using only her right hand. She put on a thick wool sweater and well-tailored tweed slacks. The red sweater gave some hint of color to her face, and her hair curled loosely just below her collar. As she bathed and dressed, she tried to rationalize last night's hallucination.

Had she even *been* at the window? Or was that part of the dream? Maybe the shade had snapped up by itself, pulling her out of a nightmare. She closed her eyes as once more the scene floated into her consciousness. It had seemed so real: the trunk light had shone directly into the trunk on the staring eyes, the long hair, the high-arched eyebrows. For one instant it had seemed so clear. That was what frightened her: the clarity of the image. The face had been familiar even in the dream.

Would she talk to Molly about that? Of course not. Molly had been worried about her lately. "Katie, you're too pale. You work too hard. You're getting too quiet." Molly had bullied her into the scheduled operation. "You can't let that condition go on indefinitely. That hemorrhaging can be dangerous if you let it go." And then she'd added, "Katie, you've got to realize you're a young woman. You should take a real vacation, relax, go away."

From outside, a horn blew loudly as Molly pulled up in her battered station wagon. Katie struggled into a warm beaver jacket, turning the collar up around her ears, and hurried out as fast as her swollen knees would allow. Molly pushed open the door for her and leaned over to

kiss her. She eyed her critically. "You're not exactly blooming. How badly *were* you hurt?"

"It could have been a lot worse." The car smelled vaguely of peanut butter and bubble gum. It was a comforting, familiar smell, and Katie felt her spirits begin to lift. But the mood was broken instantly when Molly said, "Our block is some mess. Your people have the Lewis place blocked off, and some detective from your office is going around asking questions. He caught me just as I was leaving. I told him I was your sister and we did the number on how wonderful you are."

Katie said, "It was probably Phil Cunningham or Charley Nugent."

"Big guy. Beefy face. Nice."

"Phil Cunningham. He's a good man. What kind of questions were they asking?"

"Pretty routine. Had we noticed what time she left or got back—that kind of thing."

"And did you?"

"When the twins are sick and cranky, I wouldn't notice if Robert Redford moved in next door. Anyhow, we can barely see the Lewises' house on a sunny day, never mind at night in a storm."

They were driving over the wooden bridge just before the turn to Winding Brook Lane. Katie bit her lip. "Molly, drop me off at the Lewis house, won't you?"

Molly turned to her, astonished. "Why?"

Katie tried to smile. "Well. I'm an assistant prosecutor, and for what it's worth, I'm also adviser to the Chapin River Police Department. I wouldn't normally have to go, but as long as I'm right here, I think I should."

The hearse from the Medical Examiner's office was just backing into the driveway of the Lewis home. Richard was in the doorway watching. He came over to the car when Molly pulled up. Quickly Molly explained: "Katie's having lunch with me and thought she should stop by here. Why don't you come over with her, if you can?"

He agreed and helped Katie out of the car. "I'm glad you're here," he said. "There's something about this setup I don't like."

Now that she was about to see the dead woman, Katie felt her mouth go dry. She remembered the image of the face in her dream. "The husband is in the den," Richard said.

"I've met him. You must have too. At Molly's New Year's Day party. No. You came late. They'd left before you arrived."

Richard said, "All right. We'd better talk about it later. Here's the room."

She forced herself to look at the familiar face, and recognized it instantly. She shuddered and closed her eyes. Was she going crazy?

"You all right, Katie?" Richard asked sharply.

What kind of fool was she? "I'm perfectly all right," she said, and to her own ears her voice sounded normal enough. "I'd like to talk to Captain Lewis."

When they got to the den, the door was closed. Without knocking, Richard opened it quietly. Chris Lewis was on the phone, his back to them. His voice was low but distinct. "I know it's incredible, but I swear to you, Joan, she didn't know about us."

Richard closed the door noiselessly. He and Katie stared at each other. Katie said, "I'll tell Charley to stay here. I'm going to recommend to Scott that we launch a full investigation." Scott Myerson was the Prosecutor.

"I'll do the autopsy myself as soon as they bring her in," Richard said. "The minute we're positive it was the cyanide that killed her, we'd better start finding out where she got it. Come on; let's make the stop at Molly's a quick one."

Molly's house, like her car, was a haven of normality. Katie often stopped there for a glass of wine or dinner on her way home from work. The smell of good food cooking; the kids' feet clattering on the stairs; the blare of the television set; the noisy young voices, shouting and battling. For her it was re-entry into the real world after a day of dealing with murderers, kidnappers, muggers, vandals, deviates, arsonists and penny-ante crooks. And dearly as she loved the Kennedys, the visit made her appreciate the serene peace of her own home. Except, of course, for the times that she would feel the emptiness of her house and try to imagine what it would be like if John were still alive and their children had started to arrive.

"Katie! Dr. Carroll!" The twins came whooping up to greet them. "Did you see all the cop cars, Katie? Something happened next door!" Peter, older than his twin by ten minutes, was always the spokesman.

"Right next door!" John chimed in. Molly called them "Pete and Repeat." "Get lost, you two," she ordered now. "And leave us alone while we eat."

"Where are the other kids?" Katie asked.

"Billy, Dina and Moira went back to school this morning, thank God," Molly said. "Jennifer's in bed. I just looked in and she's dozed off again. Poor kid still feels lousy."

They settled at the kitchen table. The kitchen was large and cheerfully warm. Molly produced Reubens from the oven, offered drinks, which they refused, and poured coffee. Molly had a way with food, Katie thought. Everything she fixed tasted good. But when Katie tried to eat, she found her throat was closed. She glanced at Richard. He had piled hot mustard onto the corned beef and was eating with obvious pleasure. She envied him his detachment. On one level he could enjoy a good sandwich. On the other, she was sure that he was concentrating on the Lewis case. His forehead was knitted; his thatch of brown hair looked ruffled; his blue-gray eyes were thoughtful; his rangy shoulders hunched forward as with two fingers he lightly drummed the table. She'd have bet that they were both pondering the same question: Who had been on the phone with Chris Lewis?

She remembered the only conversation she'd had with Chris. It had been at the New Year's party, and they'd discussed hijacking. He'd been interesting, intelligent, pleasant. With his rugged good looks, he was a very appealing man. And she remembered that he and Vangie had been at opposite ends of the crowded room and he'd been unenthused when she, Katie, congratulated him on the coming baby.

"Molly, what was your impression of the Lewises—I mean their relationship to each other?" she asked.

Molly looked troubled. "Candidly, I think it was on the rocks. She was so hung up with being pregnant that whenever they were here she kept yanking the conversation back to babies, and he obviously was upset about it. And since I had a hand in the pregnancy, it was a real worry for me."

Richard stopped drumming his fingers and straightened up. "You had *what?*"

"I mean, well, you know me, Katie. The day they moved in, last summer, I went rushing over and invited them to dinner. They came, and right away Vangie told me how much she hoped to have a baby and how upset she was about her best childbearing years being over because she'd turned thirty."

Molly took a gulp of her Bloody Mary and eyed the empty glass regretfully. "I told her about Liz Berkeley. She never was able to conceive until she went to a gynecologist who's something of a fertility expert. Liz had just given birth to a little girl and of course was ecstatic. Anyhow, I told Vangie about Dr. Highley. She went to him and a few months later conceived. But since then I've been sorry I didn't keep out of it."

"Dr. Highley?" Katie looked startled.

Molly nodded. "Yes, the one who's going to . . ."

Katie shook her head, and Molly's voice trailed off.

Edna Burns liked her job. She was bookkeeper-receptionist for the two doctors who staffed and ran the Westlake Maternity Concept team. "Dr. Highley's the big shot," she confided to her friends. "You know, he was married to Winifred Westlake and she left him everything. He runs the whole show."

Dr. Highley was a gynecologist/obstetrician, and as Edna explained, "It's a riot to see the way his patients act when they finally get pregnant; so happy you'd think they invented kids. He charges them an arm and a leg, but he's practically a miracle worker.

"On the other hand," she'd explain, "Highley is also the right person to see if you've got an internal problem that you *don't* want to grow. If you know what I mean," she'd add with a wink.

Dr. Fukhito was a psychiatrist. The Westlake Maternity Concept was one of holistic medicine: that mind and body must be in harmony to achieve a successful pregnancy and that many women could not conceive because they were emotionally charged with fear and anxiety. All gynecology patients consulted Dr. Fukhito at least once, but pregnant patients were required to schedule regular visits.

Edna enjoyed telling her friends that the Westlake Concept had been dreamed up by old Dr. Westlake, who had died before he acted on it. Then, eight years ago, his daughter Winifred had married Dr. Highley, bought the River Falls Clinic when it went into bankruptcy, renamed it for her father and set up her husband there. "She and the doctor were crazy about each other," Edna would sigh. "I mean she was ten years older than he and nothing to look at, but they were real lovers. He'd have me send her flowers a couple of times a week, and busy as he is, he'd go shopping with her for her clothes. Let me tell you, it was some shock when she died. No one ever knew her heart was that bad.

"But," she'd add philosophically, "he keeps busy. I've seen women who never were able to conceive become pregnant two and three times. Of course, a lot of them don't carry the babies to term, but at least they know there's a chance. And you should see the kind of care they get. I've seen Dr. Highley bring women in and put them to bed in the hospital for two months before a birth. Costs a fortune, of course, but buhlieve me, when you want a baby and can afford it, you'll pay anything to get one. But you can read about it yourself, pretty soon," she'd add. "*Newsmaker* magazine just did an article about him and about the Westlake Maternity Concept. It's coming out Thursday. They came last week and photographed him in his office standing next to the pictures of all those babies he's delivered. Real nice. And if you think we're busy now, wait till that comes out. The phone'll never be on the hook."

Edna was a born bookkeeper. Her records were marvels of accuracy. She loved receipts and took a sensual pride in making frequent and healthy bank deposits in her employer's account. A neat but prominent sign on her desk let it be known that all payments must be made in cash; no monthly bills would be rendered; retainer fees and payment schedules would be explained by Miss Burns.

Edna had been told by Dr. Highley that unless specifically instructed otherwise, she was to be sure to make follow-up appointments with people as they left; that if for any reason a patient did not keep the next appointment, Edna should phone that patient at home and firmly make a new one. It was a sound arrangement and, as Edna gleefully noted, a financial bonanza.

Dr. Highley always complimented Edna on the excellent records she maintained and her ability to keep the appointment book full. The only time Dr. Highley really gave her the rough side of his tongue was when she was overheard talking to one patient about another's problems. She had to admit that had been foolish, but she'd allowed herself a couple of Manhattans for lunch that day and that had lowered her guard.

The doctor had finished up his lecture by saying, "Any more talking and you're through."

She knew he meant it.

Edna sighed. She was tired. Last night both doctors had had evening hours, and it had been hectic. Then she'd worked on the books for a while. She couldn't wait to go home this evening, and wild horses wouldn't drag her out again. She'd put on a robe and mix herself a nice batch of Manhattans. She had a canned ham in the refrigerator, so she'd make that do for supper and watch television.

It was nearly two o'clock. Three more hours and she could clear out. While it was quiet she had to check yesterday's calendar to make sure she'd made all the necessary future appointments. Frowning nearsightedly, she leaned her broad, freckled face on a thick hand. Her hair felt messy today. She hadn't had time to set it last night. She'd been kind of tired after she had a few drinks.

She was an overweight woman of forty-four who looked ten years older. Her unleavened youth had been spent taking care of aging parents. When Edna saw pictures of herself from Drake Secretarial School she was vaguely surprised at the pretty girl she'd been a quarter of a century ago. Always a mite too heavy, but pretty nevertheless.

Her mind was only half on the page she was reading, but then something triggered her full attention. She paused. The eight-o'clock appointment last night for Vangie Lewis.

Last night Vangie had come in early and sat talking with Edna. She was sure upset. Well, Vangie was kind of a complainer, but so pretty Edna enjoyed just looking at her. Vangie had put on a lot of weight during the pregnancy and, to Edna's practiced eye, was retaining a lot of fluid. Edna prayed that Vangie would deliver that baby safely. She wanted it so much.

So she didn't blame Vangie for being moody. She really wasn't well. Last month Vangie had started wearing those moccasins because her other shoes didn't fit anymore. She'd shown them to Edna. "Look at this. My right foot is so bad, I can only wear these clodhoppers my cleaning woman left behind. The other one is always falling off."

Edna had tried to kid her. "Well, with those glass slippers I'll just have to start calling you Cinderella. And we'll call your husband Prince Charming." She knew Vangie was nuts about her husband.

But Vangie had just pouted and said impatiently, "Oh, Edna, Prince Charming was Sleeping Beauty's boyfriend, not Cinderella's. Everybody knows that."

Edna had just laughed. "Mama must have been mixed up. When she told me about Cinderella she said Prince Charming came around with the glass slipper. But never mind—before you know it, you'll have your baby and be back in pretty shoes again."

Last night Vangie had pulled up that long caftan she'd started wearing to hide her swollen leg. "Edna," she'd said, "I can hardly even get this clodhopper on. And for what? God Almighty, for what?" She'd been almost crying.

"Oh, you're just getting down in the dumps, honey," Edna had said. "It's a good thing you came in to talk to Dr. Fukhito. He'll relax you."

Just then Dr. Fukhito had buzzed and said to send Mrs. Lewis in. Vangie started down the corridor to his office. Just as she left the reception area, she stumbled. She'd walked right out of that loose left shoe. "Oh, to hell with it!" she cried, and just kept going. Edna had picked up the moccasin, figuring Vangie would come back for it when she finished with Dr. Fukhito.

Edna always stayed late Monday nights to work on the books. But when she was ready to go home around nine o'clock, Vangie still hadn't come back. Edna decided to take a chance and ring Dr. Fukhito and just tell him that she'd leave the shoe outside the office door in the corridor.

But there was no answer in Dr. Fukhito's office. That meant that Vangie must have walked out the door that led directly to the parking lot. That was crazy. She'd catch her death of cold getting her foot wet.

Irresolutely Edna had held the shoe in her hand and locked up. She went out to the parking lot toward her own car just in time to see

Vangie's big red Lincoln Continental with Dr. Highley at the wheel pull out. She'd tried to run a few steps to wave to him, but it was no use. So she'd just gone home.

Maybe Dr. Highley had already made a new appointment with Vangie, but Edna would phone her just to be sure. Quickly she dialed the Lewis number. The phone rang once, twice.

A man's voice answered: "Lewises' residence."

"Mrs. Lewis, please." Edna assumed her Drake Secretarial School business voice, crisp but friendly. She wondered if she was talking to Captain Lewis.

"Who's calling?"

"Dr. Highley's office. We want to set up Mrs. Lewis' next appointment."

"Hold on."

She could tell the transmitter was being covered. Muffled voices were talking. What could be going on? Maybe Vangie had been taken sick. If so, Dr. Highley should be told at once.

The voice at the other end began to speak. "This is Detective Cunningham of the Valley County Prosecutor's office. I'm sorry, but Mrs. Lewis has died suddenly. You can tell her doctor that he'll be contacted tomorrow morning by someone on our staff."

"Mrs. Lewis died!" Edna's voice was a howl of dismay. "Oh, what happened?"

There was a pause. "It seems she took her own life." The connection was broken.

Slowly Edna lowered the receiver. It wasn't possible. It just wasn't possible.

The two-o'clock appointments arrived together: Mrs. Volmer for Dr. Highley, Mrs. Lashley for Dr. Fukhito. Mechanically Edna greeted them.

"Are you all right, Edna?" Mrs. Volmer asked curiously. "You look upset or something."

She knew that Mrs. Volmer had talked to Vangie in the waiting room sometimes. It was on the tip of her tongue to tell her that Vangie was dead. But some instinct warned her to tell Dr. Highley first.

His one-thirty appointment came out. He was on the intercom. "Send Mrs. Volmer in, Edna." Edna glanced at the women. There was no way she could talk on the intercom without their hearing her.

"Doctor, may I step in for a moment, please? I'd like to have a word with you." That sounded so efficient. She was pleased at her own control.

"Certainly." He didn't sound very happy about it. Highley was a bit scary; still, he could be nice. She'd seen that last night.

She moved down the hall as fast as her overweight body would allow. She was panting when she knocked at his office door. He said, "Come in, Edna." His voice was edged with irritation.

Timidly she opened the door and stepped inside his office.

"Doctor," she began hurriedly, "you'll want to know. I just phoned Mrs. Lewis, Vangie Lewis, to make an appointment. You told me you want to see her every week now."

"Yes, yes. And for heaven's sake, Edna, close that door. Your voice can be heard through the hospital."

Quickly she obeyed. Trying to keep her voice low, she said, "Doctor, when I phoned her house, a detective answered. He said she killed herself and that they're coming to see you tomorrow."

"Mrs. Lewis what?" He sounded shocked.

Now that she could talk about it, Edna's words crowded in her mouth, tumbling out in a torrent. "She was so upset last night, wasn't she, Doctor? I mean we both could see it. The way she talked to me and the way she acted like she didn't care about anything. But you must know that; I thought it was the nicest thing when I saw you drive her home last night. I tried to wave to you, but you didn't see me. So I guess of all people you know how bad she was."

"Edna, how many people have you discussed this with?"

There was something in his tone that made her very nervous. Flustered, she avoided his eyes. "Why, nobody, sir. I just heard this minute."

"You did not discuss Mrs. Lewis' death with Mrs. Volmer or anyone else in the reception area?"

"No . . . no, sir."

"And not with the detective on the phone?"

"No, sir."

"Edna, tomorrow when the police come, you and I will tell them everything we know about Mrs. Lewis' frame of mind. But listen to me now." He pointed his finger at her and leaned forward. Unconsciously, she stepped back. "I don't want Mrs. Lewis' name mentioned by you to anyone—*anyone*, do you hear? Mrs. Lewis was an extremely neurotic and unstable woman. But the fact is that her suicide reflects very badly on our hospital. How do you think it's going to look in the papers if it comes out that she was a patient of mine? And I certainly won't have you gossiping in the reception room with the other patients, some of whom have very tenuous holds on the fetuses they are carrying. Do you understand me?"

"Yes, sir," Edna quavered. She should have known he'd think she'd gossip about this.

"Edna, you like your job?"

"Yes, sir."

"Edna, do not discuss with anyone—*anyone,* mind you—*one word* about the Lewis case. If I hear you have so much as mentioned it, you're finished here. Tomorrow we'll talk with the police, but no one else. Mrs. Lewis' state of mind is confidential. Is that clear?"

"Yes, sir."

"Are you going out with friends tonight? You know how you get when you drink."

Edna was close to tears. "I'm going home. I'm not feeling well, Doctor. I want to have my wits about me tomorrow when the police talk to me. Poor little Cinderella." She gulped as easy tears came to her eyes. But then she saw the expression on his face. Angry. Disgusted.

Edna straightened up, dabbed at her eyes. "I'll send Mrs. Volmer in, Doctor. And you don't have to worry," she added with dignity. "I value our hospital. I know how much your work means to you and to our patients. I'm not going to say one single word."

The rest of the afternoon was busy. She managed to push the thought of Vangie to the back of her mind as she talked with patients, made future appointments, collected money, reminded patients if they were falling behind in their payments.

Finally, at five o'clock she could leave. Warmly wrapped in a leopard-spotted fake-fur coat and matching hat, she drove home to her garden apartment in Edgeriver, six miles away.

CHAPTER 9

In the clinically impersonal autopsy room of the Valley County Morgue, Richard Carroll gently removed the fetus from the corpse of Vangie Lewis. His long, sensitive fingers lifted the small body, noting that the amniotic fluid had begun to leak. Vangie Lewis could not have carried this baby much longer. He judged that it weighed about two and a half pounds. It was a boy.

The firstborn son. He shook his head at the waste as he laid it on an adjacent slab. Vangie had been in an advanced state of toxemia. It was incredible that any doctor had allowed her to progress so far in this condition. He'd be interested to know what her white-cell count had been. Probably terrifically high.

He'd already sent fluid samples to the laboratory. He had no doubt that the cyanide killed the woman. Her throat and mouth were badly burned. She'd swallowed a huge gulp of it, God help her.

The burns on the outside of her mouth? Carefully Richard examined them. He tried to visualize the moment she'd drunk the poison. She'd started to swallow, felt the burning, changed her mind, tried to spit it out. It had run over her lips and chin.

To him it didn't wash.

There were fine white fibers clinging to her coat. They looked as though they'd come from a blanket. He was having them analyzed. It seemed to him that she had been lying on a chenille spread. He wanted to compare the fiber from the spread with those taken from the coat. Of course, the coat was pretty tired-looking, and they might have been picked up at any time.

Her body had become so bloated that it looked as though Vangie had just put on whatever clothes she could find that would cover her.

Except for the shoes. That was another incongruous note. The shoes were well cut and expensive. More than that, they looked quite new. It was unlikely Vangie could have been outdoors on Monday in those shoes and have them in such mint condition. There were no water spots or snow marks on them, even though the ankles of her panty hose had spatters of dirty snow. Didn't that suggest that she must have been out, come in, decided to leave again, changed her shoes and then committed suicide?

That didn't wash either.

Another thing. Those shoes were awfully tight. Particularly the right foot. She could barely lace the shoe, and the vamp was narrow. It would have been like putting on a vise. Considering the rest of the way she was dressed, why bother to put on shoes that will kill you?

Shoes that will kill you . . .

The phrase stuck in Richard's mind. He straightened up. He was just about finished here. As soon as they had a lab report he could tell Scott Myerson what he had found.

Once more he turned to study the fetus. The cyanide had entered its bloodstream. Like its mother, it must have died in agony. Carefully Richard examined it. The miracle of life never ceased to awe him; if anything, it grew with every experience he had with death. He marveled at the exquisite balance of the body: the harmony of its parts, muscles and fibers, bones and sinews, veins and arteries; the profound complexity of the nervous system, the ability of the body to heal its own wounds, its elaborate attempt to protect its unborn.

Suddenly he bent over the fetus. Swiftly he freed it from the placenta and studied it under the strong light. Was it possible?

It was a hunch, a hunch he had to check out. Dave Broad was the man for him. Dave was in charge of prenatal research at Mt. Sinai. He'd send this fetus to him and ask for an opinion.

If what he believed was true, there was a damn good reason why Captain Chris Lewis would have been upset about his wife's pregnancy.

Maybe even upset enough to kill her!

CHAPTER 10

Scott Myerson, the Valley County Prosecutor, scheduled a five o'clock meeting in his office for Katie, Richard and the two Homicide Squad detectives assigned to the Lewis suicide. Scott's office did not fit the television world's image of a prosecutor's private chambers. It was small. The walls were painted a sickly yellow. The furniture was battered; the ancient files were battleship gray. The windows looked out on the county jail.

Katie arrived first. Gingerly she eased into the one reasonably comfortable extra chair. Scott looked at her with a hint of a smile. He was a small man with a surprisingly deep voice. Large rimmed glasses, a dark, neat mustache and meticulously tailored conservative suit made him look more like a banker than a law enforcer. He had been in court all day on a case he was personally trying and had spoken to Katie only by phone. Now he observed her bandaged arm and the bruise under her eye and the wince of pain that came over her face as she moved her body.

"Thanks for coming in, Katie," he said. "I know how overloaded you are and do appreciate it. But you'd better take tomorrow off."

Katie shook her head. "No. I'm okay, and this soreness will probably be a lot better in the morning."

"All right, but remember, if you start feeling rotten, just go home." He became businesslike. "The Lewis case. What have we got on it?"

Richard and the detectives came in while she was talking. Silently they settled in the three folding chairs remaining.

Scott tapped a pencil on his desk as he listened. He turned to the detectives. "What did you come up with?"

Phil Cunningham pulled out his notebook. "That place was no honeymoon cottage. The Lewises went to some neighborhood gatherings." He looked at Katie. "Guess your sister tried to have them included. Everyone liked Chris Lewis. They thought Vangie was a pain in the neck—obviously jealous of him; not interested in getting involved with any activities in the community; not interested in *anything.* At the parties she was always hanging on him; got real upset if he talked more than five minutes to another woman. He was very patient with her. One of the neighbors said her husband told her after one of those parties that if he were married to Vangie, he'd kill her with his bare hands. Then when she got pregnant she was really insufferable. Talked baby all the time."

Charley had opened his notebook. "Her obstetrician's office called to set up an appointment. I said we'd be in to talk to her doctor tomorrow."

Richard spoke quietly. "There are a few questions I'd like to ask that doctor about Vangie Lewis' condition."

Scott looked at Richard. "You've finished the autopsy?"

"Yes. It was definitely cyanide. She died instantly. The mouth and throat were badly burned. Which leads to the crucial point."

There were a water pitcher and paper cups on top of the file. Walking over to the file, Richard poured a generous amount of water into a paper cup. "Okay," he said, "this is filled with dissolved cyanide. I am about to kill myself. I take a large gulp." Quickly he swallowed. The paper cup was still nearly half full. The others watched him intently.

He held up the paper cup. "In my judgment, Vangie Lewis must have drunk at least the approximately three ounces I just swallowed in order to have the amount of cyanide we found in her system. So far it checks out. But here's the problem. The outside of her lips and chin and even neck were burned. The only way that could have happened would have been if she spat some of the stuff out . . . quite a lot of it out. But if she swallowed as much as she did in one gulp, it means her mouth was empty. Did she then take another mouthful and spit it out? No way. The reaction is instantaneous."

"She couldn't have swallowed half of the mouthful and spat out the rest?" Scott asked.

Richard shrugged. "There was too much both in her system and on her face to suggest a split dose. Yet the amount spilled on the spread was negligible, and there were just a few drops at the bottom of the glass. So if she was holding a full tumbler, she'd have had to splash some of it all over her lips and chin, then drink the rest of it to justify the amount expended. It *could* have happened that way, but I don't believe it. The other problem is the shoes she had on."

Quickly he explained his belief that Vangie Lewis could not have walked comfortably in the shoes that had been laced to her feet. While she listened, Katie visualized Vangie's face. The dead face she had seen in the dream and the dead face she'd seen on the bed slid back and forth in her mind. She forced her attention back to the room and realized Charley was talking to Scott. ". . . Richard and I both feel the husband noticed something about the body that he didn't tell us."

"I think it was the shoes," Richard said.

Katie turned to him. "The phone call Chris Lewis made. I told you about that before, Scott."

"You did." Scott leaned back in his chair. "All right. You two"—he pointed to Charley and Phil—"find out everything you can about Captain Lewis. See who this Joan is. Find out what time his plane came in this morning. Check on phone calls Vangie Lewis made the last few days. Have Rita see Mrs. Lewis' doctor and get his opinion of her mental and physical condition."

"I can tell you about her physical condition," Richard said. "If she hadn't delivered that baby soon, she could have saved her cyanide."

"There's another thing," Scott said. "Where did she get the cyanide?"

"No trace of it in the house," Charley reported. "Not a drop. But she was something of a gardener. Maybe she had some stashed away from last summer."

"Just in case she decided to kill herself?" Scott's voice was humorless. "Is there anything else?"

Richard hesitated. "There may be," he said slowly. "But it's so far out . . . and in light of what I've just heard, I think I'm barking up the wrong tree. So give me another twenty-four hours. Then I may have something else to throw on the table."

Scott nodded. "Get back to me." He stood up. "I believe we all agree. We're not closing this as a suicide." He looked at Richard. "One more question. Is there any chance that she died somewhere else and was put back in her bed?"

Richard frowned. "Possible . . . but the way the blood congealed in her body tells me she was lying in the position in which we found her from the minute she drank that cyanide."

"All right," Scott said. "Just a thought. Let's wrap it up for tonight."

Katie started to get up. "I know it's insane, but . . ." She felt Richard's arm steadying her.

"You sure look stiff," he interrupted.

For an instant she'd been about to tell them about the crazy dream she'd had in the hospital. His voice snapped her back to reality. What a fool she'd have appeared to them. Gratefully she smiled at Richard. "Stiff in the head mostly, I think," she commented.

He could not let Edna destroy everything he'd worked for. His hands gripped the wheel. He could feel the trembling in them. He had to calm down.

The exquisite irony that she of all people had seen him drive the Lincoln out of the parking lot. Obviously she'd assumed that Vangie was with him in the car. But the minute she told her story to the police, everything would be over. He could hear the questions: "You drove Mrs. Lewis home, Doctor. What did you do when you left her? Did you call a cab? What time was that, Doctor? Miss Burns tells us that you left the parking lot shortly after nine P.M."

The autopsy would certainly prove that Vangie had died around that time. What would they think if he told them he'd walked back to the hospital in that storm?

Edna had to be silenced. His medical bag was on the seat next to him. The only thing in it was the paperweight from his office desk. He didn't usually bother to carry a bag with him anymore, but he'd taken it out this morning planning to put the moccasins in it. He'd intended to drive into New York for dinner and leave the shoes in separate litter cans to be collected in the morning.

But this morning Hilda had come in early. She'd stood in the foyer talking to him while he put on his gray tweed overcoat. She'd handed him his hat and the bag. It was impossible to transfer the moccasins from the Burberry to the bag in front of her. What would she have thought? But no matter. The Burberry was to the back of the closet. She had no reason to go near it, and tonight when he finished with Edna he would go home. He'd get rid of the shoes tomorrow night.

It was a stroke of luck that Edna lived so near the hospital. That was why he knew her apartment. Several times he'd dropped off work for her when she was laid up with sciatica. He'd just had to check the apartment number to be sure. He'd have to make it look like a murder committed during a felony. Katie DeMaio's office would be involved, but would certainly never connect the homicide of an obscure bookkeeper with either her employer or Vangie Lewis.

He'd take her wallet, grab any bits of jewelry she had. Racking his brain, he remembered that she owned a butterfly-shaped pin with a minuscule ruby and an engagement ring with a dot of a diamond in it. She'd shown them to him when he'd left some work at her place a few months ago.

"This was my mother's ring, Doctor," she'd said proudly. "Dad and she fell in love on their first date and he brought it to her on their second date. Would you believe they were both in their early forties then? Dad gave it to me when Mom died. That was three years ago, and you know he didn't live but two months without her. Of course, Mom had smaller fingers; that's why I wear it on my pinkie. And he gave her the pin on their tenth anniversary."

He'd chafed through the tiresome recital, but now realized that like everything else, it was potentially useful. He'd been sitting by her bed. She kept her cheap plastic jewelry box in the night-table drawer. That ring, the pin and the wallet from her handbag would be easy to carry and would clearly establish a robber-connected murder.

Then he'd get rid of them and the shoes and that would be the end.

Except for Katie DeMaio.

He rubbed the underside of his lower lip over his upper lip. His mouth was dry.

He had to think about Edna's apartment. How would he get in? Did he dare ring the bell, let her admit him? Suppose she wasn't alone?

But she would be alone. He was sure of it. She was going home to drink. He could tell from the nervous, eager movements she made while he watched her from the corridor. She'd been excited, agitated, obviously filled with the stories she wanted to tell to the police tomorrow.

Freezing perspiration drenched him at the thought that she might have decided to talk to the patients in the reception room before she talked to him about Vangie. The Ednas of this world want an audience. Listen to me. Notice me. I exist!

Not for long, Edna, not for long.

He was driving into her apartment area. Last time he'd left the car behind her apartment in one of the visitor stalls. Did he dare drive right there now? It was cold, windy, dark. Few people would be standing around. Anyone who was coming in would be hurrying, not noticing a perfectly ordinary dark, medium-priced car. Last time he'd walked around the end of her apartment-building unit. She lived on the ground floor of the last apartment. Thick bushes tried to hide a rusting chain-link fence that separated the complex from a steep ravine which dropped down a dozen feet and terminated in railroad tracks, a spur of the main line.

Edna's bedroom window backed onto the parking lot. There were high untrimmed bushes under her window. The window was ground level—quite low, if he remembered correctly. Suppose that window was unlocked? By now, if he had any judgment, Edna would be very drunk. He could go in and out by the window. That would lend credence to the burglary. Otherwise, he'd ring the bell, go in, kill her and then leave.

Even if he were found out, were seen, he'd simply say that he'd stopped by to drop off papers, then decided not to leave them because she was drinking. Some intruder must have come in later. No one in his right mind would accuse a wealthy doctor of robbing a penniless book-keeper.

Satisfied, he slowed down as he approached the apartment complex. The double units, all exactly the same, looked stark and forlorn in the cold February night.

The parking area had a half-dozen cars in it. He drove between a camper and a station wagon. His car disappeared into the cavelike space the larger vehicles provided. He pulled on his surgical gloves and put the paperweight in his coat pocket. Sliding cautiously out, he closed the door noiselessly and disappeared into the deep shadows cast by the building. Silently he thanked the gods that Edna lived in the very last apartment. Absolutely no chance of his mistaking where to go.

Her bedroom shade was pulled down most of the way, but she had a plant in the window. The shade rested on the top of the plant, and he could see in clearly. The room was lighted by a foyer fixture. The window was open a crack. She must be in the living room or dining area. He could hear the faint sound of a television program. He would go in through the window.

Glancing rapidly about, he once again assured himself that the area was deserted. With steely-strong gloved fingers he raised the window, noiselessly pulled up the shade, quietly lifted the plant out onto the ground. Later it would be clear proof of the method of entry. He hoisted himself onto the windowsill. For a big man he was surprisingly agile.

He was in the bedroom. In the dim light he absorbed the virginal tidiness, the candlewick bedspread, the crucifix over the bed, the framed photos of an elderly couple, the lace runner on the scarred top of the mahogany-veneer dresser.

Now for the necessary part, the part he detested. He felt for the paperweight in his pocket. He had decided to bludgeon her. Once he had read that a doctor had been proved guilty of murder because of the flawlessly accurate stabbing. He could not risk having his medical knowledge reveal him. It was his medical knowledge that had brought him to this place.

He began to tiptoe down the short foyer. Bathroom to the right. Living room six feet ahead to the left. Cautiously he peered into it. The television set was on, but the room was empty. He could hear the sound of a chair creaking. She must be at the dinette table. With infinite care he moved into the living room. This was the moment. If she saw him and screamed . . .

But her back was to him. Wrapped in a woolly blue robe, she was slumped in a chair at the head of the table. One hand was next to an outsized cocktail glass, the other folded in her lap. A tall pitcher in front of her was almost empty. Her head was on her chest. Faint, even breathing told him she was asleep. She smelled heavily of alcohol.

Quickly he appraised the situation. His eye fell on the hissing radiator to the right of the table. It was the old-fashioned kind with sharp, exposed pipes. Was it possible he didn't need the paperweight after all? Maybe . . .

"Edna," he whispered softly.

"Wha . . . oh . . ." She looked up at him with bleary eyes. Confused, she began to rise, twisting awkwardly in her chair. "Doctor . . ."

A mighty shove sent her smashing backward. Her head cracked against the radiator. Blinding lights exploded in her brain. Oh, the pain! Oh, God, the pain! Edna sighed. The soothing warmth of her gushing blood floated her into darkness. The pain spread, intensified, peaked, receded, ended.

He jumped back, careful to stay clear of the spattered blood, then bent over her carefully. As he watched, the pulse in her throat flickered and stopped. He held his face close to hers. She had stopped breathing. He slipped the paperweight into his pocket. He wouldn't need it now. He wouldn't have to bother robbing her. It would look as though she'd fallen. He was lucky. He was meant to be safe.

Quickly retracing his steps, he went back into the bedroom. Scanning to assure himself that the parking area was still empty, he stepped out the window, remembered to replace the plant, pulled down the shade and closed the window to the exact place where Edna had had it.

As he did, he heard the persistent chiming of a doorbell—*her doorbell!* Frantically he looked around. The ground, hard and dry, offered no evidence of his footprints. The windowsill was meticulously clean. No disturbed dust there. He'd stepped over it, so no sign of his shoes marred the white surface.

He ran back to his car. Quietly the engine started. Without turning on his headlights he drove out of the apartment complex. As he approached Route 4, he turned on the lights.

Who was standing on Edna's doorstep? Would that person try to get in? Edna was dead. She couldn't gossip about him now. But it had been so close, so terribly close.

Adrenaline pounded through his veins. Now there was only one possible threat left: Katie DeMaio.

He would begin to remove that threat now. Her accident had given him the excuse he needed to start medication.

It was a matter of hospital record that her blood count was low. She had received a transfusion in the emergency room.

He would order another transfusion for her on the pretense of building her up for the operation.

He would give cumadin pills to her. They would short-circuit her clotting apparatus and negate the benefits of the transfusion. By Friday when she came into the hospital she'd be on the verge of hemorrhaging.

It might be possible to perform emergency surgery without administering further anticoagulants. But if necessary he would inject her with heparin. There would be a total depletion of the coagulation precursors. She would not survive that surgery.

The initial low blood count, the cumadin and the heparin would be as effective on Katie DeMaio as the cyanide had been on Vangie Lewis.

 *CHAPTER 12*

Richard and Katie left Scott's office together. She had known he'd be annoyed if she suggested calling a cab to take her home. But when they got into his car, he said, "Dinner first. A steak and a bottle of wine will set your juices running."

"What juices?" she asked cautiously.

"Saliva. Stomach. Whatever."

He chose a cabin-type restaurant that perched precariously on the Palisades. The small dining room was warmed by a blazing fire and lit by candles.

"Oh, this is nice," she said.

The proprietor obviously knew Richard well. "Dr. Carroll, a pleasure," he said as he guided them to the table in front of the fireplace and pulled out a chair for Katie.

She grinned as she sat down, thinking that either Richard rated or she must look as chilled and woebegone as she felt.

Richard ordered a bottle of St. Emilion; a waiter produced hot garlic bread. They sat in companionable silence, sipping and nibbling. Katie realized it was the first time she had been with him like this, across a small table, separated from everyone else in the room, looking at each other.

Richard was a big man with a wholesome, thoroughly healthy look that was manifested in his thick crop of dark brown hair, his strong, even features and broad, rangy shoulders. When he's old, he'll have a leonine quality, she thought.

"You just smiled," Richard said. "The usual penny for your thoughts."

She told him.

"Leonine." He considered the word thoughtfully. "A lion in winter. I'd settle for that. Are you interested in what I'm thinking?"

"Sure."

"When your face is in repose, your eyes are very sad, Katie."

"Sorry. I don't mean them to be. I don't think of myself as being sad."

"Do you know I've been wanting to ask you out for the last six months but it took an accident that might have killed you to make it happen?"

"You never asked me out," she said evasively.

"You never *wanted* to be asked out. There's a definite signal you release. 'Do Not Disturb.' Why?"

"I don't believe in going out with anyone I work with," she said, "just on general principles."

"I can understand that. But that's not what we're talking about. We enjoy each other's company. We both know it. But you're having none of it. Here's the menu."

His manner changed, became brisk. "*L'entrecôte* and the steak *au poivre* are the specialties here," he told her. When she hesitated, he suggested, "Try the *poivre*. It's fantastic. Rare," he added hopefully.

"Well done," Katie said.

At his look of horror she laughed out loud. "Of course rare."

His face cleared. He ordered salads with house dressing and baked potatoes, then leaned back and studied her.

"Are you having none of it, Katie?"

"The salad? The steak?"

"No. Don't keep weaving and dancing. All right, I'm not being fair. I'm trying to pin you down and you're a captive audience. But tell me what you do when you're not at the office or the Kennedys'. I know you ski."

"Yes. I have a college friend who's divorced. The winter after John died, she dragged me up to Vermont with her. Now she and I and two couples rent a condominium in Stowe during the ski season. I go weekends as often as I can. I'm not a great skier, but I enjoy it."

"I used to ski," Richard said. "Had to give it up because of a twisted knee. I should try it again. Maybe you'll invite me up sometime with you." He did not wait for an answer. "Sailing is my sport. I took my boat to the Caribbean last spring and went from island to island . . . 'brilliance of cloudless days with broad bellying sails, they glide to the wind tossing green water. . . .' Here's your steak," he finished lightly.

"And you also quote William Carlos Williams," she murmured.

She had secretly expected him to be impressed that she knew the quotation, but he didn't seem surprised. "Yes, I do," he said. "The house dressing is good, isn't it?"

They lingered over coffee. By then Richard had told her about himself. "I was engaged during med school to the girl next door. I think you know I grew up in San Francisco."

"What happened?" Katie asked.

"We kept postponing the wedding. Eventually she married my best friend, whoever he is." Richard smiled. "I'm joking, of course. Jean was a very nice girl. But there was something missing. One night when for the fourth or fifth time we were discussing getting married, she said, 'Richard, we love each other, but we both know there's something more.' She was right."

"No regrets; no second thoughts?" Katie asked.

"Not really. That was seven years ago. I'm a little surprised that the 'something more' didn't happen along before now."

He did not seem to expect her to comment. Instead he began to talk about the Lewis case. "It makes me so angry; any waste of life affects me like that. Vangie Lewis was a young woman. She should have had a lot of years ahead of her."

"You're convinced it wasn't a suicide?"

"I'm not *convinced* of anything. I'll need to have much more information before I pass judgment."

"I don't see Chris Lewis as a murderer. It's too easy to get a divorce today if you want to be free."

"There's another angle to that." Richard pressed his lips together. "Let's hold off talking about it."

It was nearly ten-thirty when they turned into Katie's driveway. Richard looked quizzically at the handsome fieldstone house. "How big is this place?" he asked. "I mean how many rooms have you got?"

"Twelve," Katie said reluctantly. "It was John's house."

"I didn't think you bought it on an assistant prosecutor's salary," Richard commented.

She started to open the car door. "Hold it," he said. "I'll come around. It may still be slippery."

She had not planned to invite him in, but he did not give her the chance to say good night at the door. Taking the key from her hand, he put it in the lock, turned it, opened the door and followed her in. "I'm not going to stay," he said, "but I do admit to an overwhelming curiosity as to where you keep yourself."

She turned on the light and watched somewhat resentfully as he looked over the foyer and then the living room. He whistled. "Very, very nice." He walked over to John's portrait and studied it. "From what I heard, he was quite a guy."

"Yes, he was." Uncomfortably, Katie realized that on nearly every table there was a picture of herself and John. Richard went from one to the next. "A trip abroad?"

"Our honeymoon." Her lips were stiff.

"How long were you married, Katie?"

"One year."

He watched as a look of pain flickered over her face; it was more than that: an expression of surprise too, as though she were still puzzled about what had happened. "When did you find out that he was sick? It was cancer, I understand."

"Shortly after we got back from our honeymoon."

"So you never really had more than that trip, did you? After that it was a deathwatch. Sorry, Katie; my job makes me blunt—too blunt for my own good, I guess. I'll take off now." He hesitated. "Don't you believe in drawing these drapes when you're alone here?"

She shrugged. "Why? No one's going to come barging in on me."

"You, of all people, should be aware of the number of home burglaries. And in this location you'd be a prime target, especially if anyone knew you're alone here. Do you mind?"

Without waiting for an answer he went over to the window and pulled the draperies shut. "I'll be on my way. See you tomorrow. How are you going to get to work? Will your car be ready?"

"No, but the service people are going to lend me one. They'll drop it off in the morning."

"Okay." For a moment he stood with his hand on the knob, then in a highly credible brogue said, "I'll be leavin' ye, Katie Scarlett. Lock your door, now. I wouldn't want anyone tryin' to break into Tara." He bent down, kissed her cheek and was gone.

Smiling, Katie closed the door. A memory raced through her mind. She was five years old, joyously playing in the muddy backyard in her Easter dress. Her mother's outraged cry. Her father's amused voice doing his Gerald O'Hara imitation: "It's the land, Katie Scarlett"— then, in a wheedling voice, to her mother: "Don't get mad at her. All good Micks love the land."

The clock chimed musically. After Richard's bear-warm presence, the room seemed hollow. Quickly she turned out the light and went upstairs.

The phone rang just as she got into bed. Molly has probably been trying to get me, she thought as she lifted the receiver. But it was a man's voice who responded when she said hello.

"Mrs. DeMaio?"

"Yes."

"This is Dr. Highley. I hope I'm not calling too late, but I've tried several times to reach you this evening. The fact that you were in an accident and were in our hospital overnight has come to my attention. How are you feeling?"

"Quite well, Doctor. How nice of you to call."

"How is the bleeding problem? According to your records you had a transfusion here last night."

"I'm afraid it's about the same. I thought I was over my period, but it started again yesterday. I honestly think I may have been a bit light-headed when I lost control of the car."

"Well, as you know, you should have taken care of this condition at least a year ago. Never mind. It will all be behind you by this time next week. But I do want you to have another transfusion to build you up for the surgery, and I also want you to start in on some pills. Can you come to the hospital tomorrow afternoon?"

"Yes. As a matter of fact, there was a chance I was coming anyhow. You've heard about Mrs. Lewis?"

"I have. A terrible and sad situation. Well, then, I'll see you tomorrow. Call in the morning and we'll arrange a definite time."

"Yes, Doctor. Thank you, Doctor."

Katie hung up. As she turned out the light, she reflected that Dr. Highley hadn't really appealed to her on her first visit. Was it because of his reserved, even aloof attitude?

It shows how you can misjudge people, she decided. It was very nice of him to personally keep trying to get in touch with me tonight.

CHAPTER 13

B ill Kennedy rang the bell of the Lewis house. An orthopedic surgeon at Lenox Hill Hospital, he had been operating all day and did not hear about Vangie Lewis' death until he returned home. Tall, prematurely white, scholarly and somewhat shy in his professional life, Bill became a different person when he entered the warm haven of the home Molly created for him.

Her bustling presence made it possible for him to leave behind the problems of his patients and relax. But tonight the atmosphere had been different. Molly had already fed the children and given them strict orders to stay out of the way. Briefly she told him about Vangie. "I called and asked Chris to come to dinner and to sleep in the den tonight rather than be alone over there. He doesn't want to, but you go drag him here. I'm sure he'll at least come to dinner."

As he walked between the houses, Bill considered the shock it would be to come home and find he had lost Molly. But it wouldn't be the same for Chris Lewis. No one in his right mind could think that that marriage had been anything like his and Molly's. Bill had never told Molly that one morning when he was having coffee at a drugstore near the hospital he'd seen Chris in a booth with a very pretty girl in her early twenties. It was written all over the two of them that they were involved with each other.

Had Vangie known about the girl? Was that why she'd committed suicide? But so violently! His mind flashed back to the summer. Vangie and Chris had been over for a barbecue. Vangie had started to roast a marshmallow and gotten her hand too near the heat. Her finger had blistered and she'd carried on as though she'd been covered with third-degree burns. She'd gone shrieking to Chris, who had tried to calm her down. Embarrassed for her, Chris had explained, "Vangie has a low pain tolerance." By the time Bill got salve and applied it, the blister was practically nonexistent.

Where would a person of Vangie's emotional makeup get the courage to take cyanide? Anyone who'd read anything about that poison would know that even though death was almost instantaneous, one died in agony.

No. Bill would have sworn that Vangie Lewis committing suicide would have swallowed sleeping pills and fallen asleep. Showed how little anyone knew about the human mind . . . even someone like himself who was supposed to be a pretty good judge of people.

Chris Lewis opened the door. Ever since he'd spotted him with the girl, Bill had been somewhat reserved with Chris. He just didn't cotton to men who ran around when their wives were pregnant. But now the sight of Chris's drawn face and the genuine sadness in his eyes called up Bill's compassion. He gripped the younger man's arms. "I'm terribly sorry."

Chris nodded woodenly. It seemed to him that like an onion peeling layer by layer, the meaning of the day was sinking in on him. Vangie was dead. Had their quarrel driven her to kill herself? He couldn't believe it, and yet he felt lonely, frightened and guilty. He allowed Bill to persuade him to come to dinner. He had to get out of the house—he couldn't think clearly there. Molly and Bill were good people. Could he trust them with what he knew? Could he trust *anyone*? Numbly reaching for a jacket, he followed Bill down the street.

Bill poured a double Scotch for him. Chris gulped it. When the glass was half-empty he forced himself to slow down. The whiskey burned his throat and chest, making a passage through the tension. Calm down, he thought, calm down. Be careful.

The Kennedy kids came into the den to say good night. Well-behaved kids, all of them. Good-looking too. The oldest boy, Billy, resembled his

father. Jennifer was a dark-haired beauty. The younger girls, Dina and Moira, were fair like Molly. The twins. Chris almost smiled. The twins looked like each other. Chris had always wanted children. Now his unborn child had died with Vangie. Another guilt. He had resented her pregnancy. His child, and he hadn't wanted it, not for one single second. And Vangie had known it. What had, *who* had driven her to kill herself? Who? That was the question. Because Vangie hadn't been alone last night.

He hadn't told the police. It would be opening up a can of worms, *begging* them to start an investigation. And where would that lead? To Joan. The other woman. To him.

The clerk had seen him leave the motel last night. He'd started to come home, to have it out with Vangie. He'd even jotted down figures to discuss with her. She could have the house. He'd give her twenty thousand a year, at least until the baby was eighteen. He'd carry a large insurance policy on his life for her. He'd educate the baby. She could keep on going to that Japanese psychiatrist she was so crazy about. Only let me go, Vangie. Please let me go. I can't spend any more of my life with you. It's destroying both of us. . . .

He'd gotten as far as the house. Somewhere around midnight he'd arrived. He'd driven in and the minute the garage door opened, knew something was up. Because he'd almost rammed the Lincoln. She'd parked in his space. No, someone else parked her car in *his* space. Because no way would Vangie ever try to drive that wide car into the area between the posts and the right wall. The garage was an oversized one. One side could hold two cars. That was the side Vangie always used. And she needed every inch. She was a lousy driver, and her peripheral vision probably wasn't that great either. She simply couldn't judge space well. Chris always parked his Corvette in the narrower side. But last night the Lincoln had been expertly parked there.

He'd gone in and found the house empty. Vangie's handbag was on the chaise in their room. He'd been puzzled but not alarmed. Obviously she'd gone off with someone to stay overnight. He'd even been pleased that maybe she had a girlfriend to confide in. He'd always tried to make her develop friends. And Vangie could be secretive. He wondered if she'd forgotten her handbag. Vangie was forgetful, or maybe she'd packed an overnight bag and didn't want to bother with the heavy purse.

The house depressed Chris. He decided to go back to the motel. He hadn't told Joan about coming home. He was careful to say as little as possible to Joan about Vangie. To Joan, any mention of Vangie was a continuing reminder of what she saw to be her own position as an interloper.

If he'd told Joan this morning that he and Vangie had quarreled and Vangie had obviously been so upset she'd gone to stay with someone rather than be alone, Joan would have been heartsick.

But then this morning he'd found Vangie dead. Somebody had parked the car for her before midnight. Somebody had driven her home after midnight. And those shoes. The one day she'd worn them she'd complained endlessly about them. That was around Christmas when he'd taken her to New York, trying to give her some fun. Fun! God, what a miserable day. She hadn't liked the play. The restaurant didn't serve veal piccata and she'd set her heart on it. And she'd talked incessantly about how the shoe dug into her right ankle.

For weeks now she'd worn nothing but those dirty moccasins. He'd asked her to please get some decent shoes, but she'd said these were the only comfortable ones. Where were they? Chris had searched the house thoroughly. Whoever drove her home might know.

He hadn't told the police any of this. He hadn't wanted to involve Joan. "I checked into a motel because my wife and I had quarreled. I wanted a divorce. I decided to come home and try to reason with her. She wasn't here and I left." It hadn't seemed necessary to drag all this in. Even the shoes really weren't that important. Vangie might have wanted to be fully dressed when she was found. That swollen leg embarrassed her. She was vain.

But he should have told the cops about his being here, about the way the car was parked.

"Chris, come into the dining room. You'll feel better if you eat something." Molly's voice was gentle.

Wearily, Chris looked up. The soft hallway light silhouetted Molly's face, and for the first time he could see a family resemblance between her and Katie DeMaio.

Katie DeMaio. Her *sister.* He couldn't discuss this with Bill and Molly. It would put Molly in the middle. How could she honestly advise him whether or not to keep quiet about his coming home last night when her own sister was in the Prosecutor's office? No. He'd have to decide this on his own.

He brushed a hand over burning eyes. "I would like to have something, Molly," he said. "Whatever it is, sure smells good. But I'll have to leave pretty quickly. The funeral director is coming to the house for Vangie's clothes. Her mother and father want to be able to see her before the interment."

"Where will it be?" Bill asked.

"The coffin will be flown to Minneapolis tomorrow afternoon. I'll be on that plane too. The service will be the next day. The Medical Examiner released her body late this afternoon." The words hammered in his ears . . . Coffin . . . Body . . . Funeral . . . Oh, God, he thought, this had to be a nightmare. *I wanted to be free of you, Vangie, but I didn't want you to die. I drove you to suicide. Joan's right. I should have stood by you.*

At eight he went back to his house. At eight thirty, when the funeral director came, he had a suitcase with underwear and the flowing caftan Vangie's parents had sent her for Christmas.

The funeral director, Paul Halsey, was quietly sympathetic. He requested the necessary information quickly. Born April 15. He jotted down the year. Died February 15—just two months short of her thirty-first birthday, he commented.

Chris rubbed the ache between his eyes. Something was wrong. Even in this unreal situation where *everything* was wrong, there was something specific. "No," he said, "today's the *sixteenth,* not the *fifteenth.*"

"The death certificate clearly states that Mrs. Lewis died between eight and ten P.M. last night, February fifteenth," Halsey said. "You're thinking the sixteenth because you *found* her this morning. But the medical examiner who performed the autopsy can pinpoint the time of death accurately."

Chris stared at him. Waves of shock dissolved his sense of exhaustion and unreality. He had been home at midnight and the car and Vangie's purse had been here. He'd waited around for about half an hour before he drove back to the motel in New York. When he'd come home this morning, he'd assumed that Vangie had come in sometime after he left and killed herself.

But at midnight she'd already been dead three or four hours. That meant that sometime after midnight, after he left, someone had brought her body here, put it on her bed and laid the empty glass beside her.

Someone had wanted to make it seem that Vangie had committed suicide.

Had she killed herself somewhere else? Had someone brought her back who simply didn't want to be involved? Of course not. Vangie had never inflicted the pain of cyanide poisoning on herself. Her murderer had staged the suicide.

"Oh, Christ," Chris whispered. "Oh, Christ." Vangie's face filled his vision. The wide, thickly lashed, petulant eyes; the short, straight nose; the honey-colored hair that fell over her forehead; the small, perfectly formed lips. At the last moment she must have known. Someone had held her, forced that poison into her, viciously killed her and the baby she was carrying. She must have been so frightened. A tearing wrench of pity brought tears to his eyes. No one, no *husband,* could be silent and let those deaths go unpunished.

But if he told the police; if he started an investigation, there was one person they would inevitably accuse. As the funeral director stared at him, Chris said aloud, "I have to tell them, and they're going to blame it on me."

⟨≈⟩ *CHAPTER 14*

He hung up the phone slowly. Katie DeMaio suspected nothing. Even when she mentioned Vangie Lewis' name there hadn't been any hint that her office wanted anything more than to discuss Vangie's emotional state with him.

But Katie's accident had happened barely twenty-four hours ago. She was probably still experiencing a certain amount of shock reaction.

Her blood count was already low. Tomorrow when the cumadin was introduced into her system, the clotting mechanism would begin to collapse, and with the further hemorrhaging she'd begin to feel disoriented, light-headed. Certainly she would not be analytical enough to separate a supposed nightmare from an actual event.

Unless, of course, there were too many questions about the suicide. Unless the possibility of Vangie's body's having been moved was introduced and discussed in her office.

The danger was still so great.

He was in the library of the Westlake home—his home now. The house was a manorlike Tudor. It had archways and built-in bookcases and marble fireplaces and hand-blocked antique wallpaper and Tiffany stained-glass windows: the kind of home impossible to duplicate today at any price. The craftsmanship wasn't available.

The Westlake House. The Westlake Hospital. The Westlake Maternity Concept. The name had served him well, given him immediate entrée, socially and professionally. He was the distinguished obstetrician who had met Winifred Westlake on a transatlantic sailing, married her and relocated in America to carry on her father's work.

The perfect excuse for having left England. No one, including Winifred, knew about the years before Liverpool at Christ Hospital in Devon.

Toward the end she had started to ask questions.

It was nearly eleven o'clock and he hadn't had dinner yet. Knowing what he was going to do to Edna had robbed him of the desire to eat.

But now that it was over, the release had come. Now the need for food had become a craving. He went into the kitchen. Hilda had left dinner for him in the microwave oven: a small Cornish hen with wild rice. He just needed to heat it up for a few minutes. When he had time he preferred to cook his own meals. Hilda's food was without imagination, even though it was well enough prepared.

She was a good housekeeper, too. He liked coming home to the elegant orderliness of this place, to sip a drink, to eat when he chose, to spend hours working on his notes in the library, unthreatened by the possibility of someone's dropping in, as occasionally happened at his hospital laboratory.

He needed the freedom of the house. He'd gotten rid of the live-in housekeeper Winifred and her father had had. Hostile bitch, looking at him with sour, sullen eyes, swollen with weeping. "Miss Winifred was almost never sick until . . ."

He'd stared at her and she hadn't finished. What she was going to say was "until she married you."

Winifred's cousin resented him bitterly, had tried to make trouble after Winifred's death. But he couldn't prove anything. There hadn't been one shred of tangible evidence. They'd dismissed the cousin as a disgruntled ex-heir.

Of course, there hadn't been that much money at all. Winifred had sunk so much into purchasing the hospital. Now his research was taking staggering amounts, and most of it had to come directly from the practice. He couldn't apply for a grant, of course. But even so, he could manage. Women were willing to pay anything to conceive.

Hilda had set the table for him in the small dining room off the pantry—the morning room it used to be called. He would not eat any meal in the kitchen, but the twenty-by-thirty-foot dining room was ostentatious and ridiculous for a solitary diner. This room with its round pedestal table, Queen Anne cabinet and view of the tree-filled side lawn was far more appealing.

Selecting a chilled bottle of Pouilly-Fuissé from the refrigerator, he sat down to eat.

He finished dinner thoughtfully, his mind running over the exact dosage he would give Katie DeMaio. The cumadin would not be suspected in her bloodstream after death. Failure of coagulation would be attributed to the transfusions. If he had to administer the heparin, traces of it and the cumadin might show if there was a thorough autopsy. But he had an idea of what he could do to circumvent that.

Before going to bed, he went out to the foyer closet. He'd get those moccasins safely in his bag now, not risk a recurrence of this morning's

annoyance. Reaching back into the closet, he put his hand in one pocket of the Burberry and pulled out a misshapen shoe. Expectantly he put his free hand in the other pocket—first matter-of-factly, then urgently. Finally he grabbed the coat and rummaged frantically all over it. Then he sank to his knees and pawed through the overshoes neatly stacked on the closet floor.

Finally he stood up, staring at the battered moccasin he was holding. Again he saw himself tugging the shoe off Vangie's right foot.

The *right* shoe.

The shoe he was holding.

Hysterically he began to laugh—noisy, rattling sounds wrenched from the frustrated fury of his being. After all the danger, after the ignominious crawling around the parking lot like a dog sniffing to pick up a scent, he had botched it.

Somehow in the dark, probably that time he'd shrunk against the shrubbery when the car roared into the parking lot, the shoe had fallen out of his pocket. The shoe he'd *found* was the one he'd already *had*.

And somewhere, the battered, shabby, ugly left moccasin that Vangie Lewis had been wearing was waiting to be found; waiting to trace her footsteps back to him.

CHAPTER 15

Katie had set the clock radio for six A.M., but was wide awake long before the determinedly cheery voice of the CBS anchorman wished her a bright morning. Her sleep had been troubled; several times she'd almost started to jump up, frightened by a vague, troubling dream.

She always turned the thermostat low at night. Shivering, she ran to adjust it, then quickly made coffee and brought a cup back upstairs to bed.

Propped against the pillows, the thick comforter wrapped around her, she eagerly sipped as the heat of the cup began to warm her fingers. "That's better," she murmured. "And now, what's the matter with me?"

The antique Williamsburg dresser with its oval center mirror was directly opposite the bed. She glanced into it. Her hair was tousled, a dark brown smudge against the ivory eyelet-edged pillowcases. The bruise under her eye was now purple tinged with yellow. Her eyes were swollen with sleep. Deep crescents accentuated the thinness of her face.

As Mama would say, I look like something the cat dragged in, she reflected.

But it was more than the way she looked. It was even more than the overall achiness from the accident. It was a heavy feeling of apprehension. Had she started to dream that queer, frightening nightmare again last night? She couldn't be sure.

Vangie Lewis. A line from John's funeral service came to her: "We who are saddened at the certainty of death . . ." Death was certain, of course. But not like that. It was bad enough to think of Vangie taking her own life, but it seemed impossible that anyone would choose to kill her by forcing cyanide down her throat. She simply didn't believe Chris Lewis was capable of that kind of violence.

She thought of Dr. Highley's call. That damn operation. Oh, there were thousands of D-and-C's performed every year on women of every age. It wasn't the operation itself. It was the reason for it. Suppose the D-and-C didn't clear up the hemorrhaging? Dr. Highley had hinted that eventually it might be necessary to consider a hysterectomy.

If only she had become pregnant during the year with John. But she hadn't.

Suppose she did remarry someday. Wouldn't it be a bitter, miserable trick if by then she couldn't have children? Knock it off, she warned herself. Remember that line from *Faust?* We weep for what we may never lose.

Well, at least she was getting the operation over with. Check in Friday night. Operation Saturday, home Sunday. At work Monday. No big deal.

Molly had called her after she got to the office yesterday. She'd said, "Katie, I could tell you didn't want me to talk in front of Richard, but don't you think it would be better to postpone going to the hospital till next month? You got a pretty good shaking up."

She'd been vehement. "No way. I want to be through with this; and besides, Molly, I wouldn't be surprised if this darn business contributed to the accident. I felt light-headed a couple of times Monday."

Molly had been distressed. "Why didn't you tell me?"

"Oh, come on," Katie had said. "You and I both hate complainers. When it's really bad, I swear I'll yell for you."

"I hope so," Molly said. "I guess you might as well get it over with." Then she'd asked, "Are you going to tell Richard?"

Katie had tried not to sound exasperated. "No, and I'm not going to tell the elevator operator or the street-crossing guard or Dial-a-Friend. Just you and Bill. And that's where we leave it. Okay?"

"Okay. And don't be a smart-ass." Molly had hung up decisively, her tone a combination of affection and authoritativeness, the warning-signal voice she used when one of the kids was getting out of line.

I'm not your child, Molly, girl, Katie thought now. I love you, but I'm not your child. But as she sipped the coffee she wondered if she was leaning too much on Molly and Bill, drawing emotional support from them. Was she indeed coasting on their coattails out of the mainstream of life?

Oh, John. She glanced instinctively at his picture. This morning it was just that, a picture. A handsome, grave-looking man with gentle, penetrating eyes. Once during that first year after his death she'd picked up that picture, stared at it, then slammed it face down on the dresser crying, "How could you have left me?"

The next morning she'd been back on balance, ashamed of herself, and had made a resolution never to have three glasses of wine when she was feeling low. When she'd straightened the picture, she'd found a gouge in the lovely old dresser top which had been caused by the embossed silver frame. She'd tried to explain to the picture. "It isn't just self-pity, Judge. I'm angry for *you*. I wanted you to have another forty years. You knew how to enjoy life; how to do something worthwhile with life."

For who hath known the mind of the Lord? Or who hath been His counsellor? That phrase from the Bible had flitted across her mind that day.

Remembering, Katie thought, I'd better think along those lines now.

Stripping off her pale green nightgown, she went into the bathroom and turned on the shower. The nightgown trailed over the bench at her dressing table. In college she'd favored striped drop-seat p.j.'s. But John had bought her exquisite gowns and peignoirs in Italy. It still seemed appropriate to wear them here in this house, in his bedroom.

Maybe Richard was right. Maybe she was keeping a deathwatch. John would be the first one to blast her for that.

The hot shower helped to pick up her spirits. She had a plea-bargaining session scheduled for nine, a sentencing at ten and two new cases to begin preparing for trial for next week. And she had plenty of work to do on this Friday's trial. It's Wednesday already, she thought with dismay. I'd better get a move on.

She dressed quickly, selecting a soft brown wool skirt and a new turquoise silk shirt with full sleeves that covered the bandage on her arm.

The loan car from the service station arrived as she finished a second coffee. She dropped the driver back at the station, whistled as she saw the extensive damage to the front of her car, counted her blessings that she hadn't been seriously injured and drove to the office.

It had been a busy night in the county. A fourteen-year-old girl had been raped. People were talking about a drunken-driving accident that had resulted in four deaths. A local police chief had called requesting that the Prosecutor help set up a lineup for the victim to view suspects who had been picked up after an armed robbery.

Scott was just coming out of his office. "Lovely night," Katie observed.

He nodded. "Son of a bitch—that jerk who rammed into the car with all those kids was so blotto he couldn't stand up straight. All four kids were killed. They were seniors at Pascal Hills on the way to a prom-committee meeting. Incidentally, I was planning to send Rita over to talk to the doctors at Westlake Hospital, but she's covering the rape case. I'm especially interested in the psychiatrist Vangie Lewis was going to. I'd like his opinion as to her mental state. I can send Charley or Phil, but I think a woman would be less noticeable over there, might be able to drift around a bit and see if Mrs. Lewis talked to the nurses or became friendly with other patients. But it'll have to wait until tomorrow. Rita's been up all night, and now she's driving around with that kid who was raped to see if she can spot her attacker. We're pretty sure he lives near her."

Katie hesitated. She had not planned to tell Scott that she was Dr. Highley's patient or that she'd be checking into Westlake Friday night. But it would be unthinkable to have someone from the office report that to him. She temporized. "Maybe I can help out. Dr. Highley is my gynecologist. I actually have an appointment with him today." She pressed her lips together, deciding there was no need to go into a tiresome recital about her scheduled operation.

Scott's eyebrows shot up. As always when he was surprised, his voice became deeper. "What are your impressions of him? Richard made some crack yesterday about Vangie's condition; seemed to think that Highley was taking chances with her."

Katie shook her head. "I don't agree with Richard. Dr. Highley's specialty is difficult pregnancies. He's practically considered a miracle man. That's the very point. He tries to bring to viable term the babies other doctors lose." She thought of his phone call to her. "I can vouch for the fact that he's a very concerned doctor."

Scott's frown made deep crease lines in his forehead and around his eyes. "That's your gut-level reaction to him? How long have you known him?"

Trying to be objective, Katie thought about the doctor. "I don't know him long or well. The gynecologist I used to go to retired and moved a couple of years ago, and I'd just not bothered about another one. Then when I started having trouble—well, anyhow, my sister Molly knew about Dr. Highley because her friend raves about him. Molly goes to someone in New York, and I didn't want to bother with that. So I made

an appointment last month. He's very knowledgeable." She remembered her examination. He had been gentle but thorough. "You're quite right to have come," he'd said. "In fact, I must suggest that you should not have ignored this condition for over a year. I think of the womb as a cradle that must always be kept in good repair."

The one thing that had surprised her was that he did not have a nurse in attendance. Her other gynecologist had always called the nurse in before he began an examination; but then, he'd been from another generation. She judged Dr. Highley to be in his mid-forties.

"What's your schedule today?" Scott asked.

"Busy morning, but this afternoon is adjustable."

"All right. You go see Highley, and talk to the shrink too. Get a feeling of whether or not they think she was capable of suicide. Find out when she was over there last. See if she talked about the husband. Charley and Phil are checking on Chris Lewis now. I was awake half the night and kept thinking that Richard is right. Something about that suicide stinks. Talk to the nurses too."

"Not the nurses," Katie smiled. "The receptionist, Edna. She knows everybody's business. I wasn't in the waiting room two minutes last month before I found myself giving her my life history. In fact, maybe you ought to hire her to interrogate witnesses."

"I ought to hire a lot of people," Scott commented drily. "Talk to the Board of Freeholders. All right, I'll see you later."

Katie went into her own office, grabbed her files and rushed to her appointment with a defense attorney about an indicted defendant. She agreed to drop a heroin charge from "possession with intent to distribute" to simple "possession." From there she hurried to a second-floor courtroom where she reflectively listened as a twenty-year-old youth she had prosecuted was sentenced to seven years in prison. He could have received twenty years for the armed robbery and atrocious assault. Of the seven years, he'd probably serve one-third the term and be back on the streets. She knew his record by heart. Forget rehabilitation with this bird, she thought.

In the sheaf of messages waiting for her, there were two phone calls from Dr. Carroll. One had come in at nine fifteen, the other at nine forty. She called back, but Richard was out on a case. Her feeling of slight pressure at the two calls was replaced by a sensation of disappointment when she couldn't reach him.

She phoned Dr. Highley's office fully expecting to hear the nasal warmth of Edna's voice. But whoever answered was a stranger, a crisp, low-spoken woman. "Doctor's offices."

"Oh!" Katie thought swiftly and decided to ask for Edna. "Is Miss Burns there?"

There was a fraction of a minute's pause before the answer came. "Miss Burns won't be in today. She called in sick. I'm Mrs. Fitzgerald."

Katie realized how much she was counting on talking to Edna. "I'm sorry Miss Burns is not well." Briefly she explained that Dr. Highley expected her call and that she'd also like to see Dr. Fukhito. Mrs. Fitzgerald put her on hold and a few minutes later came back on the line.

"They'll both see you, of course. Dr. Fukhito is free fifteen minutes before the hour anytime between two and five, and Dr. Highley would prefer three o'clock if it is also convenient for you."

"Three o'clock with Dr. Highley is fine," Katie said, "and then please confirm three forty-five with Dr. Fukhito." Lowering the phone, she turned to the work on her desk.

At lunchtime, Maureen Crowley, one of the office secretaries, popped her head in and offered to bring a sandwich to Katie. Deep in preparation for Friday's trial, Katie nodded affirmatively.

"Ham on rye with mustard and lettuce and dark coffee," Maureen said.

Katie looked up, surprised. "Am I really that predictable?"

The girl was about nineteen, with a mane of red-gold hair, emerald-green eyes and the lovely pale complexion of the true redhead. "Katie, I have to tell you, about food you're in a rut." The door closed behind her.

"You look peaked." "You're on a deathwatch." "You're in a rut."

Katie swallowed over a hard lump in her throat and was astonished to realize she was close to tears. I *must* be sick if I'm getting this thin-skinned, she thought.

When the sandwich and coffee arrived, she ate and sipped, only vaguely aware of what she was having. The case on which she was trying to concentrate was a total blur. Vangie Lewis' face was constantly before her. But why had she seen it in a nightmare?

CHAPTER 16

Richard Carroll had had a rough night. The phone rang at eleven o'clock, a few minutes after he got home from Katie's house, to inform him that four kids were in the morgue.

He replaced the receiver slowly. He lived on the seventeenth floor of a high-rise north of the George Washington Bridge. For moments he stared out the wall-length picture window at the New York skyline, at the cars darting swiftly down the Henry Hudson Parkway, at the blue-

green lights that revealed and silhouetted the graceful lines of the George Washington Bridge.

Right now phones were ringing to tell the parents of those youngsters that their children wouldn't be coming home.

Richard looked around his living room. It was comfortably furnished with an oversized sofa, roomy armchairs, an Oriental rug in tones of blue and brown, a wall bookcase and sturdy oak tables that had once graced the parlor of a New England ancestor's farmhouse. Original watercolors with sailing themes were scattered tastefully on the walls. Richard sighed. His deep leather reclining chair was next to the bookcase. He'd planned to fix a nightcap, read for an hour and turn in. Instead he decided to go to the morgue to be there when the parents came to identify those youngsters. God knew there was precious little anyone could do for those people, but he knew he'd feel better for trying.

It was four A.M. before he got back to the apartment. As he undressed he wondered if he was getting too saddened by this job. Those kids were so messed up; the crash impact had been terrific. Yet you could see how attractive they'd all been in life. One girl particularly got under his skin. She had dark hair, a slim, straight nose, and even in death she was graceful.

She reminded him of Katie.

The thought that Katie had been in an automobile accident Monday night jolted Richard anew. It seemed to him that they'd progressed light-years in their relationship in the couple of hours they'd spent together at dinner.

What was she afraid of, poor kid? Why couldn't she let go of John DeMaio? Why couldn't she say "Thanks for the memory" and move on?

As he got into bed he felt bleakly grateful that he'd been able to help the parents a little. He'd been able to assure them that the youngsters had died instantly, that they probably never knew or felt anything.

He slept restlessly for two hours and was in the office by seven. A few minutes later a summons came that an old lady had hanged herself in a deteriorating section of Chester, a small town at the north end of the county. He went to the death scene. The dead woman was eighty-one years old, frail and birdlike. A note was pinned to her dress: *There's nobody left. I'm so sick and tired. I want to be with Sam. Please forgive me for causing trouble.*

The note brought into focus something that had been nagging Richard. From everything he'd heard about Vangie Lewis, it seemed in character that if she'd taken her life, she'd have left a note to explain or to blame her action on her husband.

Most women left notes.

When he got back to the office Richard tried phoning Katie twice, hoping to catch her between court sessions. He wanted to hear the sound of her voice. For some reason he'd felt edgy about leaving her alone in that big house last night. But he was unable to reach her.

Why did he have a hunch that she had something on her mind that was troubling her?

He went back to the lab and worked straight through until four thirty. Returning to his office, he picked up his messages and was absurdly pleased to see that Katie had returned his calls. Why wouldn't she? he asked himself cynically. An assistant prosecutor wouldn't ignore calls from the Medical Examiner. Quickly he phoned her. The switchboard operator in the Prosecutor's section said that Katie had left and wouldn't be back today. The operator didn't know where she was going.

Damn.

That meant he wouldn't get to talk to her today. He was having dinner in New York with Clovis Simmons, an actress on one of the soaps. Clovis was fun; he always enjoyed himself with her, but the signs were that she was getting serious.

Richard made a resolve. This was the last time he'd take Clovis out. It wasn't fair to her. Refusing to consider the reason for that sudden decision, he leaned back in his chair and scowled. A mental alarm was sending out a beeping signal. It reminded him of traveling in the Midwest when the radio station would suddenly announce a tornado watch in effect. A *warning* was the sure thing. A *watch* suggested potential trouble.

He had not been exaggerating when he'd told Scott that if Vangie Lewis had not delivered that baby soon she wouldn't have needed the cyanide. How many women got into that same kind of condition under the Westlake Maternity Concept? Molly raved about the obstetrician because one of her friends had had a successful pregnancy. But what about the failures over there? How many of *them* had there been? Had there been anything unusual about the ratio of deaths among Westlake's patients? Richard switched on the intercom and asked his secretary to come in.

Marge was in her mid-fifties. Her graying hair was carefully bubbled in the style made popular by Jacqueline Kennedy in the early sixties. Her skirt was an inch over her plump knees. She looked like a suburban housewife on a television game show. She was in fact an excellent secretary who thoroughly enjoyed the constant drama of the department.

"Marge," he said, "I'm playing a hunch. I want to do some unofficial investigating of Westlake Hospital—just the maternity section. That maternity concept has been in operation for about eight years. I'd like to know how many patients died either in childbirth or from complications of pregnancy and what the ratio is between deaths and the number of patients treated there. I don't want to let it out that I'm interested. That's why I don't want to ask Scott to have the records subpoenaed. Do you know anybody over there who might look at the hospital records for you on the quiet?"

Marge frowned. Her nose, not unlike a small, sharp canary's beak, wrinkled. "Let me work on it."

"Good. And something else. Check into any malpractice suits that have been filed against either of the doctors over at Westlake Maternity. I don't care whether the suits were dropped or not. I want to know the reason for them, if any exist at all."

Satisfied at getting the investigation under way, Richard dashed home to shower and change. Seconds after he left his office, a call came for him from Dr. David Broad of the prenatal laboratory at Mt. Sinai Hospital. The message Marge took asked that Richard contact Dr. Broad in the morning. The matter was urgent.

CHAPTER 17

Katie left for the hospital at quarter to three. The weather had settled into a tenacious, somber, cloudy cold spell. But at least the warmth of the cars had melted most of the sleet from the roads. She deliberately slowed down as she rounded the curve that had been the starting point of her accident.

She was a few minutes early for her appointment, but could have saved her time. The receptionist, Mrs. Fitzgerald, was coolly pleasant, but when Katie asked if she filled in for Edna very often, Mrs. Fitzgerald replied stiffly, "Miss Burns is almost never absent, so there's very little need to substitute for her."

It seemed to Katie that the answer was unduly defensive. Intrigued, she decided to pursue the issue. "I was so sorry to hear that Miss Burns is ill today," she added. "Nothing serious, I hope?"

"No." The woman was distinctly nervous. "Just a virus sort of thing. She'll be in tomorrow, I'm sure."

There were several expectant mothers sitting in the reception area, but they were deep in magazines. There was no way Katie could feasibly strike up a conversation with them. A pregnant woman, her face puffy, her movements slow and deliberate, came from the corridor that led to the doctors' offices. A buzzer sounded at the desk. The receptionist picked up the phone.

"Mrs. DeMaio, Dr. Highley will see you now," she said. She sounded relieved.

Katie walked quickly down the corridor. Dr. Highley's office was the first one, she remembered. Following the printed instructions to knock and enter, she opened the door and stepped into the medium-sized office. It had the air of a comfortable study. Bookshelves lined one wall. Pictures of mothers with babies nearly covered a second wall. A club chair was placed near the doctor's elaborately carved desk. Katie remembered that the examining room, a lavatory and a combination kitchen/instrument-sterilizing area completed the suite. The doctor was behind his desk. He stood up to greet her. "Mrs. DeMaio." His tone was courteous; the faint British accent, barely perceptible. He was a medium-tall man, about five feet eleven inches. His face, smooth-skinned with rounded cheeks, terminated in a plump oval chin. His body gave the impression of solid strength, carefully controlled. He looked as though he could easily put on weight. Thinning sandy hair, streaked with gray, was carefully combed in a side part. Eyebrows and lashes, the same sandy shade, accentuated protruding steel-gray eyes. Feature by feature he was not an attractive man, but his overall appearance was imposing and authoritative.

Katie flushed, realizing that he was aware of her scrutiny and not pleased by it. She sat down quickly and to establish rapport thanked him for the phone call.

He dismissed her gratitude. "I wish you had something to thank me for. If you had told the emergency-room doctor that you were my patient, he would have given you a room in the west wing. Far more comfortable, I assure you. But just about the same view," he added.

Katie had started to fish in her shoulder bag for a pad and paper. She looked up quickly. "View. Anything would be better than the one I thought I had the other night. Why . . ." She stopped. The pad in her hand reminded her that she was here on official business. What would he think of her talking about nightmares? Unconsciously she tried to straighten up in the too-low, too-soft chair.

"Doctor, if you don't mind, let's talk about Vangie Lewis first." She smiled. "I guess our roles are reversed at least for a few minutes. I get to ask the questions."

His expression became somber. "I only wish there were a happier reason for our roles to be reversed. That poor girl. I've thought of little else since I heard the news."

Katie nodded. "I knew Vangie slightly, and I must say I've had the same reaction. Now, it's purely routine, of course, but in the absence of a note, my office does like to have some understanding of the mental state of a suicide victim." She paused, then asked, "When was the last time you saw Vangie Lewis?"

He leaned back in the chair. His fingers interlocked under his chin, revealing immaculately clean nails. He spoke slowly. "It was last Thursday evening. I've been having Mrs. Lewis come in at least weekly since she completed the halfway point of her pregnancy. I have her chart here."

He indicated the manila file on his desk. It was tabbed LEWIS, VANGIE. It was an impersonal item, Katie decided, a reminder that exactly one week ago Vangie Lewis had lain in the examining room adjoining this office having her blood pressure checked, the heartbeat of her fetus confirmed.

"How was Mrs. Lewis," she asked, "physically and emotionally?"

"Let me answer as to her physical condition first. It was a worry, of course. There was danger of toxic pregnancy, which I was watching very closely. But you see, every additional day she carried increased the baby's chance of survival."

"Could she have carried the baby to full term?"

"Impossible. In fact, last Thursday I warned Mrs. Lewis that it was highly likely that we would have to bring her in within the next two weeks and induce labor."

"How did she respond to that news?"

He frowned. "I expected Mrs. Lewis to have a very valid concern for the baby's life. But the fact is that the closer she came to the potential birth, the more it seemed to me that she feared the birth process. The thought even crossed my mind that she was not unlike a little girl who wanted to play house, but would have been terrified if her doll turned into a real baby."

"I see." Katie doodled reflectively on the pad she was holding. "But did Vangie show any specific depression?"

Dr. Highley shook his head. "I did not see it. However, I think that answer should come from Dr. Fukhito. He saw her on Monday night, and he's better trained than I to recognize that symptom if it's being masked. My overall impression was that she was getting morbidly fearful of giving birth."

"A last question," Katie asked. "Your office is right next to Dr. Fukhito's. Did you at any time Monday night see Mrs. Lewis?"

"I did not."

"Thank you, Doctor. You've been very helpful." She slipped her pad back into her shoulder bag. "Now it's your turn to ask questions."

"I don't have too many. You answered them last night. When you've finished talking with Dr. Fukhito, please go to room 101 on the other side of the hospital. You'll be given a transfusion. Wait about a half hour before driving after you've received it."

"I thought that was for people who gave blood," Katie said.

"Just to make sure there's no reaction. Also . . ." He reached into the deep side drawer of his desk. Katie caught a glimpse of small bottles in exquisite order in the drawer. He selected one containing about nine or ten pills. "Take the first one of these tonight," he said. "Then one every four hours tomorrow; the same on Friday. Take four pills in all tomorrow and Friday. You have just enough here. I must stress that it's very important you don't neglect this. As you know, if this operation does not cure your problem, we must consider more radical surgery."

"I'll take the pills," Katie said.

"Good. You'll be checking in around six o'clock Friday evening."

Katie nodded.

"Fine. I'll be making my late rounds and will look in on you. You're not worried, I trust?"

She had admitted her fear of hospitals to him on the first appointment. "No," she said, "not really."

He opened the door for her. "Till Friday, then, Mrs. DeMaio," he said softly.

CHAPTER 18

The investigative team of Phil Cunningham and Charley Nugent returned to the Prosecutor's office at four P.M. exuding the strained excitement of hounds who have treed their quarry. Rushing into Scott Myerson's office, they proceeded to lay their findings before him.

"The husband's a liar," Phil said crisply. "He wasn't due back till yesterday morning, but his plane developed engine trouble. The passengers were off-loaded in Chicago, and he and the crew deadheaded back to New York. He got in Monday evening."

"Monday evening!" Scott exploded.

"Yeah. And checked into the Holiday Inn on West Fifty-seventh Street."

"How did you get that?"

"We got a list of his crew on the Monday flight and talked to all of them. The purser lives in New York. Lewis gave him a ride into Manhattan and then ended up having dinner with him. Lewis told some cock-and-bull story about his wife being away and he was going to stay in the city overnight and take in a show."

"He told the purser that?"

"Yeah. He parked the car at the Holiday Inn, checked in; then they went to dinner. The purser left him at seven twenty. After that Lewis got his car, and the garage records show he had it for over two hours. Brought it back at ten. And get this. He took off again at midnight and came back at two."

Scott whistled. "He lied to us about his flight. He lied to the purser about his wife. He was somewhere in his car between eight and ten and between midnight and two A.M. What time did Richard say Vangie Lewis died?"

"Between eight and ten P.M.," Ed said.

Charley Nugent had been silent. "There's more," he said. "Lewis has a girlfriend, a Pan Am flight attendant. Name's Joan Moore. Lives at 201 East Eighty-seventh Street in New York. The doorman there told us Captain Lewis drove her home from the airport yesterday morning. She left her bag with him and they went for coffee in the drugstore across the street."

Scott tapped his pencil on the desk, a sure sign that he was about to issue orders. His assistants waited, notebooks in hand.

"It's four o'clock," Scott said crisply. "The judges will be leaving soon. Get one of them on the phone and ask him to wait around for fifteen minutes. Tell him we're having a search warrant sworn out."

Phil sprinted from his chair and reached for the telephone.

"You"—Scott pointed to Charley—"find out what funeral director picked up Vangie Lewis' body in Minneapolis. Get to him. The body is not to be interred, and make damn sure Chris Lewis doesn't decide to cremate it. We may want to do more work on it. Did Lewis say when he was coming back?"

Charley nodded. "He told us he'd return tomorrow immediately after the services and interment."

Scott grunted. "Find out what plane he's coming in on and be waiting for him. Invite him here for questioning."

"You don't think he'll try to skip?" Charley asked.

"No, I don't. He'll try to brazen it through. If he has any brains he'll know that we have nothing specific on him. And I want to talk to the girlfriend. What do you know about her?"

"She shares an apartment with two other flight attendants. She's planning to switch to Pan Am's Latin American Division and fly out of Miami. She's down in Fort Lauderdale right now signing a lease on an apartment. She'll be back late Friday afternoon."

"Meet her plane too," Scott said. "Invite her here for a few questions. Where was she Monday night?"

"In flight on her way to New York. We're absolutely certain."

"All right." He paused. "Something else. I want the phone records from the Lewis house, particularly from the last week, and when you do the search see if there isn't some kind of answering machine on one of the phones. He's an airline captain. It would make sense to have one."

Phil Cunningham was hanging up the phone. "Judge Haywood will wait."

Scott reached for the phone, swiftly dialed Richard's office, asked for him and softly muttered, "Damn. The one day he leaves early has to be today!"

"Do you need him right now?" Charley's tone was curious.

"I want to know what he meant by saying there was something else that didn't jibe. Remember that remark? It might be important to know what it is. All right, let's get busy. And when you search that house, search it with a fine-tooth comb. And look for cyanide. We've got to find out fast where Vangie Lewis got the cyanide that killed her.

"Or where Captain Lewis got it," he added quietly.

CHAPTER 19

By contrast with Dr. Highley's office, Dr. Fukhito's seemed more spacious and brighter. The writing table with long, slender lines occupied less space than Dr. Highley's massive English desk. Graceful cane-backed chairs with upholstered seats and arms and a matching chaise substituted for the clubby leather chairs in the other office. Instead of the wall with framed pictures of mothers and babies, Dr. Fukhito had a series of exquisite reproductions of Ukiyo-e woodcuts.

Dr. Fukhito was tall for a Japanese. Unless, Katie thought, his posture was so upright that he seemed even taller than he probably was. No, she judged him to be about five feet ten.

Like his associate, Dr. Fukhito was expensively and conservatively dressed. His pin-striped suit was accentuated by a light blue shirt and silk tie in muted tones of blue. His jet-black hair and small, neat mustache complemented pale gold skin and brown eyes more oval than almond-shaped. By either Oriental or Occidental standards he was a strikingly handsome man.

And probably a very good psychiatrist, Katie thought as she reached for her notebook, deliberately giving herself time to absorb impressions.

Last month her visit with Dr. Fukhito had been brief and informal. Smiling, he'd explained, "The womb is a fascinating part of the anatomy. Sometimes, irregular or inordinate flowing may indicate an emotional problem."

"I doubt it," Katie had told him. "My mother had the same problem for years, and I do understand it's hereditary, or can be."

He'd queried her about her personal life. "And suppose a hysterectomy becomes necessary someday? What would you feel about that?"

"I would feel terrible," Katie had replied. "I've always wanted a family."

"Then have you any plans to be married? Have you a relationship with someone?"

"No."

"Why not?"

"Because right now I'm more interested in my job." She had terminated the interview abruptly. "Doctor, you're very kind, but I don't have any big emotional hang-ups, I can assure you. I'm looking forward very much to being relieved of this problem, but I assure you it's a purely physical one."

He had acceded gracefully, standing up at once and holding out his hand. "Well, if you're to become Dr. Highley's patient, please remember I'm right here. And if a time comes when you'd like to talk things out with someone, you might want to try me."

Several times in the past month it had fleetingly crossed Katie's mind that it might not be a bad idea to talk with him to get a professional and objective view of where she was at emotionally. Or, she wondered, had that thought sprung into being much more recently—for instance, since last night's dinner with Richard?

Pushing that thought away, she straightened in the chair and held up her pen. Her sleeve fell back, revealing her bandaged arm. To her relief, he did not question her about it.

"Doctor, as you know, a patient of yours and Dr. Highley's, Vangie Lewis, died sometime Monday evening."

She noticed that his eyebrows rose slightly. Was it because he was expecting her to positively state that Vangie committed suicide?

She continued, "Doctor, you saw Vangie at about eight o'clock that night. Isn't that true?"

He nodded. "I saw her at precisely eight o'clock."

"How long did she stay?"

"About forty minutes. She phoned Monday afternoon and asked for an appointment. I usually work until eight on Monday night and was completely booked. I told her so and suggested she come in Tuesday morning."

"How did she respond?"

"She began to cry over the phone. She acted quite distressed, and of course, I told her to come in, that I could see her at eight."

"Why was she so distressed, Doctor?"

He spoke slowly, choosing his words carefully. "She had quarreled with her husband. She was convinced he did not love her or want the baby. Physically, the strain of the pregnancy was beginning to tell on her. She was quite immature, really—an only child who had been inordinately spoiled and fussed over. The physical discomfort was appalling to her, and the prospect of the birth had suddenly become frightening."

Unconsciously, his eyes shifted to the chair at the right of his desk. She had sat in it Monday evening, that long caftan folding around her. Much as she had claimed to want a baby, Vangie had hated maternity clothes, hated losing her figure. In the last month she'd tried to conceal her outsized body and swollen leg by wearing floor-length dresses. It was a miracle she hadn't tripped and fallen the way they flapped around her feet.

Katie stared at him curiously. This man was nervous. What advice had he given Vangie that had sent her rushing home to kill herself? Or had sent her to a killer, if Richard's hunch was right? The quarrel. Chris Lewis had not admitted that he and Vangie had quarreled.

Leaning forward quickly, Katie asked, "Doctor, I realize that you want to protect the confidentiality of Mrs. Lewis' discussions with you, but this is an official matter. We do need to know whatever you can tell us about the quarrel Vangie Lewis had with her husband."

It seemed to him that Katie's voice came from far off. He was seeing Vangie's eyes terrified and staring at him. With a fierce effort he cleared his thoughts and looked directly at Katie. "Mrs. Lewis told me that she believed her husband was in love with someone else; that she'd accused him of that. She told me she had warned him that when she found out who the woman was she'd make her life hell. She was angry, agitated, bitter and frightened."

"What did you tell her?"

"I promised her that before and during the birth she would be given everything necessary to make her comfortable. I told her that we hoped she would have the baby she'd always wanted and that it might be the instrument to give her marriage more time."

"How did she react to that?"

"She began to calm down. But then I felt it necessary to warn her that after the baby was born, if her marriage relationship did not improve, she should consider the possibility of terminating it."

"And then?"

"She became furious. She swore that she would never let her husband leave her, that I was like everyone else, on his side. She got up and grabbed her coat."

"What did you do, Doctor?"

"It was clearly time for me to do nothing. I told her to go home, get a good night's sleep and to call me in the morning. I realized it was far too early for her to deal with the seemingly irrevocable fact that Captain Lewis wanted a divorce."

"And she left?"

"Yes. Her car was parked in the rear parking area. Occasionally she'd ask if she could use my private entrance in order to go out the back way. Monday night she didn't ask. She simply walked out through that door."

"And you never heard from her again?"

"No."

"I see." Katie got up and walked over to the paneled wall with the pictures. She wanted to keep Dr. Fukhito talking. He was holding something back. He was nervous.

"I was a patient here myself Monday night, Doctor," she said. "I had a minor automobile accident and was brought here."

"I'm glad it was minor."

"Yes." Katie stood in front of one of the pictures. *A Small Road at Yabu Koji Atagoshita.* "That's lovely," she said. "It's from the *Hundred Views of Yedo* series, isn't it?"

"Yes. You're very knowledgeable about Japanese art."

"Not really. My husband was the expert and taught me a little about it, and I have other reproductions from the series, but this one is beautiful. Interesting, isn't it, the concept of one hundred views of the same place?"

He became watchful. Katie's back was to him and she did not see that he pressed his lips into a rigid line.

Katie turned around. "Doctor, I was brought in here around ten o'clock Monday night. Can you tell me, is there any chance that Vangie Lewis did not leave at a little after eight o'clock; that she was still around the hospital; that at ten o'clock, when I was brought in, semiconscious, I might have seen her?"

Dr. Fukhito stared at Katie, feeling clammy wet fear crawl across his skin. He forced himself to smile. "I don't see how," he said. But Katie noticed that his knuckles were clenched and white, as if he were forcing himself to sit in his chair, not to run away, and something—was it fury or fear?—flashed in his eyes.

CHAPTER 20

At five o'clock Gertrude Fitzgerald turned the phone over to the answering service and locked the reception desk. Nervously she phoned Edna's number. Again there was no answer. There was no doubt. Edna had been drinking more and more lately. But she was such a cheerful, good person. Really loved everybody. Gertrude and Edna often had lunch together, usually in the hospital cafeteria. Sometimes Edna would say, "Let's go out and get something decent." That meant she wanted to go to the pub near the hospital where she could get a Manhattan. Those days Gertrude always tried to make her keep it down to one drink. She'd kid her along. "You can have a couple tonight, honey," she'd say.

Gertrude understood Edna's need to drink. She didn't drink herself, but she understood that hollow, burning feeling when all you do is go to work every day and then go home and stare at four walls. She and Edna laughed sometimes about all the articles that told you to take up yoga or tennis or join a bird-watching club or take a course. And Edna would say, "I couldn't get these fat legs in the cross-leg position; there's no way I'll ever touch the ground without bending my knees; I'm allergic to birds and at the end of the day I'm too tired to worry about the history of ancient Greece. I just wish that somewhere along the way I'd meet a nice guy who wanted to come home to me at night, and buh-lieve me, I wouldn't care if he snored."

Gertrude was a widow of seven years, but at least she had the children and grandchildren; people who cared about her, called her up, sometimes borrowed a few hundred bucks; people who needed her. She had her own lonely times, God knew, but it wasn't the same as it was for Edna. She'd *lived*. She was sixty-two years old, in good health, and she had something to look back on.

She could swear Dr. Highley had known she was lying when she said Edna had called in sick. But Edna had admitted that Dr. Highley had warned her about the drinking. And Edna needed the job. Those old parents of hers had cost her a mint before they died. Not that Edna ever complained. Sad thing was, she wished they were still around; she missed them.

Suppose Edna *hadn't* been drinking? Suppose she was sick or something? The thought made Gertrude catch her breath sharply. No two ways about it. She'd have to check up on Edna. She'd drive over to her house right now. If she was drinking, she'd make her stop and sober her up. If she was sick, she'd take care of her.

Her mind settled, Gertrude got up from the desk briskly. Something else. That Mrs. DeMaio from the Prosecutor's office. She'd been very nice, but you could tell she'd been anxious to talk to Edna. She'd probably phone Edna tomorrow. What could she want of her? Whatever would Edna be able to tell her about Mrs. Lewis?

It was an intriguing problem, one that kept Gertrude occupied as she drove the six miles to Edna's apartment. But she was still unable to come up with an answer by the time she drove into the visitors' parking area behind Edna's apartment and walked around to the front door.

The lights were on. Even though the shiny, self-lined drapery was drawn, Gertrude could tell that there were lights coming from the living room and dinette. As she neared the door, she heard the faint sound of voices. The television set, of course.

A momentary irritation flashed through her. She might just get really annoyed if Edna was sitting all nice and comfortable in her recliner and hadn't even bothered to answer the phone. She, Gertrude, had covered her work for her, covered her absence and now driven miles out of her way to make sure she wasn't in need.

Gertrude rang the bell. It pealed in a clanging double chime. She waited. Even though she listened hard, there was no sound of hurrying feet approaching the door, or a familiar voice calling, "Right with you." Maybe Edna was rinsing her mouth with Scope. She was always afraid that one of the doctors might drop in with emergency work to do. That had happened a few times on days Edna was out. That was how Dr. Highley had first noticed Edna's problem.

But there was no reassuring sound of voice or footsteps. Gertrude shivered as she firmly pushed the bell again. Maybe Edna was sleeping it off. It was so terribly cold. She wanted to get home herself.

By the time she'd rung the bell four times, the annoyance had passed and Gertrude was thoroughly alarmed. There was no use fooling around; something was wrong and she had to get into the apartment. The superintendent, Mr. Krupshak, lived directly across the court. Hurrying over, Gertrude told her story. The super was eating dinner and looked annoyed, but his wife, Gana, reached for the wide key ring on a nail over the sink. "I'll go with you," she said.

The two women hurried across the courtyard together. "Edna's a real friend," Gana Krupshak volunteered. "Sometimes in the evening I pop in on her and we visit and have a drink together. My husband doesn't approve of liquor, even wine. Just last night I stopped over at about eight. I had a Manhattan with her, and she told me that one of her favorite patients had killed herself. Well, here we are."

The women were on the small porch leading to Edna's apartment. The superintendent's wife fumbled with the keys. "It's this one," she murmured. She inserted the key into the lock, twisted it. "This lock has a funny little thing—you have to kind of jiggle it."

The lock turned and she pushed open the door as she spoke.

The two women saw Edna at exactly the same moment: lying on the floor, her legs crumpled under her, her blue robe open, revealing a flannel nightgown, her graying hair plastered around her face, her eyes staring, crusted blood making a crimson crown on the top of her head.

"No. No." Gertrude felt her voice rise, high, shrill, an entity she could not control. She pressed her knuckles to her mouth.

In a dazed voice Gana Krupshak said, "It's just last night I was sitting here with her. And"—the woman's voice broke—"she was pretty under the weather—you know what I mean, the way Edna could get—and she was talking about a patient who killed herself. And then she phoned that patient's husband." Gana began to sob—noisy, racking sounds. "And now poor Edna is dead too!"

CHAPTER 21

Chris Lewis stood next to Vangie's parents to the right of the coffin, numbly acknowledging the sympathetic utterances of friends. When he'd phoned them about her death, they had agreed that they would view her body privately, have a memorial service tomorrow morning followed by a private interment.

Instead, when he'd arrived in Minneapolis this afternoon, he found that they had arranged for public viewing tonight and that after the chapel service tomorrow morning a cortege would follow Vangie's body to the cemetery.

"So many friends will want to say good-bye to our little girl. To think that two days ago she was alive, and now she's gone," her mother sobbed.

Was it only Wednesday? It seemed to Chris that weeks had passed since he'd walked into that nightmare scene in the bedroom yesterday morning. *Yesterday morning.*

"Doesn't our baby look lovely?" her mother was asking the visitor who had just approached the coffin.

Our little girl. Our baby. If only you had let her grow up, Chris thought, it might all have been so different. Their hostility to him was controlled, but lurked below the surface ready to spring out. "A happy girl does not take her own life," her mother had said accusingly.

They looked old and tired and shattered with grief—plain, hard-working people who had denied themselves everything to surround their unexpectedly beautiful child with luxury, who had brought her up to believe her wish was law.

Would it be easier for them when the truth was revealed that some-one had taken Vangie's life? Or did he owe it to them to say nothing, to keep that final horror from them? Her mother was already trying to find comfort, to frame a version she could live with: "Chris was on a trip and we're so far away, and my baby was feeling so sick and she took a sip of something and went to sleep."

Oh, God, Chris thought, how people twist truth, twist life. He wanted to talk to Joan. She'd been so upset when she heard about Vangie that she'd hardly been able to talk. "Did she know about us?" He'd finally had to admit to her that Vangie suspected that he was interested in someone else.

Joan would be back from Florida Friday evening. He was going to return to New Jersey tomorrow afternoon right after the funeral. He would say nothing to the police until he'd had a chance to talk to Joan, to warn her that she might be dragged into this. The police would be looking for a motive for him to kill Vangie. In their eyes, Joan would be the motive.

Should he leave well enough alone? *Did* he have the right to drag Joan into this, to unearth something that would hurt Vangie's parents even more?

Had there been someone else in Vangie's life? Chris glanced over at the coffin, at Vangie's now-peaceful face, the quietly folded hands. He and Vangie had scarcely lived as man and wife in the past few years. They'd lain side by side like two strangers; he emotionally drained from the endless quarreling, she wanting to be cajoled, babied. He'd even suggested separate rooms, but she'd become hysterical.

She became pregnant two months after they moved to New Jersey. When he'd agreed to one more final try at the marriage, he had made a genuine effort to make it work. But the summer had been miserable. By August he and Vangie had barely been speaking. Only once, around the middle of the month, had they slept together. He had thought it an irony of fate that after ten years she had become pregnant just as he met someone else.

A suspicion that Chris realized had been sitting somewhere in his subconscious sprang full-blown to life. Was it possible that Vangie had become involved with another man, a man who did not want to take responsibility for her and a baby? Had she confronted that other man? Vangie had threatened that if she knew whom Chris was seeing, she'd make her wish she were dead. Suppose she had been having some kind of affair with a married man. Suppose she'd hurled hysterical threats at *him?*

Chris realized that he had been shaking hands, murmuring thanks, looking into familiar faces and not really seeing them: neighbors from the condominium where he and Vangie had lived before the move to New Jersey; airline friends; friends of Vangie's parents. His own parents were retired in North Carolina. Neither was well. He had told them not to make the trip to Minneapolis in the bitterly cold weather.

"I'm very sorry." The man who was clasping his hand was in his mid-sixties. He was a slightly built man, but sturdily attractive, with winter-gray hair and bushy brows over keen, penetrating eyes. "I'm Dr. Salem," he said, "Emmet Salem. I delivered Vangie and was her first gynecologist. She was one of the prettiest things I ever brought into this world, and she never changed. I only wish I hadn't been away when she phoned my office Monday."

Chris stared at him. "Vangie phoned you Monday?"

"Yes. My nurse said she was quite upset. Wanted to see me immediately. I was teaching a seminar in Detroit, but the nurse made an appointment with me for her for today. She was planning to fly out yesterday, from what I understand. Maybe I could have helped her."

Why had Vangie called this man? Why? It seemed to Chris that it was impossible to think. What would make her go back to a doctor she hadn't seen in years? She wasn't well, but if she wanted a consultation, why a doctor thirteen hundred miles away?

"Had Vangie been ill?" Dr. Salem was looking at him curiously, waiting for an answer.

"No, not ill," Chris said. "As you probably know, she was expecting a baby. It was a difficult pregnancy from the beginning."

"Vangie was what?" The doctor's voice rose. He stared at Chris in astonishment.

"I know. She had just about given up hope. But in New Jersey she started going to the Westlake Maternity Concept. You may have heard of it, or of Dr. Highley—Dr. Edgar Highley."

"Captain Lewis, may I speak with you?" The funeral director had a hand under his arm, was propelling him toward the private office across the foyer from the viewing room.

"Excuse me," Chris said to the doctor. Nonplussed by the director's agitation, he allowed himself to be guided into the office.

The funeral director closed the door and looked at Chris. "I've just received a call from the Prosecutor's office in Valley County, New Jersey," he said. "Written confirmation is on the way. We are forbidden to inter your wife's body. Your wife's body is to be flown back to the Medical Examiner's office in Valley County immediately after the service tomorrow."

They know it wasn't a suicide, Chris thought. They already know that. There was nothing he could do to hide it. Once he had a chance to talk to Joan Friday night, he'd tell the Prosecutor's office everything he knew or suspected.

Without answering the funeral director, he turned and left the office. He wanted to speak to Dr. Salem, find out what Vangie had said to the nurse on the phone.

But when he went back to the other room, Dr. Salem was already gone. He had left without speaking to Vangie's parents. Vangie's mother rubbed swollen eyes with a damp crumpled handkerchief. "What did you say to Dr. Salem that made him leave like that?" she asked. "Why did you upset him so terribly?"

CHAPTER 22

Wednesday evening he arrived home at six o'clock. Hilda was just leaving. Her plain, stolid face was guarded. He was always aloof with her. He knew she liked and wanted this job. Why not? A house that stayed neat; no mistress to constantly give orders; no children to clutter it.

No children. He went into the library, poured a Scotch and broodingly watched from the window as Hilda's broad body disappeared down the street toward the bus line two blocks away.

He had gone into medicine because his own mother had died in childbirth. His birth. The accumulated stories of the years, listened to from the time he could understand, told by the timid, self-effacing man who had been his father. "Your mother wanted you so much. She knew she was risking her life, but she didn't care."

Sitting in the chemist's shop in Brighton, watching his father prepare prescriptions, asking questions: "What is that?" "What will that pill do?" "Why do you put caution labels on those bottles?" He'd been fascinated, drinking in the information his father so willingly shared with him—the one topic his father could talk about; the only world his father knew.

He'd gone to medical school, finished in the top ten percent of his class; internships were offered in leading hospitals in London and Glasgow. Instead he chose Christ Hospital in Devon, with its magnificently equipped research laboratory—the opportunity it gave for both research and practice. He'd become staff; his reputation as an obstetrician had grown rapidly.

And his project had been held back, retarded, cursed by his inability to test it.

At twenty-seven he'd married Claire, a distant cousin of the Earl of Sussex—infinitely superior to him in social background, but his reputation, the expectation of future prominence had been the leveler.

And the incredible ignominy. He who dealt in birth and fertility had married a barren woman. He whose walls were covered with pictures of babies who never should have been carried to term had no hope of becoming a father himself.

When had he started to hate Claire? It took a long time—seven years.

It was when he finally realized that she didn't care; had never cared; that her disappointment was faked; that she'd *known* before she married him that she could not conceive.

Impatiently he turned from the window. It would be another cold, wind-filled night. Why did February, the shortest month of the year, always seem to be the longest one? When all this was over he'd take a vacation. He was getting edgy, losing grip on his nerves.

He had nearly given himself away this morning when Gertrude told him that Edna had phoned in sick. He'd grasped the desk, watched his knuckles whiten. Then he'd remembered. The fluttering pulse that had stopped beating, the unfocused eyes, the muscles relaxing in extremis. Gertrude was covering for her friend. *Gertrude was lying.*

He'd frowned at Gertrude. When he spoke he'd made his voice icy. "It is most inconvenient that Edna is absent today. I hope and expect that she will be here tomorrow."

It had worked. He could tell from the nervous licking of the lips, from Gertrude's averted eyes. She believed that he was furious at Edna's absence. She probably knew that he'd spoken sharply to Edna about her drinking.

Gertrude might prove to be an ally.

POLICE: And how did the doctor respond when you told him Miss Burns was absent?
GERTRUDE: He was quite angry. He's very methodical. He doesn't like anything that upsets the routine.

The missing shoe. This morning he'd gone to the hospital soon after dawn and once again searched the parking lot and the office. Had Vangie been wearing it when she came into his office Monday night?

He realized that he couldn't be sure. She'd been wearing that long caftan, her winter coat buttoned awkwardly over it. The caftan was too large; the coat strained at the abdomen. She lifted the caftan to show him her swollen right leg. He'd seen the moccasin on that foot, but he'd never noticed the other shoe. Had she been wearing it? He simply didn't know.

If it had fallen off in the parking lot when he carried her body to the car, someone had picked it up. Maybe a maintenance man had seen it; discarded it. Often patients who were checking out had overflowing shopping bags, stuffed with cards or plants and last-minute personal items that didn't fit in the suitcase, and lost things between the hospital room and the parking lot. He'd inquired at the lost-and-found desk, but they had no footwear. It might simply have been thrown into the rubbish bag.

He thought about lifting Vangie out of the trunk of the car, carrying her past the shelves in her garage. They had been filled with garden tools. Was it possible that the looser shoe had perhaps brushed against something protruding? If it was found on a shelf in the garage, questions would be asked.

If Vangie did *not* have the shoe on when she left Fukhito's office, her stocking sole would have become soiled. But the portico between the offices was sheltered. If her left foot was badly soiled, he'd have noticed it when he laid her out on the bed.

The horror of finding that he was carrying the *right* shoe, the shoe that he had struggled to pull off Vangie's foot, had unnerved him. The more fool he. After the terrible, terrible risk.

The right shoe was in his bag in the trunk of the car. He wasn't sure whether to dispose of it—not until he was positive the other one wouldn't still show up.

Even if the police started an intensive investigation into the suicide, there was nothing that constituted evidence against him. Her file in the office could bear intensive professional scrutiny. Her true records, all the true records of the special cases, were in the wall safe here. He defied anyone to locate that safe. It wasn't even in the original plans of the house. Dr. Westlake had installed it personally. Only Winifred had known about it.

No one had any reason to suspect him—no one except Katie DeMaio. She'd been on the verge of telling him something when he'd mentioned the view from the hospital room, but she had changed her mind abruptly.

Fukhito had come in to him just as he was locking up tonight. Fukhito was nervous. He'd said, "Mrs. DeMaio was asking a lot of questions. Is it possible that they don't believe Mrs. Lewis committed suicide?"

"I really don't know." He'd enjoyed Fukhito's nervousness; understood the reason for it.

"That interview you gave to *Newsmaker* magazine; that's going to come out tomorrow, isn't it?"

He'd looked at Fukhito disdainfully. "Yes. But I assure you I gave the distinct impression I use a number of psychiatric consultants. Your name will not appear in the article."

Fukhito was not relieved. "Still, it's going to put the spotlight on this hospital; on us," he complained.

"On *yourself*—isn't that what you're saying, Doctor?"

He'd almost laughed aloud at the troubled, guilty look on Fukhito's face.

Now, finishing his Scotch, he realized that he had been overlooking another avenue of escape. If the police came to the conclusion that Vangie had been murdered; if they *did* investigate Westlake; it would be an easy matter to reluctantly suggest that they interrogate Dr. Fukhito. Especially in view of his past.

After all, Dr. Fukhito was the last person known to have seen Vangie Lewis alive.

CHAPTER 23

After leaving Dr. Fukhito, Katie went to the east wing of the hospital for the transfusion. It was given to her in a curtained-off area near the emergency room. As she lay on top of a bed, her sleeve rolled back, the needle strapped in her arm, she tried to reconstruct her arrival at the hospital Monday night.

She thought she remembered being in this room, but she wasn't sure. The doctor who had sewed the cut in her arm looked in. "Hi, I thought I saw you at the desk. I see Dr. Highley ordered another transfusion. I hope you're looking into that low blood count."

"Yes. I'm under Dr. Highley's care."

"Fine. Let's take a look at that arm." He rebandaged it as she lay there. "Good job. Have to admit it myself. You won't have a scar to show your grandchildren."

"If I have any," Katie said. "Doctor, tell me, was I on this bed Monday night?"

"Yes, we had you in here after the X-rays. You don't remember?"

"It's all such a blur."

"You lost a lot of blood. You were in a pretty good state of shock."

"I see."

When the transfusion was finished, she remembered that Dr. Highley had told her not to drive for twenty minutes. She decided to go to the admitting office and fill out the necessary forms for an inpatient stay. Then she wouldn't have to bother with them Friday evening.

When she left the hospital it was nearly six o'clock. She found herself automatically turning the car in the direction of Chapin River. Nonsense, she thought. You're having dinner with Molly and Bill tomorrow night. Forget about dropping in tonight.

The decision settled, she made a U-turn and drove to Palisades Parkway. She was getting hungry, and the thought of going home did not appeal to her. Who was the poet who had written on the joys of solitude and then had finished the poem with the lines "But do not go home alone after five. / Let someone be waiting there."?

Well, she had learned to cope with loneliness, had taught herself to genuinely enjoy a quiet evening of reading with the stereo playing.

The feeling of emptiness that came over her lately was something new.

She passed the restaurant where she and Richard had eaten the night before, and on impulse swung into the parking area. Tonight she'd try the other specialty, the *entrecôte*. Maybe in the warm, intimate, quiet restaurant she'd be able to think.

The proprietor recognized her and beamed with pleasure. "Good evening, madam. Dr. Carroll did not make a reservation, but I have a table near the fireplace. He is parking the car?"

She shook her head. "Just me tonight, I'm afraid."

For an instant the man looked embarrassed, but recovered quickly. "Then I suspect we have made a new and beautiful friend." He led her to a table near the one she had shared with Richard.

Nodding at the suggestion of a glass of Burgundy, Katie leaned back and felt the same sense of unwinding she'd experienced the night before. Now if she could just collect her thoughts, sort out the impressions that she'd received talking to Dr. Highley and Dr. Fukhito about Vangie Lewis.

Taking out her pad, she began to scan what she had jotted down during the interviews. Dr. Highley. She'd expected him to explain or defend the fact that Vangie Lewis was obviously in serious trouble with her pregnancy. He had done exactly that, and what he told her was completely reasonable. He was going day by day to buy the baby time. The remarks he'd made about Vangie's reaction to the impending birth rang true. She'd heard from Molly the story of Vangie's hysterical reaction to a blister on the finger.

What then? What more did she want of Dr. Highley? She thought of Dr. Wainwright, the cancer specialist in New York, who had taken care of John. After John died, he'd spoken to her, his face and voice filled with pain. "I want you to know, Mrs. DeMaio, we tried everything possible to save him. Nothing was left undone. But sometimes God takes it out of our hands."

Dr. Highley had expressed regret over Vangie's death, but certainly not sorrow. But of course, he had to stay objective. She'd heard Bill and Richard discussing the need to stay objective when you practice medicine. Otherwise you'd constantly be torn in two and end up useless.

Richard. Inadvertently her eyes slid over to the table where she'd been with him. He'd said, "We both know we could enjoy each other." He was right. She did know it. Maybe that was why she usually felt unsettled with him, as though things could be taken out of her hands. Is it possible that it could happen twice in a lifetime? From the very beginning you *know* something is right, someone is right.

When she and Richard were leaving Molly's after that quick lunch yesterday, Molly had asked them both to dinner Thursday night— tomorrow. Molly said, "Liz and Jim Berkeley are coming over. She's the one who thinks Dr. Highley is God. You two might be interested in talking with her."

Katie realized how much she was looking forward to that dinner.

Again she looked down at her notes. Dr. Fukhito. Something was wrong there. It seemed to her that he'd deliberately weighed every word he said when he'd discussed Vangie's Monday-night visit. It had been like watching someone step by step through a mine field. What was he afraid of? Even allowing for the reasonable concern of protecting the doctor-patient relationship, he'd been afraid he would say something that she would pounce on.

Then he'd been openly hostile when she asked if by any chance Vangie might still have been in the hospital at ten o'clock when she, Katie, was brought in.

Suppose she *had* glimpsed Vangie? Suppose Vangie had been just leaving Dr. Fukhito's office; had been walking somewhere in the parking lot? That would explain seeing her face in that crazy nightmare.

Dr. Fukhito had said that Vangie left by his private entrance.

No one had seen her go.

Suppose she *hadn't* left? Suppose she'd stayed with the doctor. Suppose he'd left with her or followed her home. Suppose he'd realized that she was suicidal, that he was responsible in some way . . .

Enough to make him nervous.

The waiter arrived to take her order. Before she put away the pad, Katie made one final note: *Investigate Dr. Fukhito's background.*

CHAPTER 24

Even before he crossed the George Washington Bridge and drove down the Harlem River and FDR Drive Wednesday evening, Richard knew that he should have cancelled the date with Clovis. He was preoccupied about Vangie Lewis' death; his subconscious was suggesting that he had missed something in the autopsy. There had been something he'd intended to examine more closely. What was it?

And he was worried about Katie. She had looked so thin last night. She'd been extremely pale. It wasn't until she'd had a couple of glasses of wine that some color had come into her face.

Katie wasn't well. That was it. He was a doctor and should have spotted it sooner.

That accident. How carefully had she been examined? Was it possible that she'd been hurt more than anyone realized? The thought haunted Richard as he turned onto the Fifty-third Street exit from the FDR Drive and headed for Clovis' apartment one block away.

Clovis had a pitcher of very dry martinis waiting to be poured and a plate of hot crabmeat-filled puffs fresh from the oven. With her flawless skin, tall, slender body and Viking coloring, she reminded Richard of a young Ingrid Bergman. Until recently he'd toyed with the idea that they might end up together. Clovis was intelligent, interesting and good-tempered.

But as he returned her kiss with honest affection, he was acutely aware that he'd never worry about Clovis the way he now found himself worrying about Katie DeMaio.

He realized Clovis was talking to him. "... and I'm not home ten minutes. The rehearsal ran over. There was a lot of rewriting. So I fixed the drinks and nibbles and figured you could relax while I get dressed. Hey, are you listening to me?"

Richard accepted the drink and smiled apologetically. "I'm sorry. I'm on a case that won't let go. Do you mind if I make a couple of calls while you're getting ready?"

"Of course I don't mind," Clovis said. "Go ahead and dial away." She picked up her glass and started toward the foyer that led into the bedroom and bath.

Richard took his credit card from his wallet and dialed the operator. There was no way he was going to put a call to one woman on another woman's phone bill. Quickly he gave his account number to the operator. When the connection went through, he allowed the phone to ring a dozen times before he finally gave up. Katie wasn't home.

Next he tried Molly's house. Probably Katie had stopped there. But Molly had not spoken to her at all today.

"I don't really expect her," Molly said. "You're both coming tomorrow night. Don't forget that. She'll probably call me later. But I wish she'd gone home by now. She could stand taking it easy."

It was the opening he needed. "Molly, what's the matter with Katie?" he asked. "There is something wrong physically, isn't there? Besides the accident, I mean?"

Molly hesitated. "I think you'd better talk to Katie about that."

Certainty. Cold fear washed over him.

"Molly, I want to know. *What's the matter with her?*"

"Oh, not much," Molly said hastily. "I promise you that. But it's nothing she wanted to discuss. And now I've probably said more than I should. See you tomorrow."

The connection broke. Richard frowned into the dead receiver. He started to replace it on the cradle, then on impulse put through a call to his office. He spoke to the assistant on the evening shift. "Anything unusual going on?" he asked.

"We just got a call for the wagon. A body was found in an apartment in Edgeriver. Probably an accident, but the local police thought we'd better take a look. Scott's people are heading over there."

"Switch me to Scott's office," Richard said.

Scott did not waste time on preliminaries. "Where are you?" he demanded.

"In New York. Do you need me?"

"Yes. This woman who was found in Edgeriver is the receptionist Katie wanted to talk to today at Westlake. Name's Edna Burns. Supposedly she phoned in sick today, but there's no question she's been dead a good twenty-four hours. Body was found by a co-worker from Westlake. I'm trying to get Katie. I'd like her to go over there."

"Give me the address," Richard said.

He wrote it quickly and hung up the phone. Katie had wanted to question this Edna Burns about Vangie Lewis, and now Edna Burns was dead. He knocked on Clovis' bedroom door. She opened it, wrapped in a terry-cloth robe. "Hey, what's the hurry?" she asked, smiling. "I just got out of the shower."

"Clo, I'm sorry." Quickly he explained. Now he was frantic to get away.

She was clearly disappointed. "Oh, of course I understand, but I was counting on seeing you. It's been a couple of weeks—you do know that. All right. Go, but let's have dinner tomorrow night. Promise?"

Richard temporized. "Well, very soon." He started to leave, but she caught him by the arm and pulled his face down for a kiss.

"Tomorrow night," she told him firmly.

CHAPTER 25

On the way home from the restaurant, Katie turned over in her mind the conversation she'd had with Edna Burns on her first visit to Dr. Highley. Edna was a born listener. Katie was not given to discussing her personal affairs, but when Edna took the preliminary information, she had clucked sympathetically. Not quite believing her own ears, Katie had heard herself telling Edna all about John.

How much had *Vangie* told Edna? She'd been going to Westlake since last summer. How much did Edna know about Dr. Fukhito? There was something oddly intimidating about his nervousness. Why should he be nervous?

Katie pulled up in front of her house and decided not to put the car away yet. It was Wednesday and Mrs. Hodges had been here. The house smelled faintly of lemon wax. The mirror over the antique marble table in the hall was shining. Katie knew her bed had been made with fresh linen; the ceramic kitchen tile would be gleaming; the furniture and rugs had been vacuumed; her laundry would be back in the drawers or closet.

Mrs. Hodges had worked full time when John was alive. Now pensioned off, she'd begged for the chance to come in one day a week and take care of "my house."

It wouldn't last much longer. It couldn't. Mrs. Hodges was past seventy now.

Whom would she get when Mrs. Hodges no longer came in? Who would exercise the same care with the valuable bric-a-brac, the antiques, the English furniture, the lovely old Orientals?

"It's time to sell," Katie thought. "I know it."

Taking off her coat, she tossed it on a chair. It was only a quarter of eight. The night loomed long ahead of her. Edna had told her that she lived in Edgeriver. That was less than twenty minutes' drive away. Suppose she phoned Edna now? Suppose she suggested driving down to see her? Mrs. Fitzgerald had said that Edna was expected at work tomorrow, so she couldn't be too sick. If Katie was any judge, Edna would love a chance to gossip about Vangie Lewis.

Mrs. Hodges always left a freshly baked cake or pie or muffins in the bread box for Katie. She'd take whatever was there now down to Edna and have a cup of tea with her. A lot of gossip could be exchanged over a teapot.

Edna was listed in the telephone book. Quickly Katie dialed her number. It rang once and the receiver was picked up. She formed the words "Hello, Miss Burns," but never got to speak them.

A man's voice said, "Yes." The short word was delivered in a clipped, not-unfamiliar voice.

"Is Miss Burns there?" Katie asked. "This is Mrs. DeMaio from the Prosecutor's office."

"Katie!"

Now she recognized the voice. It was Charley Nugent, and he was saying, "Glad Scott got in touch with you. Can you come right down?"

"Come down?" Afraid of what she'd hear, Katie asked the question: "What are you doing at Edna Burns's apartment?"

"Don't you know? She's dead, Katie. Fell—or was pushed—into the radiator. Split her head open." His voice lowered. "Get this, Katie. She was last seen alive around eight o'clock last night. A neighbor was with her." His voice became a whisper. "The neighbor heard her on the phone with Vangie Lewis' husband. Edna Burns told Chris Lewis that she was going to talk to the police about Vangie's death."

CHAPTER 26

After he finished the second Scotch he went into the kitchen and opened the refrigerator. He had told Hilda not to prepare anything for him tonight, but had given her a long shopping list. He nodded in approval at the new items in the meat drawer: the boneless breasts of chicken, the filet mignon, the double loin lamb chops. Fresh asparagus, tomatoes and watercress were in the vegetable bin. Brie and Jarlsberg were in the cheesebox. Tonight he'd have the lamb chops, asparagus and a watercress salad.

Emotional exhaustion always compelled him to eat. The night Claire died, he'd left the hospital, to all outward appearances a husband benumbed with grief, and had gone to a quiet restaurant a dozen blocks away and eaten heavily. Then he'd trudged home masking an acute sense of well-being with the weary posture of the grief-stricken. The friends who were gathered waiting to greet him, to commiserate with him had been deceived.

"Where were you, Edgar? We were worried about you."

"I don't know. I don't remember. I've just been walking."

It had been the same after Winifred's death. He'd left her relatives and friends at the grave site, refused invitations to join them for dinner. "No. No. I need to be alone." He'd come back to the house, waited long enough to answer a few phone calls, then contacted the answering service. "If anyone phones, please explain that I'm resting and that I'll return all calls later."

Then he'd gotten into the car and driven to the Carlyle in New York. There he had requested a quiet table and ordered dinner. Halfway through the meal he looked up and saw Winifred's cousin, Glenn Nickerson, across the room—Glenn, the high school athletic coach who had been Winifred's heir until he came along. Glenn was dressed in the dark blue suit and black tie he'd worn to the funeral, a bargain-priced, ill-fitting suit obviously bought specially for the occasion. His normal garb was a sports jacket, slacks and loafers.

Nickerson was obviously watching him. He'd lifted his glass in a toast, a mocking smile on his face. He might as well have shouted his thoughts: "To the grieving widower."

He'd done what was necessary: walked over to him without the slightest sign of distress and spoken pleasantly. "Glenn, why didn't you join me when you saw I was here? I didn't realize you came to the Carlyle. This was a favorite dining spot of ours. We became engaged here— or did Winifred ever tell you that? I'm not Jewish, but I think that one of the most beautiful customs in this bewildering world is that of the Jewish faith, where after a death the family eats eggs to symbolize the continuity of life. I am here to quietly celebrate the continuity of love."

Glenn had stared at him, his expression stony. Then he'd stood up and signaled for his check. "I admire your ability to philosophize, Edgar," he said. "No. I don't consider the Carlyle one of my regular eating spots. I simply followed you here because I had decided to visit you and reached your block just as your car pulled out. I had the feeling it might be interesting to keep an eye on you. How right I was."

He'd turned his back on Glenn, walked with dignity back to his own table and not glanced in his direction again. A few minutes later he'd seen Glenn at the door of the dining room on his way out.

The next week, Alan Levine, the doctor who'd treated Winifred, indignantly told him that Glenn had asked to see Winifred's medical records.

"I threw him out of my office," Alan said heatedly. "I told him that Winifred had developed classic angina symptoms and that he would do himself a favor if he studied the current statistics on women in their early fifties' having heart attacks. Even so, he had the gall to speak to the police. I had a call from the Prosecutor's office asking in so many words if a heart ailment could be induced. I told them that being alive today was enough to induce heart trouble. They backed off immediately, said it was obviously a disinherited relative trying to cause trouble."

But you *can* induce heart trouble, Dr. Levine. You can prepare intimate little dinners for your dear wife. You can use her susceptibility to gastroenteritis to bring on attacks so strong that they register as heart seizures on her cardiogram. After enough of these the lady apparently has a fatal seizure. She dies in the presence of her own physician, who arrives to find the physician husband applying mouth-to-mouth resuscitation. No one suggests an autopsy. And even if someone had, there would have been little risk.

The only risk would have occurred if they had thought to delve into Claire's death.

The chops were nearly cooked. He expertly seasoned the watercress, removed the asparagus from the steamer and took a half-bottle of Beaujolais from the wine rack in the pantry.

He had just begun to eat when the phone rang. He debated ignoring it, then decided that at this time it was dangerous to miss any calls. Slapping his napkin on the table, he hurried to the extension in the kitchen. "Dr. Highley," he said curtly.

A sob sounded over the phone. "Doctor—oh, Dr. Highley. It's Gertrude, Gertrude Fitzgerald. Doctor, I decided to go see Edna on my way home."

He tightened his grip on the receiver.

"Doctor, Edna is dead. The police are here. She fell. Doctor, could you come here right away? They're talking about performing an autopsy. She always hated autopsies. She used to say how terrible it was to cut up dead people. Doctor, you know how Edna was when she drank. I told them that you've been here in her apartment; that you've caught her drinking. Doctor, come here and tell them how you would find her sometimes. Oh, please come here and convince them that she fell and that they don't have to cut her up."

⟩⟩⟩ CHAPTER 27

Before she left the house, Katie made a cup of tea and carried it to the car. Driving with one hand, she held the bubbling liquid to her lips with the other. She'd planned to bring cake down to Edna and have tea with her. And now Edna was dead.

How could a person she'd met only once have made such an impression on her? Was it simply that Edna was such a good person, so truly concerned with the patients? So many people were so indifferent, so noncaring. In that one conversation with Edna last month, it had been so easy to talk about John.

And Edna had understood. She'd said, "I know what it is to watch someone die. On the one hand, you want the misery to be over for them. On the other hand you don't want to let them go." She'd shared the aftermath of loss. "When both Mom and Dad died, all my friends said, 'Now you're free, Edna.' And I said, 'Free for what?' And I bet you felt that way too."

Edna reassured her about Dr. Highley. "You couldn't find a better doctor for any GYN problem. That's why it makes me so mad when I hear him criticized. And all those people who file malpractice suits! Let me tell you, I could shoot them myself. That's the trouble when people think you're God. They think you can do the impossible. I tell you when a doctor loses a patient today, he has to worry. And I don't just mean obstetricians. I mean geriatric doctors too. I guess nobody's supposed to die anymore."

What had Charley meant by telling her that Edna had phoned Chris Lewis last night? In practically the same breath Charley had suggested the possibility of foul play.

"I don't believe it," Katie said aloud as she turned off Route 4 onto Edgeriver. It would be like Edna to call Chris Lewis to express her sympathy. Was Charley suggesting Edna might have in some way *threatened* Chris Lewis?

She had a vague idea of where the apartment development was and was able to find it easily. She mused that as garden apartments went, this one was getting somewhat rundown. When she sold the house she'd probably move into a high-rise for a while. There were some buildings overlooking the Hudson that had lovely apartments with terraces. And it would be interesting to be near New York. She'd be more likely to go to the theater and museums. *When* I sell the house, she thought. At what point did *if* become *when?*

Charley had told her that Edna's apartment was the last one in units 41 through 60. He'd said to drive behind that row and park. She slowed down, realizing that a car had entered the development from another road and was pulling into that same area ahead of her. It was a black medium-sized car. For a moment the driver hesitated, then chose the first parking spot available on the right. Katie pulled around him. If Edna's apartment was the end one on the left, she'd try to get closer to it. She found a spot directly behind that building and parked. She got out of the car, realizing that she must be looking at the back window of Edna's apartment. The window was raised an inch. The shade was pulled down to the top of a plant. A faint light could be seen from inside the apartment.

Katie thought of the view from her bedroom windows. They looked over the little pond in the woods behind the house. Edna had gazed out at a parking area and a rusting chain-link fence. Yet she had told Katie how much she enjoyed her apartment, how cozy it was.

Katie heard footsteps behind her and turned quickly. In the lonely parking area, any sound seemed menacing. A figure loomed near her, a silhouette accentuated by the dim light from the solitary lamppost. A sense of familiarity struck her.

"Excuse me. I hope I didn't startle you." The cultured voice had a faint English accent.

"Dr. Highley!"

"Mrs. DeMaio. We didn't expect to see each other so soon and under such tragic circumstances."

"Then you've heard. Did my office call you, Doctor?"

"It's chilly. Here. Let's take this footpath around the building." Barely touching her elbow with his hand, he followed her on the path. "Mrs. Fitzgerald called me. She substituted for Miss Burns today and evidently she was the one to find her. She sounded terribly upset and begged me to come. I don't have any details of what happened as yet."

"Neither do I," Katie replied. They were turning the corner to the front of the building when she heard rapid footsteps behind them.

"Katie."

She felt the pressure of the doctor's fingers on her elbow tighten and then release as she looked back. Richard was there. She turned, absurdly glad to see him. He grasped both her shoulders. In a gesture that ended even as it began, he pulled her to him. Then his hands dropped. "Scott reached you?"

"No. I happened to call Edna myself. Oh, Richard, this is Dr. Edgar Highley." Quickly she introduced the two men, and they shook hands.

Katie thought, How absurd this is. I am making introductions and a few feet inside that door a woman is lying dead.

Charley let them in. He looked relieved to see them. "Your people should be here in a couple of minutes," he told Richard. "We've got pictures, but I'd like you to have a look too."

Katie was used to death. In the course of her job, she constantly held up vivid and gory pictures of crime victims. She was usually able to separate herself from the emotional aspect and concentrate on the legal ramifications of wrongful death.

But it was a different matter to see Edna crumpled against the radiator in the kind of flannel nightgown her own mother considered indispensable; to see the blue terry-cloth robe so like the ones her mother used to pick up on sale at Macy's; to see the solid evidence of loneliness—the slices of canned ham, the empty cocktail glass.

Edna had been such a cheery person, who found some small measure of happiness in this shabbily furnished apartment, and even the apartment had betrayed her. It had become the scene of her violent death.

Gertrude Fitzgerald was sitting on the old-fashioned velour couch at the opposite end of the L-shaped room, out of sight of the body. She was sobbing softly. Richard went directly into the dinette to examine the dead woman. Katie walked over to Mrs. Fitzgerald and sat beside her on the couch. Dr. Highley followed her and pulled up a straight-backed chair.

Gertrude tried to talk to them. "Oh, Dr. Highley, Mrs. DeMaio, isn't this terrible, just terrible?" The words brought a fresh burst of sobs. Katie gently put a hand on the trembling shoulders. "I'm so sorry, Mrs. Fitzgerald. I know you were fond of Miss Burns."

"She was always so nice. Such fun. She always made me laugh. And maybe she had that little weakness. Everybody has a little weakness, and she never bothered anyone with it. Oh, Dr. Highley, you'll miss her too."

Katie watched as the doctor bent over Gertrude, his face grave. "I surely will, Mrs. Fitzgerald. Edna was a marvelously efficient person. She took so much pride in her work. Dr. Fukhito and I used to joke that she had our patients so relaxed by the time we saw them that she could have put Dr. Fukhito out of his job."

"Doctor," Gertrude blurted out, "I told them you've been here. I told them that. You knew Edna's little problem. It's just silly to say she didn't fall. Why would anyone want to hurt her?"

Dr. Highley looked at Katie. "Edna suffered from sciatica, and when she was laid up I occasionally dropped off work for her to do at home. Certainly not more than three or four times. On one occasion when she was supposed to be ill, I came here unexpectedly and it was then I realized that she had a serious drinking problem."

Katie looked past him and realized that Richard had completed examining the body. She got up, walked over to him and looked at Edna. Silently she prayed:

Eternal rest grant unto her, Oh Lord. May legions of angels greet her. May she be conducted to a place of refreshment, light and peace.

Swallowing over the sudden lump in her throat, she quietly asked Richard what he had found.

He shrugged. "Until I have had a chance to see how bad the fracture is, I'd say it could go either way. Certainly it was a hell of a smash, but if she was drunk—and it's obvious she was—she might have stumbled when she tried to get up. She was a pretty heavy woman. On the other hand, there's a big difference between being run over by a car and by a train. And that's the kind of difference we have to evaluate."

"Any sign of forced entry?" Katie asked Charley.

"None. But these locks are the kind you could spring with a credit card. And if she was as drunk as we think she was, anyone could have walked in on her."

"Why would anyone walk in on her? What were you telling me about Captain Lewis?"

"The superintendent's wife—name's Gana Krupshak—was a buddy of Edna Burns. Fact is, she was with Mrs. Fitzgerald when the body was found. We let her go to her own apartment just before you came. She's shook up bad. Anyhow, last night she came over here around eight o'clock. She said Edna already had a bag on. She stayed till eight thirty, then decided to put out the ham, hoping Edna would eat something and start to sober up. Edna told her about Vangie's suicide."

"Exactly *what* did she tell her?" Katie asked.

"Nothing much. Just mentioned Vangie's name and how pretty she'd been. Then Mrs. Krupshak went into the kitchen and she heard Edna dialing the phone. Mrs. Krupshak could hear most of the conversation. She swears Edna called whoever she was talking to 'Captain Lewis' and told him she had to talk to the police tomorrow. And get this. Krupshak swears she heard Edna give Lewis directions for driving here and then Edna said something about Prince Charming."

"Prince Charming!"

Charley shrugged. "Your guess is as good as mine. But the witness is positive."

Richard said, "Obviously we'll treat this as a potential homicide. I'm beginning to agree with Scott's hunch about Chris Lewis." He glanced into the living room. "Mrs. Fitzgerald looks pretty washed out. Are you through talking to her, Katie?"

"Yes. She's in no condition to question now."

"I'll get one of the squad cars to drive her home," Charley volunteered. "One of the other guys can follow in her car."

Katie thought, I do not believe Chris Lewis could have done this to Edna; I don't believe he killed his wife. She looked around. "Are you *sure* there's nothing valuable missing?"

Charley shrugged. "This whole place would go for about forty bucks in a garage sale. Her wallet's in her pocketbook; eighteen dollars there. Credit cards. The usual. No sign of anything being disturbed, let alone ransacked."

"All right." Katie returned to Dr. Highley and Gertrude. "We're going to have you driven home, Mrs. Fitzgerald," she said gently.

"What are they going to do to Edna?"

"They must investigate the extent of her head injuries. I don't think they'll probe beyond that. But if there is even the faintest chance that someone did this to Edna, we have to know it. Think of it as a way of showing we valued her life."

The woman sniffled. "I guess you're right." She looked at the doctor. "Dr. Highley, I had an awful nerve asking you to come here. I'm sorry."

"Not at all." He was reaching into his pocket. "I brought these sedatives along in case you needed them. As long as you're being driven home, take one right now."

"I'll get a glass of water," Katie said. She went to the sink in the bathroom. The bathroom and bedroom were off a rear foyer. As she let the water run cold, she realized that she hated the idea that Chris Lewis was emerging as a prime suspect in two deaths.

Taking the water glass back to Gertrude, she again sat beside her. "Mrs. Fitzgerald, just to satisfy ourselves, we want to be positive there's no possibility of Edna's having been robbed. Do you know if she kept any valuables—any jewelry, perhaps?"

"Oh, she had a ring and a pin she was so proud of. She only wore them on special occasions. I wouldn't know where she kept them. This is the first time I've been here, you see. Oh, wait a minute. Doctor, I remember that Edna said she showed you her ring and pin. In fact, she told me she showed you her hiding place for them when you were here. Perhaps you can help Mrs. DeMaio."

Katie looked into the cold gray eyes. He hates this, she thought. He's really angry to be here. He doesn't want to be part of this.

Had Edna had a crush on the doctor? she wondered suddenly. Had she exaggerated the number of times he might have dropped off work, maybe even hinted to Gertrude that he was a little interested in her? Maybe without even meaning to shade the truth, she'd invented a little romance, fantasized a possible relationship with him. If so, it was no wonder Mrs. Fitzgerald had rushed to summon him, no wonder he looked acutely embarrassed and uncomfortable now.

"I really don't know of hiding places," he said, his voice stiff with an undercurrent of sarcasm. "One time Edna did show me a pin and ring that were in a box in her night-table drawer. I hardly consider that a hiding place."

"Would you show me, Doctor?" Katie asked.

Together they walked down the short foyer into the bedroom. Katie switched on the lamp, a cheap ginger-jar base with a pleated paper shade.

"It was in there," Dr. Highley told her, pointing to the drawer in the night table on the right side of the bed.

Using only the very tips of her fingers, Katie opened the drawer. She knew that there'd probably be a complete search for evidence and the fingerprint experts would be called in.

The drawer was unexpectedly deep. Reaching into it, Katie pulled out a blue plastic jewelry case. When she raised the lid, the bell-like tinkle of a music box intruded on the somber silence. A small brooch and a thin old diamond ring were nestled against cotton velvet.

"Those are the treasures, I guess," Katie said, "and that, I would imagine, eliminates the robbery theory. We'll keep this in the office until we know who the next of kin is." She started to close the drawer, then stopped and looked down into it.

"Oh, Doctor, look." Hastily she set the jewelry box on the bed and reached into the drawer.

"My mother used to keep her mother's old battered black hat for sentimental reasons," she said. "Edna must have done the same thing."

She was tugging at an object, pulling it out, holding it up for him to see.

It was a brown moccasin, heavily scuffed, badly worn, battered and shabby. It was shaped for the left foot.

As Dr. Edgar Highley stared at the shoe, Katie said, "This was probably her mother's and she considered it such a treasure she kept it with that pathetic jewelry. Oh, Doctor, if memorabilia could talk, we'd have a lot of stories to hear, wouldn't we?"

CHAPTER 28

At precisely eight A.M. Thursday morning, the Investigative Squad of the Homicide Division of Valley County pulled up to the Lewis home. The six-man team was headed by Phil Cunningham and Charley Nugent. The detectives in charge of fingerprinting were told to concentrate on the bedroom, master bath and kitchen.

It was admittedly a slim possibility that they would find significant fingerprints that did not belong to either Chris or Vangie Lewis. But the lab report had raised another question. Vangie's fingerprints were on the tumbler that had been lying next to her, but there was some question about the positioning of those prints. Vangie had been right-handed. When she poured the cyanide crystals into the glass, it would have been natural for her to hold the glass with her left hand and pour with her right. But only her right prints were on the tumbler. It was an inconclusive, troublesome fact that further discredited the apparent suicide.

The medicine chests in both bathrooms and the guest powder room had already been searched after the body was found. Once again they were examined in minute detail. Every bottle was opened, sniffed. But the bitter-almond scent they were looking for was not to be found.

Charley said, "She must have kept the cyanide in *something*."

"Unless she was carrying just the amount she used in the glass and then flushed the envelopes or capsule she had it in down the john?" Phil suggested.

The bedroom was carefully vacuumed in the hope of finding human hair that did not come from the head of either Vangie or Chris. As Phil put it: "Any house can have hairs from delivery people, neighbors, anybody. We're all shedding hair all the time. But most people don't bring even good friends into the bedroom. So if you find human hair that doesn't belong to the people who sleep in the bedroom, you just might have something."

Particular attention was given to the shelves in the garage. The usual half-empty cans of paint, turpentine, some garden tools, hoses, insecticides, rose powder and weed killer were there in abundance. Phil grunted in annoyance as the prong of a hand spade pulled at his jacket. That prong had been protruding over the edge of the shelf, its handle wedged into place between the end of the shelf and a heavy paint can. Bending to free his sleeve, he noticed a sliver of printed cotton hooked on the prong.

That print. He'd seen it recently. It was that faded Indian stuff; madras. The dress Vangie Lewis was wearing when she died.

He called the police photographer out to the garage. "Get a picture of that," he said, pointing to the tool. "I want a close-up of that material." When the picture was taken, he carefully removed the piece of material from the prong and sealed it in an envelope.

In the house, Charley was going through the desk in the living room. Funny, he thought. You can get a real slant on people from the way they keep their records. Chris Lewis obviously had taken care of all the bookkeeping in the family. The checkbook stubs were precisely written, the balances accurate to the penny. Bills were apparently paid in full as they came in. The large bottom drawer held upright files. They were alphabetically arranged: AMERICAN EXPRESS; BANK AMERICARD; FEDERATED ANSWERING SERVICE; INSURANCE; PERSONAL LETTERS.

Charley reached for the personal-letter file. Quickly he leafed through it. Chris Lewis maintained a regular correspondence with his mother. *Many thanks for the check, Chris. You shouldn't be so generous.* That was written only two weeks ago. A January letter began: *Got Dad the TV for the bedroom and he's enjoying it so much.* One from last July: *The new air conditioner is such a blessing.*

If Charley was disappointed at not finding more significant personal data, he did admit grudgingly that Christopher Lewis was a concerned and generous son to aging parents. He reread the mother's letters, hoping for clues to Vangie and Chris's relationship. The recent letters all ended the same way: *Sorry Vangie isn't feeling well* or *Women do sometimes have difficult pregnancies* or *Tell Vangie we're rooting for her.*

At noon, Charley and Phil decided to leave the rest of the team to complete the search and return to the office themselves. They were scheduled to meet Chris Lewis' plane at six o'clock. They had ruled out forced entry. There was no trace of cyanide in the house or garage. The contents of Vangie's stomach revealed that she'd eaten lightly on Monday; that she had probably had toast and tea about five hours before she died. A new loaf of bread in the bread box had two slices missing. The soiled dishes in the dishwasher told their own story: a single dinner plate, cup and saucer, salad dish, probably from Sunday night; a juice glass and cup, Monday's breakfast; a cup, saucer and plate with toast crumbs from the Monday supper.

Vangie had apparently dined alone Sunday night; no one had eaten with her Monday night. The coffee mug in the sink had not been there Tuesday morning. Undoubtedly Chris Lewis had made himself instant coffee sometime after the body was found.

The driveway and grounds were being searched with minute care and so far revealed nothing unusual.

"They'll be at this all day, but we haven't missed anything," Charley said flatly. "And other than the fact that she tore her dress on that prong on the garage shelf, we've come up with a big zero. Wait a minute. We still haven't checked the answering service for messages."

He got the Federated Answering Service number from the file in the desk, dialed and identified himself. "Give me any messages left for either Captain or Mrs. Lewis starting with Monday," he ordered.

Taking out his pen, he began to write. Phil looked over his shoulder: *Monday, February 15, 4:00 p.m. Northwest Orient Reservations phoned. Mrs. Lewis is confirmed on Flight 235 at 4:10 p.m. from La-Guardia Airport to the Twin Cities of Minneapolis/St. Paul on Tuesday, February 16.*

Phil whistled silently. Charley asked, "Did Mrs. Lewis receive that message?"

He held the phone slightly away from his ear so that Phil could hear. "Oh, yes," the operator said. "I was on the board myself Monday evening and gave it to her at about seven thirty." The operator's voice was emphatic. "She sounded very relieved. In fact, she said, 'Oh, thank God.' "

"All right," Charley said. "What else have you got?"

"Monday, February fifteenth, nine thirty P.M. Dr. Fukhito left word for Mrs. Lewis to call him at home as soon as she got in. He said she had his home number."

Charley raised one eyebrow. "Is that it?"

"Just one more," the operator replied. "A Miss Edna Burns called Mrs. Lewis at ten P.M. Monday. She wanted Mrs. Lewis to be sure and phone her no matter how late it was."

Charley doodled triangles on the pad as the operator told him that there were no further messages on the service for either Tuesday or Wednesday, but that she knew a call had come through Tuesday evening and had been picked up by Captain Lewis. "I was just starting to answer when he came on," she explained. "I got right off." In reply to Charley's question, she affirmed that Mrs. Lewis had not learned about either Dr. Fukhito's or Miss Burns's call. Mrs. Lewis had not contacted the service after seven thirty on Monday night.

"Thank you," Charley said. "You've been very helpful. We'll probably want a complete file of messages you've taken for the Lewises going back some time, but we'll be in touch about that later on."

He hung up the receiver and looked at Phil. "Let's go. Scott's going to want to hear all about this."

"How do you read it?" Phil asked.

Charley snorted. "How else can I read it? As of seven thirty Monday evening Vangie Lewis was planning to go to Minneapolis. A couple of hours later she's dead. As of ten o'clock Monday night, Edna Burns had an important message for Vangie. The next night Edna's dead and the last person who saw her alive heard her talking to Chris Lewis telling him she had information for the police."

"What about that Japanese shrink who called Vangie Monday night?" Phil asked.

Charley shrugged. "Katie talked to him yesterday. She may have some answers for us."

⚘ *CHAPTER 29*

For Katie, Wednesday night seemed endless. She'd gone to bed as soon as she returned from Edna's apartment, remembering first to take one of the pills Dr. Highley had given her.

She'd slept fitfully, her subconscious restless with images of Vangie's face floating through a dream. Before she woke up, that dream dissolved into a new one: Edna's face as it had looked in death; Dr. Highley and Richard bending over her.

She'd awakened with vague, troubling questions that eluded her, refusing to come into focus. Her grandmother's battered old black hat. Why was she thinking about that hat? Of course. Because of that shabby old shoe Edna obviously prized; the one she had kept with her jewelry. That was it. But why just *one* shoe?

Grimacing as she got out of bed, she decided that the soreness throughout her body had intensified during the night. Her knees, bruised from slamming into the dashboard, felt stiffer now than they had right after the accident. I'm glad the Boston Marathon isn't being run today, she thought wryly. I'd never win.

Hoping that a hot bath might soak some of the achiness away, she went into the bathroom, leaned down and turned on the taps in the tub. A wave of dizziness made her sway, and she grabbed the side of the tub to keep from falling. After a few moments the sensation receded, and she turned slowly, afraid that she might still faint. The bathroom mirror revealed the deathly pallor of her skin, the faint beads of perspiration on her forehead. It's this damn bleeding, she thought. If I weren't going into the hospital tomorrow night, I'd probably end up being carried in.

The bath did reduce some of the stiffness. Beige foundation makeup minimized the paleness. A new outfit—a shirred skirt and matching jacket in heather tweed and a crew-neck sweater—completed the attempt at camouflage. At least now I don't look as though I'm about to fall on my face, she decided, even if I am.

With her orange juice she swallowed another of Dr. Highley's pills and thought about the still-incredible fact of Edna's death. After they left Edna's apartment, she and Richard had gone to a diner for coffee. Richard ordered a hamburger, explaining that he'd planned to have dinner in New York. He'd been taking someone out. She was sure of it. And why not? Richard was an attractive man. He certainly didn't spend all his evenings sitting in his own apartment or in family situations at Molly and Bill's. Richard had been surprised and pleased when she told him that she'd gone back to the Palisades restaurant. Then he'd become preoccupied, almost absentminded. Several times he'd seemed to be on the verge of asking her a question, then apparently changed his mind. Even though she protested, he'd insisted on following her home, going into the house with her, checking that doors and windows were locked.

"I don't know why I feel uncomfortable about you alone in this place," he'd told her.

She'd shrugged. "Edna was in a garden apartment with thin walls. No one realized she was hurt and needed help."

"She didn't," Richard said shortly. "She died almost instantly. Katie, that Dr. Highley. You know him?"

"I questioned him about Vangie this afternoon," she'd hedged.

Richard's frown had lightened. "Of course. All right. See you tomorrow. I imagine Scott will call a meeting about Edna Burns."

"I'm sure he will."

Richard had looked at her, his expression troubled. "Bolt the door," he'd said. There had been no lighthearted good-bye kiss on the cheek.

Katie put her orange-juice glass in the dishwasher. Hurriedly she grabbed a coat and her handbag and went out to the car.

Charley and Phil were beginning the search of the Lewis house this morning. Scott was consciously drawing a web around Chris Lewis—a circumstantial web, but a strong one. If only she could prove that there was another avenue to explore before Chris was indicted. The trouble with being arrested on a homicide charge is that even if you prove your innocence, you never lose the notoriety. In years to come people would be saying, "Oh, that's Captain Lewis. He was involved in his wife's death. Some smart lawyer got him off, but he's guilty as sin."

She arrived at the office just before seven thirty and wasn't surprised to find Maureen Crowley already there. Maureen was the most conscientious secretary they had. Beyond that, she had a naturally keen mind and could handle assignments without constantly asking for direction. Katie stopped at her desk. "Maureen, I've got a job. Could you come in when you have a minute?"

The girl got up quickly. She had a narrow-waisted, graceful young body. The green sweater she was wearing accentuated the vivid green of her eyes. "How about now, Katie? Want coffee?"

"Great," Katie replied, then added, "but no ham on rye—at least, not yet."

Maureen looked embarrassed. "I'm sorry I said that yesterday. You, of all people, are not in a rut."

"I'm not sure about that." Katie went into her office, hung up her coat and settled down with the pad she'd used at Westlake Hospital.

Maureen brought in the coffee, pulled up a chair and waited silently, her steno book on her lap.

"Here's the problem," Katie said slowly. "We're not satisfied that the Vangie Lewis death is a suicide. Yesterday I talked with her doctors, Dr. Highley and Dr. Fukhito, at Westlake Hospital."

She heard a sharp intake of breath and looked up quickly. The girl's face had gone dead white. As Katie watched, two bright spots darkened her cheekbones.

"Maureen, is anything the matter?"

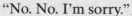

"No. No. I'm sorry."

"Did I say anything to startle you?"

"No. Really."

"All right." Unconvinced, Katie looked back at her pad. "As far as we know, Dr. Fukhito, the psychiatrist at Westlake, was the last person to see Vangie Lewis alive. I want to find out as much as I can about him as fast as possible. Check the Valley County Medical Society and the AMA. I've heard he does volunteer work at Valley Pines Hospital. Maybe you can learn something there. Emphasize the confidentiality, but find out where he came from, where he went to school, other hospitals he's been connected with, his personal background: whatever you can get."

"You don't want me to talk to anyone at Westlake Hospital?"

"Good heavens, no. I don't want anyone there to have any idea we're checking on Dr. Fukhito."

For some reason the younger woman seemed relieved. "I'll get right on it, Katie."

"It's not really fair to have you come in early to do other work and then throw a job at you. Good old Valley County isn't into overtime. We both know that."

Maureen shrugged. "That doesn't matter. The more I do in this office, the more I like it. Who knows? I may go for a law degree myself, but that means four years of college and three years of law school."

"You'd be a good lawyer," Katie said, meaning it. "I'm surprised you didn't go to college."

"I was insane enough to get engaged the summer I finished high school. My folks persuaded me to take the secretarial course before I got married so at least I'd have some kind of skill. How right they were. The engagement didn't stand the wait."

"Why didn't you start college last September instead of coming to work?" Katie asked.

The girl's face became brooding. Katie thought how unhappy she looked and decided that Maureen must have been pretty hurt about the breakup.

Not quite looking at Katie, Maureen said, "I was feeling restless and didn't want to settle down to being a schoolgirl. It was a good decision."

She went out of the room. The telephone rang. It was Richard. His voice was guarded. "Katie, I've just been talking to Dave Broad, the head of prenatal research at Mt. Sinai. On a hunch, I sent the fetus Vangie Lewis was carrying over to him. Katie, my hunch was right. *Vangie was not pregnant with Chris Lewis' child. The baby I took from her womb has distinctly Oriental characteristics!*"

Edgar Highley stared at Katie DeMaio as she stood with that shoe in her hand, holding it out to him. Was she mocking him? No. She believed what she was saying, that the shoe had had some sentimental memory for Edna.

He *had* to have that shoe. If only she didn't talk about it to the Medical Examiner or the detectives. Suppose she decided to show it to them? Gertrude Fitzgerald might recognize it. She'd been at the desk many times when Vangie came in. He'd heard Edna joke with her about Vangie's glass slippers.

Katie put the shoe back, closed the drawer and walked out of the bedroom, the jewelry box tucked under her arm. He followed her, desperate to hear what she would say. But she simply handed the jewelry box to the detective. "The ring and pin are here, Charley," she said. "I guess that shoots any possibility of burglary. I didn't go through the bureau or closet."

"It doesn't matter. If Richard suspects wrongful death, we'll search this place with a fine-tooth comb in the morning."

There was a staccato rap at the door, and Katie opened it to admit two men carrying a stretcher.

Edgar Highley walked back to Gertrude. She had drunk the water in the glass Katie had given her. "I'll get you more water, Mrs. Fitzgerald," he said quietly. He glanced over his shoulder. The others all had their backs to him, as they watched the attendants prepare to lift the body. It was his chance. He had to risk taking the shoe. As long as Katie hadn't mentioned it immediately, it was unlikely she'd bring it up now.

He walked rapidly to the bathroom, turned on the tap and slipped across the hall to the bedroom. Using his handkerchief to avoid fingerprints, he opened the night-table drawer. He was just reaching for the shoe when he heard footsteps coming down the hall. Quickly he pushed the drawer shut, stuffed his handkerchief into his pocket and was standing at the door of the bedroom when the footsteps stopped.

Willing himself to appear calm, he turned. Richard Carroll, the Medical Examiner, was standing in the foyer between the bedroom and the bathroom. His eyes were questioning. "Doctor," he said, "I'd like to ask you a few questions about Edna Burns." His voice was cold.

"Certainly." Then, in what he hoped was a casual tone, he added, "I have just been standing here thinking of Miss Burns. What a shame her life was so wasted."

"Wasted?" Richard's voice was sharply questioning.

"Yes. She actually had a good mathematical mind. In this computer age Edna might have used that talent to make something of herself. Instead, she became an overweight, gossiping alcoholic. If that seems harsh, I say it with real regret. I was fond of Edna, and quite frankly I shall miss her. Excuse me. I'm letting the water run. I want to give Mrs. Fitzgerald a glass of cold water. Poor woman, she's terribly distressed."

Dr. Carroll stood aside to let him pass. Had his criticism of Edna distracted the Medical Examiner from wondering what he was doing in Edna's room?

He rinsed the glass, filled it and brought it to Gertrude. The attendants had left with the body, and Katie DeMaio was not in the room.

"Has Mrs. DeMaio left?" he asked the detective.

"No. She's talking to the super's wife. She'll be right back."

He did not want to leave himself until he was sure that Katie did not talk about the shoe in front of Gertrude. But when she came back a few minutes later, she did not mention it.

They left the apartment together. The local police would keep it under surveillance until the official search was completed.

Deliberately he walked with Katie to her car, but then the Medical Examiner joined them. "Let's have coffee, Katie," he said. "You know where the Golden Valley diner is, don't you?"

The Medical Examiner waited until she was in the car and had started to pull out before he said, "Good night, Dr. Highley" and abruptly left.

As he drove home, Edgar Highley decided there was a personal relationship of some sort between Katie DeMaio and Richard Carroll. When Katie bled to death, Richard Carroll would be both professionally and emotionally interested in the cause of death. He would have to be very, very careful.

There was hostility in Carroll's attitude toward him. But Carroll had no reason to be hostile to him. Should he have gone over to Edna's body? But what would have been the point? He should not have pushed her so hard. Should he have robbed her? That had been his original intention. If he had, he would have found the shoe last night.

But Edna had talked. Edna had told Gertrude that he'd been at her apartment. Edna might even have made it sound more frequent, more important. Gertrude had told Katie that he knew where the pitiful jewelry was kept. If they decided Edna had been murdered, would they tie the murder to Edna's job at the hospital? What else had Edna told people?

The thought haunted him as he drove home.

Katie was the key. Katie DeMaio. With her safely out of the way there was no evidence to tie him to Vangie's death—or Edna's. The

office files were in perfect order. The current patients could bear the most minute scrutiny.

He turned into his driveway, drove into the garage, entered the house. The lamb chops were on the plate, cold and edged with grease; the asparagus had wilted, the salad was limp and warm. He would reheat the food in the microwave oven, prepare a fresh salad. In a few minutes the table would look as it had before the phone call.

As he once again prepared the food, he found himself becoming calm. He was so near to being safe. And soon it would be possible to share his genius with the world. He already had his success. He could prove it beyond doubt. Someday he would be able to proclaim it. Not yet, but someday. And he wouldn't be like that braggart who claimed to have successfully cloned but refused to offer even a shred of proof. He had accurate records, scientific documentation, pictures, X-rays, the step-by-step, day-by-day accounts of all the problems that had arisen and how he had dealt with them. All in the files in his secret safe.

When the proper time came he would burn the files about the failures and claim the recognition that was due him. By then there would surely be more triumphs.

Nothing must stand in his way. Vangie had nearly spoiled everything. Suppose he had not met her just as she came out of Fukhito's office? Suppose she hadn't told him about her decision to consult Emmet Salem?

Happenstance. Luck. Call it what you will.

But it had also been happenstance that sent Katie DeMaio to the window just as he left with Vangie's body. And exquisite irony that Katie had come to him in the first place.

Once again he sat down at the table. With intense satisfaction he saw that the dinner looked as appetizing, as delicious as when he'd first prepared it. The watercress was crisp and fresh; the chops bubbling; the asparagus piping hot under a delicate hollandaise. He poured wine into a thin goblet, admiring the delicate satiny feel of the crystal as he picked it up. The wine had the hearty Burgundy flavor he'd been anticipating.

He ate slowly. As always, food restored his sense of well-being. He would do what he must, and then he'd be safe.

Tomorrow was Thursday. The *Newsmaker* article would be on the stands. It would enhance his social as well as his medical prestige.

The fact that he was a widower lent him a specific appeal. He knew how his patients talked. "Dr. Highley is so brilliant. He's so distinguished. He has a beautiful home in Parkwood."

After Winifred's death, he had allowed his connections with her friends to lapse. There was too much hostility there. That cousin of hers kept making insinuations. He knew it. That was why these three years he hadn't bothered with another woman. Not that he found solitude a sacrifice. His work was all-absorbing, all-satisfying. The time dedicated to it had been rewarded. His worst professional critics admitted that he was a good doctor, that the hospital was magnificently equipped, that the Westlake Maternity Concept was being copied by other physicians.

"My patients are not allowed to drink or smoke during their pregnancies," he had told the *Newsmaker* interviewer. "They are required to follow a specific diet. Many so-called barren women would have the babies they want if they would show the same dedication as athletes in training. Many of the long-range health problems suffered today would have been prevented entirely if mothers had not been eating the wrong food, taking the wrong medication. We have had the visible example of what Thalidomide did to scores of unfortunate victims. We recognize that a mother on drugs may produce an infant addict; an alcoholic mother will often be delivered of a retarded, undersized, emotionally disturbed child. But what of the many problems that we consider simply the lot of man . . . Bronchitis, dyslexia, hyperactivity, asthma, hearing and sight impairment? I believe that the place to eliminate these is not in the laboratory, but in the womb. I will not accept a patient who will not cooperate with my methods. I can show you dozens of women I have treated with a history of several miscarriages who now have children. Many more could experience that same joy, *if* they were willing to change their habits, particularly their eating and drinking habits. Many others would conceive and bear a child if their emotions were not so disturbed that in effect they are wearing mental contraceptives far more efficient than any device for sale in the drugstore. This is the reason, the basis of the Westlake Maternity Concept."

The *Newsmaker* reporter had been impressed. But her next question was a loaded one. "Doctor, isn't it a fact that you have been criticized for the exorbitant fees you charge?"

"Exorbitant is *your* word. My fees, aside from rather spartan living expenses, are spent to develop the hospital and to pursue prenatal study."

"Doctor, isn't it a fact that a large percentage of your cases have been women who miscarried several times under your care, even *after* following your schedule rigidly—and paying you ten thousand dollars, plus all hospital and lab expenses?"

"It would be insanity for me to claim that I could bring every difficult pregnancy to term. Yes. There have been cases where the desired pregnancy was begun, but spontaneously aborted. After several of these occurrences, I suggest that my patient adopt a child and help to arrange a suitable adoption."

"For a fee."

"Young woman, I assume you are being paid to interview me. Why don't *you* use your time for volunteer work?"

It had been foolish to attack the reporter like that. Foolish to risk animosity, foolish to give her any reason to discredit him, to delve too deeply into his background. He'd told her that he'd been obstetrical chief in Liverpool before his marriage to Winifred. But of course he hadn't discussed Christ Hospital in Devon.

The interviewer's next question had been meant to entrap him.

"Doctor, you perform abortions, do you not?"

"Yes, I do."

"Isn't that incongruous for an obstetrician? To try to save one fetus and to eliminate another?"

"I refer to the womb as a cradle. I despise abortion. And I deplore the grief I witness when women come to me who have no hope of conceiving because they have had abortions and their wombs have been pierced by stupid, blundering, careless doctors. I think everyone—and I include my colleagues—would be astounded to learn how many women have denied themselves any hope of motherhood because they decided to defer that motherhood by abortion. It is my wish that all women carry their babies to healthy term. For those who do not want to, at least I can make sure that when they eventually want a child, they will still be able to have one."

That point had been well received. The reporter's attitude had changed.

He finished eating. Now he leaned back in the chair and poured more wine into his glass. He was feeling expansive, comfortable. The laws were changing. In a few years he'd be able to announce his genius without fear of prosecution. Vangie Lewis, Edna Burns, Winifred, Claire . . . they'd be unrelated statistics. The trail would be cold.

He studied the wine as he drank, refilled his glass and drank again. He was tired. Tomorrow morning he had a cesarean section scheduled—another difficult case that would add to his reputation. It had been a difficult pregnancy, but the fetus had a strong heartbeat; it should be delivered safely. The mother was a member of the socially prominent Payne family. The father, Delano Aldrich, was an officer of the Rockefeller Foundation. This was the sort of family whose championship would make the difference if the Devon scandal were ever to surface again.

Only one obstacle left. He had brought Katie DeMaio's file home from the office. He would begin now to prepare the substitute file that he would show to the police after her death.

Instead of the history she'd given him of prolonged periods of bleeding over the past year, he would write, "Patient complains of frequent and spontaneous hemorrhaging, unrelated to monthly cycles." Instead of sponginess of uterine walls, probably familial, a condition that would be remedied indefinitely by a simple D-and-C, he would note findings of vascular breakdown. Instead of a slightly low hemoglobin he would indicate that the hemoglobin was chronically in the danger zone.

He went into the library. The file marked KATHLEEN DeMAIO which he had taken from the office was on top of his desk. From the drawer he extracted a new file and put Katie's name on it. For half an hour he worked steadily, consulting the office file for information on her previous medical history. Finally he was finished. He would bring the revised file with him to the hospital. He added several paragraphs to the file he had taken from the office, the one he would put in the wall safe when completed.

Patient was in minor automobile accident on Monday night, February 15. At 2:00 a.m. patient, in sedated condition, observed from the window of her room the transferral of the remains of Vangie Lewis by this physician. Patient still does not understand that what she observed was a true event rather than an hallucination. Patient is slightly traumatized by accident, and persistent hemorrhaging. Inevitably she will be able to achieve clear recollection of what she observed and for this reason cannot be permitted to remain as a threat to this physician.

Patient received blood transfusion on Monday night in emergency room of hospital. This physician prescribed second transfusion on pretense of preparation for Saturday surgery. This physician also administered anticoagulant medication, cumadin pills to be taken on regular basis until Friday night.

Pursing his lips, he laid down the pen. It was easy to imagine how he would complete this report.

Patient entered the hospital at 6:00 p.m. Friday, February 19, complaining of dizziness and general weakness. At 9:00 p.m. this physician, accompanied by Nurse Renge, found the patient hemorrhaging. Blood pressure was falling rapidly. With whole blood hanging, emergency surgery was performed at 9:45 p.m.

The patient, Kathleen Noel DeMaio, expired at 10:00 p.m.

He smiled in anticipation of completing this troublesome case. Every detail was perfectly planned, even to assigning Nurse Renge to floor duty Friday night. She was young, inexperienced and terrified of him.

After putting the file in the temporary hiding place in the top desk drawer, he went upstairs to bed and slept soundly until six in the morning.

Three hours later he delivered a healthy baby boy by cesarean section to Mrs. Delano Aldrich and accepted as his due the tearful gratitude of the patient and her husband.

≈ CHAPTER 31

The funeral service for Vangie was held on Thursday morning at ten o'clock in the chapel of a Minneapolis funeral home. His heart aching with pity for Vangie's parents, Chris stood beside them, their muffled sobs assaulting him like hammer blows. Could he have done things differently? If he had not at first tried to placate Vangie, would she be lying here now? If he'd insisted that she go with him to a marriage counselor years ago, would it have helped their marriage? He had suggested that to her. But she had refused. "I don't need any counseling," she'd said. "And don't you suggest anytime I get upset about anything that there's something the matter with me. It's the other way around. You never get upset about anything; you don't care about anything or anybody. You're the problem, not me."

Oh, Vangie. Vangie. Was truth somewhere in the middle? He had stopped caring very early in their marriage.

Her parents had been outraged to hear that Vangie could not be buried, that her body was to be shipped back east. "Why?"

"I simply don't know." There was no use in answering beyond that—not now.

"Amazing grace, how sweet the sound." The soloist's soprano voice filled the chapel. "I once was lost but now am found."

Months ago, last summer, he'd felt life was bleak and hopeless. Then he'd gone to that party in Hawaii. And Joan had been there. He could remember the precise moment he'd seen her. She was on the terrace in a group of people. Whatever she'd said made them all laugh, and she'd laughed too, her eyes crinkling, her lips parting, her head tilting back. He'd gotten a drink and joined that group. And he hadn't left Joan's side again that evening.

". . . was blind and now I see." The Medical Examiner would not have released Vangie's body Tuesday night if he'd suspected foul play. What had happened to change his mind?

He thought of Edna's call. How much talking had she done to other people? Could she throw some light on Vangie's death? Before he left Minneapolis, he had to call Dr. Salem. He had to find out what he knew about Vangie that had made him react with such shock last night. Why had Vangie made an appointment to see him?

There had been someone else in Vangie's life. He was sure of it now. Suppose Vangie had killed herself in front of someone and that person brought her home? God knew she'd have had plenty of opportunity to be involved with another man. He was away from home at least half the month. Maybe she had met someone after they moved to New Jersey.

But would Vangie have caused herself pain?

Never!

The minister was saying the final prayer. ". . . when every tear shall be dried . . ." Chris led Vangie's parents into the anteroom and accepted the expressions of sympathy from the friends who had attended the service. Vangie's parents were going to stay with relatives. They had agreed that the body should be cremated in New Jersey and the urn returned to be buried in the family plot.

Finally Chris was able to get away. It was just after eleven o'clock when he arrived at the Athletic Club in downtown Minneapolis and took the elevator to the fourteenth floor. There in the solarium he ordered a Bloody Mary and took it to a phone.

When he reached Dr. Salem's office, he said, "This is Vangie Lewis' husband. It's urgent I speak with the doctor immediately."

"I'm sorry," the nurse told him. "Dr. Salem left a short time ago for the American Medical Association convention in New York. He will not be back until next week."

"New York." Chris digested the information. "Can you tell me where he's staying, please? It may be necessary for me to contact him there."

The nurse hesitated. "I suppose it's all right to tell you that. I'm sure Dr. Salem intends to get in touch with you. He asked me to look up your New Jersey phone number, and I know he took your wife's medical records with him. But just in case he misses you, you can reach him at the Essex House on Central Park South in New York City. His extension there is 3219."

Chris had pulled out the small notebook that he kept in a compartment of his wallet. Repeating the information, he wrote it down quickly.

The top of the page was already filled. On it were Edna Burns's address and the directions to her apartment in Edgeriver.

CHAPTER 32

S cott called a noon meeting in his office with the same four people
who had been present at the meeting a day and a half earlier to discuss Vangie Lewis' death.

This meeting was different. Katie could feel the heightened atmosphere as she went into the office. Scott had Maureen waiting with a
pen and paper.

"We're bringing sandwiches in here," he said. "I'm due in court again
at one thirty and we've got to move fast on Captain Lewis."

It was as she'd expected, Katie thought. Scott is zeroing in on Chris.
She looked at Maureen. The girl had an aura of nervousness around her
that was almost visible. It started when I gave her that assignment this
morning, Katie thought.

Maureen caught her glance and half-smiled. Katie nodded. "Uh-huh.
The usual." Then added, "Did you have any luck with the phoning?"

Maureen looked at Scott, but he was scanning a file and ignoring
them. "So far not much. Dr. Fukhito's not a member of the AMA or the
Valley County Medical Society. He donates a lot of his time to disturbed children at Valley Pines Psychiatric Clinic. I have a call in to the
University of Massachusetts. He attended medical school there."

"Who told you that?" Katie asked.

Maureen hesitated. "I remember hearing it somewhere."

Katie had a feeling of evasiveness in the answer, but before she could
probe further, Richard, Charley and Phil came into the office together.
Quickly they gave their lunch choices to Maureen, and Richard pulled
a chair next to Katie's. He tossed his arm over her chair and touched the
back of her head. His fingers were warm and strong as for an instant he
massaged her neck muscles. "Boy, are you tense," he said.

Scott looked up, grunted, and began to speak. "All right, by now you
all know that the baby Vangie Lewis was carrying had Oriental characteristics. So that opens two possibilities. One: with the birth imminent
it's possible she panicked and killed herself. She must have been frantic
knowing she could never pass the baby off as her husband's. The second
possibility is that Christopher Lewis found out that his wife had been
having an affair and killed her. Let's try this. Suppose he went home
unexpectedly Monday evening. They quarreled. Why was she rushing
home to Minneapolis? Was it because she was afraid of him? Don't forget, he never admitted she was going home and she expected to be gone
before he returned from his trip. From what Katie tells us, the psychiatrist claims she ran out of his office nearly hysterical.

"The *Japanese* psychiatrist," Katie said. "I have Maureen checking on him right now."

Scott looked at her. "Are you suggesting that you think there was something between him and Vangie?"

"I'm not suggesting anything yet," Katie replied. "The fact that he's Oriental certainly doesn't say that Vangie didn't know another Oriental man. But I can tell you this. He was nervous when I spoke with him yesterday, and he was carefully choosing every word he said to me. I certainly did not get the whole truth from him."

"Which brings us to Edna Burns," Scott said. "What about it, Richard? Did she fall or was she pushed?"

Richard shrugged. "It is not impossible that she fell. The alcohol level in her blood was point two five. She was blotto. She was heavy."

"What about that business of drunks and babies' being able to fall without getting hurt?" Katie asked.

Richard shook his head. "That may be true about breaking bones, but not when your skull cracks into a sharp metal object. I would say that unless someone admits killing Edna, we'll never be able to prove it."

"But it is possible she was murdered?" Scott persisted.

He shrugged. "Absolutely."

"And Edna was heard talking to Chris Lewis about Prince Charming." Katie spoke slowly. She thought of the handsome psychiatrist. Would someone like Edna refer to *him* as Prince Charming? Would she have called Chris after Vangie's death to tell him she suspected an affair? "I don't believe that," she said.

The men looked at her curiously. "What don't you believe?" Scott asked.

"I don't believe that Edna was vicious. I know she wasn't. I don't think she ever would have called Chris Lewis after Vangie died to hurt him by telling him about an affair Vangie was having."

"She may have felt sorry enough for him that she didn't want him to consider himself a bereaved husband," Richard said.

"Or she may have been looking for a few bucks," Charley suggested. "Maybe Vangie told her something Monday night. Maybe she knew Chris and Vangie had quarreled and why they'd quarreled. She had nothing. Apparently she was still paying off medical bills for her parents, and they've been dead a couple of years. Maybe she didn't think there was any harm in putting the arm on Lewis. She did threaten to go to the police."

"She said she had something to tell the police," Katie objected. "That's the way the super's wife put it."

"All right," Scott said. "What about the Lewis house? What did you turn up?"

Charley shrugged. "So far, not much. There's a phone number with a 621 area code scribbled on the pad beside the kitchen phone. It's not Vangie's parents' number, we know that. We thought we'd call it from here. Maybe Vangie was talking to a friend, gave some of her plans. The other thing is that she tore that dress she was wearing on a prong sticking out from the shelf in the garage."

"What do you mean the dress she was wearing?" Scott demanded.

"The dress she was found in. You couldn't miss it. It was a long job with one of those madras print designs."

"Where are the clothes she was wearing?" Scott asked Richard.

"The lab probably still has them," Richard said. "We were going over them on a routine check."

Scott picked up the message pad Charley had handed him and tossed it to Katie. "Why don't you dial this now? If it's a woman, you might get more out of her."

Katie dialed the number. There was a pause and then a phone began ringing. "Dr. Salem's office."

"It's a doctor's office," she whispered, her hand over the phone. To the person on the other end she said, "Perhaps you can help me. I'm Kathleen DeMaio from the Valley County, New Jersey, Prosecutor's office. We're conducting a routine inquiry into the death of Mrs. Vangie Lewis last Monday, and she had the doctor's phone number on her pad."

She was interrupted: "Oh, that is a coincidence. I just hung up with Captain Lewis. He's trying to reach the doctor too. As I explained to him, Dr. Salem is on his way to New York right now to the AMA convention. You can reach him later in the day at the Essex House Hotel on Central Park South."

"Fine. We'll do that." On a chance, Katie added, "Do you know anything about Mrs. Lewis' call? Did she speak with the doctor?"

"No. She did not. She spoke to me. She called Monday and was so disappointed that he wasn't going to be back in his office till Wednesday. I made an emergency appointment for her on Wednesday because he was going right out again. She said she had to see him."

"One last question," Katie said: "What kind of doctor is Dr. Salem?"

The woman's tone became proud. "Oh, he's a prominent obstetrician and gynecologist."

"I see. Thank you. You've been very helpful." Katie hung up the phone and reported the conversation to the others.

"And Chris Lewis knew about the appointment," Scott said, "and he wants to talk to the doctor now. I can't wait to get at him tonight. We'll have a lot of questions for him."

There was a knock at the door and Maureen came in without waiting for a response. She was carrying a cardboard tray with inserts for coffee cups and a bag of sandwiches. "Katie," she said, "that call from Boston about Dr. Fukhito is just coming in. Do you want to take it?"

Katie nodded. Richard reached over and picked up the phone, holding it out to her. As she waited for the call to be switched, Katie became aware of a slow, persistent headache. That rap against the steering wheel hadn't been hard enough for a concussion, but she realized that her head had been bothering her the last few days. I just am not operating on all cylinders, she thought. So many things were teasing her mind. What was she trying to recall? Something. Some impression.

When she explained her credentials, she was quickly switched to the head of personnel at the University of Massachusetts Medical School. The man's voice was guarded. "Yes, Dr. Fukhito graduated from U Mass in the first third of his class. He interned at Massachusetts General and later became affiliated with the hospital and also had a private practice. He left the hospital seven years ago."

"Why did he leave?" Katie asked. "You must understand a police investigation. All information will be kept confidential, but we must know if there are any factors in Dr. Fukhito's past that we should be aware of."

There was a pause; then the informant said, "Dr. Fukhito was asked to resign seven years ago, and his Massachusetts license was suspended for a period of one year. He was found guilty of unethical behavior after he unsuccessfully defended a malpractice suit."

"What was the cause of the suit?" Katie asked.

"A former patient sued Dr. Fukhito for inducing her to have a personal relationship with him when she was under psychiatric treatment. She had recently been divorced and was in great emotional difficulty. As a result of that relationship she bore Dr. Fukhito's child."

CHAPTER 33

Molly bustled around her kitchen rejoicing in the fact that all the children were back in school. Even twelve-year-old Jennifer had been well enough to go this morning; in fact, had pleaded to go. "You're just like Katie," Molly had scolded, "when you set your head to anything. Well, all right, but you can't walk. It's too cold. I'll drive you."

Bill was not going into New York until the afternoon. He was planning to attend one of the seminars at the AMA convention. They were

enjoying a rare chance to chat in peace as Bill sat at the table sipping coffee and Molly sliced vegetables. "I'm sure Katie and Richard and the Berkeleys will enjoy each other," Molly was saying. "Jim Berkeley is bright and he's a lot of fun. Why is it that most people in advertising really *are* so interesting?"

"Because their stock in trade is words," Bill suggested. "Although I must say I've met some that I wouldn't spend time looking up again."

"Oh, sure," Molly agreed absently. "Now, if Liz just doesn't spend the whole evening talking about the baby . . . Although I must say she's getting better about that. When I phoned to invite her the other day she only spent the first twenty minutes on Maryanne's latest trick . . . which, incidentally, is to blow her oatmeal all over the place as she's being fed. Isn't that cute?"

"It is if it's your first baby and you waited fifteen years to have one," Bill commented. "I seem to remember every time Jennifer blinked you recorded it in her baby book."

Molly began slicing celery. "Remember your aunt gave me a baby book to keep for the twins. I don't think I ever got the wrapping paper off it. . . . Anyhow, it should be fun. And even if Liz does rave about the baby, maybe a little of it will sink in on Katie and Richard."

Bill's eyebrows rose. "Molly, you're about as subtle as a sledgehammer. You'd better watch out or they'll start avoiding each other completely."

"Nonsense. Don't you see the way they look at each other? There's something smoldering—better than smoldering—there. My God, Richard called me last night to see if Katie was here and then wanted to know if there was something the matter with her. You should have heard how worried he sounded. I tell you he's crazy about her, but just is smart enough not to show it and scare her off."

"Did you tell him about the operation?"

"No. Katie gave me hell the other morning when I asked if she had told him. Honest to God, the way most people let everything hang out these days . . . Look, why can't she just say to Richard, 'I've got this problem, it's a nuisance, Mother had it and had to have a D-and-C every couple of years, and it looks like I'm built like her'? Instead, the poor guy is obviously worried that it's something serious. I don't think it's fair to him."

Bill got up, walked over to the sink, rinsed out his cup and saucer and put them in the dishwasher. "I don't think you have ever realized that Katie has been desperately hurt by losing the two men she loved and counted on . . . your father when she was eight, and then John when she was twenty-four. She reminds me of the last scene in *Gone with the Wind* when Rhett says to Scarlett, 'I gave my heart to you and you broke it. Then I gave it to Bonnie and she broke it. I'll not risk it a third time.' That's something of Katie's problem. But frankly, I think she's got to work it out herself. Your hovering over her like a mother hawk isn't helping her. I'd like nothing better than to see her get together with Richard Carroll. He'd be good for her."

"And he plays golf with you," Molly interjected.

Bill nodded. "That too." He picked up a stalk of celery and nibbled on it. "A word of advice. If Katie doesn't want to tell Richard about this operation, don't fill him in. That's not fair to her. If he's persistent in being concerned about her, it has to make some sort of statement to her. You've gotten them together. Now—"

"Now bug off," Molly sighed.

"Something like that. And tomorrow night when Katie goes into the hospital, you and I are going to the Met. I got tickets for *Otello* months ago and I don't plan to change them. You be there when she comes out of the recovery room Saturday morning, but it won't hurt her any to wish she had someone with her Friday evening. Maybe she'll do a little thinking."

"Go into the hospital by herself?" Molly protested.

"By herself," Bill said firmly. "She's a big girl."

The telephone rang. "Pray it isn't the school nurse saying one of the kids started with the virus again," Molly muttered. Her "Hello" was guarded. Then her tone became concerned. "Liz, hi. Now, don't tell me you're going to cancel on me tonight."

She listened. "Oh, for heaven's sake, bring her along. You have the folding carriage. . . . Sure, we'll put her up in our room and she'll be fine. . . . Of course I don't mind. So if she wakes up we'll bring her down and let her join the party. It'll be like old times around here. . . . Great. See you at seven. Bye."

She hung up. "Liz Berkeley's regular baby-sitter had to cancel and she's afraid to leave her with someone she doesn't know, so she's bringing the baby along."

"Fine." Bill looked at the kitchen clock. "I'd better get out of here. It's getting late." He kissed Molly's cheek. "Will you quit worrying about your little sister?"

Molly bit her lip. "I can't. I've got this creepy feeling about Katie, like something might happen to her."

W hen Richard returned to his office, he stood for a long time staring out the window. His view was somewhat more appealing than the one from Scott's office. Besides the northeast corner of the county jail, a distinct section of the pocket-sized park in front of the courthouse was visible to him. Only half aware of what he was seeing, he watched as a flurry of sleet-weighted snow pelted the already-slick frozen grass.

Wonderful weather, he thought. He glanced up at the sky. Heavy snow clouds were forming. Vangie Lewis' body was being flown into Newark from Minneapolis on a two-thirty flight. It would be picked up at seven and brought to the morgue. Tomorrow morning he'd re-examine it. Not that he expected to find anything more than he already knew. There were absolutely no bruise marks on it. He was sure of that. But there was something about her left foot or leg that he had noticed and dismissed as irrelevant.

He pushed that thought aside. It was useless to speculate until he could re-examine the body. Vangie had obviously been highly emotional. Could she have been induced to suicide by Fukhito? If Vangie was carrying Fukhito's child, he must have been panicked. He'd be finished as a doctor if he were found to be involved with a patient again.

But Chris Lewis had a girlfriend—a good reason for wanting his wife out of the way. Suppose he had learned of the affair? Apparently even Vangie's parents hadn't known she was planning to come home to Minneapolis. Was it possible Vangie hoped to be delivered of the baby by the Minnesota obstetrician and keep quiet about it? Maybe she'd say she'd lost it. If she wanted to preserve her marriage, she might have been driven to that. Or if she realized a divorce was inevitable, the absolute proof of her infidelity might have weighed in the settlement.

None of it rang true.

Sighing, Richard reached over, snapped on the intercom and asked Marge to come in. She had been at lunch when he returned from Scott's office and he had not collected his messages.

She hurried in with a sheaf of slips in her hand. "None of these are too important," she informed him. "Oh, yes, there was one right after you went to Mr. Myerson's office. A Dr. Salem. He didn't ask for you by name; he wanted the Medical Examiner. Then he asked if we had performed the autopsy on Vangie Lewis. I said you were the M.E. and that you'd performed it personally. He was catching a plane from

Minneapolis, but asked if you'd call him at the Essex House in New York around five o'clock. He sounded anxious to talk to you."

Richard pursed his lips in a soundless whistle. "I'm anxious to talk to *him*," he said.

"Oh, and I got the statistics on the Westlake obstetrical patients," Marge said. "In the eight years of the Westlake Maternity Concept, sixteen patients have died either in childbirth or of toxic pregnancies."

"Sixteen?"

"Sixteen," Marge repeated with emphasis. "However, the practice is huge. Dr. Highley is considered an excellent doctor. Some of the babies he's brought to term are near miracles, and the women who died had all been warned by other doctors that they were high pregnancy risks."

"I'll want to study all the fatalities," Richard said. "But if we ask Scott to subpoena the files from the hospital, we'll alert them, and I don't want to do that yet. Have you got anything else?"

"Maybe. In these eight years two people filed malpractice suits against Dr. Highley. Both suits were dismissed. And a cousin of his wife's came in and claimed that he didn't believe she'd died of a heart attack. The Prosecutor's office contacted her personal physician and he said the cousin was crazy. The cousin had been the sole heir before Winifred Westlake married Dr. Highley, so that may be why he wanted to start trouble."

"Who was Winifred Westlake's personal physician?"

"Dr. Alan Levine."

"He's a top internist," Richard said. "I'll have a talk with him."

"How about the people who filed the malpractice suits? Do you want to know who they are?"

"Yes, I do."

"I figured that. Here."

Richard looked down at the two names on the sheet of paper Marge handed him. *Anthony Caldwell, Old Country Lane, Peapack, N.J.,* and *Anna Horan, 415 Walnut Street, Ridgefield Park, N.J.*

"You do nice work, Marge," he said.

She nodded. "I know." Her tone was satisfied.

"Scott is in court by now. Will you leave word for him to call me when he gets back to his office? Oh, and tell the lab I want Vangie Lewis' clothes available to put on her first thing tomorrow morning. All tests have to be finished on the clothing by this afternoon."

Marge left, and Richard turned to the work on his desk.

It was after four before Scott returned the call. He listened to Richard's decision to interview the complainants against Dr. Highley and was clearly not impressed. "Look, today there isn't any doctor, no matter who he is, who isn't hit by malpractice suits. If Dr. Schweitzer were still alive, so help me, he'd be defending himself against them in the jungle. But go ahead on your own if you want to. We'll subpoena the hospital records when you're ready for them. I am concerned about the high number of obstetrical deaths of mothers, but even that may be explainable. He does deal in high-risk pregnancies."

Scott's voice deepened. "What I'm most interested in is what this Dr. Salem has to say. You talk with him and get back to me and then I'll get in on the act. Between you and me, Richard, I think we're going to pull a tight-enough circumstantial case around Captain Chris Lewis that we may force him to come clean. We know that his movements are unaccounted for on Monday night, when his wife died. We know Edna Burns called him Tuesday night. We now know that the funeral director left him before nine on Tuesday night. After that he was alone and could easily have gone out. Suppose he did go down and see her? He's handy. Charley tells me he's got sophisticated tools in his garage. Edna was almost blind drunk when she called him. The neighbor told us that. Suppose he drove there, slipped the lock, got into the apartment and shoved that poor dame before she knew what hit her? Frankly, that's the way my gut sees it, and we'll have him here tonight to tell us all about it."

"You may be right," Richard said. "But I'm still going to check these people out."

He caught Dr. Alan Levine just as he was leaving his office. "Buy you a drink," Richard suggested. "I'll only take fifteen minutes."

They agreed to meet at the Parkwood Country Club. A midway point for both of them, it had the virtue of being quiet on weekdays. They'd be able to talk in the bar without worry about being overheard or having people drop over to say hello.

Alan Levine was a Jimmy Stewart-at-fifty-five look-alike—a fact that endeared him to his older patients. They enjoyed the easy cordiality of professionals who respected each other, enjoyed a drink together if their paths crossed, waved to each other on the golf links.

Richard came directly to the point. "For various reasons we're interested in Westlake Hospital. Winifred Westlake was your patient. Her cousin tried to insinuate that she did not die of a heart attack. What can you tell me about it?"

Alan Levine looked directly at Richard, sipped his martini, glanced out the picture window at the snow-covered fairway and pursed his lips. "I have to answer that question on a couple of levels," he said slowly. "First: Yes, Winifred was my patient. For years she'd had a near-ulcer. Specifically, she had all the classic symptoms of a duodenal ulcer, but it never showed up on X-ray. When she'd periodically experience pain, I'd have the usual X-rays done, get negative results, prescribe an ulcer diet, and she experienced relief almost immediately. No great problem.

"Then the year before she met and married Highley she had a severe attack of gastroenteritis which actually altered her cardiogram. I put her in the hospital for a suspected heart attack. But after two days in the hospital the cardiogram was well within the normal range."

"So there might or might not have been a problem with her heart?" Richard asked.

"I didn't think there was. It never showed up in the standard tests. But her mother died of a heart attack at fifty-eight. And Winifred was nearly fifty-two when she died. She was older than Highley by some ten years, you know. Several years after her marriage she began to come to me more frequently, constantly complaining of chest pains. The tests produced nothing significant. I told her to watch her diet."

"And then she had a fatal attack?" Richard asked.

The other doctor nodded. "One evening, during dinner, she had a seizure. Edgar Highley phoned his service immediately. Gave them my number, the hospital's number, told them to call the police. From what I was told, Winifred keeled over at the dining-room table."

"You were there when she died?" Richard queried.

"Yes. Highley was still trying to revive her. But it was hopeless. She died a few minutes after I arrived."

"And you're satisfied it was heart failure?" Richard asked.

Again there was the hint of hesitation. "She'd been having chest pains over a period of years. Not all heart trouble shows up on cardiograms. In the couple of years before she died she was suffering periodically from high blood pressure. There's no question that heart trouble tends to run in families. Yes. I was satisfied at the time."

"At the time." Richard underscored the words.

"I suppose the cousin's absolute conviction that something was wrong about her death has troubled me these three years. I practically threw him out of my office when he came in and as much as accused me of falsifying records. Figured he was a disgruntled relative who hated the guy who took his place in the will. But Glenn Nickerson is a good man. He's coach at Parkwood High, and my kids go there now. They're all crazy about him. He's a family man, active in his church, on the town council; certainly not the kind of man who would go off half-cocked at being disinherited. And certainly he must have known that Winifred would leave her estate to her husband. She was crazy about Highley. Why, I never could see. He's a cold fish if ever I met one."

"I gather you don't like him."

Alan Levine finished his drink. "I don't like him at all. And have you caught the article about him in *Newsmaker?* Just came out today. Makes a little tin god of him. He'll be even more insufferable, I suppose. But I've got to hand it to him. He's an excellent doctor."

"Excellent enough to have chemically induced a heart attack in his wife?"

Dr. Levine looked directly at Richard. "Frankly, I've often wished I'd insisted on an autopsy."

Richard signaled for the check. "You've been a great help, Alan."

The other man shrugged. "I don't see how. What possible use is any of this to you?"

"For the present, it gives me insight when I talk to some people. After that, who knows?"

They parted at the entrance to the bar. Richard fished in his pocket for change, went over to the public telephone and phoned the Essex House Hotel in New York. "Dr. Emmet Salem, please."

There was the jabbing sound of a hotel phone ringing. Three, four, five, six times. The operator broke in. "I'm sorry, but there's no answer there."

"Are you sure Dr. Salem has checked in?" Richard asked.

"Yes, sir, I am. He called specifically to say that he was expecting an important phone call and he wanted to be sure to get it. That was only twenty minutes ago. But I guess he changed his mind or something. Because we are definitely ringing his room and there's no answer."

⟜ CHAPTER 35

When she left Scott's office, Katie called in Rita Castile and together they went over the material Katie would need for upcoming trials. "That armed robbery on the twenty-eighth," Katie said, "where the defendant had his hair cut the morning after the crime. We'll need the barber to testify. It's no wonder the witnesses couldn't make a positive identification. Even though we made him wear a wig in the lineup, he didn't look the same."

"Got it." Rita jotted down the barber's address. "It's too bad you can't let the jury know that Benton has a long juvenile record."

"That's the law," Katie sighed. "I sure hope that someday it stops bending backward to protect criminals. That's about all I have for you now, but I won't be coming in over the weekend, so next week will really be a mess. Be prepared."

"You won't be coming in?" Rita raised her eyebrows. "Well, it's about time. You haven't given yourself a full weekend off in a couple of months. I hope you're planning to go someplace and have fun."

Katie grinned. "I don't know how much fun it will be. Oh, Rita, I have a hunch that Maureen is upset about something today. Without being nosy, is there anything wrong that you know about? Is she still down about the breakup with her fiancé?"

Rita shook her head. "No, not at all. That was just kid stuff, and she knew it. The usual going-steady-from-the-time-they-were-fifteen, an engagement ring the night of the prom. They both realized by last summer that they weren't ready to get married. He's in college now, so that's no problem."

"Then why is she so unhappy?" Katie asked.

"Regret," Rita said simply. "Just about the time they broke up she realized she was pregnant and had an abortion. She's weighted down with guilt about it. She told me that she keeps dreaming about the baby, that she hears a baby crying and is trying to find it. Said she'd do anything to have had the baby, even though she would have given it out for adoption."

Katie remembered how much she had hoped to conceive John's child, how furious she'd been when after his death someone commented that she was lucky not to be stuck with a baby. "Life is so crazy," she said. "The wrong people get pregnant, and then it's so easy to make a mistake you have to live with for the rest of your life. But that does explain it. Thanks for telling me. I was afraid I'd said something to hurt her."

"You didn't," Rita said. She gathered up the files Katie had assigned her. "All right. I'll serve these subpoenas and hunt for the barber."

After Rita left, Katie leaned back in her chair. She wanted to talk again with Gertrude Fitzgerald and Gana Krupshak. Mrs. Fitzgerald and Edna had been good friends; they'd often lunched together. Mrs. Krupshak had frequently dropped into Edna's apartment at night. Maybe Edna had said something to one of them about Dr. Fukhito and Vangie Lewis. It was worth a try.

She called Westlake Hospital and was told that Mrs. Fitzgerald was home ill; requested and got her home phone number. When the woman answered she was obviously still distraught. Her voice was weak and shaking. "I have one of my migraines, Mrs. DeMaio," she said, "and no wonder. Every time I think of how Edna looked, poor dear . . ."

"I was going to suggest that we get together either here or at your home," Katie said. "But I'll be in court all day tomorrow, so I guess it will have to wait until Monday. There's just one thing I would like to ask you, Mrs. Fitzgerald. Did Edna ever call either of the doctors she worked for 'Prince Charming'?"

"*Prince Charming?*" Gertrude Fitzgerald's voice was astonished. "Prince Charming? My goodness. Dr. Highley or Dr. Fukhito? Why would anyone call either of them Prince Charming? My heavens, no."

"All right. It was just a thought." Katie said good-bye and dialed Mrs. Krupshak. The superintendent answered. His wife was out, he explained. She'd be back around five.

Katie glanced at the clock. It was four thirty. "Do you think she'd mind if on my way home I stopped to talk to her for a few minutes? I promise I won't be long."

"Suit yourself," the man answered shortly, then added, "What's going on with the Burns apartment? How long before it gets cleared out?"

"That apartment is not to be entered or touched until this office releases it," Katie said sharply. She hung up, packed some files in her briefcase and got her coat. She'd have just enough time to talk to Mrs. Krupshak, then go home and change. She wouldn't stay late at Molly's tonight. She wanted one decent night's sleep before the operation. She knew she wouldn't sleep well in the hospital.

She was just ahead of the evening traffic, and Mrs. Krupshak was home when she rang her bell. "Now, isn't that timing?" she exclaimed to Katie. The shock of discovering Edna's body had begun to wear off for this woman, and clearly she was beginning to enjoy the excitement of the police investigation.

"This is my bingo afternoon," she explained. "When I told my friends what happened they could hardly keep their cards straight."

Poor Edna, Katie thought, then realized that Edna would have been delighted to be the center of an active discussion.

Mrs. Krupshak ushered her into an L-shaped living room, a mirror image of the unit Edna had lived in. Edna's living room had been furnished with an old-fashioned velour couch, matching straight-backed fireside chairs, a fading Oriental rug. Like Edna, the apartment had had its own innate dignity.

The superintendent's wife had an imitation-leather couch and club chair, an oversized cocktail table topped by an exactly centered plastic flower arrangement and an orange-toned autumnal print over the couch that picked up the wildly vivid shade of the carpeting. Katie sat down. This place is ordinary, she reflected. It's unimaginative, yet it's clean and comfortable and you get the feeling that even if her husband is brusque and unsociable, Gana Krupshak is a happy woman. Then Katie wondered why she was suddenly so concerned with defining happiness.

With a mental shrug she turned to the questions she wanted to ask. "Mrs. Krupshak," she said, "we talked last night, but of course, you were so shocked. Now I wonder if you would go over with me very carefully what happened Tuesday night: how long were you with Edna; what did you talk about; did you get the impression that when she spoke to Captain Lewis she made an appointment with him."

Gana Krupshak leaned back in her chair, looked past Katie, half-closed her eyes and bit her lip.

"Now, let's see. I went over to Edna's right at eight o'clock, because Gus started to watch the basketball game and I thought, To hell with the basketball game, I'll pop over to Edna's and have a beer with her."

"And you went over there," Katie encouraged.

"I did. The only thing is, Edna had made a pitcher of Manhattans and they were about half gone and she was feeling pretty rocky. You know, like, sometimes she'd get in moods, kind of *down,* if you know what I mean, and I thought she was in one of those. Like, last Thursday was her mother's birthday and I stopped in then and she was crying about how much she missed her mother. Now, I don't mean she'd take it out on you, no way, but when I popped over there Thursday she was sitting with her folks' picture in her hands and the jewelry box on her lap and tears rolling down her cheeks. I gave her a big hug and said, 'Edna, I'm going to pour you a nice Manhattan and we'll toast your maw and if she was here she'd be joining us.' So if you know what I mean, I kind of kidded her out of the blues and she was fine, but when I went over Tuesday night and saw her under the weather I figured she really wasn't over the lonesome spell."

"Did she tell you she was still depressed Tuesday night?" Katie asked.

"No. No. That's it. She was kind of excited. She talked in a sort of rambly way about this patient who had died, how beautiful she'd been, like a doll, and how sick she'd been getting and how she—Edna, I mean—could tell the cops a lot about her."

"Then what happened?" Katie asked.

"Well, I had a Manhattan, or two, with her and then figured I'd better get home because Gus gets in a snit if I'm still out when he goes to bed. But I hated to see Edna drink much more, because I knew she'd be feeling real bad in the morning, so I got out that nice canned ham and opened it and cut off a few slices for her."

"And that was when she made the call?"

"Just like I told you last night."

"And she talked to Captain Lewis about Prince Charming?"

"As God is my witness."

"All right, but one last thing, Mrs. Krupshak: do you know if Edna kept any articles of clothing of her mother's as a sentimental keepsake?"

"Clothing? No. She did have a lovely diamond pin and ring."

"Yes, yes, we found those last night. But—well, for example, my mother used to keep her mother's old black felt hat in her closet for sentimental reasons. I noticed an old moccasin in Edna's jewelry drawer. It was quite shabby. Did she ever show it to you or mention it?"

Gana Krupshak looked directly at Katie. "Absolutely not," she said flatly.

CHAPTER 36

The *Newsmaker* article was on the stands Thursday morning. The phone calls began as soon as he went to his office after delivering the Aldrich baby. He instructed the switchboard to ring through directly to him. He wanted to hear the comments. They were beyond his expectations. "Doctor, when can I have an appointment? My husband and I have longed for a baby. I can fly to New Jersey at your convenience. God bless you for your work." The Dartmouth Medical School phoned. Would he consider a guest lecture? An article writer for *Ladies' Home Journal* wanted to interview him. Would Dr. Highley and Dr. Fukhito appear together on *Eyewitness News?*

That request troubled him. He'd been careful to give the *Newsmaker* reporter the impression that he worked with a number of psychiatrists, in the same sense a family lawyer might have his clients consult with any one of a dozen counselors. He had clearly suggested that the program was entirely under his control, not a joint effort. But the reporter had picked up Fukhito's name from a number of the safe patients he'd given her to interview. Now the reporter credited Fukhito as the psychiatrist who seemed to be primarily involved with Dr. Edgar Highley in the Westlake Maternity Concept.

Fukhito would be desperately troubled by the publicity. That was why he'd been chosen. Fukhito had to keep his mouth shut even if he ever started to get suspicious. He was in no position to allow a breath of scandal to hit Westlake. He'd be permanently ruined if that happened.

Fukhito was becoming a distinct liability. It would be easy enough to get rid of him now. He was giving a lot of time on a voluntary basis to the clinic at Valley Pines. He could undoubtedly become staff there now. Probably Fukhito would be glad to scramble for cover. Then he could start to rotate psychiatrists; he knew enough of them by now who weren't competent to counsel anyone. They'd be easy enough to dupe.

Fukhito would have to go.

The decision made, he signaled for his first patient to come in. She was new, as were the two scheduled after her. The third patient was an interesting case: a womb so tipped that she'd never be able to conceive without intervention.

She would be his next Vangie.

The phone call came at noon just as he was leaving for lunch. The nurse covering the reception desk was apologetic. "Doctor, it's a long-distance call from a Dr. Emmet Salem in Minneapolis. He's in a phone booth at the airport now and insists on speaking with you at once."

Emmet Salem! He picked up the phone. "Edgar Highley here."

"Dr. Highley." The voice was icy cold. "Dr. Highley from Christ Hospital in Devon?"

"Yes." A chill, sickening fear made his tongue heavy, his lips rubbery.

"Dr. Highley, I learned last night that you treated my former patient, Mrs. Vangie Lewis. I'm leaving for New York immediately. I'll be at the Essex House Hotel in New York. I must tell you that I am planning to consult with the Medical Examiner in New Jersey about Mrs. Lewis' death. I have her medical records with me. In fairness to you I suggest we discuss her case before I level accusations."

"Doctor, I'm troubled by your tone and insinuations." Now he could talk. Now his own voice hardened into chips of granite.

"My plane is boarding. I'll be checking into room 3219 of the Essex House Hotel shortly before five o'clock. You can call me there." The connection was broken.

He was waiting in the Essex House when Emmet Salem emerged from the cab. Swiftly he disappeared into an elevator to the thirty-second floor, walked past room 3219 until the corridor turned in a right angle. Another elevator stopped at the floor. He listened as a key clicked, a bellman said, "Here we are, Doctor." A minute later the bellman emerged again. "Thank you, sir."

He waited until he heard the elevator stop at the floor for the bellman. The corridors were silent. But that wouldn't last long. Many of the delegates to the AMA convention were probably staying here. There was always the danger of running into someone he knew. But he had to take the chance. He had to silence Salem.

Swiftly he opened his leather bag and brought out the paperweight that only forty-eight hours ago he had intended to use to silence Edna. Incongruous, impossible—that he, the healer, the doctor, was repeatedly forced to kill.

He slipped the paperweight into his coat pocket, put on his gloves, grasped the bag firmly in his left hand and knocked on the door.

Emmet Salem pulled the door open. He'd just removed his suit jacket. "Forgot something?" His voice trailed off. Obviously he'd expected the bellman had come back.

"Dr. Salem!" He reached for Salem's hand, walking forward, backing the older man into the room, slipping the door closed behind him. "I'm Edgar Highley. It's good to see you again. You got off the phone so abruptly that I couldn't tell you I was having dinner with several colleagues who are attending the convention. I have only a very few minutes, but I'm sure we can clear up any questions."

He was still walking forward, forcing the other man to retreat. The window behind Salem was wide open. He'd probably had the bellman open it. The room was very hot. The window was low. His eyes narrowed. "I tried to phone you, but your extension is out of order."

"Impossible. I just spoke to the operator." Dr. Salem stiffened, his face suddenly cautious.

"Then I do apologize. But no problem. I'm so anxious to go over the Lewis file with you. I have it in my case here." He reached for the paperweight in his pocket, then cried, "Doctor, behind you, watch out!"

The other man spun around. Holding the paperweight in his fist, he crashed it on Salem's skull. The blow sent Emmet Salem staggering. He slumped against the windowsill.

Jamming the paperweight back into his pocket, Edgar Highley cupped his palms around Emmet Salem's foot and shoved up and out.

"No. No. Christ, please!" The half-conscious man slid out the window.

He watched dispassionately as Salem landed on the roof of the extension some fifteen floors below.

The body made a muffled thud.

Had it been seen? He had to hurry. From Salem's suit coat on the bed, he pulled out a key ring. The smallest key fitted the attaché case on the luggage rack.

The Vangie Lewis file was on top. Grabbing it, he shoved it into his own briefcase, relocked Salem's bag, returned the keys to the suit-coat pocket. He took the paperweight from his pocket and placed it in his own bag with the file. The wound had not spurted blood, but the paperweight was sticky.

He closed his own bag and glanced around. The room was in perfect order. There was no trace of blood on the windowsill. It had taken less than two minutes.

He opened the door cautiously and looked out. The corridor was empty. He stepped out. As he closed the door, the phone in Salem's room began to ring.

He did not dare be seen getting on the elevator on this floor. His picture was in the *Newsmaker* article. Later people might be questioned. He might be recognized.

The fire-exit stairway was at the end of the corridor. He descended four levels to the twenty-eighth floor. There he reentered the carpeted corridor. An elevator was just stopping. He got on it, his eyes scanning the faces of the passengers. Several women, a couple of teen-agers, an elderly couple. No doctors. He was sure of that.

At the lobby he walked rapidly to the Fifty-eighth Street exit of the hotel, turned west and then south. Ten minutes later he reclaimed his car from the park-and-lock garage on West Fifty-fourth Street, tossed his bag into the trunk and drove away.

〜 *CHAPTER 37*

Chris arrived at the Twin Cities airport at ten minutes of one. He had an hour to wait before his plane left for Newark. Vangie's body would be on that plane. Yesterday, coming out here, he'd thought of nothing except that coffin in the hold of the plane. He'd held on to some semblance of normality by reassuring himself that soon it would be over.

He had to see Dr. Salem. Why had Dr. Salem been so upset? Tonight when he got off the plane at Newark, the Medical Examiner's office would be waiting for Vangie's body.

And the Prosecutor's office would be waiting for him. The certainty haunted Chris. Of course. If they were suspicious in any way about Vangie's death, they were going to look to him for answers. They'd be waiting to bring him in for questioning. They might even arrest him. If they'd investigated at all, they knew by now that he'd returned to the New Jersey area Monday night. He had to see Dr. Salem. If he was detained for questioning he might not be able to talk to him. He did not want to talk to the Prosecutor's office *about* Dr. Salem.

Once again he thought of Molly and Bill Kennedy. So what if Molly was Katie DeMaio's sister? They were good people, honest people. He should have trusted them, talked to them. He had to talk to someone.

He had to talk to Joan.

His need for her was a hunger. The minute he started to tell the truth, Joan became involved.

Joan, who in this sleazy world still held such inviolate principles, was about to be dragged through the mud.

He had the phone number of the stewardess with whom she was staying in Florida. Not knowing what he would say, he went to the phone, automatically gave his credit-card number, heard the ring.

Kay Corrigan answered. "Kay, is Joan there? It's Chris."

Kay knew about him and Joan. Kay's voice was concerned. "Chris, Joan has been trying to phone you. Tina called from the New York apartment. The Valley County Prosecutor's office has been around asking all kinds of questions about you two. Joan is frantic!"

"When will she be back?"

"She's over at the new apartment now. It doesn't have a phone. From there she has to go to the company personnel office in Miami. She won't be here till about eight tonight."

"Tell her to stay in and wait till I call her," Chris said. "Tell her I've got to talk to her. Tell her . . ." He broke the connection, leaned against the phone and pushed back a dry sob. Oh, God, it was too much, it was all too much. He couldn't think. He didn't know what to do. And in a few hours he'd be in custody, suspected of killing Vangie . . . maybe *charged* with killing Vangie.

No. There was another way. He'd get the flight into LaGuardia. He could still make it. Then he'd be in Manhattan and able to see Dr. Salem at almost the same time he reached the hotel. The Prosecutor's office wouldn't realize he wasn't on the Newark flight until six o'clock. Maybe Dr. Salem could help him somehow.

He barely made the LaGuardia flight. The coach section was full, but he bought a first-class ticket and was able to get on the plane. He didn't worry about his luggage, which was checked through to Newark.

On the plane he accepted a drink from the stewardess, waved away the food and listlessly thumbed through *Newsmaker* magazine. The page opened to SCIENCE AND MEDICINE. His eye caught the headline: "Westlake Maternity Concept Offers New Hope to Childless Couples." *Westlake.* He read the first paragraph. "For the past eight years, a small privately owned clinic in New Jersey has been operating a program called the Westlake Maternity Concept which has made it possible for childless women to become pregnant. Named after a prominent New Jersey obstetrician, the program is carried on by Dr. Edgar Highley, obstetrician-gynecologist, who was the son-in-law of Dr. Franklin Westlake . . ."

Dr. Edgar Highley. Vangie's doctor. Funny she never talked very much about him. It was always the psychiatrist. "Dr. Fukhito and I talked about Mama and Daddy today . . . he said it was obvious I was an only child . . . Dr. Fukhito asked me to draw a picture of Mama and Daddy as I visualized them; it was fascinating. I mean it really was interesting to see how I visualized them. Dr. Fukhito was asking about you, Chris."

"And what did you say, Vangie?"

"That you worshiped me. You do, don't you, Chris? I mean underneath that put-downy way you have with me, aren't I your little girl?"

"I'd rather you thought of yourself as my wife, Vangie."

"See, I can't talk with you about anything. You always get nasty. . . ."

He wondered if the police had talked to either of Vangie's doctors.

This last month she had looked so ill. He had suggested that she have a consultation. The company doctor would have recommended someone. Or Bill Kennedy would surely have been able to suggest someone from Lenox Hill. But of course, Vangie had refused to have a consultation.

Then on her own she'd made an appointment with Dr. Salem.

The plane landed at four thirty. Chris hurried through the terminal and hailed a cab. One of the few breaks of this rotten day was that he'd be ahead of the five-o'clock rush.

"The Essex House, please," he told the driver.

It was just two minutes of five when he reached the hotel. He headed for a lobby telephone. "Dr. Emmet Salem, please."

"Thank you, sir."

There was a pause. "That line is busy, sir."

He hung up. At least Dr. Salem was here. At least he'd have a chance to talk to him. He remembered he'd written Dr. Salem's extension in his notebook, opened it and dialed "3219." The phone rang . . . again . . . again. After six rings he broke the connection and dialed the operator. Explaining that the line had been busy only a few minutes before, he asked the operator to try it for him.

The operator hesitated, spoke to someone, then came back. "Sir, I just gave this message to another party. Dr. Salem checked in, contacted me to say that he expected an important call and be sure to reach him and then apparently stepped out. Why don't you try again in a few minutes?"

"I'll do that. Thank you." Irresolutely Chris hung up the phone, walked over to a lobby chair facing the south elevator bank and sat down. The elevators opened and dislodged passengers, filled again, disappeared in a streak of ascending panel lights.

One elevator caught his attention. There was something vaguely familiar about someone on it. Dr. Salem? Quickly he scanned the passengers. Three women, some teen-agers, an elderly couple, a middle-aged man with a turned-up coat collar. No. Not Dr. Salem.

At five thirty Chris tried again. And at quarter of six. At five past six he heard the whispers that ran through the lobby like a flash fire. "Someone jumped from a window. The body spotted on the roof of the extension." From somewhere along Central Park South the wail of an ambulance and the yip-yip of police cars were frantic explosions of increasing sound.

With the certainty of despair, Chris went to the bell captain's desk. "Who was it?" he asked. His tone was crisp, authoritative; suggested he had a right to know.

"Dr. Emmet Salem. He was a big shot in the AMA. Room 3219."

Walking with the measured gait of an automaton, Chris pushed through the revolving door at the Fifty-eighth Street entrance. A cab was cruising from west to east. He hailed it, got in and leaned back in the seat closing his eyes. "LaGuardia, please," he said; "the National Airlines terminal."

There was a seven-o'clock flight to Miami. He could just make it.

In three hours he'd be with Joan.

He had to get to Joan, try to make her understand before he was arrested.

⪻ *CHAPTER 38*

Twelve-year-old Jennifer threw open the door as Katie came up the walk. "Katie, hi." Her voice was joyous, her hug sturdy. The two smiled at each other. With her intense blue eyes, dark hair and olive skin, Jennifer was a younger version of Katie.

"Hi, Jennie. How do you feel?"

"Okay. But how about you? I was so worried when Mom told me about your accident. You sure you're okay now?"

"Let's put it this way: by next week I'll be in great shape." She changed the subject. "Anybody here yet?"

"Everybody. Dr. Richard is here too.... You know what his first question was?"

"No."

" 'Is Katie here yet?' I swear he's got a case on you, Katie. Mom and Dad think so too. I heard them talking about it. How about you? Have you got a case on him?"

"Jennifer!" Half laughing, half irritated, Katie started up the short staircase toward the den in the back of the house, then looked back over her shoulder. "Where are the other kids?"

"Mom shipped them off with a baby-sitter to eat at McDonald's and then to a movie. She said the Berkeley baby would never sleep if the twins were around."

"Good thinking," Katie murmured. She started down the foyer to the den. After leaving Gana Krupshak, she'd gone home, showered and changed. She'd left the house at quarter of seven thinking, Very soon Chris Lewis will be in Scott's office being questioned. . . . What explanation could he give for not admitting that he was in the New Jersey area Monday night? Why hadn't he volunteered that immediately?

She wondered if Richard had spoken to the Minnesota doctor yet. He might have cleared up a lot of questions. She'd try to get Richard aside and ask him.

Driving over, she had resolved to put the case out of her mind for the rest of the evening. Maybe *not* thinking about it for a while would help her to follow up the elusive threads that kept escaping her—

She reached the den. Liz and Jim Berkeley were seated on the couch, their backs to her. Molly was passing hors d'oeuvres. Bill and Richard were standing by the window talking. Katie studied Richard. He was wearing a navy blue pin-striped suit that she'd never seen before. His dark brown hair had touches of gray she'd never noticed. His fingers on the stem of the glass he was holding were long and finely shaped. Funny how this past year she'd seen him as a composite, never noticing details. It seemed to her that she was like a camera that had been locked into one position and was just beginning to focus again. Richard looked serious. His forehead was creased. She wondered if he was telling Bill about the Lewis fetus. No, he wouldn't discuss that even with Bill.

At that moment Richard turned his head and saw her. "Katie." His smile matched the pleased tone in his voice. He came hurrying over to her. "I've been listening for the doorbell."

So often in these three years she'd entered a room where she was the outsider, the loner, amidst couples. Now here tonight, Richard had been waiting for her, listening for her.

Before she had time to consider her feelings, Molly and Bill were saying hello, Jim Berkeley had stood up and the usual confusion of greetings was taking place.

On the way to the dining room she did manage to ask Richard if he'd reached Dr. Salem. "No. Apparently I just missed him at five," Richard explained. "Then I tried again from my place at six, but there was no answer. I left this number with the hotel operator and with my answering service. I'm very anxious to hear what that man has to say."

By tacit agreement, none of them brought up the Lewis suicide until dinner was almost over. And then it came about because Liz Berkeley said, "What luck. I have to admit I've been holding my breath that Maryanne wouldn't wake up and be fussy. Poor kid, her gums are so swollen she's in misery."

Jim Berkeley laughed. He was darkly handsome with high cheekbones, charcoal-brown eyes and thick black eyebrows. "When Maryanne

was born, Liz used to wake her up every fifteen minutes to make sure she was still breathing. But since she's teething, Liz has become like every other mother." He imitated her voice, "Quiet, dummy, don't wake up the baby."

Liz, a Carol Burnett type, with sinewy slenderness, an open, pleasant face and flashing brown eyes, made a face at her husband. "You have to admit I'm calming down to being normal. But she *is* a miracle to us. I'd just about given up hope and then we tried to adopt, but now there just aren't babies. Especially with the two of us in our late thirties, they told us to forget it. And then Dr. Highley. He's a miracle maker, that man."

Katie watched as Richard's eyes narrowed. "You genuinely think that?" Richard queried.

"Positively. I mean, Dr. Highley isn't the warmest person on earth—" Liz began.

"What you mean is that he's an egocentric son of a bitch and as cold a fish as ever I've met," her husband interrupted. "But who gives a damn about that? What matters is that he knows his business, and I have to say he took excellent care of Liz. Put her to bed in the hospital almost two months before the delivery and personally checked on her three or four times a day."

"He does that with all his difficult pregnancies," Liz said. "Not just me. Listen, I pray for that man every night. The difference that baby has made in our lives, I can't even begin to tell you! And don't let this one fool you"—she nodded in the direction of her husband—"he's up ten times a night to make sure that Maryanne is covered and that there's no draft on her. Tell the truth." She looked at him. "When you went up to the john before, didn't you look in on her?"

He laughed. "Sure I did."

Molly said what Katie was thinking. "That's the way Vangie Lewis would have felt about her child."

Richard looked at Katie questioningly and she shook her head. She knew he was wondering if she'd told Molly and Bill that the Lewis baby was Oriental. Deliberately Richard pulled the conversation from Vangie. "I understand that you used to live in San Francisco," he said to Jim. "I grew up there. In fact, my father still practices at San Francisco General. . . ."

"One of my favorite towns," Jim replied. "We'd go back there in a minute, wouldn't we, Liz?"

As the others chatted, Katie listened with half a mind, contributing enough to the conversation that her silence wasn't noticeable. She had so much thinking to do. These few days in the hospital would give her time for that too. She was feeling light-headed and fatigued, but did not want to make a move too soon for fear of breaking up the party.

Her chance came as they left the table to go into the living room for a nightcap. "I'm going to say good night," Katie said. "I have to admit I haven't slept well this week and I'm really bushed."

Molly looked at her knowingly and did not protest. Richard said, "I'll walk you to the car."

"Fine."

The night air was cold, and she shivered as they started down the walk. Richard noticed immediately and said, "Katie, I'm worried about you. I know you're not feeling up to par. You don't seem to want to talk about it, but at least let's have dinner tomorrow night. With the way the Lewis case is breaking, the office will be a zoo tomorrow."

"Richard, I'm sorry. I can't. I'm going away this weekend." Katie realized her tone was apologetic.

"You're *what?* With all that's happening at the office? Does Scott know that?"

"I . . . I'm committed." What a lame, stupid thing to say, Katie thought. This is ridiculous. I'm going to tell Richard that I'll be in the hospital. The driveway lights were on his face, and his expression of mingled disappointment and disapproval was unmistakable.

"Richard, it's not something I've talked up, but . . ."

The front door was thrown open. "Richard, Richard!" Jennifer's shout was rushed and excited. "Clovis Simmons is on the phone."

"Clovis Simmons!" Katie said. "Isn't she the actress on that soap opera?"

"Yes. Oh, hell, I was supposed to call her and forgot. Hold on, Katie. I'll be right back."

"No. I'll see you in the morning. You go ahead." Katie got into the car and pulled the door closed. She fished for the ignition key in her handbag, found it and inserted it into the lock. Richard looked irresolute for an instant, then hurried into the house, listening as Katie's car drove away. Hell, he thought, of all the times. His "Hello, Clovis" was brusque.

"Well, Doctor, it's a shame I have to track you down, but we did discuss dinner, didn't we?"

"Clovis, I'm *sorry*." No, Clovis, he thought, *you* discussed dinner. *I* didn't.

"Well, obviously it's too late now." Her tone was cool. "Actually, I just got in from the taping and wanted to apologize in case you'd kept the evening. I should have known better."

Richard glanced at Jennifer, who was standing at his elbow.

"Clovis, look, let me call you tomorrow. I can't talk very well now."

There was a sharp click in his ear. Richard hung up the phone slowly. Clovis was angry, but more than that, she was hurt. How much we take people for granted, he thought. Just because I wasn't serious about her, I didn't bother to think about her feelings. Tomorrow he could only call and apologize and be honest enough to tell her that there was someone else.

Katie. Where was she going this weekend? Was there someone else for her? She'd looked so troubled, so worried. Was it that he'd been misreading her all along? He'd put her reticence, her lack of interest in him to the probability that she was living in the past. Maybe there was someone else in her life. Was he being as much a fool about her feelings as in a different way he'd been with Clovis?

The possibility sheared away the pleasure of the evening. He'd make his excuses and go home. It still wouldn't be too late to try Dr. Salem again.

He went into the living room. Molly, Bill and the Berkeleys were there. And swathed in blankets, sitting straight up on Liz's lap, was a baby girl.

"Maryanne decided to join the party," Liz said. "What do you think of her?" Her smile was proud as she turned the baby to face him.

Richard looked into solemn green eyes set in a heart-shaped face. Jim Berkeley was sitting next to his wife, and Maryanne reached over and grabbed his thumb.

Richard stared at the family. They might have posed for a magazine cover: the smiling parents, the beautiful offspring. The parents handsome, olive-skinned, brown-eyed, square-featured; the baby fair-complexioned, red-blond, with brilliant green eyes.

Who the hell do they think they're kidding? Richard thought. That child has to be adopted.

⤙⤚ *CHAPTER 39*

Phil Cunningham and Charley Nugent watched in disgust as the final stragglers filed through the waiting room at Newark Airport's Gate 11. Charley's perpetually mournful expression deepened.

"That's it." He shrugged. "Lewis must have figured we'd be waiting for him. Let's go."

He headed for the nearest pay phone and dialed Scott. "You can go home, boss," he said. "The Captain didn't feel like flying tonight."

"He wasn't on board? How about the coffin?"

"That came in. Richard's guys are picking it up. Want us to hang around? There are a couple of indirect flights he might be on."

"Forget it. If he doesn't contact us tomorrow, I'm issuing a pickup order for him as a material witness. And first thing in the morning, I want you to go through Edna Burns's apartment with a fine-tooth comb."

Charley hung up the phone. He turned to Phil. "If I know the boss, I'd say that by tomorrow night at this time there'll be a warrant out for Lewis' arrest."

Phil nodded. "And after we get Lewis, I hope we can hang something on that shrink if he was the one who made that poor gal pregnant."

The two men wearily started down the stairs to the exit. They passed the baggage area, ignoring the people clustered around the carousels waiting for their luggage. A few minutes later the area was deserted. Only one unclaimed bag circled forlornly on the ramp: a large black carryall, properly tagged, in accordance with airline regulations, CAPT. CHRISTOPHER LEWIS, NO. 4, WINDING BROOK LANE, CHAPIN RIVER, N.J. Inside the bag, placed there at the last minute, was the picture Vangie's parents had pressed on Chris.

It was a nightclub photo of a youthful couple. The inscription read, *Remembrance of my first date with Vangie, the girl who will change my life. Love, Chris.*

 CHAPTER 40

Richard phoned the Essex House Hotel as soon as he reached his apartment after leaving the Kennedys'. But once again there was no answer on Dr. Salem's number. When the operator came back on the line, he said, "Operator, did Dr. Salem receive my message to phone me? I'm Dr. Carroll."

The woman's voice was oddly hesitant. "I'll check, sir."

While he was waiting, Richard reached over and flipped on the television set. *Eyewitness News* had just begun. The camera was focusing on Central Park South. Richard watched as the marquee of the Essex House Hotel was featured on the screen. Even as the telephone operator said, "I'm connecting you with our supervisor," Richard heard reporter Gloria Rojas say, "This evening in the prestigious Essex House Hotel, headquarters for the American Medical Association convention, a prominent obstetrician-gynecologist, Dr. Emmet Salem of Minneapolis, Minnesota, fell or jumped to his death."

CHAPTER 41

Joan Moore sat distractedly by the telephone. "Kay, what time did he say he'd phone?" she asked. Her voice trembled, and she bit her lip.

The other young woman looked at her with concern. "I told you, Joan. He called about eleven thirty this morning. He said he'd be in touch with you tonight and that you should wait in for his call. He sounded upset."

The doorbell rang insistently, making them both jump from their chairs. Kay said, "I don't expect anybody." Some instinct made Joan run to the door and yank it open.

"Chris—oh, my God, Chris!" She threw her arms around him. He was ghastly white, his eyes were bloodshot, he swayed as she held him. "Chris, was is it?"

"Joan, Joan." His voice was nearly a sob. Hungrily he pulled her to him. "I don't know what's happening. There's something wrong about Vangie's death, and now the only man who might have told us about it is dead too."

CHAPTER 42

He had planned to go directly home from the Essex House, but after he drove out of the parking lot and started up the West Side Highway in the heavy traffic, he changed his mind. He was so terribly hungry. His stomach had been empty all day. He never ate before operating, and this morning the call from Salem had come just before he would have left for lunch.

He didn't want to take the time to prepare food tonight. He'd go to the Carlyle. Then if the question ever arose as to his whereabouts tonight, he could truthfully admit he had been in New York. The maître d' would emphatically reassure the police that Dr. Edgar Highley was a valued and frequent patron.

He would have smoked salmon, vichyssoise, a rack of lamb . . . His mouth salivated in anticipation. The sudden, terrible depletion of energy now that it was over needed to be corrected. There was still tomorrow. Inevitably there'd be a thorough investigation when Kathleen

DeMaio died. But her former gynecologist had retired and moved away. No one would loom from the past with old medical records to challenge him.

And then he'd be safe. Right now, all over the AMA convention, doctors were probably discussing the *Newsmaker* article and the West-lake Maternity Concept. Their remarks would be tinged with jealousy, of course. But even so, there would be offers for him to speak at future AMA seminars. He was now on the path to public fame. And Salem, who might have stopped him, was finished. He was anxious to go through Vangie's medical history in the file he'd taken from Salem. He'd incorporate it with his own records. That history would be invaluable in his future research.

The last new patient this morning. She would be next. He parked on the street in front of the Carlyle. It was nearly six thirty. Parking would be legal at seven. He'd just wait in the car until then. It would give him a chance to calm himself down.

His bag was locked in the trunk. Vangie's file, the paperweight and the shoe were in it. How should he dispose of the shoe and the paperweight? Where should he dispose of them? Any one of the overflowing trash baskets in this city would do. No one would fish them out. They'd be collected in the morning together with the tons of garbage that accumulated every twenty-four hours in this city of eight million, lost in the smell of decaying food and discarded newspapers. . . .

He'd do it on the way home, under cover of darkness, never noticed.

A sense of buoyancy at the anticipation of how well it was going made him suddenly straighten up in his seat. He leaned over and looked into the rearview mirror. His skin was glistening, as if with perspiration about to burst through the pores. His eyelids and the skin under his eyes were accumulating fatty tissue. His hairline still showed no sign of receding, but the dark sandy hair was shot with silver now . . . He was starting to age. The subtle change that began in the mid-forties was happening to him. He was forty-five now. Young enough, but also time to become aware of the swift passage of years. Did he want to remarry? Did he want to father children of his own? He'd wanted, expected them from Claire. When they hadn't come he'd checked his own sperm count, found it surprisingly low, secretly blamed himself all those years for Claire's inability to conceive. Until he learned that she'd made a fool of him.

He would not have minded having a child by Winifred. But she was virtually past childbearing years when they married. After she became suspicious of him, he didn't bother to touch her. When you are planning to eliminate someone, she is already dead to you, and sex is for the living.

But now. A younger woman, a woman unlike Claire and Winifred. Claire, haughtily demeaning him with her sneering comments about his father's apothecary; Winifred the do-gooder, with her causes and charities. Now he needed a wife who would not only be socially at ease, but also like to entertain, to travel, to mingle.

He hated those things. He knew his contempt showed. He needed someone who would take care of all that for him, soften his image.

One day he would be able to carry out his work publicly. One day he would have the fame he deserved. One day the fools who said his work was impossible would be forced to acknowledge his genius.

It was seven o'clock. He got out of the car and carefully locked it. He walked to the entrance of the Carlyle, his dark blue suit covered by a blue cashmere coat, his shoes shined to a soft luster, his silver-tipped hair unruffled by the biting night drafts.

The doorman held the door open for him. "Good evening, Dr. Highley. Pretty bad weather, isn't it, sir?"

He nodded without answering and went into the dining room. The corner table he preferred was reserved, but the maître d' quickly switched the expected diners to another table and led him to it.

Wine warmed and soothed him. The dinner gave him the strength he was anticipating. The demitasse and brandy restored him to total balance. His mind was clear and brittle. He reviewed each step of the procedure that would lead Katie DeMaio to death by hemorrhage.

There would be no mistakes.

He was just signing his check when the maître d' came to his table, his footsteps uncharacteristically hurried, his manner agitated. "Dr. Highley, I'm afraid there's a problem."

His finger gripped the pen. He looked up.

"It's just, sir, that a young man was observed prying the trunk of your car. The doorman saw him just as he got it open. Before he could be stopped, he had stolen a bag from the trunk. The police are outside. They believe it was a drug addict who chose your car because of the MD license plates."

His lips were rubbery. It was hard to form words. Like an X-ray machine he mentally examined the contents of the bag: the blood-stained paperweight; the medical file with both Vangie and Salem's names on it; Vangie's moccasin.

When he spoke, his voice was surprisingly steady. "Do the police believe that my bag will be recovered?"

"I asked that question, sir. I'm afraid they just don't know. It might be discarded a few blocks from here after he's taken what he wants from it, or it might never show up again. Only time will tell."

CHAPTER 43

Before she went to bed, Katie packed an overnight bag for her stay in the hospital. The hospital was halfway between the house and the office, and it would have been an unnecessary waste of time to return home for the bag tomorrow.

She realized that she was packing with a sense of urgency. She'd be so glad to get this over with. The heavy sense of being physically out of tune was wearing her down mentally and emotionally. Tonight she'd felt almost buoyant setting out for Molly's. Now she felt depleted, exhausted, depressed. It was all physical, wasn't it?

Or was the nagging thought that maybe Richard was involved with someone contributing to the feeling of depression?

Maybe when this wasn't hanging over her, she'd be able to think more clearly. It felt as though her mind were being plagued by half-completed thoughts like swarms of mosquitoes, landing, biting, but gone before she could reach them. Why did she have the sensation of missing threads, of not asking the right questions, of misreading signals?

By Monday she'd be feeling better, thinking straight.

Wearily, she showered, brushed her teeth and hair and got into bed. A minute later she pulled herself up on one elbow, reached for her handbag and fished out the small bottle Dr. Highley had given her.

Almost forgot to take this, she thought as she swallowed the pill with a gulp from the water glass on her night table. Turning off the light, she closed her eyes.

CHAPTER 44

Gertrude Fitzgerald wearily let the water run cold in the bathroom tap and opened the prescription bottle. The migraine was beginning to let up. If it didn't start in on the other side of her head, she'd be all right by the morning. This last pill should do it.

Something was bothering her . . . something over and beyond Edna's death. It had to do with Mrs. DeMaio's call. It was so silly, asking if Edna had ever called Dr. Fukhito or Dr. Highley Prince Charming. Perfect nonsense.

But *Prince Charming*.

Edna *had* talked about him. Not in relation to the doctors, but somehow in the last couple of weeks. If she could only remember. If Mrs. DeMaio had asked if Edna had ever mentioned him, it might have helped her remember right away. Now it was eluding her, the exact circumstance.

Or was she imagining it? Power of suggestion.

When this headache was finished, she'd be able to think. Really think. And maybe remember.

She swallowed the pill and got into bed. She closed her eyes. Edna's voice sounded in her ears. "And I said that Prince Charming won't . . ."

She couldn't remember the rest.

 CHAPTER 45

At four A.M. Richard gave up trying to sleep, got out of bed and made coffee. He had phoned Scott at home about Emmet Salem's death, and Scott had immediately alerted the New York police that his office wanted to cooperate in the investigation. More than that it had been impossible to accomplish. Mrs. Salem was not at home in Minneapolis. The doctor's answering service could only supply the emergency number of the doctor covering the practice and did not know how to reach his nurse.

Richard began writing notes. *1. Why did Dr. Salem phone our office? 2. Why did Vangie make an appointment with him? 3. The Berkeley baby.*

The Berkeley baby was the key. Was the Westlake Maternity Concept as successful as had been touted? Or was it a cover-up for private adoptions for women who either couldn't conceive or could not carry babies to term? Was the fact that they were being put to bed in the hospital two months before the supposed delivery nothing but a cover-up for what would become an obvious nonpregnant condition?

Babies were hard to adopt. Liz Berkeley had openly admitted that she and her husband had tried that route. Suppose Edgar Highley had said to them, "You'll never have your own child. I can get you a child. It will cost you money and it will have to be absolutely confidential."

They'd have gone along with it. He'd stake his life on that.

But Vangie Lewis had been pregnant. So she didn't fit into the adoptive pattern. Granted she was desperate to have a child . . . but how the hell did she expect to pass off an Oriental baby on her husband? Was there any chance that there was Oriental blood in either family? He'd never considered that.

The malpractice suits. He had to find out the reason those people sued Highley. And Emmet Salem had been Vangie's doctor. His office would have her medical records. That would be a place to start.

Vangie's body had come back on the plane that Chris Lewis did not take. It was in the lab now. First thing in the morning he'd review the autopsy findings. He'd go over the body again. There was something . . . It had seemed unimportant at the time. He'd brushed over it. He'd been too involved with the fetus and the cyanide burns.

Could Vangie have simply spilled the cyanide on herself? Maybe she'd been frantically nervous. But the glass would have had more prints. She'd have picked it up, refilled it; there'd be something—an envelope, a vial—that she'd have used to hold more cyanide.

It hadn't happened like that.

At five thirty Richard turned out the light. He set the alarm for seven. At last sleep came. And he dreamed of Katie. She was standing behind Edna Burns's apartment looking in the window, and Dr. Edgar Highley was watching her.

CHAPTER 46

As befits a bookkeeper, Edna had kept meticulous records. When the search team headed by Phil Cunningham and Charley Nugent descended on her apartment on Friday morning, they found a simple statement in the old-fashioned breakfront:

> *Since my one blood relative never bothered to inquire about or send a card to my dear parents in their illness, I have decided to leave my worldly goods to my friends, Mrs. Gertrude Fitzgerald and Mrs. Gana Krupshak. Mrs. Fitzgerald is to receive my diamond ring and whatever household possessions she cares to have. Mrs. Krupshak is to receive my diamond pin, my imitation fur coat and whatever household possessions Mrs. Fitzgerald does not wish to have. I have discussed my funeral with the establishment that handled my parents' arrangements so beautifully. My $10,000 insurance policy less funeral expenses is assigned to the nursing home which took such fine care of my parents and to whom I am still financially indebted.*

Methodically the team dusted for fingerprints, vacuumed for hair and fibers, searched for signs of forced entry. A smear of dirt on the bottom of the windowsill plant in the bedroom caused the crinkles around Phil's eyes and forehead to settle into a deep frown. He went around the back of the apartment building, thoughtfully scraped a sample of frozen dirt into an envelope and with his fingertips pushed up the bedroom window. For an average-sized person, it was low enough to step over.

"Possible," he said to Charley. "Someone could have come in here and sneaked up on her. But with the ground so frozen, you'd probably never be able to prove it."

As the final step, they rang the doorbells of all the neighbors in the courtyard. The question was simple: had anyone noticed any strangers in the vicinity on Tuesday night?

They had not really expected success. Tuesday night had been dark and cold. The untrimmed shrubbery would have made it possible for anyone who did not want to be seen to stay in the shadows of the building.

But at the last apartment they had unexpected success. An eleven-year-old boy had just come home from school for lunch. He heard the question asked of his mother.

"Oh, I told a man which apartment Miss Burns lived in," he reported. "You remember, Ma, when you made me walk Porgy just before I went to bed, after *Happy Days . . .*"

"That would be around nine thirty," the boy's mother said. "You didn't tell me you spoke to anyone," she said accusingly to her son.

The boy shrugged. "It was no big deal. A man parked at the curb just when I was coming back down the block. He asked me if I knew which apartment Miss Burns was in. I pointed it out. That's all."

"What did he look like?" Charley asked.

The boy frowned. "Oh, he was nice-looking. He had sort of dark hair and he was tall and *his car was neat.* It was a 'Vette."

Charley and Phil looked at each other. "Chris Lewis," Charley said flatly.

On Friday morning, Katie got into the office by seven o'clock and began a final review of the case she was trying. The defendants were eighteen- and seventeen-year-old brothers accused of vandalizing two schools by setting fires in twelve classrooms.

Maureen came in at eight thirty carrying a steaming coffeepot. Katie looked up. "Boy, I'm going all out to nail those two," she said. "They did it for kicks—*for kicks.* When you see the way people are struggling to pay taxes to keep up the schools their kids go to, it's sickening; it's more than a crime."

Maureen reached for Katie's coffee cup and filled it. "One of those schools is in my town, and the children next door go there. The ten-year-old had just finished a project for the science fair. It was fantastic—a solar heating unit. Poor little kid worked on it for months. It got burned in the fire. There was just nothing left of it."

Katie jotted a note on the side of her opening statement. "That gives me some extra ammunition. Thanks."

"Katie . . ." Maureen's voice was hesitant.

Katie looked up into troubled green eyes. "Yes?"

"Rita told me that she told you about . . . about the baby."

"Yes, she did. I'm terribly sorry, Maureen."

"The thing is I can't seem to get over it. And now this Vangie Lewis case . . . all the talk about that . . . only brings it back. I've been trying to forget. . . ."

Katie nodded. "Maureen, I'd have given anything to have had a baby when John died. That year I prayed I'd get pregnant so I'd have something of him. When I think of all the friends I have who elect never to have children or who have an abortion as casually as they have their hair set, I wonder about the way life works out. I just pray God that someday I will have children of my own. You will too, of course, and we'll both appreciate them because of not having the ones we wanted before."

Maureen's eyes were filled with tears. "I hope so. But the thing about the Vangie Lewis case is—"

The telephone rang. Katie reached for it. It was Scott. "Glad you're in, Katie. Can you run over here for a minute?"

"Of course." Katie got up. "Scott wants me now. We'll talk later, Maureen." Impulsively she hugged the girl.

Scott was standing by the window staring out. Katie was sure he was not seeing the barred windows of the county jail. He turned when she came in.

"You're on trial today—the Odendall brothers?"

"Yes. We have a good case."

"How long will it take?"

"Most of the day, I'm sure. They're bringing character witnesses from their kindergarten teacher on up, but we'll get them."

"You usually do, Katie. Have you heard about Dr. Salem yet?"

"You mean the doctor from Minneapolis who called Richard? No, I haven't spoken to anyone this morning. I went straight to my office."

"He fell—or was pushed—out a window in the Essex House last night a few minutes after he checked into the hotel. We're working with the New York police on it. And incidentally, Vangie Lewis' body arrived from Minneapolis last night, but Lewis wasn't on the flight."

Katie stared at Scott. "What are you saying?"

"I'm saying that he probably took the flight that went into LaGuardia. It would have gotten him into New York about the time Salem checked in. I'm saying that if we find he was anywhere in the vicinity of that hotel, we may be able to wrap this case up. I don't like the Lewis suicide, I don't like the Edna Burns accidental death and I don't like the idea that Salem fell from a window."

"I don't believe Chris Lewis is a murderer," Katie said flatly. "Where do you think he is now?"

Scott shrugged. "Hiding out in New York, probably. My guess is that when we talk to his girlfriend she'll lead us to him, and she's due in from Florida tonight. Can you hang around this evening?"

Katie hesitated. "This is the one weekend I have to be away. It's something I can't change. But I'll be honest, Scott. I feel so absolutely lousy that I'm not even thinking straight. I'll get through this trial . . . I'm well prepared; but then I will leave."

Scott studied her. "I've told you all week that you shouldn't have come in," he said, "and right now you look paler than you did Tuesday morning. All right, get the trial over with and clear out of here. There'll be plenty of work on this case next week. We'll go over everything Monday morning. You think you'll be in?"

"Positively."

"You should have a complete checkup."

"I'm going to see a doctor this weekend."

"Good."

Scott looked down at his desk, a signal that the meeting was over. Katie went back to her own office. It was nearly nine, and she was due in the courtroom. Mentally she reviewed the schedule of the pills Dr. Highley had given her. She'd taken one last night, one at six o'clock this morning. She was supposed to take one every three hours today. She'd better swallow one now before going down to court. She washed it down with the last sip of coffee from the cup on her desk, then gathered her file. The sharp edge of the top page of the brief slit her finger. She gasped at the quick thrust of pain and popping a tissue from her top drawer wrapped it around the finger and hurried from the room.

Half an hour later as, with the rest of the people in the courtroom, she rose to acknowledge the entrance of the judge, the tissue was still wet with blood.

 CHAPTER 48

E dna Burns was buried on Friday morning after an eleven-o'clock Mass of the Resurrection at St. Francis Xavier Church. Gana Krupshak and Gertrude Fitzgerald followed the coffin to the nearby cemetery and, holding hands tightly, watched Edna placed in the grave with her parents. The priest, Father Durkin, conducted the final ceremony, sprinkled holy water over the coffin and escorted them back to Gertrude's car.

"Will you ladies join me for a cup of coffee?" he asked.

Gertrude dabbed at her eyes and shook her head. "I really have to get to work," she said. "I'm taking Edna's place until they find a new receptionist, and the doctors both have office hours this afternoon."

Mrs. Krupshak also declined. "But Father, if you're on your way back to the rectory, would you drop me off? Then I won't take Gertrude out of her way."

"Of course."

Gana turned to Gertrude. Impulsively she said, "Why don't you come by for dinner with us tonight? I have a nice pot roast I'm cooking."

The thought of going back to her own solitary apartment had been upsetting Gertrude, and she quickly accepted the offer. It would be good to talk about Edna tonight with the other person who'd been her friend. She wanted to express to Gana what a crying shame it was that neither of the doctors had come to the Mass, although at least Dr. Fukhito had sent flowers. Maybe talking it out with Gana would help her to think clearly and she'd be able to get a handle on that thought which kept buzzing around inside her head—about something that Edna had said to her.

She said good-bye to Gana and Father Durkin, got into her car, turned on the ignition and released the brake. Dr. Highley's face loomed in her mind: those big, fishlike, cold eyes. Oh, he'd been nice enough to her Tuesday night, giving her the pill to calm her down and what-have-you. But there was something funny about him that night. Like when he went to get her a drink of water, she'd started to follow him. She didn't want him waiting on her. He'd turned on the water tap, then gone into the bedroom. From the hall she'd seen him take out his handkerchief and start to open Edna's night-table drawer.

Then that nice Dr. Carroll had started to walk down the hall and Dr. Highley had closed the drawer, stuffed the handkerchief in his pocket and backed up so it looked like he was just standing in the bedroom doorway.

Gertrude had let Dr. Carroll pass her, then slipped back into the living room. She didn't want them to think she was trying to overhear what they were saying. But if Dr. Highley wanted something from that drawer, why didn't he just say so and get it? And why on earth would he open the drawer holding a handkerchief over his fingers? Certainly he didn't think Edna's apartment was too dirty for him to touch. Why, it was immaculate!

Dr. Highley always was a strange man. Truth to tell, like Edna, she'd always been a little afraid of him. No way would she agree to take over Edna's job if it was offered to her. Her mind decided on that point, Gertrude steered the car off the cemetery road and onto Forest Avenue.

CHAPTER 49

The lifeless body of Vangie Lewis was placed on the slab in the autopsy room of the Valley County Medical Examiner. His face impassive, Richard watched as his assistant removed the silk caftan that was to have been Vangie's burial robe. What had seemed soft and natural in the gentle light of the funeral parlor now resembled a department-store mannequin, features with a total absence of life.

Vangie's blond hair had been carefully coiffed to flow loose on her shoulders. Now the hair spray had begun to harden, separating the hairs into thin, strawlike groups. Fleetingly, Richard remembered that St. Francis Borgia had given up a life at court and entered a monastery after viewing the decaying body of a once-beautiful queen.

Sharply, he pulled his mind to the medical problem at hand. He had missed something about Vangie's body on Tuesday afternoon. He was

sure of that. It had something to do with her legs or feet. He would concentrate his attention there.

Fifteen minutes later he found what he was seeking: a two-inch scratch on Vangie's left foot. He had dismissed it because he'd been so involved with the cyanide burns and the fetus.

That scratch was fresh. There was no sign of healing skin. That was what had bothered him. Vangie's foot had been scratched shortly before her death, and Charley had found a piece of the cloth from the dress she was wearing when she died protruding from a sharp implement in the garage.

Richard turned to his assistant. "The lab is supposed to be finished with the clothes Mrs. Lewis was wearing when we brought her in. Will you please get them and dress her in them again. Call me when she's ready."

Back in his office, he scribbled on a pad: *Shoes Vangie was wearing when found. Sensible walking shoes, cut fairly high on sides. Could not have been wearing them when foot was scratched.*

He began to examine the notes he'd made during the night. The Berkeley baby. He was going to talk to Jim Berkeley, get him to admit that the baby was adopted.

But what would that prove?

Nothing of itself, but it would begin the investigation. Once that admission was made, the whole Westlake Maternity Concept would be exposed as a gigantic fraud.

Would anyone kill to prevent that fraud from being exposed?

He needed to see Dr. Salem's medical records on Vangie Lewis. By now, Scott must have reached Dr. Salem's office. Quickly, he dialed Scott. "Have you spoken to Salem's nurse?"

"Yes, and also to his wife. They're both terribly broken up. Both swear he had no history of high blood pressure or dizziness. No personal problems, no money problems, a full schedule of lecturing for the next six months. So I say, forget both the suicide and the accidental-fall angles."

"How about Vangie Lewis? What did the nurse know?"

"Dr. Salem asked her to get out Vangie's file yesterday morning in his office. Then, just before he left for his plane, he made a long-distance phone call."

"That might have been the one to me."

"Possibly. But the nurse said that he told her he had other long-distance calls to make, but he'd use his credit card from the airport after he checked in for his flight. Apparently he had a thing about getting to the airport with a lot of time to spare."

"Is she sending Vangie's file to us? I want to see it."

"No, she's not." Scott's voice hardened. "Dr. Salem took it with him. She saw him put it in his attaché case. That case was found in his room. But the Lewis file wasn't in it. And get this: After Dr. Salem left, Chris Lewis phoned his office. Said he had to talk to Salem. The nurse told him where Dr. Salem would be staying in New York, even to giving him the room number. I'll tell you something, Richard: by the end of the day I expect to be swearing out a warrant for Lewis' arrest."

"You mean you think there was something in that file that Chris Lewis would kill to get? I find that hard to believe."

"Someone wanted that file," Scott said. "That's pretty obvious, isn't it?"

Richard hung up the phone. *Someone* wanted the file. The medical file. Who would know what was in it that might be threatening?

A doctor.

Was Katie right in her suspicions about the psychiatrist? What about Edgar Highley? He'd come to Valley County with the imprimatur of the Westlake name, a name respected in New Jersey medical circles.

Impatiently, Richard searched on his desk for the slip of paper Marge had given him with the names of the two patients who had filed malpractice suits against Edgar Highley.

Anthony Caldwell, Old Country Lane, Peapack.
Anna Horan, 415 Walnut Street, Ridgefield Park.

Turning on the intercom, he asked Marge to try to phone both people.

Marge came in a few minutes later. "Anthony Caldwell is no longer at that address. He moved to Michigan last year. I got a neighbor on the phone. She told me that his wife died of a tubal pregnancy and that he filed suit against the doctor, but it was dismissed. She was anxious to talk about it. Said Mrs. Caldwell had been told by two other doctors that she'd never conceive, but that as soon as she started the Westlake Maternity Concept program she became pregnant. But she was terribly sick all the time and finally died in her fourth month."

"That gives me enough information for the moment," Richard said. "We're going to subpoena all the hospital records. What about Mrs. Horan?"

"I caught her husband home. He's a law student at Rutgers. Says she's working as a computer programmer. Gave me her phone number at the job. Shall I get her for you now?"

"Yes, please."

Marge picked up Richard's phone, dialed and asked for Mrs. Anna Horan. A moment later, she said, "Mrs. Horan, one moment please. Dr. Carroll is calling."

Richard took the phone. "Mrs. Horan."

"Yes." There was a lilting inflection in her voice, an accent he could not place.

"Mrs. Horan, you filed a malpractice suit last year against Dr. Edgar Highley. I wonder if I might ask you some questions about that case. Are you free to talk?"

The voice on the other phone became agitated. "No . . . not here."

"I understand. But it's urgent. Would it be possible for you to stop by my office after work today and talk with me?"

"Yes . . . all right." Clearly, the woman wanted to get off the phone.

Richard gave the office address and offered directions, but was interrupted.

"I know how to get to you. . . . I'll be there by five thirty."

The connection was broken. Richard looked at Marge and shrugged. "She's not happy about it, but she's coming in."

It was nearly noon. Richard decided to go to the courtroom where Katie was trying the Odendall case and see if she'd have lunch with him. He wanted to ventilate his thoughts about Edgar Highley. Katie had interviewed him. What had her reaction been? Would she agree that maybe there was something wrong about the Westlake Maternity Concept—either a baby ring or a doctor who took criminal chances with his patients' lives?

When he got to the courtroom, it was deserted except for Katie, who was still at the prosecutor's table.

Preoccupied with her notes, she barely looked up when he came over to her. At his suggestion of lunch, she shook her head.

"Richard, I'm up to my eyes in this. Those skunks have retracted their confession. Now they're trying to say someone else set the fires, and they're such convincing liars I swear the jury is falling for it. I've got to work on the cross-examination." Her eyes went back to her notes.

Richard studied her. Her usually olive skin was deadly pale. Her eyes when she'd looked up at him had been heavy and clouded. He noticed the tissue wrapped around her finger. Gently, he reached over and unwound it.

Katie looked up. "What . . . oh, that darn thing. It must be deep. It's been bleeding off and on all morning. I needed that."

Richard studied the cut. Released from the tissue, it began to flow rapidly. Pressing the tissue over the cut, he reached for a rubber band and wound it above the cut. "Leave this on for about twenty minutes. That should stop it. Have you been having any clotting problems, Katie?"

"Yes, some. But oh, Richard, I can't talk about it now. This case is running away from me and I feel so lousy." Her voice broke.

The courtroom was empty except for the two of them. Richard reached down and put his arms around her. He hugged her head against his chest and put his lips on her hair. "Katie, I'm going to clear out now. But wherever you go this weekend, do some thinking. Because I'm throwing my hat in the ring. I want you. I want to take care of you. If there's someone you're seeing now, tell him he's got stiff competition, because whoever he is, he's not watching out for you. If it's the past that's holding you, I'm going to try to break that hold."

He straightened up. "Now go ahead and win your case. You can do it. And for God's sake, take it easy this weekend. Monday, I'm going to need your input on an angle I see developing in the Lewis case."

All morning she'd felt so cold—so desperately, icy cold. Even the long-sleeved wool dress hadn't helped. Now, so close to Richard, the warmth of his body communicated itself to her. As he turned to leave, she impulsively grasped his hand and held it against her face. "Monday," she said.

"Monday," he agreed, and left the courtroom.

⟣ CHAPTER 50

Before they left the garden apartment complex where Edna had lived, Charley and Phil rang the Krupshaks' doorbell. Gana had just returned from the funeral.

"We're finished with our investigation in the apartment," Charley told her. "You're free to enter it." He showed her the note Edna had left. "I have to check on whether this constitutes a will, but all that stuff isn't worth a thousand dollars, so my guess is that we'll return that jewelry to you, and you and Mrs. Fitzgerald can divide it and the furniture. At least, you can look it over and decide it between yourselves; but don't remove anything yet."

The two investigators returned to the office and went directly to the lab, where they turned in the contents of the vacuum bag, the plant that had been on the windowsill and the traces of earth they had removed from the ground. "Run these through right away," Phil directed. "This stuff gets top priority."

Scott was waiting for them in his office. At the news that Chris had been in the vicinity of Edna's apartment on Tuesday night, he grunted with satisfaction. "Lewis seems to have been all over the map this week," he said, "and wherever he's been someone has died. I sent Rita over to New York this morning with a picture of Chris Lewis. Two bellmen positively identify him as being in the lobby of the Essex House

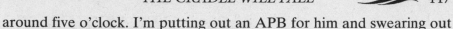

around five o'clock. I'm putting out an APB for him and swearing out a warrant for his arrest."

The phone rang. Impatiently, he reached for it and identified himself. Then his expression changed. "Put her on," he said quickly. Holding his hand over the speaker, he said, "Chris Lewis' girlfriend is calling from Florida . . . Hello, yes, this is the Prosecutor." He paused. "Yes, we are looking for Captain Lewis. Do you know where he is?"

Charley and Phil exchanged glances. Scott's forehead furrowed as he listened. "Very well. He'll be on the plane with you arriving in Newark at seven P.M. I'm very glad to know that he's surrendering voluntarily. If he wishes to consult with a lawyer, he may want to have one here. Thank you."

He hung up the phone. "Lewis is coming in," he said. "We'll crack this case open tonight."

CHAPTER 51

Through the long, sleepless night, Edgar Highley rationalized the problem of the stolen bag. It might never show up. If it had been abandoned after the thief went through it, the odds were he'd never see it again. Few people would take the trouble to try to return it. More than likely they'd simply keep the bag and throw out the contents.

Suppose the bag were recovered intact by the New York police? His name and the address of the hospital were inside it. If the police phoned him, they'd probably ask for a list of the contents. He'd simply mention some standard drugs, a few instruments and several patients' files. A medical file with the name VANGIE LEWIS on the tab would mean nothing to them. They probably wouldn't bother to study it. They'd just assume it was his. If they asked about the shoe and the bloodstained paperweight, he would deny any knowledge of them; he'd point out that obviously, the thief must have put them there.

It would be all right. And tonight the last risk would be removed. At five A.M. he gave up trying to sleep; showered, standing under the hot needle spray nearly ten minutes until the bathroom was filled with steam; wrapped himself in a heavy ankle-length robe and went down to the kitchen. He was not going in to the office until noon, and he'd make his hospital rounds just before that. Until then, he'd go over his research notes. Yesterday's patient would be his new experiment. But he hadn't yet chosen the donor.

At four o'clock, Richard, Scott, Charley and Phil studied the body of Vangie Lewis, now dressed in the clothes in which she had died. The scrap of flowered material that had been found on the prong in the garage exactly fitted the tear near the hem of her dress. The panty hose on her left foot showed a two-inch slash directly over the fresh cut.

"No trace of blood on the hosiery," Richard said. "She was already dead when her foot caught on the prong."

"How high was the shelf that prong was on?" Scott asked.

Phil shrugged. "About two feet from the floor."

"Which means that someone carried Vangie Lewis in through the garage, laid her on her bed and tried to give the appearance of a suicide," Scott said.

"Without question," Richard agreed. But he was frowning. "How tall is Chris Lewis?" he asked.

Scott shrugged. "He's a big one. Maybe six feet four. Why?"

"Let's try something. Wait a minute." Richard left the room, returning with a ruler. Carefully, he marked the wall at heights of two, three and four feet from the floor. "If we assume Chris Lewis was the one who carried Vangie in, I suggest that she would not have been scratched by that prong." He turned to Phil. "You're sure the shelf was two feet off the ground?"

Phil shrugged. "Within an inch." Charley nodded in agreement.

"All right. I'm six feet two. Gently, Richard put one arm under the dead woman's neck, the other under her knees. Picking her up, he walked over to the wall. "Look where her foot touches. She was small. It wouldn't have been grazed by any object lower than three feet on the shelf *if* she was carried by a tall man. On the other hand . . ." He walked over to Phil. "How tall are you . . . About five feet ten?"

"Just about."

"All right. Chris Lewis has over six inches on you. Take her and see where her foot falls when you hold her."

Gingerly, Phil accepted the body and walked by the wall. Vangie's foot trailed against the first mark Richard had made. Quickly, Phil laid her back on the slab.

Scott shook his head. "Inconclusive. Impossible to figure. Maybe he was bending over, trying to hold her away from him." He turned to the attendant. "We'll want those clothes as evidence. Take good care of them. Get some photos of the cut, the stocking and the dress."

He walked with Richard back to his office. "You're still thinking about the psychiatrist, aren't you?" he asked. "He's about five ten."

Richard hesitated and decided not to say anything until he had spoken with Jim Berkeley and the woman patient who had pressed the malpractice suit. He changed the subject. "How's Katie doing?"

Scott shook his head. "Hard to say. Those bums are blaming the vandalism on one of their friends who was killed on his motorcycle last November. Their new story is they took the rap for him because they felt sorry for his folks, but now their minister has persuaded them for the sake of their own family they have to tell the truth."

Richard snorted. "The jury isn't falling for that, is it?"

Scott said, "It's out now. Listen, no matter how hard you try to pick your jury, there's always one bleeding-heart on it who will fall for a sob story. Katie's done a great job, but it could go either way. Okay. I'll see you later."

At four thirty, Jim Berkeley returned Richard's call. "I understand you've been trying to reach me." His voice was guarded.

"Yes." Richard matched the other man's impersonal tone. "It's important that I speak with you. Can you stop in my office on your way home?"

"Yes, I can." Now Jim's voice became resigned. "And I think I know what you want to talk about."

<h1 style="text-align:center;"> CHAPTER 53</h1>

Edgar Highley turned from the girl on the examining table. "You may get dressed now."

She had claimed to be twenty, but he was sure she wasn't more than sixteen or seventeen. "Am I . . ."

"Yes, my dear. You are very definitely pregnant. About five weeks, I should think. I want you to return tomorrow morning and we will terminate the pregnancy."

"I was wondering: do you think I should maybe have the baby and have it adopted?"

"Have you told your parents about this?"

"No. They'd be so upset."

"Then I suggest you postpone motherhood for several years at least. Ten o'clock tomorrow."

He left the room, went into his office and looked up the phone number of the new patient he had chosen yesterday. "Mrs. Englehart, this is Dr. Highley. I want to begin your treatment. Kindly come to the hospital tomorrow morning at eight thirty and prepare to spend the night."

⌇ *CHAPTER 54*

Whrile the jury was deliberating, Katie went into the courthouse cafeteria. She carefully chose a small table at the end of the room and sat with her back to the other tables. She did not want anyone to either join or notice her. The light-headed feeling was persistent now; she felt fatigued and weak, but not hungry. Just a cup of tea, she thought. Mama always thought that a cup of tea would cure all the ills of the world. She remembered coming back to the house from John's funeral, her mother's voice concerned, gentle: "I'll make you a nice hot cup of tea, Katie."

Richard. Mama would love Richard. She always liked big men. "Your dad was a skinny little one, but oh, Katie, didn't he seem like a big man?"

Yes, he did.

Mama was coming up for Easter. That was just six weeks from now. Mama would be so delighted if she and Richard got together.

I do want that, don't I? Katie thought as she sipped the tea. It's not just because I'm so aware of loneliness this week.

It was more than that. Much more. But this weekend in the hospital, she'd be able to sort things through, to think quietly.

She sat for nearly an hour, absently sipping the tea, reviewing every step of her summation. Had she convinced the jury that the Odendall boys were lying? The minister. She'd scored there. He'd agreed that neither boy was a churchgoer; that neither boy had ever consulted him for any reason before. Was it possible that he was being used by them to bolster their story? "Yes," he agreed. "It is possible." She had made that point. She was sure of it.

At five o'clock she returned to the courtroom. As she entered, the jury sent word to the judge that it had reached a verdict.

Five minutes later, the foreman announced the verdict: "Robert Odendall, not guilty on all counts. Jonathan Odendall, not guilty on all counts."

"I don't believe it." Katie wasn't sure if she had spoken aloud. The judge's face hardened into angry lines. He dismissed the jury curtly and told the defendants to stand up.

"You are very lucky," he snapped, "luckier than I hope you'll ever be again in either of your lives. Now clear out of my courtroom, and if you're smart you'll never appear before me again."

Katie stood up. No matter if the judge clearly felt the verdict was erroneous, she had lost the case. She should have done more. She felt rather than saw the victorious smile the defense attorney shot at her. A thick, hard lump burned in her throat, making it impossible to swallow. She was within inches of tears. Those two criminals were about to be released on the streets after flouting justice. A dead boy had been labeled a criminal.

She stuffed her notes into her briefcase. Maybe if she hadn't felt so lousy all week she'd have conducted a better case. Maybe if she'd had this hemorrhaging problem taken care of a year ago instead of delaying and putting it off with this crazy, childish fear of hospitals, she wouldn't have had the accident Monday night.

"Will the State please approach the bench?"

She looked up. The judge was beckoning to her. She walked over to him. The spectators were filing out. She could hear delighted squeals as the Odendalls embraced their gum-chewing, braless girlfriends.

"Your Honor." Katie managed to keep her voice steady.

The judge leaned over and whispered to her: "Don't let it get you down, Katie. You proved that case. Those little bastards will be back here in two months on other charges. We both know it, and next time you'll nail them."

Katie tried to smile. "That's just what I'm afraid of, that they will be back. God knows how much damage they'll be doing before we can nail them. But thanks, Judge."

She left the courtroom and went back to her office. Maureen looked up hopefully. Katie shook her head and watched the expression change to sympathy. She shrugged. "What can you do, huh?"

Maureen followed her into her office. "Mr. Meyerson and Dr. Carroll are in a meeting. They don't want to be disturbed. But of course, you can go in."

"No. I'm sure it's the Lewis case, and I'd be of no use to them or anyone else right now. I'll catch up on Monday."

"All right. Katie, I'm sorry about the Odendall verdict, but try not to take it so hard. You really look sick. Are you all right to drive? You're not dizzy or anything?"

"No, really, and I'm not going far. I'll be driving just fifteen minutes and then I won't budge till Sunday."

As she walked to the car, Katie shuddered. The temperature had gotten up to about forty degrees in the afternoon, but was dropping rapidly again. The wet, damp air penetrated the loose sleeves of her red wool wraparound coat and pierced her nylon hose. She thought longingly of her own room, her own bed. How great it would be to be able to go there now, to just go to bed with a hot toddy and sleep the weekend away.

At the hospital, the admitting office had her completed forms waiting. The clerk was briskly bright.

"My goodness, Mrs. DeMaio, you certainly rate. Dr. Highley has given you the bedroom of Suite One on the third floor. That's like going on a vacation. You'll never dream you're in a hospital."

"He said something about that," Katie murmured. She was not about to confide her fear of hospitals to this woman.

"You may be a bit lonesome up there. There are just three suites on that floor, and the other two are empty. And Dr. Highley is having the living room of your suite redecorated. Why, I don't know. It was done less than a year ago. But anyhow, you won't need it. You'll only be here till Sunday. If you want anything, all you have to do is press the buzzer. The second-floor nursing station takes care of both the second- and third-floor patients. They're all Dr. Highley's patients anyhow. Now, here's your wheelchair. If you'll just get into it, we'll whisk you upstairs."

Katie stared in consternation. "You don't mean I have to use a wheelchair now?"

"Hospital regulations," the admitting clerk said firmly.

John in a wheelchair going up for chemotherapy. John's body shrinking as she watched him die. John's voice weakening, his wry, tired humor as the wheelchair was brought to his bed: "Swing low, sweet chariot, coming for to carry me home." The antiseptic hospital smell.

Katie sat down in the chair and closed her eyes. There was no turning back. The attendant, a middle-aged, solidly plump volunteer, pushed the chair down the corridor to the elevator.

"You're lucky to have Dr. Highley," she informed Katie. "His patients get the best care in the hospital. You push that buzzer for someone and you'll have a nurse at your beck and call in thirty seconds. Dr. Highley is strict. The whole staff trembles when he's around, but he's good."

They were at the elevator. The attendant pushed the button. "This place is so different from most hospitals. Most places don't want to see you until you're ready to deliver, and then they shove you out when the

baby is a couple of days old. Not Dr. Highley. I've seen him put pregnant women to bed here for two months just as a precaution. That's
why he has suites, so people can have a homelike atmosphere. Mrs.
Aldrich is in the one on the second floor. She delivered by cesarean yesterday and hasn't stopped crying. She's that happy. Her husband's just
as bad. He slept on the sofa in the living room of her suite last night. Dr.
Highley encourages that. Well, here's the elevator."

Several other people got on the elevator with them. They glanced at
Katie curiously. Observing the magazines and flowers they were carrying, she decided they were obviously visitors. She felt oddly removed
from them. The minute you become a patient you lose your identity,
she thought. You become a case.

They got off at the third floor. The corridor was carpeted in a soft
green shade. Excellent reproductions of Monet and Matisse paintings
enhanced by recessed framing were scattered along the walls.

In spite of herself, Katie was reassured. The volunteer wheeled her
down the corridor and turned right. "You're in the end suite," she
exclaimed. "It's kind of far off. I don't think there's even any other
patients on this floor today."

"That's all right with me," Katie murmured. She thought of John's
room. The two of them wanting to absorb each other, to stockpile
against the separation. Ambulatory patients coming to the door, looking in. "How's it going today, Judge? He looks better, doesn't he, Mrs.
DeMaio?"

And she, lying, "Indeed he does." Go away, go away. We have so little time.

"I don't mind being alone on the floor," she repeated.

She was wheeled into a bedroom. The walls were ivory; the carpet,
the same soft green as the corridor. The furniture was antique white.
Printed draperies in shades of ivory and green matched the bedspread.
"Oh, this is nice," Katie exclaimed.

The attendant looked pleased. "I thought you'd like it. The nurse will
be in in a few minutes. Why don't you just put your things away and
make yourself comfortable?"

She was gone. Somewhat uncertainly, Katie undressed, put on a
nightgown and warm robe. She put her clothes in the closet. What in
God's name would she do for the long, dreary evening that stretched
before her? Last night at this time she'd been dressing to go to Molly's
dinner party. And when she'd arrived, Richard had been waiting for her.

She realized she was swaying. Instinctively, she reached for the
dresser and held on to it. The light-headed feeling passed. It was probably just the rushing, and the aftermath of the trial and—Let's face it,
she thought: apprehension.

She was in a hospital. No matter how she tried to push away the thought, she was in a hospital. Incredible, childish, that she could not overcome her fear. Daddy. John. The two people she'd loved best in the world had gone into the hospital and died. No matter how she tried to intellectualize, rationalize, she could not lose that terrible feeling of panic. Well, maybe this stay would get her over it. Monday night hadn't been that bad.

There were four doors in the room. The closet door, the bathroom door, the one leading to the corridor. The other one must go into the living room. She opened it and glanced in. As the admitting clerk had told her, it was pulled apart. The furniture was in the middle of the room and covered with painter's drop cloths. She flicked on the light. Dr. Highley surely was a perfectionist. There was nothing the matter with the walls that she could see. No wonder hospital costs were so outrageous.

Shrugging, she turned off the light, closed the door and walked over to the window. The hospital was U-shaped, the two wings parallel to each other at right angles behind the main section.

She'd been on the other side Monday night, exactly opposite where she was now. Visitors' cars were beginning to fill the lot. Where was the parking stall she'd dreamed about? Oh, of course—that one, over to the side, directly under the last light post. There was a car parked there now, a black car. In her dream it had been a black car. Those wired spokes; the way they glinted in the light.

"How are you feeling, Mrs. DeMaio?"

She spun around. Dr. Highley was standing in the room. A young nurse was hovering at his elbow.

"Oh, you startled me. I'm fine, Doctor."

"I knocked, but you didn't hear me." His voice was gently reproving. He came over to the window and drew the drapery. "No matter what we do, these windows are drafty," he commented. "We don't want you catching cold. Suppose you sit on the bed and let me check your pressure. We'll want to take some blood samples too."

The nurse followed him. Katie noticed that the girl's hands were trembling. She was obviously in awe of Dr. Highley.

The doctor wrapped the pressure cuff around her arm. A wave of dizziness made Katie feel as though the walls of the room were receding. She clutched at the mattress.

"Is there anything wrong, Mrs. DeMaio?" The doctor's voice was gentle.

"No, not really. I'm just a touch faint."

He began to pump the bulb. "Nurse Renge, kindly get a cold cloth for Mrs. DeMaio's forehead," he instructed.

The nurse obediently rushed into the bathroom. The doctor was studying the pressure gauge. "You're a bit low. Any problems?"

"Yes." Her voice sounded as though it belonged to someone else, or maybe as though she were in an echo chamber. "My period started again. It's been dreadfully heavy since Wednesday."

"I'm not surprised. Frankly, if you hadn't scheduled this operation, I'm quite sure you'd have been forced to have it on an emergency basis."

The nurse came out of the bathroom with a neatly folded cloth. She was biting her lower lip to keep it from quivering. Katie felt a rush of sympathy for her. She neither wanted nor needed a cold compress on her forehead, but leaned back against the pillow. The nurse put it on her head. The cloth was soaking, and she felt freezing water run down her hairline. She resisted the impulse to brush it away. The doctor would notice, and she didn't want the nurse to be reprimanded.

A flash of humor raised her spirits. She could just see telling Richard, "And this poor, scared kid practically drowned me. I'll probably have bursitis of the eyebrows from now on."

Richard. She should have told him she was coming here. She wanted him with her now.

Dr. Highley was holding a needle. She closed her eyes as he drew blood from a vein in her right arm. She watched him put the blood-filled vacu-tubes on the tray the nurse held out to him.

"I want these run through immediately," he said brusquely.

"Yes, Doctor." The nurse scurried out, obviously delighted to get away.

Dr. Highley sighed. "I'm afraid that timid young woman is on desk duty tonight. But you won't require anything special, I'm sure. Did you complete taking the pills I gave you?"

Katie realized that she had not taken the three-o'clock pill and it was now after six.

"I'm afraid I skipped at three o'clock," she apologized. "I was in court and everything but the trial went out of my mind, and I guess I'm overdue for the last one."

"Do you have the pills with you?"

"Yes, in my handbag." She glanced at the dresser.

"Don't get up. I'll hand it to you."

When she took the bag from him, she unzipped it, fished inside and brought out the small bottle. There were just two pills in it. The night table held a tray with a carafe of ice water and a glass. Dr. Highley poured water into the glass and gave it to her. "Finish these," he said.

"Both of them?"

"Yes. Yes. They're very mild, and I did want you to have them by six." He handed her the glass and dropped the empty jar into his pocket.

Obediently, she swallowed the pills, feeling his eyes on her. His steel-rimmed glasses glinted under the overhead light. The glint. The spokes of the car glinting.

There was a blur of red on the glass as she laid it down. He noticed it, reached for her hand and examined her finger. The tissue had become damp again.

"What's this?" he asked.

"Oh, nothing. Just a paper cut, but it must be deep. It keeps bleeding."

"I see." He stood up. "I've ordered a sleeping pill for you. Please take it as soon as the nurse brings it."

"I really prefer not to take sleeping pills, Doctor. They seem to cause an overreaction in me." She wanted to sound vehement. Instead, her voice had a lazy, weak quality.

"I'm afraid I insist on the pill, Mrs. DeMaio, particularly for someone like yourself who is likely to spend the night in sleepless anxiety without it. I want you well rested in the morning. Oh, here's your dinner now."

Katie watched as a thin, sixtyish woman carrying a tray came into the room and glanced nervously at the doctor. They're all petrified of him, she thought. Unlike the usual plastic or metal hospital tray, this one was made of white wicker and had a side basket that held the evening newspaper. The china was delicate, the silverware gracefully carved. A single red rose stood in a slender vase. Double loin lamb chops were kept hot by a silver dome over the dinner plate. An arugula salad, julienne string beans, small hot biscuits, tea and sherbet completed the meal. The attendant turned to go.

"Wait," Dr. Highley commanded. He said to Katie, "As you will see, all my patients are served fare that compares favorably with the food in a first-class restaurant. I think one of the abiding wastes in hospitals is the tons of institutional food that are thrown out daily while patients' families bring in CARE packages from home." He frowned. "However, I think I would prefer if you did not eat dinner tonight. I've come to believe that the longer a patient fasts before surgery, the less likelihood she will experience discomfort after it."

"I'm not at all hungry," Katie said.

"Fine." He nodded to the attendant. She picked up the tray and hurried out.

"I'll leave you now," Dr. Highley told Katie. "You *will* take the sleeping pill."

Her nod was noncommittal.

At the door he paused. "Oh, I regret, your phone apparently isn't working. The repairman will take care of it in the morning. Is there anyone you expect to call you here tonight? Or perhaps you'll be having a visitor?"

"No. No calls or visitors. My sister is the only one who knows I'm here, and she's at the opera tonight."

He smiled. "I see. Well, good night, Mrs. DeMaio, and please relax. You can trust me to take care of you."

"I'm sure I can."

He was gone. She leaned back on the pillow, closing her eyes. She was floating somewhere; her body was drifting, drifting like . . .

"Mrs. DeMaio." A young voice was apologetic. Katie opened her eyes. "What . . . oh, I must have dozed." It was Nurse Renge. She was carrying a tray with a pill in a small paper cup. "You're to take this now. It's the sleeping pill Dr. Highley ordered. He said I was to stay and be sure you took it." Even with Dr. Highley gone, the girl seemed nervous. "It always makes patients mad when we have to wake them up to give them a sleeping pill, but that's the way it works in the hospital."

"Oh." Katie reached for the pill, put it in her mouth, gulped down water from her carafe.

"Would you like to get settled in bed now? I'll turn down your covers for you."

Katie realized she'd been sleeping on top of the spread. She nodded, pulled herself up and went into the bathroom. There she removed the sleeping pill from under her tongue. Some of it had already dissolved, but she managed to spit out most of it. No way, she thought. I'd rather be awake than have nightmares. She splashed water on her face, brushed her teeth and returned to the bedroom. She felt so weak, so vague.

The nurse helped her into bed. "You really are tired, aren't you? Well, I'll tuck you in, and I'm sure you'll have a good night's sleep. Just push the buzzer if you need me for anything."

"Thank you." Her head was so heavy. Her eyes felt glued together.

Nurse Renge went over and pulled down the shade. "It's started to snow again, but it's going to change to rain. It's a wicked night, a good night to be in bed."

"Open the drapes and raise the window just about an inch, won't you?" Katie murmured. "I always like fresh air in my bedroom."

"Certainly. Shall I turn off the light now, Mrs. DeMaio?"

"Please." She didn't want to do anything except sleep.

"Good night, Mrs. DeMaio."

"Good night. Oh, what time is it, please?"

"Just eight o'clock."

"Thank you."

The nurse left. Katie closed her eyes. Minutes passed. Her breathing became even. At eight thirty, she was not aware of the faint sound that was caused when the handle on the door from the living room of the suite began to turn.

Gertrude and the Krupshaks lingered over Gana's pot roast dinner. Gratefully, Gertrude acceded to Gana's urgings to have seconds, to have a generous slice of homemade chocolate cake. "I don't usually eat this much," she apologized, "but I haven't swallowed a morsel since we found poor Edna."

Gana nodded soberly. Her husband picked up his coffee cup and dessert plate. "The Knicks are playing," he announced. "I'm gonna watch." His blunt tone was not ungracious. He settled himself in the living room and switched on the dial.

Gana sighed. "The Knicks . . . the Mets . . . the Giants . . . One season after the other. But on the other hand, he's *here.* I can look across the room and there he is. Or if I come home from bingo, I know I'm not going into an empty place, like poor Edna always had to."

"I know." Gertrude thought of her own solitary home, then reflected on her oldest granddaughter. "Gran, why not come to dinner?" or "Gran, are you going to be home Sunday? We thought we'd drop in to say hello." She could have it a lot worse.

"Maybe we should go in and take a look at Edna's place," Gana said. "I don't want to rush you . . . I mean, have more coffee, or another piece of cake . . ."

"No. Oh, no. We should go in. You kind of hate to do it, but it's something you can't avoid."

"I'll get the key."

They hurried across the courtyard. While they were at the table, the wet, cold combination of snow and rain had once again begun to fall. Gana dug her chin into her coat collar. She thought of Edna's lovely imitation-leopard coat. Maybe she could take it home tonight. It was hers.

Inside the apartment, they became quiet. The finger-printing powder the detectives had used was still visible on the tabletops and door handles. Inadvertently, they both stared at the spot where Edna's crumpled body had lain.

"There's still blood on the radiator," Gana muttered. "Gus'll probably repaint it."

"Yes." Gertrude shook herself. Get this over with. She knew her granddaughter's taste. Besides the velour couch, Nan would love those matching chairs, the tall-backed ones with mahogany arms and legs. One was a rocker, the other a straight chair. She remembered Edna's telling her that when she was a child, they'd been covered in blue velvet with a delicate leaf pattern. She'd had them redone inexpensively and always sighed, "They never looked the same."

If Nan had them re-covered in velvet again, they'd be beautiful. And that piecrust table. Altman's had copies of that in the reproduction gallery. Cost a fortune, too. Of course, this one was pretty nicked, but Nan's husband could refinish anything. Oh, Edna, Gertrude thought. You were smarter than most of us. You knew the value of things.

Gana was at the closet removing the leopard coat. "Edna loaned me this last year," she said. "I was going to a social with Gus. I love it."

It did not take them long to finish sharing the contents of the apartment. Gana had little interest in the furniture; what Gertrude did not want she was giving to the Salvation Army; but she was delighted when Gertrude suggested she take the silver plate and good china. They agreed that Edna's wardrobe would also go to the Salvation Army. She had been shorter and heavier than either of them.

"I guess that's it," Gana sighed. "Except for the jewelry, and the police will give that back to us pretty soon. You get the ring, and she left the pin to me."

The jewelry. Edna had kept it in the night-table drawer. Gertrude thought of Tuesday night. That was the drawer Dr. Highley had started to open.

"That reminds me," she said: "we never did look there. Let's make sure we didn't forget anything." She pulled it open. She knew that the police had removed the jewelry box. But the deep drawer was not empty. A scuffed moccasin lay at the bottom of it.

"Well, as I live and breathe," Gana sighed. "Now, can you tell me why Edna would save that thing?" She picked it up and held it to the light. It was out of shape; the heel was run down; white stains on the sides suggested it had been exposed to salted snow.

"That's it!" Gertrude cried. "That's what had me mixed up."

At Gana's mystified expression, she tried to explain. "Mrs. DeMaio asked me if Edna called one of the doctors Prince Charming. And that's what confused me. Of course she didn't. But Edna did tell me how Mrs. Lewis wore terrible old moccasins for her appointments. Why, she pointed them out to me only a couple of weeks ago when Mrs. Lewis was leaving. Edna said that she always kidded Mrs. Lewis. The left shoe was too loose, and Mrs. Lewis was always walking out of it. Edna used to tease Mrs. Lewis that she must be expecting Prince Charming to pick up her glass slipper."

"But Prince Charming wasn't Cinderella's boyfriend," Gana protested. "He was in the 'Sleeping Beauty' fairy tale."

"That's what I mean. I told Edna that she had it mixed up. She just laughed and said that Mrs. Lewis told her the same thing, but that her mother told her the story that way and it was good enough for her."

Gertrude reflected. "Mrs. DeMaio was so anxious when she asked about that Prince Charming talk. And Wednesday night—I wonder:

could Mrs. Lewis' shoe be what Dr. Highley wanted from this drawer? Is that possible? You know, I've half a mind to go to Mrs. DeMaio's office and talk to her, or at least leave a message for her. Somehow I just feel I shouldn't wait till Monday."

Gana thought of Gus, who wouldn't have his eyes off the set until nearly midnight. Her acquisitive desire for excitement surged. She'd never been in the Prosecutor's office. "Mrs. DeMaio asked me whether Edna kept her mother's old shoe for sentimental reasons," she said. "I'll bet she was talking about this moccasin. Tell you what: I'll drive over there with you. Gus'll never know I'm gone."

CHAPTER 56

Jim Berkeley parked his car in the courthouse lot and went into the main lobby. The directory showed that the Medical Examiner's office was on the second floor in the old wing of the building. He had seen the expression on Richard Carroll's face last night when he'd looked at the baby. Anger and resentment had made him want to say, "So the baby doesn't look like us. So what?" But it would have been stupid to do that. Worse, it would have been useless.

After several wrong turns in the labyrinth of the building, he found Richard's office. The secretarial desk was empty, but Richard's door was open, and he came out immediately when he heard the reception-area door snap shut. "Jim, it's good of you to come." Obviously, he was trying to be friendly, Jim thought. He was trying to make this seem a casual meeting. His own greeting was reserved and cautious. They went inside. Richard eyed him. Jim stared back impassively. There was none of the easy humor of last night's dinner.

Obviously, Richard got the message. His manner became businesslike. Jim stiffened.

"Jim, we're investigating Vangie Lewis' death. She was a patient at Westlake Maternity Clinic. That's where your wife had the baby."

Jim nodded.

Richard was obviously picking his words carefully. "We are disturbed at some problems that we see coming out of our investigation. Now, I want to ask you some questions—and I swear to you that your answers will remain in this room. But you can be of tremendous help to us, if—"

"*If* I tell you that Maryanne is adopted. Is that it?"

"Yes."

The anger drained from Jim. He thought of Maryanne. Whatever the cost, she was worth having. "No, she is not adopted. I was at her birth. I filmed it. She has a small birthmark on her left thumb. It shows in those pictures."

"It is quite unlikely for two brown-eyed parents to have a green-eyed child," Richard said flatly. Then he stopped. "Are you the baby's father?" he asked quietly.

Jim stared down at his hands. "If you mean would Liz have had an affair with another man? No. I'd stake my life and my soul on that."

"How about artificial insemination?" Richard asked. "Dr. Highley is a fertility expert."

"Liz and I discussed that possibility," Jim said. "We both rejected it years ago."

"Might Liz have changed her mind and not told you? It's not that unusual anymore. There are some fifteen thousand babies born every year in the United States by that means."

Jim reached into his pocket and pulled out his wallet. Flipping it open, he showed Richard two pictures of Liz, himself and the baby. In the first one, Maryanne was an infant; her eyes were almost shut. The second was a recent Kodachrome. The contrast between the skin tone and eye color of the parents and the baby was unmistakable.

Jim said, "The year before Liz became pregnant, we learned that it was almost impossible for us to adopt. Liz and I discussed artificial insemination. We both decided against it, but I was more emphatic than she. Maryanne had light brown hair when she was born, and blue eyes. A lot of babies start out having blue eyes and then they turn the parents' color. So it's just the last few months that it's become obvious that something is wrong. Not that I care. That baby is everything to us." He looked at Richard. "My wife won't even tell a social lie. She's the most honest person I've ever known in my life. Last month I decided to make it easy for her. I said that I'd been wrong about artificial insemination, that I could see why people went ahead with it."

"What did she say?" Richard asked.

"She knew what I meant, of course. She said that if I thought she could make a decision like that and not tell me, I didn't understand our relationship.

"I apologized to her, swore I didn't mean that; went through hell trying to reassure her. Finally, she believed me." He stared at the picture. "But of course, I know she was lying," he blurted out.

"Or else she wasn't aware of what Highley did to her," Richard said flatly.

D annyboy Duke zigzagged across Third Avenue, racing toward Fifty-fifth and Second, where he had the car parked. The woman had missed her wallet just as he got on the escalator. He'd heard her scream, "That man, the dark-haired one—he just robbed me."

He'd managed to slide through the wall of women on Alexander's main floor, but that bitch came rushing down the escalator after him, shouting and pointing as he went out the door. The security guard would probably chase him.

If he could just get to the car. He couldn't ditch the wallet. It was stuffed with hundred-dollar bills. He'd seen them, and he needed a fix.

It had been a good idea to go into Alexander's fur department. Women brought cash to Alexander's. It took too long to get a check or credit card cleared. He'd found that out when he worked as a stock boy there while he was still in high school.

Tonight he'd worn a coat that made him look like a stock boy. Nobody had paid any attention to him. The woman had one of those big, open pocketbooks; she'd held it by one strap as she rummaged through the coat rack. It had been easy to grab her wallet.

Was he being followed? He didn't dare look back. He'd call too much attention to himself. Better to stay against the sides of the buildings. Everyone was hurrying. It was so lousy cold. He could afford a fix; plenty of fixes now.

And in a minute he'd be in the car. He wouldn't be a man running in the street. He'd drive away, over the Fifty-ninth Street Bridge, and be home in Jackson Heights. He'd get his fix.

He looked back. No one running. No cops. Last night had been so lousy. The doorman had almost grabbed him when he broke into that doctor's car. And what did he get for his risk? No drugs in the bag. A medical file, a messy paperweight and an old shoe, for Christ sake.

The pocketbook he'd grabbed later from the old lady. Ten lousy bucks. He'd barely been able to get enough stuff to tide him over today. The pocketbook and bag were in the back seat of the car. He'd have to get rid of them.

He was at the car. He opened it, slipped in. Never, never, no matter how bad off he was, would he get rid of the car. Cops don't expect you to drive away. If you're spotted, they check the subway stations.

He put the key into the ignition, turned on the engine. Even before he saw the flashing dome light, he heard the siren of the police car as it raced the wrong way up the block. He tried to pull out, but the squad car cut him off. A cop, his hand on the butt of his pistol, jumped out. The headlights were blinding Danny.

The cop yanked open his door, looked in and removed the ignition key. "Well, Dannyboy," he said. "You're still at it, right? Don't you never learn any new tricks? Now get the hell out, keep your god-damned hands where I can see them and brace so I can read you the goddamned *Miranda.* You're what—a three-time loser? I figure you got ten to fifteen coming, we get lucky with a judge."

CHAPTER 58

T he plane circled over Newark. The descent was bumpy. Chris glanced at Joan. She was holding his hand tightly, but he knew it had nothing to do with flying. Joan was absolutely fearless in a plane. He'd heard her argue the point with people who hated to fly. "Statistically, you're much safer in a plane than in a car, a train, a motorcycle or your bathtub," she'd say.

Her face was composed. She'd insisted they have a drink when cock-tails were served. Neither one of them had wanted dinner, but they'd both had coffee. Her expression was serious but composed. "Chris," she'd said, "I can bear anything except thinking that because of me Vangie committed suicide. Don't worry about dragging me into this. You tell the truth when you're questioned and don't hold anything back."

Joan. If they ever got through this, they'd have a good life together. She was a woman. He still had so much to learn about her. He hadn't even realized he could trust her with the simple truth. Maybe he'd got-ten so used to shielding Vangie, from trying to avoid arguments. He had so much to learn about himself, let alone Joan.

The landing was rough. Several passengers exclaimed as the plane bounced down. Chris knew the pilot had done a good job. There was a hell of a downwind. If it kept up, they'd probably close the airport.

Joan grinned at him.

"The stewardess must have brought us in." It was an old airline gag.

"Or at least was doing a little lap time."

They were silent as the plane taxied over to the gate. People meeting passengers had to wait past the security gate. But Chris was not sur-prised to see the two detectives who had been at the house after he found Vangie waiting for him.

"Captain Lewis. Miss Moore."

"Yes."

"Please come with us." Ed's voice was formal. "It is my duty to inform you that you are a suspect in the death of your wife, Vangie Lewis, as well as in several other possible homicides. Anything you say may be used against you. You are not required to answer questions. It is your right to call a lawyer."

Joan answered for him. "He doesn't need a lawyer. And he'll tell you everything he knows."

CHAPTER 59

Molly settled back as the orchestra began the few bars of music that signaled the beginning of *Otello*. Bill *loved* opera. She *liked* it. Maybe that was part of the reason she couldn't relax. Bill was already totally absorbed, his expression serene and thoughtful. She glanced around. The Met was packed as usual. Their seats were excellent. They should be. Bill had paid seventy dollars for the pair. Overhead the chandeliers twinkled, glistened and then began to fade into silvery darkness.

She should have insisted on going to see Katie in the hospital tonight. Bill didn't, *couldn't* understand Katie's dread of hospitals. No wonder. Katie was ashamed to talk about it. The awful part was that there was a basis for her fear. Daddy *hadn't* gotten help in time. The old man who was in the room with him had told them that. Even Bill admitted that a lot of mistakes were made in hospitals.

With a start she heard applause as Placido Domingo descended from the ship. She'd heard nothing of the opera so far. Bill glanced over at her, and she tried to look as though she were enjoying herself. After the first act, she'd phone Katie. That would help to reassure her. Just hearing Katie's voice that she was all right. And by God, she'd be at that hospital early in the morning before the operation and make sure Katie wasn't too nervous.

The first act seemed interminable. She had never realized it was so long. Finally, intermission came. Impatiently refusing Bill's suggestion of a glass of champagne from the lobby bar, she hurried to a phone. Quickly, she dialed and jammed in the necessary coins.

A few minutes later, white-lipped, she rushed to Bill. Half sobbing, she grabbed his arm. "Something's wrong, something's wrong . . . I called the hospital. They wouldn't put the call through to Katie's room. They said the doctor forbade calls. I got the desk and insisted the nurse check on Katie. She just came back. She's a kid, she's hysterical. Katie's not in her room. Katie's missing."

🙢 *CHAPTER 60*

He left Katie's room and a smile of satisfaction flitted across his face. It was going very well. The pills were working. She was beginning to hemorrhage. The finger proved that her blood was no longer clotting.

He went down to the second floor and stopped in to see Mrs. Aldrich. The baby was in a crib by her bed. Her husband was with her. He smiled aloofly at the parents, then bent over the child. "A handsome specimen indeed," he proclaimed. "I don't think we'll trade him in."

He knew his attempts at humor were heavy-handed, but sometimes it was necessary. These people were important, very important. Delano Aldrich could direct thousands of dollars of research funds to Westlake. More research. He could work in the laboratory with animals, report his successes. Then, when he publicly began work with women, all the experimentation of these years would make immediate success inevitable. Fame deferred is not necessarily fame denied.

Delano Aldrich was staring at his son, his face a study in awe and admiration. "Doctor, we still can't believe it. Everyone else said we'd never have a child."

"Everyone else was obviously wrong." It was her anxiety that had been the main problem. Fukhito had spotted that. Muscular dystrophy in her father's family. She knew she might be a carrier. That and some fibroid cysts in her womb. He'd taken care of the cysts and she'd become pregnant. Then he'd done an early test of the amniotic fluid and had been able to reassure her on the dystrophy question.

Still, she was a highly emotional, almost hyperactive personality. She'd had two early miscarriages over ten years ago. He'd put her to bed two months before the birth. And it had worked.

"I'll stop in in the morning." These people would be fervent witnesses for him if there was any question that Katie DeMaio's death was suspicious.

But there shouldn't be any question. The dropping blood pressure was a matter of hospital record. The emergency operation would take

place in the presence of the top nurses on the staff. He'd even send for the emergency-room surgeon to assist. Molloy was on tonight. He was a good man, the best. Molloy would be able to tell the family and Katie's office that it had been impossible to stop the hemorrhaging, that Dr. Highley had headed a team working frantically.

Leaving the Aldriches, he went to Nurse Renge's desk. He had carefully manipulated the schedule so that she was on. A more experienced nurse would check on Katie every ten minutes. Renge wasn't that bright.

"Nurse Renge."

"Doctor." She stood up quickly, her hands fluttering nervously.

"I am quite concerned about Mrs. DeMaio. Her blood pressure is in the low normal limit, but I suspect the vaginal bleeding has been heavier than she realizes. I'm going out for dinner, then will come back. I want the lab report on her blood count ready. I did not want to distress her—she has a lifelong fear of hospitals—but I should not be surprised if we have to operate tonight. I'll make that judgment when I come back in about an hour. I persuaded her not to eat dinner, and if she requests any solid food, do not give it to her."

"Yes, Doctor."

"Give Mrs. DeMaio the sleeping pill, and do not in any way intimate to her that emergency surgery may be necessary. Is that clear?"

"Yes, Doctor."

"Very well."

He made a point of speaking to several people in the main lobby. He'd decided to have dinner at the restaurant adjacent to the hospital grounds. It wasn't bad. One could get a quite decent steak, and he wanted to be able later to present the image of a conscientious doctor.

I was concerned about Mrs. DeMaio. Instead of going home, I had dinner next door and went directly back to the hospital to check on her. Thank God I did. At least we *tried.*

And another important point. Even on a dismal night like this, it would not be unusual to walk over to the restaurant. That way no one would be quite sure how long he'd been gone.

Because while he was waiting for coffee to be served, he'd take the last necessary step. He had left Katie at five past seven. At quarter of eight he was in the restaurant. Katie was going to be given the sleeping pill at eight o'clock. It was a strong one. Thanks to her weakened condition, it would knock her out immediately.

By eight thirty it would be safe for him to go up the back stairs to the third floor, go into the living room of the suite, make sure Katie was asleep and give her the shot of heparin, the powerful anticoagulant drug, which combined with the pills would send her blood pressure and blood count plummeting.

He'd come back here and finish coffee, pay his bill and then return to the hospital. He'd take Nurse Renge up with him to check on Katie. Ten minutes later Katie would be in surgery.

She had made it so easy by not having visitors tonight. Of course, he'd been prepared for that possibility. He'd have slipped the heparin into the transfusion she'd be receiving during the operation. That would have been just as effective, but riskier.

The steak was adequate. Odd how hungry he became at times like this. He would have preferred waiting until after it was over to eat, but that would be almost impossible. By the time Katie's sister was reached it would be well after midnight, since she was at the opera. He'd wait at the hospital for her, to console her. She'd remember how kind he'd been. He wouldn't get home until two or three. He couldn't fast that long.

He permitted himself one glass of wine. He'd have preferred his usual half-bottle, but that was impossible tonight. Nevertheless, the one glass warmed him, made him more alert, helped his mind to rove over the possibilities, to anticipate the unexpected.

This would be the end of the danger. His bag had not shown up. It probably never would. The Salem threat had been eliminated. The papers reported his death as "fell or jumped." Edna was buried this morning. Vangie Lewis had been interred yesterday. The moccasin in Edna's drawer would mean nothing to the people who disposed of her shabby belongings.

A terrible week. And so unnecessary. He should be allowed to openly pursue his work. A generation ago artificial insemination was considered outrageous. Now thousands of babies were born that way every year.

Go back hundreds of years. The Arabs used to destroy their enemies by infiltrating their camps and impregnating their mares with cotton soaked with the semen of inferior stallions. Remarkable genius to have planned that.

The doctors who had performed the first successful in vitro fertilization were geniuses.

But his genius surpassed them all. And nothing would stand in the way of his reaping the rewards due him.

The Nobel Prize. Some day he would receive it. For contributions to medicine not imagined possible.

He had single-handedly solved the abortion problem, the sterility problem.

And the tragedy was that if it were known, like Copernicus he would be considered a criminal.

"Did you enjoy your dinner, Doctor?" The waitress was familiar. Oh, yes, he had delivered her some years ago. A boy.

"Very much indeed. And how is your son?"

"Fine, sir. Simply fine."

"Wonderful." Incredible this woman and her husband had met his fee, giving him the money saved for a down payment for a home. Well, she'd got what she wanted.

"I'd like cappuccino, please."

"Certainly, Doctor, but that will take about ten minutes."

"While you're getting it, I'll make some phone calls." He'd be gone less than ten minutes. Now the waitress wouldn't miss him.

Through the window he noticed that the snow had stopped. He couldn't, of course, take his coat from the checkroom. Slipping out the side door near the hallway with the telephones and rest rooms, he hurried back across the path. The cold bit at his face, but he scarcely noticed it. He was planning every step.

It was easy to keep in the shadows. He had his key to the fire exit in the rear of the maternity wing. No one ever used those stairs. He let himself into the building.

The stairway was brightly lighted. He turned off the switch. He could find his way through this hospital blindfolded. At the third floor he opened the door cautiously, listened. There was no sound. Noiselessly he stepped into the hall. An instant later he was inside the living room of Katie's suite.

That had been another problem he'd considered. Suppose someone accompanied her to the hospital: her sister, a friend? Suppose that person asked to stay overnight on the sofa bed in the living room? The Westlake Clinic openly encouraged sleeping in if the patient desired it. By ordering this living room repainted, he'd effectively blocked that possibility.

Planning. Planning. It was everything, as useful and necessary in life as in the laboratory.

This afternoon he had left the needle with the heparin in a drawer of an end table under the painter's drop cloth. The light from the parking lot filtered through the window, giving him enough visibility to find the table at once. He reached for the needle.

Now for the most important moment of all. If Katie woke up and saw him, he'd be exposed to danger. Granted, she would probably fall back asleep immediately. Certainly she'd never question the injection. But when he returned with Nurse Renge later, if she was by some chance still conscious, if she said anything about the shot, it would be easy enough to explain: she was confused; she meant when I took the blood samples. Even so. Better if she didn't wake up now.

He was in the room, bending over her. He reached for her arm. The drapery was partly open. Faint light was coming into the room. He

could see her profile. Her face was turned from him. Her breathing was uneven. She was talking in her sleep. He could not catch the words. She must be dreaming.

He slipped the needle into her arm, squeezed. She winced and sighed. Her eyes, cloudy with sleep, opened as she turned her head. In the dim light he could see the enlarged pupils. She looked up at him puzzled. "Dr. Highley," she murmured, "why did you kill Vangie Lewis?"

 CHAPTER 61

S cott Myerson was more tired than angry. Since Vangie Lewis' body had been found Tuesday morning, two other people had died. Two very decent people—a hard-working receptionist who deserved a few years' freedom after supporting and caring for aged parents and a doctor who was making a real contribution to medicine.

They had died because he had not moved fast enough. Chris Lewis was a murderer. Scott was sure of that. The web drawing around Lewis was unbreakable. If only they had realized immediately that Vangie Lewis' death was a homicide. He'd have brought Lewis in for questioning immediately. They might have cracked him. And if they had, Edna Burns and Emmet Salem would be alive now.

Scott couldn't wait for the chance to get to Lewis. Any man who could murder his pregnant wife was capable of any cold-blooded murder. Lewis proved that. He was the worst kind of criminal. The one who didn't look or sound the part. The one you trusted and turned your back on.

Lewis and his girlfriend were landing at seven. They should be here by eight. Lewis was cool, all right. Knew better than to run. Thought he could brazen it out. Knows it's all circumstantial. But circumstantial evidence can be a lot better than eyewitness testimony when properly presented in court. Scott would try the case himself. It would be his pleasure.

At seven fifty, Richard walked into Scott's office. He did not waste time on preliminaries. "I think we've uncovered a cesspool," he said, "and it's called the Westlake Maternity Concept."

"If you're saying that the shrink was probably playing around with Vangie Lewis, I agree," Scott said. "But I thought we decided that this afternoon. Anyhow, it's going to be easy enough to find out. Get blood samples from the fetus and we'll bring Fukhito in. He can't refuse to have his blood tested. If he does, it's an open admission of guilt, and he'd be finished with medicine if another paternity case was proved."

"That's not what I'm talking about," Richard broke in impatiently. "It's Highley I'm after. I think he's experimenting with his patients. I just spoke to the husband of one of them. There's no way he's the baby's father, but he was present at the birth. He's been thinking that his wife agreed to artificial insemination without his permission. I think it goes beyond that. I think Highley is performing artificial insemination without his patients' *knowledge.* That's why they're able to produce miracle babies under his care."

Scott snorted. "You mean to say you think Highley would inject Vangie Lewis with the semen of an Oriental father and expect to get away with it? Come on, Richard."

"Maybe he didn't know the donor was Oriental. Maybe he made a mistake."

"Doctors don't make mistakes like that. Even allowing your theory to be true . . . and frankly, I don't buy it . . . that doesn't make him Vangie's murderer."

"There's something wrong with Highley," Richard insisted. "I've felt it from the first minute I laid eyes on him."

"Look, we'll investigate Westlake Maternity. That's no problem. If there's any kind of violation there, we'll find it and prosecute it. If you're right and he's inseminating women without their consent, we'll get him. That's a direct violation of the Offense Against the Person Act. But let's worry about that later. Right now Chris Lewis is my first order of business."

"Do this," Richard persisted. "Go back further with the check on Highley. I'm already looking into the malpractice suits against him. Some woman, a Mrs. Horan, will be here shortly to tell why she pressed a suit. But the *Newsmaker* article says he was in Liverpool, in England, before he came here. Let's phone there and see if we can find any trace of impropriety. They'll give you that information."

Scott shrugged. "Sure, go ahead."

The buzzer on his desk sounded. He switched on the intercom. "Bring him in," he said. Leaning back on his chair, he looked at Richard.

"The bereaved widower, Captain Lewis, is here with his paramour," he said.

Dannyboy Duke sat in the precinct house hunched miserably forward in a chair. He was perspiring; his nerves were on edge. His arms were trembling. It was hard to see. In another thirty seconds he'd have been away. He'd be in his apartment now, the blissful release of the fix soaring through his body. Instead, this steamy, sweaty hell.

"Give me a break," he whispered.

The cops weren't impressed. "You give *us* a break, Danny. There's blood on this paperweight, Danny. Who'd you hit with it? Come on, Danny. We know it wasn't the old lady whose pocketbook you grabbed last night. You pushed her down. She's got a broken hip. That's pretty lousy when you're seventy-five, Danny. Odds are she'll end up with pneumonia. Maybe die. That makes it murder two, Dannyboy. You help us, we'll see what we can do for you, you know?"

"I don't know what you're talking about," Danny whispered.

"Sure you do. The doctor's bag was in your car. So was the pocketbook. The wallet you just grabbed in Alexander's was in your pocket. We know you stole the bag last night. We've got the call right here. The doorman saw you do it in front of the Carlyle Hotel. He can identify you. But who'd you hit with that paperweight, Danny? Tell us about it. And what about that shoe, Danny? Since when do you save beat-up shoes? Tell us about that."

"It was in the bag," Danny whispered.

The two detectives looked at each other. One of them shrugged and turned to the newspaper on the desk behind him. The other dropped the file he had been examining back into the bag. "All right, Danny. We're calling Dr. Salem to find out just what he had in this bag. That'll settle it. It could go easier if you'd cooperate. You've been around long enough to figure that out."

The other detective looked up from the paper. "Dr. Salem?" His voice was startled.

"Yeah. That's the name on the file. Oh, I see. The nameplate says Dr. Edgar Highley. Guess he had a patient's file from some other doctor."

The younger detective came over to the table carrying the morning *Daily News*. He opened the file and examined the sheaf of papers with the name EMMET SALEM, M.D. printed across the top. He pointed to page three of the *News*. "Salem's the doctor who was found on the roof of the Essex House extension last night. The Valley County Prosecutor is working with our people on that case."

The police officers looked at Dannyboy with renewed interest and narrowed, suspicious eyes.

CHAPTER 63

He watched as Katie's eyes closed and her breathing became even. She'd fallen asleep again. The question about Vangie had come from somewhere in her subconscious, triggered perhaps by a duplication of her mental state of Monday night. She might not even remember asking the question, but he couldn't take the chance. Suppose she talked about it again in front of Nurse Renge or the other doctors in the operating room before they anesthetized her? His mind groped for a solution. Her presence at the window last Monday night could still destroy him.

He had to kill her before Nurse Renge made her check, in less than an hour. The heparin shot would act to anticoagulate her blood immediately, but it would take several hours to complete the procedure. That was what he had planned. Now he couldn't wait. He had to give her a second shot, immediately.

He had heparin in his office. He didn't dare go near the hospital dispensary. He'd have to go down the fire stairs to the parking lot, use the private door to his office, refill the hypodermic needle and come back up here. It would take at least five minutes. The waitress would start to question his absence from the table, but there was no help for that. Satisfied that Katie was asleep, he hurried from the room.

CHAPTER 64

The technician in the Valley County Forensic Lab worked overtime on Friday evening. Dr. Carroll had asked him to compare all microscopic samples from the home of the presumed suicide Vangie Lewis with all microscopic samples from the home of the presumed accident victim Edna Burns. Carefully he had sifted the vacuum-bag contents of the Lewis home and the Burns apartment and painstakingly searched for substances that might be out of the ordinary.

The technician knew he had a superb instinct for microscopic evidence, a hunch factor that rarely failed him. He was always particularly interested in loose hair, and he was fond of saying, "We are like fur-bearing animals. It's astonishing how much hair we are constantly shedding, including people who are virtually bald."

In the exhibits from the Lewis home he found an abundance of strands of the ash-blond hair of the victim. He'd also found medium brown hair, a fair quantity of it, in the bedroom. Undoubtedly the husband's, since those same hairs were in the den and living room.

But there were also a number of silverish-sandy hairs in the victim's bedroom. That was unusual. In the kitchen or living room, strands of hair could easily come from a visitor or deliveryman, but the bedroom? Even in this day, there were few non-family members who were invited to enter the bedroom. Shafts found there assumed special significance. The hair had come from a man's head. The length suggested that automatically. Some of the same strands were on the coat the victim had been wearing.

And then the technician found the connection Richard Carroll had been seeking. Several sandy hairs with silver roots were clinging to the faded blue bathrobe of Edna Burns.

He placed the samples of hair under powerful microscopes and painstakingly went through the sixteen points of comparison check.

There was absolutely no doubt. One person had been close to both dead women; close enough to have held a head near to Edna Burns's chest and to have brushed a head on Vangie Lewis' shoulder.

The technician reached for the phone to call Dr. Carroll.

 ## CHAPTER 65

She tried to wake up. There was a click: a door had closed. Someone had just been here. Her arm hurt. Dr. Highley. She dropped off. . . . What had she said to Dr. Highley? Katie woke up a few minutes later and remembered. Remembered the black car and the shiny spokes and the light on his glasses. She'd seen that Monday night. Dr. Highley had carried Vangie Lewis to his car Monday night. Dr. Highley had killed Vangie.

Richard had suspected something. Richard had tried to tell her. But she wouldn't listen.

Dr. Highley knew she knew about him. Why had she asked him that question? She had to get out of here. He was going to kill her too. She'd always had nightmares about hospitals. Because somehow she'd known that she would die in a hospital.

Where had Dr. Highley gone? He'd be back. She knew that. Back to kill her. Help. She needed help. Why was she so weak? Her finger was

bleeding. The pills he had given her. Since she'd been taking them she'd been so sick. The pills. They were making her bleed.

Oh God, help me, please. The phone. The phone! Katie fumbled for it. Her hand, weak and unsteady, knocked it over. Shaking her head, forcing her eyes to stay open, she pulled it up by the cord. Finally she had the receiver at her ear. The line was dead. Frantically she jiggled the cradle, tried dialing the operator.

Dr. Highley had said the phone was being repaired. She pushed the bell for the nurse. The nurse would help her. But the click that should have turned on the light outside her door did not happen. She was sure the signal wasn't lighting the nurse's panel either.

She had to get out of here before Dr. Highley came back. Waves of dizziness nauseated her as she stood up.

She had to. Vangie Lewis. The long blond hair, the petulant, little-girl eagerness for a child. Dr. Highley had killed Vangie, killed her baby. Had there been others?

She made her way from the bed, holding on to the footrail. The elevator. She'd go down in the elevator to the second floor. There were people there—other patients, nurses.

From nearby a door closed. He was coming back. *He was coming back.* Frantically Katie looked at the open door to the corridor. He'd see her if she went out there. The bathroom door had no lock. The closet. He'd find her there. Through sheer willpower she managed to stumble to the door leading to the living room, open it, go inside, close it before he came into the bedroom.

Where could she go? He'd look for her immediately. She couldn't stay here. If she tried to go out into the foyer, she'd pass the open door of the bedroom. He'd see her. She had to go down the foyer and turn left, then down the long hall to the elevator. She was no match for him. Where could she go? She heard a door open inside. He was in the bedroom looking for her. Should she try to hide under the drop cloth? No. No. She'd be trapped there. He'd find her, drag her out. She bit her lip as dizziness clawed at the space behind her eyes. Her legs were rubbery, her mouth and skin spongy.

She stumbled to the door of the living room, the one that led to the hall. There was another door there, the fire exit. She'd seen it when she was wheeled in. She'd go down that to the second floor. She'd get help. She was in the hall. In a minute he'd be behind her.

The door to the fire stairs was heavy. She tugged at it . . . tugged again. Reluctantly it gave way. She opened it, stepped inside. It closed so slowly. Would he see it closing? The stairs. It was so dark here, terribly dark. But she couldn't turn on a light. He'd see it. Maybe he was running down the corridor toward the elevator. If he did that, she'd have an extra minute. She needed that minute. Help me. Help me. She grabbed onto the banister. The stairs were steep. Her bare feet were silent. How many stairs in a flight? Thirteen. No, that was a house. There was a landing here after eight steps. Then another flight. Eight more steps, then she'd be safe. Seven . . . five . . . one. She was at the door, tried to turn the handle. It was locked. It opened only from the other side.

From upstairs she heard the third-floor door open and heavy footsteps coming down the stairs.

~ CHAPTER 66

C hris refused to call a lawyer. He sat opposite the Prosecutor. He had been so worried about this encounter, so afraid they wouldn't believe him. But Joan believed him; Joan had said, "It just makes sense that they'll be suspicious of you, Chris. Tell every single thing you know. Remember that quote from the Bible, 'The truth shall make you free.' " Chris looked from the Prosecutor to the two detectives who had met him at the airport. "I have nothing to hide," he said.

Scott was unimpressed. A bookish-looking young man carrying a stenographer's pad came into the room, sat down, opened the pad and took out a pen. Scott looked directly at Chris. "Captain Lewis, it is my duty to inform you that you are a suspect in the deaths of Vangie Lewis, Edna Burns and Dr. Emmet Salem. You may remain silent. You are not required to answer any questions. At any point you may refuse to continue answering questions. You are entitled to the services of a lawyer. Any statement that you make can be used against you. Is that perfectly clear."

"Yes."

"Can you read?"

Chris stared at Scott. Was he being sarcastic? No, the man was deadly serious.

"Yes."

Scott shoved a paper across the desk. "This is a copy of the *Miranda* warning you have just heard. Please read it carefully. Be sure you understand it and then, if you are so disposed, sign it."

Chris read the statement swiftly, signed it and handed it back.

"Very well." Scott pushed the paper to one side. His manner changed, became somehow more intense. Chris realized the formal questioning was about to begin.

Funny, he thought, every night of your life, if you wanted to, you could watch some form of cops-and-robbers or courtroom drama show and you never expect to get involved in one yourself. The Prosecutor obviously believed that he had killed Vangie. Was he crazy not to have legal counsel? No.

The Prosecutor was talking. "Captain Lewis, have you been in any way ill-treated or abused?"

"I have not."

"Would you care for coffee or food?"

Chris rubbed his hand over his forehead. "I would like coffee, please. But I am ready to answer your questions fully."

Even so, he was not prepared for Scott's question. "Did you murder your wife, Vangie Lewis?"

Chris looked directly at him. "I did not murder my wife. I do not know if she was murdered. But I do know this. If she died before midnight Monday night, she did not kill herself in our home."

Scott, Charley, Phil and the stenographer were startled into unprofessional astonishment as Chris calmly said, "I was there just before midnight Monday. Vangie was not home. I returned to New York. At eleven the next morning I found her in bed. It wasn't until the funeral director came to the house for clothes to dress my wife for burial and told me the time of death that I realized that her dead body must have been returned to our house. But even before that I knew something was wrong. My wife would never have worn or even tried to put on the shoes she was wearing when she was found. For six weeks before her death the only shoes she could wear were a pair of battered moccasins a cleaning woman had left. Her right leg and foot were badly swollen. She even used those moccasins as bedroom slippers. . . ."

It was easier than he had expected. He heard the questions coming at him: "You left the hotel at eight P.M. Monday night and returned at ten. Where did you go?"

"To a movie in Greenwich Village. After I got back to the motel I couldn't sleep. I decided to drive home and talk to Vangie. That was shortly after midnight."

"Why didn't you stay and wait for your wife?" And then the one that was a hammerblow to his stomach: "Did you know your wife was carrying a Japanese fetus?"

"Oh, my God!" Horror somehow mingled with a sense of release flooded Chris's being. *It hadn't been his baby.* A Japanese fetus. That psychiatrist. Was he louse enough to do that to her? She'd trusted him so. Oh, God, the poor kid. No wonder she was getting so frightened to give birth. That must have been why she called Dr. Salem. She wanted to hide. Oh, God, she was such a child.

The questions came: "You were not aware your wife was involved with another man?"

"No. No."

"Why did you go to Edna Burns's apartment Tuesday night?"

The coffee came. He tried to answer. "Wait, please—can we take this just the way it happened?" He began to sip the coffee. It helped. "It was Tuesday night, just after I realized that Vangie had died before she was brought home, that that woman, Edna Burns, called. She was almost incoherent. She rambled on about Cinderella and Prince Charming, said she had something for me, something I'd want to have, and she had a story for the police. I thought she might know who Vangie had been with. I thought if she told me, I might not have to admit that I'd been home Monday night. I wanted to keep Joan out of this."

He set down the coffee cup, remembering Tuesday night. It seemed so long ago. Everything was so out of proportion. "I drove to Miss Burns's housing development. Some kid was walking his dog and pointed out her apartment to me. I rang the bell and knocked on the door. The television was on, the light was on, but she didn't answer. I figured she'd passed out and there was no use trying to talk to her, that maybe she was just a crank. I went home."

"You never went in?"

"No."

"What time was that?"

"About nine thirty."

"All right. What did you do then?"

The questions, one after another; he drank more coffee. Truth. The simple truth. It was so much easier than evasion. Keep the future in mind. If they believed him, he and Joan would have a life together. He thought of the way she'd looked at him, thrown her arms around him last night in her apartment. For the first time in his entire life, he'd known there was someone he could go to in trouble; someone who would want to share it with him. Everyone else—Vangie, even his parents—had always leaned on him.

For better, for worse.

It would be *better* for them. Joan, my darling, he thought. He took a deep breath. They were asking about Dr. Salem.

Richard sat at Katie's desk as he waited for the staff director of Christ Hospital, Devon, to answer his phone. Only by emphasizing the urgency of his need to talk to someone in authority who had been at the hospital more than ten years had he been given the man's private number.

While he waited, he looked around. The table behind Katie's desk was filled with files she was working on. It was no wonder she hadn't taken any time off after her accident. But no matter how busy, she should have stayed home. This afternoon she'd looked lousy. And losing that case today must have upset her terribly. He wished he'd seen her before she left.

The phone continued to jab. The guy must be out or asleep. Maybe it could wait till morning. No. He wanted to find out *now*.

There were snapshots in a frame on Katie's desk. Katie with an older woman, probably her mother. He knew the mother lived in Florida somewhere. Katie with Jennifer, Molly's oldest. Katie looked like Jen's big sister. Katie with a group of people in ski outfits. These must be the friends she stayed with in Vermont.

No picture of John DeMaio. But Katie wasn't the kind to subtly remind people at work that she was the widow of a prominent judge. And there certainly were plenty of pictures of him around that house.

The phone continued to ring. He'd give it another minute.

Richard realized he was pleased to note that there were no pictures of any other guy either. He'd been analyzing his reaction to Katie's announcement that she'd be away for the weekend. He'd tried to make it look as though he were surprised that she wouldn't be available with a big case breaking. Hell. That had nothing to do with it. He was worried that she was with some other guy.

"Yes." An angry, sleepy voice had answered the phone.

Richard straightened up, tightened his grip on the receiver. "Mr. Reeves? Mr. Alexander Reeves?"

"Yes."

Richard went directly to the point. "Sir, I apologize profusely for calling you at this hour, but the matter is vital. This is a transatlantic call. I'm Dr. Richard Carroll, the Medical Examiner of Valley County, New Jersey. I must have information about Dr. Edgar Highley."

The sleepiness vanished from the other man's voice. It became intense and wary. "What do you want to know?"

"I have just spoken with Queen Mary Clinic in Liverpool and was surprised to learn that Dr. Highley had been on staff there a relatively short time. We had been led to believe otherwise. However, I was told that Dr. Highley was a member of the Christ Hospital staff for at least nine years. Is that accurate?"

"Edgar Highley interned with us after his graduation from Cambridge. He is a brilliant doctor and was invited to become staff, specializing in obstetrics and gynecology."

"Why did he leave?"

"After his wife's death he relocated in Liverpool. Then we heard he had emigrated to the United States. That's not uncommon, of course. Many of our physicians and surgeons will not tolerate the relatively low pay structure of our socialized medicine system."

"There was no other reason for Dr. Highley's resignation?"

"I don't understand your question."

Richard took a chance. "I think you do, Mr. Reeves. This is, of course, totally confidential, but I can't waste time being discreet. I believe that Dr. Highley may be experimenting with his pregnant patients, perhaps even with their lives. Is there any justification that you can offer to support that possibility?"

There was a long pause. The words that came next were slow and deliberately enunciated. "While he was with us, Dr. Highley was not only a practicing physician, but was deeply involved in prenatal research. He did quite brilliant experiments on embryos of frogs and mammals. Then a fellow doctor began to suspect that he was experimenting with aborted human fetuses—which is, of course, illegal."

"What was done about it?"

"It was kept very quiet, of course, but he was being watched very carefully. Then a tragedy occurred. Dr. Highley's wife died suddenly. There was no way we could prove anything, but the suspicion existed that he had implanted her with an aborted fetus. Dr. Highley was asked to resign. This is, of course, absolutely confidential. In no way is there a shred of proof, and I must expect that you treat this conversation as inviolable."

Richard absorbed what he had heard. His hunch had been right. How many women had Highley killed experimenting on them? A question came into his mind—a wild, long-shot possibility.

"Mr. Reeves," he asked, "do you by any chance know a Dr. Emmet Salem?"

The voice warmed immediately. "Of course I do. A good friend. Why, Dr. Salem was visiting staff here at the time of the Highley scandal."

CHAPTER 68

Silently Katie ran down the stairs to the main floor. Desperately she grasped the knob, tried to open the door. But it would not give. It was locked. Upstairs, the footsteps had paused. He was trying the second-floor knob, making sure that she had not escaped him. The footsteps started again. He was coming down. No one would hear her if she screamed. These heavy doors were fireproof. No hospital sounds could be heard here. On the other side of the door, there were people: visitors, patients, nurses. Less than six inches away. But they could not hear her.

He was coming. He would reach her, kill her. She felt heavy, dull pain in her pelvic area. She was flowing heavily. Whatever he had given her had started the hemorrhaging. She was dizzy. But she had to get away. He had made Vangie's death look like suicide. He still might get away with that. Wildly she began rushing down the staircase. There was one more flight. It probably led to the basement of the hospital. He'd have to explain how and why she'd gotten there. The farther she got, the more questions would be asked. She stumbled on the last stair. Don't fall. Don't make it look like an accident. Edna had fallen. Or had she?

Had he killed Edna too?

But she'd be trapped here. Another door. This one would be locked too. Helplessly she turned the knob. He was on the mid landing. Dark as it was, she could see movement, a presence rushing down at her.

The door opened. The corridor was dimly lit. She was in the basement. She saw rooms ahead. Quiet. It was so quiet. The door snapped closed behind her. Could she hide somewhere? Help me. Help me. There was a switch on the wall. She pressed her hand on it. Her finger smeared it with blood. The corridor disappeared into blackness as a few feet behind her the door from the stairwell burst open.

CHAPTER 69

Highley was suspected of causing his first wife's death. Winifred Westlake's cousin believed he had caused Winifred's death. Highley was a brilliant researcher. Highley may have been experimenting on some of the women who were his patients. Highley may have injected Vangie Lewis with the semen of an Oriental male. But why? Did he hope to get away with it? Undoubtedly he knew Fukhito's background. Would he try to accuse him? Why? Had it been an accident? Had he used the wrong semen? Or had Vangie been involved with Fukhito? Was Dr. Highley's possible experimentation only incidental to Vangie's pregnancy?

Richard could not find the answer. He sat at Katie's desk twirling her Mark Cross pen. She always carried this. She must have rushed out of here this evening and forgotten to pick it up. But of course, she'd been upset. Losing that case must have rattled her badly. Katie would take that hard. Katie took a lot of things hard. He wished he knew where she was. He wanted to talk to her. The way her finger bled. He'd have to ask Molly if she knew whether or not Katie had a low platelet count. That could be a real problem.

A chill made Richard's fingers stiffen. That could be a sign of leukemia. Oh, God. Monday, he'd drag Katie to a doctor if he had to tie her up to do it.

There was a soft knock on the door and Maureen looked in. Her eyes were emerald green, large and oval. Beautiful eyes. Beautiful kid.

"Dr. Carroll."

"Maureen, I'm sorry I asked you to stay. I thought Mrs. Horan would be here long ago."

"It's all right. She did phone. She's on her way. Something came up at work and they needed her. But there are two women here. They're friends of the Miss Burns who died. They wanted to see Katie. I told them she was gone, and one of them mentioned your name. She met you the other night when you were at the Burns apartment; a Mrs. Fitzgerald."

"Fitzgerald? . . . Sure. Mrs. Fitzgerald is a part-time receptionist at Westlake Hospital." As Richard said "Westlake," he stood up. "Tell them to come on in. Maybe you'd better call Scott."

"Mr. Myerson is absolutely not to be disturbed. He and Charley and Phil are still questioning Captain Lewis."

"All right. I'll talk to them. Then if it's anything much, we'll make them wait."

They came in together, Gana's eyes snapping with excitement. She had regretfully decided not to wear Edna's leopard coat. It just seemed too soon. But she had her story ready to tell.

Gertrude was carrying the moccasin in a paper bag. Her neat gray hair was every inch in place. Her scarf was knotted at her throat. The good dinner had faded into memory, and now more than anything she wanted to get home and to bed. But she was glad to talk to Dr. Carroll. She was going to tell him that the other night in poor Edna's apartment,

Dr. Highley had been pulling open the night-table drawer. There was nothing in that drawer except the shoe. Did Dr. Carroll think that Dr. Highley wanted to get that shoe for any reason?

Mrs. DeMaio had been so interested in that Prince Charming business. Dr. Carroll might want to know about that too. He could tell Mrs. DeMaio when she came in Monday. Dr. Carroll was looking at them expectantly.

Gertrude leaned forward, shook the bag, and the shabby moccasin fell onto Katie's desk. Primly she began to explain, "That shoe is the reason we are here."

 *CHAPTER 70*

She zigzagged down the corridor. Would he know where the light switch was? Would he dare to turn it on? Suppose there was someone down here? Should she try to scream?

He knew this hospital. Where would she go? There had been a door at the end of the hall. The farthest door. Maybe he'd try the others first. Maybe she could lock herself in somewhere. She might miss the doors on the side. But if she ran straight, she'd have to touch that far wall. The door was in the middle. Her finger was bleeding. She'd try to smear blood on the door. When the nurse made her rounds, they'd start to search for her. Maybe they'd notice the bloodstains.

He was standing still. He was listening for her. Would he see a shadow when the door opened? Her outstretched hand touched a cold wall. Oh, God, let me find the door. Her hand ran down the wall. She touched a doorframe. Behind her she heard a faint squeaking sound. He had opened that first door. But now he wouldn't bother to look in that room. He'd realize he hadn't heard that squeak, that she hadn't tried that door. Her hand found a knob. She turned it deliberately, grinding her cut finger against it. A heavy formaldehyde smell filled her nostrils. From behind her she heard rushing feet. Too late. Too late. She tried to push the door closed, but it was shoved open. She stumbled and fell. She was so dizzy, so dizzy. She reached out. Her hand touched a pants leg.

"It's all over, Katie," Dr. Highley said.

CHAPTER 71

"Are you sure this is your wife's shoe?" Scott demanded. Wearily Chris nodded. "I am absolutely certain. This is the one that was so loose on her . . . the left one."

"When Edna Burns phoned you, did she tell you she had this shoe?"

"No. She said she had something to tell the police and that she wanted to talk to me."

"Did you get an impression of blackmail . . . of threat?"

"No, drunken garrulousness. I knew she was from Westlake Hospital. I didn't realize then that she was the receptionist Vangie used to talk about. She said Edna was always kidding her about her glass slippers."

"All right. Your statement will be typed immediately. Read it carefully, sign it if you find it accurate and then you can go home. We'll want to talk with you again tomorrow morning."

For the first time Chris felt as though the Prosecutor had begun to believe him. He got up to go. "Where is Joan?"

"She's completed a statement. She can go with you. Oh, one thing: what impression do you have of Dr. Highley?"

"I never met him."

"Did you read this article about him?" Scott held up *Newsmaker* magazine.

Chris looked at the article, at the picture of Dr. Highley. "I saw this yesterday on the plane into New York."

Memory jogged.

"That's it," he said. "That's what I couldn't place."

"What are you talking about?" Scott asked.

"That was the man who came down in the elevator at the Essex House last night when I was trying to reach Dr. Salem."

He switched on a light. Through the haze she could see his full-cheeked face, his eyes protruding as he stared down at her, his skin glistening with perspiration, his sandy hair falling untidily on his forehead.

She managed to stumble to her feet. She was in a small area like a waiting room. It was so cold. A thick steel door was behind her. She shrank back against the door.

"You've made it so easy for me, Mrs. DeMaio." Now he was smiling at her. "Everyone close to you knows about your fear of hospitals. When Nurse Renge and I make rounds in a few minutes, we'll assume you left the hospital. We'll call your sister, but she won't be home for several hours, will she? We won't start looking for you *in* the hospital until much later. Certainly no one will dream of looking for you here.

"An old man died in the emergency room tonight. He's in one of those vaults. Tomorrow morning when the undertaker comes for his body, you'll be found. It will be obvious what happened to you. You were hemorrhaging; you became disoriented, almost comatose. Tragically, you wandered down here and bled to death."

"No." His face was blurring. She was so dizzy. She was swaying.

He reached past her and opened the steel door. He pushed her through it, held her as she slid down. She had fainted. Kneeling beside her, he injected the last shot of heparin. She probably wouldn't recover consciousness again. Even if she did, she couldn't get out. From this side the door was locked. He looked at her thoughtfully, then got to his feet and brushed the smudge of dust from his trousers. At last he was finished with Katie DeMaio.

He closed the steel door that separated the vaults from the receiving area of the morgue and turned out the light. Cautiously he opened the door into the corridor and hurried down it, letting himself out into the parking lot of the hospital by the same door through which he'd come in fifteen minutes before.

A few minutes later, he was drinking lukewarm cappuccino, waving away the offer of the waitress to bring him a hot cup. "My calls took a bit longer than I expected," he explained. "And now I must hurry back to the hospital. There's a patient there about whom I'm quite concerned."

～～ *CHAPTER 73*

"Good night, Dr. Fukhito. I feel much better. Thank you." The boyish face managed a smile.

"I'm glad. Sleep well tonight, Tom." Jiro Fukhito got up slowly. This young man would make it. He'd been in deep depression for weeks, nearly suicidal. He'd been doing eighty miles an hour in a car that crashed. His younger brother was killed in the accident. Regret. Guilt. Overwhelming, more than the boy could handle.

Jiro Fukhito knew he had helped him through the worst of it. His work could be so satisfying, he reflected as he walked slowly down the corridor of Valley Pines Hospital. The work he did here, the volunteer work—this was where he wanted to practice.

Oh, he'd done enough for many of the patients at Westlake. But there were others he hadn't helped, hadn't been *allowed* to help.

"Good night, Doctor." A number of the patients in the psychiatric ward greeted him as he walked toward the elevator. He'd been asked to come full time on staff here. He wanted to accept that offer.

Should he start the investigation that would inevitably destroy him?

Edgar Highley wouldn't hesitate to reveal the Massachusetts case if he suspected that his associate had discussed his patient with the police.

But Mrs. DeMaio already suspected something. She'd recognized his nervousness when she questioned him the other day.

He got into his car, sat in it irresolutely. Vangie Lewis did not commit suicide. She absolutely did not commit suicide by drinking cyanide. She had gotten on the subject of the Jones cult during one of their sessions when she was talking about religion.

He could see her sitting in his office, hear her earnest, shallow explanation of her religious beliefs. "I'm not one for going to church, Doctor. I mean I believe in God. But in my own way. I think about God sometimes. That's better than rushing off to a service you don't pay attention to anyhow, don't you think? And as for those cults. They're all crazy. I don't see how people get involved in them. Why, remember all those people who killed themselves because they were told to? Did you hear the tape of them screaming after they drank that stuff? I had nightmares about it. And they looked so *ugly*."

Pain. Ugliness. Vangie Lewis? Never!

Jiro Fukhito sighed. He knew what he had to do. Once again his professional life would pay for the terrible mistake of ten years ago.

But he had to tell the police what he knew. Vangie had run out of his office into the parking lot. But when he left, fifteen minutes later, her Lincoln Continental was still in the lot.

There was no longer any doubt in Jiro Fukhito's mind that Vangie had gone into Edgar Highley's office.

He drove out of the hospital parking lot and turned in the direction of the Valley County Prosecutor's office.

S cott held the moccasin. Richard, Charley and Phil sat around his desk.

"Let's try to put this together," Scott said. "Vangie Lewis did not die at home. She was taken there sometime between midnight and eleven A.M. The last known place she visited was Dr. Fukhito's office at the hospital. Vangie was wearing the moccasins Monday night. Somewhere in the hospital she lost one of them, and Edna Burns found it. Whoever brought her home put other shoes on her to try to cover up for the missing ones. Edna Burns found the shoe and was talking about it. And Edna Burns died.

"Emmet Salem wanted to reach you, Richard. He wanted to talk to you about Vangie's death. He came to New York and fell or was pushed to his death a few minutes later, and the file he was carrying on Vangie Lewis disappeared."

"And Chris Lewis swears that he saw Edgar Highley in the Essex House," Richard interjected.

"Which may or may not be true," Scott reminded him.

"But Dr. Salem knew about the scandal in Christ Hospital," Richard said. "Highley wouldn't want that to come out just when he's getting national publicity."

"That's no motive to kill," Scott said.

"How about Highley trying to get that shoe out of Edna's drawer?" Charley asked.

"We don't *know* that. That woman from the hospital claimed he was opening the drawer. He didn't touch anything." Scott frowned. "Nothing hangs together. We're dealing with a prominent doctor. We can't go off half-cocked because he was involved ten years ago in a hushed-up scandal. The big problem is motive. Highley had no motive to kill Vangie Lewis."

The intercom buzzed. Scott switched it on. "Mrs. Horan is here," Maureen said.

"All right, bring her in, and I want you to take down her statement," Scott directed.

Richard leaned forward. This was the woman who had filed the malpractice suit against Edgar Highley.

The door opened and a young woman preceded Maureen into the room. She was a Japanese girl in her early twenties. Her hair fell loosely on her shoulders. Bright red lipstick was an incongruous note against her tawny skin. Her delicate, graceful carriage gave a floating effect even to the inexpensive pantsuit she was wearing.

Scott stood up. "Mrs. Horan, we appreciate your coming. We'll try not to keep you too long. Won't you sit down?"

She nodded. Clearly nervous, she wet her lips and deliberately folded her hands in her lap. Maureen unobtrusively sat behind her and opened her steno book.

"Will you state your name and address?" Scott asked.

"I am Anna Horan. I live at 415 Walnut Street in Ridgefield Park."

"You are or were Dr. Edgar Highley's patient?"

Richard turned quickly as he heard Maureen gasp. But the girl quickly recovered herself and, bending her head, resumed taking notes.

Anna Horan's face hardened. "Yes, I was that murderer's patient."

"*That murderer?*" Scott said.

Now her words came in a torrent. "I went to him five months ago. I was pregnant. My husband is a second-year law student. We live on my salary. I decided I had to have an abortion. I didn't want to, but I thought I had to."

Scott sighed. "And Dr. Highley performed the procedure at your request and now you're blaming him?"

"No. That's not true. He told me to come back the next day. And I did. He took me to an operating room in the hospital. He left me, and I knew—I *knew*—that no matter how we managed, I wanted my baby. Dr. Highley came back; I was sitting up. I told him I'd changed my mind."

"And he probably told you that one out of two women say the same thing at that moment."

"He said, 'Lie down.' He pushed me down on the table."

"Was anyone else in the room? The nurse?"

"No. Just the doctor and me. And I said, 'I know what I'm saying.' And—"

"And you allowed him to persuade you?"

"No. No. I don't know what happened. He jabbed me with a needle while I was trying to get up. When I woke up, I was lying on a stretcher. The nurse said it was all over. She said I should rest for a while."

"You don't remember the procedure?"

"Nothing. Nothing. The last I remember is trying to get away." Her mouth worked convulsively. "Trying to save my baby. I wanted my baby. Dr. Highley took my baby from me."

A harsh, pained cry echoed Anna Horan's heartbroken sobs. Maureen's face was contorted, her voice a wail. "That's exactly what he did to me."

Richard stared at the weeping young women: the Japanese girl; Maureen with her red-gold hair and emerald-green eyes. And with absolute certainty he knew where he had seen those eyes before.

⌒ *CHAPTER 75*

He got off at the second floor of the hospital and instantly felt the tension in the air. Frightened-looking nurses were scurrying in the hall. A man and woman in evening dress were standing by Nurse Renge's desk.

Quickly he walked over to the desk. His voice was disapproving and brittle as he asked, "Nurse Renge, is there something wrong?"

"Doctor, it's Mrs. DeMaio. *She's missing.*"

The woman was in her mid-thirties and looked familiar. Of course! She was Katie DeMaio's sister. What had made her come to the hospital?

"I'm Dr. Highley," he said to her. "What does this mean?"

Molly found it hard to talk. Something had happened to Katie. She knew it. She'd never forgive herself. "Katie . . ." Her voice broke.

The man with her interrupted. "I'm Dr. Kennedy," he said. "My wife is Mrs. DeMaio's sister. When did you see her, Doctor, and what was her condition?"

This was not a man to be easily deceived. "I saw Mrs. DeMaio a little more than an hour ago. Her condition is not good. As you probably know, she's had two units of whole blood this week. The laboratory is analyzing her blood now. I expect it to be low. As Nurse Renge will tell you, I expect to perform a D-and-C tonight rather than wait for the morning. I think Mrs. DeMaio has been concealing the extent of her hemorrhaging from everyone."

"Oh, God, then where is she?" Molly cried.

He looked at her. She'd be easier to convince. "Your sister has an almost pathological fear of hospitals. Is it possible that she would simply leave?"

"Her clothes are in the closet, Doctor," Nurse Renge said.

"*Some* clothes may be in the closet," he corrected. "Did you unpack Mrs. DeMaio's bag?"

"No."

"Then you don't know what other articles of apparel she had with her?"

"It's possible," Bill said slowly. He turned to Molly. "Honey, you know it's possible."

"We should have been here," Molly told him. "How bad is she, Doctor?"

"We must find her and get her back here. Would she be likely to go to her own home or to yours?"

"Doctor"—Nurse Renge's timid voice had a tremor—"that sleeping pill should have made Mrs. DeMaio fall asleep. It was the strongest one you ever ordered."

He glowered at her. "I ordered it for the very reason that I understood Mrs. DeMaio's anxiety. You were told to see that she swallowed it. She did not want the pill. Did you watch her take it?"

"I saw her put it in her mouth."

"Did you watch her swallow it?"

"No . . . not really."

He turned his back on the nurse in a gesture of contempt. He spoke to Molly and Bill, his voice reflective, concerned. "I hardly think Mrs. DeMaio is wandering around the hospital. Do you agree that she might have left of her own volition? She could simply have gotten on the elevator, gone to the lobby and walked out with the visitors who are coming and going all evening. Do you agree that's possible?"

"Yes. Yes. I do." Molly prayed, Please let it be that way.

"Then let's hope and expect that Mrs. DeMaio will be home very shortly."

"I want to see if her car is in the parking lot," Bill said.

The car. He hadn't thought about her car. If they started looking for her in the hospital now . . .

Bill frowned. "Oh, hell, she's still got that loan car. Molly, what make is it? I don't think I've even seen it."

"I . . . I don't know," Molly said.

Edgar Highley sighed. "I think even if you could identify her car, you'd be wasting your time looking in the parking lot. I would suggest that you phone her home. If she's not there, go and wait to see if she comes in. She's scarcely been gone an hour now. When you do contact her, please insist she return to the hospital. You can stay with her, Mrs. Kennedy. Doctor, if you feel it will comfort Mrs. DeMaio, I would be glad to have you with me in the operating room. But we must not allow that hemorrhaging to continue. Mrs. DeMaio is a very sick girl."

Molly bit her lip. "I see. Thank you, Doctor. You're very kind. Bill, let's just go to Katie's house. Maybe she's there now and not answering the phone."

They turned from him. They believed him. They would not suggest searching the hospital for several hours at least. And that was all he needed.

He turned to the nurse. In her own stupid, blundering way she had been an asset. Of course Katie had never swallowed that sleeping pill. Of course he was justified in having ordered it.

"I am sure that we'll be hearing from Mrs. DeMaio shortly," he said. "Call me immediately when you do. I'll be at my home." He smiled. "I have some records to complete."

～～ CHAPTER 76

"We must seize Dr. Highley's records before he has a chance to destroy them. To the best of your knowledge, does he keep all his records in his office?"

Jiro Fukhito stared at Richard. He had gone to the Prosecutor's office prepared to make a statement. They had listened to him almost impatiently, and then Dr. Carroll had outlined his incredible theory.

Was it possible? Jiro Fukhito reviewed the times when suspicions had formed in his mind, then were calmed by Highley's obstetrical genius. *It was possible.*

Records. They had asked him about records. "Edgar Highley would never keep records that suggest malfeasance in his office at the hospital," he said slowly. "There is always the danger of a malpractice subpoena. However, he frequently takes files to his home. I never could understand why he did that."

"Have search warrants sworn out immediately," Scott told Charley. "We'll hit the office and his home simultaneously. I'll take the squad to the house. Richard, you come with me. Charley, you and Phil take the office. We'll pick up Highley as a material witness. If he's not there, I want a stakeout on the house and we'll nab him as soon as he gets home."

"What worries me is that there may be someone he's experimenting on now," Richard said. "I'll say odds are that the hair shafts the lab found on Edna and Vangie's bodies came from Highley." He looked at his watch. It was nine thirty. "We'll wrap this up tonight," he predicted.

He wished Katie were here. She'd be relieved to know that Chris Lewis was about to be eliminated as a suspect. Her hunch about Lewis had been right. But his own hunch about Highley had been right too.

Dr. Fukhito stood up. "Do you need me any longer?"

"Not right now, Doctor," Scott said. "We'll be in touch with you. If by any chance you happen to hear from Dr. Highley before we arrest him, please do not discuss this investigation with him. You understand that?"

Jiro Fukhito smiled wearily. "Edgar Highley and I are not friends. He would have no reason to call me at home. He hired me because he knew he would have a hold over me. How right he was. Tonight I shall analyze my own conduct and determine how many times I have forced back suspicions that should have been explored. I dread the conclusion I shall reach."

He left the room. As he walked down the corridor, he saw a nameplate on a door: MRS. K. DEMAIO. Katie DeMaio. Wasn't she supposed to have gone into the hospital tonight? But of course, she never would go through with her operation while Edgar Highley was under investigation.

Jiro Fukhito went home.

 *CHAPTER 77*

She was drifting down a dark corridor. Way at the very end there was a light. It would be warm when she got there. Warm and safe. But something was holding her back. There was something she had to do before she died. She had to make them know what Dr. Highley was. Her finger was dripping blood now. She could feel it. She was lying on the floor. It was so cold. All these years she'd had nightmares that she'd die in the hospital. But it wasn't so bad after all. She'd been so afraid of being alone. Alone without Daddy, then alone without John. So afraid of risking pain. We are all alone. We're born alone and die alone. There's really nothing to be afraid of. Couldn't she possibly smear Dr. Highley's name on the floor with her finger? He was insane. He had to be stopped. Slowly, painfully, Katie moved her finger. Down, across, down again. H . . .

He got home at quarter past nine. The gratifying sense of having at last eliminated the final threat gave him a sense of total buoyancy. He had finished eating less than an hour ago, but somehow could not even remember the meal. Perhaps Hilda had left something for a snack.

It was better than he had hoped. Fondue. Hilda made remarkably good fondue. It was perhaps her best culinary accomplishment. He lit the Sterno can under the pot, adjusted it to a low flame. A crisp loaf of French bread was in a basket, covered by a damask napkin. He'd make a salad; there was sure to be arugula. He'd instructed Hilda to buy some today.

While the fondue heated, he would complete Katie DeMaio's file. He was anxious to be finished with it. He wanted to think about the two patients tomorrow: the donor and the recipient. He was confident that he could duplicate his success.

But was that enough? Wouldn't it be more interesting if the recipient were given twins to carry? Two alien fetuses from separate donors?

The immuno-reactive theory he'd perfected might break down. Almost certainly it would. But how long would it take? What specific problems would develop?

He went into the library, opened the desk drawer and withdrew Katie DeMaio's file from the hidden compartment. On the last page he made a final entry:

> *Patient entered hospital at approximately 6:00 p.m. with blood pressure 100/60, hemoglobin no more than 10 grams. This physician administered the final two cumadin pills at 7:00 p.m. At 8:30 this physician returned to Mrs. DeMaio's room and administered 5 ml. heparin by injection. Mrs. DeMaio awakened briefly. In a near-comatose state she asked this physician, "Why did you kill Vangie Lewis?"*
>
> *This physician left Mrs. DeMaio to obtain more heparin. Obviously it was impossible to allow Mrs. DeMaio to repeat that question before witnesses. When this physician returned, patient had left room. Probably realizing what she had said, she tried to escape. Patient was apprehended and another 5 ml. of heparin was administered. Patient will hemorrhage to death tonight in Westlake Hospital.*
>
> *This file is now closed.*

He put down his pen, stretched, walked over to the wall safe and opened it. Bathed in light from the crystal sconces, the buff-colored files took on an almost golden sheen.

They *were* golden: the records of his genius at his fingertips. Expansively he lifted them all out, laid them on his desk. Like a Midas savoring his treasure, he ran his fingers over the name tabs. His great successes. Berkeley and Lewis. His fingers stopped and his face darkened. Appleton, Carey, Drake, Elliot . . . failures. Over eighty of them. But not really failures. He had learned so much. They had all contributed. Those who had died, those who had aborted. They were part of the history.

Lewis. An addendum was necessary. To Vangie's file he added an account of his meeting with Emmet Salem.

The fondue must be ready. Irresolutely he looked at the files. Should he put them away now or give himself the pleasure of reading some of them? Perhaps he should study them. This week had been so difficult. He needed to refresh himself concerning some of the drug combinations he would want to use in the new case.

From somewhere in the distance a sound was beginning to penetrate the library: the wailing shriek of police sirens carried by the bone-chilling wind. The sound crescendoed into the room, then abruptly ceased. He hurried to the window, snatched back the drapery and glanced out. The police were here!

Had Katie been found? Had she been able to talk? With lightning movements he ran to the desk, stacked the files, replaced them in the still-open safe, closed it and slid back the panel.

Calm. He must be calm. His skin felt clammy. His lips and knees were rubbery. He must control himself. There was one last desperate card in the deck that he could always play.

If Katie had talked, it was all over.

But if the police were here for another reason, he might still be able to outwit them. Maybe Katie was already dead and her body had been found. Remember the questions and accusations when Claire died. They'd come to nothing. There had been absolutely no proof.

All the possibilities and consequences were exploding in his mind at once. It was exactly the same as during an operation or a delivery when something abruptly went wrong and he had to make an irrevocable decision.

And then it came. The icy, deliberate calm, the sense of power, the godlike omniscience that never failed him during difficult surgery. He felt it flowing through his body and brain.

There was a sharp, authoritative rap at the door. Slowly, deliberately, he smoothed his hair. His fingers, now miraculously dry and warm, tightened the knot in his tie. He walked to the front door and opened it.

～ CHAPTER 79

As the squad car raced toward Edgar Highley's home, Scott methodically reviewed the statements he'd heard in the past few hours from Chris Lewis, Gertrude Fitzgerald, Gana Krupshak, Jiro Fukhito, Anna Horan and Maureen Crowley.

Seemingly they pointed in one direction: to Dr. Edgar Highley, placing him under grave suspicion of malpractice, malfeasance and murder.

Not three hours ago, most of this same circumstantial evidence had pointed to Chris Lewis.

Scott thought of Pick Up Sticks, the game he'd played as a kid. You had to remove the sticks from the pile, one by one, without disturbing the rest of them. If you so much as jiggled another stick, you lost. It was a game Scott had played skillfully. But the trouble was that almost always, no matter how much care he took, the pile would collapse.

Circumstantial evidence was like that. Piled up, it looks impressive. Take it apart piece by piece and it caves in.

Richard was sitting beside him on the back seat of the squad car. It was because of Richard's insistence on slanting all the evidence against Edgar Highley that they were here now rushing through Parkwood with sirens screeching. Richard had heated this investigation to fever pitch by arguing that Highley might destroy evidence if he knew he was under suspicion.

Edgar Highley was a prominent physician, an excellent obstetrician. A lot of important people were fervently indebted to him because of the babies he had delivered in their families. If this turned out to be a witch-hunt, the Prosecutor's office would be under attack from the press and the public.

"This stinks." Scott did not realize he'd spoken aloud.

Richard, deep in thought, turned to him frowning. "What stinks?"

"This whole business: this search, this assumption that Highley is a combination of genius and murderer. Richard, what proof have we got? Gertrude Fitzerald *thinks* Highley was going into the night-table drawer for the shoe. Chris Lewis *thinks* he caught a glimpse of Highley in the Essex House. You *think* Highley has performed medical miracles.

"Look, even if the grand jury returns an indictment, which I doubt it will, a good lawyer could have this whole mess dismissed maybe without a trial. I've half a mind to turn around right now."

"Don't!" Richard grasped Scott's arm. "For God's sake, we've got to seize his records."

Scott hunched back in the seat, pulling his arm free.

"Scott," Richard urged, "forget everything except the number of maternity deaths at Westlake. That alone is sufficient reason for an investigation."

The squad car swerved around a corner. They were in the elegant west section of Parkwood. "All right," Scott snapped. "But remember, Richard, by tomorrow morning the two of us may be regretting this excursion."

"I doubt it," Richard said shortly. He wished he could overcome the growing worry that was grinding the pit of his stomach. It had nothing to do with this moment, this case.

It was Katie. He was desperately, irrationally worried about Katie. Why?

The car pulled into a driveway. "Well, this is it," Scott said sourly. The two detectives who were in the front seat jumped out of the car. As Richard started to get out, he noticed the movement of a drapery in a window at the far right of the house.

They had parked behind a black car with MD plates. Scott touched the hood. "It's still warm. He can't have been here long."

The younger detective who had driven the car rapped sharply on the front door. They waited. Scott stamped his feet impatiently, trying to warm them. "Why don't you ring the doorbell?" he asked irritably. "That's what it's there for."

"We were seen," Richard said. "He knows we're here."

The young investigator had just raised his finger to the bell when the door opened. Edgar Highley was standing in the foyer. Scott spoke first. "Dr. Highley?"

"Yes?" The tone was cold and questioning.

"Dr. Highley, I'm Scott Myerson, the Valley County Prosecutor. We have a search warrant for these premises, and it is my duty to inform you that you have become a suspect in the wrongful deaths of Vangie Lewis, Edna Burns and Dr. Emmet Salem. You have the right to consult a lawyer. You can refuse to answer questions. Anything you say may be used against you."

Suspect. They weren't sure. They hadn't found Katie. Every shred of evidence had to be circumstantial. He stepped aside, opening the door wider to allow them to enter. His voice was brittle with controlled fury as he said, "I cannot understand the reason for this intrusion, but come in, gentlemen. I will answer any questions you have; you are welcome to search my home. However, I must warn you, when I consult a lawyer it will be to bring suit against Valley County and against each one of you personally."

When he'd left Christ Hospital in Devon, he'd threatened to sue if any word of the investigation was leaked. And for the most part it had been kept quiet. He'd managed to see his file in the Queen Mary Clinic in Liverpool and there was no reference to it.

Deliberately he led them into the library. He knew he made an imposing figure sitting behind the massive Jacobean desk. It was vital that he unnerve them, make them afraid to question too closely.

With a gesture that barely escaped being contemptuous, he waved them to the leather couch and chairs. The Prosecutor and Dr. Carroll sat down; the other two men did not. Scott handed him the printed *Miranda* warning. Scornfully he signed it.

"We'll proceed with the search," the older detective said politely. "Where do you keep your medical records, Dr. Highley?"

"At my office, of course," he snapped. "However, please satisfy yourselves. I'm sure you will. There is a file drawer in this desk with personal papers." He stood up, walked over to the bar and poured Chivas Regal into a crystal tumbler. Deliberately he added ice and a splash of water. He did not go through the ritual of offering a drink to the others. If they'd come even minutes sooner he would still have had Katie's file in the desk drawer. They were trained investigators. They might notice the false bottom in that drawer. But they would never discover the safe—not unless they tore the house apart.

He sat down in the high-backed striped velvet chair near the fireplace, sipped the Scotch and eyed them coldly. When he'd come into the library he'd been so preoccupied that he hadn't noticed the fire Hilda had laid for him. It was burning splendidly. Later he'd have the fondue and wine here.

The questions began. When had he last seen Vangie Lewis?

"As I told Mrs. DeMaio . . ."

"You are sure, Doctor, that Mrs. Lewis did not enter your office Monday night after leaving Dr. Fukhito?"

"As I told Mrs. DeMaio . . ." They had no proof. Absolutely no proof.

"Where were you Monday night, Doctor?"

"Home. Right where you see me now. I came home directly after my office hours."

"Did you receive any phone calls?"

"None I recall." The answering service had taken no message Monday night. He'd checked.

"Were you in Edna Burns's apartment on Tuesday night?"

His smile, contemptuous. "Hardly."

"We'll want some hair samples from you."

Hair samples. Had some been found on Edna or in that apartment? How about Vangie? But he'd been in Edna's apartment with the police on Wednesday night. Vangie always wore that black coat to the office. Even if strands of his hair had been found near the dead women, they could be explained.

"Were you in the Essex House Hotel last night after five P.M.?"

"Absolutely not."

"We have a witness who is prepared to swear that he saw you get off the elevator there at approximately five thirty."

Who had seen him? He had glanced around the lobby as he got off the elevator. He was certain that no one he knew well was there. Maybe they were bluffing. Anyhow, eyewitness identification was notoriously unreliable.

"I was *not* in the Essex House last night. I was in New York at the Carlyle! I dine there frequently; in fact to my dismay my medical bag was stolen while I was dining there."

He'd give gratuitous information; make it seem as though he were becoming cooperative. It had been a mistake to mention Katie DeMaio's name. Would it be natural to tell these people that she was missing from the hospital? Obviously they didn't know she was a patient there. The sister had not yet contacted them. No. Say nothing about it. Doctor-patient confidentiality. Later he'd explain, "I would have told you, but of course assumed that Mrs. DeMaio had fled the hospital in nervous anxiety. I thought she would be troubled to have that fact a matter of record on her job."

But it was foolish to have mentioned the theft.

"What was in your bag?" The Prosecutor's interest seemed perfunctory.

"A basic emergency kit, a few drugs. Hardly worth the thief's effort." Should he mention that it contained files? No.

The Prosecutor was hardly listening. He beckoned to the younger investigator. "Get that package out of the car."

What package? Edgar Highley's fingers gripped the glass. Was this a trick?

They sat in silence, waiting. The detective returned and handed a small parcel fastened with a rubber band to Scott. Scott yanked the rubber band and pulled off the wrapping paper, revealing a battered shoe. "Do you recognize this moccasin, Doctor?"

He licked his lips. Careful. Careful. Which foot would it fit? Everything depended on that. He leaned over, examined it. The *left* shoe, the one that had been in Edna's apartment. *They had not found his bag.*

"Certainly not. Should I recognize this shoe?"

"Vangie Lewis, your patient, wore it continually for several months. She saw you several times a week. And you didn't ever notice?"

"Mrs. Lewis wore a pair of rather shabby shoes. I certainly do not address my attention to specifically recognizing one particular shoe when it's placed before me."

"Did you ever hear of a Dr. Emmet Salem?"

He pursed his lips. "Possibly. The name seems familiar. I'd have to go through my records."

"Wasn't he on staff with you at Christ Hospital in Devon?"

"Of course. Yes. He was visiting staff. Indeed, I do remember him." How much did they know about Christ Hospital?

"Did you visit Dr. Salem last night at the Essex House?"

"I believe that question has already been answered."

"Were you aware that Vangie Lewis was carrying an Oriental baby?"

So that was it. Smoothly he explained: "Mrs. Lewis was becoming terrified at the prospect of giving birth. That explains it, does it not? She knew that she could never make anyone believe her husband was the father."

Now they were asking about Anna Horan and Maureen Crowley. They were coming close; too close; like dogs baying as they closed in on their quarry.

"Those two young women are typical of many who demand abortions and then blame the physician when they experience emotional reactions. It's not uncommon, you know. Check with any of my colleagues."

Richard listened as Scott persisted in his questioning. Scott was right, he thought bleakly. Together everything added up. Separately everything was refutable, explainable. Unless they could prove wrongful death in the maternity cases, it would be impossible to charge Edgar Highley with anything and make it stick.

Highley was so composed, so sure. Richard tried to think how his father, a neurologist, would react if he were questioned about the wrongful death of one of his patients. How would Bill Kennedy react? How would he, Richard, react both as a person and as a doctor? Not like this man—not with this sarcasm, this scorn.

It was an act. Richard was sure of it. Edgar Highley was acting. But how could they prove it? With sickening certainty he knew they'd never find anything incriminating in Highley records. He was far too clever for that.

Scott was asking about the Berkeley baby. "Doctor, you are aware that Mrs. Elizabeth Berkeley gave birth to a baby who has green eyes. Isn't that a medical impossibility when both parents and all four grandparents have brown eyes?"

"I would say so, but clearly Mr. Berkeley is not the father of that baby."

Neither Scott nor Richard had expected the admission. "That doesn't mean I know who the father is," Edgar Highley said smoothly, "but I seriously doubt that it is the obstetrician's business to delve into matters such as that. If my patient wishes to tell me that her husband is her baby's father, then so be it."

A shame, he thought. He would have to defer fame a little longer. He'd never be able to admit the success of the Berkeley baby now. But there would be others.

Scott looked at Richard, sighed and stood up. "Dr. Highley, when you go to your office tomorrow you will learn that we have seized all your hospital and office records. We are deeply concerned at the number of maternity deaths at Westlake Hospital, and that matter is under intensive investigation."

He was on safe ground. "I invite the most minute scrutiny of all my patients' records. I can assure you that the Westlake Maternity death ratio is remarkably low in consideration of the cases we handle."

The smell of the fondue was filling the house. He wanted to eat it. He was so hungry. Unless it was stirred, it would surely burn. Just a few minutes more.

The phone rang. "I'll let my service take it," he said, then knew he could not. Undoubtedly it would be the hospital saying that Mrs. DeMaio had not yet returned home and her sister was frantic. It might be the perfect opportunity to let the Prosecutor and Dr. Carroll know about Katie's disappearance. He picked up the phone. "Dr. Highley here."

"Doctor, this is Lieutenant Weingarden of the Seventeenth Precinct in New York. We've just arrested a man who answers the description of the person who stole a bag from the trunk of your car last night."

The bag.

"Has it been recovered?" Something in his voice was giving him away. The Prosecutor and Dr. Carroll were watching him curiously. The Prosecutor stalked over to the desk and openly reached for the other extension.

"Yes, we have recovered your bag, Doctor. That's exactly the point. Several of the items in it may lead to far more serious charges than theft. Doctor, will you describe the contents of your bag?"

"Some medicine—a few basic drugs; an emergency kit."

"What about a patient's file from the office of a Dr. Emmet Salem, a bloodstained paperweight and an old shoe?"

He could feel the hard, suspicious stare of the Prosecutor. He closed his eyes. When he spoke, his voice was remarkably controlled. "Are you joking?"

"I thought you'd say that, sir. We're cooperating with the Valley County Prosecutor's office concerning the suspicious death of Dr. Emmet Salem last night. I'll call the Prosecutor now. It looks as though the suspect might have killed Dr. Salem in the process of a theft. Thank you, sir."

He heard Scott Myerson's order to the New York policeman: "Don't hang up!"

Slowly he replaced the receiver he was holding on the cradle. It was all over. Now that they had the bag, it was all over. Whatever chance he had had of bluffing his way through the investigation was finished.

The paperweight sticky with Emmet Salem's blood. The medical file on Vangie Lewis that contradicted the information in his office records. The shoe, that miserable filthy object.

If the shoe fits . . .

He stared down at his feet, objectively contemplating the patina of his handsome English cordovans.

They'd never stop searching now until they found the true files.

If the shoe fits wear it.

The moccasins had never fit Vangie Lewis. The supreme irony was that they fit *him*. As clearly as though he had walked in them, they tied him to the deaths of Vangie Lewis, Edna Burns, Emmet Salem.

Hysterical laughter rumbled inside him, shaking his stolid frame. The Prosecutor had completed the call. "Dr. Highley," Scott Myerson's voice was formal, "you are under arrest for the murder of Dr. Emmet Salem."

Edgar Highley watched as the detective sitting at the desk stood up quickly. He hadn't realized the man had been taking notes. He watched as the detective pulled handcuffs from his pocket.

Handcuffs. Jail. A trial. Blobs of humanity passing judgment on *him*. He who had conquered the primary act of life, the birth process, a common prisoner.

He drew himself up. The indomitable strength was returning. He had performed an operation. Despite his brilliance the operation had failed. The patient was clinically dead. There was nothing left to do except turn off the life-sustaining apparatus.

Dr. Carroll was looking at him curiously. From the moment of their Wednesday night meeting, Carroll had been hostile. Somehow Edgar Highley was sure that Richard Carroll was the man who had become suspicious of him. But he had his revenge. Katie DeMaio's death was his revenge on Richard Carroll.

The detective was approaching him. The handcuffs caught the glint of the fire.

He smiled politely at him. "I have just remembered that I do have some medical records that might interest you," he said. He walked over

to the wall, released the spring that held the panel in place. The panel slid back. Mechanically he opened the wall safe.

He could gather up the records, make a dash for the fireplace. The fire Hilda had laid was fairly brisk now. Before they could stop him, he could get rid of the most important files.

No. Let them know his genius. Let them mourn it.

He lifted the files out of the safe, stacked them on the desk. They were all staring at him now. Carroll walked over to the desk. The Prosecutor still had his hand on the phone. One detective was waiting with the handcuffs. The other detective had just come back into the room. Probably he'd been going through the house snooping into his possessions. Dogs hounding their quarry.

"Oh, there is another case you'll want to have."

He walked over to the table by the fireplace chair and reached for his Scotch. Carrying it to the safe, he sipped it casually. The vial was there, right in the back of the safe. He'd put it away Monday night for possible future use. The future was now. He'd never expected it to end this way. But he was still in control of life and death. The supreme decision was his alone to make. A burning smell was permeating the room. Regretfully he realized it was the fondue.

At the safe he moved quickly. He slipped the vial open and dumped the crystals of cyanide into his glass. As understanding swept over Richard's face, he held up the glass in a mocking toast.

"Don't!" Richard shouted, throwing himself across the room as Edgar Highley raised the glass to his lips and gulped down the contents. Richard knocked the glass away as Highley fell, but knew it was too late. The four men watched futilely, helplessly, as Highley's screams and groans died into writhing silence.

"Oh, God!" the younger detective said. He bolted from the room, his face green.

"Why'd he do it?" the other detective asked. "What a lousy way to die."

Richard bent over the body. Edgar Highley's face was convulsed; foaming bubbles were blistering his lips. The protruding gray eyes were open and staring. He could have done so much good, Richard thought. Instead, he was an egocentric genius who used his God-given skill to experiment with lives.

"Once I got on the line with the New York police, he knew he couldn't lie or murder his way out anymore," Scott said. "You were right about him, Richard."

Straightening up, Richard went over to the desk and scanned the names on the files. BERKELEY. LEWIS. "These are the records we're looking for." He opened the Berkeley file. The first page began:

Elizabeth Berkeley, age 39, became my patient today. She will never conceive her own child. I have decided that she will be the next extraordinary patient.

"There's medical history here," he said quietly.

Scott was standing over the body. "And when you think that this nut was Katie's doctor," he muttered.

Richard looked up from reading Liz Berkeley's file. "What did you say?" he demanded. "Are you suggesting that Highley was treating Katie?"

"She had an appointment with him Wednesday," Scott replied.

"She had a *what?*"

"She happened to mention it when—" The phone interrupted him. Scott picked it up. "Yes," then said, "I'm sorry, this is not Dr. Highley. Who is calling, please?" His expression changed. Molly Kennedy. "Molly!"

Richard stared. Apprehension strangled his neck muscles. "No," Scott said. "I can't put Dr. Highley on. What's the matter?"

He listened, then covered the mouthpiece with his hand. "Oh, Jesus," he said, "Highley admitted Katie to Westlake tonight and she's missing."

Richard yanked the phone from him. "Molly, what's happened? Why was Katie there? What do you mean she's missing?"

He listened. "Come on, Molly. Katie would never walk out of a hospital. You should know that. Wait."

Dropping the phone, he frantically scattered the files on the desk. Near the bottom of the pile he found the one he dreaded to see. DeMaio, Kathleen. Opening it, he raced through it, his face paling as he read. He came to the last paragraph.

With the calm of desperation, he picked up the phone. "Molly, put Bill on," he ordered. As Scott and the detectives listened, he said, "Bill, Katie is hemorrhaging somewhere in Westlake Hospital. Call the lab at Westlake. We'll need to hang a bottle of O negative the minute we find her. Have them ready to take a blood sample and analyze for hemoglobin, hematocrit and type and cross-match for four units of whole blood. Tell them to have an operating room ready. I'll meet you there." He broke the connection.

Incredible, he thought. You can still function knowing that already it may be too late. He turned to the detective at the desk. "Call the hospital. Pull the search team from Highley's office and have them start looking for Katie. Tell them to look everywhere—every room, every closet. Get all the hospital personnel to help. Every second counts."

Without waiting for instructions, the younger investigator ran to start up the car. "Come on, Richard," Scott snapped.

Richard grabbed Katie's file. "We have to know what-all he's done to her." For an instant he looked at Edgar Highley's body. They'd been seconds too late preventing his death. Would they be too late for Katie?

With Scott he hunched in the back of the squad car as it raced through the night. Highley had given Katie the heparin over an hour ago. It was fast-acting.

Katie, he thought, why didn't you tell me? Katie, why do you feel you have to go it alone? Nobody can. Katie, we could be so good together. Oh, Katie, we could have what Molly and Bill have. It's there waiting for us to reach out for it. Katie, you felt it too. You've been fighting it. Why? Why? If you'd only trusted me, *told* me you were seeing Highley. I'd never have let you go near him. Why didn't I see that you were sick? Why didn't I *make* you tell me? Katie, I want you. Don't die, Katie. Wait. Let me find you. Katie, *hang on.* . . .

They were at the hospital. Squad cars were roaring into the parking lot. They ran up the stairs into the lobby. Phil, his face drawn into deep lines, was commanding the search.

Bill and Molly came running into the lobby. Molly was sobbing. Bill was deadly calm. "John Pierce is on his way over. He's the best hematologist in New Jersey. They've got a reasonable supply of whole blood on hand here, and we can get more from the blood bank. Have you found her?"

"Not yet."

The door to the fire stairs, partly ajar, burst open. A young policeman ran out. "She's on the floor in the morgue. I think she's gone."

Seconds later, Richard was cradling her in his arms. Her skin and lips were ashen. He could not get a pulse. "Katie. Katie."

Bill's hand gripped his shoulder. "Let's get her upstairs. We'll have to work fast if there's any chance at all."

≈ *CHAPTER 80*

She was in a tunnel. At the end there was a light. It was warm at the end of the tunnel. It would be so easy to drift there.

But someone was keeping her from going. Someone was holding her. A voice. Richard's voice. "Hang on, Katie, hang on."

She wanted so not to turn back. It was so hard, so dark. It would be so much easier to slip away.

"Hang on, Katie."

Sighing, she turned and began to make her way back.

On Monday evening Richard tiptoed into Katie's room, a dozen roses in his hand. She'd been out of danger since Sunday morning, but hadn't stayed awake long enough to say more than a word or two.

He looked down at her. Her eyes were closed. He decided to go out and ask the nurse for a vase.

"Just lay them across my chest."

He spun around. "Katie." He pulled up a chair. "How do you feel?"

She opened her eyes and grimaced at the transfusion apparatus. "I hear the vampires are picketing. I'm putting them out of business."

"You're better." He hoped the sudden moisture in his eyes wasn't noticeable.

She had noticed. With her free hand she gently reached up and brushed a finger across his eyelids. "Before I fall asleep again, please tell me what happened. Otherwise I'll wake up about three in the morning and try to put it together. Why did Edgar Highley kill Vangie?"

"He was experimenting on his patients, Katie. You know about the test-tube baby in England, of course.

"Highley was far more ambitious than to simply produce in vitro babies for their natural parents. What he set out to do was take fetuses from women who had abortions and implant those fetuses in the wombs of sterile women. And he did it! In these past eight years he learned how to immunize a host mother from rejecting an alien fetus.

"He had one complete success. I've shown his records to the fertility research lab in Mt. Sinai Hospital, and they tell me that Edgar Highley made a quantum leap in blastocyst and embryonic research.

"But after that success, he wanted to break new ground. Anna Horan, a woman he aborted, claims that she changed her mind about the abortion, but that he knocked her out and took her fetus when she was unconscious. She was right. He had Vangie Lewis in the next room waiting for the implant. Vangie thought she was simply having some treatment to help her become pregnant with her own child. Highley never expected Vangie to retain the Oriental fetus so long, although his system had become perfected to such a degree that the race issue was really not a consideration.

"When Vangie didn't abort spontaneously, he became so fascinated by his own research that he couldn't bear to destroy the fetus. He decided to bring it to term, and then who would blame him if Vangie had a partly Oriental child? The natural mother, Anna Horan, is married to a Caucasian."

"He was able to suppress the immune system?" Katie remembered the elaborate charts in college science courses.

"Yes, and without harm to the child. The danger to the mother was much greater. He's killed sixteen women in the last eight years. Vangie was getting terribly sick. Unfortunately for her, she ran into Highley last Monday evening just as she left Fukhito. She told him she was going to consult her former doctor in Minneapolis. That would have been a risk, because a natural pregnancy for Vangie was a million-to-one shot, and any gynecologist who had treated her would have known that.

"But it was when she mentioned Emmet Salem's name that she was finished. Highley knew that Salem would guess what had happened when Vangie produced a half-Oriental child, then swore that she'd never been involved with an Oriental man. Salem was in England when Highley's first wife died. He knew about the scandal."

"And now," Richard said, "that's enough of that. All the rest can wait. Your eyes are closing again."

"No. . . . You said that Highley had *one* success. Did he actually transfer a fetus and have it brought to term?"

"Yes. And if you had stayed five minutes longer at Molly's last Thursday night and seen the Berkeley baby, you could guess now who the natural mother is. Liz Berkeley carried Maureen Crowley's baby to term in her womb."

"Maureen Crowley's baby." Katie's eyes flew open, all sleepiness gone. She tried to pull herself up.

"Easy. Come on, you'll pull that needle out." Gently he touched her shoulder, holding her until she leaned back. "Highley kept complete case histories of what he did from the moment he aborted Maureen and implanted Liz. He listed every medication, every symptom, every problem until the actual delivery."

"Does Maureen know?"

"It was only right to tell her and the Berkeleys and let the Berkeleys examine the records. Jim Berkeley has been living with the belief that his wife lied to him about artificial insemination. You know how Maureen felt about that abortion. It's been destroying her. She went to see her baby. She's one happy girl, Katie. She would have given it out for adoption if she had delivered it naturally. Now that she's seen Maryanne, sees how crazy the Berkeleys are about her, she's in seventh heaven. But I think you're going to lose a good secretary. Maureen's going back to college next fall."

"What about the mother of Vangie's baby?"

"Anna Horan is heartbroken enough about the abortion. We saw no point in having her realize that her baby would have been born if Highley hadn't murdered Vangie last week. She'll have other children."

Katie bit her lip. The question she'd been afraid to ask. She had to know. "Richard, please tell me the truth. When they found me, I was hemorrhaging. How far did they have to go to stop the bleeding?"

"You're okay. They did the D-and-C. I'm sure they told you that."

"But that's all?"

"That's all, Katie. You can still have a dozen kids if you want them."

His hand reached over to cover hers. That hand had been there, had pulled her back when she was so near to death. That voice had made her want to come back.

For a long, quiet moment she looked up at Richard. Oh, how I love you, she thought. How very much I love you.

His troubled, questioning expression changed suddenly into a broad smile. Obviously he was satisfied at what he saw in her face.

Katie grinned back at him. "Pretty sure of yourself, aren't you, Doctor?" she asked him crisply.

About the Author

MARY HIGGINS CLARK is the beloved author of eleven novels. Her bestsellers include *Remember Me, I'll Be Seeing You, All Around the Town, Loves Music, Loves to Dance, While My Pretty One Sleeps* and the novels in her first Wings Books omnibus, *Weep No More, My Lady, Stillwatch* and *A Cry in the Night.* Her collection of short stories is entitled *The Anastasia Syndrome and Other Stories.* Mary Higgins Clark's books have sold more than twenty-five million copies in the United States.

Mary Higgins Clark began writing for a living after her husband died, leaving her a widow with five children. In 1979 she graduated from Fordham University at Lincoln Center with a B.A. in philosophy; nine years later she received an honorary Ph.D. from her alma mater. In 1980, she was awarded the Grand Prix de Literature of France. In 1987 Mary Higgins Clark served as president of the Mystery Writers of America.